Lucy Smith

AUTUMN DECEPTION

Two Bestselling Novels Complete in One Volume

Seasons of Intrigue

To Catch the Summer Wind
The Race for Autumn's Glory

DORIS ELAINE FELL

Inspirational Press, New York

First Inspirational Press edition published in 2000.

Inspirational Press
A division of BBS Publishing Corporation
386 Park Avenue South
New York, NY 10016

Inspirational Press is a registered trademark of
BBS Publishing Corporation.

Published by arrangement with Crossway Books, a division of
Good News Publishers.

Library of Congress Control Number: 00-132381

ISBN: 0-88486-283-6

Printed in the United States of America.

CONTENTS

To Catch the Summer Wind 1

The Race for Autumn's Glory 369

To Catch the Summer Wind

SEASONS OF INTRIGUE

BOOK FIVE

To Catch the Summer Wind

Doris Elaine Fell

*Why should we
be in such
desperate haste to succeed,
and in such
desperate enterprises?
If a man does not keep pace
with his companions,
perhaps it is because
he hears
a different drummer.
Let him step to
the music which he hears,
however measured
or far away.*

—Henry David Thoreau

To Howard and Elsie
my brother and his wife

· · · ·

When I count my blessings and my friends,
you shine brightly among them.

Prologue: London

May, 1986. Olivia Renway waited alone in the Chelsea dining room, her slender, well-manicured hands clasped tightly in front of her. She was a striking, genteel woman of sixty-two with russet hair and intense blue eyes framed by velvet black lashes. She sat with her back straight in the brocade chair, feeling out of place in this restaurant that catered to a lunch crowd of corporate executives and rakish artists. Even the masculine paintings on the paneled walls were of fox hunts and men riding to hounds. Somber waiters in crimson cummerbunds moved soundlessly across the plush red carpet, balancing trays of steaming broccoli and roast lamb trimmed with parsley and mint jelly.

She sent her platter back, untouched, leaving only a rosebud lying in the center of the linen cloth where her grandson had tossed it; its pink petals were taut except for the one Ian had torn free. Olivia wanted to grab her Burberry and briefcase and flee out into the rain-drenched city and never come to London again; but Ian would come back to the table looking for her, trusting her to be there. He was too young to abandon even though leaving him might save his life.

The man from Prague who had followed them this morning sat across the room, still wearing his damp raincoat and defiantly tapping the ashes of a thin cigar into his cup as he met her gaze. She placed him at twenty-six to thirty, a not unattractive man with a narrow face and hair so blond that it looked snow-white. At once Olivia glanced down at the wedding band with the five-carat diamond sparkling on her finger. Above the ring the sapphire bracelet—a fragile memory of the war years—pinched the skin of her narrow wrist. These were Olivia's two worlds—the life with Uriah Kendall and her hidden past.

Her knuckles blanched as she reached out to rearrange the crumbs around the fallen petal. Why had she insisted on going to London without Uriah? His finely chiseled face and handsome smile stayed locked in her memory. Thoughts of him sent tiny ripples along her spine, arousing her need for him. She longed to fly home to Maryland, to those tender, wide-open arms, but it would be better for all of them if she could outrun the man from Prague and slip away into oblivion. Then Uriah and Ian would never bear the humiliation of her past. Escape? But what would become of her promise to meet Uriah at their Cotswold cottage in June?

As she fingered the lone rose petal, soft and fragrant as her own skin, Olivia saw her thirteen-year-old grandson bounding back from the loo. Somehow she had to get him safely to Heathrow and on a plane back to Maryland as quickly as possible.

"I was worried about you, Ian," she said.

He flopped into the chair scowling, a rangy lad with one trousered leg swinging impatiently. Olivia loved him fiercely and felt fury at the new threats that might distance her from her grandson. He was her jeans and T-shirt boy, looking miserable in a suit and tie. And yet the two of them were so much alike—both tall and fair with piercing blue eyes—Ian with sandy red hair, her own beginning to gray at the temples, his unruly with one wavy lock slipping over his forehead and almost hiding his scowl. He had Uriah's cheeks and jawbone and strength of character, but that stubborn streak and his narrow nose and sensitive mouth were so like her own.

His lips twisted as he tugged at the tie. "Are we going to sit here all day, Grams, just because it's raining?" he asked.

"Just until the waiter brings the check."

She fumbled for her credit card. Thoughts of last night's phone caller with his distinct Czechoslovakian accent wiped the beginnings of a smile from her face. In those years before Uriah, she had faced trouble head-on with a Beretta tucked safely at the bottom of her bag or a Bren automatic hidden in the boot of her car. But she would never risk carrying a gun in Ian's presence.

"What took you so long?" she asked.

"I went to the bathroom."

"Twenty minutes ago."

He met her concern with silence and then said, "There was a man in the loo asking about you."

"That stranger across the room?"

His glance was obvious, his nose screwed up in boredom. "That's him. I think he followed us this morning."

"He seemed to be everywhere we went," she admitted.

"Are you afraid, Grams?"

Yes, I'm frightened, she thought. *Frightened for both of us.* But she smiled and said, "Not when you're with me."

"I told him you were my grandmother, but he said you were Olivia Renway, the suspense novelist."

"Not Olivia *Kendall?*"

"Don't think he knew that."

"I'm always running into people who think they know me."

"Dad hates that. Says you never had time to be his mother."

"Aubrey exaggerates," she said.

But Aubrey was right. Mothering had been difficult at best. Even now in his mid-thirties, Aubrey still sulked in her presence.

"Ian, your father was a demanding child," she said.

"But Dad said you spent all your time writing books—that you never had time for him."

"Aubrey exaggerates," Olivia said again. "I gave him everything money could buy—the best clothes, the best private schools, the opportunity to travel." *But what was all of that when she had failed so miserably at being his friend, his mother?*

"He thinks you should go by your married name."

"I do. That's who I am. Olivia Kendall. But Uriah wants me to keep my professional life separate."

Ian shrugged. "I like you both ways."

Aubrey's resentments had passed on to Ian's older brother, but Ian had wormed his way into Olivia's heart from the day he was born. She didn't want anything to weaken the bond between them. Motherless from birth, Ian had needed her in a way that Aubrey and Grover never had.

"Ian," she whispered, "I'm sorry I disappointed your father."

"Doesn't matter. Gramps is proud of you."

"He's proud of you, too. He wants you to go to Sandhurst."

"Can't. I'm not a Brit."

She smiled again. He was more English and more loyal to his grandfather's country than he realized. "Uriah will think of a way."

"No. I want to be a cyclist, not a Grenadier Guard."

"Couldn't you be both?"

"No." Clear, definite.

At thirteen he was already racing and doing well in the junior classics. Ian was committed to a career in cycling when he grew up so he could be an American hero like Greg LeMond—even if he had to defy family traditions to make his own mark in life. "Maybe you'll win the Tour de France for me someday, Ian."

He cocked his head, giving her the Kendall appraisal. "Will you be there?"

Her throat tightened. "Just try and stop me."

"You won't get too old?"

"No. I'll always be young." *And I'll always love you, always pray for you, no matter what happens.*

Unexpectedly he said, "Gramps will like your new dress."

She touched the jeweled neckline of the stylish dinner dress with its Italian label. "Uriah won't like the price."

"He'll like you in it. Wear it when we meet him next week."

"Ian, he won't be coming. I'm sending you home."

He stared in disbelief. "Grams, what did I do wrong?"

"Nothing. You've been an angel, but I'm going back to Czechoslovakia."

"I'll go with you."

"It's a business trip this time. Next summer maybe or even in the fall, we'll go to all the places we planned to go." She knew even as she made the suggestion that there would be no trip—next summer, in the fall, ever. "I'm sorry, Ian."

"But we always do something special in June."

"I know. I promised you a summer filled with rainbows, four weeks together in Italy and the Greek islands and then to Paris to watch Greg LeMond ride in the Tour de France. Honey, I want that as much as you do, but we'll go some other time."

"Don't send me home. I won't get in your way."

Her despair matched the gloom and disappointment on his face, a look of betrayal so intense that she stood and slipped into her Burberry as a bolt of lightning flashed behind the church spires. She had to calm herself. She would have the chauffeur drop her off at Westminster Abbey so she could slip inside for a moment of solitude. Then she would walk the rest of the way to Downing Street for her appointment with the prime minister.

As the waiter picked up her credit card, the man from Prague was paying his bill, too. "Ian, I have an appointment on Downing Street. After that we'll drive out to Heathrow."

"Aren't we going back to Stratford first?"

"No, I want you to catch a flight out of Heathrow this afternoon. I'm certain I can get you on board."

He shuffled to his feet, his lip quivering. "Don't send me away, Grams. Dad will think I made you mad."

She touched his cheek with her gloved fingers. "I'll call Uriah and explain everything. He'll let Aubrey know. Maybe you and Uriah could go on down to Disney World."

"That's kids' stuff."

"Then go camping in the Blue Ridge Mountains."

"Gramps always forgets the matches."

"Then have him take you to one of the junior classics."

"No! I don't want to watch a race. I want to ride in it, and I can't do that again until I get my new bicycle."

She had promised him a racing cycle for Christmas—yellow like the one Greg LeMond rode. From the corner of her eye, she saw the white Towncar emerge through the downpour and brake to a stop in front of the restaurant; its windshield wipers were swishing rhythmically, working overtime. Across the River Thames, another crooked streak of lightning flashed above the Albert Bridge. "Ian, dear, we have to leave now."

She put her hands on his shoulders for what she knew would be the last time and leaned down and kissed the top of his head. "I love you, Ian. You must always remember that."

Tears balanced on her lashes as she flicked the bracelet from her wrist and tucked it into his pocket. Before he could protest, she touched his lips. "Take care of it for me, Ian."

"Until you get back from Czechoslovakia?"

"Until I ask you for it."

Across the vast room, the man with the cigar stood and began wending his way toward the revolving doors. "Hurry, Ian," she said. "We must not keep Charles waiting."

"I don't like Charles."

"Honey, I know he's not our regular driver, but Michaels is sick. Charles is just filling in for the day."

"I still don't like him."

Outside the Fox Hunt Restaurant, she hesitated, protected by the canopied arch above her. As Ian shivered beside her, Olivia heard the man from Prague coming through the revolving door. She gripped Ian's hand and ran toward the waiting limousine.

The chauffeur tipped his cap as they slid across the back seat. "Westminster Abbey, Charles," she said. "While I'm there, take Ian to the cycle shop. He's interested in a yellow racer." A lump rose in her throat. "I promised him one for Christmas."

"Very good, Miss Renway."

As he eased the car from the curb, the London traffic darted in every direction, merging and doubling back on itself. Charles studied Olivia in the rearview mirror, his shrewd hawk-eyes fixed on her face. "When should Ian and I be back?" he asked.

"By two. I'll be at Downing Street. Meet me there."

Olivia stood inside the hallway as the door to number 10 Downing Street closed behind her. Beyond the narrow entryway, two houses had been joined together with a stairway that rose to the prime minister's small but well-kept flat at the top of the building. She knew from her last visit that the prime minister's personal touches were everywhere: a porcelain collection on display and art treasures like the Turner painting that hung in the White Drawing Room. British history cried out from the very walls of this building with striking portraits of Nelson and Wellington and a lifelike painting of Churchill in the Cabinet Room that had made Olivia feel as though she were facing the man himself.

Near Olivia a magnificent sculpture fit perfectly into the alcove. Above it hung a picture of Londoners asleep in the underground during the Blitz. Olivia had lived through a blitz of her own, a frightening escape from Czechoslovakia, a poignant memory that came crashing back as the painting stirred the remembrance of air raid sirens and Luftwaffe planes roaring overhead.

She turned at the sound of the secretary's light footsteps in the hallway. "Miss Renway, I'm Cynthia. We're sorry to keep you waiting. The prime minister had an unexpected phone call."

Someone protesting my visit. Butterflies kicked at Olivia's stomach as she followed Cynthia up the stairs to the private flat in the rafters. Cynthia left her at the study door where one of the most powerful women in the world sat at the desk poring over briefs that affected scores of nations, an empty coffee cup pushed off to one side. As the woman tugged at a pearl earring, the desk light cast a golden sheen on her reddish brown hair.

"Should I come back another time?" Olivia asked softly.

The prime minister stood, her face serious, her hands outstretched in welcome. "It's been a long time, Olivia."

"Two years," Olivia said. On previous occasions, Olivia had been an invited guest, the first time with Uriah, grandson of Lord and Lady Kendall. On her second visit, she had sat with the prime minister for an hour, reminiscing about Oxford. But two years ago, a brunch at the Chequers estate had ended in a bitter debate over Uriah's removal from British Intelligence.

"Please sit down, Olivia."

As she eased into a chair across from the prime minister, she glanced around. The study had been repapered since her last visit. The ugly sage-green wallpaper was gone, and a cream stripe brightened the room. Their eyes met again. "You've had a busy year. The G7 Summit in Tokyo earlier this month, wasn't it?"

The prime minister flicked a thread from her gray tweed suit. "Yes, along with a quick visit to South Korea, and I'm just back from that trip to Israel. It will be Camp David in November."

"I almost called you when you came to Washington a year ago."

"Why didn't you? We're old friends, Olivia."

"My friendship may have cost you that bombing in Brighton. I've been afraid that something I wrote risked your safety—"

"Since when have you teamed up with the Irish Republic?" There was a tongue-in-cheek pause. "Brighton was an IRA bombing."

Olivia snatched another glance at the striped wallpaper. "Czech terrorists may be the next real threat."

"To Brighton or Chelsea?"

"To you," Olivia said.

"And you've come here to warn me?" The prime minister pushed the empty cup farther away. As the seconds passed, a mixture of independence and wisdom, of amusement and annoyance, of concern and kindness showed in those alert eyes. "We're on good terms with Czechoslovakia. I have no briefs to the contrary, no word on any Czech subversives in the country. But, Olivia, I'll pass your concerns on to Dudley Perkins over at MI5."

"Perkins won't believe you. If it weren't for your intervention, he would keep the Kendalls banned from this country forever. Now he's convinced Uriah works for the CIA."

"Does he?"

"That would amuse Uriah. You know that he's retired."

"Isn't Langley just across the Potomac?"

Olivia shook her head. "Not from our place."

"Have you had tea, Olivia? We don't keep a live-in, but the deep freeze is well stocked. Or I can stir up a poached egg on Bovril toast if you prefer."

"I've eaten. I didn't want to take up much of your time."

The smile went back to quick and friendly. "That's right. You have a book signing this afternoon."

"That was canceled. Actually I have an appointment with my publisher. That's why I'm in London." She snapped her briefcase open and handed an autographed copy of her novel across the desk. "This is the one on industrial sabotage and chemical weapons snaking their way out of Europe into Asia." She tapped the unfinished manuscript in her case. "This will be a sequel to it."

"Uriah must be bursting with pride."

"Yes, but he's against my writing on a steel plant that produces chemical weapons for mass destruction. But I knew I had hit upon the truth when the phone threats started a week ago."

The prime minister's hand went involuntarily across the folder in front of her as Olivia slid a single sheet across the desk. "Are you familiar with these companies?" Olivia asked.

With a quick appraisal, the PM said, "Nishokura Steel? No, but this steel plant in Munich, Germany—I recognize that one."

"And the old Van Rindin architectural firm?"

"I don't believe I've heard of that one either."

"Also in Germany—also a family-run business with a branch facility not far from Prague." Olivia's voice turned bitter. "They're both thriving and prosperous since the late 1930s, but someone should have put them out of business a long time ago."

The warmth between them chilled. "A personal grudge, Olivia?"

Olivia's throat spasmed. "I'm convinced the Russelmanns and Van Rindins helped design the concentration camps of World War II. If it hadn't been for them, my father would still be alive."

"The war has been over for more than forty years, Olivia."

"No, it's very fresh for me. But what a marvelous excuse. They made the bomb, but they didn't drop it. They designed the ovens, but they didn't stoke them."

The prime minister's quiet reserve seemed to shout across the desk that separated them, saying, *You've gone quite mad, Olivia.*

Olivia continued, "Otto Russelmann founded a steel company in the Ruhr Valley in the early thirties. He prospered throughout the war designing weapons of death—and died of a stroke before they could drag him into the Nuremberg trials. The whole family was acquitted of war crimes. Only God knows why. It was so unfair."

"You speak as though you knew them personally."

I did. But I can't tell you that, not without risk to Uriah. Accountability. She was demanding accountability of others when she had never rendered her own. She touched the blanched line around her wrist where the sapphire bracelet had been and felt the racing drumbeat of her own heart.

"I know enough about them to know they were evil, and it passed down through the generations." *Oh, Uriah—dear family of mine—what unhappiness my life has cost you.*

"Olivia!" The clear enunciation of her name drew her back. "Perhaps collaboration was the only way the Russelmanns and the Van Rindins could survive in Nazi Germany."

"They could have fled from Germany—left it all." *As I fled from Prague.*

Across the shiny desk their eyes met again, the prime

minister's steady and unblinking. The corner of Olivia's mouth twitched. She said, "I don't know about the factories in Munich and the Ruhr Valley—but after the war Otto Russelmann's family enlarged the steel plant in Czechoslovakia."

"State-controlled, wasn't it?"

"No longer, not since the Communists left. But for some reason the Russelmanns fared well even during the Communist rule. I know. I just came back from Prague. Jarvoc actually—the village where I was born."

"You promised Uriah you would never go there again."

"My brother Dorian's wife died. I went home for the funeral. While I was there, I hit upon this idea for a book sequel when I recognized someone I had known in the war."

"Did that person recognize you?"

"I didn't think so at the time. But last night there was another threatening phone call—all in Czech. And this morning someone followed me. I'm frightened for my grandson Ian. He's with me today." Olivia paused. "I'm certain that I saw that same man at the factory where my brother Dorian works."

"At the Russelmann Steel factory in Jarvoc?"

"I'm certain of it. The Russelmanns have contracts with Nishokura in Japan and with the office of Jon Gainsborough."

"The steel magnate here in England?" the PM asked.

"Yes. I can't let history repeat itself. If it's the last thing I do, I have to buy my brother's way out of the Czech Republic." She rubbed her blanched wrist. "I have something that the Russelmanns want. That's why I'm going back to Prague. I'll barter with them for Dorian's freedom— before I expose them."

Olivia studied the cream stripes on the wall again as she tried to stop her fears from leapfrogging within her mind. Her facial muscles drew tight. "I have an old account to settle. Uriah knows nothing of my plans, but I'm telling you, dear friend, in case something goes wrong."

"I'm afraid for you, Olivia."

"Don't be. I don't expect you to understand, but it goes

back a long ways—to the assassination of Reinhard Heydrich."

"The head of the German protectorate in Czechoslovakia?"

"Yes. The Germans retaliated by destroying Lidice—and most of my family. It's still a bitter pill for Dorian and me to swallow. . . . When I saw that man in Jarvoc, it all came back."

"If you're in danger, Olivia, I'll call Scotland Yard."

"Please don't. My brother and childhood nanny are the ones in danger. I brought her back with me, but Dorian refused to come. At least my old nanny is safe from the younger generation of Russelmanns and Van Rindins." *Safe from Altman Russelmann.*

The prime minister's smile turned sympathetic. "You were always imaginative—even back at Somerville—and totally absorbed by novels of intrigue, especially Dorothy Sayers's, as I recall. But don't hold the younger generations guilty for the past. Trust me, Olivia. I keep abreast of the threats worldwide."

Disappointment flushed Olivia's cheeks. "What if the Russelmanns are still stockpiling toxic nerve gases?"

"British Intelligence will keep me informed. If there's a problem in Jarvoc, they'll contact Czech Intelligence for me."

"No. For the first time since I married Uriah, I may be able to prove that the things Dudley Perkins said about me were lies."

"Dudley was just an ambitious junior officer back then. Trying to do what he thought was right."

"He ruined Uriah's career. Robbed him of his honor, his knighthood."

The coffee cup was repositioned. "Leaving M15 was Uriah's choice. It was that or not marry you—a difficult decision at best. But if it helps, I never believed the rumors."

"Then why didn't you come to our wedding? Never mind. Some of those rumors were true, but I never spied against Britain. I want my husband's good name cleared. I want Uriah's title restored." Olivia snapped her briefcase shut. "If anything happens to me, the research in here will be proof enough."

They both stood, like strangers now. "We must keep in touch, Olivia. The next time Uriah is with you, why don't you have Sunday brunch with us out at Chequers again?"

In spite of Olivia's last visit there, the invitation struck a pleasant chord. She loved the prime minister's Elizabethan country manor with its highly polished furniture and antique treasures—a weekend refuge from the pressures and formality of London. Mostly Olivia remembered holding hands with Uriah as they enjoyed the tangy smell of a winter log burning in the fireplace.

"Oh, we'd love to come," she said.

As the phone rang, Olivia added, "I'll see myself out."

"You could leave by the back way through the gate."

"No. I have a ride waiting. Besides, if someone saw me come in, they'll be waiting for me to leave the same way."

"Not your Czechoslovakian terrorists?" the PM asked kindly.

"Perhaps."

🪲🪲🪲

The nervous tapping of Olivia's heels against the rain-washed sidewalk mirrored her thumping heart. She felt anger at her chauffeur for parking the Towncar at the end of the block. As she hurried toward it, a gangly young man with a large black umbrella elbowed her to the curb. She stepped aside to let him pass, but as he came abreast he said, "Miss Renway, may I have your autograph?"

Her grip on the briefcase tightened. "You've mistaken me for someone else," she said.

His amicable grin faded, leaving a puzzled expression on his face as though once confronting her, he was suddenly speechless. And then he shook his head. "No," he stammered, holding up the book. "See, this is your picture here on the back cover. I'd know you anywhere. I've read all your books."

In the picture, her hands rested on the chair back, the

sapphire bracelet in full view. She pushed around him and hurried on toward Whitehall. He turned and fell into step with her, holding his umbrella over her head. "Please. Just sign it for me. I've waited out here in the rain for an hour."

Reluctantly, she set down her briefcase and took the book.

"Name's Nedrick Russelmann," he volunteered.

As she repeated his name, the dryness in her mouth came back. Could it be—but, no, there couldn't be any connection.

Russelmann ran the back of his hand across his lower lip, those black-browed, dark eyes tugging at Olivia's past. She had to reach the safety of the Towncar. She opened the book jacket, scrawled her signature, and shoved the novel back into his hand. "Nedrick, I must go," she said, but her voice trembled.

He stepped back. "Here, Miss Renway, take my umbrella."

Olivia took it and picked up her briefcase. As she stepped off the curb, she saw him raise the book and wave it in the air.

She heard the gunning of an engine and tilted the umbrella back just in time to see the gray Renault bearing down on her. The impact of the vehicle sent her hurtling into the air and slammed her into the gutter—the back of her head striking the curb. The tires squealed as the car turned on a dime and fled back toward Whitehall.

For a moment, she felt nothing; then all of her nerve endings awakened in a thrust of pain so severe that she gasped. In her blurred vision, she saw Russelmann kick the twisted umbrella aside and grab her leather case. *My book draft and my notes on Prague!*

As pain ravaged her body, she cried out, "Why, Nedrick?"

Nedrick turned back, his face chalky white, his eyes desperate. He tossed the case toward her and fled along Downing to Whitehall as the passersby gathered around her broken body.

The stagnant smell of a cigar overwhelmed her as the man from Prague leaned over her. His raincoat lay open, his rich brown tie almost touching her cheek. His powerful fingers dug deep into her limp wrist. "Where is it?" he demanded. "Where is it?"

My bracelet. He wants my sapphire bracelet. "It's gone."

He stood, snatched the briefcase, and merged into the gathering crowd. Next week, next month he would stalk someone else. In the distance, she heard the plaintive wail of a siren and knew that it would not arrive in time.

"Help is coming," a uniformed bobby said as he knelt beside her and put his hand gently on her shoulder.

"My briefcase?" she cried.

He took a quick survey. "We'll find it. Tell me your name."

She gazed around dazedly. Where was Charles and the Towncar? Surely her chauffeur would come to her rescue. Wait . . . there was Charles. He was walking away. She struggled to lift her head and uttered the single word, "Charles."

Olivia caught a glimpse of him stepping into the limousine. She heard the door slam and the motor rev. She stared after him. As the car sped away, Ian's terrified face pressed against the back window, his hands pounding against the glass.

"I love you, Ian," she whispered.

Rain pelted her face, but a glimmer of sunlight broke through the darkened clouds, touching the sky with pastel ribbons of a rainbow. Beneath her breastbone something exploded. Her breathing was cut off. Spurts of blood filled her mouth and trickled down her chin. As the constable patted her hand, the excruciating pain eased. Olivia felt herself floating, drifting away. The solitude of her moments in Westminster Abbey flashed back. She mouthed the prayer again. The constable's face blurred. For a moment she thought she saw her beloved Uriah, and then her tunnel vision glimpsed a dazzling white light. Her fingers relaxed. She felt no fear, only peace. A peace like the calm that had swept over her in the Abbey.

As the bobbies cordoned off the area, the emergency phone at the prime minister's residence rang with a third warning. The brittle Czechoslovakian voice on the other end said coldly, "A bomb is set to go off at number 10 Downing in the next fifteen minutes. . . . "

Moments later the gates on the property swung open, and a limousine sped down the driveway, the prime minister and her personal secretary shielded on the backseat.

Chapter 1

June 1, 1986. A low mist hung over the city as Uriah Kendall's Rolls Royce followed the stark white hearse bearing Olivia's body. The small procession wound its way slowly along the River Thames as his beloved Olivia took leave of London for the last time.

Uriah sat in the backseat with his grandsons huddled silently beside him. He could offer the boys no comfort; he had none to give. As Ian kicked at the upholstery, streaking it with brown shoe polish, Grover glared up at Uriah, wide-eyed, visibly annoyed, as though his grandmother had deliberately betrayed him by dying.

Uriah felt numb, his dark blue eyes almost as lifeless as Olivia's. He was distinguished looking, a well-groomed man meticulously attired with not a strand of his thick sandy hair out of place. Uriah's despair deepened as he thought about Olivia's five-carat diamond lying in his pocket, securely wrapped in a white linen handkerchief. Not stolen, but safe. He fixed his gaze on the gloves and walking stick on his lap and asked himself for the hundredth time, *Why, Olivia? Why? Why have you left me?*

Another lump rose in his throat as he listened to the thump, thump, thump of Ian's shoe. It was impossible for Uriah to swallow. Impossible to think clearly. There were so many words left unsaid, so many dreams unfinished. Behind the closed doors at Scotland Yard the constable had given Uriah a detailed report of the accident. Everything had blurred for Uriah when he read the medical report: Olivia's body bruised, battered, crushed by a hit-and-run driver. Olivia dead on a rain-swept London street with a man's umbrella by her broken body.

Dudley Perkins of MI5 had been there, coldly stating that Olivia's death had not been accidental. Perkins was right. Olivia would never step blindly from the curb without looking both ways.

"Can you explain the man's umbrella, Uriah?" Perkins had asked. "We must know the name of the man who accompanied her."

Without answering, Uriah had signed a release for Olivia's possessions, her beautiful things stuffed into a white plastic bag. He listened mechanically as the constable read off each item. The expensive dress stained with her blood. Red shoes with a broken heel. Her watch cracked. Her rings undamaged. *And the ugly black umbrella.* Uriah had taken the rings and refused the rest. He kept silent about Olivia's missing sapphire bracelet and leather attaché case, the one he had given her.

The funeral procession moved steadily over the motorway, following the river that Olivia had loved back toward its source. Uriah insisted that the procession take the hour's drive to Oxford to the academic world where Olivia had graduated from Somerville College—and where she had found her measure of peace in the college chapel at Christ's Church, not far from the narrow footpaths that edged the winding Cherwell.

In the deadly silence of his own heart, he pictured Olivia as he had first seen her standing in the rain on the Cotswold bridge, turning in slow motion to face him—cautious, watchful even then. At first all he had seen was a young woman in a charcoal gray trench coat leaning desolately against the railing, her slender feet pressed into beige pumps, her russet hair damp against her cheek. Startled by his sudden appearance, she had stood her guard, wary, ready to take flight, her delicate features like a mirage, her enormous blue eyes swallowed up in sadness.

Days later she told him that she had come to England as

a Czech refugee, stealing over the back streets of war-torn London, creeping around elusively like the fog that crept over the Thames. But once she became his wife, Uriah lavished on her the good things of London: art galleries and concerts and wild spending sprees on Oxford and Regent Streets.

In the front seat of the car, Aubrey gripped the steering wheel. "Dad, we should have taken Mom home to Maryland," he said grudgingly. "Why are we leaving her in England?"

"We've been over that already, Aubrey. I want to bury your mother in Kendallshire—in the village where we met."

"Away from the prying eyes of her fans—away from her family?"

"That's enough, Aubrey."

Ian stirred and leaned against Uriah. "There are only five cars following us, Grandpa. I thought Grandma had a lot of friends."

Uriah reached out and drew the boy closer, and then his eyes riveted once again on the white hearse. *Six cars and a hearse. We make a strange lot of summer mourners,* he thought. *Family and a few close friends and Dudley Perkins.*

Perkins was riding in the fourth car, there on behalf of the prime minister. Edwin Wallis, a young constable from Scotland Yard, rode with him. Wallis was an alert thirty-year-old with horn-rimmed glasses and little interest in the funeral itself. *He doesn't know about the missing briefcase or bracelet,* Uriah thought. *How could he? I haven't reported the loss.*

Miles beyond Oxford, they left the steep hills and gullies and passed through the thick woodland into the village of Kendallshire where old friends lined the main road. The hearse led the way on through the gated cemetery to the knobby knoll where Uriah would bury Olivia beside his parents. During the graveside service, the vicar tried to offer Uriah comfort, but his words fell on deaf ears. Uriah stared into the dirt crevice as they lowered Olivia's casket into it and vowed that he would allow nothing to tarnish her memory. A sudden breeze blew gently over the flowers on the grave, scenting the air with the sweet fragrance of the lilacs and roses that she had loved; it was as though she had opened her slender hand and blown him one final kiss.

Afterwards Aubrey broke their silence. "Dad, the boys and I are driving back to London. Will you go with us?"

"And leave Olivia?"

Aubrey licked his lip, the tip of his tongue touching his thick mustache. Aubrey's eyes were wide and brooding, blue and intense like Olivia's, but his skin was coarse and ruddy from too much sun and too much drinking. Uriah stared off at the gentle valley with a Cotswold river running through it. The rustic bridge where he had first seen Olivia spanned the rippling water. "Your mother and I were happy here, Aubrey," he said.

"I know, Dad. I grew up here—remember? But there's nothing more you can do for Mother."

You're wrong. I can stay with her a little longer. "Son, there's room at the cottage. Come, spend some time with me."

The Kendalls' charming two-story cottage with its brick chimneys and steep thatched roof had once belonged to his great-grandparents. A dry stone wall surrounded the garden—Olivia's garden filled with the smell of wild thyme and marjoram and alive with colorful roses and lilacs. "Stay," Uriah urged.

"We can't, Dad. Ian saw what happened to Mother. Please fly back to the States with us."

"I'll stay at the cottage for a few weeks." His heart ached as he tried to lift his head to face his son. "I wish the Gregorys had come."

"Miriam's doctor wouldn't release her from the hospital. 'Pneumonia,' she said. I promised I'd call the minute I got home."

"Does Drew know yet?" Uriah asked.

"We still haven't reached him. Miriam's lawyer tried. I tried."

Uriah sighed. "I wish the prime minister had come."

"She sent flowers."

"They were friends. Did she have to send Dudley in her place?"

"She had to stick with the business in London. There was a bomb threat at the residence shortly after—" Aubrey cleared his throat. "Shortly after Mother was killed."

"But it proved a hoax."

"The bomb in the financial district wasn't. A Czech terrorist group took credit, *not the IRA.*" His mustache twitched. "Perkins says there's a connection between Mom's death and the terrorists."

Behind them Dudley Perkins's car door slammed shut. "We have to go, Dad. Perkins offered us a lift back to London, but the constable from Scotland Yard is staying on if you do."

"Edwin Wallis? Absolutely not."

"It's a precaution. Wallis knows about Mom's missing china closet and round table. He will be around if you need him."

"Your idea, Aubrey? Are you trying to find some link between the robbery at the cottage and your mother's—your mother's accident?"

"Yes. I've called the agency in London. Charles, the chauffeur, doesn't exist. They never heard of him. Edwin Wallis stays."

"Aubrey, we need to get something jolly well straightened out before you go. I make my own decisions. I'm not an invalid, son. Just—just a widower. I won't have Constable Wallis hanging around here and snooping through your mother's private papers."

"Do we have something to hide, Dad?"

Uriah swayed. For a moment it looked as though Aubrey would put one of his broad, sun-freckled hands on Uriah's shoulder. Uriah would have welcomed the grip. When it didn't happen, he glanced past Aubrey and saw Perkins drumming his fingers on the car window.

"You'd better go, son."

As he walked Aubrey to the car, Ian flung himself at his grandfather. Uriah lifted Ian's quivering chin. "Ian, no one is blaming you for what happened."

"Gramps, I couldn't go to her. Charles wouldn't let me."

Charles, the chauffeur. "I know, Ian." Uriah leaned down and embraced the boy. "We'll talk when I get home."

Aubrey glowered. "You're not to mention the accident to Ian again. He's to erase it from his memory. That's what I plan to do."

🕯️🕯️🕯️

The next morning tears stung Uriah's eyes as he left the bedroom he had shared with Olivia. He went into the empty sitting room. The walls were faded where the antique china closet and end table had once stood, but Olivia's desk sat by the window as neat as she had left it. Why would a thief steal her favorite treasures from her childhood home in Czechoslovakia? No, a thief would not be so selective. But if Olivia sent those treasures away herself, she never intended to come back to him.

He moved mechanically across the room to the desk. As he rummaged through the drawers, his housekeeper came into the room. "I've made you a cup of tea, Mr. Kendall, and some of those scones you love. You just sit yourself down."

He obeyed because he was too tired to argue after working late into the night, poring over boxes of Olivia's private papers. As she arranged the tray, he asked, "Maddie, did my wife tell you why she was going into London?"

The wizened eyes glanced toward the spot where the china closet had stood. "No, Mr. Kendall. But a few days before—before the accident—your wife and grandson took a place over near Stratford to be near an old family friend from Prague."

Beatrice Thorpe? Alive? Startled, he asked, "Whereabouts?"

"Mrs. Kendall said it was best if I didn't know. Told me not to worry about the cottage for a few days. I was just to leave it unattended. Of course, I couldn't do that." She swiped at a speck of dust with her gnarled fingers. "Your wife seemed different after her trip to Prague for the family funeral."

"I begged her not to go."

"That's what she said, but she was better when the boy

arrived. They were a special pair, those two. And the last thing she told me was to have the cottage spotless for your arrival and fresh flowers in the bedroom. I know she was pleased that you were coming."

"Then why did she call and tell me not to come?"

Maddie picked up his empty cup. "When your wife went away, she took boxes of her manuscripts with her. I've been thinking maybe that's what you've been looking for." She cleared her throat before saying, "I carried a box of family pictures out to the car for her. She said that friend of hers wanted to see them."

The pictures from Prague. Beatrice?

"There were other papers, Maddie. Private records. Her birth certificate. Some insurance papers. I can't find them—"

"She must have taken them with her. It's a good thing. That Mr. Wallis from Scotland Yard was asking about them yesterday—before you came back from the cemetery."

"What?"

"It's all right, Mr. Kendall. I sent him scudding off. Told him he ought to be ashamed coming here with his questions on a day like that. Especially with you grieving so."

"He'll be back, Maddie."

Uriah waited until Maddie went into the kitchen before he began another frantic search. He flung open the doors in the cadenza and checked the hall closet. No more boxes. Even the backup files on Olivia's computer had been wiped clean. These, like Olivia, were gone. She had left little behind to tarnish her name or reveal the truth about her last few days in London. Comforted with that thought, he left the house and made the lonely trek to Olivia's grave. He could lock the memory of the accident on Downing Street away even as it was already locked in Ian's mind.

Four weeks later Uriah left the Rolls Royce at the gate of the cemetery and went once more to the knobby knoll where Olivia lay. He shed no tears as he knelt and placed an orchid there. "My darling, I have to leave you now. I have burned the few papers that I found. I can do no more for you."

When he returned to the gravel road, a young man in jeans and a threadbare sweater was running his hand over the bonnet of the Rolls Royce, envy in his dark eyes. A well-worn backpack lay on the ground beside him. As Uriah approached, he reared back on his worn sneakers and jerked his thumb toward the car. "Yours, mister?"

"Mine," Uriah told him. "My London car."

"What I'd give to have a Rolls!" Using his sweater, he wiped a smudge from the chrome and then with unexpected bluntness said, "I'm sorry about your wife, Mr. Kendall."

"You know about Olivia?"

"Everybody in the village does."

"But you're not from here."

"No, I was born in Czechoslovakia. I've been bumming across Europe ever since I dropped out of school. But I always carry a couple of Miss Renway's books in my pack here."

He grinned, an amicable grin, as he bent down and flipped his canvas pack open. He held the book out and said, "See, your wife signed this one for me the other day in London."

A burst of rage shook Uriah. What right did this stranger have to boast of seeing Olivia alive? Alive in London. The image of Olivia on the rusty bridge here in the village— Olivia vibrant and beautiful—taunted him. He no longer wept at the thought of her dying. Tears had exhausted him. But inside he cried out. To be the last to see her alive—that was Uriah's right, Uriah's privilege, taken from him violently on Downing Street.

When he saw Olivia's signature in the front of the book, Uriah felt as though he would retch and empty his gut while the boy watched. He pushed the book away and walked around to the driver's side of the car.

The boy's watchful gaze followed him. "Don't be angry with me, mister," he said. "I'm like you. I lost my family, too."

Something about the sensitive mouth and the piercing dark eyes reminded Uriah of Olivia. She had looked that way when he first met her—an aloof young woman with velvet-lashed eyes, someone who needed a friend. This young man, eighteen or nineteen at best, was a loner like Olivia, a boy in need of a friend. Someone who read Olivia's books.

Impulsively, Uriah opened his wallet and took out a twenty-pound note. "I'm leaving now, but get yourself something to eat."

"You don't have to do that, Mr. Kendall."

"I want to."

The long fingers wrapped around the money. "I'd like to drive a car like this someday." As Uriah slid into the driver's seat, the boy asked, "Could you use a chauffeur, mister?"

Uriah laughed as the engine hummed. He hadn't laughed since Olivia's death, and the release was overwhelming. "I don't make my home in England anymore. You'd have to move to Maryland."

"That'd be okay. Anything to drive a car like this."

Uriah tapped his forefinger on the steering wheel. His mind had never cleared since the funeral, and now it seemed even more befuddled. If he drove away—left this stranger in the dust—he was leaving something of Olivia behind. This stranger had seen Olivia alive. Alive like Uriah wished she could be. He reached across and opened the passenger's door. "I'm driving back to London today. Right now. Would you like to ride along with me?"

"That would beat walking."

Dumping his backpack onto the backseat, he slid into the car beside Uriah and bounced on the leather cushion. "Like I told you, if you're looking for a chauffeur, I'm good with engines. Oh, by the way, Mr. Kendall, my name's Ned. Nedrick Russelmann."

Chapter 2

New York City, spring, 1996. It was Chase Evans's kind of day—a marvelous spring morning with the heat of seasonal changes nipping at the calendar, threatening the city with the early onset of a broiling Manhattan summer. Chase strolled lazily over the Columbia campus, her light-weight beige sweater tossed jauntily over one shoulder, a load of textbooks balanced in her suntanned arms. The pressure was off, her oral comprehensives behind her, and the plans for a summer abroad rapidly coming together.

As she drew abreast of the students sprawled on their backs on the south lawn, she realized that one of the classes had spilled out from the stuffy building into the freshness of an outdoor lecture. Instead of awakening the bespectacled student near her, the blistering sun was lulling him toward slumber. He lay with his head pillowed on a pair of dirty Nikes, a blade of grass dangling limply from his mouth. She allowed her gaze to wander back to the speaker. He wasn't the usual bearded professor with horn-rimmed glasses riding the tip of his nose, but a striking marine captain in full-dress blues. From head to toe he was spotless, his military cap tucked in the crook of his arm and his voice deep and sad as he vividly described his bitter years in the jungles of Laos.

She nudged the student, the sharpness of her polished toenail digging into his arm. Squinting up at her—his alert eyes magnified by thick lenses—he brushed her sandaled foot away. The blade of grass in his mouth raced from corner to corner as he grumbled, "What's your problem? You've got the whole lawn. Sit down."

She slid down and dropped her books on the ground between them. "What's a marine doing on campus?" she asked.

The blade of grass got a fresh gnaw. "He's just talking about the old conflict in Southeast Asia."

"The Vietnam War? The political club won't like that."

"*You* in particular?"

"He's probably off the wall."

Ignoring scowls for silence, he rolled to his side and braced himself on his elbow. "You got something against the military?"

"I believe in peaceful settlements."

"Wars don't work that way." With a flick of his finger, he opened one of her books. "Chase Evans, eh? I'm Kelly Carlson. You named for the old Chase Manhattan Bank or something?"

"No, for a close family friend."

"Some friend. Our marine hero up there has a tag, too. His old man is a retired admiral."

"Is that what got him on campus?"

"That or having an ex-father-in-law in the Senate."

"So he's political? Has he said anything worthwhile yet?"

"A bit on the blunders in Washington. That should please you. Bet you'd like to see a woman in the White House. Right?"

"Why not? If she qualifies." Chase was convinced that a woman would be there one day, a conviction that had sprouted at Vassar and intensified at Columbia. "I keep up an ongoing correspondence with senators and congressmen," she admitted.

"Demanding equality for women?"

"Lately I've been defending the rights of the elderly in nursing homes and fighting for more funding for AIDS patients."

"Like I said, you'd like that top office."

"Not really, but I want my vote to count when the time comes."

The blade of grass was back in Kelly's mouth, slurring his words. "Maybe that's why our marine hero went back to Vietnam three times—to make his vote count."

As a glowering student sought a quieter spot on the lawn, Kelly turned back to Chase. "I feel sorry for the captain. Some turncoat left him for dead in the Laotian jungles twenty years ago."

"Then he's the marine in the news lately?"

"Yeah. Caught in a government cover-up. Even took the rap for being a traitor. But he's an American hero now. That's politics for you. That's why I'm in chemistry. Science makes sense."

Chase swept her hair from the nape of her neck and felt the air cool her skin. "Why the uniform? Is he running for Congress?"

"It didn't help Ollie North any. I don't think this Luke Breckenridge will fare any better even if he is an admiral's son."

"Kelly, he's got good looks going for him."

"If you like older men with somber, unsmiling faces."

Yes, she could easily like this one. The marine captain had handsome, well-chiseled features. His sandy hair fringed with gray at the temples added to his good looks. And the deep scar that cut along his neck intrigued her.

Breckenridge's voice stayed well modulated as he said, "We could have won that war."

"Why didn't you, Captain?" Chase challenged from the rear.

Captain Breckenridge's piercing dark eyes fixed steadily on her. "I've asked myself that for twenty years."

"Then why did you go back there? Vietnam was a lost cause."

"Patriotism, ma'am," he said. "That's what motivated me."

With a chuckle, Kelly shouted, "Patriotism gets you killed."

Chase saw mocking indifference on the faces of the students around her, the response that she often gave her father when he spoke of Vietnam. She was willing to put odds on it—if these grad students had joined any war, it would likely have been on the side of the protest marchers. She wanted to unmuddy the waters and take back her own sarcastic comments, but it was too late.

She turned to Kelly. "The captain has walked into a den of lions. Like I did when I took my comprehensives."

"Breckenridge's choice. He was supposed to lecture us on the restored diplomatic relations with Vietnam. Instead he's defending America's right to be there twenty or thirty years ago." Kelly shrugged. "Forget the captain, Chase. What'cha doing this evening?"

She did another quick appraisal. Not bad looking, but his Nike laces were frayed and dirty, his T-shirt smudged. Her father would never approve. "I'm on my way home to Long Island," she said.

"With a stopover at the Halverson House?"

"How did you know about that?"

"I know Jeff Carlson."

"Oh, no. You're Jeff's brother!" she exclaimed.

"Yeah. I'm the brother *without* AIDS."

"You should see Jeff more. He talks about you all the time."

Kelly stretched on his back again. "Nothing to talk about. He got himself into that. I didn't."

"He needs you, Kelly."

"Why? Doc says he'll be dead in a few weeks." Kelly spewed the blade of grass from his mouth. It stuck to his T-shirt. "Jeff never was very smart."

He chewed hard on his lower lip and drew blood. Embarrassed, he looked away and then faced her again. "You can't save him. You can't make him well. Why waste your time?"

"I'm just trying to make a difference."

"Yeah, nurse said Jeff would have been gone weeks ago if you hadn't befriended him, but I don't think you did him a favor." His words startled her.

"Your brother is afraid to die."

"Aren't we all? How can you hack it? You're just wasting your time trying to right the wrongs in that place."

"I just read to Jeff and the others or play music for them."

"High classical stuff, Jeff tells me." He plucked another blade of grass and chewed it thoughtfully. "I think you sat in on one of my poly sci classes last semester, didn't you?"

She did a double take. "Yes, I had to drop out a week later for a business trip to Geneva with my father."

"You should have stayed with us. Then you'd understand what the man up front is trying to say."

"Do you?"

"I'm not interested in Vietnam or in any American company hog-jumping on business opportunities in Hanoi. We should account for the MIAs first." Kelly rolled to his side again and picked up the book with Dorothy L. Sayers's name in neon green. "*The Mind of the Maker?* What are you, Chase? Some kind of a religious zealot?"

She laughed, an easy ripple that turned more eyes their way. "I'm doing my doctorate on Miss Sayers and Olivia Renway—women novelists who tried to make a difference."

"To dying people like you do? You are an idealist."

"That's what my father says."

Kelly ran his fingers over Sayers's book again. "Don't you have any interests in life besides working on a Ph.D.?"

"Tennis. Sailing. Concerts. Dinner shows."

"Then have dinner with me tonight."

The idea repulsed her. "I have to get back to Long Island. I promised your brother that I'd drop by to see him this evening."

"Chase, don't you date?"

She glanced at Captain Breckenridge. "Older men preferably."

That wasn't true, but she'd never see Kelly again unless she ran into him at Jeff's bedside. She dated all the time, young men in their middle-to-late twenties who often bored her. She took Sayers's book from his hand. "And I study a lot, too."

"So you can't squeeze in time for a hamburger tonight?"

"Not really."

Captain Breckenridge had finished his speech and cut the crowd off on their seventh question. He took his visored cap and squared it on his well-shaped head. "Thank you for your time," he said.

He was booed from the rear as an unenthusiastic applause echoed in the crowd. Chase put her own hands lightly together and then, pitying the handsome captain, began to applaud loudly. Over the heads of the other students their eyes met momentarily.

Kelly swung to a sitting position, pushed himself to his feet, and brushed the grass from his patched jeans. He held out his hand and jerked Chase to her feet. "Well, I guess you'll be off then to right my brother's wrongs?"

What Chase wanted to do was apologize to Luke Breckenridge. She said, "Kelly, you could help Jeff if you visited him more."

"Sorry. Count me out. I get all choked up when I see him." He hoisted his book pack and Nikes to his shoulder. "I don't even plan to go to Jeff's funeral."

He started to walk off barefooted and then turned back to face her. "That's not true. I just don't know what to say to him."

"Jeff said you were close as kids."

"Real close." His eyes shadowed. "If he died in a war—died for some cause like that marine talked about—maybe I'd understand."

🦂🦂🦂

As Luke Breckenridge watched the crowd break up, he knew he didn't want to lecture about Vietnam and Laos ever again. He wanted to pack his uniform and ribbons away in mothballs and never put them on again. He needed to get on with his life. More than anything, he wanted to fly back to Europe—back to Sauni in Busingen, to the only woman he had ever loved.

Today's attempt to stretch the minds of these students and give them a glimpse of the hard choices made twenty years ago had failed, but strangely enough, he felt like saluting their backs as they sauntered away. His moment of jubilation was snatched from him as he saw a young woman push her way through the crowd toward him. He recognized her—the charming heckler who had applauded him. There was a fashionable simplicity to her outfit. She wore a short skirt and an orange tank top with a thin black belt pulled snugly against her narrow waist—and, Luke noted, she wore them well.

But don't come, he thought. *Not if you want to argue about the lost cause of Vietnam.*

The crowd was gone. It was just the two of them now. She stood there eyeing him from her five-foot-five vantage point, her long bare arms a copper tan. The sun gave a golden luster to her light chestnut hair. It fell in a stylish blunt cut, chin-level. He disliked hair hanging in a woman's eyes, but this girl's bangs had been swept back in a single wave above her left brow. He cocked his head, studying her as she studied him, feasting his eyes on a face that had surely been touched by an artist's brush. She was stunning in a wholesome way. Her wide brown eyes were open and direct, the long lashes curled up, the brows thinly arched like Sauni's.

"Did you miss my narrow Bartholomew nose, Captain?"

That was something Sauni might say, off-the-wall, direct, challenging. "I didn't know it belonged to the Bartholomews."

"Something I inherited on my mother's side. Satisfied?"

"Very much so."

With a quick comeback she said, "You're not bad yourself. Or maybe it's the uniform you're wearing."

He chuckled with a total sense of freedom.

"It wasn't that funny."

"No, but you are delightful."

"You didn't think so during the lecture." Without apology she said, "I'm Chase Evans. Bet you're glad that speech is over."

"The heckling was worse than going into battle."

She gave him a do-or-dare smile. "But you drew up the wrong battle lines, Captain. The students around here only remember the Bosnian war and the one in the Persian Gulf. So forget *your* war. You'll never convince my fellow Columbians that the American position was justified. I'm not sure you've convinced yourself."

He saw something of Sauni in those eyes, heard the challenge that Sauni had thrown at him so many years ago. "I believed in it back then. And you?"

The suntanned shoulders shrugged. "It's my father's opinion that America is rarely wrong. He was a marine there, too." Luke forced himself to concentrate on her words as she went on. "Captain, I'm afraid some of the Columbians of the Vietnam era are remembered for their protest marches, not their patriotism. It's passed down to my generation. Let's forget it and go have coffee."

"I am thirsty," he admitted.

She thrust her books into his arms and with a light, happy-go-lucky step walked through the campus with him. They ended up in a small cafe where Luke ordered orange freezes instead of coffee.

As they sat there, Chase said, "It would have gone better for you, Captain, if you hadn't worn that uniform."

"Are you all anti-military?"

She considered that. "No. I just thought you were using the uniform to impress us. Are you running for Congress?"

He choked on his drink. "I'm not interested in politics."

"You must have been twenty years ago."

"That was different, Chase."

She twisted her straw. "No. That war was all politics."

"At the time I thought it was all patriotism."

"You and my dad both. But you have Lyndon Johnson to thank for your tours of duty in Vietnam." Without missing a breath, she said, "Captain, has it been rough since you've been back home?"

Lightly, he said, "The last two months have been a nightmare. I felt like a nameless case number in hospital pajamas."

"Walter Reed Medical Center?"

"Germany first."

That's where military doctors had thumped and

pounded his body and taken pictures until he felt X-rated. Shrinks with placid smiles did their best to squeeze Luke's twenty years of exile into capsule form. High-ranking brass with gold braid on their shoulders interrogated him for hours, their mental calculators running at quad-speed. Things looked hopeless right on up to the day when the *Washington Post* headlines started the Associated Press wires sizzling. "Marine Hero Exonerated—Full Pardon Expected." Within days public opinion at home rallied to his defense, forcing his immediate transfer to Walter Reed in Washington.

"You don't talk much, do you, Captain?"

"Not about myself," he said.

"Were you this quiet when you first hit the States? Or did you at least show a little emotion?"

"I cried," he said honestly. "I came back to America on a medical evac." With a passport in his own name and with an honor guard standing at attention when his plane arrived. Langley intended for it to be a quiet reentry, but the public acclaimed him as a hero. "And then I was admitted to Walter Reed and had to face more debriefing and thumping and pounding and X-rays. And those endless couch-potato interviews."

"The shrinks, eh? Did it help?"

"In a way. But my mom says I'll get the most help on my knees."

"Praying?"

He laughed. "It's not a foreign language."

They sipped their orange freezes slowly and were lingering on a refill when her smile turned impish. "Why don't you dump that uniform and do something you really want to do?"

"Chase, I'm not sure what that something else is. I was trained as a military advisor."

"Haven't you heard about the military cutbacks?"

"Senator Summers, my ex-father-in-law, keeps me posted."

"That old filibusterer? How do you stand him?"

"He's changed. He's been supportive since I came home."

"So what does the ex-son-in-law of Senator Summers want to do with his life besides talk about Southeast Asia?"

"I honestly don't know. But no more speeches after today."

"Smart move. But you could make a mint writing that book on your lost years. At least that's what the news commentators say."

"I'm not lost anymore—so I didn't sign the book contract."

Whatever I do, he thought, *I don't want to do it without Sauni.* He pushed his frosty glass away. "Now tell me about you, Chase."

"There's not much to tell." She grinned. "I've spent *my last twenty years* living in New York. For the last six of them I've been a professional student. Dad calls it bumming around in the ivy halls. He wants me to get a permanent nine-to-five job. Pronto."

"So why don't you go to work, Chase?"

"I will next June when I finish my doctorate. I want to teach at the university level, Captain. If I can convince my father."

Luke couldn't see her confined to a stuffy classroom with a chalkboard behind her, but he said, "Then go for it."

"Over my father's dead body?"

He grinned. "I wouldn't get that drastic."

She held his attention talking casually about the Bartholomews, neither apologizing nor bragging about her family wealth. She spoke warmly of her friends in the nursing home. And then she grew heated as she told Luke that someone had to find a cure for AIDS.

"Let's try abstinence and higher moral standards," he suggested.

"What about babies born with the disease?" she countered. "Or innocent hospital patients who get it through blood transfusions. No, Captain, I'm concerned about people dying with an illness, not in lecturing them on cause and effect."

Luke took her rebuke quietly. He found her intelligent and sensitive, yet political; knowledgeable about her study program, but too idealistic. And he found her attractive, very attractive. He said, "You've sparked my interest in literature again. I'm going to read up on Sayers and Renway—and on AIDS."

She tugged at a tiny teardrop earring. "Then we can discuss them the next time we meet. Will you be in New York City long?"

"I'm leaving for Ocean City this afternoon."

She sighed. "How sad. I love New York City."

"Somehow that doesn't surprise me."

"I was seven before I realized that not everyone lived in a lovely old brownstone house and had a father working in the financial world." She took a final swallow through her straw. "I'm going to London this summer. I'll miss all of this."

"Then why go?" he teased.

"It's part of my research project on Olivia Renway. She left an unfinished manuscript behind—a lost manuscript. So I'm off to merry ole England to dig in the news files."

"Don't take on something you can't finish," he warned.

"I won't. I'm stubborn that way."

"I'll be in Europe myself. Look me up. I'll introduce you to my friends." He named them and added, "The Gregorys live in London." He wrote down Sauni's Busingen number. "Phone me when you get to Europe."

Chase's brilliant eyes sparkled. "You won't mind?"

"Of course not." *Funny kid,* he thought, but as she flushed with anticipation, the warning flags unfurled again. *Sauni won't like this.* Still he said, "I'd love to see you again, Chase."

Kendall residence, Maryland. For Uriah Kendall thoughts of Olivia's death were always the same. Senseless. Unfair. Too soon. So long ago. That moment ten years ago still lay half-submerged in his memory, all but forgotten for weeks at a stretch. Then some wisp of wind stirred the leaves outside their bedroom window. Or sounds of the London symphony playing *Fantasia* called Olivia back to him—her face so vivid in his mind that he reached out to touch her soft cheek.

The letter on the mantel had brought Olivia back this time, intensifying the thoughts of her that always flooded his mind toward the end of May. He was staring over at the letter when he heard Nedrick Russelmann coming into the study, a quick bounce to his steps, that friendly flash of a grin on his lean face.

At twenty-eight Ned was a gangly man with wistful dark eyes and a persistent troubled frown that wedged between his thick black brows. The frown and the wistfulness disappeared when he smiled. "Sorry, I'm late. I lost track of time."

"I thought you were out tinkering in my workshop or polishing that car again. Kept hoping you'd come in for a game of chess."

Ned averted his gaze. "I took the car for a spin."

To Washington again? Uriah wondered. Often without a word Nedrick left the house to cruise up and down the streets of Washington where the embassies were located. Calmly Uriah asked, "Did you drive on Linnean Avenue today?"

"On Reservoir Road this time. Saw a German diplomat arrive."

The car was Ned's territory—where he went, Ned's business. But Nedrick's intense interest in foreign embassies worried Uriah. They'd been together—the car, Uriah, and Ned—ever since Olivia's death. Ever since Ned ran his hand over the other Rolls Royce in England and asked, "Could you use a chauffeur, mister?"

Ned had dropped into Uriah's life at a time when life itself had come to a standstill. Now Uriah thought of him more as a son than a chauffeur, as part of the family—someone more loyal and dependable than Aubrey had ever been. "What about that game of chess, Ned? Or checkers?"

"Later."

Uriah's throat constricted as Ned went straight to the mantel and thumbed through the pile of mail. "Looking for something special?" Uriah asked.

"Yes, this letter from Chase Evans. She has no right bothering us about Olivia."

Us? Uriah thought. He often felt a strange closeness to Ned, a tie that he could not define, as though Ned were his son and not Aubrey. In unexplained ways, Ned reminded him of Olivia—solitary, sensitive, and fiercely independent. Ned had devoured Uriah's friendship as though he had been starved for it all his life. They brought out the best in each other, Ned refusing to allow Uriah to slip into permanent mourning. He'd miss Ned if he ever moved away.

Nedrick shook the long white envelope. "Have you done anything about getting rid of this Chase Evans yet?" he asked.

"My lawyer has called her twice now. Three times maybe."

"Is she blackmailing you, Mr. Kendall?"

"Blackmailing me? For what? No, money isn't the problem. Miss Evans is one of the New York Bartholomews." Weariness gripped him again. "What she really wants is to read Olivia's last manuscript."

Nedrick spun around, his dark eyes solemn. He ran his hand through the thick dark hair that whipped back from his high forehead. "Her unfinished novel? I thought it was lost."

"More likely stolen. Olivia had her attaché case with her when she left the prime minister's residence moments before her death."

"That was ten years ago. How can you be so certain?"

"She always carried it. It's the one I gave her."

Ned tapped the letter in his hand. "May I?" he asked.

Uriah stirred in his leather chair as though he were sitting on tenterhooks. He had no doubt that Ned had already seen the letter, but he said, "Of course, read it. Miss Evans seems to know everything about my family. The war. London. Olivia's days at Oxford. She even knows Ian is in Gascony preparing for the Tour de France." *But I pray she hasn't found some link to Prague that would tarnish Olivia's memory.*

Ned's scowl deepened. He slapped the letter. "She can't be serious. She plans to see Ian in France. Can't you stop her?"

"From writing her dissertation on the works of Olivia Renway? No. In a way it's flattering. But I won't let her disturb Ian and bring his grandmother's death back to him."

Ned forced a good-humored smile. "Ian can hold his own as long as he keeps his mind on winning that yellow jersey."

"Lately my grandson doesn't have the mind-set of a winner."

Ned grabbed the telephone as it rang. "Kendall residence," he said. "Oh, it's you, Gregory. Yes, Uriah's here. Just a sec."

Uriah bellowed into the phone, "Drew, where are you?"

"In Paris on my honeymoon."

"Then why are you calling me?" Without waiting for Drew's answer, he said, "I'm sorry I couldn't make the wedding."

"We understood. This time of year is rough for you."

"Yes, it's hard without Olivia. But Ian was there."

"We're worried about your grandson, Uriah. There are rumors that he's dropping out of the race. That he doesn't have the stomach for it since the death of his friend Alekos."

"Ian can't drop out. It won't matter if he doesn't win."

"It does to Ian. Why don't you fly over and be with him? Bring Nedrick with you. Or are those two still at odds?"

"They have their problems."

Uriah glanced at the letter back on the mantel. "Drew, there's a young student doing her doctorate dissertation on Olivia."

"Good choice."

Uriah reserved his opinion. "I'd like you to stop her, Drew. Her name's Chase Evans. She's bound to ask Ian where he was when Olivia was killed."

"But I'm on my honeymoon, man. Well—maybe Miriam and I can detour by way of the hills of Gascony for a visit with Ian."

"I'd be grateful. So would Ian."

"Gotta go, Uriah. Miriam is coming."

Uriah cradled the receiver and turned to Ned. "Could you

spare a month or two for a trip to Europe? I'd like to see Ian."

"Ian and I don't get on, Mr. Kendall."

"You could try for my sake."

Ned braced against the mantel, his hands in his pockets, his eyes dark with despair. "It's not just Ian, is it? You want to find your wife's missing attaché case before Miss Evans does."

"I've never wanted to find it," Uriah said. "The contents of that case may have cost Olivia her life."

"Why should I be interested then?"

Uriah closed his eyes trying to shut out the expression on Nedrick's face—trying to ward off the prickling doubt that rose again. Sometimes Uriah pondered on their chance meeting in the Cotswold cemetery. He wondered again now and heard himself saying, "I'd think you'd be very interested in the contents of that case."

🜊🜊🜊

Uriah knows. Ned wanted to cry out and defend himself. *I was there, but I left your wife's leather case behind when I fled.*

Nedrick dropped into Olivia's old chair and stretched his legs toward an unlit fireplace. Beside him Kendall looked suddenly old. "What did Gregory have to say, Uriah?" Ned asked.

"He said Ian blames himself for the death of his friend in Sulzbach. That's worrisome. When Olivia died, he withdrew for a time, lost in his own grief. We can't let that happen again."

A new threat, Ned acknowledged silently. Shock might force Ian's memory of Downing Street to surface, but it seemed unlikely that he could place Ned at the scene. The Towncar had been parked half a block away. Yet any risk was too great to take.

"What about it, Ned? Will you go to Europe with me?"

Ned dragged his heels across the rug. "I have other plans."

"I know, but I need your help." Uriah pressed his fingertips together, his smile faint. "I'm homesick for England, but I can't face going alone. Ned, will you put your own plans on hold and go with me?"

Nedrick greeted the question with silence. If he went to England, he risked losing everything. Ned glanced around the study. He'd come to love this old, well-furnished place. Ten years of good living. He owed Uriah something. "Okay, I'll go with you, and if Miss Evans gets to be a problem, I'll take care of it for you," he promised. *The Russelmanns always took care of problems.*

Chapter 3

Miriam came back into the room looking lovely in her sheer white dressing gown, her creamy skin glowing as she stepped gracefully toward Drew. Her hazel-brown eyes were radiant, her smile full and expectant. He took her in his arms and caressed her, his chin resting against her lightly scented hair. *"Liebling,"* he said, "I never dreamed I could be so happy again."

They began to dance without music, Drew humming the song so familiar to both of them. "Yes," she whispered, "I will be your partner for the rest of our lives."

He whirled her around the room, and they fell breathless on the edge of the bed, sitting there facing each other. Laughing, smiling. "You're such a gorgeous woman," he said.

She cupped his cheeks with her slender hands. "I love the way you stretch the truth." A frown touched her brow. "Drew, you were on the phone. It wasn't Langley, was it?"

"No."

"Don't tell me Troy Carwell knows we're here in Paris."

"Carwell won't bother us."

As CIA station-chief, Carwell tended to isolate himself within the embassy walls, a man committed to doing a job well. Drew knew that Troy's wife might be out climbing the steps to the Eiffel Tower, but Carwell would hold to his twelve-hour days on the Avenue Gabriel.

Miriam lured Drew back. "How can you be so sure?"

"He'd have to call every hotel in Paris to find us."

Drew had promised that there would be no evasive answers this time around. They'd go into marriage with the Agency on the back burner. He'd be up front with her as much as he dared without revealing Company secrets. Why was he finding it so hard to break old patterns? He gave himself a mental thrashing and said, "I was talking to Uriah Kendall."

"You called Uriah on our honeymoon?"

"That's what he asked. I told him Ian needs him."

She tightened the sash on her gown. "Did he believe you?"

"He will. Ian's his whole life."

"Drew, he has Aubrey and Grover."

Useless assets, Drew thought. "Yes, a grumpy, disagreeable son and a greedy grandson. Bet they make Uriah's life miserable."

"You do go on about them. I always got on with them both."

"You're diplomatic, *Liebling.*"

"I did it for Olivia. She never forgave herself for not faring well with Aubrey. She gave him everything."

Everything except herself. She struggled there. Drew smiled. "Olivia and I both had trouble giving ourselves."

"You're doing better," Miriam said softly.

"Miriam, when we leave Paris, let's hit the hills of Gascony and check on Ian."

"Uriah's idea?"

"I agreed to it. Uriah is worried about a young grad student who's researching Olivia's life and writings."

Miriam's dazzling eyes widened. "He should be pleased."

"Hardly. He doesn't want the girl anywhere near Ian. And he definitely doesn't want her digging into Olivia's past."

"Is that why Uriah ignored me after Olivia died? It wasn't until I opened the art gallery in Beverly Hills that we were in touch again. Even then he sent Aubrey to pick out the pictures."

"And you don't sell the cheapest paintings."

Those well-set brows arced above her brilliant eyes.

"Drew, if it doesn't sell for a million, I feel like I've been cheated."

He ran his finger gently across her lips. Miriam—gifted and beautiful. Would he ever have her completely to himself, or would a part of Miriam always be committed to the art world?

"Uriah wants us to meet the student," he said.

"Just for a friendly chat? Or in full battle armor?"

"Whatever it takes to keep Chase Evans from stirring up haunting memories for the Kendalls. Uriah doesn't want her to bother Ian. And he definitely doesn't want Miss Evans to know that marriage to Olivia cost him his career with British Intelligence."

"I always thought it quite romantic that Uriah gave up so much for the woman he loved."

"He didn't give up the British throne—just his career."

Her lips parted and then closed again. Drew was grateful that she didn't remind him of what his own job had cost them. "The Kendalls had a good marriage, Miriam."

"I used to envy them." She stroked his arm. "I wish Olivia knew that we were back together again. She wanted that for us."

"Not half as much as I wanted you back again," Drew said. "Back then we troubled the Kendalls. And now they worry me. I know that Uriah is hiding something about Olivia's past, something so important to him that he was willing to sacrifice our friendship."

Her joy slipped to a half smile. "Let Uriah work it out."

Drew's grin stretched the somber lines around his gray-blue eyes. "Bad idea, eh? Especially with us still on our honeymoon."

"I'm glad you remembered."

"I did. I even made reservations for us on the Riviera."

"Oh, Drew, a day or two in the sun, and I'll look like a lobster. Why don't we go to Prague instead? I promised one of my clients that I'd look into some paintings there."

Business. Miriam's business. Miriam's career. Drew sprang to his feet, leaving her alone on the bed. He paced across the room to the window with its magnificent view of the Seine.

Drew could sketch a map of Europe with his eyes closed, even the changing boundaries that had come with the fall of communism. He'd hit so many of the main cities in the Cold War, often in the dead of night. But the logistics were impossible even with open borders. Prague and the Riviera were miles apart.

He turned to argue. He was not willing to let her job come between them, but from across the room she met his gaze, her eyes shining. He couldn't marshal any enthusiasm for Prague, but he said, "If that's what you want, I'll cancel our reservations on the Riviera."

"It was just an idea, Drew."

"I'll have you on the Charles Bridge before you know it. But I thought he Riviera would please *you*." His smile swept away. It was happening all over again—this tiptoeing over eggshells. "Miriam, I thought we were going to be up front with each other."

She brushed her hair back from her forehead. "I'm sorry. I want you to be happy, and yet I really want to go to Prague. For Olivia in a way. I've been thinking of her a lot lately."

Miriam and Olivia had been special friends, their age difference insignificant, their love of the art world a strong bond. He hadn't been there for Miriam when her best friend died.

"*Liebling*, you can't bring Olivia back."

"She's never been far away, Drew. I can't tell you how often I've thought of her and our special times together."

"Promise me you won't do anything foolish in Prague."

"Like looking up her brother Dorian?"

"Let's just stay at the Adria a couple of days."

Prague would make their schedule tight; it might even prevent them from sidetracking to Germany for a surprise visit with Robyn. He'd planned a special surprise for Miriam and his daughter. The Von Tonner Art Museum was opening soon, and he planned to be there when Pierre and Robyn cut the ribbon.

"*Liebling*, I have to be back in London by the first of July and back at the embassy bright and early the next morning. That was the agreement with Troy Carwell."

"Is that what you really want—to go back to the embassy?"

No, he thought. *I want to spend a lifetime with you, whatever lifetime I have left. But I know you so well. You need space to move in—an art gallery to run.* "Langley is counting on me staying on at the embassy for a while. I told them I would."

The old code of silence rose between them. He could not tell her that there were problems at the embassy—that Langley wanted an insider checking it out. The trail of betrayals that Porter Deven and Aldrich Ames had left behind was still turning up rough edges with the threat of other betrayals in the ranks. This new threat of more traitors would keep him at his post in London.

"I don't want to think about getting back to England. Right after that, Drew, I have to fly home."

"London is home now, Miriam," he reminded her.

Her cheeks flushed. "Yes, and I'm anxious to get our new apartment in Chelsea looking just right for you."

"For *us*. And to rescue me from my old dark, dismal flat."

"It is dreary."

"Except for the painting you gave me."

She laughed. "Don't forget the hearth rug."

"I won't be happy seeing you off to Los Angeles."

"But, Drew, we agreed that I'd take frequent trips back to Beverly Hills until the gallery is running smoothly without me."

He held out his hands. She went to him, and their fingers entwined. "I'm sorry I can't fly to Los Angeles with you."

She leaned against his broad chest. "It's all right."

It wasn't all right. He knew she was terrified of flying alone. America was being plagued by terrorism now. He had never told her that a college friend—a former CIA officer—had died in the Oklahoma City bombing. The less she knew, the less she worried. But the worry shoe was on his own foot. Miriam's gallery on Rodeo Drive was an easy target for terrorists. He didn't want to lose Miriam, not when he had just found her again.

"It'll work out, Miriam," he said, trying to pour confidence into his words. "We'll make it work this time."

"We already have. I love you, Drew Gregory."

She reached up on tiptoe, and he leaned down to encircle her in his arms. "Drew, I always liked our reunions—even in the old days. I'll expect roses on my desk when I get to California."

"Yes. Eleven red ones," he promised.

🔔🔔🔔

Jarvoc, several miles west of Prague. Hanz Russelmann spaded the soil by the back porch, turned it over for the third time, and then stood up as tall as his hunched shoulders would permit. A proud man by birth and family tradition, his once-handsome profile remained strong, the bony German features distinct, well-chiseled. As his sun-weathered hands rested on the shovel, sweat streaked down his bristly cheeks and dropped on his gray work shirt. As far as he could see, the land was his own. The Russelmann farm spread out over the rolling hills and dipped down through the valley to a narrow winding branch of the Vltava River, and yet he was miserably unhappy. Despondent.

"*Guten Morgen*, Uncle Hanz," Mila called.

He looked up. His niece was leaning out an upstairs window, her face filled with more sunshine than the sky itself.

He waved as she exclaimed, "I love this time of year!"

Indeed, the bleakness of winter had ended, and the countryside had turned chartreuse green with the spring rains adding both life and color to the land. The distant slopes were blotched with yellow buttercups, and the wilting red geraniums in the window boxes had perked up.

"Oh, Uncle Hanz, just think—in a few weeks the hills will be an emerald green."

He envied her. Mila Van Rindin saw everything in golden hues and brilliant greens. His own sense of color had dimmed to grays. Sadly he said, "And then all too soon, winter will strike again."

"You worry too much about winter," she told him.

And why wouldn't he? In six months he would move reluctantly into another decade, ten years past his three-score-years-and-ten. Mila was twenty-six, but the winters of

Russelmann's life were running out. He shifted on his lame leg. The shattering war wound had made him an inch shorter and left him even now with throbbing pain at night. The ugly scar ran from his hip to his ankle, a constant reminder that he had once worn the uniform of a Luftwaffe pilot—that he had once dropped bombs over London, killing men who may well have walked the halls of Cambridge and studied with him before he was called home to serve on the losing side of the war. *Friends at university. Enemies at war.*

"Come down and help me. Tilling the soil is a lonesome job."

"I don't like gardening," she said.

"Then we'll pick berries."

"Some other time. . . . You miss her, don't you, Uncle Hanz?"

"Blanca?" The truth was, he rarely thought of her. He had been widowed for almost as many years as he had been married to her. She had been blinded by a stroke, wheelchair-bound, but Blanca had been a good companion. Yet he had never loved his wife. Even in marriage, his memories often strayed back to an air raid shelter in London and the girl he had left behind. His hasty departure from London in the dead of night during one of the worst air raids of the war robbed him of the chance to say a proper goodbye to his beloved British spy. Hanz had never forgotten Olivia Renway and never forgiven her. She had cost him half a million dollars in Kashmir sapphires.

"Uncle Hanz, do you think Nedrick remembers how beautiful it is in Jarvoc in the springtime?"

If it were not for the shovel, Hanz's legs would have buckled. His grandson was coming home. Yesterday's cable from Nedrick lay crumpled in his back pocket. Nedrick had disappeared from their lives ten years ago, his interest in the Russelmann factories in the Ruhr Valley, Poland, and Jarvoc nonexistent. Mila would never leave the farm, not when she was hoping that Nedrick would come back to her again. They had planned to run off together—second cousins, friends and dreamers—but Nedrick had gone without her.

Hanz felt her pain. His hope for the Russelmann family had always lain in Nedrick—Altman's only son. But Altman would not welcome Nedrick's return. Gruffly Hanz said, "Don't shed tears for my beloved grandson. It's best if he never comes back to us."

Mila disappeared behind the curtain, leaving him alone again, still leaning on his shovel. He felt beaten by time. His sons Altman and Josef considered him too old to make company decisions at the mill, but his mind was good, set in concrete against all war and all destruction. Only his body— that once sturdy six-foot-two frame—failed to keep pace with the demands of the Russelmann steel plant.

Hanz had only to turn to the south—as he did now—to see the gray ghostlike buildings. Funnels of black smoke rose from the chimneys of the far plant, curling up innocently toward the cerulean blue sky. It was eerie—like the rings of smoke and stench that had risen from the ovens and darkened the Czech skyline. Fifty years had slipped from him, but not the memory of the ovens. His factory? No, his son's now, but on paper Hanz was still the head of the family inheritance that had reaped devastation in the thirties and forties. He could never remove the stain of the evil that his father and grandfather had permitted. He could not even stop what was happening now.

As time grew closer for Hanz to render up an account of his own life, his flawed past haunted him. In recent months, Hanz had sought to find the peace of his Lutheran boyhood. Always when it seemed within reach, peace eluded him. The curling black smoke, the stench of the ovens, the blast of bombs took it away. He was certain there could be no peace for Hanz Russelmann, but he must stop Nedrick from coming back to Jarvoč. For Ned's own safety.

As Mila came out the door with a tray in her hands, Hanz propped the shovel against the wall of the house. "Here, let me take that for you, Mila."

She hesitated, her glance dropping to his lame leg. "It's heavy. I'm taking it to my father and the others."

Hanz shaded his dark eyes with one hand and stared out

toward the barn where the others were meeting. Then he reached out. "I was going out there anyway."

She pulled back, uncertain. "Then let me get another cup."

He waited, the wonderful aroma of hot coffee filling his nostrils. Mila came back at once and put another mug on the tray. She patted his hand. "Will you be all right, Uncle Hanz?"

Like Nedrick, Mila was filled with wanderlust and misgivings about the future. She had the Van Rindins' harsh German features, and the sun on her skin had robbed her of real beauty, yet she had an inner sensitivity, an unspoiled honesty. Impulsively he kissed her cheek, and then Hanz limped off toward the barn, the agony of the walk tearing at his limb.

His youth was playing itself out in the lives of his sons. Altman—the bastard son of the only woman Hanz had ever loved—and Josef the son of Blanca. He saw in them some of the old Nazi love of power—so gripping that they would do anything as long as they became rich in the process. For too long he had turned a blind eye to his sons' nefarious transactions with third world countries that wanted nuclear power. His sons were pleasant-appearing men, but they were trapped in the unforgivable scurvy of deficient minds—men capable of the atrocities of past generations of Russelmanns.

Hanz's hip felt on fire, his leg dragging at his commands. Still he walked proudly. *I am walking into hell itself*, he thought. *But I will beat my sons at their own game.*

Somehow. Some way.

🐞🐞🐞

Altman Russelmann stood in the open barn door, his back to the others. He toed out his cigarette, grinding the butt angrily into the ground, and turned to face Jiri Benak and Gustav Van Rindin, Mila's father. Gustav's two sons were there, too—Pavel who looked browbeaten and Franz with the brooding, dark face.

"My father is coming," Altman told them.

"Good," Gustav said. "Do you want me to tell him that he is no longer in charge?"

"No, Gustav. I can handle my father."

Gustav smirked. "You haven't done a good job of it lately."

Altman tossed a pack of cards on the table. "Shuffle those, Franz, and, Charlie," he told Pavel, "go and help my father before he stumbles with that bum leg of his."

"Isn't that the scar of the old Fatherland?"

"Don't let Hanz hear you say that, Charlie."

Pavel glowered through his tinted silver-rimmed glasses. "Don't call me Charlie. My name is Pavel. I hate your constant reminders that I botched that job in London."

Gustav's fat jowls bobbed as he looked at his son. "That was a long time ago, Pavel. Ten years. You just weren't cut out to be a chauffeur. We know that now."

Pavel's bitterness festered as he fingered his thick mustache with angry strokes. "Altman, you never told us you planned to kill Olivia Renway."

"How many times have I told you—that wasn't the original plan? Franz got out of control. We just wanted the Russelmann sapphires back." He thumbed their attention to the blond man at the end of the table. "But Jiri blundered that one."

Jiri tapped his cigar against the chair arm. "Renway wasn't wearing the bracelet that day. At least I grabbed her briefcase."

"What good did it do us?" Gustav asked. "It's rotting in Altman's safe with none of the rest of us privy to its contents. And for what? Renway wasn't as well-informed as we thought."

Wrong, Altman knew. *But we won't go into that.* A copy of his own birth certificate had been in the briefcase, proving that he was the son of Olivia Renway. And the manuscript pages and notes were full of veiled references to the Russelmann factory with their Japanese and Iranian interests clearly marked out. But how had she known? Hanz? Had his father confided in her?

Altman tried to speak, but for a moment hostility controlled his tongue. He could never be reasonable where Olivia Renway was concerned. Even her death had not alleviated his constant suspicions. She remained in his mind, not as his mother, but as a threat to his financial empire. His mandates had destroyed her—his own hands left pure white as Franz and the others obeyed his orders. But Altman had not destroyed what his mother knew about the Russelmann family.

His voice wavered. "We couldn't risk what she knew."

"You set us all up, Altman," Pavel said. "Renway's young grandson saw the accident. He saw what happened to her."

"Forget it, Charlie. It happened a long time ago."

"Do you think the years erased it for that boy?" He nodded toward the open door. "Go carry your own father's tray, Altman."

Jiri's narrow face grimaced. "It's Nedrick who should be angry, not you, Charlie. He didn't know who she was. I just said, 'Talk to her, Ned. If she's Olivia Renway, get her autograph.'"

"I have no doubt that my son knew that she was his grandmother. Nedrick and my father were always close. Always sharing things," Altman said. "I should never have trusted Nedrick—never have allowed him to be there when Renway died."

Franz rubbed his temples. "He got even taking refuge in Uriah Kendall's home. But, Altman, doesn't it bother you? Renway was your mother!"

In the split-second silence that followed, Altman's rage burned hotly against Olivia again. "She deserted me because I was the son of a German pilot."

Gustav overlapped the chair as he sat down. "We may be cousins, but let me remind you—thanks to your mother, you are half Jewish. If you had been in Germany during the war, you would have been tossed into a concentration camp."

"I am not Jewish," Altman shouted.

"Deny it then, but Olivia Renway was part Jewish. Never mind, Altman, being British was bad enough."

Altman forced himself to ignore Gustav as Hanz entered the barn and limped across the room. As Hanz spanned the distance between them, coffee sloshed over the edge of the tray.

Hanz's eyes looked dark and sad as though life had cheated him of its best treasures. Perhaps death would come sooner than Altman expected. With any luck they would not have to wait long for his demise. But in truth, he was reluctant to lose his father. The old man's approval still meant something to him.

Hanz glanced around at the others. "Well, what is it this time? Has another Japanese contract gone awry?"

"The opposite," Gustav said. "Foreign sales are up—especially with our Nishokura account. No thanks to your vote."

Altman raised a hand, silencing the threat of another verbal duel between the two men. "Father," he said, "Gustav and I have been discussing your resignation."

"Your takeover plans, you mean? Wait a few years and I'll be dead. You won't need my resignation then."

"Father, it's time to sign over your responsibilities to me. You've earned the right to just putter in your garden."

"Apparently your brother is not in agreement. Where is he?"

"Josef is at the plant overseeing new orders."

"Orders for steel or orders for warheads?"

Altman stiffened. "That's preposterous."

"That's what I thought." Hanz didn't know, but he said, "I know about the stockpile of weapons now. And about the sarin."

"We don't manufacture nerve gas. We're a steel industry."

"That's what my father and grandfather said of the family business in the thirties. But they lied. I know they lied."

Gustav pounded the table. "Hanz, we had nothing to do with those Tokyo disasters—nor the one in Korea."

"And you haven't tried to break the embargo on Iraq?"

Gustav lumbered from his chair, his fat cheeks scarlet.

"Sit down, Gustav." Altman's voice steadied as he turned back to Hanz. "We have legitimate contracts, Father, worldwide. Check the records if you want. But we've never sold any nerve gas or any of its components to the Orient."

"But perhaps one of the countries you do business with did."

Altman watched his father's gaze go slowly around the table to the faces of the men he had come to despise. Hanz was right. They were all clever, power-hungry men, himself included. Jiri had been given too much power, Pavel too little. But his father's contempt seemed to bypass Gustav and the others and settle once more on Altman. He braced himself for more ridicule.

"Don't get involved in sabotage, Altman."

"That's strange coming from you, Father."

Gustav butted in again. "You've gone mad, Hanz. One way or the other, we plan to take over the plant."

"No, you may need me at the helm a little longer."

Hanz took Nedrick's cable from his pocket and slid it across the rough tabletop within inches of Altman's long fingers. "Go on, son. Read it."

Altman snatched it up and read it. "It's from Nedrick. My son is coming here to Jarvoc." He held the cable in his fist and shook it at the others. "Some nonsense about a young woman who wants to research Olivia Renway's life and find her missing manuscript. But she won't find it. It's safe."

Hanz rested his head in his hands as though he could no longer sit upright in the chair and face his illegitimate son. Behind them a clucking hen scratched her claws against the straw. "Do you think Olivia was so unwise as to have only one copy of that manuscript?" he asked.

Gustav's scowl deepened. "She was clever enough to marry a former British agent, but Pavel and Jiri found none of her manuscripts at the Kendall cottage in the Cotswolds. Altman, I'm against your son coming to Jarvoc again. He'd just be trouble."

Altman flicked his fingers, willing the numbness to ease. "No, my son comes. If Ned has betrayed us, we'll deal with that later. If necessary, we'll destroy him."

Hanz lifted his face, his voice strained as he said, "Altman, don't you understand? Nedrick is concerned about us. Why else would he contact us after all these years?"

"He contacted *you*, Father. The cable is addressed to you."

"No, Nedrick is reaching out to all of us. That should be warning enough that this girl—this Chase Evans—cannot be trusted. Perhaps Evans is a plant—or worse a CIA agent herself."

"Then we'll silence her, Father. But all of this is of no consequence to you. Your beloved Olivia is dead."

"Son, to me she was dead long before she died."

But for Altman, his mother would never be dead. She haunted his memories. He was part of her. He had tried to destroy her—but she was there. Her marriage to Uriah Kendall had locked her into intelligence work. Now with terrorism spreading throughout the world—and the family coffers growing as a result—he would not risk Chase Evans uncovering the facts that Olivia had gathered.

Slowly Hanz pushed himself up, balancing on his lame leg. "Was there anything else, Altman? Did you want me for anything else?"

"We want your resignation, Father."

The older man shook his head. "I'm staying on at least until I talk with Nedrick. If there is anything that I can still do for this family, it is to keep that boy away from the rest of you."

"Father, he is not a boy. He'd be twenty-eight by now."

"I'd forgotten. He's still eighteen when I think of him."

"No, he's a grown man now." Altman suddenly brightened. He thumped the cable in triumph. "There's a slim hope. He's a Russelmann, Father, and he's coming home. Coming back where he belongs. He can be most useful to us."

Hanz's craggy face, lined with years, paled. "Altman," he said, "I've regretted the day I went to Cornwall and found you. I would have been better off if I had never known you existed."

"We would have both been better off, Father."

Chapter 4

Early Wednesday morning Chase Evans left her home on Long Island and stopped off at the Willowglen Nursing Center before catching the train into New York City. The Willowglen was a three-winged single-story building buffed white by the annual paint job. For the ninety-nine residents inside, the fresh coat of paint and the smell of a newly mown lawn did little to lift their spirits. Two days ago old man Wellington had died in his sleep, and, surprisingly, his bed was still empty. The ninety-nine simply waited as Joe Wellington had waited for the toes-up departure that would eventually come to each one.

As Chase walked down the wide corridor, a lump rose in her throat. Just a week ago she had sat beside Joe Wellington in the chapel service, strangely moved by the hymns that had lulled Joe to sleep. For hours afterwards she had chewed on the words of the squat, round-faced young preacher with fuzzy blond hair. With a booming voice for one so stunted, he had described the wide and narrow paths on which he seemed certain the residents of Willowglen tottered. His face had turned purple as they dozed off, and Chase, out of kindness, had given him her attention, even nodding in agreement as he spoke of heaven and hell. Heaven had been whispered softly around the Evans's household—a question mark behind it—when her grandmother Callie died; but hell seemed always channeled to the ravages of war and the battlefields of Vietnam, which her father described as "hell itself."

Lately Chase found herself caught up with growing uncertainty. What could she offer to her friends here at Willowglen or to the AIDS patients at Halverson Wayside House? She could hold their hands while they died, but she could not promise them an eternal tomorrow; she didn't even know whether anything existed beyond this life. She never held Callie Bartholomew's hand, not until the last day. Callie, Chase's maternal grandmother—although she never dared call her that—had spent the last few weeks of her life at the Willowglen, refusing visits from her oldest and dearest friends.

At seventy-three, while still a glamorous woman, Callie left the oncologist's office, canceled her world cruise, and put her much-loved brownstone home in New York City on the market. Without a word to her family, she had moved to Long Island and admitted herself into a private room at the Willowglen. Even as the tentacles of death encircled Callie, she had tried to convince herself that when you died, you died. Nothingness. Chase hated thinking about it. What if Callie had been wrong? If so, all the Bartholomew millions didn't gain her entry into what lay beyond.

On her last visit in that antiseptic room, Callie had held out her thin hand, and Chase ran across the room to take it. "Dear Chase, I've been a foolish woman," she had said, her glazed eyes full of fear. "Hold my hand, child. I'm so afraid."

"It'll be all right," Chase had promised.

"No, it's too late to prepare for tomorrow. Too late—"

Then having turned her back on family care and spiritual comfort, Callie had done her toes-up in the middle of the night when the private duty nurse had stepped briefly from the room.

Willowglen did nothing but remind Chase of Callie and those spur-of-the-moment flights to Paris and Milan to buy a fashionable outfit for the latest New York ball. Chase had inherited much of Callie's vivaciousness and her unrelenting devotion to causes, even if it meant stepping on the toes of the wealthy. Callie was stinking rich herself, the

Bartholomew name as well known as Rockefeller or Kennedy.

What Chase had liked the most about Callie was her marvelous sense of humor. At the dedication of the Bartholomew Library in memory of her late husband, Callie had tripped on the way to the podium. Strong arms had lifted her up and set her back on her feet. With a flick of her jeweled wrist she had said, "My beloved husband would have been embarrassed, but he's not here—at least I don't think he is—so let's get on with cutting the ribbon, and you students can get on with your lives."

But it hadn't been an accident. Hours later pain seared through Callie's leg, setting off the alarm that would end in a diagnosis of bone cancer. After Callie's death—or perhaps because of it—Chase had gone back to Willowglen to fill the lonely hours of others.

She turned into the west wing and found her friends in the back dining room, lined up in rows on both sides of the table—mouths sagging, lips parted for a spoonful of lumpy mush. Marie spotted her first. One by one the youthful faces of yesterday turned her way. Chase tried to imagine how they must have looked before the wrinkles appeared, before they had grown inevitably old and were confined in wheelchairs. Peg must have been tall and stately, not hunched and toothless as she was now. Maude squinted through half-blinded eyes that were once a brilliant blue. They were all there—all but Joe Wellington. Alice with the angelic smile, Daphine with the arthritic fingers, and dear Marie. How could Chase tell them that she planned to be gone for the summer? How could they tell her that they, too, might be gone before she got back?

She managed a quick "hi" for Alice, a hug for Daphine, a whispered "I love you" for the new little lady with the vacant stare. Then she pulled up a chair beside Marie and met those faded blue eyes with a smile. Marie's yellow-white hair had been pulled back from her face into a single ponytail that hung to her waist. Her face seemed thinner this morning, her grip on Chase's hand feeble. "I missed you, Marie, but I'm only here for a few minutes. I'm on my way to the university," she said as she offered her some juice. "But I'll come back."

At least once more before I leave for London.

Twenty minutes later she was on her feet, squeezing the blue-veined hand. She pressed Marie's head against her, and then, with a quick wave to all of them, she left the Willowglen in tears.

She indulged in a self-pity party as the train rattled into New York City. A subway ride later she was on the Columbia campus making her way to Doc Hampton's windowless cubicle with a slit of light showing beneath the door. Chase stopped and knocked. She rapped again seconds later. Hampton, she was certain, would be glaring down at some student's final exam, a red marker in his hand, his mood aggravated by the disturbance outside his door.

She risked a third brusque rap and heard his gravelly response, "Come in. I have all the time in the world."

Chase thrust the door open. "Good morning," she said. "I'm sorry I'm late. I stopped off at the Willowglen again."

He thumped the papers on the desk. "I wasn't going anywhere."

Nigel Hampton was not her image of a British don strolling leisurely across the lawns and walkways of Oxford in a black flowing robe—hair windblown, conversation philosophical, his honors too numerous to mention. The truth was, he had little hair to be wind-tossed; thin strands of washed-out brown stretched across his balding head, secured in place by something with a pleasant, albeit unfamiliar, scent. Chase had no doubt that he could easily match the intellect of C. S. Lewis and handle hours in the pub dissecting literary topics and wars and politics. Sometimes in the classroom, Hampton scared her half to death, but she liked the man and admired his brilliance and wit.

"You wanted to see me? About my prelims?"

"If you could have stuttered on paper, you would have."

Her heart sank. "Doc Hampton, I didn't—"

"You did well. Four major exams, and you did well."

He seemed both surprised and pleased. She heaved a

sigh, but he still didn't smile. "It's not my comprehensives?" she asked.

His voice seemed as grave as his expression. "I should never have persuaded the committee to hear your orals early. You could have used another week or two to prepare."

"But you're leaving for England."

"Someone in the department could have filled in for me."

"Yes, one of Prof. Marsten's old cronies."

"A prospect that's shaky at best," he admitted.

Chase's long legs locked at the knees. "Prof, didn't I make it?"

He seemed determined to extract something from the old-fashioned inkwell on his cluttered desk. Chase fixed her own gaze on the crook in his wide nose and then on the cleft in his chin.

His narrow face drew down to his long, sagging jowls. "I warned you to be confident when you took your orals. You looked terrified," he said.

"What did you expect with the six of you throwing all those curves my way? It was like a lion's den."

He chuckled. "And Prof. Marsten put up quite a roar."

"Professor Hampton, what about my orals?" she persisted.

"They went well. You're a good student, Chase, but sit down. Let's salvage your research project."

She lowered into the chair. "I thought you approved it."

"I did provisionally, but Marsten put thumbs down on any comparative study of Olivia Renway and Dorothy L. Sayers. She says you're putting too much emphasis on Renway's missing novel."

"They both had unfinished works. Sayers left an unfinished biography of a nineteenth-century novelist. Someone else finished that. But Renway! No one knows where her last manuscript is."

"Do you?" he asked.

"No, but it's important to my research project. I know it sounds brazen, but I'd like to find it and finish it for her."

He gave her a hard, brittle laugh. "That's unlikely, Chase."

Involuntarily, Chase's imagination went wild. Had Olivia Renway been carrying that thirtieth novel in her briefcase as she walked down the rain-soaked street, an umbrella clutched in her other hand? In her mind's eye, Chase could see the London rain splashing against Renway's ankles and could hear the horrible screech of brakes and the final cry of pain as Renway's battered body was crushed by the speeding car.

She tried to calm the frustration in her voice, saying, "Prof, two weeks ago I wrote a letter to Olivia Renway's widower to ask his help. I heard from Mr. Kendall's lawyer instead."

"Not good," Hampton said.

"Mr. Kendall refused any interviews, but the attorney did say that Kendall is going to London for the summer. Probably to his Cotswold cottage." She crossed one slender leg over the other, her sandal balanced on her big toe. "I haven't figured out how yet, but I'd really like to look him up when I get there."

Hampton shuffled through the mess on his desk, finally finding his thick spectacles in the clutter. He scowled as he put them on, making deep horizontal lines across his forehead and three vertical lines between his brows. "Pry too much and you'll need a lawyer of your own."

She shrugged indifferently. "I'm a Bartholomew, sir. I don't let lawyers scare me off."

He stared absently at the old-fashioned inkwell again. "Chase, are you certain you don't want to consider a project on Thoreau instead?"

Hampton seemed to be backing away from her. Without his support, Marsten would tear her project apart. "Is the committee going to reject my proposal after all the work I've put in?"

"With a bit of a rewrite, I'm certain we can get it passed."

"But you're flying back to England." She could never muddle through without him. "I wish they'd extend your sabbatical another year."

"My wife doesn't. But don't worry, Chase. I've convinced Marsten that we'd have your revised proposal back on her desk in a fortnight. That's the best I can do for you. So there's nothing stopping your trip to Europe."

"My summer abroad is dependent on my dad's funding."

The three vertical lines on his forehead became one. "Isn't it time you paid your own way? You're twenty-three now, aren't you?"

"Twenty-four. In another nine months I'll cash in on my inheritance that's been tied up in the courts for months."

Hampton's mouth twisted as he asked, "What would happen to you if your father's financial world collapsed?"

"You don't know my father. Everything he touches turns to gold—at least, into stocks and bonds and mutual funds."

Seymour Evans's calculated risks had taken him the whole nine yards—a CEO in the aircraft industry, a mansion on Long Island, a Blue Water sailing yacht for his weekend pleasure, banking reserves in Switzerland, and a foreign account in London. Chase felt a sudden urge to defend her father, to trace his long journey from barefoot boy to wealthy Long Islander.

"I won't apologize for my father's success. He's worked hard for it. Dad grew up in poverty and joined the service to put clothes on his back and three meals a day in his stomach."

"Is that why he married into the Bartholomew family?"

"He didn't marry the family—just my mother. Dad came out of the marines twenty-nine years ago before the Vietnam War had gone full scale and persuaded my mom to marry him."

Hampton's chair squeaked as he turned. "Posthaste—before her parents found out, according to Marsten."

"Marsten wasn't there. But she's right. The Bartholomews were outraged," she admitted. "But my dad earned every dime he has himself. And I'm not letting a doctorate slip between my fingers just because I'm Seymour Evans's daughter."

Her outburst seemed to please Hampton. "Good," he said. "And after your doctorate, what then, Chase?"

"I'll teach at the university level like you do. You keep

telling me there's nothing more promising than to touch a student's life and mold his mind."

Hampton's smile turned generous. "So you have been listening to me! Can I tell Marsten that you'll be getting back to her in a fortnight with a revised proposal?"

"Yes, but when I tell my dad I'll be in Europe, he'll have fits worrying about me driving on the wrong side of the street."

"I'm prepared to make you an offer that he can't resist." She met Hampton's twinkling gaze across the desk as he said, "You can stay with my wife and me at Oxford, safely out of the traffic jams in London. I'll be your mentor. Marsten approves of that."

"Oxford? Why would you do that for me?"

He looked away. "I considered voting with Marsten to stop your project. I wanted to stop you," he said darkly. "Marsten wanted me to persuade you to do your dissertation on the Inklings—Tolkien and C. S. Lewis with Sayers thrown in—"

"And omit Olivia Renway?"

"Yes, but whatever your reasons, you have to choose your own study." His eyes were back on her, his expression full of concern. "I won't try to stop you," he promised. "I can only pray that nothing happens to you while you're abroad."

Pray? She had never thought of him as a man who prayed. "You're not making sense, Dr. Hampton."

"Renway's tragic death was a topic of conversation at Oxford. She was one of our own, a Somerville graduate, you know. Whatever skeletons lie in her closet are best left there."

"You sound like you dislike her."

Again he hesitated. "You'll learn soon enough that Lord and Lady Kendall disapproved of Renway marrying their son."

"Why?"

"There were questions about her background that threatened to ruin their son's career. In the end it did."

"Prof, I'm interested in Renway's writings and in Dorothy Sayers's influence on her life and career."

"You're a stubborn one, but then if you took my advice and studied Thoreau, you wouldn't be coming to Oxford this summer. No, the committee won't stand in your way if I support you," he said, giving way to a faint smile. "But, Chase, you're going to have to decide how to handle Sayers's belief in a deity."

"Do you mean God?" she asked, surprised. "Marsten is tough enough."

"Sayers wrote more than mysteries. Among other things, she was a persuasive theologian." He slapped the desk. "Enough. What about Oxford? You'll find us a bit more traditional."

"You're not a totally hip campus?" she teased, glad that his mood had lightened.

"We didn't exactly rush out and get wired, so don't expect a new million-dollar computer lab at your disposal."

"Will I have access to the libraries?"

"I'll arrange it."

"Will your wife mind my coming?"

"She's fond of my students. She'll be particularly fond of you, once we tell her about your friends at Willowglen."

He ran his fingers through his thinning hair, his green eyes turning merry. "You and my wife will get on quite well," he said. "She drives about an hour each day to an elderly residence. The Eagle's Nest, they call it. Half of them can't walk, let alone fly, but my wife spends all of her time there where no one has any recollection of Chaucer or C. S. Lewis."

The literary ignorance at the Eagle's Nest seemed an affront to him. Chase said, "It sounds as if you don't like them because they don't remember."

"My wife accuses me of that." He was suddenly back to extracting thoughts from the inkwell. "Yes, you'll find my wife's place of business most interesting."

"Is it like Willowglen?"

"The residents are. Some of them are a pathetic lot." He thumped the marker against his hand, streaking his palm with red. "You'll want to get to know one of them. I think she's batting ninety-five. A jolly, independent old thing with nothing to do but knit multicolored lap robes. A dowager as old as the London Bridge."

"Don't make fun of her, Professor Hampton."

His bristly chin got a pensive rub. "You'll know what I mean when you see her. She sits in her private room in fancy clothes and a high felt hat as though she's stepping out any minute."

"Is her memory good?"

"At ninety-five? Better than mine will be. She's happy dwelling in the past. She may not know anything about Chaucer or C. S. Lewis, but she definitely remembers Prague."

"I don't understand, Prof."

"You will when you meet her. She knew Olivia Renway."

Chapter 5

Long Island, New York. At seven on the button, Chase came out of a fuzzy nap at the sound of her father's footsteps in the hallway. She had come into his private study after supper and taken over his sofa. She closed her eyes again, measuring his steps as he crossed the marbled hallway. Silence. He'd be by the stairs now, setting his attaché case down and hooking his hat—that he never wore but always carried in the car—on the shiny brass knob at the foot of the cream rail. Precisely, keeping the folds perfect, he'd lay his suit coat neatly over the railing. She heard his warm, muffled words to the dachshund puppy that had somehow won favor with him and taken up residence inside the family mansion. Puddles and all.

He called up the stairwell. "Nola, it's me. I'm home."

He'd forgotten, as he always did, that Nola was never home ahead of him on Wednesdays. Her Wednesdays were crammed full with committee meetings—she chaired four of them—or with playing bridge, which she hated losing.

That confident thud of Seymour's steps came closer as he entered the study and brushed past the sofa without pausing. His leather chair squeaked as he sat down and slapped his case on the desk. Chase thought of her father as heart-attack prone, a man in a pressure cooker, but his blood pressure only shot sky high when he talked about her inability to settle on a permanent career.

She was not afraid of her father, but she could not please

him—not unless she quit being a professional student and landed a top position in some corporate office in New York City as her brother Tad had done. It frustrated Chase that her father always came out on Tad's side. The only other way to long-lasting approval would be to marry a wealthy New York attorney as her sister Adele had done.

Chase's father was a marvelously successful man himself: self-made, well-disciplined, professionally groomed. He was as predictable as the seasons. His day started at 5:00 in the morning when he slipped out of his king-sized bed, showered, dressed, and took breakfast alone: one egg, two pieces of rye toast—one with jam, one with butter—and two cups of black coffee, sugarless as he was. Promptly at 5:45, he would leave the house, toss one of the two morning papers into the car with his hat, and drive off to work in his Lincoln Towncar, arriving well ahead of his employees. Except for phone calls and one luncheon date a week with Nola, Seymour stayed out of touch with the family until seven in the evening.

In spite of his demanding schedule, Nola had adapted to dinner at eight and a companionable evening sitting together in the family room, Nippy the dachshund nestled on one lap or the other. At eleven straight up, Seymour flipped on the evening news. At midnight Chase's parents went up the wide steps arm in arm. They'd talk—and sometimes laugh—for another fifteen minutes, and then silence until Seymour's loud snoring echoed through the walls.

Saturday was reserved for his wife's social calendar, Sunday for an eighteen-hole round of golf with three of his friends. On lucky Sundays he would invite Chase to go along to fill in for a missing partner. She played well, somehow pleasing him.

For another minute or two, Chase heard him rattle papers on his desk, and then across the room from behind his large mahogany desk, he said, "I assume you want to talk to me, Chase?"

She swung to a sitting position. "Do you have time, Dad?"

Curtly he snapped, "I always have time for my family."

She didn't argue. At unexpected moments, he did set

aside his work, however briefly, to talk with them. Into his rigid schedule, he sometimes reserved a slot for family matters—his wife's guest list, Tad's latest speeding ticket, Adele's marital disharmony, or Chase's endless aspirations. She realized that this was one of those golden moments as he asked, "Well, what is it?"

"I'm going to Oxford this summer on a study program."

Only one brow lifted. "How do you propose to pay for that?"

"I was hoping you'd help me."

A twinkle glinted in his eyes. "You mean, pay your way. Your last study program in Europe was a total fizzle."

"That doesn't count, Dad. I was seventeen then, off to a year of finishing school in Switzerland."

"It about finished us. You almost flunked out."

Chase took the old fight with her dad good-naturedly. "Dad, I was majoring in social activities. And I did learn French."

"And I paid through the nose—a heavy endowment to the school to keep you there and an outlandish fee for two tutors, *not one,* to thump something into that featherbrain of yours."

She smiled. "My I.Q. is much higher than that."

"When you choose to capitalize on it as you did at Vassar."

He didn't mention Nathan, but she felt a flush in her cheeks. Nathan, that gorgeous thirty-five-year-old Swiss tutor, had spent more time flirting with her than teaching her calculus. When her father caught on, Nathan had been dismissed. Once Chase came home and entered Vassar—a miracle in itself—she did a complete turnaround, taking honors, and pleasing herself as well as her parents. She was hooked. Learning was addictive.

She walked across the room and sat down in the chair facing her father's desk. He was meticulous in his wrinkle-free blue shirt with a navy silk tie knotted in place. He looked every inch the CEO of his own company, the commander-in-chief of his own household. Chase could never decide whether he was handsome or not with his silver-foxed hair

and Grecian skin; his eyes were so dark brown that they
appeared black as she looked at him.

"Dad, I'll have my doctorate in another year."

"Do you have to go to England to get it?"

"I'm studying up on two novelists who lived there."

He straightened a pile of work sheets, already in perfect
order, and placed them in his attaché case. Then he drew
the household ledger toward him—each dime, each purchase neatly penned in the appropriate column.
Accounting records were essential to Seymour—as though
at any moment the poverty of his youth would catch him
unawares. He seemed always braced for his own financial
crash. The crash of '29—she'd heard it a thousand times—
had left his family unemployed and his mother in long
bread lines.

He opened the ledger. "How much will it cost? Ten
thousand?"

Hopefully she said, "Fifteen, maybe. And then I'll need an
expense account and my air fare."

The figure Chase named was small—her father dealt in
million-dollar contracts. He folded his hands on top of the
ledger. "I suppose you've discussed this with your mother?"

"Once or twice."

Chase saw the first hint of defeat in her father's face. "It
doesn't worry your mother—your constant chasing after the
wind, your endless schooling. But it worries me that a
daughter of mine still doesn't know what she wants to do
with her life."

She didn't want to hear a repeat of her father's rise from
emptying wastebaskets to a top position in the corporate
world. The thought of her teaching at the university level
would blow him straight out of his leather chair. He wasn't
into tenure and long-haired students, musty libraries and
research papers. Teaching, she knew, wouldn't offer the
advancements that he coveted for her.

"Chase," he demanded, "these British authors—are they
accomplishing something worthwhile with their writings?"

"They did before they died."

"Two dead novelists? What started you on this wild idea?"

"I've been wondering what happened to Olivia Renway's missing manuscript."

"And who is Olivia Renway?"

Chase's mother answered from the doorway. "If you read books for mere pleasure, you'd know. She was a British-born novelist. Quite well known. And, dear, very rich! That should impress you."

No, Czechoslovakian, Chase thought.

Nola crossed the room to the cushioned chair near Seymour's desk. Her soft brown hair was cut short; the blue-gray eyes wide, the skin folds above them puffy. She looked tired, but then she slept poorly, catching most of her sleep after Seymour stopped snoring. She had a built-in time clock that made her spring from the bed by 7:30 and be on the go, full speed ahead within the hour. Nola loved the out of doors—swimming and sailing, golfing and gardening. Long hours in the sun had taken their toll on her skin, leaving it coarse and blotched with wrinkles long ahead of time. But what Chase loved about her mother was her happy smile and the straight, open gaze that met hers now.

Nola sat down and crossed her legs, one open-toed slipper tapping the air. She folded her large-knuckled hands, one on top of the other, her chin resting on them. "I gather that you and Chase have been discussing London," she said.

"So this is another of *your* schemes, Nola?"

"Why not?" his wife asked. "I want you to fund Chase's summer. If you don't, Seymour, I will."

Her threat was real. She had become financially independent again with the Bartholomew inheritance. Seymour leaned back in his chair, his interest finally aroused. "How will a summer abroad prepare Chase for the business world?"

"If you mean investments, it won't. Your Dow Jones averages don't interest her. Nor me, really."

"They should. My wise investments keep us in luxury."

"Don't take all the credit, my dear. My parents taught me about wise investments long before you came along."

"Nola," he said patiently, "writing a dissertation that sends her chasing off to England is a waste of time. She could just as well pick a political theme like America's involvement in the war in Southeast Asia. She could even include that marine hero who lectured at Columbia the other day."

"Luke Breckenridge?" Chase asked, clearly remembering that handsome face. "Dad, he wasn't anything spectacular. Oh, he's a handsome hunk, but he's no football or basketball star or pop singer. Strip away that marine uniform and what do you have?"

"May I remind you, Chase, I was a marine."

"You remind us often enough," Nola said.

"And Vietnam was my war. It would make a good topic for your dissertation."

Chase shrugged. "And you didn't even start that conflict. It doesn't matter, Dad. I don't want to research Breckenridge's life. He's been out of circulation for twenty years." The memory of Luke's sad smile filled her mind. "Dad, he was kind of shy and out of place in twentieth-century USA!"

"Twenty years of captivity does that," Seymour said. "Never mind, Chase, with your mother on your side, you win. Forget the marine hero."

"I may see him again. He told me he's going back to Europe."

"What's wrong with the good old USA? When I came back from Vietnam, America was good enough for me."

"He hates the crowds and the news media, so he's going to help set up some art museum in Germany. And," she said with an air of mystery, "he expects me to call him when I get to Europe."

Seymour unbuttoned one shirt sleeve with jerking motions and folded it above his wrist. "I don't want you contacting him over there."

Nola laughed. "So now you don't trust the marines. Then why don't you laser off that *semper fidelis* tattoo of yours?"

Her mother had scored. Seymour almost always wore long-sleeved shirts, even in the sizzling summer, anything to hide his tattooed biceps in public. He still boasted about his days with the marines, but he withdrew when his wife or daughters pressed him for tales of his wild and woolly days as an off-duty marine.

"Chase, phone the captain and let your father talk to him."

Seymour gave the idea a quick thumbs down. There was no appeasing him. "Dad, Prof. Hampton invited me to stay in his home in Oxford. He's offered to be my mentor for the summer."

Seymour stared at her, more disgruntled than ever. "I trust that's all. Attend Oxford? What will that cost me?"

In that flash Chase decided that if she ever married, it would be on the run. She wouldn't dare wait for her father's approval. "It's a private arrangement. Prof. Hampton promised me access to the libraries there. It's a chance of a lifetime, Dad."

"So is getting a permanent job."

Nippy chose that moment to enter the room and piddle on the plush ash-blue carpet. For a second no one moved, and then Seymour pointed angrily at the dachshund. "Get that dog out of my study. I have work to do. We'll talk about Oxford later."

Without even glancing at Nola, Chase went to the door and mopped the damp rug with her sweatshirt. She scooped Nippy up into her arms as she left the room. His squat body and drooping ears draped over her arm as she hurried down the long, spacious hall and skidded to her listening post. The intercom system went throughout the house. She flicked on the button into the study—a trick that Tad had taught her when they were children.

Her mother's voice came through clearly. "Seymour, don't say that again. Our daughter is not lazy. She chalks up twenty hours a week volunteering. And that on top of her studies."

"All at my expense."

"It costs less than Tad's speeding tickets, and it doesn't hurt your reputation. I constantly hear about Seymour Evans's lovely daughter—the good she does for the abused elderly in nursing homes, her hours with children on the pediatric ward."

"It's her time at the Halverson Wayside House that bothers me. Risking her health with those AIDS patients."

"Sometimes, Seymour, I think you are totally witless. She will not contact the virus by reading to them."

"She's a stubborn one, that girl."

"She is, unfortunately, a chip off the old Evans block."

"Hardly," he groused. "You won't find me in any AIDS march. I wish Chase would keep her political convictions to herself."

"You never did."

"Nola, I can't support this Oxford whim of hers."

"She'd have her own money if you hadn't talked my mother into adding that codicil to her will—just before she died. It was unfair to delay Chase's inheritance—to want her treated differently from Tad and Adele."

"I simply suggested that none of the children should inherit until they were twenty-five. Your mother agreed."

"Callie loved Chase. You took advantage of mother's ill health. You used her to try and force Chase to stop going to university and find a permanent job. But I'm proud of Chase. She's the only one of our children who will have a Ph.D.!"

"She's the only one without gainful employment. I don't want her to be thirty and jobless. I can't foot her bills forever."

"Funny," Nola said sadly. "You never stand in Tad's way."

"He's always made the right choices."

"Your choices for him. It has left him a social disaster." Pain crept into her voice. "In case you've forgotten, Chase never went off on drugs like Tad did. She's a good girl, Seymour."

"She's a woman."

Chase kept her hand cupped around the puppy's mouth and heard her father drumming his pen on the desk. "Tad's okay now. I'm proud of him."

"Are you proud of his divorce, too? Seymour, she can't be like Tad, and surely you wouldn't want another Adele. Give it nine months; then Chase will have her own money. Thanks to my mother. But help her now, please."

The pen clapped more loudly. "A doctorate won't change her."

"Oh, Seymour, if only Chase could please you."

He coughed. "You said that about me once to your mother."

"Callie came around in the end. 'My self-made son-in-law,' she called you. She just wanted the best for you."

"I want the best for Chase. I want her to marry well."

"That may not mean marrying into money, Seymour. We had nothing when we started out."

Chase expected her father to explode. Instead, he said huskily, "I hated it when your parents cut you off. It took me so many years to provide for you the way they did."

"It didn't matter. We had each other."

"Your mother never forgave me for not taking you on a proper honeymoon. She told me that a day or two before she died."

Nola's laugh turned merry. "That did eat at Callie's pride. Dear mother! She never admitted to her friends that we went off for six days to a broken-down summer cabin."

Seymour's voice lightened. "And we came back flat broke without even the foggiest notion of how we would survive or where we'd live. When your father called me in for that Bartholomew lecture, I could have thrashed him for suggesting an annulment."

"I almost fainted when you told him that it was too late for that. But I did think he would offer you a job."

"You know I refused it. I told him I'd make it on my own."

"Yes, you earned your own way from the day I married you. Chase is so much like you. She'll be all right, Seymour."

Chase predicted what would happen next and heard her Dad's husky voice saying, "Nola, I love you."

"That's why I've stayed with you all these years, Seymour." With a breezy laugh Nola said, "Wouldn't you like a summer alone? Just the two of us again?"

Chase pictured Nola slipping behind the desk and leaning her sun-browned cheek against Seymour's. "I'm sorry. I am guilty of spoiling our children."

"You win again," he said quietly. "Chase can have her

way. Pack her up. I'll open another account for her in London."

"Can we send a new laptop computer with her?"

"What about that state-of-the-art system in her bedroom?"

"She can't carry that on board the plane."

"Anything, Nola. I'll have my secretary tend to it. At least I won't have to be embarrassed with Chase waving banners on some street corner in Long Island for three whole months. She can take her causes to the streets of London."

Chase was about to switch off the intercom when he added, "But, Nola, I'm uneasy about her trip abroad. All alone."

"You always worry about Chase, darling."

"It's different this time. It's not just the money. I keep thinking back to that Oklahoma City bombing and the disasters in the Tokyo subways. I couldn't bear it if anything happened to Chase." His voice faltered. "I'm quite fond of her, you know."

"Then why don't you tell her that?"

"I don't know how." He sighed heavily. "It's easier to write out a check."

Chapter 6

Ocean City, New Jersey. Luke Breckenridge stood at the attic window in the bedroom he had once shared with his brother Landon and stared across Asbury Avenue. The media trucks were gone. Not a single out-of-town visitor gawked up at the shingled two-story house with its front porch spotless from his mother's scrubbing. He swung open the shutters and sucked in the ocean air, wondering if he'd soon be free to walk the boardwalk of his hometown and not be recognized. He longed for anonymity, even for the isolation that he had known for all those years when people thought he was dead in the Laotian jungles. A dead traitor.

Betrayal in the jungles of Laos remained a vivid memory. His captivity had left his back and jaw scarred, his mind often in the torture mode. His stateside reentry process and the long weeks of tests and interrogation had added to the pressure. If Luke had appreciated any of the top brass who grilled him, it was the lanky shrink with the bushy eyebrows and half-mast eyelids that hid an amused twinkle. Sid Grozfelt had a slow drawl and a backwoods approach that didn't win ribbons from his fellow officers, but they won Luke's approval.

Even now Luke smiled at their last interview. As Grozfelt had come into the hospital room at Walter Reed, Luke had snarled, "Is the black crepe for a traitor still hanging on my door?"

"Didn't notice," Sid said as he sat down by the window.

"I'm fed up with these four walls that separate me from my family." *Sequestered even from Sauni.* "I might as well be dead."

"Nothing wrong with the view from this window, Captain."

"It would look better from the outside."

Sid turned, grinning. "That's what I told the committee after another phone call from your wife. She sent her love."

"You heard from Sauni? I haven't."

"The switchboard is still monitoring your incoming calls. The operator gave Mrs. Breckenridge a bit of a run-around before transferring her call to my office." He chuckled. "I wouldn't want to cross wires with your wife often, Captain."

In his slow drawl, he quoted Sauni, "'All this political maneuvering—they've been holding Luke's family in mourning for twenty years now, and they still won't let him go. Do I have to fly to Washington and talk to the president himself?'"

Grozfelt leaned back in the chair, a silly grin on his face. "Captain, your wife thinks I'm your chaplain. I do make a rather good confessional sometimes."

Before Luke could react, two officers from Langley barged straight into Luke's private room. Chad Kaminsky shut the door and leaned against it as Harv Neilson, the better groomed of the two, stormed toward the bed where Luke was sitting.

"CIA big boys," Luke hissed.

Grozfelt unraveled from his chair and placed himself firmly in Neilson's path. "Sir, may I help you?"

"We're here to see Breckenridge about his escape from Laos," Neilson said. "And his time at the mercenary camps in Europe."

Sid took a small notebook from his shirt pocket and flipped to a blank page. "No need. We've already discussed those issues. Besides, when Captain Breckenridge leaves here, he goes with a clean bill of health from Walter Reed. *A free man.*"

"But we're from Langley."

"So Breckenridge tells me."

"It's all right, Grozfelt. Sooner or later they'll track me down." *Or have me killed*, Luke thought. "Let's hear them out."

Neilson was a bookish man with law degrees and a brusque manner that turned nasty as he said, "We'd like to speak with Breckenridge alone."

Sid's voice remained calm. "I'm his doctor. I stay."

As Neilson glared down at him, Luke asked, "Are you here to discuss my CIA mission in Laos?"

"No, but if you were held in Southeast Asia against your will—as you claim—how did you escape from there?"

Luke had answered that question a hundred times already in the hours of interrogation. Again he stuck consistently to his belief that his escape from Laos had been Russian-orchestrated.

"Russian?" Neilson mocked.

"If not Russia, then it was the work of the CIA."

"Next you'll tell me Porter Deven arranged your freedom."

"No," Luke said. "Porter Deven wanted me dead."

Though Neilson hounded him, Luke remained guarded about his time at the mercenary camp in the foothills of the Pyrenees.

Neilson's eyes hardened. "You were the brigadier commander there."

Luke's response remained polite, clipped. "Yes, sir."

"You were there for monetary gain?"

"No, sir."

"Where are the men you served with?"

"I don't know, sir."

Neilson no longer denied Luke's brief association with the CIA, but he didn't admit to it either. Luke could imagine the detailed triplicate reports that would follow the Neilson-Kaminsky visit. At the door as they left, Neilson's gaze slipped past Grozfelt and settled angrily on Luke. "Porter Deven was a good man. You ruined his career, Breckenridge."

"He was a traitor, Neilson—the traitor who betrayed me."

The muscles on Neilson's jaw throbbed. "You should have died in that mercenary camp, Breckenridge."

"Nice chaps," Grozfelt said as the door slammed behind them. "But, Breckenridge, you really got to them with that 'Yes, sir. No, sir. I don't know, sir.' Where are those men now?"

"In Africa perhaps or bloody-well wounded or dead, many of them lying in unmarked graves in Bosnia or Chechnya."

"And you think you owe those men something?"

My silence mostly and only sketchy recollections for the record. Aloud he said, "There have always been foreign legions, Sid, filled with misfits and renegades willing to fight another man's war for a price. That wild riffraff of mercenaries trusted me. No matter what price I have to pay, Sid, I won't expose them." But he would, as he did often now in the deep quiet of his soul, pray for their safety.

"Well, Breckenridge," Grozfelt had said on discharging him the following morning, "I've talked the brass into setting you free. You've got a good mind, Captain. Forget Porter Deven's betrayal. Don't let the bitterness of lost years destroy you."

With an unmilitary stance, Grozfelt extended his freckled hand and gave Luke a phone number. "If you ever want to talk things out again, call me. We can't give you back the years you lost, Captain, but make the time that's left count."

Luke didn't even wait for his parents to drive down to Walter Reed to pick him up. He rented a car and sped home to Ocean City, a resort town already bracing for the summer crowds, home to the best set of parents a man could have. As he settled into the familiar environment, his thoughts often strayed far from the Jersey shore to Sauni in Busingen, Germany. Sauni Summers was the only woman he had ever loved, the gal he had married, the young wife who had left him when he went back to Vietnam for a third tour of duty. Since coming back home, he had racked up enormous phone bills with his transatlantic calls just to hear her say, "I still love you, Luke."

His solitary musings were interrupted by the sound of

the front doorbell ringing. He dreaded the thought of another reporter with a new angle on the Luther Breckenridge story.

"Luther. Luther." The soft, mellow voice of Amy Breckenridge echoed up the narrow stairs. "Luke, dear."

He went to the top of the stairs and smiled down at his mother, a genteel woman, her kindly eyes full of love for him. "Dinner won't be until seven. But you have company."

"I was afraid of that." Luke ducked his head to avoid the low-pitched ceiling and made his way down the steps. He kissed Amy on the cheek. "Who is it, Mom?"

"Said he was a friend of yours. A stranger to me."

Luke found his guest engrossed in the rogue's gallery that went the length of the hallway. "You have to see this to believe it," Sid Grozfelt said staring up at the generations of Breckenridges in uniform. "I take it that this one is the admiral."

Luke nodded toward the sitting room. "That's him in person."

Luke's dad dozed in his maroon leather chair, his stocking feet on the hassock, his unused pipe on the table beside him. He looked old and beaten sitting there, aged in the long years of Luke's absence. He was no longer the proud, rigid man that Luke had known as a boy.

"Let's not disturb him," Grozfelt said. "Why don't we take a drive, Luke? Or a stroll on that boardwalk of yours?"

"What's wrong, doctor? Or do you always make house calls?"

"I haven't heard from you since you left Walter Reed. Thought I'd drop by and check on you myself."

"A three-hour drive?"

Luke's mother watched them from the kitchen door. "I'll be back in a couple of hours, Mom," Luke promised. He waved and followed Sid to the porch. "Where to?" he asked.

"Your brother's grave. Your high school. And the boardwalk."

Luke didn't question Grozfelt. His therapeutic approach didn't fit the textbook. "Let's hit the boardwalk first," Luke said. "It's just a few blocks walk from here."

"How's your recovery program, Luke?" Sid asked as they strolled along.

"I'm better. This is the first day without the news media. But I don't feel like a hero. I don't even want to be one. Maybe I should have stayed back at the mercenary camp."

"That kind of retreat would be like going back to the leeks and garlic in Egypt."

Luke sighed. "Mom tells me that life will get back to normal. But when, Sid? I've spent half of my life in exile."

"Vietnam wasn't your fault, Luke."

"But the mercenary camp in Spain was my choice."

"Understandable. You had no place to go. No legal papers to identify you. Porter Deven robbed you of a lot of years. But don't forget you have a full pardon now."

"Are there any other decisions in Washington I should know about?" Luke asked.

"Besides balancing the budget and giving tax advantages to the wealthy? Some good news for you. Public opinion swayed Spain to drop the charges against you."

Luke grabbed Grozfelt's arm. "I've been expecting the worst, but this means I'm really free to go back to Europe."

"I'd say so. But there's still some concern in the House about your training of mercenary soldiers. It'll take time."

Grozfelt sauntered over to a hamburger stand, ordered, and went heavy on the mustard and relish. He spoke with his mouth full. "Luke, what about those book contracts—in seven figures, right?"

"Is that why you're here? Do you have a problem with that?"

Sid almost choked laughing. "No, just my curiosity."

"I turned them down. I don't want to repeat the Laotian story ever again. I don't even want to remember it."

Sid stopped in the middle of the boardwalk. "Is your wife behind your decision to drop the book contracts?" he asked.

"Not really. But a university student thought I was crazy."

Chase Evans—that was her name. A pretty, young woman with chestnut hair and tiny earrings at her well-shaped ears. He ran down the fragmented recollections: lipstick that matched her polished nails; a stylish, low-cut tank top; and a voice light and quick like a summer breeze. "We had a chat after I blew a lecture at Columbia University. She spent the next hour trying to convince me that my speech hadn't been all that bad. Nice girl, Sid. You'd rate her high on your scale."

Sid wiped the mustard from his mouth. "What's important is whether she means something to you or not."

"Just friends. She's to call me when she gets to Europe."

Grozfelt let that one ride as they ambled over to the railing and stood there watching the four-foot waves wash away the top layer of the beach. In the deafening roar of the water, as the waves crashed beneath the boardwalk, Luke tried to recapture the carefree days of his boyhood. But his thoughts kept somersaulting back to sea, trying to beat the raging Atlantic to the other side of the world where Sauni lived.

"Any more trouble with nightmares, Luke?"

Luke gave Grozfelt a twisted grin. "Coming home was just what the doctor ordered. I feel as safe as a little kid again."

"No flashbacks? No anger?"

"Will they ever go away, Sid? Sometimes I think I still hate Porter Deven. He ruined my whole life."

"He can only destroy what you let him destroy. Tell me, Luke, is your former wife still in the picture?"

Luke wiped his palms on his jeans. Miserable flashbacks of Southeast Asia and Spain—those faces from the past— kept Sauni at a distance. "I can't ask her to share the torment of my personal battles."

"Do the battles have faces?" Sid asked.

Luke couldn't voice them: the bamboo cage in the Laotian jungle, the roving Pathet Lao troops that hunted him down, the mercenary camps in Europe where he trained men to kill, and his unrelenting rage at Porter Deven—the CIA officer who had betrayed him. "Sid," Luke confided at last, "I can think of Vietnam and Laos now and dwell more on Neng Pao's friendship than on the betrayal. Without my friend Neng, I would never have made it. Maybe it will be that way with Porter Deven in time."

"A day at a time, Luke. Use some of those mental gymnastics that helped you survive in Southeast Asia. You'll come through, especially with that young woman in Busingen rooting for you."

Luke turned. "You've been in touch with Sauni again?"

Grozfelt's eyelids opened wider, his amusement more apparent. "Several times. She still thinks I'm the chaplain. Imagine—a nice, little Jewish boy like me! Mrs. Breckenridge is quite a woman! When will you two get back together?"

"I don't feel good enough for her."

"There you go again, putting yourself down. Look at the bright side. She never remarried. She went to great lengths to clear your name. You're still young, Breckenridge—vibrant and virile. Getting back with your wife is quite feasible."

Grozfelt didn't wait for an answer, but said, "I won't ask about your financial state, but Congress and the military are still dragging their heels. They did make one decision—seems like nothing will be done about the life insurance policy. They voted against asking your parents to pay it back."

"I have some back pay coming to me from the marines. That will tide me over for now."

"Twenty years' worth?"

"That hasn't been decided. But at least I'm covered for the captivity time in Laos."

It was 7:15 before they got back to the house. "Come in and have dinner with us," Luke suggested.

"No, I need to get back to Washington."

"And turn in your reports on me?"

"No reports. We'll just chalk this up as a visit with an old friend." Sid's handclasp was firm as he said, "Keep in touch, Captain. Call me collect if you have to, even from Europe."

Luke waited until Grozfelt drove away, and then he went back inside the house. He paused at the sitting room, a lump rising in his throat as he saw his father still sleeping in the chair. Luke longed to walk across the room and put his arm around the admiral's shoulders. He smiled instead and left him undisturbed.

When he reached the kitchen, he grabbed an apple and leaned against the sink watching his mother. She searched Luke's face. "You've decided, haven't you, son?"

He met her honest gaze. "Yes. I'm going back to Europe."

"You're not happy here?"

"Sauni's over there."

"Your dad and I will miss you. Dreadfully. We like having you up there in your old room or spending your evenings with us."

"Europe may not be permanent. It depends on Sauni."

"There's something even more important for you to consider."

He touched her wrinkled cheek. "I know. Your prayers haven't been wasted. Nor Sauni's. I'm sorting all of that out, too. But I'm still having trouble believing in God's Son when He took yours."

Tears filled her eyes. "Don't, Luke. Landon was so ill. I prayed that God would set him free."

Luke couldn't buy that. "Did you pray that way about me?"

"No." She turned on the faucet and filled the teakettle. "Even when we buried what we thought was your body, I didn't want it to be true. Not when you weren't at peace."

"Landon was at peace," Luke said. "I want that, too."

"It's all right, Luke. Even if you don't believe completely yet, at least believe the miracles. Your honorable discharge. The miracle of your survival. Surely God had a purpose in this."

"You talked about miracles when Landon and I were boys."

"I'd forgotten."

"I didn't. I thought of it often these last twenty years."

Her hands looked dishwater red, her steps slow as she took her kettle to the stove. Inside, Luke knew, she was a tower of strength. She'd always been there—for all of them.

She turned on the burner and looked back at him. "Luke, do we have much longer with you?"

"Several days. I'm scheduled to speak at the graduation at Ocean City High before I can leave."

"And you're to be introduced at the Tabernacle."

The Tabernacle was as familiar to him as the boardwalk and Shriver's salt water taffy. The old building had been replaced with modern architecture with a cross on top; it was as much a part of his mom's roots as the house they lived in. Her pride was wrapped up in his speaking to the town where she could hold her head up—now that he was no longer called a traitor. He winked. "I'll spend those fifteen minutes bragging about my parents."

She picked up his apple core and threw it in the garbage bag. "Did you go over to Landon's grave again today?"

"Yes. Grozfelt went with me. He's my shrink, Mom. He was assigned to help me sort out the last twenty years."

"But the cemetery is a private matter, Luke."

"I told Grozfelt that I could always talk things out with my brother. He knows I still miss Landon. Like you do, Mom."

Her lip trembled as she lifted the lid on the vegetables. "Luke, work it out with Sauni. If you get back together, we'll come to see you." She sighed. "Have you told your father yet?"

"No. He'll worry about not being here when I get back."

"Your father is good for a number of years. We both are. Having you alive and back in our lives was all we ever wanted." She brushed strands of her silvery hair away from her face. "I'll fret about you being alone over there. What will you do while Sauni teaches all day?"

"Drew Gregory's daughter offered me a job at the Von Tonner Art Museum for a few weeks." He grinned, confident now. "I promised her four days a week making picture frames. That leaves my weekends free to drive up to Busingen."

"Luke, you won't get involved with Drew Gregory, will you?"

"I thought you liked him."

"I do. Very much. But, Luke dear, he's still with the CIA. Dad and I don't want anything to happen to you."

"Mom, I'll be careful, but I can't forget that Drew saved

my life—at least he gave it back to me. I was CIA once. Remember? Briefly in that one big mission in Laos."

She swayed and had to lean against him. Wiping her hands on her apron, she said, "Oh, Luke, we're going to miss you. You won't leave until after that visit to the White House?"

"No, Dad's counting on it. I think he'll get more kick out of shaking the president's hand than I will. I think this full pardon was forced on the president."

"It won't hurt his political position either."

"While I'm in Washington, maybe he can get me an invitation to Annapolis before I leave." Luke tried not to sound bitter. "I'm not exactly their favorite son in spite of my full pardon."

"But, Luke dear, you're my favorite son."

Chase waited by the phone, hoping that Luke Breckenridge, the tall, handsome marine hero, would call her. She kept picturing the distinguishing gray strands that edged his thick sandy hair and those dark eyes, one moment sad, the next hypnotic in their intensity. The uniform with all its ribbons had set him apart, making him appealing, easy to think about.

They would meet again! Even if she lost all of her luggage on the flight, Chase had no intention of losing Breckenridge's address. Luke reminded her of the strengths that she most admired in her father, someone who would surely go places. Luke was far more exciting than her usual dates— and there were plenty of them: Tom who saw dating Seymour Evans's daughter as an open invitation for a day on board the family yacht, Randy who hated it when she won at golf, and Calvin the bookworm who was dry as dust even on a dinner date.

Captain Luther Breckenridge had not been boring.

She closed her suitcases and locked them. As she reached the stairs, her father glanced up at her. "Well," he said, frowning at her oversized bags, "I see you packed lightly this time."

He met her halfway up the steps and took her luggage. "You won't change your mind, Chase?"

"About the trip? No, Dad."

"I hate to see you go. It's an unsettled world out there."

As they reached the porch, she touched her father's cheek in a rare show of affection. "Once I get my Ph.D., I'll go to work. You'll see. If all else fails, I'll get a job sweeping floors."

"You don't have any experience with a broom, Chase."

He was right. "You don't mind driving me to Kennedy?"

"I insist on it. But hurry. Nola is in the car waiting."

Ten minutes later he pulled to a stop in front of the Willowglen Nursing Center. "Chase, Mother and I thought you'd like to say goodbye to your friends one more time."

"And I'm going in with you," Nola announced.

"It won't bother you, Mother?"

"Of course, it will. I haven't been back to this wretched place since your grandmother died."

Seymour drummed his fingers on the steering wheel. "Don't be long. I want to get to Kennedy International on time."

Nola took Chase's arm. "Your father has a business appointment at two. We don't want him to miss that."

As they passed the room where Callie had died, Nola said, "I hate this place."

"Mom, coming here to live was Callie's choice, not yours."

Marie's arms were already outstretched when they reached her, the thin face lighting with joy at the sight of Chase. "I'm going away for the summer, Marie, but I'll come to see you as soon as I get back."

The old woman's frail grasp tightened.

"Honest, Marie. I'll be back." *But you won't be here. You're thinner than last week. You're failing rapidly.*

Unexpectedly, Nola crouched down beside Marie's wheelchair. "I'll come to see you while Chase is gone," she offered.

The watery eyes fixed on Nola. "Really, Marie. I'll come and bring you flowers and read Chase's letters to you."

What letters? Chase wondered. *I usually telephone.*

They left Marie and walked to the car in silence, their sad mood weighing them down all the way to Kennedy. Tears still pricked Chase's eyes as they stood at the departure gate.

"Write," Nola told her.

"Just call us collect," Seymour advised. "That way we'll know you aren't lost on the back of beyond."

"I'll do both, Dad. How's that?"

"I still don't like you traveling alone."

"You're old-fashioned."

"I'm cautious. I don't even like Tad going off alone."

"Tad seldom does."

"Chase, your ticket is *round* trip," Nola reminded her.

"I'll keep that in mind. And thanks for Paris, Dad."

"I don't approve of you going there first, not alone, not after that series of bombings there last year."

"But the last time I saw Paris—"

Her father's face went gray as the boarding gate opened. "No jokes, Chase. This is it. I want you back here in September to finish your studies. Please be careful. Stay out of the way of bombs and strangers and don't leave your luggage unattended."

His fears came at her like leeches. She had an uneasy feeling that unless she looked both ways all the way to England, she was in for trouble. She scolded herself and said, "Stop worrying, Dad. Nothing's going to happen to me."

Gruffly, her father pulled her to him, hugged her, and said what she had never heard him say before. "I love you, Chase."

Chapter 7

Paris lay far behind the Gregorys as they rode over the winding hills of Gascony and crested the steepest elevation. Below them was another quaint village nestled in the verdant valley. Drew let up on the gas and coasted toward the village, avoiding the children at play and the sheep lazily crossing the dusty road that ran through the center of town. He crept past the white-steepled church and headed toward the stone hotel with three chimneys poking up from its slate roof. A cobblestone path led to the door where colorful flower boxes hung in each window.

"Oh, Drew. Let's stay there!" Miriam exclaimed.

He smiled—he'd been doing a lot of that in the last few days—and said amiably, "Why not? We're at least within earshot of Ian Kendall. I'm sure of it."

"Does he know we're coming?"

"I thought we'd surprise him."

"He might surprise us and be gone."

He answered her arched brows with a shrug of his broad shoulders. "No, Jon Gainsborough gave me Ian's schedule. He's the British industrialist who sponsors Ian's cycling team."

"You don't sound as though you like him."

"Jon's all right, but he and Dudley Perkins are thick."

She patted his arm. "Reason enough to be careful."

They parked in the rear and entered through the patio dining room where the tables were set with sparkling pink goblets and freshly picked flowers. Stepping cautiously over the mopped tiles, they found the hostess dozing in a rocker, the mop bucket still at her side. She came to with a jerk and fired such a quick round of French at them that even Drew had to listen intently.

Within minutes she escorted them up a narrow stairway to the only unoccupied room on the second floor, *a chambre sur la cour.* Outlandish green wallpaper ran in wide strips from ceiling to floor. A sink and a bidet stood beside the tub in the corner, as old-fashioned as the mahogany wardrobe with its chipped finish.

Before he could suggest traveling on, his bride who loved luxury ran her fingers over the porcelain pitcher and wash basin as though she had been ushered into the queen's palace.

"Take the room, Drew. I love it."

He wanted nothing more than to please her. "We'll take it," he said, and feeling a bit romantic at the isolation, nodded appreciatively to their hostess. "Make that two nights."

Drew regretted it five minutes later when he flopped down on a bed as hard as a limestone slab. The pillow roll felt equally rigid and unyielding beneath his neck.

"Miriam, we'll never sleep on this four-poster."

She laughed and tossed her cashmere sweater to him. As he tucked it under his head, she said, "Darling, it's just for two nights. But forget the bed. Come here and look at this view."

Reluctantly, he struggled to his feet to stand with her by the open shutters. The air smelled sweet and fresh, as though they had just come through a rainstorm. A thick vine framed the window, and red geraniums poked their colorful heads up from the window box below. The far-flung slopes rose and fell in patterns of emerald and jade and loden greens. Trees and bushes, flowers, and more stone houses dotted the verdant hillsides.

"Miriam, let's look for Uriah's grandson while we still have daylight in our favor."

She leaned back against his chest. "I'd forgotten about Ian. I'll have to freshen up a bit first."

"And I need a bath after that long drive." He stepped away from the window and started to strip down.

"Where's the bathroom?" she asked.

"The water closet is at the end of the hall and the tub," he said, thumbing toward the corner of the room, "is there."

"But there's not even a shower curtain."

"Doesn't look that way. But," he said, running his finger under the tap and sinking lower into the tub, "the water's steaming. Care to join me?"

🜂🜂🜂

The Gregorys left their charming room an hour later and followed the scribbled map to a large chalet on the other side of town. They were directed to a private room in the back, an odoriferous enclosure that accommodated exercise equipment and five metal tables, all occupied. Riding gear and helmets lay piled against the wall, the outfits emblazoned with the red and blues of the Jon Gainsborough cycling team.

Ian was easy to spot with his lanky body and flaming reddish hair. He lay facedown on the middle table, a sheet draped over his buttocks and thighs, his upper torso gleaming with sweat, his bare feet toes down. A physical therapist stood by his side working his back muscles, taut after a long day's drive.

"Keep your eyes straight ahead," Drew teased as he led Miriam to Ian. He stooped down. "Kendall, it's Drew Gregory."

Ian looked like he would sprint from the table with a backward flip. "Don't get up, Ian," Drew warned. "Miriam is with me."

Ian stretched his arm back and blindly gripped her fingers. "How's this character treating you, Miriam?"

"Like royalty."

"Good. Then I won't get up and settle accounts for you."

She laughed softly. "No, Ian, I'm more than happy."

"Good," he said again, and there was a catch in his voice. "If you're here for the race, you're six weeks early."

"No," Drew assured him. "We're just doing the country-side, so we swung by to see you."

Ian's answer vibrated as the masseur dug deeper into his shoulder muscles. "A hundred kilometers out of your way? A deliberate detour? How'd you find me?"

"Gainsborough gave us your schedule. How are you doing?"

"Coach Skobla said my timing was better today. But yes-terday—dismal at best. I'm still considering dropping out."

"The Kendalls never quit," Drew told him.

Ian nodded toward the other tables. "The team won't thank me if I lose. And Gainsborough would have coach's head if I did."

"Give it your best. It doesn't matter whether you win."

"It does to me, Drew."

"Just go for it. If you don't win the yellow jersey this time, try again next year. You're a young rider. You have time."

"A rider without friends. Orlando and Chris don't wait around for me anymore, not since Alekos died at Sulzbach." His shoulders arched. "They think Alekos would be alive if it hadn't been for me. I really messed up."

Drew slipped his arm around Miriam, his thoughts on sixteen missing years in his marriage. "We all make mis-takes, Ian."

Kendall rolled to his side and swung himself upright, maintaining his modesty with the sheet over his lap. He waved the masseur off with the flip of his hand. "What hap-pened to Alekos in Sulzbach really *was* my fault."

"No," Drew said, "Alekos made some careless choices."

"He just wanted to win the race—to beat me."

"Then go out there and race for him," Miriam said gently.

"I promised my grandmother that I'd win the Tour de France for *her*." Ian wiped his eyes with his sun-freckled hand, allowing Drew relief from those probing blue eyes so much like Olivia's. Ian's voice dropped to a husky low. "Sometimes I almost forget my grandmother, and then at other times she seems to be in the next room, influencing me like she always did."

"Ian, you were so close to her."

"Yeah, Miriam, but I was angry with her the day she died. She told me she was sending me back to Maryland." His jaw tightened. "Once she made up her mind, nothing stopped her. I almost hated her for breaking her promise to me. It didn't matter to her that I was counting on going to Italy and the Greek islands with her."

Long ago Drew had broken a promise to his own daughter. Now he tried to see Ian's hurt from the perspective of a child. But his friendship had been with Uriah and Olivia. He couldn't call up more than a time or two when he'd paid attention to the thin-lipped, scrawny Ian. Ian had been a nice-looking kid but withdrawn and sensitive. Drew had bought him a baseball mitt and tossed a ball or two his way. He'd bought him a chocolate ice cream cone that Ian had dripped over the red leather seat of Drew's new car. And he had pushed him on a swing at a Kendall picnic back when Ian was six or seven—because Miriam had told him to.

Now Drew faced a stranger sitting there on the metal table in front of him. The brief openness that Ian had shown in Sulzbach when Alekos had died was gone. There was a barrier between them again, a wall that said, *Come no further, Drew Gregory.*

The room had emptied slowly—Ian's teammates grabbing up their clothes from the floor and slipping out without even a glance at him. Drew knew he should leave the past buried in that Cotswold cemetery, but as he tossed a towel around Ian's shoulders, he asked, "Ian, what really happened on Downing Street ten years ago? I want to hear it from you."

Ian jerked his head toward Drew. "You want a rerun?"

"I want to help you."

The agony on Ian's face was fresh; his blue eyes darkened even more. "Drew, I saw the car hit my grandmother. I couldn't even reach her."

"Uriah told us it was an unwitnessed hit-and-run."

"Come on, Gregory. I was there."

"You were just a kid."

"A thirteen-year-old with two eyes. My grandfather rarely

talks about it. It's as though Downing Street never happened."

A mask of indifference settled on Ian's face, but his roupy voice gave him away. "You won't believe me, but Dudley Perkins still insists my grandmother was an enemy agent— that she was deliberately killed on Downing because of it."

Miriam braced herself on the metal table. "Not Olivia! Not my best friend," she whispered.

Ian gave her a cursory glance. "Your husband wants the gory details. Does your Agency want to ruin my grand- mother's reputation, Drew?"

"If she was killed, it's time we found out the truth."

A hard sneer distorted Ian's fine facial features. "Perkins accused my grandmother of being involved in espionage back in the war. We could live with that. But Perkins would like to take my grandfather down with her. He insists that she was still an agent until the day she died."

Miriam linked her arm in Drew's and leaned against him. Drew felt numb. "Perkins wants to connect Uriah with acts of espionage? Tell me, Ian, what did you see that day on Downing?"

Ian rubbed his forehead. "Not much. Enough. I don't know."

"Try us. Did Olivia pass her attaché case to anyone?"

His puzzled frown deepened. "No. I don't think so. At first it was just my grandmother walking along the street— and then the stranger and the crowds and the siren—"

"Back up. What happened first?"

"We had lunch together. That's when she told me she was sending me home. I thought she was mad at me for taking so long in the loo, but she kept asking me about some man sitting across the dining room from us."

"What restaurant?"

"It was in Chelsea somewhere."

"It's important, Ian. Her death was well publicized. Some waiter might remember her."

"How? I can't remember what Charles the chauffeur looked like or the man in the dining room. I try, but they're always faceless." He pondered. "I think I could take you there. I'm sure it was a popular restaurant—the kind my grandmother liked—but this one had a horse motif and thick red carpets."

"The Fox Hunt?"

"Yeah, that may have been the name."

Drew grabbed a pen from his pocket and jotted it down. "Did anyone follow you to Downing Street?"

"I don't know. My grandmother went alone. She was visiting the prime minister."

Drew and Miriam exchanged glances. "You met her there?"

He frowned, forcing his thoughts back to something he didn't want to remember. Finally he said, "Charles and I were parked at the end of Downing, on Whitehall. We saw my grandmother coming toward us, but I was still mad at her—almost hoping that something would happen to her because she was sending me away."

He wiped perspiration from his face. "She was halfway to Whitehall when she put down her attaché case to autograph a book for a stranger. Imagine signing a book in the blinding rain."

Ian stared beyond Miriam and Drew as though part of the veiled mist on Downing Street was clearing for him. "The stranger gave her his umbrella, and then my grandmother stepped off the curb." He focused on Miriam. "Maybe I'm crazy—I'm not sure."

Drew tightened his hold on Miriam's arm and waited.

"I—I think that man waved the book in the air as if he were signaling someone. Yeah! That's when that Renault gunned its engine and moved in on my grandma, full speed." Ian's cold expression wavered. He swayed on the metal table. "And then the car hit her. If only I could have warned her—"

Miriam considered it a plaintive cry, as if Ian had just heard the thud of the Renault slamming into Olivia. At twenty-three, in spite of the misery on his face, he was a handsome young man, good looking as Olivia had been. "Ian," she said softly, "it could have been accidental."

"It wasn't."

Coldly Drew asked, "You've known this all these years and said nothing?"

"When I was a kid, I used to think it was my fault. I was so angry with her. I wanted something to happen—"

"You've thought about it a lot since Alekos died. Right?"

"Until then, Drew, I didn't want to remember. But they were both cut down deliberately."

The fragrance of Miriam's French perfume barely offset the smell of Ian's sweaty body, but she broke free from Drew and put her cheek against Ian's bristly cheek. "Whatever Olivia's reason for sending you home that day, I know she loved you, Ian."

He pushed her away. "She was going to Prague without me."

"Why Prague?" Drew asked.

"Something to do with her unfinished novel. She wasn't supposed to go back there. She'd just come back from a family funeral. She promised Gramps that after the funeral, she'd never go there again."

Drew sighed. "Sometimes I think we never really knew her."

"We knew her and we loved her," Miriam said. "We just didn't know everything about her."

Miriam thought about Olivia, the guarded part that sometimes kept her distant. They had met at an arty luncheon in New York City, a dining room teeming with artists and museum curators and art buyers. Olivia was a beautiful woman, elegantly turned out, poised and graceful. Age had separated them, and yet immediately they had been caught up with their mutual love for Rembrandt paintings. Even now she still mourned Olivia. Missed her maturity and wisdom. Missed her friendship. She was not prepared to discover another side to her old friend. She didn't want to know the truth about Olivia.

She tilted her head, studying Ian. His troubled gaze and

features were so much like Olivia's. "You remind me of your grandmother," she said.

"Because I'm moody and pigheaded?"

"Because you're gentle and kind under that mask of yours. You have her depth and sensitivity, Ian, those special strengths that I so admired in her." She squeezed his hand. "It's a good thing I see Uriah in you, too. He's flying over in a few days."

"Just for the Tour de France?"

"He's coming just for *you*, Ian."

Drew hand-brushed his silver-streaked hair and laughed. "Maybe he's coming to protect you from Chase Evans."

"Huh? Chase Evans? A girl by that name checked into the hostel where we're staying." He grinned. "This one is kind of pretty. Comes from Long Island." His facial muscles had relaxed, allowing his wry grin to widen. "Orlando was tongue-tied around her, so I took her out for a soft drink."

"The famous Kendall rescue?" Drew asked.

"You might call it that. I suggested that she go back to England with me." He pointed to his cycling gear on the floor. "But she's out of my class. Quite a dresser."

"Sounds like the girl we're talking about. Did you tell her about yourself?"

"Guilty. We flirted a bit. Talked about the Tour de France."

"And about Uriah and Olivia?"

"I never even mentioned them. Too busy getting to know her." He considered. "I think she said she's here for the summer. Yeah, that's it—some kind of project that her father is funding. But what's my grandfather's interest in a young woman like that?"

"She wanted your grandfather's help. She's doing a comparative study on two novelists."

"Oh, that's right. She's going on to Oxford. Wants a Ph.D.—like I said, that's out of my line. I don't care what she writes about. Once she leaves here, I'll never see her again."

"You will. She's researching your grandmother's story."

"Why didn't she tell me?" Ian wet his lips. "Does she

know about Prague? Has she been in touch with Dudley Perkins?"

"You'll have to ask Miss Evans. But according to Uriah, she'd contact the queen if she thought it would help her. Now get showered and dressed, Ian, and we'll take you to dinner."

❦❦❦

Chase Evans was sitting on the steps when Ian got back to the hostel. She was pretty even in the evening shadows, her chin cupped in her slender hands as she looked up at him and smiled. She was wearing white slacks and a teal turtleneck sweat top, her hair falling softly around her face.

"Hello. I wondered if you were coming home."

"I've been out," he said guardedly.

"I thought we were going to have a Coke together."

"I wasn't thirsty this evening."

He remembered last night and his quick heartbeat as he had sat across from her. Resentment and disappointment filled him now.

"Ian, are you angry with me?"

He put one foot on the step and paused. "Yes. About New York and your Columbia University study program—"

"I meant to tell you."

"After you quizzed me about my grandmother?"

"I didn't plan it that way."

"Yeah, I'm sure of it." He took another step.

"Don't go."

"I need my sleep if I'm going to ride in the morning."

"Will I see you tomorrow?"

"We won't be coming back this way." *I'll make sure of it.*

"But you invited me to travel back to England with you."

"I changed my mind."

She actually looked hurt, as though he had let her down. "I'm still going to stay over and watch you ride off in the morning," she said.

He swung his sweater over his shoulder. "Don't bother."

"Ian, I'm sorry. Really. I would have told you, but it was too soon. Please, why not introduce me to your friends?"

"Orlando and Chris? You've already met them."

"No, I mean the couple you had dinner with this evening. Orlando said they were close friends of your grandfather's."

"Leave the Gregorys alone. I don't want you pumping them with your questions."

"But I can't blow my doctoral dissertation, not when I've gone this far." She shook her head. "I don't understand your family. Most people would be pleased to have their grandmother remembered. You act like there's something to hide."

The door had almost slammed shut when he heard her mumble, "Don't help me then. But I'll find out my own way."

Chapter 8

Nedrick Russelmann made his way across the Westminster Bridge and walked briskly along the River Thames, idly pausing now and then to watch a swirling whirlpool or to stare at the quiet waters pooled by the embankment. Three hours ago when he left Uriah Kendall alone at the Cotswold cottage, he had said, "Uriah, I have business in London."

Wise, cagey Uriah. His smile had turned marginal as he dropped the car keys into Nedrick's hand and said, "Do what you must then." *As though betrayal no longer mattered.*

In despair Ned had followed the river as it wound its way gently around the scenic country roads into the center of London. This River Thames coursed through Uriah's veins, this great city of London, this country—all of it part of Uriah's makeup, part of his strength. Nedrick tossed a stone into the water and watched its rippling effect spreading out, forming its own little whirlpool. One lie. One lie to Uriah had led to another, churning the little eddies into a violent maelstrom, a raging undercurrent in Ned's mind that was luring him back to Prague.

The resonant, deep chimes of Big Ben sounded out the hour, narrowing the time until Nedrick kept his appointment with Jiri Benak, the Russelmanns' errand boy. Ten years ago Nedrick had turned his back on the prosperous Russelmanns and had gone off as a determined eighteen-year-old to find his own way, to find the gentler side of himself, as his grandfather had called it.

"You'll never be a true Russelmann," Popshot had said, and there had been both sadness and pride in Hanz Russelmann's voice.

For Nedrick, his grandfather's words were the ultimate rejection. Even as a boy Nedrick had wondered why the Russelmann Steel factory prospered when other businesses failed during those long years under communism. The Russelmanns' success dated back to Otto and Karl Russelmann in World War I, but the struggling engineering company suddenly flourished in the Nazi regime, turning out steel for a nation at war. After his war injury, Hanz had been assigned to the facility in Prague. Now Nedrick's father Altman and his Uncle Gustav vied for leadership. Engineers and architects. Men poring over blueprints and architectural plans. And why? Did a steel factory require all of that?

As Nedrick reached the age of accountability, the twisted thinking of his father took a tighter grip on him. He saw a whole lifetime spread out in front of him that wouldn't cut beyond the Prague borders. He'd be saddled permanently with the generational commitment to the steel mill—Altman would see to that.

The plant nearest the forest always had dark smoke rising from its chimney, a twisted black funnel that Popshot hated. Nedrick came to hate it himself. Not knowing why, not even caring. Its curling mass had engulfed Ned emotionally, leaving him with the inner urge to cut the family ties before greed and power meshed him into a Russelmann statistic.

He tossed another stone into the Thames, pebble-size this time, and then turned from the river and made his way toward St. James Park. Of all the family, he most admired his grandfather Hanz Russelmann—Popshot, his own nickname for the man. He longed to see him again, but perhaps the old man had died. Perhaps there would never be another chance to go fishing together; Hanz had taught him to cast a line and to hike for long hours in the woods, sighting a rabbit or deer—not for the kill but for the pleasure.

Maybe it was already too late to plow through another winter snowstorm, his grandfather limping beside him.

Nedrick grew up believing that his grandfather had been
a flying ace. Then the bitter truth came to the surface. Hanz
had not been a Czech pilot defending Czechoslovakia, but
a Luftwaffe pilot—a German, a Nazi, both still hated in the
country in which Nedrick had grown up. He had gone to
Hanz to question him about the veiled secrecy that surrounded the family business.

"Popshot always tells me the truth," he told his cousin.

Pavel laughed. "Uncle Hanz knows nothing of truth; your
hero has lived a lie all these years, and you've swallowed it."

Weeks later Nedrick quit school, packed up, and, without
even saying goodbye to Mila, left. Plain-faced Mila, his second cousin, his friend, the girl who trusted and loved him.
Mila, the girl with shiny dark hair, dark eyes, and a sad,
whimsical smile, had made his boyhood tolerable, romping
the fields with him, casting a better fishing line than he
could himself. In his own self-centered way, he had loved
her. At sixteen he had promised her the world, at seventeen
himself. At eighteen he had looked out the farm window
and watched her happily planting flower seeds beside his
grandfather. Nedrick left her to find her own way out of life
on the Russelmann farm.

But he realized as he elbowed the crowd on the busy
London street that his most nostalgic memory of Prague
always went back to his grandfather in the garden—a man's
man turning the soil, planting flowers and vegetables and
finding pleasure in the color and crops that resulted. And
he remembered Popshot's library. They'd often strolled the
streets of Prague, browsing in bookstores to add to the collection. He was with Hanz that day in Prague when Hanz
found one of Olivia Renway's novels.

Popshot had grasped that book and stared at the picture
on the back cover, his eyes hardened to an iceberg blue.
"Olivia," he cried. "Olivia. She's still alive."

Nedrick snatched up a second copy and ran his fingers
over the color photo. She was a well-dressed, stylish woman,

unsmiling and elegant—with eyes like his own—and a beautiful bracelet on her slender wrist. "Popshot, who is she?"

"She was part of my past."

After that Hanz scoured the bookstalls in Prague in search of all her books to display in his vast library. Those he couldn't find, he ordered. He read and reread them and for a time slipped from the self-assured head of the family into a brooding shell of a man, his sadness evident even when he spaded the flowers. Nedrick read Olivia's books, too, sometimes thinking that he had heard the stories before on fishing trips and on those hikes in the woods or on that vacation trip in Spain.

"Who is she really?" Ned had asked days before leaving Prague.

"Your grandmother—the gentler side of you, boy."

🦚🦚🦚

Nedrick left the crowded streets of the city and approached St. James Park along Birdcage Walk. Through the magnificent oak and beech trees he could see the Whitehall rooftops, and yet the roar of traffic had mellowed in the serenity of the gardens. Mothers sat in hired deck chairs near the water's edge watching their children toss bread crumbs to the ducks. Contentment surrounded Ned— pigeons, pelicans, and people, and the heady fragrance of summer flowers in bloom. Unlike the murky waters of the Thames, the pond seemed clear, bluish. He passed the beds of azaleas and tulips that edged the walks before he spotted Jiri Benak leaning against an ageless shade tree, his thick head of hair so blond that it gleamed snow-white in the sun.

Jiri was wearing his familiar beige trench coat, his hands thrust deep in his pockets, one no doubt wrapped carefully around the revolver he always carried. His sardonic grin twisted like a gnarled tree branch. "Nedrick, who is that man following you?"

Nedrick's gaze followed Jiri's to the English gentleman in the pinstriped suit. A black bowler hat rode low on his brow shadowing wide, inquisitive eyes in a gaunt face. His

starched white shirt was loose at the neck, the tie ridicu-
lously plain. He leaned on his umbrella like a walking stick
and took a sudden interest in the pelican at his feet.

"I don't know him," Nedrick said.

"It's all right. Pavel is nearby if we need him. We'll walk
along and see whether the man still finds us interesting."

Jiri set the pace, an easy, unconcerned gait that aggravated Nedrick even more. Jiri had been right. In their
silence, he heard the Englishman's long-stemmed umbrella
tapping against the sidewalk, dogging their steps. Jiri's
mood remained unperturbed; he bit into danger like one
biting into rich chocolate cake, savoring the moment, wanting more. Nedrick had no stamina for counting on his wits
to outmaneuver an enemy.

Or was Jiri—as he had always done—mocking the weak-
ness of Hanz Russelmann's grandson? Nedrick ran the tip
of his tongue across his upper lip and still it felt dry and
cracked. He had forgotten that the Russelmann clan
depended on force and weapons to achieve their purposes.
Those who stood in their way were removed. Why then had
they never found him in Maryland and destroyed him? Jiri
would delight in the assignment, seeing it as an opportunity to clear the path for his own promotion. Jiri despised
the favored sons—finding both Nedrick and Pavel obstacles
to his own success, but Jiri found no threat in Franz. Franz
was a weak, powerless man, a follower, a loser.

Nedrick had thrived on the luxury and comfort of the
Kendall home in Maryland, enjoying the amiable friendship with Uriah, and eager for those rare moments when
Uriah spoke openly about Olivia. Ned never risked identi-
fying himself—never made claims to the blood line that was
rightfully his own. But lately he had come to fear being discovered for who he was, threatened by an unknown honor
student determined to unravel Olivia's past. Kendall was a
reasonable man, but he would never tolerate Nedrick living
a lie.

Jiri nudged him back saying, "Do you remember your
Czech, Nedrick?"

"Some."

"Then we'll speak in Czech. Did Uriah Kendall question your coming to London this morning?"

"Why would he? He gives me free range," Nedrick said.

"And the girl? Has she contacted Kendall yet?"

"We haven't heard from her again, but she could be a problem."

"Don't tell me the old blood line is flowing again? Loyalty to the Russelmann clan never motivated you."

Not like it influenced you, Nedrick thought.

No, Nedrick's fear of being discovered, his own cowardice, had put wings to his feet. If Chase Evans unveiled Olivia's past, it would lead back to the Russelmann farm and straight to Hanz Russelmann—a past that included Nedrick, a threat that might disrupt the shrewd practices of the family business. It had never mattered before whether the business toppled, but the blood line had a new hold on him. He didn't want to see his family come to ruin, no matter how unscrupulous their dealings. Again he ran the tip of his tongue across his dry lip, searching his memory for the language of his boyhood. "Once a Russelmann, always a Russelmann," he said.

His words did not please Jiri. "Why did you come back— stirring up trouble about Renway's missing manuscript again? We know she wrote about some steel factory in Czechoslovakia—but we're not the only steel mill in the country."

"She meant the Russelmanns. I'm certain of it. Why else would she have mentioned the plant in the village where she was born?"

"She's dead, Nedrick. The book died with her."

"She died because of that book. And I'm convinced that you ordered that hit-and-run, Jiri."

"Hanz gives the orders. Always has."

Nedrick sucked in his breath and stopped in the middle of the crowd. The tapping of the Englishman's umbrella against the pavement ceased. "Popshot would not give that kind of order."

"Ask him yourself when you reach Jarvoc."

"Then my grandfather is still alive?"

"He's too obstinate to die. Besides he wants to see you—and Miss Evans. She's flying into London from Paris. Pavel will be going out to Heathrow any minute now to meet her plane."

"What was she doing in France?"

"Contacting Kendall's grandson. With a few phone calls, we traced Evans to the Bartholomew family and then to the Evans mansion on Long Island, but she outsmarted us by going to Paris first. What does she have, Nedrick, that worries you so?"

"A healthy curiosity."

"That's no problem."

"It will be, Jiri, if she stirs up the old memories that Ian Kendall has blocked out for ten years. And it's a problem if she finds the missing manuscript. Renway's death is still on file at Scotland Yard. Trace that stolen manuscript back to you, Jiri, and they have the one who murdered her."

A sneer disfigured his thin face. "Franz drove the car."

"But you planned it."

They had circled around and retraced their steps to the Birdcage Walk. "That manuscript is not a problem to us," Jiri said. "If it had been, your father would have destroyed it. But there may be missing pages, segments, notes on the steel mill. She would never have destroyed them. We must find them."

"What could she possibly have known?"

"Nothing. Everything. She must have passed them on to someone—Kendall, for instance."

"Impossible. Uriah Kendall destroyed anything that threatened his wife's reputation."

"Renway was in Prague days before her death. Talking about the tunnels."

"Perhaps she played in them as a child," Nedrick suggested.

"Or maybe she walked through them when the war ended—when the Russians liberated the people." Jiri's mocking tone was as cold as his expression. "According to her brother, she wanted to link the mill and the tunnels to the old internment camps of the forties. So she nosed around. Took notes. She may have photographed some important papers that could link us to chemical sales like those used in the subway disaster in Tokyo. Now after all these years of cooperating, Nishokura is threatening to stop doing business with us unless we triple their fees for doubling their risks."

Nerve gas? Nedrick's throat constricted as he thought of the black smoke at the waste plant that had evoked unsettling feelings in his grandfather and uneasy stirrings in himself as a boy. "But we only sell steel to Nishokura. Always have."

"We have other business interests at stake. Renway urged Dorian to stop working for us. Told him we were nothing but modern-day designers of death."

Nedrick fought off his boyhood apprehensions about his father's business. "Was there any truth in what she said?"

"She thought so. She told Dorian that she knew something might happen to her. She planned ahead."

"Meaning?" Nedrick asked.

"That she would have trusted someone with her research—someone who would finish her work for her."

"Her brother?"

"Someone outside of Prague."

"She was friends with the British prime minister."

"Someone less obvious, Nedrick. A friend left Prague with Renway ten years ago. We've never been able to locate her. They were in the resistance movement together." They were nearing the end of the path. "Whatever Chase Evans learns about Renway could be helpful to us. Let me know when Evans contacts you."

"Are the missing notes really that important? My grandmother is dead. You act like she could still destroy the Russelmanns."

Jiri held out his hand and offered Nedrick a cold-fish shake. "We can't take that chance, can we?"

Dudley Perkins watched the men shake hands and take their leave in separate directions, the blond going casually up the walkway past the azaleas toward the main boulevard. He had understood snatches of the conversation, enough to know that the man was foreign-born, straight from Prague, no doubt. *But*, thought Perkins, *you made no effort to hide that, and you were aware of my presence.*

He nodded to Lyle Spincrest standing nearby in his stark white tennis shorts. Lyle took Perkins's signal and started out on a jog behind the man in the trench coat.

With a toss of bread crumbs to the pelican, Perkins brushed his hands clean and left St. James Park, his pace casual as he lagged behind Uriah Kendall's chauffeur. Kendall's man seemed in no haste now, aimless and dejected, and then suddenly he ran for a double-decker bus, swung aboard, and managed to leave Dudley standing on the sidewalk, hands on his hips.

Twenty minutes later, Perkins walked into Scotland Yard. "Constable Wallis is expecting me," he said.

He was ushered into a compact room where Edwin Wallis sat buried under a mound of paperwork. At forty Wallis still wore his thick horn-rimmed glasses and his dark blue letterman sweater from his Oxford days—for rowing or cricket, if Perkins remembered correctly.

"Edwin," he said impatiently.

Wallis looked up. His cheeks were full, his nose long and narrow like a bobsled run. His sleepy gaze belied a sharp awareness. "Perkins," he said. "How can I help you?"

"I'd like you to open an old case for me."

Interest lit in the sleepy eyes. "Not without just cause or the queen's edict."

"It was a hit-and-run ten years ago. On Downing Street."

Wallis swiveled in his chair, the tip of his pen to his lips. "Not Olivia Renway?"

"I tried to convince you that it was more than an accident back then—that it was tied in with the bomb threat on the prime minister's residence. I still think so."

Dudley had struck the right button. Wallis reached out to a microfiche on his desk and began to flip the dials. "I went along with you to her funeral. Married to an American, wasn't she?"

"No, British. They made their home in America."

"Here it is. Never solved. Uriah Kendall's wife. Kendall was a friend of yours, wasn't he?"

"We worked together after the war."

"Oh, yes. He was washed out of MI5 because of you." Wallis's grin was wary. "Now I remember. I was new to the force. You dragged me off to the woman's funeral."

"For the protection of the Kendall family, Edwin. The prime minister's idea. The Kendalls were personal acquaintances of hers."

Wallis leaned back in his chair. "So you are still trying to connect the bombing in the financial district with Renway's death?"

"Edwin, the Czechs claimed credit. And Renway was Czech."

The intelligence reports back at Dudley's office pointed toward a new problem—Czech-oriented and ill-defined threats from an unidentified splinter group. Bomb threats. Several in Paris. London could be next. Even the Cotswolds were threatened. Dudley had put little stock in it until Uriah Kendall phoned and said, "Perkins, I want you to check up on my chauffeur. I met him ten years ago, and this morning for the first time I'm not sure I really know him. . . . "

Uriah's Czechoslovakian chauffeur.

Wallis rolled his pen across the desk. "Perkins," he said, "it's unlikely that we'll ever find the driver of the car that killed Renway. There are unsolved hit-and-runs all the time."

"But what if this one was murder?"

Chapter 9

Chase arrived at the airport just in time for her short flight to Heathrow. She had dressed in what she considered to be a simple, eye-catching outfit—her Saks Fifth Avenue ecru blazer, the off-white lace shell, and a soft voile skirt—guaranteed to be wrinkle-proof. Yet she had followed her grandmother's axiom to be classy and stunning head to toe.

She hurried to the VIP line and was given prompt, courteous service, as she knew she would be. Even the passenger who had rushed up to the check-in counter beside her watched Chase with an unblinking gaze, not particularly flattering, but not unusual either. He was thirtyish, his eyes darkly brooding in an otherwise attractive face. Without taking his eyes from her, he shoved cash across the counter and insisted on upgrading his ticket to first class. "I would like a seat near this young lady," he said.

Displeased at his brashness, Chase hurried off to the boarding gate. She had grown accustomed to the amenities of traveling first class and liked boarding early and having ample room for her long legs. As she sank into the wide-cushioned seat, a smiling flight attendant dropped a hot white towel into her hands. It felt refreshing as she held it against her cheek and leaned back against the soft cushions of her window seat.

The economy passengers pushed and shoved their way along the narrow aisle as the attendant squeezed her way

back to Chase. "I'm Angeline Melbourne," she said smiling.
"There's time for a glass of wine before we take off." She
held out the wine list.

Chase, who had never acquired a taste for alcoholic beverages, ordered a glass of iced tea instead. A gooey French
torte came with it. She was a muncher at heart—chips and
dips, mixed nuts, and low-salt pretzels—with too much
boundless energy to let the fat stick to her ribs or to ever tip
the scale at more than 118. She forked the French pastry
politely, savoring each bite, but as she did so, her spiral notebook toppled to the floor. It was impossible to retrieve it
with the tray on her lap. As she waited for the hostess, she
glimpsed the last passenger boarding—the brash, young
man from the ticket counter. His sly, sullen eyes sought hers
as he handed his canvas satchel to the attendant and strode
to the seat behind Chase.

By the time her teacup was empty, the seat belt sign was
on, and the aircraft door had been secured, leaving the seat
beside her unoccupied. She buckled her strap as the plane
taxied down the runway—smothering her disappointment
that her phone calls had failed to reach Luke Breckenridge.
Even her contact with Ian Kendall had ended on the hills of
Gascony when he pedaled off at the head of the pack without saying goodbye. Ian was, she decided, not a man of his
word. After all, he had invited her to ride the English
"Chunnel" with him.

Until yesterday Chase's goal had been literary, a search
for intriguing facts about Olivia Renway for her dissertation. Ian changed all that. There was something about
Olivia Renway that his family wanted to keep buried with
her. But what? Renway's death had been accidental, so why
had Ian warned her off? As preposterous as it sounded, she
wondered if Ian had asked the man on the plane to follow
her.

The seat belt light was off. She unsnapped her belt and
with growing concern scanned the floor for her missing
notepad. Nothing! She snapped open her attaché case and
thumbed through the contents. One spiral notepad was def-

initely gone, but she grabbed a postcard and began to write as the plane leveled off.

Dear Mom and Dad,

We just left Paris behind. London next. It's goodbye to the Eiffel Tower and Notre Dame and hello Big Ben and Westminster Abbey. It seems unreal not having Callie traveling with me and fussing about the scant snack they're serving to us now. Hugs to Marie. And, if you don't mind, could you call Halverson House and see how Jeff Carlson is doing?

Bushels of love from your wind-chaser.

With two days in London, she would have time to check old newspapers and even to walk Downing Street. Then it would be off to Oxford and the Cotswolds to visit some of the places where Olivia Renway had spent her life.

The flight attendant was back, serving a second drink to the man behind Chase. Again Chase glanced down at the floor, wondering whether he had picked up her notepad. Impulsively she got up and followed Angeline to the galley. "Could I have a cup of coffee?" she asked.

She took a sip, hating the bitter taste.

"Is something wrong?" Melbourne asked.

"Yes. I've misplaced one of my notebooks." She held up her hands, designating the size. "It's small, but important to me."

"Let me help you look."

"No, don't. I was just wondering—what do you know about the gentleman sitting behind me?"

"I know he likes his Bloody Mary strong."

Chase allowed herself a casual glance around first class, her eyes settling on him. Dark hair. A faint stubble of beard. Denim shirt and brown leather jacket. Receding hairline. Ears flat against his head.

Melbourne leaned against the galley counter. "If he's

bothering you, the pilot could call ahead and have someone from British Airways escort you through customs to a taxi."

"Thanks, but I'll just catch a taxi direct to my hotel." She put the cup down. "Do you know the man's name?"

Angeline hesitated before glancing at her passenger list. "Franz Van Rindin." Her smile was ambiguous, her eyes watchful. "You'd better sit down, Miss Evans. We'll be landing soon."

As Chase went back to her seat, she deliberately met the man's gaze. He was poker-faced, unblinking, his expression empty, as though he had little hope of happiness along the way.

"Good flight," he said to her, and even his voice sounded wooden, unimpassioned.

☙ ☙ ☙

Franz Van Rindin took the last sip of his drink and allowed the flight attendant to whisk his glass away. As she moved on down the aisle, he dropped Chase Evans's notebook on the floor and toed it under the seat in front of him. Then he fastened his seat belt and put his hands over his kneecaps, his fingers blanching as he held on. His uncle Hanz Russelmann still treasured his medals from his days as a Luftwaffe pilot—still loved flying. Franz hated it, especially taking off and landing. As the airliner lowered beneath the clouds and the British Isles stretched out below them, he focused on the passenger in front of him. She seemed to be making a last-minute search for her missing notebook; bending down for a final quick check, she retrieved it.

It's all there, he thought. *I didn't touch your shorthand scribblings on Olivia Renway.*

Like Altman, Franz was convinced that the girl was CIA. They'd already checked. Evans was a Columbia University honor student with strong political opinions; the CIA had tapped an intelligent young woman to serve them.

His grip on his knees tightened as the earth came up to meet him. In spite of the order from the Russelmann farm,

Franz had never intended to kill Olivia Renway on Downing Street. His plan had been to frighten her—as he was frightened now—allowing Jiri Benak just enough time to snatch her briefcase and the Russelmann bracelet. But Renway's visit to the prime minister changed all of that. She had gone too far! As she stepped from the curb, Franz had gunned his idling engine and roared toward her, his foot to the floorboard. She had frozen at the sound of his car. Franz could still recall the stark horror etched in her lovely face and then the impact of her body against the hard metal of his vehicle.

For ten years nothing had come of Renway's threat to destroy the Russelmanns. Had she fooled them all? Or was Altman right? The CIA had chosen Evans to take up Olivia's crusade and bring them all to ruin. What was worse in Franz's mind was the fact that Evans had contacted Uriah Kendall, an ex-MI5 officer. That meant the British and Americans were in this together.

Evans looked harmless enough, but then the Americans liked a pretty face—as Franz did. Still he found it hard to believe that they would send their intelligence agents first class. As the plane banked over the English Channel, he caught another glimpse of her profile reflected in the window. *Young*, he thought again. *Chic, smartly styled.* Maybe that made for a good agent. Her appearance did not arouse suspicion. The only second glance you'd give this girl would be with romance in mind. She had an easy smile, a breezy, jaunty gait that was both feminine and confident, and clothes too form-fitting to hide a weapon.

The flight attendant stood in the aisle, pleasantly announcing their momentary arrival at Heathrow. She frowned at Franz and then sat down for the landing. He closed his eyes and fought nausea, his muscles taut as he braced for the runway. The plane hit hard, bounced, and then they were earthbound, the wheels braking and squealing across the tarmac.

Melbourne shot to her feet. Chase Evans sat quietly, her seat belt still buckled. It was his time to fool them both. He'd be the first one off the plane. With no luggage to worry about except his empty canvas satchel, he'd signal his brother and disappear into the waiting room. Let Pavel take up the watch.

⚜ ⚜ ⚜

Chase's soft, sheer skirt swished as she moved through the passenger line, her bone t-strap pumps snug on her tired feet. Her grandmother would have looked on her with favor, pleased that she was following the Bartholomew cardinal rule to look first class when she traveled and wrinkle-free when she arrived. Callie Bartholomew had chosen her wardrobe from Paris and Milan and always accented it with expensive jewelry. Chase was more content with selections from Neiman Marcus and Saks Fifth Avenue. She often kept her accessories modest as she had done today—pierced earrings, her ruby ring, a single strand necklace. Right now Chase longed for comfort—her familiar Koret City Blues and a bright tank top—but these were at the bottom of the suitcase that would any minute be torn open for customs inspection.

Security had increased following an upsurge of IRA terrorism—leaving Chase and other foreigners in a long line. For all of his haste to disembark, Van Rindin was being delayed, arguing loudly in a Slavic accent, "The satchel is all I have. My luggage was stolen in Paris. Gone," he repeated, his wide palms extended.

"Sir," the agent countered, "why is your satchel empty?"

It was her turn now. Chase smiled at the dour customs agent. He fitted her father's image of a British official—tight-faced and aloof, a decent sort of man with serious eyes and actions more assertive than his words. It seemed as though the exposed newspaper headlines near his elbow had been deliberately placed there: "Bomb Threat Against Whitehall." Heathrow was on full alert.

She handed him her passport and snapped her pullman open. She'd learned another traveling tip from Callie. "Customs agents have big hands. Give them room to poke around. And allow yourself a chance to close your case again without sitting on it." Or losing ummentionables as Callie had done on a flight to Munich.

"Security seems heightened this morning," she said.

"Just precaution," he assured her.

Her attention was drawn back to Franz Van Rindin arguing heatedly a few feet from her. Was he making a deliberate scene? *Yes*, Chase decided. *He wants to be noticed.* He had turned his face toward the crowd, and she caught that flicker of recognition in his expression, that indiscernible nod toward her.

Was he signaling someone that things were not going well at the customs table? Or warning them that the young woman five passengers behind him was the one to follow? She searched the faces in the crowd for Van Rindin's contact without success. Fresh fury at Ian Kendall rose with the nigglings of doubt.

"Your destination?" the agent asked.

"Oxford."

"To study?"

"For the summer. I'll be staying with friends."

That was another family axiom, and she'd just blown it. Never offer information before it is needed. She considered using Nigel Hampton's name and decided she could just as well say Chaucer or Shelley and get the same response. The Londoner looking up at her right now didn't care where she stayed as long as she wasn't carrying stolen jewels or a lethal weapon.

From the corner of her eye, she saw Van Rindin resisting restraint as he was led into a small room. At once the agent relaxed. "Your destination in London, Miss Evans?" he asked, returning her passport.

"The Ritz for two days and then Oxford."

He shoved the lid down, ignoring the rest of her luggage, and flashed what proved to be a charming smile. He pushed her suitcases toward her. "Have a good stay. Next."

A burly porter loaded her luggage and led the way through the terminal, making a wide path for her with his luggage cart. As they reached the exit and stepped out on the sidewalk, two men cut across their path—a young man light on his feet and a serious-faced man with thick black hair and tinted glasses.

The younger man, with a boyish, lopsided grin, reached her first. "Miss Evans," he said, his accent clipped and British, "I'm Peter Quincy. I'm sorry I'm late."

The second intruder hesitated, spun abruptly, and disappeared back into the terminal. Alarmed, she brushed past Quincy and followed the porter to a waiting taxi.

"But, Miss Evans," Quincy protested, "I'm to drive you to Oxford. Mr. Hampton—"

She cut Quincy off with a shrug. Nigel Hampton knew she was staying in London a few days. *Take someone else with you,* she thought, *not me.* She turned her back to Quincy and faced the taxi driver. "The Ritz, please," she whispered. "And hurry."

He shoved the wad of gum to his other cheek. "Right on, miss," he said.

"Did he follow us?" she asked as they left the terminal.

"No, he's still standing there looking jilted. Lover's quarrel?" he asked.

"Just someone who wanted to take me for a ride."

She rode the rest of the way to the hotel in silence, taking in the familiar sights of London. The winding Thames. Westminster Abbey. Piccadilly Circus. But as they pulled up in front of the Ritz Hotel, Chase thought back to the strangers at Heathrow. The one had walked away abruptly; the other knew her name. Try as she could, she didn't recall which one had the mustache.

🪔🪔🪔

The Ritz doorman recognized her as he held out his gloved hand. As she stepped to the sidewalk and glanced up at him, he smiled. "Miss Evans, welcome back. Where is your grandmother?"

Chase choked as she said, "She died—months ago."

He let go of her hand apologetically. "I'm so sorry."

As she regained her composure, he averted his gaze and snapped his fingers for a bellman.

She would have settled on a quaint hotel on the other side of the Thames, but the Ritz was her father's choice. He fussed about spending money on her, but he always went high class. And this was—as her grandmother always said—blue blood at its best. Chase could picture her father confiding in a friend at a business luncheon, "My youngest daughter? She's staying at the Ritz in London, and then she'll go on for a summer at Oxford."

It wasn't that Seymour Evans was keeping up with the Joneses; he was simply striving to surpass the Bartholomews.

The inside of the Ritz was even more imposing—a restaurant with gilded chandeliers suspended from a painted ceiling, rooms that were marbled and French-styled, and the opulent Palm Court where she had had tea with Callie on their last trip to London. Chase was dressed for afternoon tea, thanks to Callie's traveling wisdom. As soon as she rested, she'd go down to the Palm Court for cucumber sandwiches and scones dripping with jams and cream.

Her room was spacious, well lit, pink, and feminine. She emptied her smaller case on the bed and hung up the items she would need over the next two days. Tomorrow would be full. She'd search out the newspaper morgues for clippings on Olivia Renway's death, and after that she'd walk to Downing Street.

With the suitcase stowed in the closet, she fluffed her pillows and stretched out on the queen-sized bed. She kicked off her pumps and wiggled her toes, staring out the hotel window on the city of London and thinking about the three lives that had brought her here: Olivia Renway, Dorothy Sayers, and her grandmother Callie Bartholomew. The Ritz was not a quiet reflective place, cornered as it was on a busy street. Outside she heard a double-decker bus roar by and the sound of a church bell chiming the hour. From her bed she could see the spire-topped cathedral in the Gothic architectural style that had fascinated her grandmother.

Callie had loved Paris and Milan, Florence and Vienna, but she had always been drawn back to the city of London. They both loved the afternoon teas at the Ritz, the tennis play-offs at Wimbledon, and the limitless spending sprees at Harrods. Mostly they loved browsing in art museums, never tiring of the Somerset House or the Turner Collection at the Tate Gallery. It struck Chase that she must see these alone now. She could never again bask in the beauty of the Cotswolds or the white cliffs of Dover with her grand-mother. Never again would they stand on a rocky cliff at Land's End on Cornwall and thrill to the wild sea waters splashing their faces. She had shared so much with Callie, and yet some aspects of her grandmother remained a mystery. Callie rarely went into Westminster Abbey or St. Paul's, but when she did, she came out strangely moved, refusing to speak.

This was Callie's England, her London—the London that Olivia Renway would have recognized, a spectacular city spread out from the banks of the Thames. But it would have been unfamiliar to Dorothy Sayers; she had known the London that existed between the world wars. Sayers, a plain-faced vicar's daughter with pincher glasses and short, thin hair, had been a woman of independence and intellect, far ahead of her society. She threw off Victorian restraints— Callie would have applauded—and entered into the jazz and swing era just before the global depression of the thirties. In Sayers's life and her books she broke the rules, finding innovative ways to commit murder in her Peter Wimsey novels—and often wearing outrageous clothes or smoking cigars as she spurned her privileged background. Her career had spanned both wars, but she would not live to see much of postwar London and would not be alive for the Beatles or Margaret Thatcher's rise to power.

As Chase lay puzzling over the similarities between Renway and Sayers, she saw only differences. Renway had been glamorous, well-styled, politically oriented, but rarely outgoing; yet in the libraries of Oxford Renway had discovered comfort in the life and writings of the outspoken Sayers.

But why? Chase asked herself again. What linked the two? The London blitz? Their alma mater? The love of London? Their writings? There was no whimsical detective, no short, pampered Lord Peter Wimsey in Renway's books. Renway leaned toward the historical, her characters deadly serious and sometimes autobiographical. Chase's grandmother would have liked both women, but she would have liked Sayers best for her break with society, but definitely not for her religious convictions. Chase reached out to her bed table and picked up the book she had started on the flight from America, Sayers's *The Mind of the Maker.* The book was filled with Sayers's pursuit of the Trinity. Perhaps it was this part of Sayers's journey that had touched Olivia Renway's life.

Chapter 10

*L*ondon. Vic Wilson finally persuaded Jon Gainsborough to lunch with him at the Fox Hunt, the restaurant where Olivia Renway had taken her last meal. When Vic arrived, he requested a table with a window view of London. The waiter led him to a straight-back brocade chair that faced the entry, seating him close to where Olivia had sat ten years ago.

Above Vic hung the massive painting *Riding to the Hounds,* the level of energy visible in the taut neck muscles of the horses and in the faces of the men who rode them. Vic thought of something Ian Kendall had told him. The boy remembered sitting beneath that painting, but why not? It was striking, vivid in color, full of action—something that would have caught the eye of Renway's curious thirteen-year-old grandson.

Kendall had confided something else to Vic. His grandmother had been afraid of someone sitting across the dining room from her. Involuntarily, Vic glanced around and was startled to see Dudley Perkins sitting nearby. So Gainsborough had alerted Perkins. Once again Drew had put his thumb on trouble. Vic would take it a step at a time. Outsmarting MI5 had been one of the fringe benefits of working at the American embassy.

He ordered a lemon and water, his stomach no longer tolerating alcoholic beverages. *Drew,* he decided, *would be proud of me, but for all the wrong reasons.* Vic's old lifestyle—

a charming date in every city with too many one-night stands—had brought him up short. Gone now even the small comfort that liquor had once given him. Vic hadn't admitted to anyone that he tired more easily. Add night sweats and little blackouts, and the picture looked glum. He hadn't risked telling his cousin Brianna about the new symptoms. She'd force him to go for another blood test, a test that might come up AIDS positive.

Wilson grabbed his lemon and water and cooled his parched throat with four great gulps. Over the brim of his glass, he saw Gainsborough standing between the potted palms, blocking the way of other guests. He was a short, squat man, his three hundred pounds squeezed into a Saville suit. The coat hung unbuttoned, his oversized trousers covering that portly belly.

Gainsborough took a quick survey of the room, turning first toward Dudley Perkins before he allowed his gaze to track the window row of tables. Vic gave him a quick salute, and Gainsborough barreled toward him, a business power-house, a steel magnate whose money did most of his talking. He came with a bold stride for such a big man, his hairpiece in front not quite matching the gray-streaked dark hair that fringed his head.

The waiter pulled the chair back, and Gainsborough lowered his hulking frame down with a thud. In a booming voice that carried to the tables around them, he asked, "Wilson, where's Drew Gregory?"

"Honeymooning. I'm filling in for him. Gregory sent word that you owe him one."

"The Sulzbach affair." He managed to soften his volume. "An unhappy recollection for all of us. I lost one of my cycling team there. Alekos Golemis—he was a good lad."

"That's why I'm here—to discuss your cycling team."

The sharp eyes narrowed. Jon hooked his umbrella over a palm branch and picked up the menu. "I didn't know Gregory was interested in cycling."

"He's interested in your plans for Ian Kendall. A drink first?" Vic asked.

"Business first. Ian's teammates don't want him to race."

"And you? Is that your way of punishing him, too?"

Gainsborough slid a glance toward Perkins who was nonchalantly munching his salad, a thick book in his free hand.

"Is it up to Perkins?" Vic asked.

"No, it's up to Kendall, but he's racing poorly."

"Ian has the weight of a dead friend on his cycle."

The fat jowls wobbled. He nodded toward Perkins. "I was just doing an old friend a favor. Coach Skobla opposed it. Never dreamed it would cost Alekos his life."

"Risky, wasn't it, breaking from their regular training?"

"It was that or Perkins would make certain Kendall didn't ride. I couldn't let that happen. Kendall is still our best chance for winning the Tour de France."

Vic felt contempt for the man drumming his fingers on the table. They were well-groomed hands with flashy rings squeezing the fat fingers. Gainsborough was buying his own margin of safety, bumping heads with Perkins, kowtowing to him. *It can mean only one thing,* Vic thought. *Perkins has a file on him.*

Where had Gainsborough gone wrong? In his business dealings? In his investments? Or was it something personal between the two men? He was nothing but a big, gutless man controlled by the staid Englishman across the room. MI5 was internal security, Perkins one of their top men. Had Gainsborough breached the security line just far enough for Dudley to find him useful?

"You have only a few weeks to decide, Gainsborough."

"Up until Sulzbach, Kendall had a real shot at winning."

"Your opinion or the coach's?"

"I depend on the men I hire. But Kendall's record is good. Montreal's Grand Prix. The Chambery Race. The Dupont Tour. He had good standings in all of them." Gainsborough's face sparkled. "You should have seen him take those cobbled climbs in the Het Volk. No question about it. The boy's good."

"You call the shots then? What about it, Gainsborough? Will Kendall ride in the Tour? He rode well in last year's race."

"Especially in the Pyrenees. He took those mountain curves at top speed, never braking once."

"Sounds crazy."

"It was. The coach was furious. But Kendall wanted to win, and he would have if that Italian hadn't crashed into him."

"I saw that crash on TV. Heartbreaking for Kendall."

Gainsborough rubbed his neck with his ringed hand. "It was disappointing for all of us. He'd taken three of the stages, but my boys are trained for team racing, not individual glory."

"And you think Kendall is racing for himself?"

"Kendall doesn't always go for structure. He wants space. That's Ian's weakest point, not always riding with the team in mind. If Orlando Gioceppi beats him at the Coors Classic, he's our next choice." Again his gaze shifted toward Perkins. "Ian has serious problems. It's as though the fight has gone out of him since Sulzbach."

"Kendall thinks you blame him for Alekos's death."

"Who else would I blame?"

"Yourself perhaps or Perkins. Why not square it away with Kendall? He needs to know you're not holding that accident against him."

"He's not the one with the threat of a lawsuit. Alekos's family is out to destroy the team now. Look, I'm hungry. Why don't we order?"

"Are you ready for that drink?"

"No, I want something solid." Gainsborough took time to study the menu and then reskimmed it before ordering a double portion of steak-and-kidney pie with roast potatoes, broccoli, and Yorkshire pudding. "And," he added, "I want creamy baked custard for dessert."

Vic kept his order simple. Eggs and toast and a pot of steeping tea. It was about all his stomach could handle.

They spent the next several minutes staring across the table at each other, starting a phrase or two and letting them go. When the food arrived, Vic said, "Gregory thinks Ian has lost his winning spirit."

"We'll know at the Coors Classic. He blows it there, and he's off the team. I can't support a loser."

"Perkins's idea or yours?"

He finished his first bite. "We were counting on Ian. The kid's a world pro. If I have to let him go, another team will snap him up. If I could only convince Perkins—"

"It's not up to Perkins. Your steel plant supports the team."

"True, but if Kendall goes, Coach Skobla will split with him. I'd lose everything."

What would you lose? Vic wondered. *Maybe you'd have Perkins off your back.* "Ludvik Skobla is new, isn't he?"

"Since the last Tour de France. One of my steel contacts in Prague recommended Skobla. He's been our best coach yet."

Vic wanted a name for the contact in Prague. He picked one from the hat and asked, "Not Cliff Harriman?"

Gainsborough's scowl made his fat face more homely. "No," he said. "The man's name is Altman Russelmann. The Russelmanns gave me my own start in the steel business. Altman knew Coach Skobla personally."

"Was he a good choice?"

"I think so. I trust Altman's recommendations. Skobla befriends the boys, but he trains them at high intensity. He's well organized and technical. Kendall needed that."

When the baked custard and coffee came, Vic nodded at the picture on the wall. "That fox hunt is one of Ian's favorite paintings."

"How would you know?"

"He came to this restaurant with his grandmother."

Food bulged in Gainsborough's cheek. He spoke with his mouth full. "Dead, isn't she?"

As you well know. "Afraid so, Gainsborough. She's the reason Kendall intends to win the Tour de France. He wants to wear the yellow jersey for her."

"We're a team, Wilson. If Kendall wears the yellow jersey, it's for the Gainsborough team. Not some dead woman."

Vic let that one ride. "When I talked with Gregory, he said that Ian raced well yesterday."

"One day is not enough. There are no miracles in cycling without good hard work. You can tell Gregory it all depends on the Coors Classic. If Ian wins that one, he will be our best choice for the Tour since Greg LeMond."

"Perkins won't try to stop Ian again?"

Gainsborough stuffed his mouth with the last spoonful of custard, his mood suddenly determined. "I won't let him."

"Drew has another request."

"I told you, there are no miracles in cycling."

"This one's under your control. He wants to ride in the team car next month."

"During the Tour de France? That's for the staff."

"It's a safety precaution. The men who killed Alekos were never picked up. They must know about the race."

Gainsborough's spoon clattered to the plate. He shoved the dish aside. "I'll check with Coach Skobla."

And who is he taking his orders from? Vic wondered.

Gainsborough held out his hand and tapped his wrist-watch. "I must be going. I'll pass your concerns onto the coach."

And to Perkins, I bet.

Even as Gainsborough stood, Perkins went on reading his book, making no effort to move. "I'm looking forward to the Coors Classic, Jon. It will be televised, won't it?"

"At least it will make the sports page." Gainsborough opened his wallet and pulled out several pound notes.

"No need," Vic said. "My treat. I'll walk you out."

They parted on the sidewalk, the big man taking off with full strides. Vic stood and watched him until that massive body was swallowed up in the pressing crowds. Then he craned his neck and glanced up at the shop sign, a brass carving of a horse and rider with a hound at their heels. Beneath the shingle were the bold red-and-white letters: The Fox Hunt.

Wilson had found his sly fox. *Two of them,* he thought as Dudley Perkins sauntered out of the restaurant. Vic turned in the opposite direction and headed for his car whistling.

Back at Brianna's empty apartment, he dropped into the

chair and spent the next hour making several business calls. Finally he dialed the Adria Hotel in Prague. When Drew picked up the phone on the third ring, Vic said, "I'm glad I caught you."

❁❁❁

Drew Gregory smiled into the phone. "Almost didn't. We're going out to dinner."

"What's on your schedule for tomorrow, Drew?"

Miriam sat at the desk, pen poised above the travel folders spread out in front of her. "Miriam's working on that. The Prague Gallery for one. She's into Renaissance paintings this week."

"Can you add the Russelmann Steel Mill to your schedule?"

"What?"

"Jon Gainsborough does business with them."

Drew turned his back to Miriam. "Didn't Gainsborough check out?"

"I have a few question marks. He didn't like lunching at The Fox Hunt, and he didn't want to talk about Olivia Renway. But he did let it slip that the Russelmanns gave him his start in the steel industry."

"A problem?"

"I picked up copies of the *Evening Standard* and the *International Herald Tribune* on my way back to Brianna's. I wanted to check the business pages. Then I made several calls this afternoon. One to an editor friend of mine, one to the Russelmann corporate office in Munich, a third to Jarvoc, Czechoslovakia." He chuckled. "I'll save the bill for you, otherwise Brianna will have my head when the charges come."

"Get to your point, Vic."

"The families of Gainsborough's friends were in business back in Nazi Germany. After the war, they eluded the Nuremberg trials."

Drew stared across the room at the pastel walls. Vic Wilson was one of those cocky guys born to crusade, born to push his convictions on others in a Newt Gingrich style. Tell Vic that they were going to clean up Congress and the Senate, and he would be on the bandwagon with his own ten-point contract for America.

"You still there, Gregory?"

Drew moved the mouthpiece closer. "Go ahead. I'm listening."

"The Russelmanns prospered all through the war. Branched out into Poland and Czechoslovakia during the war. Forced labor. Full profits."

"Thought everything was state-run in Czechoslovakia."

"Not since the Communists moved out."

Vic had always brushed off the Cold War and Communist rule. He even scoffed at the new leadership in Russia in a cocksure way that bugged his colleagues. He viewed the home front in the same way. He didn't care who was in the Oval Office. So why this sudden interest in a steel industry?

"Where's the factory, Vic?"

"In Jarvoc. That's west of Prague, not far from Kladno."

Jarvoc. The name clicked this time. Dorian Paschek's hometown. Olivia Renway's birthplace. Had Vic picked up on this, too? "I'll see what I can do, Vic. I'll check with Miriam first."

"So that's what happens when you get married?"

"It didn't the first time around."

Five minutes later, after an earful on Gainsborough and Perkins, Drew cradled the receiver and walked over to Miriam. As he gently massaged her narrow shoulders, she placed her cheek against his hand.

"I'm surprised at how many people know where we are on our honeymoon," she said. "I didn't even give our numbers to Robyn."

"I'm sorry. That call was my fault, *Liebling.* It was Vic."

"Not Uriah Kendall this time?"

"Vic was checking into some things for me."

"Something to do with Uriah?"

"Yes."

He studied her in the mirror and marveled again at her

natural beauty. She kissed the back of his hand. "Is Vic all right?" she asked.

"Sounds cheerful enough."

"Nothing about his illness?"

"Nothing new."

Softly she said, "You're going to miss him."

"He's not dead yet."

"Then why do you act like he is?"

Drew knew and hated knowing. Sooner or later he was going to lose his friend. He seethed at what was happening to Vic, but he couldn't alter it. And the truth was, he couldn't face it either.

He couldn't even find comfort in blaming it on Vic. Vic had made his own choices, always calling himself a free moral agent. That binding freedom had taken him on a wild journey from a girl in every port to no girls at all now. A year or two down the trail and Vic would test AIDS positive. The one thing Drew had promised himself was that nothing would spoil their friendship.

"You have been good friends, haven't you?"

"The best. We go at the job from different viewpoints, but we've always worked well together. He saved my life a couple of times. I'll always have that to remember."

"Drew, he is still alive. Don't treat him as though he is dying."

Gratefully he smiled at her in the mirror. "You won't mind having him in our home for dinners?"

"A little. The disease still frightens me."

"It frightens him, too."

She picked up her brush and ran it through her auburn hair, each stroke adding to the sheen. "I can't picture Vic afraid of anything."

"He's afraid of dying. He has no peace at all."

"But you do, Drew. Share yours."

"Right now he's not ready to listen."

"Someday he will. His illness—"

Miriam still couldn't bring herself to say the words HIV virus, as though verbalizing them would harm Vic more. Perhaps Drew was right. Vic would bear the reproach and rejection of his colleagues once the results of his blood tests reached the Agency.

Miriam cleared her throat. "His illness has polished some of his rough edges. It's like a new Vic at the helm."

"That's his cousin's doings. Brianna is like a rock. She'll stick with him all the way. But you're right. Being HIV positive has mellowed Vic." He tried to sound chipper as he added, "Thanks to Vic, I have good news for you, *Liebling*."

He stopped the brush mid-stroke, leaned down, and put his cheek against hers. "You'll be able to look up Dorian Paschek after all."

Chapter 11

Luke Breckenridge cracked his knuckles as the Swiss airliner banked over Zurich. For a moment it felt as if the jet hovered motionless against a sea of cumulus clouds, and then the gigantic bird shuddered as the wheels locked into place. Earth's patchwork fields came rapidly up to meet them. To Luke's left lay the wooded hills shadowed in deep purple and the mountaintops still crested in layers of snow. To his right stood the traffic control tower and in the distance the Zurichsee, blue and glistening.

On his last trip to Zurich, he had been in the custody of Drew Gregory, convinced that Drew would turn him over to the CIA, the victim of another man's treason. Luke had sat with Drew on the patio of the Schweizerhof Cafe in Schaffhausen contemplating a mad dash for freedom over the winding streets of the town. His thoughts had been far from ever seeing his precious Sauni again.

For twenty years she had thought him buried at Arlington. In a way he had been dead, dead inside. He had sat there unblinking, rigid in his flak jacket and khaki pants. Shiny black boots pressed against his callused feet; a one-inch stubble of beard covered his chin. And then—there at the cafe in Schaffhausen, Sauni came over the bridge that spanned the Rhine wearing a red dress and the heart-shaped locket that he had given her long ago. He would have known her anywhere—that lovely oval face, the sensitive mouth, that quick, light step of hers. From across the cafe patio, she met Luke's gaze, her dazzling blue-green eyes pained when she saw him. He knew she recognized him even though his strong features were marred by a jagged scar along his neck and by years of bitterness against the man and country that had betrayed him. In his rage, he would have destroyed Gregory for letting Sauni see him like that, but he could only voice his fury as she walked back over that bridge without him.

He hadn't counted on Drew's help. Gregory was gutsy, somber, determined, but he was a CIA officer. Luke didn't credit any of them with integrity. After all, one of them had betrayed him in the jungles of Laos. But Drew went doggedly after the truth. In the end he bought Luke's pardon at the cost of an old friendship with the CIA station-chief in Paris. Luke still found it hard to believe he was a free man, a man with his own passport, his name cleared of treason, the country hailing him as a hero. It seemed now that Gregory was the one who had come up short, condemned by his own Company, his friends blatantly against him. Gregory made no demands on Luke, expressed no regrets for helping him. Luke wondered whether he would have done the same for Gregory.

Sauni. Going on in life without Sauni held no meaning for Luke. His stomach knotted as the plane lined up with the runway. The pilot was committed to landing. Was Luke committed to facing Sauni once again? She had every reason to reject him. They were divorced, and he had allowed her to think he was dead for twenty years. Yet she stood with him through the roughest part of the journey back to freedom—had even threatened to storm the White House on his behalf. But when he was honored there on the lawn of the White House, she had not come to share his glory.

The wheels hit the touchdown zone, the belly of the plane shuddering as the tires burned the runway. The jet braked and came to a jarring stop at the terminal, its wing lights blinking. He let the others scramble to their feet and tug luggage from the rack as they fought for standing space in the aisle. Finally Luke stood, his lanky legs numb after the long flight.

One of the attendants made her way to him. "Sir, everyone is off the plane. Are you all right?"

He smiled down at her, his facial muscles tight. "I wasn't up to fighting the crowd."

"But you're all right? Someone is meeting you?"

"I hope so," he said.

He grabbed his briefcase and raincoat and followed her to the exit. She stepped aside, and he ducked as he left the cabin.

"Have a nice time in Zurich, sir."

I'd like that, he thought. "Thanks for a good flight."

He took off with long strides and caught up with the stragglers at the baggage roundabout. He had his luggage key and passport in his hand, but he was ushered rapidly through the customs line with only a cursory glance. Inside the noisy terminal, he envied the laughter and boisterous reunions.

As he searched for Sauni's familiar face, his neck scar pulsated, the sharp pain searing into his jaw and tracking its way to his temples. The violent onset of a headache startled him. He shouldered his raincoat and merged with the crowd, his disappointment so physical that he thought he would spill his guts as he had done in Laos when dysentery almost killed him.

She hadn't come. His sense of rejection was unbearable. He moved mechanically, inches taller than the passengers around him as they fought for space in the crowded corridor. The drone of voices sounded like the roar of a turbojet in his ears.

"Luke."

The voice sounded far away, distant like a memory.

"Luke. LUKE! *LUKE!*"

As he turned, people spread thin and walked around him. He saw Sauni hurrying toward him. He dropped his coat and briefcase. She was running now, her flimsy red dress restricting her speed. He held out his arms, his longing for her overwhelming.

She was there, looking up at him, breathless with an apology. "They told me the wrong gate," she said.

"I thought you weren't coming."

Her eyes smiled first. "Luke, you know me better than that."

He touched her cheek to make certain she was real, to make certain he was still alive himself.

"I was at the wrong gate for thirty minutes—and then I heard them announce your flight. I—"

He cupped her face and came down hard on those well-shaped lips, silencing her apology. For a moment she responded as warmly and passionately as he did. Then abruptly she pushed him away, her soft hands trembling against his broad chest.

"Luke, we'd better go." He heard panic and embarrassment in her voice. "I want to avoid the traffic."

"I'll drive," he offered.

"Oh, no. It's Annabelle's car."

Sauni kept up a nervous flow of chatter from the escalator to the parked car. She seemed relieved to get her hands on the steering wheel, to fix her eyes on the traffic. She glanced at him as they left the airport. "Luke, you look wonderful."

"My mother's cooking," he said casually.

"I'm afraid she spoiled you. You won't even like my meals."

"Mom said you've turned into an excellent cook."

A happy ripple of laughter swept through the car. "How would Amy know? We took most of our meals out when they visited me."

"She said you don't do burnt offerings anymore."

"Luke, how did you ever stand my first attempts at cooking?"

"I filled up at the mess hall before coming home."

She sobered with another glance his way, and then she was back to concentrating on the traffic. She drove defensively—the way he had taught her—and he was pleased.

"I called your mother this morning. Amy said your plane got off on time. She sent her love—said they miss you already."

"They were good about my coming. I had to see you, Sauni."

She cut him off, her voice gentle. "I told Amy I've taken a couple of days off from summer school to show you around."

"You didn't have to do that."

"I wanted to. You missed so much of Busingen the last time."

"We had that walk by the river."

"That's all we had, wasn't it, Luke?"

All we'll ever have, he thought. "Are you staying on at the school in Busingen?"

"I signed on for another term—after talking with the chaplain. He thought it was a good idea to go on with my life." To his silence she whispered, "I'm happy here."

"Teaching theology?"

"Oh, Luke."

He had always loved the way she laughed—from the day he met her on the steps of the Capitol. But this time he feared she was laughing at him.

"Luke, I teach literature—French and biblical both. My students come from all over Europe. Two even from the States."

She was still cutting him off, keeping her distance, choosing a life where there was no room for him. "Sauni, I'll stay at the hotel in Schaffhausen."

"Hotel? No, you're staying with my friends in Busingen. Right next door to me. We can wave from our bedroom windows."

It wasn't what he had in mind. Was she afraid of being near him? Or was there someone else? "I don't want to put anyone out."

"Luke, it's all arranged." Her laughter had slipped to impatience. "They're my friends. You'll like them."

His spine stiffened. These days he still didn't take to strangers and particularly to theologians. He didn't want her friends sharing the burden of his arrival. He wanted time alone with Sauni. "Will you be free to spend time with me, Sauni?"

"I told you—I took a few days off to show you around."

They covered several miles of beautiful countryside before she asked, "Did things go well for you at Walter Reed?"

"My debriefing and endless X-rays? I'm grateful it's over."

"Was it that rough?"

"The interviews with Langley were the worst."

"But Chaplain Grozfelt was nice to you, wasn't he?"

He started to say, "Sid is my shrink." But it might push her further away. "He's a good man—the easiest part of Walter Reed."

"He's the gentleman who—who told me to go on with my life."

Luke fought anger at Sid. "That's strange, Sauni. Sid is the one who told me to fly over and be with you."

☙❦☙

Sauni Breckenridge paced the living room for an hour after Luke left her, and then she crawled between the sheets and cried herself to sleep. She awakened in the middle of the night, her cheeks flushing in the darkness at the thought of Luke's kiss.

She had promised herself—no, she had promised Sid Grozfelt not to push their relationship. In a way, Grozfelt had snatched away the hope of any permanent reunion with Luke. He had warned her that Luke was on a long journey back, struggling to accept himself and society once again. Sauni had in those two long phone calls with Grozfelt confided her deep feeling for Luke, her longing to go back twenty years when they were the happiest, her willingness to marry Luke again.

Grozfelt's answer had been slow, like his Southern drawl. "There's no going back. It's one day at a time for both of you. Just remember Captain Breckenridge is walking a fragile line that cannot be hurried." Gently, he had added, "Luke is well physically, Mrs. Breckenridge, but coming back emotionally will take longer. The captain may never feel free to marry again."

"But you said he's well."

"His debriefing was not easy. There are some in Washington who would punish Captain Breckenridge for his time at the mercenary camps. An understandable concern, Mrs. Breckenridge."

"Luke had nowhere to go, Chaplain Grozfelt."

She heard him chuckle, but his words were sobering. "Right now he's finding it hard to forgive himself. . . . Celibacy could be one way of self-punishment."

No, Sauni knew Luke better than that. Deep inside Luke would always be a warm and caring man, expressive and romantic. Surely God hadn't brought Luke this far to walk a solitary journey. She wanted to call Luke and reassure him that she loved him no matter what. She propped herself up on one elbow and turned on the bedside light. The answering machine blinked, indicating two incoming calls. Had the phone rung twice while she was showering?

She pushed the message button and smiled at the sound of Luke's voice. "Sauni, I just wanted to say good night again."

But as she turned her attention to the second message, her happiness faded. "Luke," a cheerful young voice said, "it's Chase Evans. I've been trying to reach you for days. I'm in Europe. When can we get together? Please *call* me."

In Jarvoc the last whistle had blown. Except for a skeleton night crew, Russelmann Steel Mill had shut down. Hanz Russelmann stood by his office window in the air-conditioned facility and watched the lights dim on each floor. Outside, the parking lot emptied rapidly as the cars and bikes and trucks headed toward town and a round of drinks at the local pubs.

He longed for that kind of freedom, but those merry days of laughter and drinking belonged to his Cambridge years and the Oktoberfests in Munich—before the war and the twists and turns that had brought him to Prague—before

these long, lonely years of living in isolation from the land
of his birth. Fifty-five years ago seemed like forever.

Hanz had another twenty minutes before his office
would begin to overheat. Still he waited in the dark, listening, trying to determine whether Altman and Gustav had
left the building. He heard the elevator door shut and open.
Shut and open. He used up ten of his twenty minutes, and
then he moved quickly, for a man of such bulk and height,
into the deserted corridor. His luck held. Using his passkey,
he entered the well-furnished boardroom; the long oval
table was covered with fingerprints from today's conference. Altman still allowed him to sit in on the daily meetings, but Hanz no longer voiced his opinions. Even when
they discussed Nedrick and his usefulness to them, Hanz
kept his tongue, listening. If there was anything good left in
the Russelmann clan, it was Nedrick; it was up to Hanz to
protect him.

By morning the boardroom would be spotless, the table
highly polished, the plants freshly watered—and Altman,
Gustav, and Josef ready to discuss Nedrick's fate. Time was
running out for Hanz, too, but he had to beat his sons at
their own game. He had to stay alive long enough to salvage
his grandson even at the sacrifice of the factory. And by
morning Hanz intended to know more about the contracts
with Nishokura Steel in Tokyo.

From the boardroom he could work his way into
Altman's spacious quarters. He closed the door cautiously,
the click of the latch resounding like a drumbeat. He had
been prepared to stand until his eyes adjusted to the darkness, but a wide streak of light came through the door that
led into Altman's office.

The plush carpet allowed Hanz to move closer to a better
vantage point. Eerie shafts of light from the desk lamp
reflected against the massive painting of a Napoleon battle.
The painting had been swung aside, and the safe on the
wall lay open.

Altman sat at his desk deep in thought, the tip of a pen to
his lips, a report of some kind in his hand. His suit coat had
been discarded, the knot of his tie loosened, the cuffs of his

lavender shirt rolled up. In profile Altman was an attractive man, fifty something now, not at all frightening as he was when people faced those cruel, unfeeling eyes.

Sitting there so pensively, he didn't look brutish, implacable, cold-blooded. With a fresh burst of remorse Hanz regretted the day he had found his son in Cornwall, England. Things might have turned out differently if he had never known the boy existed. Until that moment Altman had no past, no history, no known parentage, no one to claim him. The boy had been told that he was an orphan, the victim of the London bombings, his heritage lost in the rubble.

Five years after the war, Hanz had gone to England to finalize the arrangements with Jon Gainsborough for a satellite steel factory north of Oxford. Once the papers were signed, Hanz set out on a futile search to find Olivia Renway. He found no trace, no clues to Olivia's whereabouts—he heard only a persistent rumor that there had been a child.

Standing motionless in the boardroom in Jarvoc, he remembered back to Olivia vomiting morning after morning. He had comforted her, telling her not to be afraid of the air raids. He was there with her. She had said nothing, nothing about the baby. But if there had been a baby, she would have gone back to the Renways in Cornwall. Yes, that is where he would find Olivia's child. He remembered that day as if it were yesterday. . . .

January 1950. Hanz took the train to Cornwall, retracing the familiar journey to the Renways' tiny fishing village. He had known Warren and Millicent Renway since Cambridge, their political thinking strongly aligned with his own. He had recruited them for the cause that was sweeping over Europe, convinced himself that the Nazi movement would restore Germany to power and lift her from the throes of a dying economy.

Hanz had considered it in his favor that Warren Renway

was a close friend of the Duke of Windsor, the man who had abdicated the British throne. Like the duke, Renway had many relatives born into German families and had been a frequent visitor in that country. Hanz soon learned that Renway and his wife had taken offense at the royal family's rejection of the duke once he married the American divorcee. Hanz nurtured Renway's resentments, playing mind games with him until Renway was convinced that England could best be served by siding with the cause that would unite the two countries and restore the duke to the English throne under German control. Warren's wife, Millicent, whose German roots went even deeper, agreed.

While war was still a rumor, Hanz had set the Renways up with a shortwave transmitter and put them in touch with German Intelligence. They wanted to avoid war at all costs, but if German pilots crashed in England, the Renways would help them escape by signaling German subs off the coast. Hanz, as it turned out, was one of the first Luftwaffe pilots to seek their help when his plane crashed during the early weeks of the Blitz. The decision from Berlin was for Hanz to remain in England to gather information that would bring the British Isles to her knees.

As his plane had limped toward the coast, the crash imminent, he had seen the futility of war and the bombs' destruction of the city of London. Hanz loved England. While he stood on the Cornish cliffs with the angry sea crashing against the boulders, he had resented the orders that would keep him there as a spy. It was then, in the darkest hour of his life, that he met Olivia face to face. He had known about her, the Renways' "adopted" daughter, but he had not met her until she came out to the cliff that day to call him home.

"Henri," she had said, "supper is ready."

Hanz turned, startled by the unexpected recognition. He had seen her once before in his life—the day the Germans moved into Prague. He had watched her flee with her father and take refuge inside the church, and he had let her go.

She was barely sixteen then, and now at seventeen her face was still waiflike, pale and thin, but her eyes were blue and beautiful. She wore a leather jacket, stolen no doubt from a downed pilot, men's trousers, and scuffed boots. The top two buttons of her white shirt were open with a floral print scarf knotted at her neck. The russet brown hair hung in loose strands, blown back from her face by the strong sea breeze. As he stared at her, her narrow chin jutted forward.

"You must be Olivia. I wondered if we'd ever meet."

"I've been in Czechoslovakia," she said.

Taking messages to the resistance fighters in Prague, he guessed. He knew at that moment that she knew nothing of the Renways' political leanings; and he knew that if she had, she would have hated them. Olivia had simply sought refuge in the home of family friends.

She came to supper that evening in a dress, her hair brushed and tied back from her face with the same scarf she had worn at her neck. Meeting her trusting, admiring gaze over the supper table, he made the decision to use her. She had already given a year of her life to the resistance movement in Prague. He would persuade her to help him. Instead he fell in love with her.

Now he had come back to Cornwall, not to find Olivia, but to find the child that she had borne him. The stone church and the orphanage attached to it were set off from the sturdy seafarers' homes that nestled securely in the towering cliffs. A shingle with the weather-beaten words "St. Michael's Children's Cove" squeaked in the wind. The orphanage had been overcrowded with children during the war, but now only fifty unwanted youngsters made their home there.

Hanz followed the robed nun inside. An hour later another somber-faced nun shook her head for the third time. "I'm sorry, Mr. Russelmann. The birth records of the children are sealed."

"Surely you can tell me whether there is a child here by the name of Renway. He—she—would be around nine or ten."

The Mother Superior folded her hands on the ledger in front of her. "The children go by their first names. Perhaps if you could be more specific about the child."

He went hopelessly to the window and stared out on the children at play. Taking the miniature binoculars from his pocket, he studied their faces. He was just about to give up when he saw the young boy standing by the stone fence. There was nothing about his solemn, morose face that reminded him of Olivia, but he saw himself in the boy.

"Sister," he said, "the boy over there—what's his name?"

She came to stand at Hanz's side, her long habit swishing at her ankles as she moved. "That's Altman," she said. "He's such a gloomy little boy. Rejected by the others."

Hanz sucked in his breath. *Altman was his middle name.* He could not take his eyes off the child. "Why do the others reject him?" he asked.

She folded her hands in front of her. "This late it shouldn't matter, but it still does. His father was a German— a soldier, I believe. And his mother partly Jewish."

He winced, remembering his own revulsion when Olivia admitted to her Jewish heritage. His throat tightened as he asked, "The boy's mother—is she dead?"

The nun glanced up at him. "Mr. Russelmann, I've told you, we don't discuss the children's records."

"It's important."

"To you perhaps. But not to the boy."

"Could I see the child and talk with him?"

"I see no harm in that, Mr. Russelmann."

As they walked to the playground together, he hounded her with questions. The boy's age? His likes and dislikes? His scholastic rating? The possibility of taking the boy out of England and raising him?

And then he faced his son, Olivia's son. Thick hair and eyes like his own with features that surely belonged to a Russelmann.

"It seems strange, Mr. Russelmann," the nun said as Altman chased after the soccerball. "You've asked many questions about the boy. But never once have you asked me who his father was."

Hanz felt as though he were back in the Luftwaffe uniform standing rigidly at attention, his commanding officer ripping the Iron Cross from his neck. He turned slowly, stiffly, and met her steady gaze. "Sister," he said with a catch in his throat, "I already know all about his father."

Hanz stood in the shadows of the boardroom, balancing painfully on his game leg, wondering what had become of that boy he had found in Cornwall, England. He tried to recall what his first impressions had been. They were vague. An angry child, raging like the seawaters on the Cornish coast. An unsmiling, sullen child chasing a soccer-ball. When Hanz told the boy he was taking him back to Germany with him, Altman shrugged and went on drawing lines with a black crayon. He showed no emotion at all when the nuns packed up his few belongings and he walked down the steps of the orphanage with Hanz to a new life. They had flown to Germany as strangers. They were still strangers.

Altman had grown from a child into a self-sufficient, power-hungry adult who still hated the mother who had rejected him. From where Hanz stood, he could see the muscles on his son's face contorting. The room had become suffocating with the air conditioner turned off, but Altman seemed unaware of the discomfort as he continued to browse through the thick report.

Unexpectedly Altman's fist came down hard on the desk, scattering the papers. As he shoved back his leather chair and struggled to his feet, one page drifted unnoticed to the floor. With the precision so characteristic of him, he put the report into the briefcase, placed it in the safe, and twirled the dial. Squaring the painting on the wall to his satisfaction, Altman snatched up his coat, switched off the lights, and left the room.

As Altman's footsteps faded, Hanz felt his way to the fallen sheet of paper and picked it up. He snapped the desk light back on and stared disbelievingly at the paper in his hand.

Olivia Renway's name ran across the top of the page, the title of her unfinished novel beside it.

Chapter 12

Prague. Early the next morning the Gregorys left their hotel room with its cheery yellow walls, took the stairs down to the Adria's marble-tiled reception room, and turned in the passkey. The electric doors slid open, and Drew and Miriam walked through them, out under the bright yellow awning onto Wenceslas Square. The hotel doorman, waiting politely by their rental car, opened the door of the Skoda with his gloved hand and wrapped his fingers around the tip that Drew gave him.

Drew maneuvered through the tangled web of one-way streets, then drove along the Vltava River not far from the Charles Bridge, honking impatiently at a horse-drawn wagon of manure and narrowly missing a nun on a motorcycle.

"Shades of New York," he complained.

"Have you forgotten, Drew? It's a heavy on-the-spot fine if they stop you for a traffic violation."

"It will probably be life if I topple that load of manure."

"Or, heaven forbid, hit that poor nun."

"Hmm." His thoughts turned back to the farm of his childhood in upstate New York, the Gregory Dairy Farm with its manure and shovels and hundreds of cattle. He could visualize the woods and the river where his brother Aaron had fished, but the face of his mom, the woman who had so molded him, blurred in his memory. He tried even harder to sketch the features of Wallace Gregory, the dad he had dearly admired.

Briefly the church of his boyhood laid claim to his memory. St. Bonaventure had been a small parish, later closed for lack of parishioners. He remembered the priest and his own days as an altar boy, but he could not remember any nun, and certainly not one on a motorcycle. The faith he had ignored and stomped on for years had become real to him once again in a simple transaction on a Sulzbach mountain slope. He'd made peace with God there, but what gripped him at this moment was the confident prospect that he would see his parents again. No one had told him that an eternal reunion was a fringe benefit, but the conviction had come on the same mountain.

Drew smiled as they left the crowded city of a hundred spires and drove west though rolling hills and gentle farmlands. The Czech Republic had few modern highways, but it abounded in scenic countryside. Wild flowers filled the hillsides. Melting snows had turned to small waterfalls. Splashes of yellow and green dotted the sprawling fields.

He bypassed Kladno, a thriving steel center, and drove northwest to Jarvoc. The town stood backed by a forest of spruce and firs, steep rolling hills rising toward the low-crested mountains. Railroad tracks ran along the edge of the forest where a long line of freight cars waited for loading. The river—more like a bubbling stream for trout—left the town as landlocked as the country, with no major outlet to the North Sea for shipping steel.

He could see the Russelmann factory as they drove along, black smoke curling from the farthest building. As he increased speed, Miriam said, "You passed Dorian Paschek's street, Drew."

"Did I? I thought the Pascheks owned a large farm."

"They did, but war and communism changed all that."

He shot a glance her way. "How would you know?"

"Olivia sent a card from Prague just before she was killed. She said the beautiful farmland had been turned into a factory town with crowded housing. . . . Please, let's see Dorian first."

He kept his foot heavy on the gas. "We'll still have time."

"No. You'll get to talking at the factory. Besides, in a town this small, Dorian will know all about the Russelmanns."

He gave in reluctantly as he turned the car back and bumped over the cobbled road to the Pascheks' faded yellow home. Its living quarters were still attached to the old barn. It sat beside a narrow row of newer, look-alike houses. There was a drabness, a sense of hopelessness to this part of town, as though a fresh coat of paint was out of reach. The housing still reflected the dull colors of communism. The narrow wood siding on Paschek's washboard of a place was worn and ridged, in dire need of a scrubbing. But the old barn had been turned into a shop. Ribbed glass plates and bowls were displayed in the window, another man's name on the shingle.

Drew parked at the end of the street. As they stepped from the car, he nodded to the sign. "Hon, Paschek doesn't live here."

"We have to make certain." She took his hand and tugged him along. Inside the shop, Miriam smiled at the woman behind the counter. "We're looking for our friend Dorian Paschek," she said.

The woman pointed along the side of the shop. "He keeps the cottage in the rear. Actually it's the old toolshed, but he fixed it up real nice and added a room or two." She fussed with the glass display. "No need to go back there. He's at work now."

Miriam never liked detours. "Where does he work?"

"Thought you knew him." Her sharp tone matched Miriam's.

Miriam mellowed. "We do—sort of. We knew his sister."

"His sister is dead. God rest her soul."

"I know, but we were friends. Very good friends."

The woman's interest turned to a dust speck on the counter. "Dorian won't be home for another six hours. He lives alone since his wife's death. We don't bother him. He likes it that way."

Drew picked up one of the glass bowls with its intricate design. "Where does Mr. Paschek work?" he asked casually.

"Same place everyone else does. There's my place. Four cafes. The pubs and the factory. But without the steel factory the town would have died long ago."

Drew put the bowl down. "We'll come back on our way out of town. We'd like to take a gift home to our daughter."

As Drew opened the door for Miriam, the woman repositioned a glass plate. "If you find Dorian, I wouldn't mention that sister of his to him. Not in front of anyone."

Miriam whirled around in the open doorway and put her foot against it. The door chime kept ringing. Above the clanging, the woman said, "Dorian never speaks of her anymore, not since she caused so much trouble."

"Trouble?" Drew asked. "She only came here for the funeral."

"And never when they really needed her. Dorian's wife was sick a long time. No," she said sadly, "Dorian's sister should have died back in the resistance movement. Then we could have put her name on the town monument—and forgotten her."

They walked back to the car in silence. As he slipped in beside Miriam, she said, "Why would Dorian feel that way? Olivia deposited money for him in Prague for years, ample enough to cover any medical expenses." She bit at her lips. "I should have told her we knew Olivia in America—that she was a good person."

"Somehow I don't think that woman would have believed you."

As they drew closer to the factory, the six-story air-conditioned building loomed up in front of them. The property was gated, the grounds well kept with trimmed hedges and a freshly cut lawn. Behind the modern complex lay acres of land with six or seven separate plants that surely contained the computer-controlled systems, the coke ovens and blast furnaces, the refineries and rolling mills that allowed the Russelmanns to produce tons of steel annually. The guard at the gate handed them a visitor's pass and waved them on.

Inside the main building the reception room was airy and spacious, the floors carpeted. A cushioned bench encircled the fountain in the middle of the hall, the sound of running water echoing through the empty room.

Drew strolled to the directory and scanned the long list of occupants. He knew enough German and French to know that many of the companies were foreign owned: investment and insurance companies, brokers and exporters, and one Japanese company—Nishokura Steel. Most of them were members of the European Community and had brought their businesses to Jarvoc, probably to avoid the monstrous rentals in the crowded city of Prague.

The Russelmanns' executive suites took up the entire second floor. "This explains it," Drew said, scanning the names again. "The Russelmanns may own this building, but they lease most of it to others." Grinning he said, "So let's go drop Vic's bombshell and tell them we know Jon Gainsborough."

"Is that what Vic wanted us to do?"

"It's the easiest way to look around."

"You won't forget Dorian?"

"Wouldn't think of it."

The Russelmann suite was more plush than the lobby. A tall, dignified gentleman in a gray suit stood by the receptionist's desk with *The Prague Post* in his arthritic hands. "I'm Hanz," he said, looking at Drew. "May I help you?"

"I'm Drew Gregory. We're looking for the Russelmanns."

"Which Mr. Russelmann?" the receptionist asked.

The older man cut her off, asking, "Were you interested in a shipment of steel, Mr. Gregory?"

"Not exactly. We're friends of Jon Gainsborough in London. He asked us to drop by."

Drew felt Miriam's jab to the ribs. Old habits were hard to break. He'd had years of small untruths and innocuous answers all in the line of duty, all intended to keep the code of silence demanded by the Agency. During those years, he was convinced that God and the Agency were incompatible. Now that he'd lined himself on the side of God, he still struggled with Company ethics.

Awkwardly he said, "Actually a friend told us to drop by. Said you and Gainsborough do business together."

The tired brown eyes blinked. The man's hair was gray and thin, his profile strong, his expression sad. "Gainsborough? He could be one of our long-standing accounts." The receptionist looked perplexed as Hanz slipped his I.D. badge into his pocket and said, "You'd have to check with Altman Russelmann. He handles the foreign contacts."

Drew glanced at the door marked President. "Could we see Mr. Russelmann?"

Hanz put a restraining hand on the receptionist's shoulder. "Altman is out in the welding plant. He'll be another two hours."

"Do you know Dorian Paschek?" Miriam asked, smiling up at Hanz. "Dorian's sister Olivia Renway and I were good friends."

For a moment Hanz froze. He remained stony-faced, but interest sparked in his eyes. "Dorian Paschek works for us."

Odd, Drew thought. *You don't recall an important foreign contract, and yet you immediately knew one of the employees.*

"Would it be possible to see Mr. Paschek?" Drew asked. "We're driving back to Prague shortly."

Without a word, Hanz limped toward them. Grabbing three hard hats from the hooks, he handed two of them to the Gregorys. "Dorian is in the field."

In spite of the limp he moved quickly, obviously not expecting them to accommodate their steps to his. He led them out the back entrance to a tram and shuttled them out past two more security gates directly onto the open fields. The guards saluted as he sped by them. The land seemed to stretch for miles, acres of property stockpiled with steel. A hydraulic pallet and a truck crane were parked in front of one plant, and wing pallets stood loaded with steel bars and tubes ready for shipment. Other trucks loaded with the wide-flange beams rumbled over the fields toward the freight cars.

"Wait here," he said and limped away.

As they waited for him to come back, Miriam pointed toward the building by the edge of the forest that looked like a military barracks with rings of black smoke rising from its chimneys. "Drew, what would they use that for?"

"Housing maybe, although it's a bit rundown for that."

He couldn't picture metallurgists and engineers finding the barracks satisfactory housing, especially with the railroad tracks running right past it. Drew turned back in time to see Hanz signal to a man in his middle years sitting high on the black seat of the forklift, his gloved hands gripping the wheel as he bounced along. The man braked and leaned over to listen to Hanz, then slid down from the yellow cab, and sauntered toward the Gregorys. He was a big man, solid but not tall. Fringes of straight gray hair hung beneath his hard hat.

He yanked his gloves and black-rimmed glasses off and slipped them into his pocket as he reached them. "I'm Dorian Paschek," he said.

He ignored the hand that Drew extended. "We're the Gregorys," Drew said. "Friends of your sister."

"Yes, she told me about you when she was here. What do you want?"

"Just to greet you," Miriam said. "We were fond of her."

It seemed as though his gray, lifeless eyes would brim with tears, but he looked away, toeing the dirt beneath his scuffed boot. Life had not been kind to Dorian Paschek. His work clothes were worn and patched, his mottled skin weather-beaten, his large hands rough and callused from working the forklift.

Hanz stood by the tram, his eyes unblinking as he watched them. "We won't keep you long, Paschek," Drew promised.

"Good. They'll dock my pay for every second." He looked from one to the other. "There's little lodging in Jarvoc." He was soft-spoken, his voice guarded. "And I've no room at my place."

"We're not staying," Miriam said. "We just wanted to meet you. I promised Olivia that I would visit her country one day."

"She came back once," he said. "For my wife's funeral.

Olivia should never have come. She was shocked to find the steel factory functioning again under the old leadership."

"You never told her?"

"Mrs. Gregory, we never wrote. When my wife died, I called Olivia. She was the only family I had left. I didn't expect her to come. But she insisted—"

"Is that when she discovered the Russelmanns back in business?"

"Yes, Gregory, and she didn't like what had happened to Jarvoc under Communist rule. To her it was like Lidice and the war all over again."

He shifted, turning his face from Hanz. "I've got to get back to work. But I'm telling you, Olivia was a fool coming back here." He ran the back of his big hand across his lips. "She came down to the factory with me—insisted on it. Her in all her finery. She took pictures and notes—it almost cost me my job."

Drew wanted to ask why Olivia had avoided coming home all those years. Or had she been told never to come back? What had clouded her past? Even Dorian seemed to reject her. Drew was convinced that it went back to the war years. Ian Kendall had hinted that part of Olivia's pain stemmed back to Lidice and the resistance movement—to Olivia's personal war against the Nazis. Somehow Jarvoc was part of the puzzle. On a gamble he asked, "Dorian, do you have your sister's notes on her last novel?"

Dorian's face hardened. "I refused to keep them."

"Do you know where they are?"

"I trust that they're in ashes like Olivia."

"Dorian, it's important to Olivia's family. Would you have any idea what your sister did with those notes?"

His gaze remained glum and dispirited. "We had a nanny when we were small, a governess actually."

"Beatrice Thorpe," Drew said.

Dorian seemed surprised. "She lived in Jarvoc, and when she could no longer care for herself, she moved in with my wife and me. But after my wife's death—"

Drew felt the man's pain. "Then you were glad when Olivia took Beatrice back to London."

He shrugged. "I knew Olivia would give her a good home. She'd be dead now, but she was the one person that my sister trusted."

As he turned to leave, Drew stopped him. "Why didn't you keep in touch with Olivia's family?"

"Her husband wrote right after Olivia's death." He tipped his hard hat forward. "Uriah wanted me to move to America."

"You should have taken him up on it."

He looked at Miriam. "I never answered him, Mrs. Gregory."

"Call me Miriam," she told him. "Olivia did."

"It was best for all of us to forget Olivia. You, too."

"*Never*, Dorian."

Drew slipped his arm around Miriam. "Paschek, we've taken up enough of your work time. I'm sorry. But look—is there anything that Uriah could do for you? Or my wife and I?"

"You can leave us alone," Dorian said.

He walked away, his grief evident in his slow gait back to the forklift. They watched him climb up into the leather seat and maneuver the truck backwards. He was scooping the prongs under a load of steel when Hanz pulled the tram up in front of them.

"I'll drive you to your car," he offered.

Drew nodded. *Good shot,* he thought. *A clever detour from any contact with Altman Russelmann.*

They were back in the Skoda, Drew with his hand on the key. He sat there, not turning on the engine. "The way Dorian acts, the economy here would be nothing without the Russelmann factory. The Russelmanns must control this town."

"At least they employ it."

"But, Miriam, Kladno is one of the major steel industries in the Czech Republic. Why competition like this so close by?"

"There are a lot of people in the surrounding areas, Drew. Competition is healthy. I'm not the only art gallery on Rodeo Drive, you know."

"It's a wild shot, *Liebling*, but if the Russelmanns control Jon Gainsborough, they may have a stake in the cycling team."

She looked horrified. "Ian!" was all she could say.

"When I talked with Vic, he said the Russelmanns set Gainsborough up in business. That means they backed him with plenty of pound notes and crowns."

He shifted his gaze. "That building in the rear—the one that looks like a Quonset hut—has been around a long time. The rest of the compound is modern, updated. But they left that one standing."

"The Russelmanns must like antiques."

"Maybe it's connected to underground tunnels. Maybe it's a reminder to the people of a bitter past."

"You're talking circles, Drew. And if we don't get out of here, the security guards will be ticketing us for loitering."

He ducked beneath the sun shield. "I'm more concerned about the gentleman up there on the second floor watching us."

She squinted through her dark glasses. "Who is he?"

"I'd say Altman Russelmann."

"But Hanz said he was out in the welding shop."

"I don't think the receptionist agreed."

"You're right! She was surprised when he said Russelmann was unavailable."

With a flick of Drew's wrist the engine hummed. "That's when Hanz took off his I.D. badge, Miriam."

"He didn't need a badge, Drew. He wasn't the custodian or some flunky. Everyone recognized him. And that suit was high-priced. Same for the shoes. I notice those things."

"My guess is he's part of executive row. Another Russelmann perhaps, so he'd be aware of the Gainsborough contracts."

👁👁👁

The city of more than a hundred spires lay ahead, a city intricate in design. Modern and medieval. Landlocked, yet a crossroads of Europe. "Oh, Drew, Olivia loved this old city," Miriam said. "I understand why."

"Why?" he teased.

"Prague is everything—a modern city, a Bohemian countryside. Romanesque and Gothic architecture. Peaceful gardens." She laughed. "And those tangled one-way streets that you despise."

"Don't forget Prague's history."

"It wasn't all glorious," she said. "But I don't think I'll ever forget my time here. Because of Olivia. Because of *you*."

They could see some distinctive landmarks now. St. Vitus's Cathedral with the rose window between its twin spires. The Prague Castle high above the Left Bank of the Vltava River. The gold-crested National Theater. "I love this city," she said.

"Sounds like you're not ready to leave it, *Liebling*."

"I'd like one more day."

"Oh, sweetheart, I couldn't look at another museum. We've accomplished what we came for, did what Vic wanted us to do. Met Dorian Paschek. I'd rather leave."

"But, Drew, I came to enjoy Olivia's city."

"One more day," he agreed reluctantly.

"You won't make me check out of the Adria?"

"Why would I do that?"

She glanced at the sideview mirror. "Because that car in the distance has been following us ever since we left Jarvoc."

He patted her knee. "We'll be all right. We came into Prague as tourists. I plan for us to leave the same way."

"And if they keep following us?"

He winked. "We'll lose them by the third museum."

Drew fell into a moody silence as he turned the car over to the doorman at the Adria and took Miriam's hand. It was too late to take action this evening, without rousing her suspicions. But Drew was an early riser—always downing two or three cups of black coffee before sociability caught up with him. Tomorrow he'd let Miriam sleep in. It would give him time to contact Leos Cepek, an old friend with Czech Intelligence. He wanted to warn Leos that the Jarvoc steel mill bore watching. The call to Dudley Perkins in London would have to come later. He dreaded that one. Perkins wouldn't thank Drew for questioning the business integrity of Jon Gainsborough, the British steel magnate who was especially useful to Perkins.

As they reached their room, Miriam asked, "Drew, why do you think Dorian hates Olivia so?"

"He doesn't. He's troubled by bad memories. Somehow Olivia made it difficult for him. Maybe Hanz let it slip when he said they built the Russelmann factory on the ruins of Jarvoc."

Chapter 13

Chase groaned as the microfilm spun off its reel and fell on the table in a crumpled mess in front of her. Three hours ago she had hit a gold mine when a jaunty cameraman on the university campus tapped his camera bag and said, "I'm Andrew Forrestal. I'd like to take your picture."

Startled she had asked, "Whatever for?"

"For the evening news." He peeked under the brim of her hat. "Tell me you've done something newsworthy today, Miss—"

"Not a thing," she said. "I'm just here for the summer. And I'm Chase Evans. From Long Island, New York, before you ask."

"That's it, Miss Evans. The influx of tourists."

His voice and face seemed to smile at the same time. Somehow it pleased her. She had taken long enough to dress this morning, finally settling on the white-trimmed navy dress, a French design her grandmother had bought for her on their last visit to Europe. She had forgotten an umbrella, and at the last minute grabbed the wide-brimmed red hat that she had worn to the Royal Ascot races. It sat low on her forehead, putting the emphasis on her dark-lashed eyes. "I'm more of a student than a tourist," she said still laughing up at him. "But no pictures."

"A pity. You'd make such a splendid subject."

"Are you the roving campus photographer?"

He chuckled. "I'm ten years post-college, and even then I didn't graduate. But I'm good with this camera." He whipped it from its case and flashed another of his easygoing grins. "I just did a session with one of the retiring dons at Imperial College. Caught him at just the right angle. He won't even look bald."

"Is he part of the evening news?"

"Will be. Now, your turn."

He aimed the camera, and she pushed his hands away. "No pictures, Mr. Forrestal."

"Such a pity. But call me Andy." His voice rang with amusement as he fell into step with her. "Americans usually take their cameras to Piccadilly and Trafalgar Square. So what are you doing at London University with an attaché case in your hand?"

"Putting my International Student Card to good use. This is a marvelous campus."

"Another piece of British history like Westminster Abbey. Which piece of history are you looking for?"

"The death of Olivia Renway."

"An accident?"

"Yes."

"That's my usual beat. Accidents. Homicides. Murders. You know—the grisly scenes. Twisted metal. Grotesque bodies—"

"That's gross, Andy."

"I'm sorry. Forgive me. . . . Who was your friend? This Renway?"

"A novelist. She married a Britisher—and ended up dead on Downing Street ten years ago."

"Because of her marriage?"

"No! Her husband wasn't even in London the day she was killed. I'm researching her life. Yesterday I went bleary-eyed looking at microfilms and microfiche at the newspaper morgue."

She had browsed until her shoulders ached from standing in front of the Business Newsbank drawers searching out clippings. She flexed her angel wings as they walked along trying to ease the kinks that were still there. "And this morning I was back at the library looking at more film and records, but I haven't put my finger on what I want yet."

For a moment he actually looked sympathetic, his face serious. Then he gave her that sly grin of his. "At least you didn't have to thumb through a stack of yellowed newspapers. But try the Public Record Office. They might be able to help you."

She brightened. "I might try them in the morning."

"So what are you tracking down?"

"Olivia Renway's reason for being on Downing Street. If I could just get into the BBC files and find out what happened—"

"Sorry, the broadcasting center is closed to the public."

"And no amount of persuasion changed their minds."

They had reached the street corner, not far from her subway station. "I have to be going now, Andrew."

He slung his camera over his shoulder and pulled her back from the curb, his grip possessive. "Don't go. I can help you. I work for an independent television station. Our news files are as thorough as those stored at BBC. But my time comes costly."

She grabbed at his invitation. "How much?"

The sum had been high, but she was leaving for Oxford in the morning. *Too high,* she thought now as she stared down at the broken reel of microfilm. Andrew Forrestal would have to fix it.

She felt a surge of relief as he came back from the storage room, another film canister in his hand. Andrew's striped shirt was only half tucked in, the sleeves rolled up. His squint seemed perpetual, as though he were looking at her through his zoom lens.

As he reached her, he stared down at the twisted film. "What happened?"

"I ran the reel too hard. I'm sorry."

"No bother. I'll repair it. Did you find what you wanted?"

She tapped the frayed film. "It's the right time frame—the end of May ten years ago—but there's nothing on the accident."

"It had to be a major tragedy to make the evening news."

His indifference irritated her. "Perhaps it was only tragic to her family."

"Or some breaking news pushed it to the back page."

"Then why did I find clippings of her death over at the newspaper office?" Chase flipped her hair from the nape of her neck and bent her head back. The ceiling of the work room was drab, colorless, one strip of paint peeling away and hanging loose. Slowly her attention was drawn to the man who had arrived moments after she did. Periodically he glanced her way, an intense man with light hair and a petulant smile. He slouched forward, his trench coat thrown over the chair beside him. She pegged him as a grumpy TV news commentator pressed for time on an article for the evening broadcast.

Along the wall behind him stood four computers, the years marked at the top of each one. The last forty years of news highlights had been preserved in full text on floppy disks and CD-ROMs. With the press of a button the past came alive—four decades of breaking news stories that had pushed school plays and traffic accidents and obituaries to the back burner.

Chase spread her notes out in front of her and looked up at Forrestal again. He was checking his watch, his interest waning rapidly. "Andrew, if only this torn film were in one piece."

"I told you, I can fix it."

"Is there some other way to check the main headline for that day? I think it was something about a bombing—"

He picked up the twisted film. "Let me at that chair. Maybe I can hand-feed the film enough for us to find out."

She leaned over his bony shoulder. As he stretched the film back and forth, the bobbing pictures made Chase dizzy.

"What was that date again?" he asked.

"The twenty-seventh of May."

"Jolly good. The man over there is interested in the same date. There it is. Bomb scare at the prime minister's place. No wonder your friend's death went to the back page."

"The IRA?"

"Some Czech splinter group took credit."

She started to say, *Renway was Czechoslovakian*, but bit her tongue. "Can you run me a copy?"

"Impossible. You're the one who broke it."

"I told you I was sorry."

His attention went back to the bobbing microfilm. "Where did you say your friend was killed?"

"Downing Street—just off Whitehall on a rainy afternoon."

He grinned. "We have a lot of rain. Come back tomorrow. I could have this film spliced back together by then."

"Can't. I'm going on to Oxford in the morning."

He handed her his business card. "Be a love and leave your address. If I find anything else on this Renway, I'll let you know. I'll even drive up to Oxford and hand-deliver it."

As he pulled the torn film back and forth, she wrote the Hamptons' address on the back of his card and tucked it in his shirt pocket. "Here we go," he said. "An obituary on Renway."

She had leaned so close that her cheek was near his. "Andrew, would they have aired it over the telly?"

He picked up the canister and frowned. "American novelist . . . wife of Uriah Kendall, son of Lord and Lady Kendall . . . " He whistled. "Somebody had it ready for the evening news that night, but it was canceled."

"Why would they do that?"

His mood turned harsh. "I told you. Some late-breaking story bumped it, or someone ordered it off the air."

Someone important. She started to say, *Olivia Renway was a good friend of the prime minister*. But what difference did it make? The late-breaking news of a bomb threat had surely swept the report of Olivia's death from the evening news.

Forrestal stood and gathered up the frayed film and canisters. "Chase, why don't you let this business go?"

One of her father's cardinal rules popped into her mind. "You never stop in the middle of a project. If the answers don't come, you back up and start over."

From the look on Andrew Forrestal's face, it was time to

back off. "Andrew, I've taken far too much of your time already."

"That's not the problem," he said. "You knew all along, didn't you? That Renway's husband was with British Intelligence."

She avoided his eyes, not wanting him to know that he had just dropped a bombshell, but he saw her surprise and said, "You didn't know." Without his smile the worry lines cut deep into his face. "Chase, let me give you a bit of advice. In this country an intelligence officer is off-limits."

Chase stuffed her notes into her briefcase and swung the case off the table. She refused to take his warning. "But, Andrew, Olivia Renway and Dorothy Sayers are not off-limits."

Andrew watched her leave and then turned to face the other occupant in the room. The man was slipping into his trench coat, a perfidious sneer on his narrow face.

Unfriendly sort! Forrestal thought. *Never mind. He paid me a hefty fee for the privilege of being here.*

"Just leave the canisters on the table," Forrestal said, and then he sauntered into the storage room, his thoughts on the girl's Oxford address in his pocket.

He whistled as he spliced the split ends of the microfilm, and still whistling went to the aisle marked 1980-89. Tapping the canister against his open palm, he wondered why this sudden interest in an old hit-and-run? But the dead woman had been the wife of a former British agent. Could Chase be a security risk? He considered his options. The better part of wisdom suggested total silence. Stay out of it. Don't get involved. Don't let the staff know that bribery money burned in his hip pocket.

Or he could call Edwin Wallis over at Scotland Yard and suggest they meet at the local pub for an hour or two. He didn't always see eye to eye with Constable Wallis, but they had exchanged favors in the past. Why not now? If Wallis didn't remember the Renway incident, at least he'd have access to the records. He thumped the canister in his hand again. Even three sheets to the wind, Wallis would laugh in his face. Edwin Wallis had a unique way of cutting you down, making even your slightest suspicion seem like child's play. The first thing the constable would ask would be, "Did you get photos of her, Andy?"

Andy's whistle died, leaving the musty room unbearable. He shrugged and filed the microfilm in the empty slot.

Behind him he heard the squeaking of a shoe. He whirled around half expecting to see the girl again. He saw only the glint of the razor-sharp knife before it broke into his skin and thrust deep into his body. The scream was his own, the agony excruciating. He squinted, trying desperately to focus on the mocking face of his assailant. For a moment he clung to the bookshelf, his fingers chalk-white. As his grip weakened, he slumped to the floor.

The man in the beige trench coat knelt beside him, his fingers deftly searching Andy's pockets until he found the card with Chase Evans's address on it. His eyes were cold, unfeeling as he raised the knife once more and plunged it into Andy's abdomen. As the man fled, Forrestal gasped for air. His thoughts reeled. Blurred images like a strip of exposed film filled his vision. Indistinct silhouettes. Curled celluloid. *This is a homicide. . . . must take pictures for the evening news. . . . Constable Wallis will demand photographs.*

His hand lay limp on his chest, soaked in his own blood. He saw nothing now. Only grayness. Darkness. Utter void. He sensed the deathly silence of the room and felt the faint thump of his own heartbeat. He wanted the girl with the pretty hat to come back. He wanted her to hold his hand.

Nedrick Russelmann made a quick decision as Chase Evans left the back entry of the television studio. Jiri Benak had not followed her out. It was up to Nedrick to set out after her.

She walked with a brisk, confident step, her narrow hips swaying slightly, that gleaming hair bouncing against her slender neck. Once she reached the embankment and passed the first elegant Victorian bridge, she slowed her pace, strolling leisurely along the tree-lined walkway. Moments later she paused on the footbridge. *Evans will make her contact here,* Ned thought.

But she gazed down at the River Thames like one beholding an old friend and enjoying the visit. Ned had not expected to find her so appealing. She seemed far more sophisticated and worldly wise than Mila, trapped as she was in the simple life in Jarvoc. He waited, but Evans seemed content to simply gaze down on the meandering blue-green river with its tiny whirlpools of polluted gray. Tugboats and tour cruisers drifted with the current; moored ships bobbed along the granite embankment. And then she moved on, those long legs stepping quickly.

Nedrick followed her, pausing briefly where she had stood. No package had been left behind. No chalk markings on the railing. He shrank back when he spotted a police launch patrolling the Thames and turned in time to see Evans bypass a call-box, too distant from it to chalk a message there.

As he reached the far end of the bridge, he kept her in sight, pacing his strides to hers—one moment pushing himself rapidly through the teeming crowd, the next feeling the press of the crowd against his leaden steps. Evans's leather briefcase banged rhythmically against her thigh, forcing Ned to think back to that never-forgotten moment when Olivia Renway had set her briefcase down to autograph a book for him.

He remembered the flicker in Renway's transparent expression when he had given her his name. Her fingers had frozen around the pen. She had recognized the name. He was certain of it. He had meant to hate her when he met her, to despise her for abandoning his father and grandfather. Instead he was stunned by her elegance, by the softness of her mouth and pensive gaze. Hanz Russelmann had loved this woman. Why then had he given the order to destroy her? To murder her! Popshot?

As the rain had come down harder that day, rolling off

Renway's designer clothes, Ned had thrust his black umbrella into her hands. He ached to say, *I'm Nedrick. I'm your grandson.* Instead, he said, "Here, Miss Renway, take my umbrella."

He had not been told that Franz would take the waving of her book as a cue to power-charge the car and hurl the gentler side of Ned's life into eternity. His umbrella had blocked her vision as the car barreled down on her. Ned still remembered the bloody designer clothes, the elegant face twisted in pain. He could still see her mouthing the words, "Why, Nedrick?"

Yes, she had known. Olivia Renway had known.

Later when he came to his senses—when the sheer exhaustion of running left him—he vomited in the gutter. In that moment he despised his grandfather. Renway's murder had taken away a part of Nedrick himself. Ned would never be able to tell Renway who he was, never be able to call her grandmother.

Thinking of it once more as he tracked the American, he wondered whether Jiri had intended for Franz to run *him* down, too, to leave him dead on Downing Street with Renway. Even now he feared that Jiri had no intention of letting him ever reach Jarvoc alive.

Ned had lost sight of Evans. He quickened his pace and finally saw her crossing the street and making her way toward the north side of Whitehall. *She's leading me back to Downing Street.*

Stone barriers blocked the entry into Downing. Chase had joined the queue of people standing behind the barriers, their cameras aimed toward the bobbies on duty at the famous doorway. Nedrick fought the rush of dryness in his mouth, fought the memory of Olivia Renway coming out that door, coming toward him.

"Distract Renway while I grab her briefcase," Jiri had told him. "And if she resists—"

But she hadn't resisted.

The gray Renault with his cousin Franz at the wheel had shattered his grandmother's body on impact. With squealing tires, Franz turned the Renault on a dime, making his own roundabout in the middle of Downing. He had careened wildly up and over the curb and bounced back into the street, the bonnet of the car rattling as he winged his way into the Whitehall traffic and disappeared.

Jiri plans the same fate for you, Ned thought as his eyes settled back on Chase Evans again. She spoke to no one. Touched no one. Passed nothing. If Jiri's prediction came true—if Chase Evans really worked for the CIA—someone would contact her. The attaché case would pass from Chase's hands to another agent's.

The man standing beside Nedrick held a crackling transistor to his ear. He slapped it and listened again. Turning to his companion in the Harris Tweed jacket, he said, "Some bloke just walked into a television studio viewing room and killed a cameraman."

"In broad daylight?"

He shook the crackling radio. "Just happened within the hour. Andrew Forrestal—"

"Forrestal? The one with all those award-winning shots?"

"Maybe one of them got him killed. Sad thing—they never catch up with those blokes."

The tweed coat was more confident. "They might this time. They keep hidden video cameras in those TV viewing rooms."

The sour taste in Nedrick's mouth stung like the bite of a bitter lemon. In front of him, Evans shifted her case to the other hand. For a second Ned thought she was passing it back to the man in the Harris Tweed, but without even noticing him, she set out once more on Whitehall, strolling toward Piccadilly.

If the cameras at the studio had caught Evans and Jiri Benak on film, Ned didn't plan to be found in their company. He struck out toward the Victoria Embankment and the nearest underground station. He'd ride a few stops, then transfer to the East London tube, and go from there to his parked car—Uriah's shiny Rolls Royce.

Nedrick felt sick thinking about the dead cameraman. The Russelmann blood pulsated through his veins, a mixture of disdain and loyalty. There would be no welcome for him in Jarvoc. No, he would take the tunnel under the English Channel and escape along the French coastline, crossing the Pyrenees into Spain where he would gladly settle in Madrid or in one of the fishing villages facing Morocco. His mouth tightened. He would change his name—to Nedrick Kendall perhaps. He knew the language. Someday he would send for Mila, and she would come to him.

But Uriah Kendall's friendship dug at his inmost fiber. He knew that before Madrid—before escaping to any fishing village—he must first head back to the Cotswolds and warn Uriah that Chase Evans was pursuing Olivia's story with deadly consequences.

Chapter 14

C hase left the Ritz too tuckered out to think about the
fifty-mile drive to Oxford. As she hit the accelerator,
the sun reflected on the Thames, promising a fair
day to replace the two gloomy gray days she had spent in
London. It was that way back home, too—the weather and
the Hudson River always playing games with her.

The Hudson was her river; the Thames belonged to Olivia
Renway, and yet for now it was hers as well. The River
Thames was London. The city spread out on either side of
its banks, no longer the great commercial port but still as
much a part of the Londoner as the city's history and ceremony. Beneath one of the bridges, a fishing trawler churned
the waters between the rusty piers, cutting its path through
the blue-green foam, chugging along toward the next bend
in the river.

Outside of London a gusty spring breeze whipped
through the open car window; it brushed against her cheek,
sweeping her back in time to the windy days of her childhood—to gentle summer days on the beach with the sea
breeze blowing in off the ocean. Back to favorite snapshots.
A smiling baby, sun-baked on a cloudless day. A happy-go-
lucky child, her pretty clothes kite-whipped as she romped
around the spacious home on the hilltop. A third grader,
housebound by a winter northeasterner, sitting by a doll-
house that was bigger than any owned by her friends. A
teenager frantically manning the sails on her father's yacht

when they were caught in an unexpected squall on Long Island Sound. The Vassar student sometimes acting as mystical as the trade winds off the Atlantic. And the torn picture of her father coming to find her during last year's bitterly cold snowstorm that blew in across the Hudson. Chase wasn't even a quarter of a century old, yet they had been good years with her needs met by doting parents and her desires lavishly fulfilled by her grandmother. Chase had always been the recipient of Callie Bartholomew's favors with many trips abroad.

The wind brushed her cheek again, taking a tear with it. Something had happened to the snapshots of her teen years. Without intending to do so, Chase had taken on some of Callie's broad views of the world and her cynicism toward an afterlife. And yet at this moment as Chase drove along the River Thames—alone in England—the trips that filled her fondest memories were the family outings with her dad at the wheel as they followed the course of the Hudson River. Life had been much richer before her dad became so engrossed in the corporate world—before a good public image had become the cardinal rule in the Evans household.

Even now, in her empty car, she wanted to shout out, "Daddy, where are we going?"

"Where do you want to go?" he'd ask in his deep bass voice.

"To the Land of Oz." Surely it was just around the bend in the Hudson River.

"Pick a place closer," he would say.

"Heaven," she had suggested once innocently.

"Don't know the way."

She admitted to herself that it was not just intellectual pursuits that drove her these days. She was obsessed with an unresolved personal search for peace. In the Evans mansion one tiptoed around discussions on finances and faith. Finances were only discussed in the form of wise investments and faith and prayer only voiced at the grave. Even her older sister had married in the family garden, and if a prayer was expressed, Chase couldn't remember it.

Chase was forever stepping to a new drumbeat. In spite of having everything at her fingertips, she never felt satisfied. Something drew her to Renway and Sayers—she felt an emotional tie. Everything she read about Renway suggested restlessness and secrecy. Sayers was another woman out of step with her times, always dancing to her own music— another intellectual who broke with the mores of society as she left her mark on the literary world. Her writings spanned a wide variety of interests from the whimsical Lord Peter Wimsey to the subtle lessons on theology that would have placed Sayers behind a pulpit had she been a man in her own generation. Something had drawn Renway to an in-depth study of Sayers, something more than their degrees from Somerville.

As Chase redefined the purposes of her study program abroad, she smiled ruefully. Maybe she should call her dissertation "The Somerville Connection." Her father would like that one. Or "The Feminine Gender at Oxford." Or if she included Margaret Thatcher, she could call it "Somerville Women in the Political Arena." The political arena? Is that where Sayers and Renway belonged?

She stretched her arm out the car window and tried to cup the wind in her hand. That was as difficult as trying to link Renway and Sayers or please her father. With nostalgia she thought of those happy childhood days with her dad at the wheel calling back to her, "What are you doing, sweetie?"

"Catching the wind."

He had filled the car with his laughter. "Do that and you can do anything."

Nola, sitting close beside him, had said, "Seymour, if she wants to chase the wind, don't laugh at her."

Lately that seemed to be all she was doing—chasing the wind with her choices and rarely pleasing her father. He expected her to take top honors in grad school and to be on the competitive side of sailing and tennis, but her hours at the Halverson House and the Willowglen were an embarrassment to him. He adamantly opposed her friendship with Jeff Carlson, and he still took it as a personal affront that his affluent mother-in-law had chosen to die of cancer in a three-winged nursing home—trapped in diapers and a wheelchair in the very city where he was so well known.

Somehow Seymour Evans the airplane industrialist was not the father she remembered from her childhood, and now she faced displeasing him more. Once she had her degree and claimed her inheritance, she planned to speak out in Washington for people like Jeff Carlson and Marie at the Willowglen. She would have the Bartholomew wealth behind her and two names to flaunt. The Bartholomews of New York had been making inroads on Washington for generations, and the name Evans was not unknown. Her dad often packed a wallop at election time and was rewarded with continual government contracts. Chase didn't want government contracts. She just wanted the politicians in Washington to take up the cause of those who could no longer stand up for themselves. She wouldn't be chasing the wind then—she'd be battling a family blizzard.

Chase shifted gears and took the hill, wishing with unexpected nostalgia that Callie could be with her wending around the mighty Thames. It was from Callie that Chase had discovered the imperfect world that was left to the Bartholomews and the Evans clan to transform. Callie never doubted her own abilities to change the world. Chase had simply taken up her banner.

But the Halverson Wayside House had caused stirrings on Long Island that would have daunted even Callie. In spite of police raids and rock-throwing, loudspeakers and marches and legal maneuvering, the town's outcry against AIDS and those infected with it had been defeated. The Halverson House sat on a privately owned hill, surrounded not by gates but by well-trimmed hedges. When it came to a council debate, little could be done. The owner called the dying residents "guests in his home." The defeat in the city council infuriated Chase's father, which was reason enough for Chase to take up the rights of the residents there.

On her first visit to the Halverson House, she had arrived with only a vague plan of what she would do when someone opened the door. She was still knocking when a gaunt-faced young man peered around the partly cracked door, his dark eyes recessed and hollow. He appeared so weak that she expected him to fall forward and topple into her arms.

"Yes, ma'am?" he said in a voice without joy.

"I came to visit someone," she told him.

He opened the door farther and allowed her to step into the massive foyer. She realized then that he was barefoot, his skin as white as the painted walls behind him. "Are you a relative?"

"The truth is, I don't know anyone here. I just came—"

The hunched shoulders squared. "You from the city council?"

"No."

"You're not some reporter?"

"No, I came as a friend." She held up a book of Robert Service's poems. "Could I read to someone? Or just sit and visit?"

His eyes seemed even more sunken now, uncertain. "It's not very pleasant around here."

Down the hall she heard guitar music and a soft melancholy voice crooning a country song. "There's music," she said.

"We try to cheer each other up."

She glanced past him down the long hallway.

"Maybe you'd like to see Jeff. He ain't got no family. At least no one who comes regularly."

"And you?"

He looked at her now as he mumbled, "These guys are all the family I have now."

"Then perhaps I can visit you next time?"

"You'd come back here? We don't usually get much company."

"Where do I find Jeff?"

"He's at the end of the hall near the kitchen." He stepped back so she could pass him. "We made up a room for him on the first floor. He's too sick to climb the stairs."

"When I come back the next time, where will I find you?"

"Just ask for Mitch. I ain't planning on going nowhere."

"I'll see you later. I'll go read to Jeff now."

"You won't be afraid of him?"

She already felt creepy. "Of course not."

"He's really sick," Mitch called as she went down the hall.

At Jeff's door she panicked. Maybe she should have worn a space suit and a mask, and then she saw Jeff lying like a corpse against the sheets, struggling and gasping for each breath.

"Hi, Jeff," she said

He tried to focus on her. His eyes were an eggshell gray, his body emaciated, his long, thin fingers ghostly white. A silver earring hung from the lobe of his ear. He tried to move his lips, but they were too dry and cracked to speak.

"I'm Chase Evans," she said softly. "I came to visit you."

Before he could protest, she had crossed the room and pulled a wicker chair to his bedside. "I'm just going to sit here for a little while. If you need something—"

He lifted a limp hand and pointed to his lips.

"You're thirsty?"

He nodded.

She turned to the door and was relieved to see a nurse entering the room with a glass of ice chips. She smiled reassuringly. "Mitch told me you had a guest, Jeff. How nice. I'll leave you two alone."

The last thing Chase had wanted was to be left alone with this dying twenty-year-old. She forced herself to stay. He coughed fitfully as she rolled up his bed, but he urged her with those lifeless hands to roll him higher. Before she realized it, she was leaning against his bed reading Robert Service poems to him and spooning ice chips between those cracked lips. An hour later when she left him, he pled, "Come back again."

"I will."

She did, but not before she spent hours in the library poring over *The New England Journal of Medicine* and all the current information she could find. She wanted nothing more than a cure that would salvage Mitch and Jeff. She wasn't even afraid that second time when she knocked on the door. She had a smile ready for Mitch, but a nurse in uniform opened the door.

"Oh," she said happily. "Miss Evans, isn't it? Jeff kept hoping you'd come back."

"Where's Mitch?"

The smile of welcome clouded. "He's gone."

"He went home?"

"He's dead."

When Chase reached Jeff's room, he was holding his own glass of ice chips. Seeing her face, he said, "I didn't think Mitch would go first. He wanted to get well and go home to his family."

"What about you, Jeff? Don't you have a family?"

"My brother Kelly, but he doesn't come by here anymore."

Now Jeff was an ocean away, on the other side of the world, dead perhaps. He had cried when she left him. "Send me a picture of the Thames," he had said, "to remember you by."

As she gripped the steering wheel, she gazed off to her right where the River Thames surged with a sudden burst of energy, going from what had been a quiet stream to a rushing river. The whole fifty miles she had allowed herself to think about her childhood, her father, Halverson House—anything but Downing Street. The conclusions she had reached yesterday were too horrid to contemplate, but as she reached the Hamptons' house in Oxford, she faced them again.

Olivia Renway's last five novels had moved away from the familiar World War II settings to the threat of terrorism and chemical warfare in Asia. Chase tried to put the broken pieces together—Renway's friendship with the prime minister and the bomb threat against number 10 Downing as Olivia lay dying. Had the driver in a rented Renault been part of the Czechoslovakian terrorist group? Had news on the terrorists pushed the report of Olivia's death to the back pages of the newspaper? Chase could no longer think of Renway's death as a simple hit-and-run. *Someone had wanted Olivia Renway dead. But why?*

Jiri Benak and Pavel Van Rindin left the Ritz in London a few minutes ahead of Chase Evans. When they reached the car, Pavel peered at Jiri through his tinted silver-rimmed glasses. "I thought you were sending Franz to the Cotswolds with me."

"I sent him back to Prague. I couldn't risk him staying on, not after Heathrow security detained him for twenty-four hours."

Pavel ran a finger through his mustache. "I don't like going to Kendallshire alone," he said. "Not with all the rumors about a bombing in the Cotswolds."

"What rumors?"

"Turn on the telly. Or your car radio."

"Why would anyone broadcast our arrival? We're not the IRA with a fifteen- or sixty-minute warning before a bomb goes off."

"The news media refers to us as a Czech splinter group."

"They've narrowed it down to that? They're winging it."

"Are they, Jiri? Or is Altman wiping his hands of us both?"

Pavel's resentments against Jiri and the Russelmann family went deep. At twenty-nine he had been browbeaten and badgered too long, robbed of any leadership in the Jarvoc steel plant. He was a moody man like his brother Franz, not much for talking, but far more intelligent, quick with his mind. A real computer genius. But lately he had been given to bouts of depression with frequent glances back over his shoulder and long solitary walks in the woods behind the farm. And now this—total paranoia.

Pavel, Jiri decided, *was expendable, as Renway had been.*

"Come on, Charlie. I can join you in a day or two—"

"Cut the Charlie blather. You know my name. Use it. But I'm telling you the truth. They're publicizing bomb threats against the Cotswolds."

"They?" Jiri scoffed.

Pavel seemed near the breaking point. Jiri put a firm hand on the man's shoulder. "Nedrick is the only one who would leak information like that."

Or maybe Hanz was switching loyalties to protect the Kendalls. Or had Franz resented being shipped back to Prague?

"Just take it easy, Pavel. All you have to worry about right now is to find us a place to stay in Kendallshire. Then observe Uriah Kendall. We can wire a firebomb when I get there."

"We?" Pavel's laugh rang shrilly. "You don't plan to test the chemical compounds this time?"

Jiri toed the compact computer at Pavel's feet. "You concentrate on the remote control I will need to set off the bomb by the click of the computer keys. We'll be out of Kendallshire before they even know we've been there."

"I want no part of political terrorism, Jiri. No part of killing more innocent people."

Jiri laughed raucously. "What do you call the family business but political participation? The steel plant is nothing but a front for exporting weapons and nerve gas components to the highest bidders."

"Our company stays clean. Nishokura handles the sales to terrorists abroad."

"That is international involvement. If we were investigated, they could trace our sales through Nishokura back twenty years. That takes in a lot of terrorist activity."

"You're behind this. You and those fancy architectural drawings of yours, Jiri. Designing weapons of destruction. Uncle Altman still thinks you're the wonder boy architect. You have them all fooled."

Jiri had grown up reading blueprints and studying design in the family architectural shop in Germany. He took pride in knowing that his grandfather had been one of the architects of the Nazi extermination camps. "Don't mock it, Charlie. The skills I learned in the family shop have paid great dividends. Yes, they have served me well in Jarvoc."

"And in the end you'll take over the compound. That will be our thanks for taking you in. I've watched you, Jiri, slipping in and out of the old waste plant. I know what we store there."

There was a noticeable shrug of Pavel's shoulders. "As long as that building is left standing, the people of Jarvoc will hate us. Maybe someday my family will wake up and get rid of you before you destroy all of us."

"Not likely, Charlie." *They might want to put you to rest,* he thought, *but I'm too important to them.*

Twelve years ago when the Russelmanns ordered the vast reconstruction of the steel compound, Jiri had been invited to design it. Altman had insisted that one building by the railroad tracks not be torn down. He wanted it left standing as a gruesome reminder to the people of Jarvoc that the Russelmanns were in control of the town. And while Jiri was drawing up the blueprints for the new plant, he discovered the layout of the old labor camp.

He had been amazed. Extermination camps had existed in Poland and Germany. But in Jarvoc? Now Jiri knew the tunnels and storerooms better than Altman did—and he knew how to use every chemical stockpiled there. Jiri was a patient man. One day he would own the company and dispose of those who stood in his way.

He slipped into the driver's seat of his car. "Pavel, your orders are to go to Kendallshire. Mine—to follow the girl."

As Pavel sauntered away, defiance in his every step, Jiri wondered if he would ever reach the Cotswolds. Or would Pavel run back to Jarvoc, back to the farm?

By the time Chase came out of the Ritz Hotel and started on her trip to Oxford, Jiri's stomach burned like fire. He tensed at the sight of her, and more acid poured into his stomach. She came gracefully in her sling-back pumps, the quick bounce to her step giving no hint of caution. He found her alluring in her tailored blazer and sheer skirt. She eased into the car rental, smiled up at the doorman, and with a quick wave drove off.

Jiri followed the American at some distance, surprised at her reckless abandon as she reached the motorway. She held the car steady, but she drove like a Londoner. Twice she risked passing on the hill, and Jiri was certain she would hit head-on when she crested the top.

As he followed her through the peaceful English countryside, he drove with one hand; the other hung limply on his bony knee. At times he could picture himself taking up residence in one of the thatched cottages with sheep grazing on the hillsides—far away from the smoke-rimmed sky at Jarvoc. Considering it now, he attributed his fondness for the English countryside to the lay of the land, its intricate design and structure; its fabric and color appealed to him. Someday, when he owned the Russelmann Steel Mill, perhaps he would take a summer cottage in the Cotswolds. The cottage would be fresh and airy, the roof thatched, the grounds private. He would hire a gardener and plant a high hedge that would isolate him from his neighbors.

As they reached a bleak stretch of land, his thoughts strayed back to the dark gray storage plant at Jarvoc. It had taken him months to discover the secrets of the old plant and even longer to locate the blueprints. They were stowed in the corner in the back room as though the architect, the designer of death, had stepped from the room and would be back to complete the detailed drawings. Jiri had brushed the lacy strand of cobwebs away, unrolled the yellow sheets, and stared down at the structural drawings for an extermination camp. His grandfather's scrawled initials were still visible in the corner.

At first Jiri had felt repulsed, then later proud. It had taken a brilliant mind to contrive such an elaborate plan in the closing months of a war. It was all there. The deposits of coal. The water supply. The railroad track. Barracks designed to house hundreds of prisoners. A ventilation system had been built into the walls. Stairs—crumbled now— led directly from the train into the building. He found cracked tins that had once contained the pellets of hydrogen cyanide. Other containers—with part of the labels still on them—had once held gas crystals. And then he discovered the underground tunnel with shelves of modern containers filled with toxic components. Jiri had not one doubt that Altman Russelmann had plans to sell these to the highest bidder. Or did the plans belong to Hanz Russelmann?

The doors in the plant were airtight, the peepholes once used by the S.S. guards still there. Some of the pipes had rusted over the years, but Jiri had replaced the ducts leading into the sealed shower rooms and the old underground morgue. He planned it carefully. It would be a simple matter to remove his competition. Altman Russelmann and

Gustav Van Rindin made frequent inspections of all the buildings. When the time was ripe, Jiri would fill the ducts with gas crystals, seal Altman and Gustav in the shower room, and gas them to death in the old crematorium.

Bored, he switched on the car radio and twirled the dial. Rock music bombarded him. He liked classical—a Wagner overture or the Hungarian Rhapsody #9, music that for all of its triumphant notes had a peaceful quality to it. He rode with the windows open, chewing on his thin cigar, his brooding suddenly startled by the news commentator. "We interrupt this program . . . Yesterday's tragic slaying of Andrew Forrestal, one of London's noted photographers . . . dead at thirty-four . . . murdered in his own studio . . . Scotland Yard released the following composites."

Accurate descriptions of Chase Evans and himself followed. He had forgotten the hidden video cameras. Pulling off the motorway at the first exit, he drove to a wooded area and parked. He folded his trench coat with precision and placed it in the boot of his car along with his Gucci tie. He substituted the sweater emblazoned with "OXFORD UNIVERSITY," bought for just such an occasion.

Taking Forrestal's business card from his pocket, he memorized the girl's Oxford address and then set it ablaze with his lighter. With the ashes still warm, he knelt and replaced the license plates on the rental car with ones from his suitcase. Back in the car, he inspected himself in the mirror. The cigar had to go. He tossed it on the gravel.

Within minutes he was back on the motorway keeping his speed within the limits. If a police officer stopped him, he would tell him that he had spent the last week at Gainsborough's steel mill. Jon Gainsborough would vouch for him. Jon was cooperative that way. After all, he wanted to continue to do business with the Russelmanns.

In the distance Jiri saw a car cresting a steep hill on the wrong side of the street. Impossible. But, no, he had caught up with the crazy American.

Chapter 15

Chase parked on a side road kitty-cornered from the Hamptons' narrow street. The Hamptons' centuries-old home was brownstone in color, with a gabled roof and dormer windows, one of four units converted from what was surely a monastic building. It was brightened by flower tubs along the front filled with tulips and pink and white geraniums. She felt both disappointment and intrigue. Having no breathing space or lawn between your lodging and the neighbors' reminded her of the crowded tenements in Manhattan; yet the whole setting here was pastoral and peaceful.

In New York it would be blaring car horns, shifting gears, and angry drivers cursing. Here the squeal of bicycles and perambulators and a car or two broke the stillness. Here it was spired cathedrals in the distance; at home skyscrapers jutted into the skyline. In New York—in the city that she loved even more than Paris—the air was often polluted with smoke and bus fumes. Here on a wide patch of meadow, the air was fresh and clean.

Chase realized that the man in the gray Renault had driven by twice already. She caught a glimpse of light hair, dark sunshades, a university sweater. Perhaps she had claimed his parking space, but an unsettling thought pushed its way into her peaceful musings. The man was following her. She moved quickly and emptied the boot of her car before he could circle the block once more. She trolleyed her pullman and balanced her carry-on with her other hand. The gray Renault whisked by her again as she reached the curb on the Hamptons' side of the street.

Close up, the house seemed smaller. Where would they find room for her? She formed an unwanted picture in her mind of a worn sofa in the tiny living room and her suitcases stacked in the corner. There was no porch, no protection from rain.

The door swung open before she could knock. "Here," said a cheerful voice, "let me give you a hand with your things."

Chase recognized the boyish, lopsided grin. "Oh, no."

"Oh, yes. Peter Quincy. Remember?"

"You were at Heathrow."

"To meet you. I was supposed to show you around London."

"But you didn't say."

"You didn't give me a chance."

He gave her a mocking bow as she stepped from the stone-flagged walkway into the house. Peter was striking and robust, small of build, five-nine if he toed it. His dark tweed jacket was well cut, his shoes well shined. His lips twisted in a funny little way as though he were holding back a chuckle. Peter's hair was an oxblood brown, and those intelligent eyes must surely belong to one of Oxford's best and brightest.

"I'm embarrassed," she said.

"Don't be. Now let me take your luggage."

She glanced behind him. "Aren't the Hamptons in?"

"Dr. Hampton is with a guest. I volunteered to wait over and show you to your room."

And have a good laugh at my expense, I'll bet. "And Mrs. Hampton?"

"She's always late getting in from the Eagle's Nest."

"And you, Peter? Are you on a scholarship?"

"Yes. I plan to live at number 10 Downing Street someday, so I'm staying on—thanks to Dr. Hampton—for postgraduate studies."

"What did you do—take first honors in science?"

He smiled, not denying it, and picked up her luggage for the second time. "Let me run these up to your room. It's the first door on the left."

"Peter."

He paused halfway up, banging the cases against the rail.

"I'm sorry about the airport. I didn't know who you were."

"And you weren't taking any chances?"

"Not when my cabby told me someone was following us."

His eyes twinkled. "You'll have time here at Oxford to make it up to me. I'm your tutor for the summer."

"My tutor!" she exclaimed. Embarrassed again, she lowered her voice and said, "But Doc Hampton promised to help me."

"He'll meet with you weekly, but I'll arrange for your library privileges and any lecture classes you want to attend."

As he disappeared at the top of the stairs, she sighed. *If only you were Luke Breckenridge.*

Nigel Hampton swept into his private study with his long black gown snapping at his ankles and was pleasantly surprised to see Constable Wallis standing with his back to the window.

"Edwin!"

Edwin Wallis had been a student at the college fifteen years ago, a studious young man who took his degree at his father's old school. But at the end of the first year, he had come to Hampton saying, "My goal is Scotland Yard, not the House of Commons."

"Your father will be disappointed," Nigel had told him.

"My father followed his own career."

Wallis had to be forty now, looking older with that receding hairline and those ugly thick-rimmed glasses. He came forward at once and shook Nigel's hand in a familiar bull-like grip.

"This is a surprise," Nigel said. "But a pleasant one."

"I'm here on business."

"I gathered as much." He pointed to a chair, and they took seats facing each other.

"How did your run go in America?" Edwin asked.

"It was a good school year."

"But Mrs. Hampton didn't go with you?"

My wife is not the business at hand, he thought. She had wanted no part of his sabbatical in New York. Her world revolved around the Eagle's Nest. They had parted for the school term with an ocean between them, an unhappy arrangement for Nigel, a satisfactory one for his wife.

As Wallis clasped his broad hands behind him, Nigel said, "My wife could not get away for a whole year."

"Not even for Christmas?"

So he knew that Margot had remained in England, refusing to ruin her holiday traditions with a trip to America. "We agreed it would be best. Christmas is a lonely time at the Eagle's Nest. Without Margot, there would be no tree or presents."

He didn't add that Margot would never go anywhere as long as Beatrice Thorpe was alive. "Edwin, I hear good things about you. Your recent promotions. Your success at the Yard."

"Fortunately you don't hear about my unsolved cases."

"Sometimes," Nigel said, smiling. "So what brings you here?"

"One of your students. An American, I believe."

He's going to ask me about Chase Evans. As he crossed and uncrossed his legs, they felt like lead. "Edwin, you know the boys get a bit rowdy during Eights Week."

"I wasn't referring to the boat race."

"But our boys were 'Head of the River' again this year."

"So Peter Quincy told me when I arrived."

"He was in the winning boat. A strong rower. Fiercely competitive, as you were, Edwin."

Edwin removed his glasses and placed a stem in his mouth. Now Nigel could see the dark circles under his eyes, the weariness in his face. "You're looking tired, Edwin."

"We've been up most of the night working on a case—"

"Long term?"

"No, a homicide in London yesterday." He took a black-and-white from an envelope and handed it to Hampton. "Is this the American student who is staying with you?"

"Chase Evans. She's a grad student from Columbia."

"In New York. We already know that. Comes from quite an influential family. Why this student, Nigel? There's no place for a woman in your all-male college."

"She was in my department at Columbia. I agreed to be her mentor this summer. That picture of her—where did it come from?"

"It was taken on a video camera at the television studio. I had them blow it up for me."

"Come on, Edwin. No jokes between us."

"There's been a homicide at the television studio. We need to ask Miss Evans a few questions."

"That's disgusting, Wallis. Evans is a fine young woman."

"Is she here?"

He considered denying it, but for the last several minutes he had heard voices in the sitting room. "Let me introduce her to you, Edwin. Perhaps you can get this mess straightened out."

As they entered the room, Peter stood up, and Chase glanced their way. "I'm here," she said cheerily, tumbling out of her chair. "Drove all the way on the wrong side of the road and didn't even get a dent in my fender."

Nigel's facial muscles felt too tight to smile.

"I didn't come at the wrong time, did I, Prof?"

Still unsmiling, he said, "This is Constable Wallis from Scotland Yard. He wants to ask you a few questions."

"Oh, dear. Is something wrong?" She smiled up at Edwin and extended her hand. Edwin wrapped his burly one around it.

Quietly, patiently he said, "You were at the television studio with Andrew Forrestal yesterday, weren't you?"

"Yes, for a couple of hours."

"Had you known him long?"

Nigel marveled at her unflushed cheeks. With utter calm

she said, "We just met yesterday and—well, he offered to help me."

"How?" Edwin asked without letting her hand go.

"He had some microfilm that he thought would be of particular interest to me. He's not in trouble, is he?"

"For helping you?"

"Well, I did pay him." She wrenched her hand from his grip. "I was driving here today and, well—I wanted to find out everything I could about a novelist named Olivia Renway while I was still in London."

Wallis's bushy brows arched above his thick-rimmed glasses. Watching him, Hampton's concern grew. "Chase is doing her doctoral dissertation on Renway," he explained.

Edwin's intimidating gaze never left her face. "Were you alone at the studio with Mr. Forrestal?" he asked.

"No. There was one other employee there—a rather surly looking man. We didn't speak."

"This man?" he asked, extending a black-and-white.

The picture was blurry. "Yes, I think that's him."

"He wasn't an employee—that's been confirmed."

"Who then, sir?"

"Chase," Hampton said, "why don't you sit down?"

She shrugged off his offer. "I don't need to sit down. What's going on, Constable?"

"Mr. Forrestal is dead," he said.

Hampton saw the involuntary shudder of her shoulders as Peter lunged toward Chase. Her face had turned ghost-like, the luster in her eyes wiped clean.

"It's all right, Peter," she said. "I'm okay."

It took her only seconds to meet Constable Wallis's accusing gaze. "What happened? Andrew was fine when I left him."

"He was murdered," Edwin said calmly.

Peter kept his steadying hand on her elbow. She stared at the photograph again. Only the tremor in her voice gave her away as she said, "You mean—"

"We don't know, Miss Evans. Perhaps if you would accompany me back to London, we could get this straightened—"

Nigel flashed a warning glance at Peter. If Edwin had anything definite on Chase, he would have sent his underlings. No, he had come himself, counting on his old friendship with his professor. Hampton had no intention of letting this happen. It was more than protecting Chase Evans. Nigel couldn't risk upsetting his wife. He said, "On what charge, Edwin?"

"I'll be responsible for her."

Nigel held his ground. "No, Edwin, she's my responsibility. A guest in my home. She's safer here than in London."

Edwin dropped the photograph back in the envelope. "Can you tell us anything more about this man, Miss Evans?"

"You have his picture. What else can I tell you?"

"The sound of his voice. His height—"

She hedged. "I didn't pay that much attention. He was sitting the whole time with his back to us. We didn't speak."

Chase's fears seemed well controlled now. She seemed to sense Peter's support and Nigel's concern. She turned back to the constable. "The man had light hair—like a Scandinavian. And he was well dressed, but you could see that in the picture, Constable." She looked up at Nigel, her confidence wavering. "He'd have no way of knowing my name or whereabouts."

She knows something, Hampton thought, *but she's not going to tell Edwin. She doesn't trust him.*

Hampton remembered Edwin's granite expression back in his student days. He was more intense now, his quiet voice more overbearing than if he had shouted. His eyes hardened as he looked down at Chase and asked, "Did Mr. Forrestal know you were coming to Oxford?"

She shot an apologetic glance toward Hampton. "I'm afraid I gave him this address. Andrew promised to get in touch with me if he learned anything more about Olivia Renway."

Not a muscle twitched in Edwin's face. "Nigel, we'll want to keep in touch with Miss Evans. If we have any more questions—"

"She will be here with us." *Thank God, she will be safe with us.* "Chase, why don't you go and freshen up for dinner. My wife will be home soon."

They watched her go in silence. As she reached the top of the stairs, Nigel faced his former student again. "Was it necessary to tell her what happened?"

"That's my job. She may well have been the last one to see Forrestal alive. She was there, Hampton, as much a suspect as the man she describes. Surely you understand that." He tucked the envelope under his arm. "There was no address on Forrestal's body. Nothing in his pockets or his wallet."

"Evans wouldn't lie to you."

"I don't suppose she would, if she's innocent. But it appears that our chief suspect has Miss Evans's name and address."

Nigel heard his wife's car arriving. "I'd rather not alarm Margot," he said.

"Of course."

"Thank you for coming, Edwin."

"I wish it could have been under more pleasant circumstances. But we'll keep in touch. If Miss Evans remembers anything, you will call—"

"You know that I will."

He walked Edwin to the door and kissed his wife on the cheek as she stepped from her car. It was too late to ask Edwin about Olivia Renway, but Hampton had seen Edwin's eyes brighten at her name. Margot was right. Nigel had been unwise in bringing the girl here.

🦀🦀🦀

As the Hamptons saw Constable Wallis off, Chase crept back down the stairs again. Peter Quincy smiled up at her and caught her hand as she reached the last steps.

"You've been crying," he said.

"Yes—a little. Is the constable gone?" she asked.

"Just. Are you all right?"

"I feel awful about Andrew Forrestal."

"Try not to think about him."

"But—he's dead, Peter."

"I'm sorry—sorry you're involved."

"Peter, I'm not involved. At least I don't think I am."

He released her hand. "I was watching you. You know something about the man at the television studio."

"He may have followed me to Oxford."

Peter urged her to sit down. "Why didn't you tell the constable?"

"I didn't like him, and I didn't want to alarm Doc Hampton."

He patted her wrist. "It's all right, Chase. I'll keep your secret. You'll be safe here. I'll see to it. In a day or so you will forget all about Forrestal. And you'll think that Hampton knows half the academia in Oxford." Peter's voice filled with admiration. "He counts several of the proctors and the vice-chancellor as best friends. He lectures with some, drinks beer in the pubs with others."

"He sounds like C. S. Lewis."

"He has a brilliant mind."

"And you're his prodigy?"

He frowned. "So was Constable Wallis fifteen years ago."

"So that's how the constable tracked me down."

"He would have found you anyway." His smile seemed infinitely patient. "Chase, I'll be by in the morning. Can you bicycle?"

"Yes, but I've rented a car."

"There's enough of a traffic jam in town with all the bicycles and perambulators. Mrs. Hampton will lend you her cycle."

"Are you supposed to go everywhere with me?"

There was no embarrassment as she met his gaze. "You'll find having a tutor isn't such a bad thing. Like I said, I'll arrange your library time and show you how to use our facilities."

"I don't need a tutor."

"That's the way we do it here, Chase. We have to get on this summer. I want that and Dr. Hampton definitely does."

Out on the walkway she heard the Hamptons' voices, low and heated. Then their words were muted by the tolling of a cathedral chime. "What's that?" Chase asked.

Peter glanced at his watch. "The bell at Christ's Church. It tolls 101 strokes a night."

"Have you ever counted them?"

"No, but let's do that some evening."

"Won't you have gate hours?"

"A few of the undergraduates still do, but that's a thing of the past for me."

Peter Quincy didn't match up to Luke Breckenridge, but he did know Oxford. "Then why don't we? I think that's the church Olivia Renway mentioned in her novels. She spent a great amount of time there."

"I'll take you there for evensong."

"Oh, but I should go with the Hamptons."

His mouth puckered again with the hint of a smile. "You'll know soon enough. The Hamptons rarely go to chapel anymore—only when Nigel's position obligates him—and even then his wife rarely goes with him."

He picked up his books, silent for a moment. "The college where Dr. Hampton teaches is all-male. It will be a bit unusual having a girl on hand."

"Me?"

The front door had cracked an inch or two, too wide to shut out the Hamptons' angry voices.

"I want the truth, Nigel. What was Constable Wallis doing here?"

"Edwin was one of my students."

"We're talking about now. How can a visit from Scotland Yard be a friendly one?"

"It wasn't. He came to see Chase Evans."

"Is she in trouble?"

"I hope not," he said. "But she knew Andrew Forrestal."

They heard Margot Hampton's quick gasp before she said, "The London photographer? He's dead, isn't he?"

"Murdered."

"Oh, Nigel, you should never have brought her here."

"I know," he said sadly. "I just thought it was for the best. I did it for you, Margot."

For a moment Chase was too stunned to move. Peter

shifted his books and touched her arm. "I'm sorry you heard that."

"No wonder you're not very happy being my tutor. I'm the unwanted guest."

"Things will work out, Chase. Hampton will see to it."

"He invited me—"

"But I'm not sure his wife did. They don't always agree on everything."

Constable Wallis sat on the backseat of the unmarked police car drumming his fingers on his knock-knees as his driver merged with the motorway traffic. The attractive American, upright and quick with her answers, had irritated him. Even more he resented his old professor's defense of the girl. If it had not been for Hampton, Wallis would have insisted on the girl accompanying him back to Scotland Yard for questioning—not on the Andrew Forrestal murder but on her relationship with Hampton and her curious search into the life of Olivia Renway.

Edwin tried to put his drumming fingers on the missing elements. Nothing came together. In that brief encounter, he had seen that Chase Evans was clearly right-handed. It had been a left-handed thrust of the knife that had claimed Forrestal's life. Evans was tall and athletic, but she would not have been strong enough for the violence at the television studio.

What had brought them together—the American student, the London photographer, and Wallis's old professor? Renway linked them. Forrestal died because he had befriended the American. Edwin felt certain of it. Edwin struggled against his respect for Hampton, knowing that nothing would stop him from finding answers even if it led back to a scandal at Oxford.

He picked up the cellular phone. He rarely shared information with MI5—was rarely invited to do so—but with jerking motions he dialed Dudley Perkins's emergency line.

Chapter 16

Dudley Perkins sat alone in his drab office, his gangly hands folded on the plain, uncluttered desk. He pressed his spine against the hard-back chair and stared down at the emergency phone as though it were a coiled snake. Edwin Wallis's call had annoyed him. The death of the television cameraman was Scotland Yard's responsibility and not within Dudley's jurisdiction. He didn't even care about the possible link between Andrew Forrestal and Uriah Kendall. Dudley already knew that Kendall had reached his cottage in the Cotswolds. If the American student made contact with Uriah, Dudley would be the first to know it.

He had enough on his mind with the intelligence report on his desk marked top secret. Czech terrorists had threatened to set off a bomb in the Cotswolds—not in London. If the threat had been against the coal mines to the north or the steel factories outside of Oxford, he would have understood, but an idyllic village in the Cotswolds seemed preposterous.

He couldn't push it aside as some mental incompetent's prank. It had been too specific: west of Oxford, south of Cheltenham, north of Chipping Sodbury. A devilish plan with someone mocking from the sidelines. Dudley had pored over the map, his focus mostly on Gloucestershire with tourists at every turn. MI5 couldn't detain everyone

for questioning nor even send out warnings with so many
Cotswold villages to alert.

Dudley had run his knuckled finger over Kendallshire
until the map was almost worn thin. He believed the isolated village of Kendallshire was the real target and found
himself wishing that the terrorist's bomb would blow the
graveyard apart, scattering Olivia Renway's ashes over the
countryside. Or better yet, he wished the Czech splinter
group would obliterate Uriah Kendall and his cottage. He
flexed his long fingers over the report, hating himself for his
lingering bitterness.

The chair squeaked as he turned and placed the folder in
the file cabinet. Slamming the drawer shut, he secured the
lock and swore silently. He would have destroyed Uriah
Kendall many times, but he had failed. Failed miserably.
Involuntarily he reached for his wallet. From behind the
credit cards he pulled out the faded snapshot of Olivia
Renway and laid it on the desk in front of him. A candid
shot—he had caught her unawares. She had turned and
blinked those velvet lashes, surprise in her eyes.

Dudley touched the tattered edges. "You were so
beguiling."

From the pages of his past he remembered his first visit
to Uriah's village. Yes, it was Uriah's village, founded by the
Kendalls. A Kendall had always been Lord of the Manor, a
position handed down from generation to generation.
Dudley had never known such power, not until he fought
his way to the top at MI5.

Long before the death of his son Joel in the Falklands—
long before Molly had come into his life—Dudley had taken
Olivia to Kendallshire with him. Beautiful, bewitching
temptress. When they arrived, she insisted on going to a cottage on her own—leaving him infuriated, jealous of her
every move, blinded to her past.

An hour later he went looking for her—ready to apologize,
prepared to ask her to reconsider sharing his room. He
found her on the stone bridge that spanned the river. She
stood there talking to Uriah Kendall, her russet hair blowing across her cheek. Sheep grazed contentedly on the

meadows behind them. With the hillsides ablaze with spring flowers, his colleague—his fellow officer at MI5—stole his girl. Moments later they walked away, not even noticing Dudley's presence.

After that Dudley dug into her past and with infinite patience built a case against her, convincing his superiors that Kendall bore watching. The resulting scandal cost Uriah his career with MI5. But it was true. Everything Dudley uncovered was true. Olivia Renway had been a spy.

Four months later—the day after Uriah became engaged to Olivia—Dudley did the next best thing. He married Molly—the rich, unglamorous daughter of Lord Gilmore, who threatened to disinherit his daughter if she went through with the wedding.

The door to Dudley's office opened quietly.

He looked up, drawn back to the present as his wife entered the colorless room. Molly was dressed to the nines, her homely face turning almost pretty as she smiled at him. She brought the sweet scent of her perfume with her as she crossed the room and stood behind him. He felt her warm lips on his thinning hair as she slipped her arms around his neck, her gloved hands resting on his chest. It was too late. Olivia Renway's ragged snapshot stared up at them. He glanced over his shoulder and saw the pain in Molly's deep blue eyes.

"You should have called before you came," he said.

"I did. You wouldn't take my calls."

"I've been busy."

"Too busy to come home? You haven't been there for three nights. It's lonely without you."

"We've been working long hours, Molly."

Her arms still rested around his neck as she leaned forward and studied the picture. "Olivia Renway, isn't it?"

"Yes. Uriah Kendall's wife."

"She's lovely," Molly said. "Did you love her, Dudley?"

"I thought I did."

"Why don't you let her go?"

"I thought I had."

Her cheek brushed against his, the fragrance of her perfume sensuous, overpowering. "You haven't shaved," she said.

"I had a business call from Scotland Yard. Give me a few moments to clean up, and then we can have lunch together."

"There isn't time. I'm going away, Dudley."

He took her hand and pulled her around to face him. "That's good. You need a holiday."

"It's more than that. . . . I'm leaving you." She leaned against the edge of his desk, her long-lashed eyes still on the snapshot. "I think you knew it was coming."

No, he hadn't even guessed. Molly was always there for him—defending him, supporting him, loving him. She was his rock, his mainstay. All through those bitter months after their son's death, no matter how grave the situation, Molly stood by him.

"Don't leave me, Molly. You've always been there for me. I would never have made it through Joel's death without you."

"We needed each other then," she said.

Dudley went cold inside. "I need you now."

"Do you? You've changed, Dudley, ever since Sulzbach—ever since that Russian agent's death."

"Marta Zubkov was nothing to me. You know that."

She ran her fingers over Renway's picture. "But Olivia was."

"That was a long time ago."

"I don't think she is ever very far from your thoughts. I've watched it destroy you. First it was Uriah Kendall's career. And then his grandson. Ian is only a young man. To threaten him with his grandmother's reputation—"

"Olivia Renway betrayed this country."

"Or did she betray you? Sometimes, my darling, I think you would have destroyed Joel, too, if he had lived long enough."

She straightened, tall and elegant, the silver of her hair and the blue of her eyes picking up the colors in her dress.

"Where will you go?" he asked.

"Paris for a while. Then to the Von Tonner Art Museum.

Friends at the Tate Gallery made certain I was invited. We both were," she said sadly.

It's always been both of us. How can she leave—go her separate way? He wanted Molly to urge him to go, but it would be a month or two before he could get away. "You'll have a good time."

"Yes, it'll be grand," she said, her voice melancholy. "They're opening the ballroom again, but it won't be the same without Ingrid von Tonner there."

"She was charming."

"And devious. Do you think I am devious, Dudley?"

Listen to us, he thought. *Empty, inane words, as though talking could hold us together.*

"But there's a nice young couple—the Courtlands. They're the ones opening the museum."

Drew Gregory's daughter and son-in-law. Then the Gregorys would be there. Suddenly it was important that Molly look more sensational than Drew's wife. "Buy yourself something to wear."

"I did. Yesterday. It's a Valentino evening dress." Her eyes brightened describing it. "Shoestring shoulder straps and a lovely ruffle on the bottom."

The Valentino label meant nine thousand pounds or more of Lord Gilmore's money. "You'll look lovely in it," he said. "Molly, will you come back to me after that?"

She reached out and touched his cheek. "I've made plans to stay with friends on a Greek island. I need time away from you."

"The last three days weren't enough?"

"You'll be all right, once you let go of Olivia Renway."

His pride was at stake, his bitter memories digging at him. He wanted to yank open the file drawer and shove the Renway folder into her hands. *Olivia was dropped back into my lap,* he wanted to say. *There's a terrorist connection, and Uriah and Ian Kendall are involved.* But he didn't really believe that. He knew only that the terrorist connection pointed toward an American student and traced back in time to Olivia Renway. Even now as he watched Molly, he was certain he could stop her from going if he could just tell her the truth. Instead he licked his thin, dry lips. "Molly, does Lord Gilmore know you're leaving me?"

"My father knows I'm going to Paris. That's all."

Dudley was not a demonstrative man, so the words did not come easily, but he said, "Molly, I love you."

She stole one more glance at the picture on his desk. "I'm glad," she said softly.

On Friday morning in Jarvoc, Hanz Russelmann picked his way along the rusty railroad track at the back of the property. His blue chino shirt lay open at the neck, the sleeves rolled up to the elbows. His work trousers came loose at the top of his boots as he trudged along. He seldom came this way, but since Nedrick's cable old memories had flooded back. He wasn't even aware that the black-and-white collie had joined him until he circled the old gun-metal building that Altman had refused to tear down.

"Patek, where did you come from?" he asked.

The dog nuzzled his fingers, but as they drew abreast of the door, a low growl rumbled in her throat. The fur on the back of her neck stiffened.

"It's all right, Patek. We won't go inside. Not this time."

Next week when Altman and the others were in Prague meeting with the representatives from Nishokura Steel, Hanz would come back and force his way inside. He had not been there for years, but he remembered the general layout of the building with its thick walls and gas sensors hanging on the paneling. Vast storage space lay hidden under the structure with its labyrinthine tunnels running beneath the railroad tracks and cutting deep into the forest. It was important now to know exactly what Altman was storing there. Hanz had seen the silver thermos containers and the fifty-five-gallon drums that had been destined for the storage sheds.

For years he had been aware that Altman and Gustav had been stockpiling weapons, no doubt selling them. Hanz was not a fool. He knew that the "satchel" and "earmuff" charges and blasting caps that Jiri Benak designed had no place in the steel business. But he had protested strongly when Jiri came back from the merc camp in the Pyrenees foothills with new suggestions. "We can increase the company profits by slicing steel beams to accommodate blasting caps," he had said. "Or we can produce bomb castings for weapons. We can sell them both to third world countries."

Altman's eyes had glazed over. "No, we won't sell direct to third world countries. We'll keep on dealing with Nishokura Steel. Let them handle any circuitous route for our products."

The look that Hanz saw in his son's eyes—in Olivia's son—had been inhuman. He had seen that same look during the war in the eyes of Himmler and Heydrich as they planned the annihilation of another race. Like Heydrich and Himmler, hatred had consumed Altman. No amount of money pleased him. He wanted power. Sometimes Hanz blamed himself. He had given Altman everything. No, not quite everything. He had robbed his son of a mother. There was nothing of Olivia in Altman, not even in his facial features, but Hanz had seen Olivia's gentleness in Nedrick.

He tried to shut out the memory of Altman saying, "Jiri, I have other ideas, too, that will make the Russelmann profits soar." Altman had presented unbelievable methods of destruction in a calm, cool, meticulous way, and then looking at Hanz he had said, "You and my brother Josef must help us, Father."

For Hanz it was as though the diabolical thinking of the thirties and forties had come back to haunt his final days on earth. The possibility of his sons and nephew hiding chemical weapons at the Russelmann plant sickened him. Now with Nedrick coming home to Jarvoc, he feared for the boy's life.

With the blistering sun directly overhead, he walked slowly down the dirt trail back toward the farmhouse, the collie at his side, the daily news tucked under his arm. He tipped Altman's visored field cap to the neighbor and moved on before he could be persuaded to stay for a cup of coffee or a glass of Becherovka.

These days long walks tired him, putting added pressure on his game leg. As he limped along, dragging his 180 pounds, he felt as though heavy steel plates had been slung across his back, the weight of them cutting painfully into his thoughts.

Reaching the front porch, he dropped down on the top step and whipped open the paper. The stray collie panted in front of him, her woeful eyes on Hanz.

"Let me rest a bit, Patek, and then I'll get you some water."

Hanz skipped the bold headlines and thumbed on to the stock and business reports. Running his eyes down the export columns, he was grateful that foreign sales on steel and iron ore were high again. The Czech Republic continued to gain recognition abroad with the Russelmann profits listed among them.

In the far column a small headline caught his attention. A subway disaster had been averted in Tokyo with a renewed crackdown on the purchase of chemical weapons from other countries. For anyone caught, punishment would be swift. Hanz tried to imagine how nerve gas components could be shipped abroad in steel bar packaging or how his sons Altman and Josef might be involved. Sixty-foot steel rails and forty-foot beams or cylinders would be shipped unpackaged, but specialty parts—the smaller welded bars and flanged steel tubes—could be crated or shipped in barrels, allowing room to hide chemical components.

My sons have gone mad, he thought. *No, not Josef.* Josef was a simple man, hardworking and industrious like his Slovakian mother. Josef had Blanca's fine features and dark hair and some of her shyness and wisdom. Surely Josef had not been taken in by Altman's schemes. Josef had worked hard for his degrees in chemistry, but, sadly, he was still the son who had always lived in the shadow of his half-brother Altman. Hanz glanced toward the sky, wishing at the moment that he knew how to pray.

The only one who seemed to be listening was the collie at his side. "Josef is not a cruel man," he told the dog.

If Nedrick had been the son of Josef, Hanz would have understood it better. They were more alike, less greedy, less power-hungry. Of all the Russelmann-Van Rindin clan in residence at the farm, only Josef was welcomed in the local pubs. The people of Jarvoc would drink with him and to him as the Russelmann who stood up for the men in the plant.

Hanz's hand proved unsteady as he tore the Tokyo article from the paper and stuffed it in his pocket.

"Here," he said to the collie. "Give me a hand."

Patek drew closer and allowed Hanz to balance himself as he stood. The dog whimpered as she followed Hanz past the compost pile to the area where he burned the leaves and trash.

Pain seared through his sciatic nerve as he knelt on one knee. He touched his lighter to the damp twigs and leaves until they sparked. As Hanz fueled the fire with page after page of grimy newsprint, Mila Van Rindin came around the corner of the house. "Uncle Hanz, where have you been?"

"About," he said. "Good day for walking."

"Altman was looking for you."

"He's sure to find me."

She wiped soot from his face with the corner of her apron. "I see you found the collie."

"She's adopted me."

"Of course. It's Friday. You always find her on Fridays."

"Maybe it's the only day she breaks loose."

Mila picked up the hose and filled the bowl with water. "Here, Patek," she said.

"Treat her like that and she'll stay around."

"We'd both like that, wouldn't we?"

Of all the Van Rindins, Mila was the gentlest, genuine and caring. Hanz saw behind the harshness of her square, bony features, the protruding cheeks, the sun-weathered skin. Her eyes said it all—lit as they were now with compassion and kindness.

"Uncle Hanz, was there any word from Nedrick?"

"Not today."

"But he is coming home?"

He stumbled back to his feet, refusing the hand that she extended his way. "Yes, he'll fly into Ruzyne Airport soon."

Shyly she asked, "And then he'll come to Jarvoc. I have his old room ready. I want him to stay with us."

"It's been ten years, Mila. He may have changed."

"You don't know that."

"You're second cousins," he reminded her.

"I don't care. He promised we'd spend our lives together."

Hanz smothered his exasperation and ran his gnarled knuckles down her cheek. "Nedrick is in London with Jiri right now."

"Then I'll go to him. I fear for Ned when Jiri is with him."

"Let's wait and see what happens," Hanz said.

Her saucer eyes seemed troubled—for herself, for him. "You're unhappy, Uncle Hanz. You're worried about Nedrick, too."

"I'm just old and weary. I walked too far for an old man."

"You could retire. Father says—"

"That I'm useless?" He smiled. "What else does Gustav say?"

"That you hold the factory back from foreign sales."

"Do I?" As he shifted the weight to his good leg, he heard the crackle of the newsprint in his pocket. "We are high on the charts on foreign sales, Mila."

"But you're still unhappy."

He turned his back on Mila, not wanting her to know how despondent he felt. He shaded his eyes and looked off toward the factory. The glare of the sun fell across the railroad tracks. It struck him now that certain days and certain points in history came back, each time with greater intensity. You could not erase the black days, anymore than you could relive the joyful ones. He had tried often to picture those months with Olivia in London. She was only seventeen when he had met her, seven years younger than himself. Her family was in Czechoslovakia. Alone and beautiful, she was in a foreign country, as he was, and he had loved her.

The joyful moments with Olivia had been overshadowed with betrayal, darkened by their last moments together in the Blitz. He had left her during an air raid, left her with a sapphire bracelet—a family heirloom he had called it. But if it had been found in her possession, it would have cost Olivia her life.

"Uncle Hanz," Mila asked, "did I say something wrong?"

He shook his head, still unable to speak.

Hanz had never seen Olivia again. Months later in May of 1942, he was in Prague, sitting on his bunk polishing his shoes, struggling with mixed emotions about the honor of flying Reinhard Heydrich into Berlin in the morning. He despised Heydrich, as he detested all loyal Nazis. But he particularly mistrusted the German-appointed head of the protectorate of Czechoslovakia, a man who led with bloody cruelty. Shortly before leaving for an evening concert with his wife, Heydrich—a towering six-footer, resplendent and arrogant in his S.S. uniform—had strolled into Hanz's room. He turned to the Luftwaffe pilot and said, "Russelmann, why don't you join us this evening for the concert?"

Hanz had remained at the castle where the Germans were quartered. The underground resistance network in Prague was extensive. So were the rumors about a possible assassination attempt on Heydrich. Hanz feared that Olivia's family might be involved. He had traced them to the Paschek farm where a wiry little woman with an English accent had insisted that Olivia had been parachuted back into Czechoslovakia. It could mean only one thing. Olivia was part of the assassination team. He must stop her.

The following morning when Heydrich's unescorted Mercedes slowed on a sharp bend of a hill, gunfire erupted. Heydrich took the fatal bullets. In the wake of his death, hundreds of Czechs were arrested and executed. As the hunt for the assassins continued, Hanz slipped out of Prague and went to Jarvoc to search once more for Olivia. The Paschek farm was empty. Fearful for their own lives, the neighbors told him that Olivia's father had remained in Prague with the resistance movement; the rest of the family had fled to

Lidice. The perky little woman with the English accent—Beatrice, they had called her—had disappeared into the hills. Five days after Heydrich's assassination, trains began the journey from Prague to extermination factories.

Hanz shuddered as Mila touched his hand. He shook himself free. In his mind's eye, he saw again the Prague train pulling into the Jarvoc station. Heard the hobnailed boots running. Heard the S.S. guards shouting, "Out. Out. *Achtung! Achtung!*"

Olivia's father was part of the human cargo on that train. Hanz remembered him stepping unassisted from the boxcar. With a sense of Czech pride, the man had placed his shoes and spectacles in the boxes provided and then went down those seven steps to his death.

"I didn't mean to add to your unhappiness," Mila said.

"You didn't, child. I was just thinking back—"

"A long ways back?"

"Yes. To when I first came to Prague."

She eased back into her favorite topic. "I'm glad you did, Uncle Hanz. Otherwise I would never have known Nedrick. Are you eager for him to come home?"

"Of course. I've missed him."

"And if he stays on and works at the plant, will that make you happy again?"

He mustn't. "It would not be easy to work for his father."

"Nor for mine," she said sadly.

"Altman and Gustav will always be hard taskmasters, Mila."

"Then I'll go away with Nedrick. You can come with us."

His tightened knuckle took another gentle run down her pitted cheek. "Nedrick will do what is best for you."

"What's all this talk about Nedrick?" Altman asked as he walked up behind them. "Surely you have better things to discuss, Mila, than my son."

As she glanced up into Hanz's weathered face, some of the brightness in her eyes clouded. "Do you want me to get your hoe for you, Uncle Hanz?" she asked.

He brushed the dirt from his hands. "Not now, Mila. The garden can wait. I think I'll have a word with Altman first."

"About what, Father?" Altman asked coldly.

Hanz pointed toward the gloomy structure by the railroad track. "About tearing down that old storage building over there."

Chapter 17

Chase unchained Margot Hampton's bike from the drain spout and stared beyond the cobbled pathway. It wasn't like Peter to be late. He kept to a strict time schedule. She wheeled the bike to the corner. Still no Peter. Beyond this quiet neighborhood lay the willow-lined Cherwell and the ancient university spires that stretched toward the cloudy sky.

In the ten days with the Hamptons, Chase had tried to put Andrew Forrestal's death from her mind, but since dawn this morning, his face had crept stealthily into her thoughts. He was dead. She accepted this, but it was frightening to think that she was one of the last persons to see him alive. If she had stayed at the station another twenty minutes, she may well have died with him.

As the days merged, she stopped looking over her shoulder for the man who had followed her to the Hamptons' house. Peter and the academic community kept her too busy to worry about strangers. She was becoming well acquainted with the city of Oxford. She could make her way through the medieval streets without getting lost now and distinguish between St. Michael's Saxon tower and the fifteenth-century bell tower of Magdalen College.

She had marked off certain landmarks for herself—the Bridge of Sighs would take her to the Hertford Quad; the Sheldonian Theatre was the place where Peter's honors degree had been conferred; and the Bodleian Library was the place to be at six because Peter didn't like to be kept waiting. She could make her way to High Street and Broad Street without Peter pedaling beside her. But mostly he refused to let her out of his sight until she was tucked away safely in one of the cubicles in the library.

As she gripped the handlebars, she looked around again for him and then remembered a book she wanted to take with her. She wheeled the bike back to the house, ran inside, and took the stair steps on the run, her heart racing as she reached her nook of a room on the second floor. She found the book on the dresser and was about to lower her window in case of an afternoon shower when she heard the Hamptons on the back patio.

She leaned out the window to interrupt their breakfast with a cheery hello, but she muzzled the greeting when she heard Margot ask, "Nigel, have you heard from Edwin Wallis?"

"Almost daily. He's like a dog gnawing a bone—insisting that Chase was the last one to see Andrew Forrestal alive."

"Is Edwin accusing her?"

"He won't go that far, but sooner or later he expects her to remember something. Or someone."

"Has she said anything to you about it?"

"She tried. I stopped her. Edwin would be bound to drag it out of me." His voice lowered. "And I forbade Peter to discuss it with her."

"Oh, Nigel, would you rather have Edwin think her guilty?"

"I would rather not involve us in any way."

Chase had disliked Constable Wallis from the moment they met. Now she was angry. *I'm practically a suspect in a murder case,* she thought. *And now even the Hamptons distrust me.* She stepped back from the window and kept her tongue, silenced by the memory of the stranger with the snow-blond hair. *Sooner or later Chase will remember.* She had to tell someone that the man from the television studio had followed her from London. If she could get into town without Peter shadowing her, she would call Luke

Breckenridge and beg him to come take her away from Oxford.

She felt as limp as the curtain as she heard Nigel say, "Margot, try not to worry. Peter keeps close tabs on Chase. He's certain that no one has followed them. She'll be fine."

Margot's cup and saucer clattered. "What about *our* safety?"

Impatiently he snapped, "Nothing will happen to us."

"I'm alone on the motorway two hours every day. Since this Forrestal tragedy, I jump every time a driver cuts in too closely."

"Chase could go with you tomorrow. She wants to visit the Eagle's Nest."

"No, Nigel. What she wants is to quiz Beatrice Thorpe."

He ran his hand through his thinning hair. "Beatrice could help Chase in her research on Olivia. What harm could that be?"

"She's an old woman. You can't depend on what she says."

"Chase is good with people like that."

"I won't be at rest until she's gone."

"The old woman or Chase, Margot?"

"Both of them. You were foolish to bring Chase here."

"Don't you like her?"

"I've always liked your students."

"Is this one so different because she's a girl?"

"You've spent your whole academic life teaching men."

"Chase is a refreshing change," he said.

"You usually bring your students home for meals, not for a whole summer. Why did you ever tell that girl about Beatrice?"

"Chase would have found out. She's very thorough."

"Too thorough. Even Edwin knows she's researching Olivia's life. No wonder there's such renewed interest in her death."

The air in Chase's bedroom stood still as Margot's voice rose to a high pitch. "Wallis and Chase will drag us through the mud before this is over."

"And in the end you and the Kendalls will be free, my

dear. I've longed for that for ten years. I lost you when Olivia died."

Margot scraped back the wrought-iron chair and gathered up the dishes. "Isn't it all best forgotten?"

Not wanting the Hamptons to come into the house and discover her still there, Chase fled down the steps and back out the front door. Peter would be annoyed when he arrived and found her gone, but she grabbed the bike and pedaled off without waiting for him.

In town she was so anxious to find a BT phone box that she didn't see the small boy dart out in front of her. She slammed on her brakes, missed the child, and collided with another student, a dishwater brunette wearing tortoise-shell glasses. The girl glared at Chase as they tried to unlock their front wheels.

"I'm sorry," Chase told her. "Are you all right?"

She examined her skinned knee. "I think so. And you?"

"Okay." Chase pointed toward a nearby cafe. "Perhaps I could make it up to you with a cup of tea?"

Inside, with cups of steaming tea in front of them, the young woman said, "I'm Anna Walker. Somerville College."

"That's Margaret Thatcher's school."

"And a hundred others."

"I'm Chase Evans. Peter—that's my tutor—promised to take me to Somerville this afternoon."

Anna sipped her tea and studied Chase. "You're American?"

"Yes. New York. I'm just here for the summer."

"Why don't you ride over to Somerville Manor with me? That's one of our houses for upperclasswomen. Ten of us presently."

"I'd like that—but let me make a phone call first."

The answering machine at the Busingen number clicked in, and a sweet voice invited Chase to leave a message. She glanced at Anna over the mouthpiece. "No one is home."

"Leave a message."

Chase forced a cheerful smile as she hung up the phone and pocketed her father's credit card. "What I wanted was

Luke's number in Germany. Never mind. I'll see him next week anyway."

"Boyfriend?"

"Just a friend."

"Hmm."

The Somerville Manor, a narrow, three-story house on a cobbled street in the heart of Oxford, had been claimed by Somerville students for a number of years. The sitting room was filled with overstuffed sofas and several beanbag chairs that one of the American students had brought with her. Six bespectacled residents sprawled about the room poring over their books.

"Forget them," Anna said. "Let me introduce you to some of Somerville's better-known achievers."

Pictures of five women hung in the hallway. "None of them ever lived at the Manor," Anna admitted as they paused by the portrait of Suzanee Cumbertain. "They were all like Thoreau. They danced to their own music. I think that's what made them special. At least some of them."

Suzanee Cumbertain had gained recognition in science. Madelaine Louberry's short career was in the film industry—seven major French films before her death in Flight 103 over Lockerbie, Scotland. Olivia Renway held the middle spot and most of Chase's attention. Anna gave Chase an apologetic glance. "I don't like Renway hanging here. She wasn't British. In fact, she spent a good bit of her life in America."

"Two strikes and you're out?" Chase asked.

"It's not that. The residents here at the Manor know little about her personal life. She wrote a few books. That's all."

"I've read them all."

Anna shrugged and moved on to Dorothy Sayers's plain, bespectacled face. "Another writer," she said.

The close-up photograph of Margaret Thatcher completed the gallery of Somerville's best. Pride rang in Anna's voice. "I think of all our grads, Lady Thatcher has had the most influence."

Beside Thatcher hung an empty frame. "That's our constant challenge," Anna said, tucking a lock of hair behind her ear. "We hope someone from the Manor hangs in this frame someday."

"You perhaps?"

Anna grinned. "I came to Somerville because of Prime Minister Thatcher. I'm even majoring in chemistry." As she tossed her head, the long hair swept across her neck again. "She's always been my role model."

"One of mine, too," Chase said. "I've always admired her."

Chase left that magnificent portrait and moved back to look up into Renway's pensive face. She was struck by Olivia's beauty, but unlike Thatcher's bright, alert gaze, Renway seemed lost in her own thoughts. "That's a remarkable painting, Anna."

"Renway's husband donated it to the Manor when she died."

"I've been studying her life."

Anna shot Chase a cold glance. "Have you found the skeletons yet? She and Sayers both had a dark past. You won't find much on Renway. Her private life seemed just that. Extremely private."

"Perhaps that's why I find her so intriguing."

"Apparently the man across the street finds *you* quite intriguing," another girl said as she joined them. "He's been there ever since you came. A secret admirer?"

"Oh, that's probably Peter. My tutor." *My shadow.*

When she reached the open window, she stepped back in horror. The blond man across the street was much older than Peter. Andrew Forrestal and a beige trench coat tossed over a chair back flashed in her mind. The dryness in her mouth came at once.

"Are you all right?" Anna asked.

All right? Hardly. She was sure it was the man from the television station in London, the stranger who had been outside the Hamptons' house ten days ago—possibly Andrew Forrestal's murderer. "I don't want that man to see me leave here."

"Well, let's jolly well get rid of him," Anna offered. "Or we can call the police if you want."

Chase nodded. "Would you? I think—"

"While we do that, you cut out the back way to Holywell Street. Can you find your way to the library from there?"

"Yes, Anna. Yes, of course."

"We'll detain the gentleman and give you time to disappear. By then the police should be here."

But even through the thin curtains they could see that the stranger had already slipped away.

❁❁❁

The library was a massive room, its seventeenth-century architecture encasing a morgue-like stillness. The arched windows were high, the broad center aisle filled with oriental throw rugs, the vaulted ceiling like padded velvet. Mahogany bookcases crowded with musty volumes lined both sides of the room. The only sound besides her own breathing was being made by a student with dark hair and tinted glasses as he idly twirled one of the world globes. *Squeak. Squeak. Squeak.*

Chase sat in an isolated cubicle, trying to erase the annoying sound from her mind. She glanced down at her notes, a column marked "Renway" and one marked "Sayers." Both women were meticulous scholars and loners. Both had the advantages of private tutors and boarding schools. She ran her finger down the notations, comparing them as she had done day after day. Like herself, they had come from privileged backgrounds, rational thinkers with strong political views. Renway was a stylish woman, Sayers at times in her earlier years outrageously dressed.

She ticked off her list, searching for links between them: voracious readers, graduates of Somerville, gifted writers. Was she hunting for something that did not exist? The world globe twirled again. *Squeak. Squeak. Squeak.*

Chase tugged at the heavy volume chained to the library table, trying to bring it closer to her tired eyes. She scanned the article on Sayers's bohemian days when she incurred moral outrage at the birth of an illegitimate son. Whamo!

Chase ran her pencil under the words: "the birth of a son."
A child born out of wedlock.

Squeak. Squeak. Squeak. This time the sound came from
footsteps. Leather shoes. The globe spun by itself now. The
student had stepped from view, but he made no effort to
hide his approach as he walked over the hardwood floors.
From the next alcove of books, she heard his heavy
breathing.

"Who's there?" she cried out.

Behind her more footsteps. She whirled around ready to
defend herself by yanking the book from its chain. "Oh, Doc
Hampton—it's you!"

Hampton gently released her grip from the chain. "That's
how we protect our ancient volumes from slippery fingers,"
he said.

"Where's Peter?"

"At the house." He put his finger to his lips, grabbed her
books and notes, and led her out the back way. Outside he
took her elbow and hurried her along.

"Doc Hampton, we've forgotten your wife's bicycle."

"Peter will see to it in the morning."

"Is something wrong?"

"When the library is empty, don't stay in there alone."

"There was a student there. Didn't you notice him?"

"He ducked out of sight when I came in. Don't ever leave
the house without Peter again."

"Was Peter angry with me?"

"No, worried about you. Someone is looking for you,
Chase. He found Peter instead."

The man who murdered Andrew Forrestal. She sucked in
her breath. "Is Peter all right?"

"He'll feel better in the morning. We've talked to
Constable Wallis. He suggests that you leave Oxford for
now."

She dragged her feet and stared up at him. *Be honest with
me,* she thought. *Your wife wants me out of your lives.* But
where would she go? To the Cotswolds? Uriah Kendall had
surely reached there by now. "Tell him I'll go to the
Cotswolds," she said.

"Delay that visit until someone can go with you."

"Well, I won't delay attending the opening of the Von Tonner Art Museum in Germany next week."

"Is Peter going with you?"

"He wasn't invited. I'm going with Luke Breckenridge—at least I'm meeting Luke there." *And I won't have Luke see me with Peter,* she thought. *No way.* "It's by invitation only."

"Until then I'll send you to the Eagle's Nest with my wife."

"Will your wife mind?"

"Peter will mind."

He struck out toward the outskirts of town, his long robe snapping at his ankles. Hampton walked briskly, striding as though he had a man at his side. She took a deep breath and increased her speed.

As they strolled along, he said, "Chase, I took the liberty to mail your revised proposal back to Professor Marsten. We had to meet her deadline—or else."

"Oh, Doc Hampton, I left it on your desk. I forgot to mail it."

His words were as quick as his steps. "You and Peter have been busy. Besides, I added a long letter. I doubt that Marsten and her committee will give you any trouble." More seriously, he asked, "How's your project coming?"

"I'm filling my notebooks with bits and pieces. Sayers played a violin quite well, and Renway came from a country that's known for making violins. Little things like that."

"You don't sound very enthusiastic, Chase."

"I don't like thinking about them being cut down in the prime of their lives. Sayers with a thrombosis—"

"And Renway with a hit-and-run," he said hastily.

"No, Prof, I don't believe that anymore. I think someone killed her. She died and never finished her life's work."

"We all die with unfinished dreams, Chase."

"Not me. I don't intend to let this one go."

Relief swept across Margot's face as Chase and Nigel walked into the kitchen, but Peter looked miserable. He sat at the table, an ice pack in his hand. His right eye was swollen and bruised, the side of his face red, the cheek puffy. Crusted blood clung to his upper lip. Chase rushed across the room to him.

He winced as she touched his bruised face. "What happened?"

"Tell her," Margot said.

He peered at Chase with his good eye. "I came by for you this morning, but you had gone off without me. I set off alone, so angry with you that I didn't hear the rider come up behind me."

Margot lifted his hand and made him place the ice pack over his eye. "His bike collided with Peter's," she said. "Deliberately."

"Who would do a thing like that?"

"Chase, he didn't give his name and address. When I tried to stand up, he pounded my face."

She leaned closer. "Peter, I'm sorry."

He licked his swollen lip and tried to smile. "He wanted to know where you were. Said crazy things like—wanting to know what the CIA agent had given me."

"*You,*" Margot said indignantly, her voice back at high pitch. "The man who accosted Peter thinks you're with the CIA."

Nigel stood with his back to the sink, a cup of hot tea in his hands. "You should have told me, Chase. If I had known about your CIA connection, I would never have invited you here."

She sank into the chair beside Peter. "Where would he get a crazy idea like that? I don't even know anyone in the CIA."

The silence in the room was deadly. Peter repositioned the ice pack. Margot rubbed her hand on the side of her skirt. Nigel turned to the stove and poured himself another cup of tea.

His back was still turned to her when he asked coldly, "Is it true? Are you with the CIA and sworn to some code of silence?"

"Prof, you know I'm a student. Why would I work for American Intelligence?"

He faced her once more, his jaw set, his gaze unfriendly, suspicious. "They've been known to recruit students before."

She tried to picture him back at Columbia smiling, joking, challenging her. The lines under his eyes had deepened. His phone contacts with Edwin Wallis were turning him against her.

"Prof, I didn't kill Andrew Forrestal."

He sighed. "I want to believe you—I do believe you—but you were there at the television station with him."

"That doesn't make me a murderer. Andrew was just trying to help me."

"Were you old friends?"

"Not friends at all. I told you before—I met Andrew at the university that morning." She glanced cautiously at Peter. "Forrestal flirted with me and then asked to take my picture."

"A total stranger?" Peter asked, disappointed. "And you simply went off with him?"

"Chase." Nigel again. "The constable said that Forrestal had a hundred dollars in his pocket."

"It should have been more than that," she said. "I paid him to show me some old news reels on Olivia's accident."

Nigel's displeasure was apparent. "Did you give Forrestal anything else?"

She felt the way she did when her father cornered her and demanded answers. She resented the embarrassment as she admitted, "He promised to get in touch with me if he found any information on Olivia—that's when I gave him your name and address here."

Nigel drained his cup. "When I told Wallis about Peter's beating, he was not happy at all. He believes you know more about the man in the television studio than you've told us—"

"I tried to tell you about that day in the television studio, but you wouldn't hear me out." She rubbed her eyes. *Sooner or later she will remember.* "He was blond. Possibly your height, Dr. Hampton. Fortyish. Harsh looking. Carrying a trench coat."

Peter leaned forward, the painful effort obvious. "Chase, except for the coat, that describes my assailant."

"I told Peter a man followed me here from London. For several days I didn't see him." Fear. Blind fear. The kind that she could taste and feel up and down her spine. "And then today—I saw him again."

"The man at the library?"

"No. I never saw him before. There's something else. The man who was in the studio may have overheard Andrew Forrestal tell me that Mr. Kendall was British Intelligence."

From across the table, Margot asked, "Is Kendall working for American Intelligence now?"

"I don't know who he's working for," Chase said. "He's retired as far as I know."

Margot sat with her hands clasped. "Chase, Peter says you've been making long distance calls from town. You could have made your calls here."

Chase closed her eyes, trying to block out the nightmare. The hot flushing in her cheeks was more anger than embarrassment. She had wanted to keep her calls to Luke private. "I've been calling a gentleman friend," she said. "I tried to call him again today. I wanted him to come and take me away from Oxford. But it doesn't matter. It's all falling into place now. Dead as Olivia Renway is, she's involved in this somehow. Otherwise, there wouldn't have been such opposition to my writing about her."

She opened her eyes in time to see the Hamptons exchange glances again. "Margot," Nigel said, "Edwin is not available for a day or two. That makes us responsible for Chase's safety. I want you to take her to the Eagle's Nest in the morning."

"No, I forbid it. I'm more concerned about you, Nigel. You've worked hard for your career. We can't risk a scandal, not here at Oxford. It would ruin you."

"It's all right, Margot."

"No, it isn't."

"I've upset all of you," Chase said. "It all has to do with Olivia Renway, doesn't it? She really was killed. And it's best if we never know why. Is that how you feel, Mrs. Hampton?"

The resentment on Margot's face softened as Nigel walked over and took her hand. "Margot, Chase is leaving for Germany in a few days. Until then find her a place at the Eagle's Nest."

She tried to pull away, but he held on tightly. "For just a few days, Margot."

"Please don't ask me to do that. If I take Chase to the Eagle's Nest, Edwin will come looking for her. Won't he, Nigel?"

As he nodded, she yanked her hand free and turned on Chase. For a moment she just sat there, desolate, twisting the rings on her finger, and then sadly she said, "Tomorrow, my dear Miss Evans, you will have your way. You will meet Beatrice Thorpe."

Chapter 18

At seven the next morning Margot Hampton and Chase drove on the motorway in a companionable silence. Even so, Chase saw tiny ridges furrow her brow as she glanced in the rearview mirror. Without warning, Margot swung the wheel to the right. Horns blared as their car careened across two lanes and skidded inches behind a minivan. With another jerk of the wheel, Margot spun them on the curve of the off-ramp on three wheels.

"We lost him," she gasped as the car righted itself.

Chase caught her breath. "What was that all about?"

Margot's hands had blanched against the wheel. "I didn't wait to find out. He's been behind us for the last hour. I had to do something."

"You almost got us killed. He'll just go to the next turn-around and come back after us."

"But he won't know which country road to follow." Chase heard the tremor in Margot's voice as she warned, "Now we must forget that little encounter, or it will ruin our whole day."

Easy for you to say, Chase thought.

"Chase, you must not tell Nigel about my daring little maneuver."

"I promise. Not a word. I'll probably still be speechless."

Her touch of humor pleased Margot. "You're not a bad sort, Chase. We should have met on different terms. I think we would have been friends."

Leaving the rush of the motorway behind, Margot bumped over the last few kilometers to the tranquillity of the Eagle's Nest. As they left the car, a lazy breeze drifted across the sleepy valley, stirring the tops of the meadow's wild flowers.

They approached a low shingled building sheltered by tall shade trees and a tangle of thickets. The grounds had flowers planted everywhere and baskets of bougainvillea hung on the screened porch. White-painted benches faced the bird bath. As they hurried up the paved walkway, they heard the sweet, plaintive song of a goldfinch as it splashed in the shallow water.

Inside, several listless residents sat serenely in the lobby. Others still sharp of mind recognized Margot, waved, and returned her smile.

Putting her finger in a vase of flowers, she called to the nearest aide. "Charlene, freshen this up a bit and pick a fresh bouquet for the receptionist's desk."

Margot led Chase to the left wing. "Beatrice Thorpe has a private room," she said. "You'll be staying in the guest room next to hers. Beatrice doesn't take to strangers, but Nigel insists on your meeting her."

"And you don't agree?"

"She's an old woman. If you barge in there asking about Olivia Renway, she may throw you out. I don't want her upset."

"I'll do my best."

"To annoy her?"

"No, to be nice to her."

Margot smiled, her tired face pleasant for the moment. "She will try to talk you into having lunch in her room. She latches onto every excuse to stay in that old chair of hers. It's a fight every day to get her to the dining room."

As they walked the corridor, Margot ran her finger along the ledge. A few steps later she scooped up a swirl of lint from the floor. "I expect this place to be kept clean and neat for the residents. Except you will find Beatrice's room outrageous. All clutter. But clean."

"Most of the rooms we passed had two beds in them."

"I know. Beatrice has the only single room. I insisted on it. Otherwise, the staff would have quit long ago."

"But you're the administrator, Mrs. Hampton."

"Yes, and I'm determined to keep my staff happy. Beatrice wore down two roommates in the beginning, always afraid someone was going to take her possessions. I had three resignations on my desk in a week."

She stopped and tapped gently on the door before swinging it open. "Beatrice, good morning. It's Margot."

Beatrice Thorpe sat in a cushioned rocker by an open window, surrounded by antique collections. The knitting needles in her ringed hands clicked in constant motion. She was dressed in an old-fashioned royal blue blouse and a long beige skirt that matched the high derby hat on her head. She looked up, her Mediterranean eyes pale blue, innocent as a child's.

"Oh, Margot, did you bring Olivia with you today?"

"No, not today, Bea. But I brought another guest. Someone who likes Olivia."

Thorpe's hair was the same shiny color as her silver-rimmed glasses. Dangling earrings hung from the wide lobes of her pierced ears.

"Is she going out?" Chase whispered.

"No. She's always dressed to the nines. She was very fashionable in her day. And after those two years in the concentration camp, clothes meant even more to her."

Chase's mind raced. *Where? When? What concentration camp?* But she resisted asking. Instead she whispered, "She's lovely. She doesn't look ninety."

"She's not. She's ninety-five. You're on your own now until lunch."

The door closed behind Margot, leaving Chase alone with the old woman. She glanced around the cluttered room—a single bed with the side rails down, a china closet filled with treasures, a high round table with a lamp and candy dish on it. China plates and a magnificent Botticelli painting of the Madonna and the Child hung on the wall. On the crowded shelves beneath the Botticelli, books were piled on top of one another. Drawers and the open closet were jammed with boxes and papers.

"Stop gawking, young lady."

"I'm sorry."

Beatrice squinted. "What's your name?"

"Chase Evans. I'm from New York."

"New York. Then come," she said, kicking the threads of her unfinished afghan with her laced shoes. "I'm Bea. My friends call me Bea. Sit down beside me. I want to go to New York. Maybe I'll go after the war."

War? As Chase pulled up a straight-back chair, her own shoes caught in the lap robe. She reached out and touched the aged hand with the tips of her fingers and thought of Marie back at Willowglen, more fragile than Beatrice Thorpe, Marie's days little more than endless hours.

"Well, why are you here?" Beatrice asked. "You should be off helping Olivia. The boys need a safe route out of Prague."

Deep wrinkles cut from the corners of Beatrice's mouth to her double chin. Chase couldn't be sure whether those lines were twisting into a smile. The faded blue eyes stayed wide and direct, demanding an answer.

"W-What boys?" Chase stammered.

"The men of Anthropoid. We can't leave them in the church. The Gestapo will find them."

Chase touched the wrinkled hand again, at a loss for words. Beatrice pushed her fingers away and went on knitting. "You've got to get word to Olivia. I can't go. I'm a prisoner here."

Anxious to appease her, Chase said, "I'll try. Tell me how."

Beatrice bent over her knitting needles and whispered urgently, "They're hiding in the catacombs at the Karel Boromejsky Church."

"I don't know where that is."

Bewildered, Beatrice tapped Chase with a needle. "Think, child. It's in the center of Prague. Now be on your way."

Chase considered running, taking off before the eccentric old woman went completely off her rocker. The imploring look on Thorpe's face stopped her. Chase wanted to explain that they were in England—that "the boys" were undoubtedly dead now.

Thorpe's agitation turned quickly to tears. "Don't you understand? The soldiers are searching the city door by door. Margot and Olivia can't hold them off much longer.... We've got to rescue them. There's a price on their heads.... We've got to get those boys across the border."

As gently as she could, Chase said, "She's gone, Beatrice."

"Gone. Olivia's not coming back?"

"She died in a traffic accident a long time ago."

"Oh! I'd forgotten about that. Then I have nothing left."

"Bea, she left her books for you. I've read all of them."

"Not the last one. You didn't read the last one on Czechoslovakia. She was killed for that one." Beatrice had come back to the present as calmly as she had left it, her rambling thoughts back in focus. She pulled the multicolored lap robe up around her waist. "No one believes me," she said, "but Olivia was killed for that manuscript."

Chase's chest tightened. "I believe you. That's why I came to see you, Miss Thorpe, to find out how she died."

Beatrice cackled. "It's Mrs. Thorpe. No one ever questioned Olivia's traffic death before except me. *And you.* And the boy."

"What boy?"

"Ian Kendall."

Ian Kendall! "You know Olivia's grandson?"

Confusion wrapped around Thorpe again. "There's no grandson. Olivia left her baby boy at St. Michael's Cove in Cornwall before she went back to Prague."

The breeze from the windows blew the long lace curtains back against a row of war photographs on the wall. A gentle wind. A fragile mind. Chase watched a troubled expression flicker on Thorpe's face again. "Can you take a message to Olivia for me?"

"I can tell Margot."

"Yes, she'll help us. Tell her the boys from the Czech Brigade need help. They've been training in England near Warwick. They did us proud, didn't they."

Chase nodded. "I'm sure they did."

"You understand, don't you? The German head of the protectorate of Prague was ruthless to our people. He had to die."

"A Nazi?" Chase asked.

"Yes. So proud and arrogant even when he played the violin. Did you know he liked music?"

"I don't know anything about him."

Beatrice leaned forward and whispered urgently, "We've got to get the boys out of the church before the Gestapo find them."

From the doorway a deep voice said, "Josef Gabcik is dead, Bea. And Jan Kubis, too."

Her features sharpened. "Dead? No, Olivia was with them when they parachuted in from England. Josef only hurt his ankle."

"Yes, I know."

Chase recognized Ian's voice before she turned to face him standing in the doorway. She was struck again by his handsome features. He looked even more athletic and muscular than she remembered in his thigh-hugging cycling shorts and the Assos jersey with the Gainsborough logo. The sun caught the brilliance of his reddish hair—the streaks of light emphasizing the stubborn set of his jaw and his obvious displeasure at seeing her. As he yanked off his dark glasses, his piercing blue eyes bore down on her. "What are you doing here, Chase?" he asked. "Did Beatrice invite you?"

"No, Margot Hampton did."

He scowled. "Does she know what you're up to?"

"She should. She's watching me closely enough."

Ian seemed perfectly at home in the room. He strode up to Beatrice and gave her an affectionate peck on the cheek. "It's all right, Bea. Gabcik and Kubis completed their mission. Remember? And Reinhard Heydrich is dead."

"But why Josef Gabcik? I liked him."

Ian cupped her cheeks in his strong hands. "There were so many reprisals after the assassination. Jan and Josef had to sacrifice themselves."

"Olivia could have hidden them in Jarvoc."

"She couldn't, Bea," he said quietly. "The Germans had taken over the steel factory."

"Did they know Heydrich was dead?"

"Yes, Beatrice. They knew."

Chase heard the catch in his voice, and then, uninvited, he flopped on top of the unmade bed. Across the small room their eyes met again. "Don't keep frightening Bea with the past."

Startled Chase said, "Ian, I didn't. She asked me to help Kubis and whatever his name was."

"Gabcik. They were part of the Czech Brigade fifty years ago." He stared at the ceiling. "They were friends of my grandmother, but I suppose you already know that."

"I guessed as much. I've uncovered some other interesting things about your grandmother, Ian. I saw a lovely portrait of her in Oxford and found several articles on her in the library."

He glared back. "Things you intend to incorporate in your dissertation? I told you on the hills of Gascony that I'd stop you."

Her patience exploded. "If I ever find your grandmother's missing manuscript, I'll finish that novel for her."

"If I can't stop you, my grandfather or the publisher will. Besides there is no manuscript and certainly no need for a sequel to her last book."

Beatrice pointed a knitting needle at him. "Then why was Olivia writing it?" she asked.

He gave her a quizzical grin. "Was she?"

"If she wasn't," Chase asked, "then why are so many people trying to stop me from finding it?"

He pillowed his head on his locked fingers, an amused smirk tugging at his mouth. "I bet you chased after leaves when you were a kid or tried to pluck the rainbow from the sky. I did."

"Actually, I tried to catch the wind—especially on a cold day on Long Island or when we were out on a family drive." Before she realized it, she was confiding, "As a little girl, I used to think if I could catch the wind, I'd somehow find

God. But since I've grown up, I don't go for that God stuff any more."

He cocked his head toward Thorpe. "Don't let the old sage hear you saying that. She counts God as one of her best friends." He seemed to be counting the squares in the ceiling. "Your quest for my grandmother's story is like chasing the wind."

Chase laughed. "You're a fine one to be talking. A whole lifetime bicycling and for what? A yellow jersey."

"My grandmother would be proud of me."

At the look on his face, she grew serious. "I would like to have known her. That's what brought me to England."

"I thought the missing manuscript brought you here. And I'm telling you, let it go."

"I'm too close to the truth, right? Her books read like the story of her life."

He swung himself back to his feet, took three steps toward her, and gripped her shoulders. "Please, Chase—let it go."

"No fighting in my room," Beatrice said, waving her knitting needles at them. "Now be good children and kiss and make up."

The pressure of Ian's fingers eased. He winked at Beatrice, and then looking deeply into Chase's eyes, he kissed her soundly.

"What—you," she sputtered. "How dare you."

"Bravo," Bea applauded. "I like to see young people happy."

As her cagey eyes fixed on them, Chase had the uncanny feeling that Beatrice Thorpe was far more aware of reality than the staff at the Eagle's Nest gave her credit for. Beatrice was still grinning when Ian planted a kiss on her own cheek.

"Behave, love," he warned her. "And stop pretending. Chase is on to you."

Bea waited until he stalked off. "I think it would be nice if you could finish Olivia's book."

"I'll have to find it first."

She chuckled. "You're closer to finding it than you think.

But it would be too painful for the Kendalls—and dangerous. Olivia was a spy, you know."

A chill shot up Chase's spine. Bea knit on as she babbled, her thoughts wandering back to the war years. "The Renways took Olivia in," she said. "They had their reasons."

She grew tired as her sentences flitted from bombings to resistance fighters, from war to air raids, from the detention camp at Jarvoc to Eduard Benes—the exiled Czech president.

"Benes could have gotten my husband safely out of Prague, but he didn't." She pointed one crooked finger at the row of war photos on the wall. "That's all I have left. Roland died as a war correspondent," she said flatly.

She met Chase's eyes as she spoke again of the assassination of Reinhard Heydrich, a look of vengeance satisfied. "The Nazis called themselves steel manufacturers and architects," she scoffed, her eyes wary. "Murderers—all of them."

She missed a stitch and trembled, saying, "Ian doesn't like me to talk about the *designers of death*—but that's what the historians called them. They're still busy."

They're still busy. Chase had to stop Ian and ask him whether Beatrice was referring to the wretched war years or remembering only the books that Olivia had written.

Bea's voice softened to a whisper as Chase stood to leave. "Henri seemed like such a nice young man," she said sadly. "Olivia protected him. She shouldn't have, you know—and then the baby. Henri never knew about the baby." For a flicker, the faded eyes brightened. "But she got even with him. She left the baby at St. Michael's Cove."

"In Cornwall?" Chase asked.

"Where else?"

The baby son left behind in Cornwall at St. Michael's Cove.

Like Sayers, Renway had held her own dark secret—a child born out of wedlock, a truth that would have no place in Chase's dissertation.

"She was a spy," Beatrice repeated. "That's why she went back to Cornwall." As suddenly as her head bobbed, her eyes closed and she slept.

🝳🝳🝳

Chase found Ian outside sitting on the lawn, his narrow-wheeled Hybrid bicycle resting against a white bench. "I've been waiting for you," he said.

"I'm glad. I was hoping to catch you. Ian, is there a steel factory in the town where your grandmother was born?"

"Yes, her brother Dorian still works there."

"Was it always a steel factory?"

"How would I know?" he asked. "I think you've been taken in by Beatrice, the keeper of the Kendall secrets."

"I think she understands far more than she lets on."

"She's old, Chase."

"I like her, Ian. I don't want you to make fun of her."

"Don't get me wrong. I'm fond of the old girl. She keeps my grandmother alive for me."

"What if she's making up all those stories, Ian?"

"It doesn't matter. It adds to what I really remember. When she dies, my grandmother will die all over again."

"You'll still have your family."

"Gramps and my dad rarely talk about her."

"What about her other children?"

He looked surprised. "What children? Forget that Cornwall legend. My grandparents only had one son—my dad, Aubrey."

He stood and swung his leg over his high-speed bike. "I was hoping to have dinner with you. We could dine out here in the woods with the saints at Eagle's Nest."

His strong face was deadly serious. It reminded her of the lovely portrait of Olivia hanging in the alcove at Somerville Manor. He had Renway's coloring and eyes and that pensive gaze, even when he smiled. She felt suddenly kindly toward him. He was, after all, fiercely protective of his grandmother's reputation and memory. "I'll pass on that dinner," she said. "We'd spend the whole time fighting over your grandmother's missing manuscript. Let's part friends instead."

"We could call a truce while we stuff down their starches."

She thought of Luke Breckenridge—as she often did these days. Particularly of his brief phone call inviting her to the Von Tonner Art Museum. "You're too young for me, Ian," she said.

"Twenty-three and I like older women."

She grinned at that. "Ask me out some other time."

"Sure. Twelve years from now when I'm old enough."

She wrapped her fingers around the handlebar. "Ian, on the back cover of one of your grandmother's books, she was wearing a beautiful blue bracelet. Was that a family heirloom?"

"I wouldn't know," he said.

He reached out and tucked a strand of hair behind her ear. "I wish I were old enough for you now, Chase," he said.

"I was talking about your grandmother's bracelet."

"I wasn't. Well, I'll be off then. I'm biking back to Kendallshire tonight."

"It'll be dark before you get there."

"I'm used to seven or eight hours of cycling a day."

"That's self-torture."

"Suffering is part of the job. I'm a professional cyclist."

"Ian, I'd like to ask you—may I come to Kendallshire and meet your grandfather?"

"He won't go for that."

"Could you at least ask him?"

"I could do that, but it will cost you."

She thought of the costly venture with Andrew Forrestal. Uneasily, she asked, "How much?"

"I'll have a few hours free on Sunday. You can have dinner with me there in Kendallshire before our team flies over to France." He pointed to the logo on his shirt. "Without Jon Gainsborough's steel company backing us, we wouldn't be riding."

He cuffed her chin playfully. "I'll talk to my grandfather and let you know whether you can come out on Sunday."

Ian rode off without looking back. He liked this girl, but he felt as if a windstorm had hit the meadow flowers. Chase was too curious, too close to a day long ago when his grandmother had trusted him with a bracelet filled with priceless Kashmir sapphires. "Take care of it for me, Ian," his grandmother had said, "until I ask for it." Three hours later she was dead.

He sped around the building and pulled up beside Margot Hampton's parked car. "Well," Margot asked, "what do you think?"

"She's determined to see my grandfather."

"Stop her."

"Should I run her down like they did my grandmother? It's up to Uriah whether Chase sees him."

"We don't want her going anywhere alone."

"Mrs. Hampton, she's harmless."

"Harmless? Not if there's a CIA connection."

He put his head back and roared, one foot still on the pedal. "Now you're sounding as nutty as Beatrice."

"I didn't start the CIA rumor."

"I'll run that one by my grandfather."

"If she goes to the Cotswolds, Peter Quincy goes with her."

"Fine, but Quincy can have dinner with my grandfather. Chase and I will be busy." He adjusted his helmet. "It's getting late. I have a long ride ahead."

"Ian, with all this renewed interest in your grandmother's death, stay away from the Eagle's Nest for a while. Even Scotland Yard is getting involved again."

He turned his eyes toward the meadow flowers, their stems dark in the twilight. "Then it's up to you to take care of Beatrice for me. I'll be at the Tour de France for three weeks in July. Will that be long enough for things to die down?"

"Chase should be gone by then."

"I hope not. But when the Tour de France is over, Mrs. Hampton, I'm coming back to discard Beatrice's papers. If a copy of my grandmother's missing manuscript is there in that pile of junk, we've got to find it before Chase Evans does."

"Do you want me to start sorting through her things?"

"She wouldn't let you."

"I don't think the sapphire bracelet is there, Ian."

Good. You don't know about the trap door in the bottom of the china closet. He winked, a triumphant twitch of his eye. "I can assure you, the bracelet is not there."

But as he pedaled away, he wondered how he could find time to slip back into Beatrice's room unnoticed and claim the sapphires. If he could just wait until the end of the race. No, he would have to get back there sooner—before the Hamptons gave Scotland Yard or Dudley Perkins an excuse to tear the room apart.

Chapter 19

Eagle's Nest, 9 A.M. Twice during the night Chase heard Beatrice whack her cane against the side rails. Twice she heard the heavy steps of the attendant going to her aid and a constrained voice arguing, reasoning, persuading, cajoling. The attendant's frustrated hissing was countered with Bea's shrill and determined protest: "I want to sit in my chair now."

There was no connecting bath between their rooms—no way for Chase to rush to Mrs. Thorpe's side. She longed to reassure Bea that they were still in the predawn hours, that morning would come. Finally the flushing of the toilet vibrated the walls between them, and quiet settled once more.

Now as she listened for some sound of wakefulness next door, she heard nothing, not even Beatrice's cane against the rail. But something had awakened Chase. She swung to a sitting position and cupped her ear. Yes, there were muffled voices coming from Thorpe's room. She had a sickening feeling that something had happened and that Beatrice was about to make her last exodus from the Nest. While Chase feared the worst, Beatrice came to life, shouting, "Get out. Get out of here."

Chase bolted across the room and cracked her door in time to see Margot Hampton and a broad-shouldered man in a tweed jacket backing hurriedly from Beatrice's room. Chase knew before he even turned that it was Edwin Wallis.

As she listened with pounding heart, they stopped just steps from her door.

"I'll get an order to tear that room apart," he said.

Margot's voice came low and strained. "Don't do that. The shock would kill her. She's just a harmless old woman."

"In this country legally or illegally, Mrs. Hampton?"

There was a marginal pause—time enough for Chase to sense a dark cloud lowering. She kept her hand on the knob, her ear pressed to the door as Hampton said, "I told you, Inspector. Beatrice was born in this country."

"Don't force me to use excessive means."

Chase curled her bare toes as the cloud darkened. Margot was fighting for more than the protection of Beatrice and her ancient possessions. Margot and Nigel felt threatened as well; they were personally involved somehow.

"She's English, Inspector," Margot said. "But she was trapped in Czechoslovakia during the war."

Chase cracked the door slightly, gambling on their anger to hide the squeak as she tried to see their faces.

Wallis rubbed his jaw, his chin cupped in his wide hand. "Thorpe. Thorpe. Roland Thorpe," he said. "A Czech war correspondent. Seems to me he was a friend of the American columnist Ernie Pyle. Maybe they worked together."

"Perhaps. But Thorpe was an excellent photographer. Beatrice took some award-winning shots herself."

"I noticed some of the black-and-whites on the wall."

"They were taken by Thorpe's husband. Ones on the downfall of Prague and the destruction of Lidice. They cost him his life."

They took a few steps away from Chase and paused again. "You still haven't answered my question, Mrs. Hampton. Is Thorpe in this country legally or illegally?"

"I told you. She was born here."

"Yes, but there was some question about her husband's loyalties. His political views."

"No one ever questioned hers. But you're wrong, Constable, about Roland Thorpe. He sacrificed his reputation feigning friendship with the German side. His camera took him into the heart of the Reichland, into Berlin itself." She shot Edwin a mocking smile. "You question his loyalty? Roland filtered back information to the resistance movement. In the end—when the Gestapo caught up with him—he was imprisoned. He died in a labor camp, but as long as Beatrice thought he was alive, she refused to leave Prague."

"Then she came back after the war? Mrs. Hampton, I have only to phone Scotland Yard, and I can have my answers."

"Olivia Renway brought her back to London ten years ago."

"Around the time Renway was killed? Why did she bother with the old woman after all those years?"

The whispered answer was barely audible. "They were friends."

"Spies?"

"I said friends. Really, Inspector, I must get back to my office. Please leave."

"But first tell me—when did she come here?"

"She's been at our facility for ten years."

"And before that?"

"Maybe with Olivia's family in Czechoslovakia. I don't know."

"I think you do."

If he had twisted her arm, Margot could not have sounded more pained. "A year after Heydrich's assassination, Beatrice exchanged her papers with a friend." Huskily, she said, "The Red Cross was securing releases for some of the foreigners in prison camps. Beatrice was on the list, but she wanted to remain in Jarvoc for her husband's sake; she thought he was still alive. The friend was pregnant—her husband also with the resistance movement; actually he was dead, but the woman didn't know it."

"I see," Wallis said. "So officially Thorpe's records are Czechoslovakian now? Her papers. I'd like to see her papers."

"There are no records."

"Perhaps in her room. Mrs. Thorpe's room is oddly furnished. Cluttered mostly."

"She chose to keep her own furnishings."

"I see," he said again.

But he didn't see, Chase was certain. And the question in her own mind must surely be in his. If Bea had returned to England—smuggled back into her own country—then how had she brought so many personal items with her?

"I'll be back. Tomorrow morning. I suggest that you don't touch anything in that room, Mrs. Hampton."

"Is it all right if we dust, Inspector? Or pick up the items you tossed around?"

"Leave everything just as it is."

"So you can exile her? She's too old to be tossed about."

His laugh came dry and brittle. "Mrs. Hampton, it is her past that interests me, not her age. I could make it quite difficult for you, harboring that woman here."

"But you won't because of Nigel."

"I'd sell my mother down the Thames if I had to. And I will find the real connection between Olivia Renway and Mrs. Thorpe."

"You'd hang them both for another promotion?"

"I'm due for one," he said calmly. "The Renway question has never been settled. It would be a gold star on my shoulder."

"But why all your interest now?"

"You have Chase Evans to thank for that. She muddied the waters. Since she reached London, MI5 has been on it. Fresh terrorist threats."

"Oh, Inspector, the next thing you'll tell me is that Chase is involved in them."

"Perhaps she is in some way. She's clever enough." To Chase it seemed that Wallis had only enough time to smack his lips before saying, "Thorpe wouldn't even budge out of that chair of hers."

"She rarely does. She'd sleep there if we'd let her."

"Why?" he insisted.

"Because she breathes better sitting up. Good day, Edwin. I'll trust you to see your own way out."

"And Miss Evans?"

"I told you in Beatrice's room—Evans is gone. To the Cotswolds, I think."

"Odd. None of my men saw her leave the Eagle's Nest."

Through the cracked door, Chase watched Margot and the inspector until they reached the end of the corridor and disappeared from view. She stole from her room and went immediately next door. Tapping lightly—so as not to startle Beatrice—she opened the door and slipped inside.

Beatrice was still in her night clothes with the derby hat on her head. "Get out. Out," she cried, waving her knitting needles frantically in the air.

"It's me, Beatrice. Chase."

Bea's eyes squinted as Chase approached. Fleetingly Chase wondered, *Do all blue eyes fade and glaze over? Do all the windows to memory cloud as Beatrice's have done? As Marie's did?* The warmth that she felt for Marie back at Willowglen spread quickly to Beatrice. Without invitation, Chase slid a straight-back chair up beside Beatrice and sat down facing her.

"You had early morning company," she said.

Beatrice was obviously agitated as she pointed toward the closet. The piles of junk seemed even more cluttered.

"That's the way the Gestapo come. In their plain clothes with all their questions. Tearing my things apart. Searching through my books."

Olivia's books. "That was Constable Wallis from Scotland Yard."

"That's what Margot told me. But I know. I know he wants Olivia's diaries."

So do I, Chase thought.

She felt like a traitor, as though she too had come in her fancy clothes, shrewdly, deceptively seeking answers—as the Gestapo had done long ago in Prague, as Constable Wallis had done only moments ago. She had come not in friendship for this old woman but for Olivia's lost manuscript. But diaries? Did she have diaries, too? As Beatrice calmed and took the start of another afghan from her knitting bag, Chase said, "Doesn't Uriah Kendall have Olivia's private papers, Beatrice?"

"Her husband?" The wrinkles turned to frowns, the puzzled gaze focused on the knitting needles. "No, Olivia wanted to protect Uriah. She wanted me to give them to the prime minister."

"To John Majors?"

"To Margaret Thatcher. Everything Olivia did was to protect Uriah. To clear his name."

Instinctively, Chase glanced around the room, shuddering at the mess that Wallis had left behind. She had to find Olivia's diary and papers before Wallis came back. *Shape up, Evans,* she told herself. *You're getting caught up in Bea's crazy stories.*

Her more rational self argued back, *What if she's telling the truth?* She managed her Willowglen smile—the happy, cheerful one that Marie loved. "Beatrice, how can you possibly know how Olivia Renway lived or what she thought?"

The knitting needles in the gnarled hands moved with lightning speed. "Who better than I? I knew that child all her life. She was so much a part of my life—still is. I know all about her—still do."

The derby hat tipped cockily on the silver hair. She poked it back in place with one of her needles and went on talking with only the loss of a stitch or two, like a wavering heartbeat kicking in and out.

"Did you really know Miss Renway?" Chase asked.

Thorpe's watery eyes brimmed over, taking on a bright glow that memory had sparked. "From the time she was born."

"Were you her nanny?"

"Her best friend."

"But you're not Czechoslovakian."

"No, I followed my husband there," she said softly. "England didn't want Roland back, so I packed up and moved to Prague to live with the Pascheks. That way I could be near my husband."

"Olivia's family? I thought her name was Renway."

The cagey eyes took refuge under the brim of the hat. "Not in the beginning. I took over for Mrs. Paschek. She had her hands full with three boys. Another baby was just too much for her. Olivia was a sickly little thing, red and ugly in the beginning—all arms and legs and double fists, not pretty like most babies."

The pictures of Olivia Renway were of a striking woman; perhaps Beatrice Thorpe had never known Olivia at all. The watery eyes brimmed over again. "She was scrawny, her face covered with downy peach fuzz. I never thought she'd grow up lovely, but then her cheeks filled in, and she stopped being fretful. She was a good baby after I took over, so easy to care for."

The ramblings of yesterday seemed more focused, the speech halting but clear, as though Beatrice were sorting out just how much to share with Chase. As they talked, Chase's fingers settled on an old-fashioned photo album on the table beside Thorpe. She flipped the cover open and immediately felt the sting of a needle across the back of her hand.

"Sorry," Chase said, her hand and her mood both smarting.

"That's Olivia's. These belonged to Olivia, too," she said, tapping her dangling earrings. "Lots of her things here."

Chase didn't move. She didn't want to damage the fragile bond between them. Why had Thorpe been permitted to keep so many possessions? The other residents were crowded together, two to a room, their possessions limited to a one-page checklist and a favorite stuffed chair. Yet Bea's room was crowded with personal belongings. Her own? Or did they really belong to Olivia Renway?

Bea paused, the knitting needles still in her hands, and leaned back in her velvety blue recliner. "She's here," Beatrice said. "In this room with me. I promised her I'd take care of her things for her."

Chase eyed the album again. "May I?" she asked.

The lips pursed. "Don't have any pictures of her childhood. They were lost in the war." She tapped her temple. "But I remember her growing up into a sweet little thing. Going to boarding school in Switzerland. And taking her for summer vacations in England—stayed with the Renways. Friends of her parents."

She rocked now, the afghan slipping to the floor. "She

should have stayed in boarding school. Been safer. She was smart as a whip, not haughty at all. Then she came back just before Prague fell—she wasn't supposed to come."

"From boarding school."

Bea groped for answers. "Yes, she was safe in Switzerland. But she came home. She was sixteen. For days she sat with her father talking about the clouds hanging over Europe."

"The war?"

She nodded. "Mr. Paschek saw it coming. Everybody did. He fought it in his own way with the underground press. I think that child knew it—she was a smart one. I think that's why she came back to work with him. He wanted to send his family to the Renways in England, but Mrs. Paschek was afraid to go, and Olivia wouldn't go, not without her father."

"But you said she had three brothers."

"She actually had four. Dorian came after Olivia. The brothers were grown up by then, except for thirteen-year-old Dorian. One of the boys was married and living in Lidice. They tried to persuade Mrs. Paschek and Olivia to go there."

"And you? Why didn't you go back to London?"

She rocked and reflected. "My husband couldn't go, and I wouldn't leave that child. I told them I'd stay and travel back to England with the rest of the family. But it was too late!"

Beatrice's past and Olivia's were tied together in this room. Olivia's private papers could be anywhere. In the bookcase. In the cluttered closet. On Beatrice's nightstand. But in spite of her confusion, she was too shrewd to reveal the hiding place. Chase paced the room with a methodical gaze. The china closet was filled with cups and plates, but were the panels hollow or solid? "The man from Scotland Yard will be back in the morning, Bea."

"To take me away?"

"Oh, no. But he plans to tear your room apart." *To destroy the things that you treasure.*

"You won't let him, will you?"

"I won't know how to stop him."

She squirmed in her chair, pathetically small, her short,

swollen legs barely touching the floor, her ankles almost lost in the ruffled trim of the recliner. "What does that man want from me?" she whispered.

"He thinks you're in this country illegally."

"But I was born in England."

"I know. And Constable Wallis wants Olivia's private papers."

"Hide them for me," Beatrice begged.

"I don't know where they are." Again Chase's gaze went slowly around the room, pausing at the clutter in the closet, lingering a second time at the bookshelves crammed with Olivia's books. Each possibility—each thought was interrupted with another glance at Beatrice. "Where are they, Bea? Tell me. I can't help you unless you tell me."

"I don't remember."

She patted the old woman's hand as she had often patted hands at Willowglen. "It's all right. It doesn't matter. I'll stay with you when the inspector comes tomorrow—"

But how can I stay? Margot told the constable that I've gone. Margot! "Beatrice latches onto every excuse to stay in that old chair of hers," she said. Under the cushion? No! Impossible!

Without asking, Chase carefully extended the leg rest. It scraped as it shot Beatrice's body into a cramped position.

Alarmed, Beatrice cried out, "I never use that leg rest. My chair is old and broken."

Chase bent down and lifted the ruffle. Beneath the rusty support rods lay a small trap door, a tiny keyhole visible on inspection. "There's a door here, Beatrice. Where's the key?"

"Olivia's diaries?" Bea asked.

"Maybe."

"You've discovered them?" Beatrice's eyes were shiny with tears. "I'd forgotten where I hid them. Oh, yes. Olivia's diaries are in there. Four of them. I remember now."

"May I read them?"

"Hide them for me. In your room."

"I won't hide something when I don't know what it says."

Her motions were frantic, her bare legs wiggling. "In here. In here," she cried as she rummaged in her knitting bag. "It's here. The key. Promise me you'll hide them after you read them."

"I promise." She took the key from Beatrice's trembling fingers. "You look tired, Beatrice. Would you like me to help you back to bed so you can take a nap?"

"No, I'm afraid of dying when I sleep. I must not die yet."

"You won't. You're just frightened. I'll stay here with you. I'll read the diaries while you rest."

Bea ran her gnarled finger over the back of Chase's hand. "Olivia would have liked you," she said.

She rose slowly to her feet, Chase's hand tight at her elbow. The steps seemed more halting than yesterday. She backed up to her bed, her knitting bag clutched in her free hand.

"Here, I'll take that for you," Chase offered.

"No, leave it by my pillow."

Chase stayed by the bed holding the fragile hand until Bea slipped into a troubled sleep. And then the soft snoring came—like a gentle wheeze. The outside wind against the curtains and Beatrice's snoring blew gently together.

As Beatrice dozed, Chase went back to the chair and fitted the key into the tiny hole. It jammed, but she struggled again, twisting and turning it, fearful that it might break before the door came loose. Finally the latch turned; the door moved. She lifted four diaries from their hiding place, lowered the leg rest, and settled in Bea's chair. She thumbed through the pages of the first diary and read: "The Germans came today. Czechoslovakia is no longer free. All I can hear is the booted step of marching men."

As Chase backed up to the first page and read through the diaries, she felt the pain and outrage of the youthful Olivia, the heartbeat of a young woman who would do anything to protect her family and her country.

> *February 24, 1939: Father has told me to stay in board-*
> *ing school and not to leave Lausanne. But I am going home*
> *in the morning before any of the others know that I have*
> *gone.*
> *February 25, 1939: The ticket agent said that the south*

border between Austria and Czechoslovakia is closed. He tells me that he must route me the long way through Munich and on into Prague. Still I have not told my father that I am coming.

February 27, 1939: I am hungry. There have been long delays. There are uniforms everywhere. No one on the train is smiling. I see fear in their faces. I am afraid. A German soldier tried to flirt with me. I pretended I could not speak his language. I wanted to cry out, "Leave me alone. I have some Jewish blood flowing in my veins."

Midnight, March 1, 1939: We spent hours at the border crossing. At last the train rumbled into my country.

March 4, 1939: Father is still angry with me. He says that I have put them all in danger, that I should have obeyed him and stayed in school. But Beatrice was glad to see me.

The farm looks different. Some of mother's favorite furniture is gone, including her small, round table and her china closet. Father has shipped them to the Renways in England while there is still time to send them. He wants the family to fly out this weekend—to go to England until Prague and Jarvoc are safe once again. I will not go unless my father goes with us.

March 13, 1939: Some of the government officials and military have fled the country. My brother Antonin went with them. I worry about Papa. I hear him leave the house each night when we are all in bed. He does not come back until dawn.

He says I am too young to help the growing resistance movement. But he is wrong. I want to work beside Papa. This is my country, too.

March 15, 1939: I am sixteen. At dawn this morning my country was invaded. The Germans have taken over Prague. Even now they are searching house by house. I think they are hunting for my father.

Chapter 20

Prague, March 15, 1939. Sixteen-year-old Olivia Paschek awakened to a foreboding silence in the tiny bedroom above her uncle's shop. She lay motionless, feeling a sudden chill sweep across the room, a nameless fear that wrapped its tentacles around her. The eerie predawn stillness was shattered by the roar of a hundred motorcycles screaming through the streets, the sound of angry voices shouting, the frightened cries of the neighbors. There was a lull in the uproar, and then she heard the booted steps against the pavement. She threw back her bedroll and pattered barefooted across the wooden boards into the other room.

On the radio beside her father, a voice droned on: "Offer no resistance . . . keep calm . . . go about your work as usual."

"Papa, what is it?" she cried.

Only his head turned, his broad stubby finger to his lips. She ran to him, and he held out his arm and pulled her close. "You should have been on the plane yesterday," he said. "Back to Switzerland. Back to safety."

"The planes weren't flying yesterday, Papa."

He cursed the weather, cursed the planes and the trains that had crossed him. His gaze went back to the window, his eyes hardened as he peered through the curtain. Now she saw what he saw. They had awakened to find their country occupied by armed forces—a Panzer division thundering down the boulevard, the neighboring streets blocked off, hundreds of billowing parachutes drifting toward the airport. The road in front of the shop was choked with armored cars and tall, broad-shouldered Germans in gray-green uniforms, their faces harsh beneath their helmets. Across the River Vltava a swastika hung from the top of the Hradcany Castle.

Dawn had brought light to their darkness. Down the street foot soldiers were searching house by house, a block at a time. In spite of the warmth of her father's strong arm around her, Olivia shivered. She knew before she asked. "Who are they, Papa?"

"The enemy." His voice filled with loathing. "They've taken us without a shot. Get dressed, Olivia. We must leave."

"They'll stop us. They're searching the houses."

"We'll be gone before they reach our shop."

"Why would they want us, Papa?"

"They are searching for the voices of opposition—political activists, the country's leaders. Teachers. Journalists."

She frowned. "But you are a friendly voice, Papa."

He smiled. "Not my words in the underground paper. These have aroused fury in Berlin."

"Then Dorian is right. You run the underground press."

"Someone had to."

Zdenek Paschek had always been her strength, her idol. She thought him old and wise, yet in truth he was only forty-five—a short, stocky man whose nose was a bit too wide, his mustache too thick and bushy, his mahogany eyes rich with kindness. Papa had been content to run the print shop and work the family farm and to spend his early evenings drinking Staropramen with his friends in the pub. He was a good provider, better off than most of their neighbors in Jarvoc, and more than willing to stretch his earnings to send Olivia to boarding school in Switzerland.

Only in recent months had his patterns changed. Now he spent long hours at his brother's shop in Prague, often taking the older boys with him. He had always been nonpolitical. Yet here he was admitting to partnership in the resistance movement; growing uprising had fanned across

Czechoslovakia ever since the Munich Agreement handed over parts of the Republic to Hitler.

Papa seemed suddenly grief-stricken. "Your mama said I have only brought danger to my family. The older boys can take care of themselves, but you and Dorian should be in Switzerland."

"He's thirteen. He can't go to a private girls' school."

"You're right," he said. "Now dress quickly. I must get you on the train. Once you reach Switzerland, promise me you will go on to England. The Renways will take care of you. I'll make certain your mama and Dorian and Beatrice come later."

"The borders will be closed, Papa."

"We can send you through Poland."

"I won't go without you."

He brushed her hair from her face with his big hands. "My stubborn one," he said. Outside, the angry shouts of the soldiers came closer. "No arguments, Olivia. Your brother Antonin is already in London. He'll take you to the Renways."

She came back from the bedroom in her brother's clothes, her own dresses shoved into a backpack. "At school they said the Nazis hurt women and girls. They raped some of my Austrian friends."

Pain ripped across his face. He nodded, unable to speak. He took her hand and led her through the storage room, past her uncle's printing press and the shelves of ink and newsprint.

🐞🐞🐞

The depot was surrounded by Wehrmacht troops, the train smoking idly on the railroad siding. Two of the third-class cars with their hard wooden benches had been cordoned off. Four bodies lay limp on the platform. "It's too late," Olivia's father cried. "I didn't get you out in time."

"It's all right, Papa. I didn't want to go without you."

They were lying in the thick grass on the knoll, hidden

behind the bushes. As her father wept, locks of raven hair fell across his creased brow.

The Kommandant ignored the lifeless bodies on the platform, his attention riveted on a frightened family trembling in front of him. "Show me your papers," he shouted in German. "Your identity papers," the Kommandant shouted again.

As the man reached into his pocket, shots rang out. He dropped in front of the Kommandant, his blood splattering over the platform. Immediately, Zdenek's hand covered Olivia's mouth. "Keep still," her father warned.

"That man didn't even resist," she cried.

"But we will."

Overhead came the drone of planes bringing the threat of bombs falling if the people of Prague resisted. Zdenek's rough hand encircled Olivia's. "Tonight—when it is dark— we will go to Jarvoc."

"We can't. They'll stop us. You heard the Kommandant. We need identity cards to prove we work in the factory at Jarvoc."

"The priest will get them for us, Olivia."

"He doesn't know we're here."

"Come, we'll hide in the catacombs of the Karel Boromejsky Church until darkness. We'll be safe there."

The Greek Orthodox church, Prague, 10 A.M. From behind the curtain, Yeurgous Papanastasious saw them steal through the sanctuary—slipping through the wall paneling to the right of the altar into the stairwell that would take them down into the crypt. The priest made no effort to stop them. They would be found soon enough. Let each man and woman in Prague grab what moments of freedom they could. Let them have these few hours or days of safety. He would not turn them away from the church. Let them find solace here. Let them set their house in order.

Yeurgous had recognized Zdenek Paschek. The Germans would be looking for him, carting him off to stand trial and die for his part in running the underground press, silencing his right to free speech. But the priest's heart went out to the young girl—and she was a girl in spite of the trousers and jacket that she wore. He had seen the red curls slipping beneath the cap, had known intuitively who she was. She was tall for her age and shapeless like her mother, but spry as she followed her father down into the crypt.

Yeurgous knelt by the altar and prayed, crying in agony for Prague, for himself, and for Zdenek Paschek and his daughter who sought refuge in the church. And in utter despair, he cried, "My God, where are You? Have You deserted even this Your sanctuary?"

It seemed to the priest that his words bounced back from the vaulted ceiling, shelling him with futility. Behind him the door burst open. Soldiers ran down the long aisle. He felt himself torn violently from his kneeling position. He cringed, shrinking back as they dragged him to his feet and thrust him against the altar. Hatred showed in their faces and boomeranged in the sharp commanding voice of their officer.

"Let the priest alone," he told them.

Luftwaffe wings shone on the lapel of the handsome blond German. "Go on with your praying, priest. Prague will need it."

Something in the eyes belied the harshness in his voice. "What would you know about prayer?" Yeurgous asked him.

In the sudden hush in the room came the answer: "It was my country—as my mother would say—that gave you 'Silent Night.'"

March 16, 1939, 3 A.M. Keeping off the main roads, Zdenek and Olivia crawled and stumbled through the rough countryside in the pitch darkness. They reached Jarvoc while it was still dark, but even in the starless night they could see that the farmhouse was under the control of soldiers. They staggered on to the dress shop owned and operated by Olivia's childhood governess. Beatrice Thorpe opened the door without a word and pulled them to safety. She held Olivia and brushed the straggly hair from her face.

"What are the Germans doing here?" Zdenek asked.

"They've taken over the factory." Her laugh was mirthless. "They've promised us food and safety in exchange for work."

"What's happened to my family?"

Beatrice was a shadowed figure in the darkness. "Your wife and Dorian have gone to Lidice to be with your oldest son."

"Good. They will be safe there. Where are the others?"

"They're waiting for you. I will take you to them. But we must go quickly. Dawn is coming." She gripped Olivia's hand. "You must come with us. We cannot leave you here alone."

🏺🏺🏺

In the caves of Jarvoc. Olivia had long suspected that her father had a mistress. Now as she faced the resistance fighters in the cavern, she knew her fears had been unfounded. She recognized most of her father's friends: Leo Padanansky and the parish priest. The farmer with six children. Margot and Ladislav Dvorak. And Beatrice's husband, Roland, the war correspondent.

"Get your daughter out of here," Leo said.

Paschek refused. "She has nowhere to go. We must take her into our confidence."

"She's only a child."

"It no longer matters," her father said. "We are at war."

"She's too young," Roland Thorpe warned.

"I'm sixteen."

Her father smiled through his sadness and held out his hand to her. "A very grown-up sixteen," he said. "We will need her. She speaks French and German fluently."

Beatrice gasped. "You're not suggesting—"

"That she run courier for us? What else can we do, Beatrice? My sons are no longer available."

"I'm quick on my feet, Papa. I know all the back roads."

"Where's your son Antonin?" Leo asked. "He's late."

"He's gone—in England by now. He flew out in the KLM plane with Colonel Moravec. Ten others made it with them."

"Impossible in that blinding spring snowstorm."

"They had to risk the storm to fool the German agents."

Leo drove his fist against the cement wall. "Then we've been deserted again. First by our ex-president, Benes. Now Moravec."

"We don't need them, Leo. We'll fight on without them."

"President Hacha is warning against that."

"Hacha is old and ill." There was a slight rustling in the cave as her father pulled a spotter's map from his pocket. "Antonin got a message through to me before he left."

You're lying, Papa, she thought. *But I see hope on Leo's face now.* "Hacha meant well, but he has sold our country out to the enemy. Moravec in London is our only hope of setting up a government in exile. If Eduard Benes joins him, they'll be dependent on our underground activities. We won't let them down."

Leo smarted. "What can a handful like us do?"

Dvorak sharpened his knife. "The same things we've been doing. Cutting brake hoses on trains and telephone lines. Spying on German agents. Maintaining our wireless listening posts."

Papa's voice was determined. "We'll keep on resisting. They'll force us to work in their factories, but we'll stage slowdowns. The intelligence files went out in the British pouch with the request for more arms and ammunition. We won't wait. We'll steal incendiary bombs from the Germans to blow up their petrol supply and destroy their equipment." Papa kept his arm around Olivia and gave her an encouraging squeeze as he said, "And we'll send couriers across the borders whenever we need to."

"What about your other sons? Can't they work for us?"

Paschek shook his head. "Torma and his family are in Lidice. Dorian and his mother are with them now."

"And your son Karol?" Roland Thorpe asked.

Paschek looked at the jaded faces. "Karol is one of the few

who listened to me. I tried to warn all of you that the Germans planned something like this."

"We didn't think it would happen so soon."

"Leo, it's been coming for months. Karol and two of his friends plan to cross the Polish border tonight—while the customs officers and police are still looking the other way."

Moodily Leo said, "And if they're lucky enough to succeed?"

"They'll make their way to the French Legion and eventually to England if Moravec can gather a Czech army around him. We'll help them. We must keep our transmitters open so we can send reports through to Czech Intelligence in Stockholm and Geneva."

Olivia had slipped from the meeting and back while the men argued. But even in the darkened cave she heard them talking. She stood before them now, still dressed in her brother's clothes, her beautiful red hair shorn to a boy's cut. "My brothers are gone," she said. "That leaves me to carry your messages. I know Geneva, Papa. And I know French and German. I can get through the lines."

☙☙☙

Eagle's Nest, England. Chase closed the last of Olivia's four diaries and leaned back in Beatrice Thorpe's recliner, her thoughts on the lovely Olivia Paschek. She could envision the youthful Olivia listening with her ear pressed against the cracks in the wall or slipping up quietly on German sentries. Chase was guilty of listening uninvited herself—ever since her brother taught her how to tune in on the intercom at their family home on Long Island. The truth was, she never lost the habit of or delight in tuning a curious ear to those around her.

As she glanced across the room, she was startled to see Beatrice's tired eyes fixed on her. "You're awake. You should have said something. I just finished reading Olivia's diaries."

Bea pulled herself up with the side rails. "You must hide

Olivia's book with the diaries—in case something happens to me."

Chase's heartbeat quickened. "The lost manuscript?"

"It was never really lost. If something happens to me," she repeated, "give it to Ian Kendall. He'll know what to do."

"Ian will be in France for three weeks. I'll put it in my father's lockbox in London. But is that what you want?"

Beatrice pointed her cane toward Olivia's end table where an old-fashioned lamp tilted precariously. "Over there," she said.

Chase popped out of the recliner and ran to the table. She felt around the edges. "Where?"

"Underneath—there's a latch."

Chase stooped down and ran her hand around the underside of the thick tabletop. Her fingernail snagged in the back as it hit a rusty latch. Once released, the drawer came free easily. Chase lifted out a thick and musty manila envelope.

"Beatrice!"

The wizened face brightened. "The nurses snooped in my bookshelves and dresser. Margot Hampton even looked in the china closet. But no one knew about the drawer in the table. 'Cept me. And Olivia. And I can trust Olivia. She won't tell a soul."

And if we had left it there until morning, Chase thought, *Constable Wallis would have found it.* Chase made some hurried decisions. She would travel to Prague to talk with Dorian Paschek about his sister. And she would leave the Eagle's Nest early in the morning, hopefully before Edwin Wallis came back.

She took the few steps back to Beatrice's bedside. The aged hand felt cold in Chase's clasp, like Marie's had felt at the Willowglen. "Thank you for trusting me, Mrs. Thorpe. May I read Olivia's manuscript before I give it to Ian?"

"Yes, do." Her eyes flickered and closed, her breathing suddenly shallow. Slowly she opened them again. "Yes, Olivia would like you," she said. Her eyes clouded. "Could you call Olivia and ask her to come have tea with us? I want her to know that the boys from Anthropoid are gone."

Her plaintive cry turned to a wail. "If only we could have gotten the assassin team safely back to London."

Chase fought the tightness in her throat. "I'll ask the nurse to get you washed and dressed."

"Oh, how nice. Dressed up for tea. I think I'll wear my derby hat today. Olivia likes that one."

"It's there on your bed—beside your knitting bag."

The Cotswolds, England. Standing here on the bridge where it had all begun, Uriah knew that he would one day come back and finish life's journey in the very place where he had been born. He had grown up in Kendallshire, one of those tranquil Cotswold villages nestled in the hills and valleys of Gloucestershire. It was sometimes missed by tourists, lying as it did on one of those roads less traveled. Thus it remained unspoiled, serene, a place to be shared by simple villagers and grazing sheep.

Uriah knew every inch of the village—the Elizabethan manor once owned by his great-grandparents, the half-timbered hotel in the middle of town, the old cloth mill where the paddles squeaked as the gentle waters of the river turned them. The village was filled with two-story cottages with steeply pitched tiled roofs, his own still thatched because he liked it that way. On the other side of the foot-bridge lay the parish church with its lancet windows where four generations of Kendalls had married.

His son Aubrey had been born here, too. Aubrey had spent his early years rollicking over the woodland paths. Even now the sun cast its golden hues on the limestone hills where sheep were grazing. Grover and Ian had only come to Kendallshire for short visits and seldom after Olivia died. Since coming back, Uriah had been calmed once again by the Cotswolds. But his peace was fragile with Nedrick attempting to shatter it with his constant warnings about trouble ahead.

For days Nedrick had tried to persuade him not to meet with the American student, but sooner or later he would be forced to face this Chase Evans—a good-looking young woman according to Nedrick—and hear her out. He would discuss Olivia's literary works, and he would answer simple questions and ask some of his own. "Yes," he would say, "Olivia was Czechoslovakian by birth. Yes, she survived the war but lived out most of it in Britain."

Some of the nasty rumors about Olivia were in public record. To deny these would be foolish, nor would he dispute them. But should he answer any questions about Cornwall? No, for Olivia's sake, he would deny these and tell Miss Evans that Olivia's British family had died before he knew her.

"I thought I'd find you here," Nedrick said.

"It's pleasant standing here—on Olivia's bridge."

"We've got to talk. The news commentator is talking about more bomb threats."

"We're safe here in the Cotswolds, Nedrick."

"They would just as soon drop bombs or nerve gas on this village as not."

"*They?*" Uriah challenged. "You seem to have some particular group in mind."

"Don't you understand, Uriah? The terrorists could just as easily target us."

"You sound so certain," Uriah said sadly. "Olivia predicted these things in her books. The use of nerve gas. The bombing of government buildings. The destructive behavior of madmen."

"Uriah, this threat is real. Some extremist group could be patterning after the subway incidents in Tokyo."

"Miserable rumors." Uriah tapped his fingers together. "I've lived with miserable rumors for years. Kaminsky and Neilson at Langley still think Olivia was connected with an extremist group. Dudley Perkins's doings, no doubt. Perkins likes to point out that Olivia's books were accurate as to time and location of bombings and terrorist threats *before they happened.*"

"What are they trying to do—blame your wife for something she wrote years ago? Or was she really involved?"

"Before our marriage we agreed not to question each

other about the past. Otherwise there would have been no marriage. But Perkins is convinced that she spied against England during the war, working directly with a German agent."

Nedrick rubbed his hands on his trouser leg. "Did your wife point her finger back at someone in Germany?"

"No," Uriah said calmly. He was aware of Nedrick's nervous movements. *I've triggered something here,* he thought. He was reminded of his concerns back in Maryland—Nedrick's keen interest in foreign embassies across the Potomac.

"There's nothing they can do now, not with your wife dead."

"But Langley and MI5 still keep close tabs on me."

"Then with Chase Evans delving into Olivia's past, it only stirs up more trouble. It's already cost Andrew Forrestal his life."

"Then out of curiosity, I will talk with Miss Evans."

"I won't stay around and watch her cut you down."

"Are you planning a holiday? Where will you go?"

Nedrick deliberated. "To a small fishing village in Spain. I was always going to do that with my grandfather."

"Spain, eh? A favorite place from your boyhood, Nedrick?"

"One of the only good recollections I have."

"I have something else you could do first. Perhaps you would like to attend the opening of the Von Tonner Art Museum. I have an invitation for myself and a guest, but I'm not going." He turned and smiled at Nedrick, wondering what twisted thoughts were running through the young man's mind. "The invitation is on my desk at the cottage. Take it if you like."

Chapter 21

Jarvoc. Altman Russelmann rallied the family out of bed for an unscheduled conference at the dining room table. Hanz limped downstairs in his tartan robe, tying the sash as he joined the others as the uninvited guest.

Altman's eyes narrowed. "No need for you to come."

Hanz remained, studying his son. Altman was well-attired as always, the shades of his tie picking up the blues in the Canali suit and linen shirt. But he seemed over-dressed for the office. Gustav sat on the other side of Altman, looking disgruntled. Josef sat at the end of the table, his eyes downcast, his sense of inferiority in Altman's presence glaring. He didn't even look up when Mila came into the room carrying a breakfast tray with an assortment of breads, stuffed eggs, and grilled sausage.

Altman rebuked her. "Where's the strudel I ordered?"

Fire lit in her dark eyes. "I'll get it," she said. As she passed Hanz, she mouthed, "I've got a surprise for you. Later."

Her smile gave Hanz boldness. "Well, what's the emergency this time, Altman?" he asked.

"Whether to continue the Nishokura accounts."

"They're our best buyer, our dumplings and roast pork."

"Forget the bread on the table, Father. They could be our downfall. Ever since the Tokyo disasters, there's been an on-going investigation."

"Nothing in the headlines about that," Gustav argued.

Altman fought back. "Behind the scenes, the finger is on Sasa Nishokura, the vice-president of foreign sales."

"And we're involved?" Hanz asked.

"We could be if we keep using them. But our records are in the clear, aren't they, Josef?"

Josef always looked miserable under pressure. "I don't know, Altman. Gustav insists on handling that lately. But Father is right. It hardly seems the time to drop a long-standing account."

"If Nishokura Steel goes down, we're not going with them."

"Why would we go with them, Altman? How could our company be in trouble for selling steel to them?" Hanz asked.

Altman ignored his father and glanced at his Omega watch. "Gunter called for a meeting at the corporate office this morning. The president from the Dortmund plant will be there. Gustav, you and I are flying in to represent Jarvoc."

Gustav bounced his unlit cigarette from one palm to the other. "Will Poland have a voice?"

"This doesn't concern their operation."

"Will Gainsborough be joining you in Munich?" Hanz asked.

"That old fool? There isn't time. The less he knows, the better for him, the better for us." Altman tugged at the button on his suit coat. "Jon is too edgy. He doesn't mind stockpiling money, but he abhors breaking the rules."

"We should at least notify Coach Skobla," Gustav suggested.

"Let him keep his mind on training the cycling team for the Tour de France."

Gustav rubbed his fat hands together. "I like that irony," he said. "Imagine Olivia Renway's grandson cycling down the Champs-Elysees in the yellow jersey next month."

"I can't imagine that at all," Altman said. "I have no intention of letting Ian Kendall win."

❁❁❁

Shortly after Altman and Gustav took off in the company jet, Hanz left the house with his toolbox and made his way slowly along the tracks to the old Jarvoc plant. It was true that the blast furnace—which smelted the iron products— belched out the ominous black smoke that often rose above the mill. But at times lately when the winds turned toward the farm, Hanz detected a different odor above Jarvoc.

Altman held the only key to the front entry of the waste plant, but Hanz made his way to the back of the ghostly gray building and went cautiously down the seven steps. He rattled the rusty lock. Time was against him. By nine the trucks and forklifts would rumble past the building toward the waiting train. He took his battery torch, shielded his eyes with goggles, and fought the chain and lock that had been bolted for fifty years.

Once inside, he was surprised at the absence of spiders. He worked his way through the numerous rooms, finding what he knew he would find. Stockpiles of weapons, drums of liquids, and a massive conveyor of rusting pipes that ran deep into the tunnels. Several gas containers bore fifty-year-old labels, the faded letters spelling out the German word for poison. *Gift gas.* He ran his hand along the bulkhead, feeling for a fissure or ruptured fault line that would allow toxic leaks to rise like a foggy mist. Poison gases seeping from the pipes could destroy everything and everyone in Jarvoc.

His uneven steps echoed loudly as he followed the pipeline to the massive steel doors that led into the tunnels. If the rusty pipes burst as the Russian pipeline had done along the Arctic Circle, any contents would spill out and destroy the underground water source for Jarvoc. Hanz could hardly imagine how far the spring thaws and flowing river might carry it.

Hanz moved on to the infamous shower rooms and glanced up at the old catwalk where the guards had once stood. His torch caught the reflection of new sensors on the wall and shiny new shower heads. Someone had been measuring the pipe's thickness to detect the cracks and corrosion that called for repairs. The doors to the shower room had been resealed and one whole section of the pipeline burnished and coated with rust-proof material. Altman? Altman never dirtied his hands. Josef? A quality chemist but spineless. Gustav was a yes-man. Jiri, the clever architect? Jiri and Altman! "Dear Lord," Hanz cried out, "what are they planning?"

Coming out of the shower room, he stopped, unwilling to go farther into the cavernous tunnels that stretched beneath the railroad tracks and forested mountains. He had walked these tunnels as a young man, recoiling then as he did now. He would not look at the chute that had sent its innocent victims into the underground morgue.

Again he regretted the day he had found his firstborn son in Cornwall. His hip throbbed as he turned and retraced his steps. The toolbox in his hand felt heavier. He stumbled and fell forward. Exhausted, he braced himself against the cold cement and wept without tears. There was only one honorable thing to do. Hanz took the old chrome-plated Smith and Wesson from his toolbox, feeling as old as the nineteenth-century weapon. He spun it on his forefinger, sensing the weight and power that it held. Better to die here alone in the tunnel than to face the shame and humiliation of what his sons had become. He lifted the revolver and pressed it against his temple.

Sunday. Chase had promised herself one sunrise at the Eagle's Nest before she left. She rolled out of bed, showered, and dressed in her Koret City Blues and a soft royal blue shell. She tiptoed from her room, stole down the corridor, and was outside when the first streaks of dawn painted their golden rays on the valley.

She was still curled in the corner of one of the white benches when Peter arrived with her car rental and the luggage she had left behind at the Hamptons. She ran to meet him and felt the roughness of his tweed jacket as he hugged her. "Peter, I'm glad you came. I hated going away without seeing you again."

His lopsided grin spread from one well-shaped ear to the other. "Jolly good. We're friends now that you're leaving. I dare say, what you hate doing is going away without your luggage."

She touched his right cheek. "Your bruises are better."

"Yes, I can even see again." He hesitated as though his thoughts were stuttering. "Chase, I kept hoping you'd fall passionately in love with England and stay forever."

"You and me?"

"That's what I had in mind."

"It would never work. You plan to take up residence at number 10 Downing someday. I'd be an embarrassment to you."

"I might only make it to the House of Commons."

"And you'd be in the Labor Party, and I'd no doubt be on the other side waving a picket sign on Whitehall. We'd argue politics all through dinner."

He caught her hand playfully and kissed it. "I really will miss you. Come back someday and maybe—"

"We'll see." But she doubted their paths would cross again.

They had run out of words, out of time. She wanted to slip the rest of her things into the car before Margot Hampton caught onto her plans, especially the suitcase with Olivia's diaries and manuscript packed in the bottom. "Peter, would you mind getting the luggage from my room?"

He held out his hand for the key. "The room beside Beatrice Thorpe's? I'm to slip in and out unnoticed. Right?"

"That gives me time to say goodbye to Beatrice."

When they reached the end of the hall, Chase broke into a run. She opened Beatrice's door without knocking. "Beatrice, I—"

She screamed. The room was in shambles. Beatrice was gone.

🏵🏵🏵

Chase was breathless when she burst into Margot Hampton's office. "Margot, where's Beatrice Thorpe?" she cried.

Margot's face went livid at the intrusion. Nigel Hampton stood behind her, his hands firmly on her shoulders. Only Constable Wallis seemed unflustered. "Miss Evans," he said with forced politeness, "they told me you had gone to the Cotswolds."

"Where is she?"

"In the infirmary," Nigel said. "But she'll be all right."

"Mrs. Thorpe was beaten rather brutally," Wallis said matter-of-factly. "At approximately one this morning."

"I was in the room next door. I never heard a thing."

"You weren't intended to hear," Wallis said. "But there were two assailants. That's all Thorpe has been able to tell us."

Nigel disagreed. "She told us they spoke to her in Czech."

Chase looked to Margot for confirmation. "I must see her."

Wallis seemed unflappable. "She's resting, and then I will see her first. You do understand the need for that." His smile was wicked. "Her room was torn apart. Apparently they didn't find what they were looking for, but we will."

Chase had the irresistible urge to stick the constable with a pin, but there wasn't one big enough to deflate his ego. The only comfort she had was that the intruders hadn't found what they were looking for. How could they? She had Olivia's diaries and manuscript in her room. "I have to talk to her, Margot."

Wallis stood and beckoned Nigel to follow him. "I'm sure your wife will want you present when I interview Mrs. Thorpe."

As they left, Margot turned angrily on Chase. "Wherever you go, trouble follows you. First it was Andrew Forrestal. Then bomb threats in Kendallshire—and now this. Poor Beatrice."

"Bomb threats, Mrs. Hampton?"

"Another Czech terrorist group, according to Edwin. They're afraid Olivia left something behind that will lead back to them. Chase, I warned Nigel if you came here, it meant trouble."

Chase glanced out the window toward the eastern horizon where the sun had come up with such brilliant colors. An hour ago? Three? Had hope been shattered that quickly with problems for the Hamptons and Bea? *Wherever you go, trouble follows you.*

Her thoughts raced to the notes from the unfinished novel—a steel factory, nerve gas, the annihilation of another generation. Which steel factory? *Who were you trying to identify? Talk to me, Olivia Renway, the way you seem to talk to Beatrice all the time. What warning were you trying to leave behind? None of it makes sense.* She groped for a link between the youthful Olivia and the genteel woman who had died on Downing Street. Czechoslovakia. It was back to the diaries. How many times had Olivia written that she would die for her country? Something had happened on her last trip to Prague and Jarvoc, a threat against her beloved country.

Chase turned back from the window and faced Margot again. "You know that I'm leaving for the Cotswolds, don't you?"

"I guessed as much. I saw Peter arrive with your car."

"Margot, I'm going to visit Ian's grandfather."

"Then Uriah will probably tell you that Edwin Wallis attended Olivia's funeral. He was a young officer back then assigned to protect the Kendall family at the graveside ceremony. The truth is, Edwin and MI5 have always linked Olivia's death to Uriah's old ties with British Intelligence. Edwin and MI5 never gave up that idea." Margot wiped her eyes with her long fingers, as though with the effort she could take away the weariness. "Ten years ago, when she came back from Prague, there were those who believed she was carrying intelligence reports—or possibly even messages to a Czech terrorist group in London. Important papers that have never been found. After her death, Uriah arranged for Beatrice to stay here in the safety of the Eagle's Nest."

Papers that Beatrice had given to Chase. She jammed her hands in her pockets. "I guess he just wanted to protect Bea."

"Because he couldn't protect his wife. He couldn't bear

the thought of his wife's friend being exiled from England again."

"Margot, do you believe the stories Beatrice tells?"

"Do you?"

"I wouldn't dare put them in my dissertation."

Margot sighed, seemingly relieved. "No, I suppose not."

"Did you know that Beatrice had a friend named Margot?"

"Did she?"

"She said she did. They ran an underground escape route in Prague during the war—rescuing the crews from downed planes."

Margot laughed, but the merriment seemed lost. "She does go on about the war days, doesn't she? But then that's what old people do. They go back to the good old days."

"They weren't good days, Mrs. Hampton. They were dreadful."

A faint smile began at the corners of Hampton's thin lips. "You are so transparent when you want answers, Chase—so obvious when you are on to something. I was named for my mother, Margot Dvorak, but I suppose Beatrice has already told you that."

"No, but I guessed." *Olivia's diaries again.*

"Beatrice, mother, and Olivia called themselves the Bronze Network. Right under the noses of the Nazis, they risked their lives leading twenty or more Allied airmen out of the country when their planes strayed over Czechoslovakia and crashed."

"Then it's true—Beatrice Thorpe and your mother were arrested."

"Yes, but, thank goodness, Olivia eluded capture. Beatrice's family here in England went through the International Red Cross trying to get her freed. She was a British citizen—British passport and birth certificate." She looked on the verge of tears. "But Beatrice and mother had already exchanged their identity papers. It was one of those humanitarian gestures in the war. Mother was pregnant, my father dead. Beatrice thought I'd have a better chance born in England."

"But their passports—they couldn't have looked alike."

"They were near in age, dark hair, haggard, war-worn faces. They had been through some rough months, sharing their limited food rationing with the men they rescued. The hoax wasn't discovered until Mother reached London. Beatrice's family was devastated, but they knew their daughter and her love for others." Margot fought to keep her voice even, unemotional. "After that there was no way out of Prague for Beatrice until Olivia found her ten years ago."

"Margot, I don't understand why Beatrice couldn't come back to England after the war. She was born here."

"Many refugees tried to leave Czechoslovakia as the Russians took control, but Beatrice had no proof of her birthright."

Margot stood up from her desk, walked across the room, and hugged Chase. "I told you once I thought we could be friends—under different circumstances. I still think that. Perhaps you can come back someday when all of this is over." Her fingers barely touched Chase's cheek. "Now go on before Edwin and Nigel get back here. But don't go without saying goodbye to Beatrice."

🪔🪔🪔

The infirmary was down the hall from Margot Hampton's office, across from the nurses' station. Beatrice lay quietly on the bed, her hand restrained so IV fluids could flow unhindered, but her fingers grasped the cane lying in the bed beside her.

She looked feeble, even smaller and shorter than her five feet. One hand was swathed in bandages; her mouth and eyes were bruised from the beating. A row of black stitches ran beneath her chin. Chase pulled up a chair and sat down. She reached through the side rails and cupped one veined hand and squeezed it.

Bea's eyelids fluttered open. Behind the large, wire-rimmed glasses, the Mediterranean blue of her eyes seemed paled by pain. Recognition came instantly. "Oh, Chase.

Chase. I was just talking to Olivia about you. She's over there in the corner."

Bea's words sounded so convincing that Chase glanced toward the corner and saw nothing.

"You don't see her?" Beatrice scolded.

"No."

"She's all in white."

Chase swallowed and swallowed again. She remembered her grandmother saying strange things like that in the closing hours of her life. *Beatrice Thorpe, don't die on me,* she thought. She tightened her grip on the wrinkled hand.

"Bea, I'm going to Prague to see Dorian."

"Oh, Olivia will like that. She can't go herself. Dorian knows the truth about Olivia and the steel mill. He'll tell you."

Her energy waned as she struggled to talk. Chase squeezed her hand again. "Don't say anymore. I'll just sit here with you."

There was a slight tap at the door, and then a nurse whisked into the room. When Chase looked down at Beatrice, the old woman's eyes had closed, the mouth lay gaping.

"Mrs. Thorpe." The sing-song voice rose an octave. "Come, dearie. Time for your medicine."

Thorpe's eyelids flicked open. "Not that again."

"Keeps you strong, dearie."

"Keeps me flustered."

The nurse put the plastic cup to her mouth, tapped the pill inside, and forced some water behind it. Beatrice pushed the glass away and swooped the pill around, her false teeth bobbing as she did so. Chase saw the tiny bulge in her cheek and smiled.

"Now come on, dearie, it's time for your morning nap."

"I want to sleep in my chair."

Again the nurse's voice rose for a deaf ear. "You're in the infirmary, Mrs. Thorpe. House rules say the side rails go up."

"You stay with me," Beatrice whispered to Chase.

The nurse tugged Thorpe's spectacles off, brushing

roughly over the bruised cheeks. "We mustn't tire you out. Mind you, Miss Evans can stay two minutes. No more. You need your rest."

"I want to go back to my own room."

"When you're better, dearie."

Thorpe tried to grip her cane and point it in the direction of the attendant as she made her way out of the room. With an angry sputter that erupted from those swollen lips, she spewed the medicine out. "That woman," Thorpe said, "is pill enough."

Chase leaned down and kissed Bea on the forehead. "I love you," she said. "I'll come back after my trip to Czechoslovakia." Even as she made the promise, she doubted that she would be back in time. "You'll be all right. Olivia will be with you."

Wearily, Thorpe turned her gaze toward the corner and smiled. "Yes, Olivia will be here."

🌑🌑🌑

The Cotswolds. When Ian came out of the house to meet her, the softly rolling hills of Kendallshire were bathed in radiant summer hues. The Kendalls' thatched cottage lay hidden at the end of the village road. Roses climbed up the old stone wall and peeked down on a charming English garden filled with wild minty thyme and brilliant geraniums. Trout frolicked in the clear running streams that rippled under an ancient stone bridge, but Chase's attention was drawn to the elderly gentleman standing there.

"Come," Ian said, "I want you to meet my grandfather."

She grabbed Ian's arm. "That's Uriah Kendall? We can't disturb him. He's too deep in thought."

"He's remembering."

She laughed. "Remembering what, Ian Kendall?"

"The day when he met my grandmother."

At the sound of their laughter, Uriah turned to face them, leaning on his cane. He was casually dressed, tufts of his sandy-gray hair dipping over his forehead. "He's handsome," she said.

"I never thought about it, but, yes, they were both good looking. They met here in the middle of this bridge."

"Then it's not right for me—"

"Now don't back out on me. Gramps agreed to see you. Said if you want to know about Olivia, this is where it all began."

No, she thought. *It began long ago in Prague and Jarvoc. In the risks that she took as a resistance fighter. On the coast in Cornwall. In the trust that she placed in a German officer.* "Your grandfather must miss her dreadfully," she said.

"She was his life."

"It's a shame the way she died. If only someone from your family had been with her." She felt Ian's arm stiffen. "Ian—Ian, you were there that day, weren't you? You saw it happen."

The muscles in his face twitched. "I was there. I couldn't do a thing to help her. We were waiting for her in the limousine on Whitehall. And then she was hit, and Charles just drove off."

"The chauffeur?"

"I was only thirteen, Chase, but I'll never forget it. If I ever see Charles again, I'll kill him with my bare hands for leaving my grandmother like that."

"Does your grandfather know about Charles?" she asked.

"We never talk about that day."

She wanted to comfort him, but she might never have another opportunity like this. "Ian, was it really an accident?"

"Does it matter?"

"To you and your family."

"You're not my family." He towered above her, his handsome face twisted with unhappiness. "I begged you to let it go."

"Ian, you weren't driving the car when Charles hit her. Don't blame yourself. You didn't kill your grandmother."

Her words stunned him. "Charles didn't hit her. We ran— but Charles didn't hit her. It was the Renault idling just in front of us. I can remember that car, but I can't remember the driver."

He spoke with his hands as though he could bring back the moment. "Someone spoke to my grandmother just before she stepped off the curb, but his face has always been a blur, too."

He gripped her elbow firmly and steered her toward Uriah. "I think we've kept my grandfather waiting long enough. But, Chase, just keep in mind that he loved Olivia Renway. Don't destroy that. It's all he has left."

She had no time to answer Ian. Uriah Kendall was holding out his hand, smiling kindly. "So this is the young woman who wants to know all about my beloved Olivia."

Chapter 22

Prague, 8:40 A.M. "A Mighty Fortress Is Our God . . ." As Hanz held the Smith and Wesson to his temple, the words from the hymn of his boyhood echoed back over the years. He lowered the revolver. He saw no hope for his sons, but his grandson had been the pride of his life. Hanz wanted to see Nedrick once more, and he wanted the Mighty Fortress to calm the turmoil raging inside him. But had God ever entered this building, this architectural death trap? He dropped the gun into his toolbox and pushed himself up, letting his back and buttocks glide over the rough wall until he had his balance.

With the fading light of his torch, he could make out the time. Ten minutes to get out of this building and back to the railroad before the forklifts rumbled his way. He dragged himself to the exit and gulped in the morning air as he hit the sunlight. The seven steps back to level ground seemed like impossible mountains. He dragged on, stumbling along the railroad tracks, his eyes riveted on the gleaming rails.

"Popshot."

Hanz shaded his eyes and stared ahead along the tracks. He recognized Mila first, and then his heart raced. The tall young man beside her was waving. Hanz dropped his toolbox and began to run, stumbling on his game leg. He staggered along the uneven ground and fell to one knee as he crossed over the tracks. Pushing himself up, he lurched forward—careening toward the only Russelmann worth knowing. The boy—the grown man—was coming lickety-split toward him. Still waving. Still running.

"Nedrick!" Unexpected tears trickled over his stubble of beard. With no strength left, he pitched forward and toppled into those strong young arms. "Nedrick. Nedrick."

"Popshot, you never greeted me like that before."

"I never missed you like I have these last ten years. I never thought I'd see you again."

Mila peered around Nedrick's shoulder. "I told you I had a surprise for you, Uncle Hanz. Oh—your leg. You're bleeding."

"It's nothing. Just a scrape."

"On a rusty rail. Sit down, Popshot. Let me have a look."

He allowed Nedrick to ease him to the ground. Strong fingers tore the trousers to the knee. "It's a nasty cut, Gramps."

"It'll heal. We'll tend it at the house. Mila here is a good nurse. Aren't you, child?"

She smiled, but Ned went on wiping the dirt from the wound.

"Nedrick has come home to us, Uncle Hanz," Mila said.

"But he can't stay."

"What kind of a welcome is that, Gramps?"

"We have serious problems at the plant."

"Nothing has changed, has it?" Nedrick asked sadly.

He watched Nedrick stare across the railroad tracks and deep into the forest. *He knows,* Hanz thought. *He remembers the tunnels. Remembers our fears as we walked along the tracks.* How many times the boy had asked him for the truth. How many times he had hidden it from him. He couldn't let him get involved now.

Hanz had wanted to protect Nedrick, a thin, frail lad, lonely as a goldfish in a pond by itself. Smart as a whip, but friendless. Over and over Nedrick had cried, "The boys in Jarvoc don't like me, Popshot. What have I done wrong?"

"Nothing," Hanz had told him. *Except to be a Russelmann. To have the blood-streaked history of Nazism on your family tree. To be related, without knowing it, to the designers of death who left a stain on Jarvoc.*

Oblivious, Mila kept smiling, content at having Nedrick by her side. "Altman doesn't know that Nedrick is here yet."

The old man's gaze went back to his grandson. "Your father is in Munich on business. But he knows. He's known every move you've made since you reached England. You should never have come back."

"I almost didn't. I planned to go somewhere else."

To the Pyrenees. To Madrid. To the fishing village where I took you as a boy. They had talked about going back there to live one day. An old man and a boy by the sea. They would fish and read Hemingway and take care of each other. It was too late for Hanz, but not for Nedrick. "You can still leave, Nedrick."

"In a few days. But I had to come back and see you. Jiri said you were well."

"Except for this lame leg of mine."

"You ran a fair race a minute ago."

He allowed Nedrick to help him stand, and then with that old independent pride taking over, he limped unassisted on the painful journey back to the farm. When they reached the house, they urged him into an easy chair. Mila ran off for some warm water and towels as Nedrick pulled the boots from his feet.

They think I've grown old, Hanz thought. *And I have.* He ruffled Ned's hair. "I'm glad you're here. But you can't stay."

"Then you and Mila must go away with me."

"Where?" Mila asked, putting the basin on the floor.

Nedrick kept his eyes on his grandfather. "To a fishing village in Spain. What about it, Popshot?"

"You and Mila go on ahead. I'll meet you there."

Nedrick shook his head. "You stay—I stay."

"These have been empty years, Nedrick. Why did you go away?"

"Popshot, you were all that ever mattered to me in this family. You and Mila." Ned cuffed her ear playfully, and then he went back to washing Hanz's wound. "After I knew about Olivia Renway, I wanted to know her, but you'd never talk about her."

Hanz gripped Nedrick's chin and tilted it up until their eyes met. "Why did you go away, Nedrick?"

"When Jiri told me that you gave the order for my grand-mother's death, I made up my mind to forget all of you."

Hanz shook his head, stunned. "Someone else gave that order." He felt reluctant to betray Altman. He groped for words and said, "Maybe it was Jiri. Believe me, Nedrick, I would never have harmed Olivia. I loved her."

"Even when you discovered she was Jewish?"

Mila sat on the floor, frowning. "Is that true, Uncle Hanz?"

"It was Warren Renway who told me Olivia was part Jewish."

"You didn't know until then, Popshot?"

"No. I didn't believe everything that Hitler taught, but I believed in the perfect Aryan race. When Warren and Millicent realized that I had fallen in love with Olivia, they tried to warn me. They knew I was going back to Berlin— that I hated saying goodbye to Olivia. I think the Renways wanted to spare us both."

"Did it bother them that she was Jewish?"

"No. She filled the void their daughter had left behind. Their families had been friends for years. I remember staring at Warren—calling him a liar. 'Ask Olivia yourself,' he told me."

"There's Jewish blood running in my veins, too, Popshot, but you've always loved me."

"Because you were all I had left of Olivia."

"You had my dad."

"Altman hated his mother. My fault, I think. I could never convince Altman that I didn't know Olivia was pregnant. If I had known, Nedrick, I would have married her."

"But you had been ordered back to Germany."

"Yes, but I would have delayed a day or two to make arrangements for her. It was cold that night, Nedrick. Bitterly cold the last time I saw her."

❀❀❀

London, February 1941. Hanz had felt miserable as he waited on the bridge for Olivia. He was dressed like an immigrant in his high-buttoned, brown-striped suit and woolen shirt. His dark visored cap was tight against his skull, his metal suitcase lying packed at his feet, a borrowed coat on top of it. But the heaviness was inside, the bitter knowledge that Olivia was Jewish. The Renways had taken the risk of telling him. Had they not considered that he would be obligated to report that they were harboring a Jew? Or had they been confident that to betray them was to betray himself?

Dusk was settling in. The entire city would be blacked out if she didn't hurry. And if she didn't come—if he didn't get to say goodbye—and then he heard her. "Henri. Henri."

He turned, but this time he did not open his arms to receive her. He watched her running toward him, her long russet hair blowing against her cheeks. Innocent. Beautiful. And Jewish. She was barely dressed warm enough in an oversized dark jacket, her thin, threadbare skirt almost to her ankles. Beneath the jacket she was layered in sweaters, Millicent's thick wool one on top.

"You're late," he scolded.

She stifled a coughing spasm before she said, "I'm sorry. I went to the doctor today."

"Are you all right?"

She pressed her head against his chest. He felt the warmth of her against him and yearned to hold her, and still he did not put his arms around her. "I have a surprise for you, Henri!"

"I have something to ask you first." He agonized for a moment. "I have to know the truth. Two days ago Millicent told me you are Jewish. Olivia, why didn't you tell me yourself?"

She pushed away from him. "I didn't think it mattered."

The wail of the sirens shattered the stillness around them. He grabbed her hand and his suitcase and began to run. "The bombers are coming early tonight," he said.

"I pray they don't hit St. Paul's Cathedral."

"They won't," he said confidently. "They use it as a beacon light when they fly in."

"I hate them. I hate the Germans."

His grip on her hand tightened. *Like I hate the Jews,* he thought. *But I don't hate this Jewess. I love her.*

As they ran, Olivia's breath came in short little gasps. He heard the drone of the lead planes flying in formation. In seconds now they would drop their firebombs, lighting the way for wave after wave of heavy bombers that would set London on fire again tonight. Tomorrow the Brits would count their casualties, bury their dead, and record the list of firemen killed in action in a ledger.

As the antiaircraft guns fought back, he prayed that nothing would happen to Olivia. And he prayed for courage to tell her he was going away. He could not tell her that he was German, and it struck him that this was no different than Olivia guarding her own nationality. They heard the hissing sounds as the bombs fell. Olivia trembled beside him. He pulled her past the crumbled walls and safely around yesterday's bomb crater, trying desperately to keep her from noticing the flames that were already ravaging the buildings east of the cathedral.

As they reached the air raid shelter, they heard the deep voice of radio announcer Edward R. Murrow saying, "This is London . . . tonight's raid is widespread . . . the city is aflame . . . buildings gutted . . ."

Hanz knew that across the city, 60,000 Londoners crowded together in underground shelters, calm and united in spite of the vibrations from bombs falling outside. In the shelter he and Olivia entered, a few people had bedded down, stretched out on their blankets, trying to sleep as a sailor led those around him in a lusty rendition of "Roll Out the Barrel." Down past a row of cots, a group of women countered with "Kiss Me Good Night, Sergeant Major."

As Hanz and Olivia went deeper into the tunnel, others made room for them. He put his suitcase down, and for the first time she seemed aware that it was his. "Henri, why the suitcase?"

He urged her to sit down and crouched down beside her.

He took her hands, Jewish hands, hands that he had caressed for five months now. "I'm going away. My country—my family needs me."

He couldn't bear the pain as she cried, "No. No, you can't."

"You slip in and out of Czechoslovakia, Olivia."

"That's different. I have to take messages back to the resistance movement for Antonin and Lieutenant-Colonel Moravec."

"Your brother Antonin should take his own messages. Your country is controlled by Germans, Olivia. If they find out that you're Jewish, it won't go well for you."

She put her hand against his cheek. "We promised not to fight about this. You know I will do anything for my country."

"I don't want anything to happen to you."

He realized now that she had not asked him where he was going or what part of England his family lived in. She had not even suggested going with him. *She knew. His little British spy knew.* He reached up and brushed a tear from her cheek.

"Try to understand," he said. "I have my orders. I have to leave you here in the shelter. I want you to go back to the Renways. Cornwall is safer."

As she leaned against the cement wall, she shivered uncontrollably. "Will you ever come back?"

"After the war—we'll be together then."

The Londoner across from them smiled, a plain-faced woman with pincher glasses and a cot blanket tossed around her shoulders. She had been reading a book by flashlight. "I come to the shelter for encouragement," she said. "Down here, watching these people, I know that the Germans cannot defeat us."

Hanz stiffened, wanting more than anything to argue with her. He recognized her now as the plain-faced vicar's daughter, the writer of detective novels. Back in college—a thousand years ago—she had come to Cambridge to lecture on medieval literature. She crawled across the floor. "I'm

Dorothy," she said as she put her blanket around Olivia's shoulders. "Are you all right?"

"I'm nauseated. I think it's the fumes down here."

"Or the smell of human bodies crowded together."

"That too," Olivia agreed.

Hanz wanted the woman to leave them alone, but Olivia found comfort in her presence. "Do you have children, Dorothy?"

"Yes," she said softly. "One son."

"Was he fun to raise, Dorothy?"

"As a baby? I'm afraid he was fostered out to my cousin Ivy." She offered a faint smile and left them.

As Olivia looked up at Hanz, he saw the distress on her face. "I could never give my child away," she whispered.

With the blanket around her and her head pillowed in Hanz's lap, Olivia finally slept. Next week he would once again be flying planes—perhaps dropping bombs on London. His fear for Olivia's safety knotted his stomach. He needed a reason to send her away, perhaps back to the Renways in Cornwall.

As the shelter shuddered violently again, he held Olivia against him. She stirred and then slept again. He ran his hand through her hair, tucking a lock behind her ear. Still she slept. He wanted more than anything to spend his life with this girl, but his orders had come through on the last wireless transmission. His safety was at risk. He must leave her. It was crucial that the message he carried reach Berlin. But would he live to get back there?

He had taken the family heirloom from the bank vault— before the bank itself became rubble in the bombings. Seven hundred thousand deutsche marks or more lay in his trouser pocket, money desperately needed by his family, desperately needed by the Third Reich. The coded messages on British troop movements and military buildup lay in two of the sapphire links, along with a report on the damage estimates against London and the Czech Intelligence movement near Warwick. He wanted to deliver the message in person, but if something happened to him, one way or the other he must get the message through to Berlin. As he looked down at Olivia, he knew what he had to do.

An hour later he awakened her. She sat up groggily, leaned against his shoulder, and put her cold hand in his. "Oh, Henri, the lady who loaned me her blanket is gone."

"Her name is Dorothy Sayers."

"You know her?"

"I know about her. She lectured at Cambridge once. She said she was going off to help the first aid team stitch and splinter the wounded. She'll be back—but I have to go now."

"Not before the all clear. It's still dark out there."

No, a city in flames would be light enough. "I'll be all right." He hesitated. "Olivia, on the bridge you told me you had something to tell me."

"It isn't important anymore, not with you going away."

"I love you, Olivia." From his trouser pocket he withdrew the Kashmir bracelet. "This belongs to my family. Could you take it back to the Renways for me? They'll know what to do with it." He smiled at her in the darkness. "When I come back again—after the war—I'll give it to you for a wedding present."

She stood, and he brushed a kiss across her lips, his bristly chin lingering against hers. "I have no choice, Olivia," he whispered. "My family—my country—need me."

"Go," she said. "Go quickly while I still have the strength to let you escape. Before I change my mind and turn you in."

He hunched forward, his shoulders squeezed into Renway's wool topcoat, and left the shelter against the advice of the warden standing there. With one hand thrust into his pocket, his suitcase in the other, he walked out into the smoke-filled city without looking back at Olivia. Piccadilly Circus was jammed with vehicles that had been deserted when the air raid siren sounded. Some had taken a direct hit, but one motorbike lay against the wall of a blackened building, the keys still in it. With a twist of Hanz's wrist, the engine sputtered and caught.

Above him brave RAF pilots—and he did consider them courageous young men—streaked through the sky, determined to repel the next wave of Messerschmitts roaring toward London. Incendiary bombs and heavy explosives spilled from the air, exploding on contact and forming a firestorm east of the city.

He mounted the bike and sped away over the gutted streets toward the waterfront. The River Thames that Olivia loved was strewn with debris, a tanker ablaze and sinking on its oil-coated waters. Balancing the suitcase between his knees, he accelerated and disappeared into the night as London burned behind him.

Nedrick and Hanz sat quietly for several minutes. Finally Nedrick put out his hand and gave Hanz a comforting squeeze. "It sounds like my grandmother knew where you were going."

"I think she did, Nedrick."

"She could have stopped you."

"Even as I left the shelter, I thought she would."

Chapter 23

on Tonner Art Museum, Germany. Drew Gregory grinned at Miriam. "Take a look at that sign, *Liebling.* That's Robyn and Pierre's dream coming true."

"Mostly Robyn's," she said stoutly. "And all on her own."

"Hmm," he agreed, grinning even more. "Except for Pierre's support, the baron's money, the Breckenridges' hard work, and the Klees overseeing the project."

"You know what I mean, Drew." Her voice caught. "Robyn didn't need me this time."

"Oh, she could have used your wisdom."

"My interference, you mean. Is that why you married me—to keep me out of Robyn's hair?"

"I thought I could keep you occupied."

She leaned over and kissed his rough cheek. "Thank you for making this possible. I never dreamed we'd be back in time."

"Pierre and I planned it that way."

"Does Robyn know we're coming?"

"Not if Pierre could keep it from her."

Drew took another look at the shiny new museum sign as a car whizzed past them on the narrow incline. "That's some lady driver. We'd better hightail it up the hill after her."

He hit the accelerator. Their car shot around the steep curve and sped up the winding road. The electronic gates

swung back allowing them an impressive view of the gray-
ish white mansion high on the hill.

Albert Klee, the caretaker, came rushing forward to greet
them. His keen, dark eyes shone beneath the bushy eyebrows—a warm welcome, unlike Drew's first encounter
with Albert's Mauser rifle. The old man could best be
described as agile and ugly with a mouth too wide, lips too
thin, teeth too yellow; but Albert was more faithful than an
old hound dog. Robyn and Pierre loved him, Miriam was
still in awe of him, and Drew respected him.

"I told your daughter your car was coming," Klee said.

"It's a rental," Drew laughed. "How did you know it was
us?"

Albert gripped his hand. "Got spotters all the way up the
hill. Like I told you, here she comes now."

Drew watched with fatherly pride—his arms outstretched
as Robyn came darting across the well-kept lawns. She was
so much like one of the Gregorys with her shiny auburn
hair, sea-blue eyes, and that cute upturned nose that she
hated. Robyn came straight into her father's arms and then
slipped from his bear hug with tears in her eyes as she
embraced Miriam.

"Mother, I never dreamed you'd come." She shot a scolding glance at Drew. "Daddy just wouldn't promise a thing.
Told me no man would leave his honeymoon for an art
gallery. What happened?"

"Your father is full of wonderful surprises."

Robyn's smile was one of her best assets. It made her face
and eyes sparkle, making Drew doubly glad that he had
come. He touched her cheek. "We couldn't miss your big
bash, Princess."

"Mother, your friend from the Metropolitan Museum of
Art is coming and the curator from Tate Gallery. But if you
two had not come, it would have been a big disappointment." Her eyes were like brilliant blue saucers. "Wait until
I tell Pierre you're here."

Drew winked again. "He knows."

"And he didn't tell me?"

"Robyn, who was that guest just ahead of us?" Miriam asked.

"The one running toward the stables? That's Chase Evans." Robyn didn't notice their surprise. "She's a friend of Luke Breckenridge. She could hardly wait to see him."

"Isn't Sauni here?" Miriam asked.

"Yes." Robyn arched her brows as she linked arms with her parents. "I hope Miss Evans won't cause trouble. I don't want anything spoiling this weekend."

۞۞۞

As Chase pulled through the gates and parked, she dropped the keys into the caretaker's gnarled hands and said, "Captain Breckenridge is expecting me. Where is he?"

The old man's thin lips tightened. "Humph."

He was not a pleasant-looking man with his thick-hooded brows and puffy cheeks. His body was so thin that it made him look weightless, but he was quick on his feet as he moved to the driver's side and slipped behind the wheel of her car.

"I'm Chase Evans. Luke Breckenridge really is expecting me."

"Humph. He's out in the stables with Monarch and Mrs.—"

She didn't let him finish but broke into a run. She was breathless when she burst through the stable door. The chestnut stallion reared and neighed, its nostrils flaring.

Chase drew back as a head appeared above the stall. "You trying to get us killed?" Luke asked, patting the horse's well-muscled neck, trying to calm him. "Monarch doesn't take to strangers—oh, Chase, it's you. Wondered when you'd get here."

"I just did."

"All settled in?"

"No," she said, blushing. "I came right down to see you."

He looked uneasy as another head appeared above the stall—a woman close to Luke's age, with long flaxen hair, a gentle face, and a heart-shaped locket around her slender neck.

"Er—hello," Chase said.

Luke looked embarrassed. "This is Sauni," he said as if that were explanation enough.

"Luke's ex-wife," the woman said softly. She smiled, but she avoided Luke's searching gaze. "Luke, I'll let you finish cleaning Monarch's stall. I promised to help Hedwig with supper."

She walked away, slowly at first, but when she reached the door, she began to run.

"Did I break up something?" Chase asked.

"Regretfully, the breakup occurred a long time ago."

"I didn't know you still saw your ex-wife."

"The subject never came up, did it?" He stroked Monarch's neck again. "Well, Chase," he said, leaving the stall and giving her a brotherly hug, "let me show you around."

When they reached the magnificent ballroom, he pointed to the frames around several of the paintings. "I made them," he said proudly. "It's been a new outlet for me."

"They're nicely carved—and this room is simply elegant."

"It's my favorite. Pierre and Robyn have commissioned me to turn it into a display room—after the big ball on Saturday."

"Will you save me a dance?" she asked.

"Of course. Several."

Drew noted that the entry halls had been freshly painted and the marble floors polished to a shine. The art collection that had lain hidden in the tunnels for years now brightened the walls in every room. Even Drew, who could not distinguish one artist from another, had taken a liking to the Rembrandt painting that still hung above the stairs. Robyn—bless her heart—had placed one of Miriam's favorites in the guest room where they were staying. It was one of Monet's lesser-known works of the Thames at sunrise, emphasizing Monet's skill with broken colors.

Miriam turned from the painting and faced Drew, gorgeous in the coral evening gown that he had purchased for her in a boutique in Paris. "Drew, you look absolutely smashing," she said.

"And you're more lovely than ever, *Liebling*. We'd better go down to dinner before we change our minds."

Baron von Tonner sat at the head of the table in his wheelchair, Pierre and Robyn on either side of him. Drew marveled that Felix was still alive, frail and aged as he was, but the baron seemed to sense the excitement, his dull eyes attentive. He managed to get his fork to his mouth twice before his strength failed and Robyn began to feed him.

By the third course, Miriam was engaged in a conversation with Lady Gilmore. Drew turned to Chase. "What are your plans, Miss Evans?" he asked. "Besides your research project."

"Oh, did Luke tell you about that?"

"No, Uriah Kendall."

As she raised her goblet to her lips, she asked, "Did Mr. Kendall also tell you I was going to Prague?"

Drew sputtered and almost choked. Miriam turned at once and dabbed the water with her napkin. He adjusted his cummerbund. "And what is so interesting in Prague?" he mumbled.

"It's Jarvoc that interests me. Mr. Kendall's wife was born there, you know, but something about that town frightened her. I want to find out what it was. And I hope to meet her brother there."

"Did Uriah encourage you to make this trip?"

"Not really."

"You're going all alone then?" Miriam interjected.

"So far."

But you have other plans, Drew thought. *Dangerous ones if they involve the Russelmanns and Dorian Paschek.* How much did this young woman know about Olivia's past? How much was still guesswork? "Jarvoc is a dismal town—just a few homes and a steel factory. It is not a place for tourists," he warned.

Chase's fine brows arched. "I'm not exactly a tourist. I'm researching for my doctoral program, but I keep running into obstacles. I want to know why, Mr. Gregory. And there was a man in her life. A Henri, I believe. Surely there are some people there who still remember Olivia Renway."

They remember all right, Drew thought as he lapsed into silence. He feared for this girl. He managed a couple of smiles for Robyn, but he was making mental notes for a phone call to Troy Carwell in Paris. He wanted permission to contact Czech Intelligence. But what excuse could he possibly give Troy? One way or the other, once he had Miriam safely on the plane at Heathrow, he was flying back to Prague.

At midnight as they crawled into bed, Miriam said quietly, "You're going back to Prague, aren't you?"

"I don't like Chase Evans going alone. Uriah should have stopped her, but he's too busy guarding the Kendall name. I'm afraid the Kendall secrets may disappoint us, Miriam."

"No matter what the Kendalls did, they're still my friends."

Miriam—generous to a fault. Loyal. She was not prepared for the truth. What was happening in the lives of Uriah and Ian Kendall had taken on new dimensions, new risks.

At breakfast Drew glanced across the table at Chase and Luke. "I have a project I want you to do for me if you would, Breckenridge."

"Name it."

"I'd like you to go to Jarvoc with Miss Evans."

Two mouths gaped open. Drew lifted his juice goblet and saluted them. "You'll love Prague. Miriam and I did." But his confidence wavered when he saw the look of dismay on Sauni's face.

Molly Perkins paused by the hall mirror. She had chosen a bright lavender frock that made her look more cheerful than she felt inside. She missed Dudley intensely, yet she was determined to put distance between them for a while. Still it depressed her that Dudley—engrossed in his work at MI5—might not miss her.

She adjusted her wide-brimmed spring hat with her gloved hands and practiced the smile she would use when she met Miriam Gregory for tea in the mansion dining room. Satisfied, she turned from self-inspection and made her way to the phone in the sitting room. Molly had hoped to find the room empty, but Felix von Tonner was there, decked out in a fine suit that failed to hide his frail body. He hunched forward in his wheelchair, surrounded by the ornate charm of seventeenth- and eighteenth-century furnishings. Logs were laid out in the stone fireplace—but Molly was certain they would never be burned for fear of blackening the two striking eight-foot portraits that dominated the room.

The oil paintings looked regal, frighteningly lifelike. She couldn't take her eyes from the baron's playful smile. Now his strong features were barely recognizable in the shriveled face of the old man. Felix sat in his wheelchair staring up at the portrait of his wife, Ingrid—elegant, charming, and dead now. The artist had caught her enticing dark eyes and engaging smile, but the devious heart lay hidden in this spectacular portrayal of the woman who had planned to steal the entire von Tonner collection.

Molly glanced around and spotted the phone by the bookcase. The von Tonners had posed behind the same brocade chair, the one that she eased into now. As she dialed her number in Chelsea and waited for Dudley to answer, she wondered with all of the artistic display throughout the mansion, why the young Courtlands had left this sitting room essentially unchanged. Was it fair to subject Felix to this daily reminder of life as it once was—and might have been? Ingrid and the past were best forgotten. Or was it for the past that the room remained unchanged—off limits to those who would come to the museum in the days ahead?

Dudley picked up the phone at last, his voice low as he said, "Good evening. Dudley Perkins speaking."

"Darling, I didn't expect to catch you at home."

"Then why did you call here?"

She winced, hurt by his abruptness. "How are you?"

"Lonely. I miss you, Molly. When are you coming home?"

"I don't know."

"Have you worn that lovely gown yet?"

"Tomorrow at the ball. . . . I've met Miriam Gregory."

He punished her with his silence, his disapproval.

"We've talked Rubens and Van Dyke. Raphael and Rembrandt. It's been marvelous. Refreshing actually to have someone know Constable's work. We even talked about the *Dance of the Nymphs*."

"Constable's work?"

He sounded close, as though he were no farther away than the baron. "No, darling," she laughed. "The French painter Camille Corot did that one a hundred years ago."

"I see," he said. But he didn't.

"It sounds as if you and Mrs. Gregory have talked for hours. Does she know who you are, Molly?"

She stared at the unlit fireplace wishing that the logs would burst into flames and wipe away the chill she felt. She forced herself to tell Dudley the truth. "I've been introduced as Lady Gilmore—and Miriam is politely allowing me my anonymity."

"That title belongs to your mother."

Did he realize how painful his verbal jabs were when he was angry? "Dudley, I didn't call to tell you about Miriam Gregory."

"Then why did you call?"

She considered hanging up. But she knew that his coldness was evidence of his anger and humiliation at her going away. "Dudley, Drew Gregory is sending one of his agents to Prague."

He sounded amused. "My dear Molly, did Drew tell you that?"

"I was in the library, staying out of the way of last-minute preparations. The French doors to the terrace were ajar—"

"And you listened in on someone's conversation?"

"I learned that little trick from you, Dudley."

"The library book must have been boring."

She jabbed back. "No, it was about the Greek islands. I can hardly wait to get there." She twisted the phone cord and said, "Gregory asked the American traitor to go to Prague and Jarvoc for him. You know, the marine captain who caused such a stir a few weeks ago. He's here at the mansion, too."

"Luke Breckenridge? He was cleared of all charges, Molly."

"Then why is Gregory sending him to Prague?"

She heard the tightness in her husband's voice as he said, "That's of no concern to me."

She fingered the phone with her gloved hands, running the cord through her fingers, vicariously strangling Dudley in the process. *You are my husband,* she thought. *I may be leaving you—at least for a time—but I do love you. I will help you.*

When she found her voice again, she said, "Captain Breckenridge will be going to Prague with that American student."

"Be more specific, Molly."

"Chase Evans. The girl you told me about."

"Oh yes."

"Like you told me, she seems to know everything about Olivia Renway. She came to the von Tonner celebration as a guest of Captain Breckenridge."

"Then maybe it is just some romantic entanglement."

"No. I heard Drew ask Breckenridge to accompany the girl. They're leaving the day after tomorrow. I think he's working with the CIA now, Dudley, don't you?"

"Hardly. The last time he went on a mission for the CIA, he lost twenty years of his life."

Why was Dudley belittling her like this? She was only trying to help him. "I really must go. Miriam and I are having tea together."

"Wait. Molly, would you go to Prague for me?"

"And follow Breckenridge and Miss Evans? No, my darling. I'm leaving for the Greek islands at the end of the week. Send your golden boy," she said bitterly. "Maybe Lyle

Spincrest will get lost in the Czech Republic. If he never came back, it would be too soon."

"Molly, can you get me the address in Prague where they're staying?"

How? she wondered. "The Gregorys stayed at the Adria when they were there. Perhaps Miss Evans will register there, too."

"And in Jarvoc?"

"I'm certain that you are well acquainted with Jarvoc. Olivia Renway was born there, and you seem to know everything about Miss Renway. Your files on her must be thick enough."

"Molly, will you call me again before you leave?"

"If I overhear something? Of course." Her eyes drifted across the room to the baron. She understood Felix von Tonner. They were both very lonely. Confused. "Goodbye, Dudley."

"Molly, come home. Please come home. I love you."

"Do you?" she whispered softly as the line went dead.

🏺🏺🏺

Chase browsed in the library with several guests, admiring the paintings of Rembrandt and Rubens. Luke was on the other side of the room, deep in thought beneath a large somber Rembrandt.

She heard the door open and felt the intruder's presence before he stood at her side. "I enjoy the swirling action of Rubens, don't you, Miss Evans?" His voice was accented, mocking.

She felt immediate fear. It was the man who had last seen Andrew Forrestal alive, the man who had followed her to Oxford, the man who had surely beaten Peter Quincy. Chase saw violence in Rubens's painting, cruelty in the stranger beside her.

"You're following me," she cried.

His tone was scornful. "Don't flatter yourself. I frequent art galleries. Don't you?"

He gave her a curt nod and cut across the room to Luke.

She watched in surprise as the two men embraced. Luke glanced over his shoulder, laughing. He came to her—a question in his arched brow. "I hear you think one of our guests is following you."

"Who is that man, Luke?" she demanded as the stranger left the room.

"Jiri Benak. He called me yesterday. Told me he had a ticket to the opening of the museum. I was surprised, but what can I say? He had to know the Courtlands to get an invitation here."

"You know him?"

The scar along Luke's neck pulsated. "I'm not proud of it. Jiri and I met at a mercenary camp in the foothills of the Pyrenees."

"Part of your past?" she asked.

"Part of what I want to forget. I had no problems with Benak at the camp. But I admit, I never could decide whether he was a soldier of fortune or had come to recruit a mercenary army of his own."

"I don't trust him, Luke. And he is following me. I must call the police or talk to Mr. Gregory or—"

He grabbed her hand. "Don't do that. It would only involve me again. Please." He looked down at her and smiled. "Benak is a funny guy. I'll tell him to bug off." His smile widened. "But coming to an art show! That's a new angle for Jiri. I hope you don't mind, but I promised to look him up when we get to Prague tomorrow."

She stared at Luke, sensing his betrayal. Benak. Gregory. Even Luke? Were they working together, recording her every step?

♨♨♨

Miriam was proud of her daughter. Robyn had just chalked up a glorious success at the mansion—from being the charming hostess for a hundred guests to the cutting of the ribbons that officially opened the Von Tonner Art Museum. Only three things shadowed the gala occasion: having to leave Robyn moments from now; Sauni

Breckenridge's unhappiness; and the absence of Uriah Kendall. The guest count had been accurate, but where was Uriah? Someone had come to the museum on Uriah's invitation. But who?

She put it from her mind as Sauni ran out to the car. Sauni looked vulnerable this morning, as though she had not slept at all. Miriam said, "You're so unhappy, Sauni. Is it Luke?"

Sauni tugged at a strand of corn silk hair that had caught in the chain of her heart-shaped locket. "I waited so long to find him, Miriam—and for a little while I thought—" Her smile collapsed. "But I want what will bring him happiness."

"Do you think that will be found apart from you?"

"I'll be at Busingen another school term. I'm not sure he'd be content working at the gallery that long."

"Sauni, he could join you in Busingen."

"He talked about studying there—before Chase arrived." Miriam's voice went up a surprised octave. "Theology?"

"No, economics. He'd like to get into investments."

"You've met Sherm Prescott. Sherm is high up in Kippen Investments. Drew could put in a good word for Luke."

"Do you think Drew would mind?"

"At least he'd mind Robyn. Talk with her. But what about Luke's work at the gallery?"

Her face clouded even more. "Once they get the rest of the collection framed, they won't need Luke anymore."

"Wrong. Robyn plans to rotate the paintings. The Flemish artists one quarter. The Impressionists the next. They'll always need new frames made and the old ones repaired."

"Luke is good at that, isn't he?"

"Yes, and he's too good to let him slip away." She cupped Sauni's cheeks gently. "Now you get back in there and tell him you'll be waiting for him in Busingen. If he doesn't come back, Sauni, then you'll know it was never meant to be. But don't give up without fighting for him. He's a good man. He needs you."

"I thought so—but he's going away with Chase Evans."

"Oh, dear! Didn't he tell you why?"

"I was afraid to ask him, Miriam. After all, Drew asked him to go."

Drew was coming with the last suitcase, Robyn at his side. With hugs all around, Drew helped Miriam into the car and drove away. As they reached the bottom of the hill, she said, "Drew, if ever I saw a woman still in love, it's Sauni Breckenridge."

"Did she tell you that?"

"Some things, darling, just don't have to be spoken."

"Then I've blown it, *Liebling*—insisting that Luke accompany Chase to Prague."

"You can't go yourself?"

"Not and be at the embassy first thing Monday morning."

"But you're going back to Prague, aren't you, Drew?"

"If they need me."

"They'll need you."

"I won't go until you're safely on the plane at Heathrow."

"Are you that anxious to send me away?"

"No, but I'm anxious for the day when you come back again. The sooner you go, the sooner you are mine again."

❧❧❧

Jiri Benak seethed with anger as he drove through the gates of the mansion behind Drew Gregory. He wanted to push Gregory's car right off the cliff, straight down into the Rhine. It was Gregory's fault that Breckenridge and Chase Evans were going to Prague. None of them would rest until they discovered the truth at the Russelmann factory. Jiri had to advance his time schedule.

He would fly back to Prague and set the wheels in motion for an early takeover of the Jarvoc steel mill. He would take the Russelmanns and Van Rindins out with a handful of gas pellets—with one quick twist of the "on" lever. The repairs in the waste terminal would hold—he was certain the showers would work again.

When the authorities came, he would feign regret, shock. His despair would seem real enough as he told the policie that he had found the family all dead on his return from

London. He would express horror at the use of Sarin gas in the tunnels and utter disbelief at the suicidal pact that had destroyed two families.

Altman's living trust—forged by Jiri himself—would allow Jiri to run the plant. He would admit that Altman and Gustav had boasted about high-level transactions, and he would acknowledge that Nishokura Steel was one of Altman Russelmann's private accounts. But to accept that Nishokura Steel had been selling nerve gas components to third world countries—impossible! He had known about the weapons—had tried to discourage their sale. But nerve gas! Sadly, Jiri would tell them, "In recent months Altman seemed quite mad, his father Hanz, senile."

Yes, he could pull it off. He knew he could pull it off.

Chapter 24

Kendallshire, *The Cotswolds*. When Uriah opened the door and saw Drew, he gripped his hand warmly. "Where's Miriam?"

"En route to Los Angeles. If everything is going well at the gallery, she'll be back in a few days."

"You'll be lost without her, Drew."

"I'll keep busy. Chase Evans flew to Prague to meet Dorian Paschek. I can't let her walk into trouble without helping her. I've wired Troy Carwell for an extra five days of holiday time."

He saw disapproval in Uriah's scowl and heard it more in his question. "Is the problem in Jarvoc?"

"Yes, at the steel mill where Dorian works. It could be as serious as the illegal sale of weapons to third world countries. That would link them with terrorists. A Russelmann family runs the mill."

Uriah's sky-blue eyes seemed sunken this morning, grief lines framing them. "That's Nedrick's last name," he said.

"I know. You look worried, Uriah."

"I haven't slept well these last few nights. Last week it was Dudley Perkins warning me about bomb threats against the Cotswolds. Had us all looking at every stranger in town who might fit the description of a terrorist. One lodge owner worried about one of her guests. When he left unexpectedly, they found enough explosives in his room to take out our whole village."

Uriah swung one lean leg over the other, looking suddenly weary and lost. "Now there's this thing about Nedrick leaving—if you find him in Jarvoc, be merciful to that young man, Drew."

Drew thought twice and then said, "Olivia's name is not welcomed in that town. Miriam and I thought we knew her, but these rumors about her being a spy just don't line up with her crusade against terrorism. Even her own brother Dorian condemns her with his silence. Why, Uriah?"

"He's frightened—the way Olivia was frightened the last time we spoke by phone. She had just discovered that a family she once knew ran the steel mill there in Jarvoc. I didn't have the courage to ask her if a Luftwaffe pilot was among them."

"The Russelmanns then? They were part of her past?"

"At first—when we married—we agreed that the past was our own. We'd start our lives from the moment we met here in Kendallshire. No looking back. No regrets. No questions asked." He twisted in his chair. "But Dudley Perkins kept digging into Olivia's background—and making certain that his memos crossed my desk."

He grimaced. "It was madness. But Perkins's actions drove me to it. I was desperate to prove him wrong. I looked through some of Olivia's personal effects. I'll never forget the hurt in Olivia's eyes. She crossed the room and picked out two pictures of an infant—with the cliffs of Cornwall in the background—and tossed them at my feet. 'Is this what you're searching for?'"

"Then you didn't know about the child before you married?"

He moaned. "I loved Olivia. Her past didn't matter to me."

Drew patted Uriah's arm. "I never questioned your love for Olivia. That's why I came here before going to Prague. Whatever we unravel there, we may not be able to quell those rumors about her being a spy and running messages for a German agent."

"Don't do this. We're old friends. I know where you're heading, Drew—a connection between the Russelmanns and Olivia; but let the past rest. Nedrick is too young to have been Olivia's son."

"But not too young to be her grandson."

Sadly Uriah admitted, "Nedrick always reminded me of her. Olivia never really came to terms with the war or the losses that she suffered. She never forgave herself for giving up that baby. Apparently the Renways insisted on it—reminding her of the child's German heritage."

He rubbed the back of his neck. "After our grandson Ian was born and she became so attached to him, she finally spoke of her firstborn child again—the child that she never intended to give up. The war cost her so much unhappiness, but the Nuremberg trials nearly destroyed her. She saw little justice in Nazi leaders escaping full judgment. But when she discovered that family in Jarvoc ten years ago, she was determined to expose them."

"Risky."

"She was used to taking risks—she married me."

"She took risks living with the Renways in Cornwall, especially when Warren Renway's loyalty was in question." Drew leaned forward. "Renway was a personal friend of the Duke of Windsor, wasn't he?"

"So was I, Drew. We all served in the Guards briefly."

"The woman in the glass shop there in Jarvoc told us that the duke visited Jarvoc in the forties. An odd place to visit. There are those who still ask whether the duke was an envoy for the British government or a supporter of the German side."

"Rubbish. You're a British history buff, Drew. You know those nasty rumors were not true."

"Even if they were, I would understand, Uriah. The duke had German ties—no doubt a blood line that traced back to Germany. And no one wanted war again."

"We both tried to persuade the duke not to sail for the Bahamas, but to spend the war years in Europe. Poor Warren was certain the duke would be king again."

"Under German control?" Drew asked. "A puppet government?"

"There are other rumors about the duke serving as a loyal British agent, so don't judge him too harshly, Drew."

"All right, I understand the connection between Olivia and the Renways, but I have to know the link between Olivia and the Jarvoc steel mill. She knew Hanz Russelmann, didn't she?"

"How did you find out, Drew?"

"My visit to Jarvoc set the wheels rolling. So a friend with Czech Intelligence did a rundown on the Russelmanns. Origin—Munich. Well-to-do. Art collectors. Their most prized possession—the Kashmir sapphires—was lost during the war. Half a million bucks never accounted for. Apparently the oldest son took it to England for safekeeping. It was Miriam who remembered that Olivia had a sapphire bracelet once."

"She was wearing that bracelet the day I met her, but shortly after we married, she took it off. Said it needed repairs. She called it a family heirloom. I thought she meant the Paschek family. I wanted to give Olivia something special for our twenty-fifth anniversary, so I took the sapphires from her jewelry box."

He sighed, remembering. "I took it to a gemologist to have it appraised and reset so she'd wear it. It was Lionel Shapman who told me it was one of the great pieces of art reported missing after the war. I knew it was expensive, but nine hundred thousand pounds! *And my wife had it in her possession.*"

"You didn't think Olivia had stolen it?"

"Never. But I knew then that the bracelet tied her in with the Russelmanns, and I knew which side of the war they had been on. I had to accept that someone Olivia cared about, perhaps even loved, had given it to her. She never spoke of him. I thought perhaps he was dead."

🌑🌑🌑

Lionel Shapman Jewelers, Maryland, 1974. When Uriah Kendall walked smartly into the jewelry store, he had less than an hour to pick Olivia up for their twenty-fifth anniversary celebration. He had planned a special evening—doing what they liked doing best—a candlelight dinner for two.

He waved at Shapman. "Is the bracelet ready?"

Lionel looked up, his countenance grim. He beckoned Uriah to follow him into the back room. The sapphires lay on a velvet pad—nine princely gems set in a solid gold bangle wristband.

"Magnificent job, Lionel. Olivia will be thrilled." He picked it up and spread it in the palm of his hand. He counted them for the sheer joy of counting. Nine blinding blue gems like the Sapphire of India. Beautiful. Rich and velvety, but as he turned them, a faint hint of violet crept into the end stones.

"What's wrong? The two end gems don't match the others."

"They're replacements. Tanzanites. They're as close a match as I could make. It's going to cost you more than we expected."

Shapman placed the originals under the gem scope and adjusted the lens. "Those are the two end stones that you brought in," he said. "Have a look for yourself."

Uriah's hands went clammy. "There are flaws in them."

"Fakes," Lionel said.

"But the specks—"

"Microfilm. Microdots, if you prefer. Those two fake sapphires had been lasered out by someone. Cleared of their imperfections. Impurities or inclusions as we call them in our business. Once the impurities were removed, the microdots were inserted."

"And the other seven stones?"

"Genuine Kashmir sapphires. You couldn't buy them if you tried today. The mines went dry in the twenties. I believe these are the Russelmann Kashmir sapphires missing since the war. It would be worth a mint at a Sotheby auction." Lionel scratched his head. "Once you pay me my fee, I'm going to forget that you ever brought that bracelet into my shop. What you do with those gems is your business, Kendall. I don't want to be involved."

"Destroy them for me, Lionel."

"Fake gems with wartime codes? Possibly even some of the final Allied invasion plans. German agents tried to steal those. No." He dropped them on the velvet pad. "I'll leave it with your conscience, Uriah."

"But those messages are no longer of value to any country."

An hour later he faced Olivia across the dining table and held out the bracelet to her.

"What are you doing with that, Uriah?"

"You said it was a family heirloom. I had it repaired for you."

Olivia was furious as he put the bracelet around her wrist. She counted the gems and then recounted them. "The two end stones are different. What have you done with them?" she demanded.

"Lionel Shapman replaced them. They were fakes, but the seven middle stones are the genuine Kashmir sapphires."

"Fakes?" She sat there stunned. "Uriah, why?"

"I thought it would make you happy to wear them again." Even in her anger, the gems caught the violet-blue of her eyes. "They look lovely on your wrist, Olivia."

"They belonged to a German family," she said.

"You don't have to tell me."

"I was to take it to the Renways. That's when I realized the sapphires were valuable and would be smuggled out of England."

"They're still worth nine hundred thousand pounds."

"Uriah, please believe me. I meant to give it to the Renways, but something inside me kept saying wait. Even then the end stones didn't look like the others. I'd crossed the border enough to know that coded messages were sent in many ways. By then I knew that Henri—"

"You don't have to tell me."

"I must. I love you, Uriah Kendall. I must tell you." The candlelight made the tears in her eyes glisten. "One night during a blackout I heard Warren slip out of the house. I followed him to the Cornwall cliffs. I watched him light a

lantern and wave it out over the Atlantic. That's when I realized that the Renways—my father's friends—were pro-Nazi.
I knew Warren was signaling a German sub. It made me
sick inside, but where could I go, Uriah? I was pregnant. I
needed the Renways."

"Did this Henri fellow know about the baby?"

"No."

He saw the agony on her face and whispered, "It's all
right, Olivia. I love you. If you want to find your child, we
will."

She nodded. "But he'd be a grown man by now."

"It doesn't matter. We'll try and find him." He reached
across the table and took her hands. "You haven't asked
about those two gems I replaced, Olivia."

"Did you turn them over to British Intelligence?"

"No, I destroyed them."

🝰🝰🝰

Uriah met Drew's gaze again. "That's the whole story,
Drew. She knew then that I knew, that I had forgiven her,
that I loved her." Old age crept into his voice. "We went back
to Cornwall once, but there was no trace of her son. I
thought by then that perhaps he, too, had died. But there
was no way of knowing."

"What did you do with Olivia's bracelet after her death?"

"I don't have it. When Scotland Yard showed me Olivia's
possessions, her briefcase and the sapphires were both
gone. An ordinary thief on Downing would not have known
the value of those sapphires, so for a time I thought one of
the underlings at the Yard might have stolen them." He
smiled, an exhausted the-world-on-my-shoulder smile.
"Back then I never admitted to Scotland Yard they were
missing. I knew the bracelet would condemn Olivia. I
couldn't let that happen. Whatever she had done—or been—
it was over. No lives were lost. Only her own."

"How can you be so certain?"

"Drew, the codes in the bracelet were never delivered to
the Germans. The Russelmanns in Jarvoc are the only ones

who would have benefited by taking both her briefcase and her bracelet."

"So you think the sapphires were taken to Prague?"

"Where else?"

"What do you plan to do about Nedrick, Uriah?"

"Nothing. Nedrick is gone. Perhaps it is best. Ian doesn't know about his grandmother's illegitimate child. It would be more humiliation than he could handle."

"Perhaps Ian has more strength than you realize."

"I'm fond of Nedrick, Drew. There's no way that he would have stayed with me all these years just to betray me."

Drew thought differently. He knew the mindlessness of intelligence agents. A sleeper would remain hidden five or ten years in blind obedience, waiting to be useful, waiting for instructions. "We've got to locate him. He may be in trouble."

"That's what I used to think when he drove the streets of Washington. I never told you—never told anyone—but Ned had an uncanny interest in the embassies and consulates in Washington. Particularly the ones on Spring of Freedom and Reservoir Road."

Germany and Czech Republic, Drew thought. Had Nedrick been receiving messages from Jarvoc right on embassy row?

"Drew, didn't you see him at the opening of the Von Tonner Art Museum? I gave him my guest tickets."

"He wasn't there. The count was right. A hundred guests—all accounted for, but Nedrick was not among them."

"Then someone else used my tickets."

Jarvoc, Czech Republic. Altman Russelmann looked out on his massive complex and the acres of land that were his. True, they were still in his father's name, but not for long, and Josef would be dealt with quickly once their father was gone. Nor would he allow the company to fall into the hands of Nedrick, that weak, disloyal, despised son of his.

From the time Nedrick could walk, he had always run to

his grandfather, never to Altman. From the time he could speak, his words to his father were, "No! Go away. I do it myself!" It was always Hanz he adored. Only moments ago Altman had dismissed Nedrick from the room after a heated argument about the Kashmir sapphires. If there had ever been a moment in time when he loved Nedrick, he could not remember it.

Yet he had no question about his feelings for the man beside him. He despised him, but he needed Jiri Benak more than his own family. There was a cleverness about Jiri, an architectural genius, that Altman still found useful; but he did not trust him for a minute. Someday, before Jiri tried to take control of Russelmann Steel, Altman would send him away. Or put him away.

"You've been in the waste plant again, haven't you, Jiri?"

"You have the only key."

And you know where I keep it, he thought. "Your shoes are muddied on the side."

Jiri glanced down. "I was out by the tracks checking out the Nishokura shipment."

"And was it to your specifications?"

"To yours, Altman." There was mockery in Jiri's voice as he said, "Twenty- to forty-foot steel rails and angles and 3 x 2 rectangle steel tubing. All descaled and coated with oil."

"And bound with black steel strapping?"

"Crated. Nishokura must be shipping it somewhere important."

"The destination is not our concern."

"The contents hidden in those steel cylinders is. What does he put on shipping labels—supplies for highway construction?"

"It's for a pharmaceutical plant in Libya."

Jiri laughed. "More likely a chemical weapons facility. Nishokura Steel does take risks."

"As long as we don't."

"Paschek was there loading the train. Why do you trust him?"

"I don't trust any of my underlings. Particularly Paschek.

There is too much hatred building in him. The men look up to him."

"Don't tell me you fear an uprising among the men?" Jiri scoffed.

"Best to be prepared. And Paschek, for all of his apparent weaknesses, has the potential for leadership. Why else do you think I keep him out in the yards stuck on that forklift? He's too clever to allow him to work inside one of the plants."

"You won't trust Chase Evans either, once you meet her. She's another clever one, and she's already in Jarvoc."

"Josef told me that your Miss Evans and a male companion have taken lodging at the Rosners' place. Are they married?"

"No, he's just another American. They've already tried to get in touch with Dorian Paschek."

"CIA?"

"He was once. I met him at a mercenary camp in Spain."

"A mercenary, eh? Then he's useful to us."

"Doubtful. He's the ex-marine with a hero's welcome in America."

"Any man can be bought."

"Not him."

"Will he recognize you?"

Jiri squirmed, hesitating. "Breckenridge and I spoke briefly at the Von Tonner Art Museum opening."

"You're a fool, Jiri. How much does he know?"

"He promised to get in touch with me when he got to Prague. He knows by now that I gave him a wrong number."

"Brilliant."

"I had them followed from the airport." He glanced at Altman. "While they're prowling around in Jarvoc, I'd better stay out of sight. I could have Pavel keep an eye on them."

"Pavel? We can't depend on him. He'd be taken in by a pretty face. Besides, he couldn't even manage to set off a bomb in Kendallshire."

"He did run," Jiri admitted, "but at least he got out of the Cotswolds with his life. But someone—you perhaps,

Altman—warned the British that Czech terrorists were there."

"You're a fool, Jiri."

"And you, a liar, perhaps. Never mind. What should we do about the Americans, Altman?"

"They are expendable. Do it any way you please."

👥👥👥

Hanz was working the compost pile when the girl approached, her steps confident and graceful as she came toward him. He couldn't decide what appealed to him most—her healthy complexion or her youthful good looks. Hanz couldn't even remember back to being that young and energetic. She had to be in her mid-twenties, a fair cut between wholesome and attractive, her smile a hair between shy and sly. But there was nothing cunning in her expression as she said, "Hello. You must be Mr. Russelmann."

"One of them."

"I'm Chase Evans."

She offered her slender hand, but he shrugged, showing her the dirt on his palms. He leaned against his pitchfork, easing the pain in his hip. *Chase Evans.* This was the student Nedrick had talked about. Petite and stylish. Her hair as silken as a rose, her large hazel-brown eyes compelling. But a CIA agent? If so, he would beat her at her own game.

"You're the American student who knows so much about Olivia Renway. My grandson told me about you." Before she recovered from her surprise, he said, "Renway was born in Jarvoc, one of the Paschek children. Did you know that?"

"Yes, but I didn't know you had a grandson."

"Until last week Nedrick worked for Uriah Kendall."

His hands took a tighter grasp on the pitchfork. This woman, this American, could bring them all to their knees. As much as he hated what his sons had become, he did not want them destroyed. "Why have you come to Jarvoc?" he asked coolly.

"To meet you and Dorian Paschek and to visit the

Russelmann Steel Mill as Olivia Renway did on her last visit here."

His eyes narrowed. "She was not well received in this town," he said. "Questions about her will only anger the people."

"Because she fell in love with a German pilot?"

"Did she?"

"Some of your neighbors say she was a German spy."

He put his head back and laughed. "Because she loved a German pilot? No, that little resistance fighter did not work for the Germans. Dorian knows that. He was merely tricking you." Sickened by the charade, he said, "I think you know who I am."

"You're Henri. She wrote about you in her diaries. I thought you were in love with her."

There was contempt in her voice. She despised him as Olivia had despised him that last night in the air raid shelter. "I was in love with her, but we were on opposite sides in the war."

He gripped the pitchfork, blinded by a sudden rage. Olivia had betrayed him—left written notes behind that would ruin all of them. *If this young woman is CIA, then she knows about the Nishokura accounts. She knows about the waste plant full of weapons.* Olivia had known. Olivia had died for it.

Before he could put vengeance into action, he saw Mila ambling down the path toward him. "Uncle Hanz, where are you?"

"Go, Miss Evans. I don't want anyone to see you here."

"Your niece Mila told me where you were. And, oh—I forgot. I was to tell you that Nedrick had gone to the waste plant. I didn't know he was your grandson."

Hanz recoiled. Nedrick must not discover what was hidden there. He had to get back to the plant—tomorrow, this afternoon, soon—and set explosives enough to destroy the arsenal stored there. If it took the entire steel plant, all the better; he would set a spectacular farewell fireworks and he would die with it. Anything to salvage Nedrick. Nothing mattered as long as his grandson went free.

"Mr. Russelmann, you weren't listening to me," Chase said.

"I told you to go."

"I will, but I keep wondering, why did you desert Olivia when she was expecting your child?"

He thought of explaining that he had been called back to Germany, that war necessitated obedience, that Olivia was not pure Aryan. Instead he said what he had wanted to say for years. "If I had known about the baby, I would never have left her."

🏺🏺🏺

Jiri waited in the shadows outside the local pub—waited for darkness, waited for Dorian Paschek to stop downing his lagers and go home. Paschek came out thirty minutes later with two friends—Ludvi Rosner, the town's artist, with shocks of gray hair showing beneath his skull cap, and Ivan Koch, with his curved pipe dangling from his mouth. Koch, who was barrel-bellied and barrel-chested, could out-chuckle and out-drink anyone in Jarvoc.

Jiri kept in the shadows as he followed the three of them to the corner. He knew from their slurred speech and raised voices that they had lingered too long over their Budvars. Paschek had the longest distance to go, two blocks beyond the others.

As Dorian turned down the lane to his three-room cottage, Jiri called out, "Paschek."

Dorian turned. "Mr. Benak, is something wrong at the plant?"

"No, but Altman sent me. Mr. Russelmann is unhappy about that friend of your sister's visiting you."

Perplexed, Dorian said, "I have no guests."

She's been in town twenty-four hours and hasn't contacted him? "You haven't seen Olivia Renway's friend?"

"My sister is dead."

How well I know, Jiri thought. And he knew by the coldness in Dorian's voice that he had sobered quickly. He shoved Dorian roughly against the stone wall that separated the Paschek dwelling from the neighbors. "I don't have time to waste. I'm talking about Chase Evans. The American CIA agent."

That suggestion hit its mark. In the light of the half-crested moon, he could see Paschek's bleary eyes narrowing with hatred and fear. Dorian was a big man, muscular, known to win in a pub brawl, but the pistol in Jiri's pocket was ample protection. He would actually delight in shooting Paschek at close range.

"Mr. Benak, I don't know any of Olivia's friends."

He pinned Dorian against the wall, his doubled fist tight beneath Paschek's jaw. "Don't lie, Paschek. It could cost you your job. We know about the Gregorys visiting you at the plant."

"I swear. I never met them before. They told me they were friends of Jon Gainsborough."

"Jon barely knows them."

"Go ahead. Check out my house, Benak. I'm hiding no one."

Jiri heard fear in Paschek's voice and smiled. "Mr. Russelmann does not want an American agent roaming around Jarvoc."

"I—"

Jiri's knuckles came down hard on Paschek's mouth, cutting off Dorian's protest.

From the window above the glass shop, a head appeared. "Quiet down there," the woman yelled. "Or I'll call the *policie*."

Jiri lowered his voice. "If the American shows up, you are to let me know. Arrange for her to meet me at the waste plant."

"No one ever goes there."

"Safe then."

"I can't—"

He silenced Dorian with another crashing blow to his face. Dorian doubled over, but Jiri knew he would make no attempt to fight back. He treasured living—treasured being employed. Surely Dorian was aware that he might himself end up at the waste plant where other employees had disappeared over the years.

"Don't make it necessary to meet with you again, Paschek! The Russelmanns do not tolerate opposition."

"No." Dorian turned away and spit—blood, Jiri was certain.

"As soon as she contacts you, we must know. Come to Altman's office in the morning and let us know what she said."

Dorian held his mouth and nodded.

"Good. And good night, Paschek."

Jiri watched him slouch off at an uneven gait and disappear down the alley toward the house. No lights went on. *What are you doing? Watching me now? No matter. You will do as I have asked.*

He took a Havana cigar from his pocket and lit it, puffing contentedly for a few minutes. He was confident that the longer he lingered out front, the more fear he could instill in Dorian.

۞۞۞

As Dorian reached his door, he heard a rustling sound by the bougainvillea bush. Before he could turn to investigate, a strong hand clasped his mouth, intensifying the pain of his split lip; an arm circled his chest in a Herculean grip. Jiri? No, not Jiri. The man behind him was too tall, six feet or more.

"We're friends," the stranger whispered. "Friends of your sister. You've got to help us."

Dorian nodded. He was not in a position to bargain.

"I'm going to release you, Mr. Paschek." The stranger's voice was deep, hypnotic. "But the man who beat you is still out front. Cry out and he'll come running back, and if he's armed—"

Dorian stopped struggling. The blood in his mouth and nostrils blocked off his air, gagging him, choking him, but the prospect of death at the hands of Jiri was even more terrifying.

"We've been followed to Jarvoc, Mr. Paschek, and we want to know why. Only friends knew we were coming here."

As the iron grip loosened, air stung the raw wounds on Dorian's face. He swallowed the blood in his mouth, fear souring his stomach as he turned to face his assailant.

"I'm Luke Breckenridge," said the towering man, his coal-black eyes glinting in the shadows. "And this is Chase Evans."

The American CIA agent! As she stepped from the shadows to Luke's side, Dorian could tell that she was young and beautiful, as Olivia had been. "Go away," he said. "My sister is dead."

"But the things that frightened Olivia are very much alive. And Beatrice Thorpe is still alive, too," she said.

"Still alive! How is she?"

"Someone tried to kill Mrs. Thorpe the other day, Paschek," Breckenridge said. "Czech terrorists, according to Scotland Yard. I'm voting on someone from the steel plant here in Jarvoc."

The girl was more gentle. "I saw Beatrice in the infirmary and talked with her. She told me everything about Olivia and Jarvoc—even about the night you were forced to betray Bea."

He felt the gnawing fear he had felt as a boy—the terrible pounding in his head as the secret police threw him against the wall. "Your sister. Where is your sister?" they had demanded.

He had lied and led them instead to the cave where Beatrice Thorpe and Margot Dvorak were hiding. Beatrice had wheeled around and glanced back at Dorian as the Gestapo led her away.

He didn't want to hear any more. She knew about Olivia's unfinished manuscript. Knew too much about the ruins of Jarvoc. Knew enough about the steel plant to lose her life as Olivia had lost hers.

Jiri's voice! Jiri's words. *If the American shows up, arrange for her to meet me in the waste plant.*

Dorian's hands shook as he turned and unlocked the door.

They followed him inside, the man moving stealthily around the room to draw the curtains; the girl stood motionless by the closed door, so close that Dorian could feel the warmth of her body and hear the sound of her breathing. As the lamp went on, he could see them clearly. The girl looked sympathetic as she watched him—the man alert and mistrustful, the jagged scar down his neck making him look even more fierce.

"What do you want from me, Breckenridge?"

"The Nishokura file from the steel plant."

"I work out on the grounds driving a forklift."

"Then get us a key so we can find the file ourselves," Breckenridge demanded.

"Leave," Dorian said, "while you still have a chance to leave Jarvoc alive."

Chapter 25

The next morning Dorian rode his bike to the steel compound and flashed his I.D. badge as he passed through the gate. His mind was numb, unable to make clear decisions, as he pedaled toward the six-story glass complex that housed Altman's office.

The waste terminal and six product plants lay behind the executive building. Ivan Koch worked by the blast furnace, Ludvi Rosner at the coke ovens, other old friends in the plant that made galvanized pipes. They rarely mentioned the war years; Altman had infiltrated the town and pubs with spotters who constantly threatened their jobs. Except for this privately owned steel mill, Jarvoc would still lie in ruins. After last night, Dorian felt backed against a human wall, even as the waste plant was backed against the forest of spruce and firs.

Chaining his bike, he went up the steps and into the lobby. Convinced that his legs would buckle if he took the stairs, he stepped into the elevator and pushed the button for the second floor. He owed nothing to Luke Breckenridge, nothing to Chase Evans. Yet sweat poured down his back as the door slammed shut leaving him trapped alone in a moving cell. His mind filled with old horrors. "Out. Out," the soldiers had shouted. And his father, a prisoner, had stumbled out of the crowded truck.

On these very grounds, Dorian thought. *Out by the rusty railroad track.* His sister Olivia had fought back as a resistance fighter, striking out against the enemy with a violence that frightened young Dorian: spying on troop movements, setting the radio beacon to guide the British bombers toward their targets, stealing past sentries to set explosives in the barracks. Olivia had always stepped to a different drummer. *And I've never fought back. I have gone on blindly here in Jarvoc, living out my life in fear. I have,* he thought bitterly, *been less than a man.*

As the elevator door opened soundlessly, Dorian wiped his swollen lip with the back of his hand and thought back to that time years ago when the Gestapo had swung a stick across his jaw. Staggering, he had tried to run toward his papa. As they yanked Zdenek Paschek from the truck, he had glanced over his shoulder and smiled—actually smiled—and whispered, "Be brave, son."

Dorian had fallen to the frozen ground, whimpering as his father was herded down the seven steps. In all those years since, Dorian had never felt like anything but a coward. Even now his boots felt like rocks as he stepped from the elevator into the carpeted hall across from the Russelmann suite. What right had Olivia had to make him look so small in the eyes of the people of Jarvoc—coming back in all her finery for Lisa Anne's funeral? Even his friends at the pub had insisted that she leave as hurriedly as she had come. She had brought back the bitter remembrance of reprisals in Jarvoc because of the Bronze Network. How dared Olivia come back and stir up so much trouble at the steel factory. His job had been in jeopardy ever since.

But he had been wrong to hate her. For the first time in ten years, he grieved for Olivia, mourned for the childhood that had been taken from them when the Nazis marched in. He grieved for Olivia as he still grieved for his wife, Lisa Anne!

"Someday, my beloved Dorian," Lisa Anne had said, "you will find the courage to break away from the Russelmanns' control."

Tears stung the back of his eyes; a miserable tightness rose in his throat. During her illness, she had forced him to watch a documentary film on the disposal of nuclear wastes. These had been transported by convoy truck to a freighter and over the ocean to an incinerator on an isolated island in the Pacific.

Dorian had been outraged as he snapped off their tiny television. "Fool politicians," he had said. "Endangering the lives of people all along the route."

"It had to be done," she told him. "And we must clean up the tunnels in Jarvoc. Otherwise our town risks total disaster." She had patted his rough cheek. "You will think of a way someday, Dorian. After I'm gone. You were meant for leadership."

Had the time come for resistance—for the revival of his sister's Bronze Network? Tonight. Or perhaps tomorrow. He would speak to the boys in the pub, and they would drink to freedom from the Russelmann reign.

But at this moment, Dorian had only the heart of a coward.

He stepped into the reception room without realizing he had moved. As the receptionist glanced up, he removed his hard hat and turned it in his bare, work-worn hands. "I'm here to see Mr. Russelmann and Mr. Benak," he said.

Altman stood in the door of his office, looking stern like a Gestapo agent. "Come in, Paschek. Jiri and I have been expecting you. We have something we want you to do for us."

"Did you see the girl?" Jiri asked.

"Yes, Mr. Benak." Dorian kept his eyes downcast, his heart racing. "I told Miss Evans that you would meet her at the waste plant this morning."

"Good," Jiri said. "I will be there waiting for her."

🌀🌀🌀

Chase set out on her own at dawn that morning, determined to catch Dorian at his shacklike dwelling. During the war, the Gestapo had turned the Pascheks' sprawling farm into the secret police headquarters. At war's end, Dorian sought to claim the land again, but Communist communal living took over; the vast acreage was parceled out in cubbyhole-size segments. Fields once planted by the Pascheks lay uncultivated. Look-alike houses in drab yellow were brightened only by lovely lace curtains and window boxes where summer flowers struggled to bloom. Chase found it difficult to imagine the lovely town that Olivia had described in her diaries. Had Olivia forgotten that Jarvoc was dominated by a factory with dark smoke pouring from its smokestacks?

Chase shuddered as she went down the alley, past the spot where the man had hand-whipped Dorian. The bougainvillea bush wound itself over the narrow porch rail, almost as determined to survive as Dorian was. Chase tapped lightly; the urgency of her knock increased when there was no response from inside.

From Dorian's yard, she could see the Russelmann farm and the factory with its eerie ring of smoke curling up and losing itself in the treetops. *What were you trying to tell us, Olivia? What is there about that steel mill that frightened you so?*

The Russelmann farm was an easy walking distance from where she stood. She set out, pacing herself to the heat of the summer day and was tired when she reached the house. Again her knocks went unanswered. She circled around to the garden and the compost pile where she had first found Hanz. His pitchfork was still plunged into the ground where he had left it.

Shading her eyes, she glanced up at the back bedroom window. The curtain moved—not windblown, but a man's hand letting it fall into place. Fear tingled her spine. She ran back to the road. Glancing frantically to her left and right, she knew that the factory was closer than the Rosners' lodging place. *Oh, Luke, I should have waited for you.* Behind her, she heard the sound of a car's engine turning over. She hid in the bushes and waited, too well hidden to even see the driver's face.

Five minutes later she brushed the weeds from her skirt and walked rapidly toward the freight train. The back gate to the compound was open, a forklift rumbling toward the tracks. Again she sought refuge—creeping around the ghostly building and down the seven steps. The rusty lock was broken, the door cracked. As she made a move to open it, a strong hand clamped around her mouth. She caught the whiff of chloroform and went limp against a man's muscular chest as he dragged her inside.

🟤🟤🟤

At 2 P.M. Drew Gregory dumped his overnight duffel on the chair in Luke's room. He was still gripping his laptop computer when he asked, "Where's Chase, Luke?"

"Missing."

"Missing?"

"I haven't heard from her for five hours. That's when she insisted on going back to Dorian Paschek's alone. From there—if I can believe the woman at the glass shop—Chase disappeared." With a distraught hand sweep through his disheveled hair, he said, "If I didn't leave, she threatened to call the *policie*."

"Luke, I told you not to let Chase out of your sight."

"Don't look at me like that, Drew. Chase had different plans. She was out of her room at the crack of dawn. She likes me—that's obvious, but she doesn't trust me anymore. We've got to find her."

"If she's really missing."

Drew set his computer on the table, loosened his tie, and tossed a map at Luke. "Troy Carwell alerted Czech Intelligence from Paris. Now they're taking us seriously and sending Leos Cepek and the *policie* from Kladno." As he changed his shirt, he said, "Fortunately, Dudley Perkins is staying in London. He'll check out Gainsborough's steel mill. We'll handle this end."

Luke shoved the map away. "I don't need a map to tell me there are plenty of places for Chase to disappear. The steel mill. The caves. Russelmann's farm. Dorian's place—I've been there. And a lot of tight-lipped people who won't help us."

He was on his feet, starting for the door. "We can't wait for your friend Cepek to arrive, Drew. We've got to take this town apart and find Chase. We've got to get to her before Jiri Benak does."

"That friend of yours who was at the gallery opening?"

"He works at the steel plant. Chase was afraid of Jiri. Said he was following her since London. I really didn't believe her."

"Then Chase is in serious trouble."

2:45 P.M. Drew was in no mood for politeness. He walked into the farmhouse through the open door and met an astonished Hanz coming down the stairs with a large toolbox in his hands. "Hanz Russelmann, we meet again," he said.

"Most unfortunate. This time it seems as though you have invaded both my home and my town."

"Chase Evans is missing."

"The CIA agent? But she was here earlier."

Gregory stepped toward Hanz. "She'd be flattered to hear you call her a CIA officer. Where is she, Russelmann?"

He had regained his composure. "I have no idea."

"British Intelligence is shutting down your operation in England—at least temporarily."

"Poor Jon! I assume it's my old connection with the war?"

"That will come out. That and so much more."

Hanz flashed a tired smile. "Poor Jon," he repeated as he reached the porch. "It was never Gainsborough's choice to work with us, but after the war we needed a foot back into the United Kingdom. A German family heading up a steel company there was out of the question."

"So you used Gainsborough?"

"We used what we knew about him. The Gainsborough money was gone, the family possessions dispersed." Russelmann eyed Drew impatiently. "My family didn't just sit back and wait to lose the war. We saw surrender coming. We kept our lists of collaborators. The Renways in Britain. Two of Gainsborough's family in Germany."

"So you came out of the war with your reputation and

your wealth intact—all except for the Kashmir sapphire bracelet?"

Hanz groped for the porch railing. "You'd better leave, Gregory."

"I don't intend to leave Jarvoc without Chase Evans."

"She is not here." He pointed to the woman coming toward them. She was young and smartly dressed in a belted jumpsuit, a black-and-white dog at her side. "There's my niece. Ask her."

"Uncle Hanz is right. I haven't seen Miss Evans since early this morning."

Mila stepped aside as Gregory stormed around the corner of the house, but he heard her say, "What did Mr. Gregory want?"

"The truth, Mila. The bitter, miserable truth."

"Wait—where are you going, Uncle Hanz?"

"To the waste plant to find the girl—if she's still alive."

Drew stepped back onto the path as Hanz limped away with the collie dog at his heels. Mila's expression was as black as her hair and eyes. "Mr. Gregory, we were going to leave for Spain today," she said. "Nedrick promised to take me away if his grandfather would go with us. But you have angered my uncle. Now he may never go away with us."

"Go later. The American is in danger if we don't find her."

Mila's eyes filled with mistrust. "Hanz thinks she's in the waste plant, but Altman has the only key." She plucked a flower from the bush beside her and pulled off the petals one by one. "There's another way into the tunnels. Nedrick and I played there as children. Mr. Gregory, if you help me get tickets for Spain—"

"I'll help you," he promised. "Tomorrow."

She latched onto his words. "We'll have to go through the old drainage ditch beneath the railroad tracks. We'll need a weeding hoe or sickle in case it's grown over."

As he chose a hand sickle and hedge shears from the shed beside the compost pile, she said shyly, "If you're not afraid to ride with me, we'll use Pavel's motorbike. We can beat Uncle Hanz that way; he walks slowly on that bad leg of his."

Drew clung to her narrow waist with one arm and to the tools with the other. As they bounced over the rutted ground along the railroad track, she swerved to the right. They leaped over the rails, coming to a jolting stop by a cement sewer pipe.

He could see as he swung his leg off the bike that weeds and twisted vines had formed an impassable web at the entry of the ditch. He attacked them with a vengeance, fighting time and nature with a sickle. Then he tossed the tools aside. "Let's go."

Mila scrambled ahead of him through dirt and debris and rat droppings. All he could see were the heels of her multicolored running shoes and the wild lavender shoelaces as he belly-crawled behind her. Halfway through he smelled a foul garlic-like odor in the ditch—as irritating as nerve gas! Colorless, tasteless, and deadly!

ôôô

When Luke Breckenridge reached the shimmering glass complex at the Russelmann compound, he was surprised to see Nedrick Russelmann coming out of the building.

"Nedrick," he said seriously, "Chase Evans is missing. Could she possibly be with your grandfather?"

Nedrick's gaze strayed out toward the railroad tracks and slid back again. "He might be out there. He's been trying to persuade my father to close down that waste plant. That's why Popshot keeps putting off our trip to Spain."

"Take me out there, Nedrick."

"I'll ask the receptionist for the key, but she's all upset this morning about some unexpected guests from Prague— potential customers, I think. Josef is showing them around the grounds."

Good, Luke thought. *Leos Cepek has arrived.*

Nedrick came back with the key, but he looked distressed as he said, "Pavel is out looking for my grandfather. We'd better cut through plant six—just in case anyone is watching us."

Inside plant six, Luke's attention was drawn to the man on the elevated catwalk near the blast furnace. He stood there, his cold eyes on them.

"My father," Nedrick explained.

"What's he doing in here?" Luke asked.

"Overseeing production probably. He's the boss."

Luke felt the heat of the blast furnace even from where he stood. The furnace was mounted on rockers; the molten metal was hot and glowing, ready to be shaped into beams and rods and tubing. The sealed room directly behind Altman held the computer-controlled instrument panel lined with dials and gauges.

"My father modernized the plant twelve years ago. Jiri's idea and design. It stepped up production when they installed the automated high-speed equipment and the computer system." The glaring overhead lights made Nedrick's skin look a sickly yellow. "We've got the whole works now—instrument specialists, computer programmers, engineers, metallurgists—"

"Nedrick, we can't stand here admiring your father's assembly line. We've got to find Chase Evans and your grandfather."

Ned's jaw clamped down. He gave a casual wave to his father, led the way to the exit, and headed out toward the plant by the railroad track. Above the smokestacks, streams of black smoke polluted the air. The waste plant looked like a military barracks, its gun-metal gray forming a ghostly apparition. A wheel loader, tractor, and dump truck were parked by the building with empty freight cars visible in the rear.

Behind him, Luke heard a vehicle rolling toward them. He jerked Ned to safety as the forklift bore down on them. It veered to the left—Dorian Paschek at the wheel—riding so close that Luke felt the frame brush his skin as the forklift passed them.

Paschek drove straight for the front entry of the waste plant, the carriage and forks ramming into the bolted door.

He reversed and rammed again. His face filled with rage as he slid from the forklift and mounted the cab of the wheel loader. Within seconds, he charged toward the door again, the bucket teeth and cutting edge of the blade tearing into the two-foot-thick door. Forward-reverse—he went back and forth on the heavy-duty wheels. Forward-reverse. He seemed void of expression as the truck scooped up the splintered wood into the yellow bucket.

When they reached Dorian, sweat was streaming from his face. "Dorian," Ned shouted, "Chase may be in there."

Dorian's lip curled in contempt. "I was here when she went in."

Ned held up the key. "You didn't have to wreck the door."

There was no indication that Paschek heard him. He switched vehicles again, driving off in the forklift as though nothing had happened. A few feet away, he barked out orders to Rosner and Koch. Rosner buggered off on the run, Ivan Koch taking to Ludvi's heels with his potbelly bobbing—both of them beating a retreat toward the office complex.

Dorian glanced back at Ned, loathing on his face.

"Paschek, what are you doing?"

"Resisting for the first time in my life. Nedrick, we've got to stop your family from destroying the Nishokura accounts before Jarvoc lies in ruins again. I've sent Rosner and Koch to the fifth floor to salvage the files."

"My father's office is on the second."

"Nishokura's bogus office is on the fifth. Go on," he said, pointing to the battered door. "Do what you must."

As Dorian drove away, Nedrick and Luke tore down the remaining boards with their bare hands and crawled through the opening. Inside, it was empty, the rows of windows barred and painted an opaque white. "Chase isn't here," Luke said.

When Drew and Mila entered the tunnels, Mila ran off in search of Hanz. Drew prowled more cautiously, his search for Chase turning futile, but his discoveries unnerving. When Nedrick and Luke caught up with him, Drew was in the storage room pulling down two cardboard cartons, rotted and mildewed by the years.

Nedrick choked from the dust as Drew opened the containers. The remains of shoes filled one, eyeglasses the other. Nedrick watched stony-faced as Luke helped Drew lift down a third carton—more shoes and moth-eaten clothes. Drew picked up a pair of baby shoes and slapped them into Ned's hand. "Someone—someone from your family—overlooked these at the end of the war." He pointed toward the shower room. "A room down there was the end of the line for these people."

Color drained from Luke's face. "I didn't think they had extermination camps in Czechoslovakia."

"Only on a smaller scale—never fully developed, Luke."

"No," Ned protested. "Jarvoc was a labor camp. That's all."

Drew snatched up an old blueprint from the floor; it tore as he unfolded it. "Obviously they had bigger plans for Jarvoc. I've already found the morgue chutes and the dressing rooms. And now these boxes of clothing," he said with utter contempt. "My guess would be that Jarvoc had large deposits of coal and a good supply of water—and the railroad depot at their disposal for this godforsaken factory."

Luke grabbed Drew's wrist. "Chase is in this mess somewhere."

"I haven't found any sign of her yet. Maybe she's safely back at the Rosner lodging. But come. We'll go the length of the tunnels if we have to—but prepare yourselves. There are more horrors in the tunnels."

He led them into a storage area surrounded by stockpiles of weapons, a subterranean arsenal. Rifles. Handguns. Missile heads. In the next cave were fifty-five-gallon drums on dollies, silver canisters of fertilizer, tanks filled with chemicals, and shelves with containers marked "liquid gases." The yellowed inventory list hanging on the wall was chilling: "Zyklon-B. Nitromethane. Stoff-146."

From behind them, a deep voice cautioned, "Don't pry

that lid open, Mr. Gregory. Not when we don't know what it contains or what would happen when it hits the air."

Drew looked up. Hanz Russelmann stood yards from them, an old man listing on his game leg, one hand braced against a wall carved with the names and dates of prisoners who never left the tunnels. The black-and-white collie whimpered at his side.

"What is this place?" Luke asked Hanz.

"It's what it once was that sickens me." He met Nedrick's despairing glance. "I won't be able to go to Spain with you, my boy, but you and Mila go. Go for me."

Ned started toward his grandfather. Hanz held up his hand.

"Jiri is in the tunnels somewhere. I have to find him. You go back to the house for me. Olivia's missing attaché case is in my room. Find it before Altman discovers I've taken it. It'll clear your grandmother's name." When Ned hesitated, his voice grew firm. "Go on. Miss Evans is safe. Go through the dressing room. You remember—I took you there once as a boy. It's the only way out. And take Patek with you."

The dog refused to move.

As Nedrick stumbled back through the tunnel, Drew said, "Hanz, your niece came in here with me. Where is she now?"

"She's with her brother Pavel, but Jiri found him first. He's in the shower room—dead. Miss Evans is with her— she'll be all right. Now all of you get out. I'm the one Jiri wants."

Drew thumped one of the gas containers. "Hanz, are your sons planning to blow up the steel factory or the whole world?"

"We don't discuss things like that."

"Stockpiling chemical weapons is a direct violation of the Geneva Protocol." His voice was iced, colder than the tunnels. "We should have listened when Olivia labeled the Russelmanns and Nishokura as terrorists. Is that why your family silenced her—so you could go on making your billions in profit?"

"I had no part in Olivia's death."

Drew underlined the words on one container. <u>Zyklon-B</u>. "This was used by the Nazis back in the 1940s, Hanz. And this one—innocent enough. Hydrochloric acid—alone, no problem. But by mixing it with other chemicals, your sons could make a nerve gas."

Drew caught the look of surprise on Hanz's face. The man was vacillating between loyalty to his family and utter revulsion at what his sons had become. "Pure speculation," Hanz said.

"Tell me, Russelmann, are Libya and Iraq constructing roads with your products or building underground chemical plants?"

"Very clever, Mr. Gregory." Jiri Benak's voice filled the room. "But be assured, if the Russelmanns had not come along, there would have been other terrorists." Jiri chuckled dryly. "And good afternoon, Breckenridge. I see you've discovered my place of employment."

They looked around and saw no one. All they could hear was Jiri's mocking laughter over the loudspeaker.

Luke doubled his fist. "I'm going to take you down, Jiri."

"Not likely."

Faintly and then in increasing volume the music of Wagner and Mozart echoed through the tunnel. The wall sensors began to blink red, the dials moving slowly to the right.

"He's turned something on," Drew warned.

Hanz's face went ashen as he glanced at the pipes above their heads. "Then we don't have much time."

Looking around again, Drew spotted Jiri standing on the catwalk by the control panel. He was wearing a trench coat with an unlit cigar jammed in his mouth and his snow-blond hair combed neatly in place. "My grandfather was one of the architects here," he boasted. "Tell them, Hanz. Tell them how our families helped design this facility for ethnic cleansing."

Drew retched. *The designers of death.*

Over the loudspeaker the music had changed to the triumphant notes of a hymn, "A Mighty Fortress Is Our God."

"Go," Hanz pled. "Chase needs your help to escape. She's out cold, but she's still alive. Go while there's still time."

Luke shook his head. "Jiri knows me. I'll keep him occupied. You go, Drew, and see if you can get Chase and Mila out of here."

"No," Hanz said firmly. "I'm the one to stay behind. I know these tunnels. I can keep Jiri at bay for a little while."

Jiri's mocking voice came over the loudspeaker again. "Hanz, I'll kill every one of them," he said, "unless you go into the shower room. Your life for theirs."

Hanz's smile was vague as he turned to Luke. "This has always been an evil place. I begged my son Altman to destroy this plant and these tunnels. I should have done so myself years ago."

Drew wasn't sure whether to despise Hanz or pity him. "Czech Intelligence will take care of that for you. Come on, Luke."

Hanz detained Luke, saying, "I'm not apt to come out of here alive. That hymn—'A Mighty Fortress'—I knew it as a lad. I know I don't deserve mercy—but can you tell me how to get to God?"

The muscles in Luke's face contorted. "I don't know— Hanz, I'm—I'm not a confessional. I—"

"Come with us, Russelmann," Drew called back.

"No, Jiri is armed. He would take us out one by one."

The music still played as Hanz obeyed Jiri's command, the collie staying faithfully by his side. Hanz dragged along, his limp more pronounced as though he were giving Drew and the others time to crawl to safety.

As they all entered the shower room, Chase opened her eyes, looking dazed and confused. Her face was streaked with dirt and tears, her eyes frantic as she saw Pavel's body and Mila moaning beside him. Drew and Luke knelt beside Chase.

"Someone grabbed me," she cried. "Dorian, I think, or Hanz."

"No," Luke told her. "It must have been Jiri Benak who brought you in here. And I'm getting you out."

"I thought you were working with him."

"No, Chase. No." Cutting the ropes that tied her wrists, Luke lifted her into his strong arms and held her tight against him as he ran out the door.

Drew tried to force Mila to her feet. "Come with us, Mila," he begged. "You can't help Pavel now."

She shook her head. "I won't go."

"Then I'll send Nedrick back for you."

"No, Mr. Gregory. I know he will never go to Spain without his grandfather. Let me stay with Uncle Hanz. He needs me."

Drew stepped into the dressing room, ready to charge off to find Nedrick. Behind him, he heard a metallic clanging. He whirled around and ran back. The gas-tight door to the shower room had been slammed tight and secured from the other side. He peered through the peek hole. It was fogged, steaming hot water pouring from the shower heads down on Mila and Hanz. Hanz had knelt down and pulled Mila to him as she bent over the inert body of Pavel. The collie whimpered beside them.

Drew caught the sickening sensation of an unknown odor and knew that Jiri had thrown gas crystals in through the ducts. He turned and sprinted back through the tunnel. His long legs cramped as he burst from the darkness into the glorious fresh air outside and collided with Nedrick.

"My grandfather lied to me," Ned said. "The attaché case wasn't in his room."

"He wanted to save your life, Ned."

"I'm going back in and save his."

Drew grabbed Ned and wrestled him to the ground, pinning him there. "You can't go back in there, Nedrick. It's too late. Nerve gas is pouring into the room where Hanz is."

Chapter 26

Drew waited beside Nedrick, but his attention was on Leos Cepek—standing aloof, grim-faced, his gray eyes alert as more agents poured onto the compound. Work at the steel mill had come to a standstill. Many of the employees were already herded together in holding areas for interrogation, their frightened wives and families on the other side of the locked gate begging for answers.

At a signal from Cepek, the Kladno *policie* took the Russelmanns into custody. Altman sneered. Josef kept his head downcast. Gustav's fat jowls sagged. In a strange way, Franz Van Rindin seemed relieved to have his hands cuffed behind him.

"Wait," he told the officer. "I have a confession to make."

"Shut up," Altman told him.

Franz lifted his dark, brooding eyes as they manhandled him into the car, his expression one of regret as he glanced back toward the ghostly plant with ominous smoke rings curling from its smokestacks. "I drove the car that killed Miss Renway," he said.

Drew felt no surprise. He was convinced that even if Franz were executed for the murder of Olivia Renway, he would welcome it as relief from his darkness.

Only Altman resisted. Even with his wrists restrained behind him, he scorned the others. He twisted his shoulders adjusting the fit of his Canali suit coat and then with his stern, well-shaped chin, he flicked some dust from his shoulder. He thrust the officer's hands from his arm and glared at his son.

"Father," Ned choked, "I'll find the best lawyers I can."

Altman's frigid gaze fixed on Nedrick. "Don't bother. I have never needed you. I don't need you now."

He nodded toward the officers. "Shall we go, gentlemen?" he asked. "But I must warn you, you've made a grave mistake in allowing Mr. Benak time to escape. When this is over and I'm free, I will make certain that you wallow in the gravel for a false arrest."

He gave a curt bow to the guards and slipped into the car, like a gentleman off for an evening concert at the National Theater. *Altman was probably right,* Drew thought. He had run his vast steel empire with cunning, and in spite of the billions in profit from the sale of firearms and nerve gas, the records would be in his favor. Gustav and Josef might hang, but Altman would have planned ahead for his own future.

Drew felt the convulsing of Ned's shoulders as he spun the younger man around and forced him toward the farmhouse. Ned's skin looked ash-white, like dirty soap suds left in a wash basin.

"It should have been my dad in there instead of Popshot."

"Ned, Hanz could have left the tunnels alive, but he chose to give the rest of us a chance to escape."

"But Mila didn't make it," Nedrick said, grief-stricken.

"She wouldn't leave Pavel nor your grandfather."

"Pavel is dead, too?"

"He was already dead when Jiri turned on those shower heads and fed in the gas pellets. They went quickly, Ned."

As they caught up with Luke and Chase, Ned said, "Popshot was a good man. He was the best friend a boy could have. We used to walk along the tracks and make plans to catch a train out of here to Spain. He wasn't like the others, Drew. He wanted nothing to do with the Nishokura accounts. You've got to believe me."

"The records will prove that."

Behind them a violent explosion erupted. Drew dropped to the ground, pulling Ned and Chase down beside him. He risked looking back. The explosion had come from deep within the forest, beyond the railroad tracks. Another major rumble shook the ground, spewing giant spruce and fir trees into the air; they disintegrated into dust and ash chips, thick as smoke, as they drifted back toward Jarvoc.

"What happened?" Ned asked.

"I'd say Jiri Benak just secured his escape route by blocking the tunnel with debris and doubling his chances of getting away. He most likely set the blast off by the steel shoring in the mine shaft. No one can follow him now."

Luke crawled over to them. "You okay, Drew?"

"We'll make it, but if that explosion put fissures in any of the containers in the plant, we're dead meat."

"Jiri's not that stupid, Drew. Once he turned on those shower heads, he secured the entry to the tunnels with those iron doors before he took off. He's a genius," Luke said glumly. "And that includes firearms and explosives."

Ned stumbled to his feet. "We've got to stop him."

"Ned, what we have to do," Drew said, "is get out of here. Jiri must know the exit to the caverns. He's long gone by now."

Nedrick stood his ground. "Won't Czech Intelligence want to talk to me? I'm a Russelmann. I have to face up to—"

"Leos Cepek told me to get you out of here. As far as he understands, the youngest Russelmann left Jarvoc ten years ago. Let's keep it that way."

"Cepek?"

"Czech Intelligence. He's an old friend of mine. I vouched for you, Ned. And I'd say you're more like a Kendall. Wouldn't you agree, Luke?" *Dear God,* Drew prayed. *I can only hope that Uriah agrees.*

Dorian Paschek came lumbering over the fields in the forklift. He veered toward them, pelting them with gravel and creating a dust screen as he pulled to a stop and saluted.

Paschek leaned down, his weather-beaten face streaked with soot. He pointed back toward Cepek. "He sent a message, Gregory. Said for you to leave quickly. Thought it best not to have American Intelligence involved."

Drew nodded. "Good man."

"His colleagues might not agree," Dorian cautioned. "Some of them are more touchy about American interference."

Again Drew nodded.

"I've got an old truck behind my house. Take it," Dorian offered. "Get out of here—before the town folk turn against you." He dropped the keys into Drew's hands and glanced at Chase, silent beside Drew. "We don't want any of you involved. Just leave the truck at the airport."

Ned protested, "Dorian, I can't leave. I've got to make certain my father didn't destroy the Nishokura files."

Dorian's anger flared. "They're safe. The boys and I made certain of that. And you, Nedrick—you've always had trouble taking orders—even when you were little. Like Mr. Gregory said, they don't know about you being back in town—that's the way Hanz wanted it. Now get out of here—all of you."

Drew saw new strength in the craggy face. He gripped Paschek's callused hand. "Jarvoc is at risk with all those hazardous components inside the plant."

"My wife told me what to do about that a long time ago. The boys and I used to talk about it at the pub—after a few drinks to give us courage. But we couldn't see a way to sabotage the plant or to destroy what's hidden there."

"And now?" Drew asked.

"As soon as they stop interrogating the employees, I'll have the men load those containers on the train as quickly as they can. We'll put distance between the danger of explosion and the village."

"You'd be destroying evidence."

"We're trying to save our town. Czech Intelligence agrees with me." His grin turned sly. "Mr. Cepek will help us. He has ties to this old town—married one of the girls from here. Even if he doesn't, as long as he turns a blind eye for a day or two, we can send some of those tanks and shells on a truck convoy over the back roads out of Jarvoc."

"You'd risk lives along the way," Drew warned.

"It's been done before, Mr. Gregory. We'll do what those people did to rid their towns of nuclear wastes. And we'll ask Prague for enough firefighters and riot *policie* and planes overhead to ward off any terrorist groups who might try to steal our shipment."

"You can't just leave it on the back roads."

"We won't." He brushed a tear from his eye. "I saw myself this morning for the miserable, weak man I was. But all morning at the plant we've been passing word man to man, 'Remember the Bronze Network. Remember the Bronze Network.'"

Olivia's old resistance movement, Drew thought.

"I only wish my wife and my sister could be here to see us clean up this town. We'll make it. We'll ship those chemicals and weapons to an isolated island in the Pacific. The island is nothing but a toxic wasteland, but they've got an incinerator there equipped to handle massive disposal efforts."

"You're risking international opposition."

"Better that than the whole world eventually becoming a wasteland."

"What about Jiri Benak?"

"We'll seal off the shower room, Mr. Gregory." His face was anguished, a man who had been acquainted with more than his share of grief. "Benak only had time to feed a few pellets into the room. I'm certain he didn't plan on running, Gregory. He planned on taking over the plant."

"It's too bad he didn't get locked in the shower room."

"No, Mr. Gregory, I wouldn't wish that on any man, not even the man who planned my sister's death." He cleared his throat. "Olivia was fond of your wife, Gregory."

"The friendship was mutual. Miriam was proud to have been a friend of Olivia's."

"A better friend to her than I was. Go. Please. All of you."

Still Drew hesitated. "Will you be all right, Dorian?"

"For the first time in fifty years, I'll be all right."

Drew watched him mop his sweaty brow, thinking, *Paschek, you've got the makings of a leader. If anyone here in Jarvoc could pull off salvaging the steel plant, you could.*

"Dorian, work with Czech Intelligence. You can trust Leos Cepek. He's a good man. I know him."

He nodded. "He's promised us more investigators and firefighters from Prague and Kladno. Chemical weapons experts from Munich and London. Paris, too, Cepek said. We'll get through this one. I better go back now. Cepek will have some questions for me, too."

Paschek saluted once again, then turned the forklift back toward the factory, and rumbled away. "There goes a man," Drew said, "who could use half a million dollars."

He gave Nedrick and Chase a gentle nudge. "You heard the man. Let's get out of here."

🌀🌀🌀

Ruzyne International, fifteen kilometers northwest of Prague. As the four of them sat in the airport coffee shop waiting for their flights to London and Zurich, Luke checked his watch and cracked his knuckles in disappointment. They had forty minutes more to keep a low profile, but he half expected other members of Czech Intelligence to burst into the room and detain them. Drew—typing furiously on his laptop computer—could take care of himself, but there'd be no fight left in Nedrick or Chase. She sat beside Luke, hunched forward, lost in thought. Ned was at a table alone, his eyes glazed; dust from the explosion still speckled his hair and shirt. Luke went back to looking at Chase and tried to coax a smile from her.

"You looked at me that way the first time we met," she said.

"I remember. You asked me if I had missed the Bartholomew nose. There's a streak of dirt on the tip of it right now."

She brushed it away, a tear with it.

"Don't go weepy on me. We're going to make it. Right, Drew?"

Drew grinned wryly. "Count on it. We'll be in London in a couple of hours, Chase."

"But I hate saying goodbye to Luke."

"Then don't," Luke said with more cheer than he felt.

"Just stand up when the time comes and say, 'So long, Luke. See ya.'"

"It's not that easy. You—you saved my life." She flipped the hair from the back of her neck. "I'm a mess, but poor Nedrick looks worse. I wish he would sit with us."

Drew said, "He needs space to sort out his losses."

"Will he lose Uriah Kendall, too?" she asked.

"I don't know, Chase." He pointed to his computer. "I've started my Jarvoc Report. I'll make sure Uriah gets a copy. If he understands everything that happened—"

"Ned is Olivia's grandson," Chase defended.

"Uriah will take that into account."

"I feel so badly about Hanz Russelmann," she said softly. "Imagine how Nedrick feels."

"I can't imagine," Luke told her.

Time was running out, takeoff for London getting close. He hated seeing the others fly out ahead of him. "Maybe I should tell Nedrick what happened back in the tunnel," he said.

Drew scowled. "Spare him a repeat of that. He already knows that his grandfather was gassed to death."

"That's not what I meant. Back in the tunnel, Hanz grabbed my arm and said, 'I'm not apt to come out of here alive—you've got to tell me how to get to God.'"

"What did you tell Hanz?" Chase asked.

"I called after him, 'Russelmann, my mother always says that God's Son is the way to peace.'"

"Jesus? Is that what you believe, Luke?"

"At that moment, Chase, I was never more certain of anything in my life."

"Then perhaps Hanz died with that name on his lips."

"It's for certain that I will." Luke cleared his throat as he turned to Drew. "Well, it's all over now. All behind us."

"No." Drew nodded toward Nedrick. "The half-million-dollar Kashmir sapphires are still unaccounted for."

Luke rubbed his jaw to ward off a grin. "You're looking at the wrong man, Drew. Nedrick didn't play chauffeur to Uriah Kendall for ten years with that kind of money in his back pocket. Maybe the Russelmanns invested it in the steel business."

"No. Dorian Paschek said his sister was wearing that bracelet when she attended his wife's funeral."

Luke whistled. "Imagine flying all over Europe with half a million dollars on your wrist."

"At least that much," Gregory said. "But it's not worth a thing now because no one knows where it is."

Chase rallied. "Wrong, Drew," Chase said. "I don't think it's really lost. In fact, I'm quite sure I know who has it."

Before they could argue with her, she snatched up her carry-on bag. "I'm going to go change clothes and freshen up a bit before our flight."

Luke watched her saunter away toward the lady's room. "Now what was that all about? She's all uptight about some bracelet that doesn't even belong to her."

"I'll see what I can find out on the flight to London, but, Luke, have you told her about you and Sauni yet?"

"I haven't figured out how."

"She's fond of you."

"My fault, I guess. I thought she knew we were just friends. But you're wrong about Sauni and me. That's a closed door, too."

"Not according to Miriam's predictions. She already has the wedding bells ringing."

"Hope she's right." Luke cracked his knuckles again. "Do you think Dudley Perkins will ever apologize to Uriah?"

"Unlikely. Dudley's point was well taken. Gut feeling tells me that Olivia knew Hanz was German. Does love cover that, or did she cross the line when she took that bracelet and allowed him to walk out of that air raid shelter?"

At the mention of his grandparents' names, Nedrick came out of his stupor. "Maybe that day she was praying Hanz would blow with the next bomb. There was no reason to believe that my grandfather would ever get back to Germany."

"Ned, I have to settle something before we reach London."

Nedrick looked uncertain, but he stood and moved to their table and faced Drew. "About Uriah?" he asked.

"It affects him. You spent a lot of time in Washington, riding near the foreign embassies."

Solemn eyes sought Drew's. "That always bugged Uriah."

"Was it a drop point for you, Ned?"

"What? You mean Uriah thought I left messages there—the old chalk-on-the-mailbox routine?"

"Did you? Did your family send you messages?"

A frown wedged between Ned's thick black brows. Miserably, he said, "My father was well known in Prague. Wealthy. Powerful. I hoped that if I went by the embassy, I'd have a chance to see him and settle our differences."

Chase stood beside them now looking stunning in a designer suit with tiny violet stars in its pattern, her dress pumps easily giving her another two inches.

Luke handed her a cup of coffee. "You look great."

"Too fancy for me," Drew said. "I'd better shave so you won't be embarrassed traveling with me." He set his laptop on the floor beside Luke. "Come on, Ned. Join me."

After they got up and walked away, Chase asked, "Was that planned?"

"Drew's idea—so we could talk."

"About us?"

"Chase, I'm really sorry. I never dreamed—"

"It's my fault, Luke. When you told me to look you up in Europe and you'd introduce me to some of your friends, I just thought . . . and then when you carried me out of the tunnels—"

"You thought I meant more by it?" He put his broad hand over hers, a warm brotherly gesture. "I'm twice your age."

"Not quite. Besides, I like older men."

"What about Ian Kendall?"

Her chin stuck out stubbornly. "He's too young. Besides, my dad would never approve of a cyclist."

Luke laughed. "Would I have met your dad's standards?"

"I think so. But I'm embarrassed I read you wrong—about us. My dad always asks me how come I'm so dumb when I'm so smart."

Luke watched her wide eyes swim with tears. He ran his long fingers over her hand as he did with Sauni when she was hurt. "It matters what your father thinks, doesn't it? It was that way with the admiral and me—always trying to please him."

"But no matter what I do, it never pleases my father."

Luke thought back to the Columbia campus and Chase's exuberance for life and solving problems. "You have helped wipe out a lifetime of pain for the Kendall family and given Olivia back her good name."

"And unraveled her old love affair. Uriah won't thank me for that. Seems I've messed up a lot of things this trip."

For a while Luke watched the planes landing and taking off, willing Drew to come back to his rescue again. The scar on Luke's neck throbbed as he thought about the emptiness of facing life on his own. "I understand you, Chase. We're a lot alike."

Above the brim of the coffee cups her dark eyes met his. "There'll be someone for you someday, Chase. Much better than I would have been. You'll see."

Luke pushed back his chair. "There's Drew and Nedrick. They'll be calling your flight any minute."

"Luke?"

"Yes."

"Thank you for being honest with me. Are you—are you going back to Sauni as soon as we leave Prague?"

If I'm not detained by the Czech policie *after the rest of you leave,* he reflected. "Straight to Busingen from the Zurich airport."

"Does she know you're coming?"

"She asked me to come. She's my one real chance for happiness."

As he helped Chase stand, she gripped the handle of her carry-on. "In Jarvoc I never expected to live long enough to get back to London."

"It's been hairy," he said. "But it's over now."

He slipped his arm around her shoulder as he walked her toward the boarding gate. "Chase, you're a special lady."

"As special as Sauni?" she quipped dryly.

"Almost." He leaned down and kissed the top of her head, turned, and walked away—praying that he'd still get out of Prague before Czech Intelligence stormed into the airport.

EPILOGUE

Londpon, 3 A.M. The phone in Chase's hotel suite rang on her bedside table. She lifted her head from the pillows and groped blindly in the darkness, finally knocking the receiver from its hook. Fumbling again, she muttered, "Yes . . . hello. What? Oh, Drew, what do you want at three in the morning?"

"Sorry. Just checking on you. Have you called home yet?"

"Drew, you're crazy, but, yes, I called home. That time change is a killer. This is Mother's day for golfing and committee meetings." Chase was still grumbling but awake. "I tried Dad at the office. His secretary—the glamorous Iron Lady herself—would only take a message. She protects Dad like he's Fort Knox."

"He'll explode when he finds out it was you."

She put her head back on the pillow and stretched. "He'll have fits and fire Melba on the spot; then—she's quite a looker—he'll rehire her three hours later. But don't worry, Drew, Dad has eyes only for Mother. Now what did you really call me for at three in the morning?"

"I've been up talking with Uriah. Can you be a sweet thing and be at the Hungerford Foot Bridge at eight in the morning?"

Irritably she asked, "Are we taking a walking tour?"

He remained annoyingly good-natured. "Maybe we'll go for a swim in the Thames. Now be a sweetheart and be on time, and jot yourself a note to bring Olivia's unfinished novel with you."

Suddenly she was fully awake. *How,* she wondered, *did he know about that?*

"What manuscript?" she hedged.

"The one you came to England for—the one you've been hiding."

"How—how did you know about that?"

"Ian pried the truth out of Beatrice Thorpe."

She chuckled. "Beatrice is the one who asked me to keep it safe for Ian."

"Well—Uriah wants it back."

At 6:25 A.M., still dripping from the shower, Chase toweled down and, with nothing unpacked, shook out a soft shell blouse and put back on her Escada suit. Wiggling her narrow feet into the lavender high-heeled pumps, she remembered the novel and groaned. Except for one folder with Olivia's notes and first chapter, she had placed the manuscript in the bank vault where her father held his British account. Drew would never believe her. She picked up her oversized shoulder bag and shoved the folder inside.

Outside the Ritz Hotel, London's weather was as unpredictable as ever—what was expected to be a sunny summer day was muggy with mist, the distant clouds threatening rain. She reached the embankment with four minutes to spare and leaned against the railing watching the swirling mist drift across the River Thames.

"Good morning, Chase."

She recognized the deep voice at once and turned to face Ian Kendall. The morning mist had dampened his hair, teasing it into waves. He was more attractive than ever in dark slacks and a blue tennis shirt that turned his eyes a cerulean blue. "I was expecting Drew," she mumbled. "Or Uriah."

"I was afraid you wouldn't come if I called."

"Thought you were in France with the Gainsborough team training in the Alps."

"I was, but my grandfather and I had an appointment at Scotland Yard; Constable Wallis had been in touch with Czech Intelligence. Gainsborough expects me back in

France by midnight, or I'm off the team. It doesn't matter—
I just had to see you."

"But why here at the river?"

"Drew's idea. He said it was going full circle."

"Because it's Olivia's river?"

"I think that's what he meant."

"Did Drew tell you all about Prague?"

"He said you almost got killed in Jarvoc. I'm sorry. I
should have stopped you from going. But you were so
determined."

"You couldn't have known about the Russelmanns."

"Beatrice Thorpe tried to warn me, but I didn't want to
hear bad things about my grandmother. When I was a kid,
she was the most perfect person I knew. I couldn't destroy
those memories."

"Did you really believe she was a spy?"

He nodded. "Dudley Perkins convinced me that she spied
against Britain—that she was a spy right on up to her death.
I felt it was my duty to protect the Kendall name at all costs."

"Ian, I know who has the Kashmir sapphires."

"How would you know that?"

"There was only one family member with Olivia on the
day she died. You have your grandmother's sapphire
bracelet, don't you? You've had it all along."

As surprise whipped across his lean face, the muscles in
his jaw flexed involuntarily. In that split second, he withdrew, shutting her out. *Come back,* she thought. *Don't run
away this time.* For his sake, for Olivia's, she refused to back
down. "You do have it, don't you?"

He looked down at her, the feverish intensity in his eyes
reproachful. "She gave it to me the day she died."

"It's worth half a million."

"So Beatrice told me. We often looked at it together. She
let me hide it in her room at the Eagle's Nest."

"But someone tore her room apart."

"I know—I was there to get the bracelet and move it for
safekeeping. If I hadn't scared those men off, she would be
dead, but she sent me away. Told me not to admit that I'd
been there."

"She was hurt, you know."

"I know, but in Beatrice's eyes I'm still Olivia's little grandson—someone to protect. She doesn't realize how responsible I feel toward her." His eyes seemed riveted on the Thames as though he could no longer meet Chase's gaze. "I'm the one who lifted Beatrice back into bed—and put the call light on. Then I went out the window and waited until the nurse came. Beatrice was hurt—badly I could tell—but, ironically, the sapphires were safe in the trap door beneath the china closet."

Chase watched a patrol boat cut the aquamarine waters of the Thames as it forged a billowy path under the Waterloo Bridge before admitting, "She asked me to hide Olivia's manuscript."

He stiffened. "Yes, Bea told me you had the unfinished novel."

"Yes, it's in my father's bank vault." She tapped her shoulder bag. "Except for a few pages that I brought with me."

She took them from her bag and held them up. "It's all here, Ian. Your grandmother's story—her life in espionage," she said lightly.

His reaction was swift. He knocked the papers from her hand. "Don't speak of her that way."

"Oh, no Ian," she cried. "Why did you do that? Those papers, the trip to Jarvoc—they proved her innocence."

He had no answer. The breeze caught the pages and swept them down the embankment. They drifted into the veiled white mist on the River Thames. Whirlpools formed by the patrol boat sucked them under and drenched them. They floated defiantly back to the top—white blotches against the gray-blue river. An early morning sightseeing boat cruised by, shredding the paper with its motor, leaving in its wake a surge of waves that sucked up the pages. At last Olivia's notes sank beneath the waters.

As they slipped from view, Chase squeezed Ian's freckled hand and leaned her head against his shoulder. "It's over, Ian," she said softly. "There's no need to protect your grandmother's name anymore. Now it's more important than ever that you win the Tour de France for her."

"That's what I promised the last time I saw her." He seemed suddenly shy, less tense, his smile creeping back. "I want you to be there, Chase. For me. Will you stay over for the race? I want you there cheering me on."

He seemed older somehow, mature, frightfully good looking. She blushed, remembering that stolen kiss at the Eagle's Nest.

"Well," he urged. "Will you come?"

"I'll think about it. Let me check my calendar for July," she said.

They stood quietly for a moment watching the patrol boat on its return run, cutting its engine as it moved slowly toward the dock. Then Chase asked, "Did Drew tell you about Nedrick?"

"Yes, we talked half the night through. But like I asked Drew, why didn't you leave Nedrick in Jarvoc?"

"He doesn't belong there anymore. He broke his ties with his family. Those who mattered to him are gone. Both of them dead."

"The girl?"

"Mila Van Rindin, his second cousin. They really cared about each other. . . . She died trying to help Nedrick's grandfather. Nedrick doesn't have anyone left unless your family helps him."

"Why should we?"

She ran her fingers over his freckled hand once more. "You're related actually. He's Olivia's first grandson."

"Yes, the legend of Cornwall is true. My grandmother did have another son. That's tough to swallow. My father won't like that."

"That won't change anything."

"Nedrick is nothing to my grandfather," he persisted.

She smiled as the swirls of mist rose from the river, spraying their faces with droplets. "Somehow I think Uriah won't agree with you. Nedrick is part of Olivia. That's what will matter to your grandfather."

🏺🏺🏺

Kendallshire, the Cotswolds, 9:00 A.M. Drew circled Kendall-shire, walking the willow-lined streets of the village and fin-ishing out a sleepless night at the church courtyard where Olivia was buried. He snatched up the lone weed that poked its ugly head at one corner of the grave and polished the marker with the palm of his hand. *Be at rest, old friend,* he thought. *Be at rest.*

Ambling on over the woodland trails, he breathed in the sweet fragrance of the meadows as the golden brilliance of the morning sun caressed the limestone cottages. He saw the young man standing alone on the old stone bridge and felt a knotting in his stomach as he turned into the narrow lane that led to Uriah's cottage.

He let himself in, joining Uriah in the parlor. Uriah sat in his club chair, deep in thought with his palms together as though he were praying, his fingers to his lips. A copy of the Jarvoc Report lay on the round table beside him, his wire-rimmed reading glasses on top of it. With nostalgia Drew remembered that Olivia and Uriah always had matching chairs wherever they lived; he knew with a sense of sadness that Olivia had once occupied the one he had just taken.

"Uriah," he said, "Kendallshire is most beautiful at this time of day."

"Yes. Olivia loved the early mornings."

In the quiet that followed, Maddie rolled in the teaploy with a pot of steaming tea and a plate full of scones and jam on it.

Drew and Uriah sipped companionably, not even stirring when Dudley Perkins rang the doorbell. Maddie ushered Perkins into the room and set out another cup and a fresh plate of scones for him.

"I'll be going now," she said, "and do the marketing."

Uriah barely nodded, his attention fixed on Perkins, his eyes showing neither warmth nor surprise at the new arrival.

"Uriah," Dudley said, "I didn't expect to get back to Kendallshire so soon."

"Drew's idea."

Perkins sat down facing them and placed his hat and

briefcase on the floor beside his walking stick. "I assume it's about this Jarvoc affair. I've read the report completely."

"More likely it's about Olivia," Uriah said.

Dudley focused on Maddie's freshly baked scones. "May I?"

"That is what they're there for."

This is not going well, Drew thought. He took a quick bite of another scone and said, "Dudley, everything I wrote in the Jarvoc Report is true." He glanced apologetically at Uriah. "Fifty years ago Olivia Renway fell in love—*for the first time.* Hanz Russelmann was a Luftwaffe pilot whose crash landing during the Blitz forced him into the role of a German agent."

Talking to Dudley was like trying to stir cement that had already set. Perkins kept his lank hands wrapped around his cup, his stony expression making his gaunt face even more homely. But Drew kept explaining. "Olivia knew the agent as Henri, as an Oxford graduate. As far as she knew, he was British to the core. Handsome. Adventuresome. But he was as committed to his cause as Olivia was to hers. She didn't know he was a German agent until that last day in the air raid shelter."

"You seem to be well informed, Gregory," Perkins snapped.

"Olivia's brother, and Uriah here, filled in some of the small print."

Perkins thumped the Jarvoc Report. "You're asking me to believe all of this—that I wrongfully accused Olivia Renway of spying against Britain?"

"You did. It's all there in the report. In detail."

"She should have stopped Russelmann right there in the shelter. All she had to do was cry out, 'A Nazi. He's a Nazi.'"

"And watch the fury of other people turn against him?" Drew asked. "Perhaps lynch him in front of her? She was only a kid herself—seventeen or eighteen at most."

"She was pregnant, Dudley," Uriah said calmly. "Perhaps that more than anything else affected her decision. No doubt in Olivia's mind, she was not helping a German spy escape. She was protecting the father of her child."

Dudley forked a scone and stared back, disbelieving, his mouth full. "That wasn't in Gregory's report. A baby? Not— not Altman Russelmann?"

"Yes," Drew confirmed.

Perkins wiped his fingers on his gangly knees. "That poor woman." His sympathy was short-lived. "But she did spy against Britain. The records at MI5 are against her. Some of the messages that Olivia carried reached Berlin. I have files to prove it."

Drew's tone hardened. "Olivia took intelligence reports across the channel between Britain and Czechoslovakia for the Czech Brigade in London. She made mistakes. Serious ones. We all do, but if some of those reports showed up in Berlin, Olivia was unaware of it. Up until that last day in the air raid shelter, she trusted Russelmann, loved him."

Drew was hit by silent opposition. He shot another apologetic glance at Uriah. "Russelmann and Olivia obviously spent time together. It would have been easy enough for him to make copies or memorize the codes while Olivia slept, even photograph them with a mini-camera. I'm not here to defend what Olivia did or didn't do. The facts are all in the Jarvoc Report."

Uriah said, "If your files at MI5 are accurate, Dudley, you already know she was active with the Czech resistance right up to the end of the war. Two months after the birth of her son, she flew into Czechoslovakia to help prepare the way for the Anthropoid team. That spring only a violent case of flu kept her from being part of the team that took Reinhard Heydrich down."

Uriah's quietly modulated tone was frightening, yet filled with pride. "Even toward the close of the war, she carried pre-invasion plans through to the resistance fighters. It was as though she constantly tried to make up for falling in love with a German agent." He shook his head. "But what good did it do? There has always been little recognition for resistance fighters. Even the Anthropoid team have only a small memorial in Leamington Park—nowhere near the country they fought and died for."

Perkins wouldn't quit. "I suppose you have excuses for her work with Beatrice Thorpe and Margot Dvorak, too?"

"Dudley, are you blind to everything that concerns my wife? The Bronze Network personally assisted twenty or more airmen safely back to the Allies. That's how Thorpe and Margot Dvorak were arrested and marched off to the labor camp in Jarvoc."

"But Olivia remained free," Perkins mocked. "Did the Germans protect her for working with them?"

This is not going well, Drew thought again. *My fault and it all boils down to Olivia—to the man who won her hand and the man who didn't.* He said, "She hid in the rafters in the barn covering a dying RAF pilot with her own body. You had a pilot-son, Dudley. Killed in the Falklands, right? Wouldn't you have liked someone like Olivia willing to sacrifice herself to protect him?"

Drew had touched a raw nerve. "The reprisals in Jarvoc were blamed on Olivia, Dudley. There's the possibility that if she had turned herself in—revealed the hiding place for that young pilot—perhaps there would not have been so many deaths in Jarvoc that week."

Uriah moaned and said, "But to hate my wife for that and seek vengeance all these years."

"Unfair," Drew agreed. "But emotions ran high." He turned back to Dudley. "You went to great effort to destroy the Kendalls because of Olivia."

Dudley snapped to his own defense. "When Olivia held on to those Kashmir sapphires, she kept nine hundred thousand pounds for herself."

Over the years Drew had carried a lot of things in his pockets from firearms to forged passports, from Miriam's diamond ring to surprise presents for his daughter Robyn. But this was the first time he carried something worth half a million, and it wasn't even insured. He reached deep into his pocket, wrapped his hand around the Kashmir sapphires, and placed them on the teaploy beside the empty teacups. Brilliant sparkling gems.

Shocked, Uriah asked, "Drew, how in the world did you

get that bracelet out of Prague without a hassle from customs?"

"It's been in England all along. Olivia gave it to Ian in London the day she died."

"Why would Ian hide it from me? Didn't he know its worth?"

"Money was never the issue with Ian. The bracelet was a trust from his grandmother. A few hours ago he asked me to give it back to you. He couldn't face you with it."

The light from the windows caught Uriah's strong, well-cut features. He was still a handsome man, his thick hair a distinguished gray, but the permanent grief lines around his eyes had increased in the last few weeks. "Nedrick should have this," he said. "It's a Russelmann heirloom."

Perkins stared at it as though it were venomous. He pushed himself to a standing position, his shoulders still slouched forward. He jerked his hat on and picked up his walking stick and briefcase. Gathering up as much self-respect as he could salvage, Dudley said, "I owe you an apology, Uriah, but it's too late to retrieve an old friendship."

Balancing the stick and case awkwardly under his arm, Perkins took a snapshot from his wallet and dropped it beside the sapphires. "This is rightfully yours, Uriah," he said.

The cottage door slammed closed behind him. Then came the tapping of Dudley's stick on the cobbled walkway. They watched from the window as Dudley's car rattled over the village road, stirring up dust until it disappeared in the distance.

Turning the frayed snapshot over, Uriah stared wistfully down at the face of his wife—a solemn, yet alluring look in those wide, pensive eyes. She was glancing back over her shoulder, young and beautiful in her sleek charcoal gray trench coat, the sapphire bracelet visible on her wrist as she waited on the old stone bridge in Kendallshire.

"This is the way Olivia looked the day I met her. Mystical and melancholy even then. I loved her, Drew, but I've wasted so many years trying to protect her name when she was never a German spy."

"Olivia of all people would have understood. But, Uriah, I wonder if she realized what a special person you are."

A whimsical smile touched Uriah's face, putting the old spark back in his eyes. "She told me often enough." As he stood, the weariness fell from him. "I'm going for a stroll," he said.

"To the bridge where you and Olivia met?"

"Yes, would you care to go with me?"

"No, someone is waiting out there for you."

Uriah glanced out the window. "Nedrick!" was all he said.

"I encouraged him to come back to the Cotswolds to see you. I asked you once before, Uriah, what are you going to do about Nedrick?"

The blue eyes turned misty. "We've had ten good years together—Nedrick and I. Do you expect me to throw them away?" He squared his shoulders. "That's Olivia's grandson—*my* grandson now." His voice remained husky. "Are you coming with me, Drew?"

"No, I won't intrude. I have a heavy date back in London. If I work it out right, I'll have just enough time to get home, air out the apartment, get my dirty clothes off the floor, and be at Heathrow when Miriam's plane hits the runway."

🏺🏺🏺

Drew stood by the open window reluctant to leave the peaceful scene. No wonder Uriah loved this place. The river with its moss-covered banks ran through the middle of the village, the gentle sounds of water turning the paddles of the old weaving mill. Drew would take the sights and sounds of Kendallshire away with him—the weather vane spinning on top of the whitewashed cathedral, the limestone hills filled with honey-colored villages, the Cotswold sheep nibbling contentedly in the golden meadows. And the sight of his good friend Uriah standing on the arched bridge embracing Olivia's grandson.

Drew wondered how much he would tell Miriam about Prague and the Russelmanns. He would answer her questions—be honest as much as he dared, but he would skip the details when he told her that Hanz Russelmann had died sacrificing himself for his grandson and the rest of them. But this moment between Uriah and Nedrick he would gladly share.

He was just tempting himself with the last scone on the plate when Uriah's phone rang. He picked it up. "Kendall's cottage," he said with his mouth still full.

"Drew, is that you?"

Miriam! "*Liebling*, where are you?"

"Cruising at 37,000 feet. Or higher maybe."

"You sound like you're in the next room."

"And you sound a thousand miles away."

"I was just leaving—heading back to London."

"Don't worry about dusting or airing the condo," she teased. "Just pick up your dirty clothes."

"You're coming in on time?"

"I gave the pilot strict orders when I boarded."

"*Liebling*, I'll be there. I love you." He cradled the phone, sensing her nearness. "How's everything at the gallery?"

"Everything's just fine. I'm so pleased."

"And I'm pleased you're coming home."

"You're all right, Drew?"

"Yes. Everything's fine here, too. Olivia's name is in the clear, her reputation intact."

"I'm glad. I always believed in Olivia."

He heard the catch in her voice and knew she would flood the jet with tears if he didn't give her something to smile about. "Miriam, I've got more good news. In the next few weeks—six months max—I'm expecting a wedding invitation."

"Sauni and Luke's?"

He swallowed his disappointment. "How did you know?"

"I just talked to Sauni."

"At 37,000 miles in the air?"

"I was worried about you, Drew. When I didn't reach you at the condo, I called Robyn and Pierre. No answer there either. So I called Sauni. I—"

Static. He shook the phone. He'd sue the airline if the call disconnected. "Repeat that," he shouted.

"I said Luke is already there. *Very much there.* They'll be married in the college chapel in Busingen as soon as Luke's parents can fly over." Her voice was joyful. "And, Drew darling, I'm not supposed to tell you—but I'm going to anyway. Luke wants you to be his best man."

Drew grinned as he hung up the phone. He grabbed his car keys off the round table and strode out of the house whistling. Easing into his Renault, he drove out of Kendallshire. He was a man at peace with himself, going with the flow, following the Thames from its source back toward London. *Back to Miriam.*

SEASONS OF INTRIGUE

BOOK SIX

The Race for Autumn's Glory

Doris Elaine Fell

Let us run with perseverance
the race marked out for us.

—Hebrews 12:1c (NIV)

To Bob Jugan
who introduced me to the Tour de France
for his contagious enthusiasm
. . . .
To Greg LeMond
the American winner of three Tours
for his memorable triumphs

. . . .
And in memory of Fabio Casartelli
Motorola Team, Tour de France, 1995
for his unforgettable smile

Prologue:
The Greek Islands

Salvador Contoni stood at the helm of his vessel and shoved his blue-and-white skipper's cap back from his forehead. Monique Dupree, a Renetti yacht, and the lure of the Greek Islands—what more could he ask for? The woman and the ship—both of them sleek and elegant like royalty, eye-catching and glamorous. He owned neither one, possessed neither of these two beauties that touched him most. He glanced down at Monique. She stood out on the deck, her narrow waist pressed against the rail, her shiny black hair blown back from her face by the gentle sea breeze. She turned, and those enormous brown eyes looked up at him. She was beautiful, even more lovely as she smiled.

"Sal, why are we going to the island of Corfu?" she asked.

"I have an appointment with a rich Athenian in the privacy of his villa. I'm counting on him chartering this yacht."

"A friend of yours?"

"I've never met him. His oldest son made all the contacts."

"Why such a clandestine meeting?"

"So no one will recognize him."

A dark shadow blocked Monique's smile, twisting her lovely features into a frown. "You should have stayed in your father's vineyards. You risk your safety in international waters."

"The man will pay me well."

"A few thousand lire? You take too many risks, Sal."

"But all of them for you."

The yacht and Monique—both of them *grandi Italiane*—except, of course, Monique was French-born. Her coral midriff and gleaming white leggings made her look trim and tidy, swank like a ship being launched on its maiden voyage and sailing gracefully through the turquoise waters. Odd—odd that he always saw his yacht as a beautiful woman and this beautiful woman as a magnificent, luxurious vessel.

"You take too many chances, Sal," she told him again.

The stakes are always high, my love, he thought. *But if I get involved in another arms deal, I will surely lose you.* His body quailed against the alternative—the rest of his life hiding out in his father's vineyards, harvesting grapes, being the heir to his father's winery. Yet Sal would consider returning to the vineyards just to spend his life with Monique, but not before he tracked down Drew Gregory—the American CIA officer who had struck him such a bitter blow. The whole mercenary camp in the Pyrenees had been shut down because of Gregory, and Sal's luxurious lifestyle had been snatched from him. And now the Athenian in Corfu had promised him vengeance against Gregory.

When he saw the worry in Monique's eyes, he thumbed the chain around his neck and pulled it away from his chest. "I wear my madre's St. Christopher's medal. Nothing can happen to me."

She blew him a kiss, stirring an overpowering longing inside him. He wanted to anchor the ship and let it bob in these cool, clear waters so he could run down to the deck and take Monique in his arms. He had always boasted that he took what he wanted, but he must not take this woman against her will. She must long for him as he did for her—must love him as he loved her.

"What are you thinking, Sal?"

"About you. About us," he said huskily.

"Don't. Please don't."

"Why not? My parents like you," Salvador called down to her.

"They barely know me."

"They want to know you better."

Her laugh was curious, accusing. "Did you tell them that I'm five years older than you?"

"It wouldn't matter to them. They say I've changed since you came into my life."

"I'm only here on holiday," she reminded him.

"Stay. Marry me, Monique. I'm almost thirty-four. It's time for me to settle down."

"Really? Did you tell your parents about my boys?"

"Madre saw their picture on the dresser when she put the fresh flowers in our room." He grinned. "She says, 'When your Monique sleeps, she looks like an angel.'"

"Do your parents know that I'm a widow?"

A rich widow, he thought. *A spectacular asset for my dwindling account.* "My madre asked when she saw your diamonds."

Sal's grin widened. "She said, 'Marry her, Salvador. Monique will take good care of you. You will never have to work outside your padre's vineyards again.'"

"Working? Is that what she called skippering my husband's yacht—taking him on rendezvous so he could sell arms to foreign countries and man a mercenary camp?"

"My mother doesn't know about those things, Monique. But I had to skipper the yacht for your husband. Harland made a poor sailor—always seasick himself."

Again her face clouded. "Harland never really trusted you."

"Not where you were concerned." *Harland Smith, the American millionaire arms dealer.* "He gave you everything, even the city of Paris."

"Almost," she agreed. "It was part of his promise when he rescued me from the hills of Normandy."

An innocent beauty thrilled with the promises of Paris. Why else would she have married a man twice her age? "Did you know he sold arms to foreign countries when you married him?" he asked.

"I knew little about him—but my husband adored me."

"Then why do you go by your maiden name, Monique?"

"For the boys," she admitted. "I do it for the boys."

Sal's palms felt sweaty on the wheel. Anzel was going on fourteen and ashamed of his father's past; Giles was still five and a mama's boy. Good-looking boys—more French than American. "My mother would like grandchildren," Sal said. "The boys can live with my parents in the villa. Madre would like that."

"And your padre?"

Sal's muscular shoulders tensed. "My father wants me to work with him in the family business."

"In the vineyards—away from the sea?"

"The Contonis sell the best vintage," he assured her.

She shook her head. "No," she said softly, "you are too restless for the vineyards, Salvador. Restless like Harland."

Sal resented the comparison, but a man could be softened in Monique's presence. Enticed. Trapped. Lured. Salvador understood this. Even now he'd willingly give up the old ways just to win her hand. Why then was he sailing steadily toward Corfu, risking her safety as well as his own to meet with a wealthy stranger?

"Sal, turn the yacht around. Let's go back to Athens."

"We've come too far, Monique." *I can't turn back.*

They had sailed leisurely up the western coast of Greece, and now as the bow of the ship sliced the turquoise waters, Corfu loomed ahead. Sal licked the salty taste from his lips. He was to travel to Corfu alone. *But why Corfu?* he wondered.

"Why Corfu?" she asked, startling him. "Why not meet the man in Athens where he makes his home?"

Vasille Golemis belonged to the New Democratic Party; he was an outspoken advocate for NATO and the European Union. "He's a well-known politician, Monique, an honored member of Parliament."

"All the more reason to meet him in public. Or is that a threat to the new government?"

Sal smiled at that. Papandreou had fallen from power early in 1996. Or was it longer? Time ran a fast race in the political world. The fact that Vasille Golemis had survived the takeover of the new leadership was a vote in his favor. Or maybe he was holding on to his spot in Parliament by a hair. Golemis had opposed the election of Costas Simitis as prime minister. As far as Sal understood, it was Golemis's personal aggravation that he had not fallen heir to the promotion himself. Still the prime minister had definite plans to lead Greece into a starring role in the European Union. Golemis readily backed Simitis in this, but Monique was right. Why would a deputy in the Greek Parliament plan a secret rendezvous with Sal in Corfu?

"I'll stay alert," he promised her. "No amount of money or threats from the Athenian will keep me on Corfu against my will."

She shook her head. "Of course not. Salvador Contoni does

only what pleases him. Takes only what he desires. Risks only those assignments that leave him with a pocket full of lire."

You know me so well, he thought. "We'll be safe," he said. "But I'd turn around right now if you promised to marry me."

"Sal, I won't take my boys away from France, not until this mess about Harland's estate is settled, and the bank accounts and the houses in Spain and Switzerland and Paris are legally mine."

"What about the castle in the Pyrenees?"

"I never want to see that again."

She didn't want the castle where he and others had trained mercenary soldiers. But she wanted everything else, including that fabulous luxury vessel anchored in the Monaco harbor.

"Will you ever get the yacht back?" he asked.

He saw a flicker in her eyes and knew that it was already free. But forget the houses and yacht. "I love *you,*" he said.

"Oh, Sal, I don't think you know what love is all about. No, you love the sea. You would never be happy far from it."

The sea was his life, his escape, his past, and his future. He had felt this magnetic enchantment since boyhood. From that first day, when his father took him from the city of Milan 140 kilometers to the Ligurian Sea, the power of the crystal waters had captivated him. His family wealth and the guaranteed opportunities in his father's vineyards were nothing once Sal felt the power of a yacht bobbing beneath him.

He saw the yacht and Monique as one. He had met her in Monaco, standing in a receiving line beside her husband. With Harland glaring at them, Sal had danced with Monique in the crowded ballroom on board the yacht. As he swung her around, he had blotted out every face from his mind but hers, but when the waltz was over, she went back to stand with her husband.

No other woman stirred such longings in Sal. Life without her was like being constantly seasick. The seasick feeling rose in him again now. He sought safer ground. "Sell the *Monique II* to me," he begged. "I can run charters here in the Greek Islands."

"It's not for sale. The boys want it when they grow up."

"We can buy them another one then."

If he had been standing closer, he was certain he would see tears in her eyes. "Sal," she said, "the yacht is one of those good things their father left behind. I want them to have it."

Elegant and royal like Monique.

"Then I'll come to Monaco and do charters for you there."

"You can't. Interpol is looking for you. And Spain."

"Not very aggressively," he said. "I've been quite visible. I was openly with my family in Milan."

She was silent for an instant, and then raising her voice above the sound of the sea, she asked, "Sal, what is that hollow log beside your navigation charts?"

"The one in the cabin?"

"Yes, by that mysterious black box."

"That's nothing for you to worry about, Monique."

She tilted her head back and laughed softly, her long, slender neck gleaming white in the sun. "I'm not worried—just curious."

"It's the famous Contoni interceptor," he boasted. "A bit more work on that, and I will be able to interrupt anyone's transmission and substitute my own."

Her arms went tightly against her chest. "Why would you want to do that?"

"It's my ticket to success, Monique. It will be useful at sea—listening to the frequencies, blocking them if I have to. Someone will pay me well for my system. The Athenian perhaps."

"Is it like a surgical bypass so you can escape detection?"

Sal saw her shiver. He wanted to be down there with her, holding her, hugging away her fears. "Why not?" he asked airily. "Salvador Contoni was meant to live free."

She turned away and let the open sea spray her face. "We seem to be taking forever to reach Corfu."

"I thought we had forever. But we'll be there soon."

"I think I'll fly home from Corfu. This is the longest I've ever been away from my sons." The sea breeze snatched at her words. "I need to be there to protect them from the endless taunts against Harland. They never give up—"

"They?"

"The Americans. The French. Interpol. There are those who want to silence you, too, Sal."

The Greek politician? he wondered. Vasille Golemis favored American bases in Greece and cooperation with other countries. Had Gregory or Interpol set Sal up for this rendezvous in Corfu?

He set his yacht on automatic pilot and leaned forward, listening to her as she said, "Harland never trusted you, but you have always in your rough way been a gentleman to me—ever since we met in Monaco." Was there a catch in her voice? Surprise? Caring? "And you've been so kind to my sons."

Is that all I matter to her—someone who has been kind to her children? Not someone who has fallen in love with her.

"Sal, you can't risk going back to Monaco. I won't let you. You mean more to me than that."

"But not enough."

"Not enough," she whispered.

"Then why did you come to Milan to see me?" he asked.

Her thickly lashed eyes misted. "You asked me to come."

"I asked you several times, and you refused."

"And then your madre invited me. Did she mind my sailing to the Greek Islands with you?"

"Would it matter?"

"Yes, I liked her. I want her to like me."

"She does."

"She won't. Not when she learns why I came here." A humorless ripple stuck in her throat. "Salvador, what would you say if I told you the American CIA sent me?"

"I wouldn't believe you. You hate them as much as I do."

"But my sons are quite fond of Drew Gregory."

Drew Gregory. The taste of gall filled his mouth. "Monique, why would you help Gregory?"

"To guarantee the safety of my children."

"Is that what Gregory promised you if you betrayed me?"

"You put it so coldly. But, yes, Gregory was certain you'd go back to Paris with me."

And then they'd arrest me. Her betrayal tore at his gut.

"You're not working for him?" He sensed a fresh hardness that would turn his eyes a steely gray. "Tell me it's not true."

"No, I'm not working for Mr. Gregory. I could never do that. But the CIA promised me a quick release of all of Harland's property if I helped them—if I persuaded you to go back to France with me."

"Did they pay you well?" he asked harshly.

"I didn't take their money. I just wanted to put the past to rest so I could live out my life on my parents' farm with my sons."

She struggled with her windblown hair. "The boys still talk about you, Sal."

"Do they?"

"Mostly about yachting and skiing with you."

"But the high speeds on the mountain slope frightened Anzel. That's why I bought him a soccer ball."

"I know. You were sweet to do that."

She retreated from him, backing away, wrapping her arms across her chest again. "I don't want you to risk going to Monaco or France. Ever. Promise me you won't go—please."

"Why?"

"I don't want the American to find you, Sal."

"If it meant being with you, I'd take the risk."

"And I don't want you to get involved with this Athenian. If you need money—let me bring the *Monique II* to you. You could do charters for me here in the Greek Islands where you'd be safe. Would you like that?"

"Not without a permanent arrangement with you."

Her liquid eyes swam as they met his. "Just the yacht, Sal." More gently, she warned, "Don't anchor in Corfu. You may be walking into danger."

"What does it matter? If I'm losing you, Monique, I have nothing else to lose."

Chapter 1

In silence they approached Corfu from the sea. The sun-drenched island was verdant with cypress trees and gnarled olive groves that rose from the rippling bay to the emerald hills above them. Fleecy clouds and chicory-blue waters added to the quiet enchantment as they drifted along a stretch of sandy beach toward the harbor where lesser yachts than Sal's lay anchored.

As he maneuvered their vessel into the harbor, Monique could not take her eyes off Salvador. She liked watching him. A thin fuzz of blond hair covered the back of his broad hands as he held steady to the wheel and eased the yacht between a multicolored ferry and a bobbing fishing vessel. She wanted to remember him like this at the helm of a ship, standing tall and good-looking with a white polo shirt stretched across his broad chest. The Mediterranean sun had creased his face, leaving it bronzed and weather-ridged around his eyes and mouth.

Once they docked, Sal strolled across the shiny deck to stand beside her. He was a strapping, well-muscled sailor, a rugged man who was both tender and brash, cruel and unforgiving. Long strands of sun-bleached hair brushed his forehead. Unruly like his personality; wild and windblown like his spirit. He leaned against the railing, his hands clasped, his elbow touching hers. Cool gray eyes—with no blueness to them—sought hers.

"Monique, I loved you," he said.

"Past tense?"

"I'm not sure." The old hardness marbled his profile. "I'll ask you once more. If I turned around right now, Monique, would you go back to Milan with me?"

Her pulse quickened. "I can't go back there."

"But you liked my family."

"Very much," she whispered.

The kinder his family had been to her, the more disloyal she felt. Whatever their son had become, the Contonis loved him. They had welcomed Monique into their home as Sal's potential bride. She could still hear Mrs. Contoni's words as they said good-bye. "If you love my son, Monique, don't ever betray him."

But she intended to leave him in Corfu and fly back to France. *Be truthful with yourself,* she scolded. *You wanted to be with him, to sense his need of you, to feel alive and protected with a man at your side. And now you're running away from him.*

"We were happy at dawn this morning," he said.

"I know."

That's when they had left the port of Piraeus and turned away from the roar of the Aegean waves to cruise through the Corinth Canal. Once Sal negotiated the canal, they had sailed along the western coast of Greece, north to this enchanting island.

Now as she finger-combed the hair that ran the length of his muscled arm, her skin prickled at the thought of never seeing him again. "I'll miss you," she admitted.

"Then don't go away."

"I must. It's best for both of us."

In the stillness that followed, they searched the faces on the dock—tourists and islanders in short pants and white shirts, giggling girls in sun hats, boys on bicycles, lovers arm in arm, families with small children in tow. Only one Corfiot gave them so much as a glance. He was overly dressed for the weather—a summer business suit, a starched dress shirt, a white handkerchief in his pocket, a flat briefcase in his hand.

"That must be my contact, Monique. Vasille Golemis's son."

"Is he to come on board?"

"No."

"Then what are we waiting for, Salvador?"

"For you to make a move? Isn't this where the CIA told you to bring me? 'Lure Salvador Contoni to Corfu, Madame Dupree,'" he mocked, "'and we'll have someone waiting to pick him off.'"

"I never saw that man before."

"Really? Weren't you given the same description? A handsome Greek in his mid-thirties, dressed in a business suit, and carrying an attaché case—with a multi-caliber Astra A-100 inside."

"Don't even think that, Sal. The CIA didn't know I was coming to Corfu. I didn't even know the place existed."

"You disappoint me, Monique. This is paradise to the international jet set. Surely Harland brought you here many times."

"Harland dreaded crowds."

"Or dreaded exposing you to younger men?"

"Both. But even if Corfu had been in my plans, I begged you to turn back to Athens an hour ago." *Because I knew then that I could not betray you. No matter what I promised Gregory,* she thought, *I want to protect you.* "Please believe me, Sal. I want to keep you out of the hands of the French and Americans."

"I want to believe you. But I wanted to marry you, too."

"I won't marry anyone, not until my sons are grown."

"As young as Giles is, that could be another twenty years."

"And with the risks you take, you won't be here then." Surely Salvador's flaunting the law would cut him down before his time, before he could even peak forty. "Go keep your appointment, Sal. I can catch a taxi to the airport from here," she told him.

He turned and faced her. Dark weather lines formed half-moons beneath his wistful eyes. "You really are leaving me."

"I just came for a week, Sal."

"I wanted it to be longer."

He cupped her chin and ran his thumb over her lips. She knew if he took her in his arms and kissed her—as he had been doing all week—this time he would know that she cared as much for him as he did for her. She had not fought his signs of affection; she had invited them, needed them. He made her feel alive again, fulfilled. Her husband's death had left her empty; but Salvador had brought her back from the abyss, back from the shame of Harland's dying, back from the terrible loneliness.

For a whole week she had responded to him, but it hadn't just been for herself or for Sal. She really was here on Drew Gregory's marching orders. "Beguile Salvador Contoni," Gregory had said. "But get him back to Paris so we can arrest him."

"Why would I do that, Mr. Gregory?" she had protested.

"It's the only way my Agency can help you, Mrs. Dupree." Gregory had helped her from the chair. "Do what we ask," he said. "Interpol has already released your yacht. It's yours. But it will be best if you anchor it somewhere other than in Monaco."

"And my Swiss chalet? And the house in Seville?"

"I have a man working on the house in Seville."

That would be Colin Burdock, she thought. The American Intelligence officer who had known Harland—and hated him. Burdock was younger and better-looking than Gregory, and yet at this moment Gregory seemed fixed in her mind's eye. She had looked up into Gregory's stoic face, different somehow these days. His voice kinder. His gaze softer. "Some religious experience," Burdock had told her apologetically. "The old boy went religious on us up on the mountain at Sulzbach."

In Austria? But not on the assignment in which Harland had been killed. Back then, Gregory had seemed totally committed to the CIA, but if Burdock was right, the Agency was vying with God now for Drew Gregory. And winning? She could not be certain.

As he stood to leave that day, she had asked, "What about my condo in Paris—is it still under surveillance? And the bank accounts—still frozen?"

"Give us Sal Contoni, Madame Dupree, and within six months, we guarantee that everything will be cleared. The estate closed. Otherwise," he had warned, "this can drag on in the French courts for years."

"You would like that, wouldn't you, Mr. Gregory?"

"It would be out of my hands. Everything in six months— except the castle in the Pyrenees. That's up to Spain."

"I don't want the castle."

"Not even for your boys?" he asked.

"There are some parts of Harland's life that I want to wipe out of their minds forever. The castle—that miserable mercenary camp—is one of them."

She had not even seen Gregory to the door, but had listened to it close quietly behind him. From the farm window in Isigny, she had watched him strike out over the front lawn to his car. He had stopped abruptly as her sons ran toward him. Even Anzel's face had brightened as Gregory opened his arms to them.

As she remembered the scene, a sudden chill ripped through

Monique's body; the sea breeze at Corfu felt like ice chips against her bare midriff. She didn't dare risk the possibility of Gregory stealing her sons' affection away from her. The CIA was using her. They would use her again, finding a new excuse the next time or possibly even allowing harm to come to her sons.

Gregory, she thought bitterly, *you are no better than Harland. And now I must outsmart all of you—tell lies about seeing Sal again. Keep my possessions if you must, but I will not betray Salvador Contoni. And I will not lose my sons to your Agency, no matter how many promises you make to me.*

She could taste the urgency of fleeing Corfu—of leaving Sal while he still had his freedom. For Sal's sake and for her sons, she must make Corfu the place for their final good-bye.

"Sal," she whispered, "I'll be gone when you get back from your meeting with the man from Athens."

"No, Monique. You will have to go with me. You are my safeguard out of Corfu."

"Don't use me, Sal," she begged.

"How touching coming from you." Wearily he said, "Let me check the cabin, and then we'll go."

"And if I run away while you're gone?"

"I'll find you."

When he came back on deck, she could see the gun holster outlined beneath his jacket. "Why, Sal?" she asked as he slipped a lacy cape over her shoulders.

"It's my insurance policy. I intend to leave Corfu safely." He caressed her hand. "The meeting won't last long. After that, if you still want to leave me, I'll take you to the airport."

Would he? As he helped her step from the yacht, young Golemis walked away. "Sal, he's not even waiting for us."

"Then we'll follow him."

Sal tucked her arm in his and guided her along the winding cobblestone alleyways of the Old Town, stepping to the blaring Greek music. The smells changed with each unfamiliar block— from the tempting sweet fragrance of bread baking in an outdoor oven to the stench of the fish market and from the tantalizing scent of lemon oil and garlic coming from the Venetian tenements to the foul odor of a poor drainage system. As they crossed onto the broader avenues of New Town, the man ahead stopped to haggle with a fishmonger over the price of octopus per kilo. Moments later, he disappeared through the mosaic doors of the Greek Orthodox church, the smelly sack in his hands.

They followed him inside and found him talking to a priest with a long beard as dark as his black cassock. As they stepped toward the pair, the cathedral door opened behind them. Sal went for his revolver and aimed it at the priest.

Unruffled, the priest extended his hand. "Your gun, Mr. Contoni. It is safer to travel on the island without a weapon."

As Sal waved the pistol, Monique cried, "Sal, give it to him. You can't shoot a priest. You'll have us both in trouble."

"A wise suggestion," the priest said, his kind expression magnetic. "Mr. Contoni, Thymous tells me you have an appointment with his family. The Golemis villa is always heavily guarded to ward off vandalism. They want their guests to come unarmed."

Sal backed away, half turning, his gaze fixed on the church gardener and the priest's assistant who blocked his exit.

"Just a precaution, Mr. Contoni. I am a man of peace, but you have quite a reputation." He gripped Sal's arm with surprising strength, wrestled the gun free, emptied the chamber, and slid the gun up the sleeve of his robe. As calmly, the priest said, "You are safe with Thymous."

Thymous's dark eyes mirrored deep pain. "Father Papanikos will return your weapon on your way out of Corfu."

"Without questions?" Sal asked, tight-lipped.

"Without questions. But, Mr. Contoni, you were to come to Corfu alone. Your wife's presence will displease my father."

"I'm Monique Dupree, not Mrs. Contoni!"

"Right now," Sal snapped, "there is no Mrs. Contoni."

Thymous seemed pleased. "Shall we go? My father doesn't like to be kept waiting."

"Your father could have saved time by meeting me in Athens."

"But the problem lies on this island, Mr. Contoni. Besides, we come here to oversee the family olive orchards." He led them toward the back of the church and out a narrow exit to the compact Fiat parked in the rear. "Allow me," he said, offering Monique his hand as she slipped into the backseat.

As Thymous took the coastal curves at full speed, Monique was certain they would crash into the medieval sea wall and spin off into the emerald sea. Twenty minutes outside of town, he snaked his way up the mountain road and passed through the gates of the Golemis Olive Orchard.

The isolation of the spacious whitewashed villa was guaranteed by the cypress trees that surrounded it. One armed guard stood near a fenced cemetery with a single grave, a lonely shrine in the middle of all this wealth. Catching her eye in the rearview mirror, Thymous said, "Alekos is buried there."

Alekos. Monique shuddered. *The problem lies on this island.* Monique stretched her neck for another glimpse of the grave site, hidden now by the winding tree-lined road. Who was Alekos, and how was Salvador tied in with the person lying there?

Thymous parked between two Mercedes Benzes and then led them through the house past a dining table spread with lamb and seafood, eggplant, and zucchini. Sal plucked a slice of goat's cheese and an olive from the salad and popped them into his mouth as they entered the well-lit sitting room.

Thymous's father sat behind a marble-top desk, the solemn face of the cyclist in the portrait on the wall behind him as mute as his own. Vasille Golemis was stocky, his face ashen, his hair and mustache a silvery gray. He made no effort to stand as he asked, "What kept you, Thymous?"

"Your guests were late in arriving."

Sal stepped forward. "My apologies, Mr. Golemis, but I took the liberty of bringing my friend Monique Dupree with me. We can speak freely in front of her."

"And this," Golemis said, pointing to the heavyset woman beside him, "is my wife, Olymbia."

As Monique took Olymbia's chubby hand in her own, she saw the resemblance between Mrs. Golemis and the portrait of the young man on a bicycle with his back to the sea. His thickly pursed lips and the shape of his nose were like his mother's, his drooping eyelids like the father's, his Grecian coloring and his hooded, well-set dark eyes exactly like his brother's. She knew with a mother's intuition that it was his grave they had just passed.

"That's our son Alekos," Vasille said. "He's dead." He turned to Salvador. "Mr. Contoni, I want my son's death avenged."

Sal's eyes narrowed. "That was not the agreement—"

Vasille waved his hand for silence. "Hear me out." He spread several pictures on the desk and thumped each one. "My son was to have ridden in the Tour de France this year, but he was killed in the Austrian mountains a few months ago."

"Alekos's death was an accident," Thymous said.

Golemis ignored him. "This is my son's cycling team. I want you to recognize each one of Alekos's teammates, Mr. Contoni, *especially Ian Kendall.*"

Sal sauntered over to the desk, Monique behind him. "What's so important about Ian Kendall?" Sal asked.

"If it were not for Kendall, my son would be alive." He poked the air toward Thymous. "Thymous wants no part of avenging his brother's death. That's why I need your help, Mr. Contoni."

Thymous's answer was tempered with sadness. "Kendall was Alekos's friend, Papa," he protested.

"What kind of a friend would take my son to that mountain to die? Alekos could have won the Tour de France this year."

Thymous's lips drew together, deepening the cleft in his chin. Monique imagined him weeping at his brother's death, crying even more at being displaced from his father's favor, his importance as the firstborn son fading. What good would the profitable olive orchards do this young man if he felt rejected—the son who had stood by the family business, by his father's side?

"Death is cruel," she said to Thymous's father. "But is it right to seek vengeance and put your family honor on the line?"

"What would you know about death and vengeance?" he asked.

She thought of the grief that Harland's life and death had brought to her and to her sons. "I'm a widow," she said.

She pitied him as he turned back to Sal. "Stop Kendall from winning. He has no right to take my son's place in that race."

"Papa, Alekos had no chance to beat Kendall's splendid riding record. Alekos always rode support for Ian."

Vasille pointed angrily at Thymous again. "Our family always stood by each other—" He groped for words to describe Thymous's betrayal. "And now it's as though both of my sons are dead."

Thymous stood motionless by the verandah door, looking like one of the marble statues that decorated the room. Monique saw the pain in those rich dark eyes, yet his features seemed cut from stone—the strong unbroken lines of his nose. the firm cheekbones, and the square well-chiseled jaw. It was as though his heritage went back in time beyond the Golemis bloodline to the mythical origin of Apollo and Zeus. *And what of Salvador?* she wondered, stealing a glance at him. Both of these men had been born into rich families—both primed to take over the family business. But Salvador was like Poseidon, the god of the sea. She was confident that if Salvador could sail all of the waters of the world, he would consider it nothing less than his right.

Salvador tossed the pictures back on the desk. "This was not our agreement, Mr. Golemis." His thumb pointed back to Thymous. "Ask him. Thymous promised me vengeance in another way—not against some young cyclist I've never heard about."

"I followed my father's instructions."

"Then you carry them out, Thymous, but count me out. I have no intention of killing this Ian Kendall for you."

"Sit down, Mr. Contoni," Vasille demanded. "I don't want Kendall to die. I want him to lose the race."

"Be reasonable, Golemis. If Kendall wins, then claim it as a victory for your son. If he loses—and that's a possibility—then you have accomplished what you want without breaking the law."

Vasille's mouth twitched. "I can't count on him losing." He gripped Sal's wrist and slammed it against the desk. Sal jerked free as Golemis roared, "Do you know who I am, Contoni?"

Sal nursed his wrist. "A member of the Greek Parliament, so why risk yourself politically or ruin your family business?"

"That's why I'm hiring you, Mr. Contoni." He reached into his desk drawer and passed an envelope to Salvador. "We agreed upon $250,000 to a Swiss account." He tapped the envelope. "A deposit receipt for half that amount is in here. The other half will be deposited when the job is finished."

"The terms have changed. Half a million. Everything up front— if I agree to do it." Salvador flicked the deposit receipt in Golemis's face. "The rest in cash now."

"Don't, Sal," Monique begged. "Let's leave."

"He can't, Madame Dupree. I know Mr. Contoni is wanted by Interpol . . . by the French." He snapped his fingers. "One word from me, and he will not leave Corfu except in custody. Only my money and political power can protect him right now."

As he reached for the phone, a dark-haired beauty came into the room carrying more food to the well-laden table. "I'm Zoe," she said as she stepped behind her father and rested her hands on his shoulders. "Let's eat, Papa. I'm sure our guests are hungry."

"Starving," Salvador agreed.

"We'll settle this matter first, Mr. Contoni. I can offer you $350,000. No more."

Golemis unfolded a well-worn cable, his large hands caressing it gently as he passed it to Salvador. "But perhaps this will convince you to help me."

Salvador's brows arched. "A sympathy cable from Drew Gregory. Did Gregory know your son?"

"It seems this Gregory was a tourist in Sulzbach at the time, but why would a tourist trouble himself about my son's death unless he was involved?"

"You tell me," Salvador said.

"According to my lawyers, Mr. Gregory has lived abroad for a number of years—American Intelligence, I suspect."

Monique felt the color drain from her cheeks. "Don't get involved, Sal. Let Mr. Golemis's lawyers handle it."

"Madame Dupree, we did file a wrongful death suit, but my son died in Austria. Since his death, Austria has become a member of the European Union, but now I cannot wait. Kendall rode well in the Italian race—came in second. He has every chance of winning in France when the Tour begins in three or four days."

"In six days, Papa," Zoe corrected. "My father's lawyers are trying to freeze the Kendall assets in England, but Papa will not wait for the wheels of justice to turn. That's why Papa insists that you help us, Mr. Contoni."

Monique felt numb. This whole family was diabolical in its thinking. She put her hand on Sal's arm, but he pulled away and held his hand out to Vasille. "I'll take my money now, Golemis."

Vasille snapped his fingers. "Open the safe, Thymous."

Monique cringed as Thymous swung back his brother's portrait and opened the vault. *You are fools,* she thought. *Salvador will come back someday and rob you.*

Thymous slapped the packet of bills into Sal's hand. "So my father's money has persuaded you to help the Golemis family?"

Sal caressed the money. "Why not?"

No, Monique thought. *I know you too well, Sal. This is not for the Golemis family. You see this as a chance to get even with Drew Gregory. I saw it in your face when you read Gregory's cable. Yes, you will take Golemis's money, but you may not carry out his wishes. You don't care who wins that race. All you want to do is destroy Gregory. Why do you hate him so?*

Sal didn't count it. His eyes remained fixed on Zoe as he took the deposit receipt and shoved it into his money belt along with the cash. He patted the bulge. "For you then, Miss Golemis, I will try to stop this Kendall before he gets to the race."

"No. Papa wants you to wait until Ian wears the yellow jersey. And he will wear it at some stage in the race."

"My daughter is right, Mr. Contoni," Golemis roared. "I want Kendall to taste victory. I want him to suffer. And when he's wearing that jersey—when he thinks he is winning—when he's ready to cross the finish line with arms outstretched, stop him."

"The winner's jersey? Then Ian Kendall is a good rider?"

Zoe masked her pain. "One of the best, Mr. Contoni."

🏺🏺🏺

As they stood to leave the villa, Vasille looked up and smiled. "*Buona notte. Buona fortuna,*" he said. "Take the Fiat. My son will pick it up at the dock later."

"You trust me, Mr. Golemis?" Salvador asked.

"I have friends all over the island."

As they passed the table, Salvador grabbed a plate and stacked it with eggplant and spinach and a heaping portion of Greek salad with its chunks of goat's cheese and tomatoes glistening in olive oil.

"You can't take that china with you," Monique warned.

"Why not? We can leave the dirty dishes in the Fiat."

He forked more lamb and pork for them both and threw a broiled fillet of fish on top. Grinning, he grabbed a carafe of white wine and followed her outside. As they came down the steps, Zoe called, "Mr. Contoni, I must speak with you."

Salvador turned with his mouth full. He liked beautiful women, and Zoe Golemis was exquisite in her tight knee-length

dress. Her wide, dark eyes were thick-lashed and enormous like
Monique's, her even teeth gleaming like the villa walls.

She glanced at Monique as she reached them. "I must speak to
you alone, Mr. Contoni. I only have a few minutes before my
father misses me."

Sal kissed Monique's cheek. "Wait for me in the garden."

As Monique turned the corner, Zoe said, "Salvador, I beg you,
please don't harm young Kendall."

"Has your father changed his mind?"

The same brilliant sun that put sweat beads on Sal's forehead
had put a sheen to the flecks of auburn in Zoe's long dark hair.
Strands of cultured pearls lay against her graceful neck, an emerald in the middle. "Please, Mr. Contoni, you must promise me
that you won't hurt—that you won't kill Ian."

"Your father wants vengeance."

"For an accident? Ian Kendall was my brother's friend. They
rode for the same team. Believed in the same goals."

"It didn't sound that way inside."

"My papa is sick with grieving. But if any real harm comes to
Ian, it will only double my father's grief."

Sal patted his money belt. "I promised your father."

"Do you always keep your word, Mr. Contoni?"

Seldom, he thought. "I'm committed to finding him. Your
father said Kendall just came off the Giro d'Italia; he gave me several addresses." He crammed his mouth full of fish, the boneless
piece that he had intended to give to Monique. "Zoe, I'll try and
warn Kendall off first. Scare him enough, and he will cancel out
of the race."

"Ian won't quit. He likes to win." Sadly, she added, "My brother
rode well, but not as well as Ian—and still they were good friends.
What my father wants you to do is destroy another young man.
What good would that do?"

For one, Sal thought, *it would pain Drew Gregory.* Sal popped
another piece of lamb into his mouth and licked his fingers.

"I don't understand your indifference, Mr. Contoni. Why are
you willing to destroy my brother's friend?"

It is not Kendall I want to destroy, he wanted to tell her. *It is Drew
Gregory. With Gregory gone, I would have a chance with Monique.*

Aloud he said, "If Alekos and Kendall were such good friends, why hasn't Kendall been in touch with your family?"

Her face turned crimson. "He came here to Corfu for Alekos's funeral, but my father ordered him off the property. Thymous and I were so ashamed—but what could we do?"

"Did Kendall really cause your brother's death?"

She looked surprised. "He wasn't anywhere around when Alekos fell off the cliff. Please, if it's more money you want, my brother and I will pay you not to harm Ian."

So she really thinks it was an accident! Sal mused. "And what happens when your father finds out you offered me money?"

"By the time the race is over, maybe some of his pain will be gone. . . . I promised Alekos that I would attend the Tour." She handed Sal a name and address. "This is a hotel near one of the mountain stages in the race. I have a reservation there."

"Does your father know?"

"It would break his heart if he thought I were going, but I often visit friends in France. Maybe I will see Ian there."

"And warn him about me?"

"Unless you agree to my terms."

Sal's charm went into a smile as he tucked the address in his pocket. "I never turn down a pretty lady. Why don't I meet you at that hotel, Zoe, and we can discuss your plans again?"

❦❦❦

As she waited for Salvador, Monique wandered along the flowered trails in the villa gardens where the air was scented with almond and nutmeg, lemon and sweet alyssum. Crocus and delicate violets peeked out from the rockery. Off the path a gardener dug in the soil, his side glance taking in Monique's move toward the tulip beds that formed part of his landscape.

She glanced back after passing him in time to see him lift the trowel and talk to it. A senile gardener? Or was he sending a message to the villa that there was a stranger in the gardens? She increased her pace and climbed the hill through the latticed arbor alive with fragrant wisteria and rambler roses, a glorious red in color. From the comfort of the marbled love seat she took in the stark white villas that lay scattered over the emerald hills and the tranquil sea rippling beyond the sun-baked cliffs.

She stirred as someone crunched over the gravel and came around the marbled bench to face her. "Oh, Thymous, I thought it was the gardener coming to spy on me."

"Andreas is harmless." Thymous's eyes were sad as he took her hand and kissed it. "I thought I would never see you again, but Andreas told me you were up here—alone."

He sat down beside her and stretched his lanky legs. "You don't approve of my father's plans, do you, Madame Dupree? Please forgive him. Everything ended for him when my brother died."

"He has the rest of you."

"We're not enough. You must understand, Monique, Alekos was my father's joy."

"His favorite son? But what about you, Thymous?"

"He has no reason to grieve over me. I have always done what he asked. Always."

"But to plan this revenge. Hasn't the Tour had its share of tragic deaths—including that British rider on Mount Ventoux?" She sighed. "Poor Kendall. Does he have a wife and children?"

"Zoe says there's an American girlfriend. My sister keeps up on things like that ever since Alekos introduced her to Ian."

"They were friends?"

"Good friends once."

"Then your father's plans will crush Zoe."

Thymous sat taller. "I won't let that happen."

"You can't stop Salvador. I know him. For money, he'll carry out your father's wishes—even if it means taking Ian's life."

"Contoni is just afraid of my father's threats."

"Salvador is afraid of no one. There's another problem—"

"I know. I saw Contoni's face fill with hatred when he read Drew Gregory's cable. Papa must have known that Salvador would do anything to get even with Mr. Gregory. . . . What are you doing with a man like that, Madame Dupree?"

"I've always made poor choices," she said softly. *Harland. Salvador. Listening to Gregory. Coming here.*

"Do you love Contoni?" he asked.

She smothered her embarrassment. "I told you. I often make poor choices."

"Madame Dupree, no matter what Salvador Contoni means to you, I won't let him hurt Kendall—or my sister."

"Will you go against your father's wishes?"

"I have to. My father's devotion to a dead son will kill him."

"It will destroy all of you. What can you possibly do?"

His gaze strayed toward the olive orchards. "Nothing will ever bring Alekos back, but I intend to uphold the Golemis name—until my father can remember what we have always stood for."

He broke off a rambler rose from the trellis and handed it to her. "Monique, may I see you again?"

For a second she buried her face in its sweet fragrance. "That's impossible, Thymous. I'm flying back to Paris today."

"With Salvador?"

"No. He's only taking me to the airport."

He leaned closer. "Let me take you. Tomorrow. The next day."

She smelled the rose again. "No, Salvador is a jealous man."

"Then give me your address in Paris."

"I have nothing to write it on."

"I have an excellent memory." At the sound of Zoe's footsteps tapping along the path, he said, "Quick, Monique. Tell me. The others are coming."

"After Paris, I'm going back to my parents' farm in Isigny. The Dupree farm. My sons are waiting for me there."

He showed no surprise. "Will I like them?"

"I don't know," she said, flustered.

Again he lifted her hand to his lips. "We'll be in touch. Soon."

"You can't—"

"I must. Zoe and I will be in France anyway."

Chapter 2

An hour after a light breakfast, Ian Kendall and Basil Millard rode out of Carpentras and the herb-scented hills of southeast France, leaving the rest of the cycling team on the sun-golden beaches of Provence. Ian set the pace. It was in him to ride hard as they left the lush vineyards in the valley and sped toward the peak of the glaring white granite hills.

As they neared the windswept summit of Mount Ventoux, Ian glanced back. Basil struggled behind him, his bicycle wobbling erratically, his face the twisted mask of an exhausted rider. "Just a few more kilometers," Ian called.

He noted Millard's jaw sagging as he gulped for oxygen in the mountain-thin air, his miniature Minolta bobbing against his breastbone. One false move on the hairpin curves, and either of them could plunge over the cliff into the deep gorge. Millard pedaled doggedly, as if they were actually in a race and he still had the chance to come in second. They rode alone with no cheering fans lining the road to deaden the pain of the climb.

In spite of the leg spasms, Ian forced himself to keep on pedaling. A kilometer from the crest he braked and lowered his bike to the ground. The scorching sun burned his bare arms as he walked to the marbled memorial with the silhouette of Tom Simpson engraved on the granite. Thirty years before Britain's cycling hero had struggled for a place in Tour history. Ian envisioned Simpson with his features contorted, his heart hammering, his jersey soaked with sweat. Fans had pushed his bike, trying to help him. Twice he fell. "Put me back on my bike," Simpson had begged. Moments later, a mere kilometer from the finish line, he collapsed and died.

Ian wiped his brow. It was hot—95 degrees—but not as hot as that day when Simpson rode this mountain in 110-degree heat. Ever since, the wind had roared around the granite slab; even now the dry winds chafed Ian's cheeks. Out of respect, he removed his helmet and pulled some wilted flowers from his jersey and laid them on the rock.

"You had to be crazy, Ian, wanting to come up here to this barren ash heap," Millard said. "Ventoux isn't even on the schedule for this year's Tour. Why did you come?"

Ian turned. He wanted to tell Millard about the threat taped inside his helmet—wanted to admit that a note delivered to his hotel room in Carpentras had lured him up the mountain. *Simpson never made it to the summit. Neither will you.*

He wet his lips. "I came here for Alekos, but you didn't have to come with me, Basil."

Millard sat on his saddle, one foot braced on the white gravel, his chest heaving. He was a solidly built young man from Birmingham, England—fair-skinned and blue-eyed behind those dark glasses. A sweaty mustache coated his upper lip. "You heard Coach Skobla this morning. No one was to go off on his own."

"Alekos and I came here together once. He told me that he hoped they'd put up a memorial like this for him one day."

"He always had weird ideas about missing the summit."

"Like Tom Simpson. It gets to me that Simpson didn't make it to the top."

"Ian, I think you respected him more than I did. And you aren't even British."

"Part of me is," Ian defended. "England is my grandfather's country. My dad was born there, too—in the Cotswolds." He gave a wry grin. "I think Simpson was one of the cycling greats."

Basil considered. "He would have been if he had lived longer."

"That's what I thought about Alekos."

"Thinking about them won't help you win the Tour, Ian."

"I'll shake it before the race begins. We've got five days."

"Good." Millard lifted his camera to his eyes and squinted. "Strike a pose at the rock, Ian. I'll catch this for posterity."

"Make it quick. We've got company."

Ian nodded toward a dark blue van disgorging its twelve passengers into the blistering sun. As the tourists ambled over to the monument, Ian stepped back to give them room. One man circled around the memorial. He was fortyish, as snow-blond as Millard, an acrid expression on his face as he glanced their way.

Ian picked up his bike. "We'd better go. Coach Skobla is catching a domestic flight out of Avignon in the morning. I can't miss that. I'm hooking a ride to London with him."

"When you call Chase Evans," said Millard, "tell her my wife will make room for her in the hotels along the Tour route."

"I will—if those bomb threats haven't scared her off."

Even behind the dark glasses, Ian saw surprise in Millard's eyes. "Don't take those seriously, Ian," he said. "Threats of sabotage are part of our history. Why, the first time I rode in the Tour, Basque terrorists threatened to bomb the mountain stages in the Pyrenees. The gendarmerie stopped that one."

Ian squeezed his arm. "If we ever need a new team leader, you're my choice. You've never ridden to your full potential."

"You know I'm a sprinter, Ian. I fade out in the mountains."

"You hung in there this morning."

"Better than I expected. Maybe something will inspire me, and I'll be King of the Mountains someday. My wife thinks I'd look good in the polka dot jersey." He shrugged. "But it doesn't work that way. You're the team leader. We ride *domestique* for you."

As the tour van rumbled up the road toward the summit, Ian walked his bike around the memorial, Millard close behind him. A chalk message had been scrawled on the back of the granite slab: *You will never make it to the summit, Kendall.*

Ian's flesh prickled. He grabbed for the handlebars and turned the wheel sharply as Basil stammered, "What the—? Who?"

"Maybe one of your Basque terrorists," Ian said, his tongue thick in his mouth. His gaze strayed toward the blue van already at the summit and turning around. The sweat on his neck turned cold. He sprang on his bike. "Let's make skid marks, Basil."

They descended the mountain, Ian never braking as they sped toward the safety of Carpentras. Behind them, he heard the grinding engine of the van closing the distance between them, and he pedaled faster.

❦❦❦

By the time Ian reached the lush English countryside two days later, the expectation of seeing Chase Evans neutralized the fears that had stirred at Mount Ventoux. As he turned off the motorway and bumped over the rocky, winding road toward the Eagle's Nest, he felt rhapsodic, merry as a cricket. He started whistling one of his grandmother's old favorites, "Got a Date with an Angel."

That's you, Chase Evans, he thought.

The Eagle's Nest lay upcountry, nestled in a sleepy valley north of Oxford, surrounded by shade trees and bushes of flaming bougainvillea that climbed the south wall. Ian broke the tranquillity as he roared into the parking lot in his grandfather's Rolls Royce. The powerful wheels spun against the gravel as he squealed to a stop beside Chase's rented Renault. He hit the ground running, burst through the lobby door, and struck palms with the old man with red-rimmed eyelids. "Give me five, Frank," he said.

For a second the trembling fingers locked with Ian's. Then Ian was off again. Ignoring the Quiet Please sign, he sprinted by a couple of wheelchairs and rounded the corridor on the double, slowing to a subdued walk in front of the nurse's station. "I'm here to see Beatrice Thorpe," he announced.

"You're back again! How nice, but Mrs. Thorpe has company—that young woman from America."

Thanks, nurse. That's what I wanted to hear, he thought.

He had spent the morning tracking Chase down and, dismayed, had even called her home in Long Island, New York. He counted on the maid answering the line, but it had been Chase's mother.

"Nola Evans," she had said sleepily, a middle of the night worry in her voice.

He had forgotten the time change between countries and considered hanging up, but then mumbled, "I'm looking for Chase."

"So are we," she laughed. "We're looking for her to come home soon."

"She doesn't plan that until late August."

"If you knew that, young man, why did you call Long Island?"

"I just thought you'd know where she is now. You see, I'm only in London a few hours, and then I'm flying back to France."

"Oh. Perhaps if you stayed in one place, she'd find you."

"Chase doesn't know I'm looking for her." He tried to picture the mother that Chase had described, a soft-spoken woman with a happy smile, someone with boundless energy bouncing between golfing with the girls and gardening for pleasure. He had a feeling that those blue-gray eyes could see him over the phone wire. "My name's Ian Kendall, ma'am. Maybe Chase mentioned me."

Her pause was significant enough to put sweat in his palms before she admitted, "I recognize the name." The midnight worry had crept back into her voice. "You must be the cyclist?"

It had sounded like an accusation. *I don't measure up,* he thought. "Sorry to have bothered you, Mrs. Evans."

"If you get in touch with Chase, tell her to call collect."

"I'll do that."

"And, Ian, Chase stays with the Nigel Hamptons in Oxford."

"She wasn't there."

"Well, she has a friend at the Eagle's Nest. Try there."

He had smiled into the phone. *Beatrice Thorpe.* Why hadn't he thought of that himself? "I'll try there next."

"I wouldn't suggest waking anyone up," she warned.

Right now, as he slid to a stop in front of Beatrice's room, he couldn't remember if he had even thanked Nola Evans, so anxious was he to borrow his grandfather's car and drive to the Eagle's Nest. He pocketed his Gainsborough cycling cap and popped in a breath mint before doing a quick self-inspection. He rubbed his freshly shaved chin. Finger-combed his thick hair. Straightened the collar of his polo shirt. Did a spit polish to the toes of his shoes. "Good luck, old boy," he said to himself.

He pushed the door open. Bea and Chase sat facing the window, Bea's cane and knitting needles on the table beside them. He stole across the room. "Guess who?" he said, covering Chase's eyes.

Her laugh came quick and breezy. "My cyclist in shining armor. I saw your reflection in the windowpane."

He pulled her to her feet, spun her around, and drew her into his arms. He kissed her soundly, his mouth lingering on her yielding lips. As he released her, he said, "I've missed you. I called your folks at two in the morning trying to find you."

Her wide brown eyes danced. "You didn't. If you rallied my dad from his sleep, he'll never forgive you."

"Your mom answered. You're to call her collect." He touched her cheek where the soft skin had turned a copper tan from the sun. "Have you told your parents about us yet?"

Dark lashes flickered. "I rarely write letters."

"Ian, is that you?" a gravelly voice demanded.

In the excitement, he had forgotten Beatrice. He kissed the top of her silvery hair and then knelt beside her. She was wearing her favorite royal-blue blouse and long beige skirt, her laced shoes poking out beneath the lap robe. He tilted her sagging chin toward him until he was level with those marvelous innocent blue eyes. "Where's the hat, sweetheart?"

She pointed to the derby monstrosity on the table.

"Were you out for tea?" he asked.

"We've been in the gardens looking for you."

"I've been with the cycling team. Hooked a ride to London with the coach. But I fly back to France tonight."

"So soon?" *Was that disappointment in Chase's voice?*

She had captured his heart, this attractive five-foot-five beauty, long-legged and well-figured. He outplayed her in tennis, but he found himself tongue-tied when he considered the degrees behind her name. Ian had never cared about a girl before, not like this one who seemed so intelligent and sure of herself. She was out of his league politically, too, but the whole time he raced the Giro d'Italia in the Italian Alps—and the whole preparation period for the French Tour—he couldn't get Chase out of his thoughts. "Chase," he said, "I had to see you. You didn't answer my letters."

"You didn't give me a permanent address."

She tucked a strand of hair behind her ear, hair the color of chestnuts. Unexpectedly he remembered his grandmother's last Christmas and her humming the song about chestnuts on an open fire. Huskily, he said, "Well, Chase, answer my letter now."

"About the weather?" she asked coyly.

"No."

"Oh—my research project is coming along just fine."

He checked his aggravation. "I don't remember asking you about your studies."

"Really?"

"Don't tease, Chase. I asked you to marry me."

"Oh, that."

"Well, what did you decide?"

"Ian, I can't marry you. I barely know you."

"It doesn't take all that much time to decide you love someone." He wanted to remind her that she had researched the Kendall history so thoroughly for her Ph.D. that she knew all of the family secrets. "The Kendalls aren't a bad lot," he said.

She blushed on that one. "But I need more time to know you."

"Why? You've met my blue-blooded grandfather Uriah. And you know enough about my grandmother to know that I look like her. That's my background." With a grin, he flexed his muscles. "You've seen me riding my cycle. That's my career."

"But I don't know you, Ian."

"What do you want to know?"

"Everything."

He rattled off his birth date, driver's license number, and his addresses in Belgium and Maryland. He threw in his physical statistics. "I'm five-foot-eleven, give or take a fraction, and 155 pounds, give or take an ounce. And I love skiing, tennis, and cycling—the Tours and world championships mostly."

"Don't forget gardening," Beatrice said. "You planted the bougainvillea here at the Eagle's Nest."

His grin turned crooked. "My grandmother taught me about lilacs and roses when I was a kid. Guess I never outgrew them. Sounds out of character, doesn't it?"

"No," Chase whispered. "It—it sounds nice."

They were both embarrassed. He'd be stuck with the yard work if they married. "I asked you something else."

"I told you. I'm going back to New York at the end of August."

"That leaves July. Come to the Tour with me. I need you."

"Ian, you wouldn't even see me in the crowd. I'd be a blur as you sped by. And I won't go alone."

"Some of the wives and girlfriends are going."

"I thought Gainsborough forbids distractions at the race."

"Jon sponsors the team—pays our salaries, but he doesn't own our personal lives." *Not yet.* "Basil Millard's wife and daughter will be there. And Robbie's wife."

"Standing in the crowd in the sweltering heat?"

"Or the rain. They've made reservations in some of the hotels along the way." He was hit with uncertainty as he thought of Marcus Nash, one of the last-minute replacements on the team. A dark choice. "Marcus Nash's fiancée will be there, too."

"You don't sound pleased."

"He replaced my friend Alekos. Nash is not a team player. But I'm sure the ladies will make room for you."

"I like traveling first class, Ian, with a bed to myself."

"Come down to where the rest of us live, Chase. I've holed up in some of the worst hotels in the world on the Tours. You sacrifice when you have to and you survive."

"Anything for the glory of a race?"

"It's my job."

"Researching is mine. My father would have my neck, to say nothing about wanting his credit cards back if I took off for a three-week marathon."

"Take me," Beatrice said. "I don't mind third-rate hotels."

He swooped her out of her wheelchair. "That's my girl, Bea, but the mountain air in the Alps would snatch your breath away."

And you're fighting for every breath now. He cradled her against his chest and carried her to the bed. "Nap time, Bea."

"I'd like to go in Olivia's place," Bea said wistfully. "She promised you she'd be there."

Yes. He remembered sitting across from his grandmother at the Fox Hunt Restaurant in London. "Ian, win the Tour de France for me someday," she had told him.

"Grams, will you be there?" he had asked.

"Just try and stop me." Death had stopped her.

Bea's eyes glazed with longing. "Someone has to be there to protect you. I know about the bomb threats against the race."

"I'll be all right," he said gently. He sent Chase a warning scowl. "Have you been worrying Bea about those rumors?"

The beginnings of a frown formed on Chase's brow. "Bea brought them up. How serious are they, Ian?"

He shrugged. "Every race has its crackpots."

But this was the first race where he had been personally threatened. He carried the Mt. Ventoux chalked message in his mind and another written warning in his pocket. *Kendall, if you compete in the Tour de France, you risk your own safety.*

He had hitched a ride home from Avignon with Coach Skobla, determined to discuss these threats with Drew Gregory or Dudley Perkins at MI5; in the safety of his grandfather's cottage in the Cotswolds, he had changed his mind. Why risk being pulled out of the race when he was prepared to give winning his best shot?

Her frown deepened. "Why don't you pull out of the race?"

"We'll be safe. The Tour has its own police force."

"So does New York City," she said.

"The worst that can happen to me is a flat tire or oxygen deficit."

"What about broken bones if you crash in the mountains?"

Had he mentioned his dreams in his letters? The pileup on the mountain curve and his grandmother in white waving to him? No, he was certain that he hadn't bothered Chase with that ridiculous dream—that recurrent nightmare.

"Ian, you lost a rider a couple of years ago, didn't you?"

She said it so casually, but she was talking about a man he had ridden with. He couldn't even choke out the name Fabio, so he said, "We've lost more than one man over the years."

"You knew him," she guessed. "Oh, Ian, I'm sorry."

He licked his upper lip. "Fabio was a friend. I speak enough Italian so we got on well." Once started, Ian was able to say, "He was an Olympic road race champion."

"A gold medalist, the papers said."

"Yes. I met him at the Tour of Switzerland. He was a good rider. Came in second." His voice caught. "Fabio had everything to live for—a wife and baby, a good career ahead—"

Softly Chase asked, "Then why did he come speeding down a mountainside without a helmet?"

"They aren't mandatory in European races. No one dwells on crashing. It's one of the risks we take when we ride in the mountains. Fabio knew it. I know it—"

Bea fidgeted with the button on her sleeve as she stared up at Chase. "Olivia was going to be at the race for Ian. Won't you go in her place?"

"Ian, is that why you asked me to go—in your grandmother's place?"

"I asked you because I want you there." He brushed the thin strands of hair back from Bea's wrinkled face and pulled up the side rail. The image of his grandmother dressed in white and waving at him came back forcibly. "Chase, I'd like to tell the team that my girl is there, cheering me from the sidelines."

"I'm not your girl," she reminded him.

"Then I'll tell them you're my friend."

"That's all we can be—just friends. Nothing more." Without thinking she said, "And I won't be your live-in girlfriend."

He shrugged. "All right. We'll save all that for marriage."

❦❦❦

A hot flush turned Chase's cheeks scarlet. She picked up a ball of yarn and tossed it. As Ian ducked, it fell to the floor and unraveled beneath the bed.

Bea rattled her side rails. "Now you pick that up. That was the beginnings of my next lap robe."

They both crouched down, and as Chase lunged for the yarn, Ian's hand came down on hers. "Chase, it won't be easy for me, but I'm willing to wait for you until marriage."

Another hot flush warmed her face as his sea-blue eyes watched her. "Is that what you tell all your girls?" she asked.

"There was never a girl like you before."

"And you're not like the boys back on Long Island," she admitted. Ian would never court her just to be a weekend guest on her father's yacht or a dinner guest at the family mansion.

Ian's hand tightened possessively. "Apparently not. Or you wouldn't leave them behind and travel to Europe so frequently."

Thanks to my grandmother's generosity and my father's credit cards, she thought. What would Ian say if she told him she was part of the New York Bartholomew-Evans clan, her family as well off as the Kennedys of Massachusetts? In her cramped position on the floor, she was convinced that she had put permanent dents in her kneecaps. "Ian, I have plans, and marriage isn't one of them."

"What are you going to do twenty years from now? Sit alone by the fireside with a row of framed sheepskins on the wall?"

"At least I won't be like Mom. Dad gives her the dregs of his time— a minute here, a minute there. That's all the time he can spare."

"Does he love her?"

Their eyes held. "That's why Mother puts up with his hours."

As the side rails rattled above them, Ian released her hand and scooped up the yarn. They stood again on opposite sides of the bed as Bea's gnarled fingers wrapped around the ball of yarn.

"I have to go, Bea," he said. "I have a dinner date in London before I fly out of Heathrow. Stay well, sweetheart."

He glanced across the bed at Chase, and with a shrug of his shoulders and a carefree wink, he said, "See you."

"Be careful. Stay safe, Ian."

The catch in her voice startled her. She imagined that her father had been much like Ian in his youth. Charming and cocky, stubborn and defiant. Her father had gone off to Vietnam in the early years of that conflict, a brash marine convinced that if every other man in the unit died, he wouldn't. That was like Ian—if every man on the team crashed on the riding circuit, he wouldn't. She asked lightly, "By any chance, Ian, are you having dinner at the Fox Hunt with Miriam and Drew Gregory?"

"How did you guess?"

"Miriam called this morning and insisted that I join them."

"Tonight—you're driving into London?"

"As soon as you leave the parking lot."

"Drive down with me."

She started to say no, and then told him, "I'd have to change first."

"Go on then. Pretty yourself up for the drive."

As she slipped into a dinner dress and heels, she knew that the part of Ian that she wanted to know was locked inside him in secret compartments. Come this far, no further. Ian would not admit to his fears, would never admit to defeat. An enigma. Like her father, Ian was a self-made man who faced life on his own terms. He had tossed aside the cushioned life that was his and had made his own way into the professional world of cycling. Ian seldom mentioned his father, rarely acknowledged his brother Grover, but he spoke highly of his grandparents and of his teammates who rode support for him.

But would she ever understand his need for winning?

Moments later as they drove away from the Eagle's Nest, Ian's eyes searched hers. His boy-next-door quality blurred as she pictured his pensive face grease-streaked as he repaired his cycle. And then she imagined Ian's sweaty face as he broke away from

the rest of the riders to descend a mountain curve without braking—risking his safety and life. Tears stung the back of her eyes as
she tried to visualize him crossing the finish line in Paris with his
arms held high and the fans screaming. Ian's world was full, centered as it was on international cycling, reporters, and fans.
Would there ever be room in that world of his for her?

❁❁❁

Long Island, New York. After the phone call from Ian Kendall in
London, Nola Evans turned to her husband. "That was Chase's
young man in England. He's trying to locate her."

Seymour poked his king-sized pillow and glared at the alarm
clock in the darkness. "At 2 A.M. in the morning?"

"I don't think Mr. Kendall considered the time change when he
dialed us. But he sounded nice, Seymour."

"Nothing sounds nice at this hour."

"You're just an old grump, dear." She cradled the handset. "I'm
going to have some hot milk. Care to join me?"

"Come to bed, Nola. We'll talk about Kendall's phone call in the
morning."

"I'm thinking about it now. You did things like that when you
were dating me."

"I don't remember."

"Dear, you don't remember anything but business statistics
and how to land the best contracts in Washington. But I do. I think
about the old days a lot lately." She slipped into her satin robe and
tightened the sash. "You called me from Honolulu on your way
home from Vietnam. At three in the morning."

"Did I? Really? I must have been crazy."

"No, you were in love with me then and not with your job. You
asked me to marry you as soon as you reached San Francisco."

"Then why didn't you?"

She sat beside him. "My parents tore up my plane ticket."

"That was a long time ago, Nola."

"Thirty years—but it seems like yesterday."

"It would be nice to start over again with you, Nola."

In three hours he would be the meticulous businessman again,
driven by work and power, this moment of vulnerability gone.

She liked him best now with his silver-fox hair uncombed, his dark brown eyes watching her, his attention all hers.

"Let's go away together this weekend," he suggested.

"I'd like that." But she knew it would never happen. The job would demand his time. She offered him the chance to retrieve his offer. "Seymour, maybe we should stay home in case Chase calls."

She sensed him smiling in the darkness. "Don't tell me Chase is serious about this idiot who calls at two in the morning?"

She leaned down and kissed him. "I married the idiot who called at three."

He held her cupped hand against his bristly cheek. "I've been grateful ever since."

"Then why don't you tell me more often?"

"I'll try, Nola." He kissed her palm. "Is Kendall the young man from Oxford? The brainy one?"

No, that was another young man. Forgotten now, she thought. "Kendall is the American hopeful in this year's Tour de France."

"The cyclist? What is that girl of ours up to this time?"

"I don't know. At least she isn't in Prague."

"That's true, but she could have found herself a long-haired college professor in Prague with six degrees behind his name."

"Like Nigel Hampton at Oxford?"

"No," he grumbled. "Just my luck she'd find a protest marcher. Some whippersnapper who is politically minded, antigovernment, anti-nine-to-five hours, and definitely antiestablishment."

She drew back. "You make Chase out to be such a rebel."

"Isn't that what you like about her? She's her own person."

Nola's lips tightened. "That's why I think she might marry this cyclist. She's spent her whole life doing the unexpected."

"I expect Chase to finish her doctorate. I've invested enough money in it. Come to bed, Nola. Don't worry about her."

"You do. All the time."

"I worry about her not having a full-time job. I certainly don't worry about her marrying. She's too busy to settle down."

"She's busy trying to win your approval—trying to find some hard-working man just like you to marry."

"Like me? Why would she want to do that?"

"I wish I knew. It would only make her unhappy."

Exhaustion sapped him. He stretched on his back in the mid-

dle of their king-size bed. As he drifted toward sleep, his words
grew muffled. "In her letter . . . she told us Kendall . . . was the last
. . . person on earth she'd marry."

"That's why I'm afraid she's thinking about it."

Chase had used three pages in her letter to describe Ian
Kendall. "He's spent his whole life racing," she had written, "and
he's chalked up a number of good wins: second place in the Giro
d'Italia, third in the Vuelta d'Espana." On the last page, Chase had
underlined every word. "Don't worry, Mother. We're just friends.
I'd never marry a man like him. I find him too arrogant. Cocky.
Impulsive. But he's intelligent and handsome, too."

All of the things Nola had once said about Seymour.

"Seymour. Don't go to sleep on me. Help me figure this out."

"Honey, don't fret about Chase getting married. Not now."

"But I want her to marry the right person. She inherits a lot of
money when she turns twenty-five. Seymour . . . what if Ian is a
gold digger?"

He opened his eyes, but they drooped as he muttered, "Kendall
has money of his own—big contract with Gainsborough. . . . I had
him checked out after Chase's last letter."

"You didn't! She'll be furious. We'll have to apologize."

"I'll have . . . my secretary . . . tend to it . . . in the morning." His
slurred words merged into a snore.

She shook him. "Seymour, you'll be gone all day. There'll be no
chance to talk to you. And it's not like Chase to talk so much about
some young man who doesn't have a college degree."

Seymour answered with a volcanic snort as he drifted into
deeper sleep. Nola watched him in the moonlit darkness. In less
than three hours he'd be off to work. She wouldn't see him again
until dinner at seven. That was never the hour to bring up the
children, unless they were talking about Tad and his latest business deal or Adele and the marvelous match she had made when
she married a New York attorney. But dear Chase, as determined
as Seymour himself, always made risky dinner conversation.

Nola grabbed the *Europe Magazine* from the bedside table and
went down the spiral stairs to the spacious kitchen. Seymour had
underlined several things in the magazine: the continuing IRA
struggle, the latest on the young president in Poland, the pros and
cons of the nuclear trade agreements in the European Union, and

the EU's single currency. One small paragraph on the Tour de France had been double-scored: "Ignoring a series of bomb threats, the international cycling race will go on as scheduled."

Even as Nola poured milk in the sauce pan and turned the heat high, she couldn't get Ian Kendall out of her mind. She couldn't build an image of him either, except that he was handsome and tall. But was this handsome young man in danger? Chase's letter had been filled with his adventures—in England or Belgium one moment, in France the next. It seemed to Nola that Kendall's whole life was spent living out of a suitcase, expending his energy in a career that would be over by the time he was thirty-five. What kind of life could he offer her daughter?

Nola's heated milk boiled over. The fumes filled the room. She drank the scalded milk anyway, brooding over her grown children and wishing them to be little again so she could hold and comfort them. The last place in the world Nola wanted her youngest daughter to live was in Europe, an ocean away from them. She put her head down on the table and wept. Wept for the three o'clock call from Seymour so long ago when they still had their whole lives in front of them. Wept for the call moments ago from the young man in London who would have a rocky time pursuing Chase—that dreamy, idealistic daughter who wouldn't even recognize love if it knocked on her door.

Chapter 3

The countryside flew by as Ian did double time to London with his foot to the floorboard and his grandfather's fabulous Rolls Royce tested to the limit. Chase turned toward Ian and liked what she saw—a well-chiseled profile from the broad forehead to the firm set of his jaw and an athletic body crowned with sandy-red hair that brushed the headliner. "Slow down," she cautioned. "Your granddad won't thank us for wrecking his car."

He eased off for a second, and then his foot shoved hard against the gas pedal again, his freckled hands strong on the wheel. "I'm trying to outrun the man behind us."

She looked back, her hair sweeping against one cheek. "The Renault? Isn't he just part of the London traffic?"

"He's stayed with us ever since we hit the motorway."

"Why would he follow us?"

His jaw tightened. "I could pull over and ask him."

She picked up the newspaper on the seat between them and thumped the article on bomb threats against the American riders. "Maybe he has something to do with this."

"Rumors only. Besides, I ride with a British team."

"That doesn't change your American birth certificate. Bomb threats can't be laughed off. Why don't they cancel the race?"

His gaze slid back to the sideview mirror. "The French don't scare easily. Neither do I. I've spent too long preparing for the Tour to stay home on some bomb scare." He freed a hand from the wheel and touched her cheek, his eyes as blue as the summer sky on Long Island. "Let's talk about us. I want you at the race."

"You flatter me. Won't your family be there?"

"Dad and Grover always have an excuse, and my grandfather will wait out the race in Paris. That's why I want you there."

She glanced at the paper. "Terrorism scares me. Why doesn't the Tour go through England? I would go then."

"We did my first year on the Tour—straight from Calais to the Eurotunnel."

"You rode through the Chunnel on bikes?"

A smile tugged at his mouth. "We boarded trains for that. The Englishman Chris Boardman wanted to wear the yellow jersey into England, but it didn't work out that way."

"I'm sorry for him."

"He did better than I did. I dropped out in the mountains with a lung infection." His blue eyes were on her again. "The race starts in Holland this year and goes into Belgium close to where I live seven months of the year. Chase, will you come?"

"I'll think about it."

"I'll ask Basil's wife to make room for you. Just in case."

"For three weeks? Ian, I'm in Europe on a study program."

"*Et alors?*"

"So what? It's my whole life."

"Why don't you just marry me and get your degree in Belgium? You speak French and German as well as I do."

That idea was one of those crazy, wonderful things that her grandmother would have applauded. Still she argued, "You would grow tired of my academic world."

He sped past a line of cars, putting the stranger farther behind them. "I have two years' college credit in horticulture. But," he said, his jaw set, "professional cycling is my life for ten more years. After that, I'm going into the flower business."

With me or without me, she thought. Weeks ago he had placed well in the Giro d'Italia. Within days of the spin down the Champs Elysees, he'd be off for a one-day race in Belgium. After that, to one of the classics in Spain or Switzerland. "Ian, why punish your body for ten more years just for the glory of winning?"

"It's not just for that moment on the podium. When I finish my racing career, I want to be proud of the records I set."

She felt a tug of sadness for him. The end of Ian's cycling career at thirty or thirty-five would be like the autumn of his life. He'd be burned out. All this racing for autumn glory.

"Ian, the two of us—it wouldn't work. My roots are in New York, and yours are wherever you hang your helmet. If you kept on winning races, I'd have to share you with your fans."

"But I'd always come home to you." Ian's face clouded. "It's okay, Chase. Go back to Columbia and finish your degree. Just promise me you'll think about it while you're there."

She laughed and teased, "I'll go you one better. If you win the Tour de France for me, I'll reconsider your proposal."

"And I'll hold you to that promise."

As they neared London, she steeled herself against a sudden nameless darkness. She could never be content living Ian's simple lifestyle. She liked people, but not pressing crowds; the latest fashions, not sweat togs; concerts and skiing, not dusty biking trails. She would grow envious of watching him sign autographs for his fans while she stared blankly at her Ph.D. shingle.

Even if Ian wanted to take a risk, she didn't. It would be best if she flew back to New York before the Tour began. But would she be able to forget Ian Kendall so easily? Her thoughts flashed back to the Eagle's Nest and his lips on hers. Why was she suddenly remembering that tender, lingering kiss?

🌑🌑🌑

In the American embassy in London, Drew Gregory stood in the doorway to his secretary's office, angrily gripping a steaming cup of cappuccino. Lennie glared back, struggling to focus on him out of her first pair of contact lenses. "Mr. Gregory, I most certainly did not leave a file on my desk."

The denial was worse than the act. He had found the folder there himself at 7:00 P.M. last evening. The hour—the exact moment of discovery—was as clear in his thinking as it had been last night when he wrestled the cuff of his shirt to note the time.

"Lennie, it was the Bosnia-Moscow report. I put it back in the locked cabinet myself. I covered for you."

Beneath the heavy makeup that she wore these days, he saw

her skin visibly blanch. Her voice tightened. "You know I never take chances with security, Mr. Gregory."

To keep his anger in check, he took a quick gulp of his coffee and sputtered at the sugary taste. "Lennie," he barked, "you know I like my coffee black."

"Oh, Mr. Gregory," she apologized, "Radburn likes cream and three sugar cubes. I guess I got mixed up this morning."

Radburn Parker, Lennie's new boyfriend. Her first beau as far as Drew knew. He could deal with the old Lennie; she didn't make mistakes. Lennie had always been a perfectionist, a prim and proper old maid in her dowdy clothes and rimless spectacles. Her work output had been flawless, and her manners and speech precise, British to the core. Drew had come back from his trip to Prague to find a fiftyish woman trying to look thirty-five with her new hairstyle and shorter skirt length. Only Lennie's sensible laced shoes still protruded from under the desk.

She appeared ready to rescue the offending cup, but he waved her back to her chair. "I'll have coffee with Vic Wilson. We have a nine o'clock meeting."

She frowned and ran her finger down his daily schedule. "I don't see anything listed here, Mr. Gregory. Not at nine."

He had slipped up there. The meeting was confidential. He cleared his throat, ready to confront her again with the security risk when the phone rang. She answered and covering the mouthpiece whispered, "It's the station-chief from Paris."

Troy Carwell. "I'll take it in my office." *And you'll stay on the line listening, the way you've been doing lately.* He kicked the door shut and raced to his desk. As he balanced the handset in the crook of his neck, he scrawled a memo on the scratch pad. It was time to ask for a new red phone, a line that even Lennie could not access. "Troy, it's Gregory."

"You took long enough," Carwell growled.

"I was in Lennie's room. Any word on Salvador Contoni?"

"Monique Dupree flew into Paris a few hours ago. Alone."

"Then she didn't find Contoni?"

"Find him? She just spent seven days with him, the last two cruising the Greek Islands on his yacht. She left him in Corfu."

"The island of Corfu," Drew mused, "and not in Milan?"

"That's the question mark. Everything went smoothly until their meeting with Vasille Golemis at his private villa."

Drew's spine stiffened. "Alekos Golemis's father?"

"The same. He's a member of the Parliament."

Golemis. The name tore at Drew's memory and quickly meshed with the senseless death of a young cyclist on the mountain near Sulzbach—a lad with strong Grecian features and eyes so dark they were almost black. He had been Ian Kendall's friend. The last time Drew saw Alekos, he was lying on a narrow metal table, his youthful body lifeless, those brilliant dark eyes closed. Dead. Murdered by a Russian agent. "Troy, why would Golemis meet with a man like Salvador Contoni?"

"We may know soon. Our agent shot pictures of their time together, including the Golemis villa. One agent nosing around was safer than alerting Greek Intelligence."

"So Monique couldn't persuade Contoni to come back?"

"We haven't heard from her, but the agent reports a rather cozy affair. It was your idea to use her, Drew. Never thought it would work. We got suckered in." Troy smacked his lips. "She took a taxi from Charles de Gaulle straight to her apartment on the Seine. Picked up her Renault and headed for Isigny."

"Her boys are there. Sorry, Troy. Thought she'd cooperate."

"Right now, there are more important things to deal with. Glenn Fairway—that old stickler for on-time appointments—will fill you in. How are things at the embassy?"

Drew thought of Lennie on the line, listening. "More priority files are missing. And, Troy, my secretary has become the scuttlebutt of the London embassy."

"Don't tell me your Miss Efficiency-plus has a beau?"

"Haven't met him yet, but he's turned my office life upside down." There was a faint click in Drew's ear. He switched to the scrambled line. "That was Lennie tuning out. She's one of the problems since I came back. Yesterday she was so anxious to meet Parker she left the Bosnia-Moscow file on her desk."

"If she's a security risk, get rid of her."

"I can't. I made the mistake of covering for her."

Embassy briefing room, 9:10 A.M. It was an odd gathering. Glenn Fairway, the London station-chief, sat at one end of the oval table flipping a pencil between his stubby fingers. The well-dressed American ambassador drummed his knuckles at the other end. Dudley Perkins was elbow-close to Fairway.

A meeting big enough to bring in MI5, Drew thought. *But who are the two strangers?* As Drew slipped into the chair beside Vic Wilson, Vic passed a hastily written note to him. "The man in tweeds is British, Fairway's latest asset. The thin man beside Perkins is Maurice Chambord, the new general secretary of the Societe du Tour de France."

The Frenchman's handshake was limp, the nameless Englishman's curt nod just as distasteful. Maurice Chambord was dark and wiry, his eye constantly on his watch. Drew let his gaze wander back to the big man in a tweed jacket and felt an immediate aversion to him. In contrast to Chambord, the Englishman was fair-skinned, his shrewd green eyes a shade lighter than his tie.

The ambassador nodded to Fairway. "Since this affects Intelligence, perhaps you could explain why we're here, Glenn."

Fairway relished taking over. There was little memorable about his face, just an ordinary, run-of-the mill appearance, but his voice commandeered the room. "It's those terrorist threats against the Tour de France—someone wants to stop the race."

"But France wants the race to go on," Chambord said.

"Too many French francs at stake?" Drew asked.

The Frenchman's look was censoring. "More is at stake than money, Monsieur Gregory. Lives are being threatened." His words spewed out sharp and angry. "They singled out an American—he wasn't in the original bomb threats. It could be an anti-American terrorist group going for an American hero. We don't know. We just have to take it seriously. That's why I'm here."

Dudley Perkins leaned forward, his face gloomy. "We're talking about your friend Ian Kendall, Drew."

"Not Ian!"

"Yes. He's a member of the British team, so it could be the work of the IRA aiming at the heart of Britain again."

"Then pull Kendall off the team."

Fairway shook his head. "What would that accomplish? You can't take a man's career away from him. The aim is to catch terrorists, not give in to their threats. And, Dudley, this is bigger than a threat against London's financial district."

Drew groaned. *Risk Kendall's life, and I won't be able to face his family again. I won't be able to face myself. And, Fairway, anger MI5, and we sit this one out alone.*

Drew didn't always agree with Perkins, but there was no point in aggravating him on his home turf. But Glenn was a cynical, self-centered man, too Company-minded to recognize that he was opposing a powerful man in the host country and quite possibly offending the Frenchman.

"Let's hear Chambord out," Drew suggested.

Chambord's smile was brief. "We can't lay the blame on any one terrorist group. No one has come forward and taken credit. But the threats have led us to believe—," he hesitated, "—that there is a Bosnia-Moscow connection."

"Impossible. Ian doesn't know anyone in Bosnia or Moscow."

Perkins's bushy brows scrunched together. "His grandfather knew people in both countries. Perhaps he has enemies there."

No, Uriah Kendall's ties with the past ended a long time ago. Drew thought of the file left on Lennie's desk. "If there is a Russian connection, then threatening the race could be a decoy to something bigger." *Or something as elusive as why Vasille Golemis would meet with a man like Salvador Contoni.*

An amused smile touched the Englishman's lips. "A problem in Moscow, Gregory? Must we blame everything on the Russians?"

Drew met the Englishman's arrogant gaze. He shrugged off his concern about Golemis and said, "The old desire for power is still there. Didn't they put a crack Russian unit in Bosnia as part of the NATO peacekeeping forces? Any problem with them?"

"Paratroopers. Good men," the Englishman countered.

The ambassador agreed. "We had nothing but praise for them."

Perkins sighed. "It's not the Russians who concern me, but a Serbian Intelligence officer is reportedly riding in the Tour—a Serbian war criminal with a contact here in London."

Fairway exploded, "You're usually up on those things, Dudley. If there's a known war criminal, turn him over to NATO."

Perkins rubbed his scrawny hands. "We only know the Serbian by his code name Roadrunner. And his English contact is called the Lily-trotter. But they slipped through our net."

The Englishman laughed. "A terrorist among the riders? Come now, Dudley, a Roadrunner and a Lily-trotter—that's absurd."

Chambord glanced at his watch again. "Gentlemen, the threats against the Tour are my immediate concern. France will understand if you withdraw your riders, but the race must go on."

"How can we help, Mr. Chambord?" the ambassador asked.

"By supporting the race. The Tour has its own police force, and our gendarmerie and French Intelligence are alerted." He glanced apologetically at Dudley Perkins. "Troy Carwell and the American ambassador in Paris are sending some men."

Drew turned to Fairway. "Me specifically?" he asked.

"You and Vic will ride in the caravan as inconspicuously as possible. You're there to protect the American riders. The French will cover the European teams."

Perkins said quietly, "I arranged for you and Mr. Wilson to ride with the Gainsborough team." He managed a sly smile. "I persuaded Jon—forced him actually—to allow you to ride in the team car as prospective sponsors for next year."

Drew nodded. "I'm sure Jon Gainsborough went for that idea."

Fairway grinned. "Like a hog snooting the mire. But the threats against the Tour are real. We can't ignore them. So we're with you, Chambord. We won't let anyone stop the Tour de France."

Chambord capped his pen and put it away. "I must leave now in order to make my plane on time."

"My deputy will drive you to Heathrow," the ambassador said.

Maurice Chambord smiled at last. "Thank you, gentlemen, for your time. And you, Mr. Ambassador, for your kindness." He turned to Dudley Perkins. "If there is a Bosnian war criminal riding in the Tour, we will find him."

"He won't be easily identified."

Chambord nodded. "That will make it more challenging."

Chapter 4

As the door closed behind the Frenchman, Drew massaged his temples. "What happens to Lennie while I'm gone?" he asked.

Fairway's smile did little more than twist his pointed nose and curl his lip. "If she's passing memos out of the embassy, we can't terminate her and risk her leaving the country. So, until we have proof, she goes into the secretarial pool with access to classified material."

"And under constant surveillance. Poor Lennie."

"Poor Parker," Fairway countered. "He's the one put to the task of dating her."

"Has anyone checked him out?"

"Parker isn't the problem, Gregory. He's part of our surveillance team."

"Lennie was doing her job until he came into her life. Why break her heart with a man who doesn't care one ounce for her?"

Across the table, the Englishman smiled. "It was the only way to win her confidence. Miss Applegate budded with red roses and evenings out on the town. She's turned into quite a love."

Fairway's gaze hardened. "Drew, why didn't you tell us Lennie had relatives in Bosnia?"

"That wasn't on her resumé."

"She failed to include it, but she comes from a clan of Russian Slavs."

If Drew told him he had reread Lennie's resumé two days ago, he would be admitting his own doubts about her. Annoyed, he said, "And I hail from the Irish Catholics. And Vic's mother was Hungarian or Polish. And you grew up in the Bronx, the Heinz variety. What difference does it make where we came from?"

Fairway's voice rose a notch. "She kept in touch with her relatives in Bosnia all through that long war and especially after NATO moved in."

"That doesn't make her a traitor."

The ambassador whipped out his handkerchief and swiped it across his glasses. "We're sorry, Gregory. Memos and files turned up missing at the embassy at an alarming rate while you were on your honeymoon. But the questions about Miss Applegate's loyalties came up while you were in Prague."

Drew turned to Vic. "And no one bothered to tell me."

"You were gone," Fairway said. "But we're telling you now. Everything points to Lennie."

"Thanks." His voice was so brittle that Fairway backed off.

Quietly the ambassador said, "In the last year she ran up some heavy debts and took out loans that she can't pay back."

"Maybe she needed money for the care of her sick parents."

"And for the transfer of funds to her family in Bosnia."

"From a London bank, Mr. Ambassador?"

"No, Gregory, through a Swiss account."

Drew knew that Lennie lived in a squeeze-box flat in a poor part of town, stretching her embassy salary beyond her limit. If she had just come to him and asked him for a loan. But Lennie had been tight-lipped about her private life and noncommunicative about her lifestyle. Now and then Drew had bought her tickets to a concert. Operas were her favorite. She had thanked him profusely and then gone off to the concert alone, a prim and proper lady in a drab suit and tied shoes, her hair pulled back into a bun. "Am I to ferret out my own secretary, Glenn?"

"It's our job to go after traitors."

"Unless you're working with her," the Englishman suggested.

He glanced at his watch and stood, a tall, distinguished forty-five-year-old with light hair and gray-blond brows who made ceremony of picking up his hat and gloves. "Fairway, I have a luncheon date. I'll report back to you in the morning."

Drew waited until he left and then asked, "Who is that man?"

"Radburn Parker," Fairway said. "He's working for us."

"Parker! He's a British asset? Since when, Glenn?"

"The last few weeks."

Drew's tongue turned acid. "You louse. You—"

A chill caught him between the shoulder blades. In the old days, he would have blasted Fairway with a string of expletives, but life had changed for Drew on the mountain slope in Sulzbach when he—a stubborn, willful man—had made contact with God. Still he raged inside. He could pray for Lennie, but he couldn't bring himself to pray for Parker or Fairway. Right now the blind spot in Drew's fury blocked out his sense of right and wrong. He fought against the admonition that a redeemed man should not let the sun go down on his wrath. He glanced out the window, arguing with himself on how to define sundown—when the sun slipped behind the mountain or when it was pitch dark outside? Regaining control, he asked, "Glenn, what do you know about Parker?"

"He's from a prominent London family."

The ambassador was more informative. "He was a minor secretary at the British embassy for a year. That's how Perkins and I met him. Some time back, he spent a number of years in Russia as a visiting history professor."

"It was a good relationship," Perkins said. "The whole time he was there, he fed intelligence information back to us—even sent some of the first information we had on the old Phoenix-40."

Disinformation, Drew thought. "And now?"

Perkins's grim expression lightened. "Thanks to the Parker Foundation, the Gainsborough cycling team can go to the race. Gainsborough keeps the team name, and Parker helps pay the bills."

"But whose idea was it for Parker to romance Lennie?"

There was a unanimous need to check their watches before Perkins said, "That was your idea, wasn't it, Mr. Ambassador?"

"No, Fairway's the one who came to me with it."

The London chief glared at Perkins. "It was Parker's idea."

As the meeting broke up, Drew latched onto Fairway's arm and whirled him around. "Why did you recruit Parker?"

Fairway brushed his sleeve. "With his steel plant tight on funds, Gainsborough needed money to keep the team from being pulled out of the Tour. As for me—I have odds on that American

rider. So Dudley and I had dinner with Parker to ask for money."
As if to further justify himself, he said, "Parker and I played polo
together—even played with Prince Charles a few times."

"Get to your point."

"After dinner and drinks, Radburn agreed to a loan from the
Parker Foundation. His word as much as guaranteed it happening."

"A loan had nothing to do with Lennie."

Fairway squirmed. "It had a lot to do with you, Drew. Parker
and I agreed on one thing. We want you out of the embassy."

"Why, Glenn? Are you still smarting over my working under
Carwell in Paris instead of your London station?"

"It is unusual. By the third drink Parker pledged his financial
support if we promised to check you out, Drew. It snowballed
after that, but Perkins here vouched for him. After all, the Parkers
are well respected in this country."

"And rich. That always counts with you, Fairway. So why
didn't Perkins hire him on at MI5? We don't need a man like
Radburn Parker in the American embassy."

Fairway stomped off, cutting his path out of the middle of the
corridor. In three quick strides Drew was at his side again. "How
did Parker get mixed up with Lennie?"

"He offered his services."

"You hired a rich playboy to ruin my secretary's name?"

"He didn't want money."

"Just access into the embassy? I bet you gave him top security
clearance without going through the usual channels."

"Time was important. We have a chance to win the Tour de
France, Drew." He rapped Drew's shoulder with his knuckles.
"And we can't risk a Deven or Ames showing up in the London
station."

"It sounds reasonable. Lennie is a British subject. Perkins is
internal security." His contempt aroused the old animosity
between them. "It was your chance for MI5 and the CIA to work
together—to better your relationships between the two countries.
So you agreed to run a smear campaign against Lennie."

"Lennie betrayed herself," he said hotly.

Fairway stalked off again, allowing Vic Wilson time to catch up with Drew. "Stay cool," Vic said. "Fairway has problems here at the embassy. The ambassador's on his neck—wants answers."

"I'm not the answer."

"Lennie may be—and she's your secretary; but if there's a smear campaign going on, it's against you, Drew. Fairway thinks you ruined it for the Agency when you took Porter Deven down."

"And he wishes I had gone down with him?" He ran his hands through his silver-streaked hair. "Fairway puts too much stock in Parker. We should have point men out observing his every move."

"What's the matter, Gregory? Are you just embarrassed that Lennie fooled you? She fooled all of us."

To Drew's silence, he said, "Until recently I thought Lennie was being set up, too. But everything blew apart when Radburn Parker showed up with photographs of Lennie meeting her foreign contact and passing embassy papers to him."

"Next you'll tell me I'm tied in with the whole mess."

Vic pulled him into an empty room. "You are involved, Drew."

"Make sense."

"You're trying to protect her—to cover for her. Fairway never took to your assignment to this embassy. My guess is he thought you came here because you wanted his job."

"Not for all the diamonds in Amsterdam," Drew told him. "Vic, have you seen those photographs of Lennie?"

"Yes. There's no mistaking it's Lennie Applegate. But all you can see of her contact is a man's hands taking the papers from her."

"Get me copies of Parker's pictures, Vic."

"You know Fairway's office is harder to crack than the Federal Reserve vault."

"Then charm his secretary."

"Fairway is busy doing that."

"Then blow up the vault. I want those pictures."

"Lennie isn't worth it."

The corner of Drew's mouth twitched. "She is to me."

Vic turned off at his own office with a low-tone parting. "Drew, if you have anything in those files of yours that you don't want found, clear them out today."

"Why?"

"Fairway plans a room search once you're gone. They'll fill your cabinet with substitute file folders. And—" He hesitated, and then said apologetically, "They plan to set the sprinklers off in Lennie's office."

"What if Lennie catches on?"

"Even if she gets back into the room after we're gone, her files will be waterlogged, nothing legible. She'll beeline out of there as fast as she entered, but the hidden cameras will capture everything she does."

Cameras that are already in place, he thought. *Recording my every move since I got back from Prague.* "Lennie is not the only one under surveillance, is she?"

"You, too, Drew, but I didn't dare warn you. I've checked out as loyal to the Company now. That's why I'm being sent with you to France as Fairway's eyes and ears."

"Good thing your friendship makes you half blind and deaf."

Vic grinned. "I was thinking the same thing."

❦❦❦

As Drew reached his office, Lennie stepped into the corridor. In spite of the warm weather she was wearing her lightweight Burberry belted tightly at her waist. She held one arm tight against her side, a purse clutched under the other.

"Oh, Mr. Gregory," she said, flustered, "I'm having lunch early. You don't mind, do you?"

Radburn Parker towered behind her, his eyes mocking as he looked at Drew. "Of course, he doesn't mind, my dear."

She met Drew's stern gaze, staring back at him reproachfully. "Mr. Gregory, Radburn tells me you are going on holiday again. I wish you had told me."

What else has Parker told you? "I just found out."

Parker tugged at her elbow and guided her toward the elevator, Lennie's shiny laced shoes tapping rhythmically beside him. She glanced back as they hurried away. "I didn't know you liked cycling. My nephew will be riding in the Tour, too."

A nephew? Did Lennie have a nephew? She never mentioned anyone except her ill parents. As the elevator doors slammed shut, Drew stormed into Lennie's office and stared around the empty room. *Lennie*, he thought miserably, *what is happening to you?*

He considered ransacking her desk, but it was exactly what Parker would expect him to do; and Parker, as far as Drew was concerned, was as unpredictable as a snake in the grass.

Back in his own office, he found the hidden cameras—because he knew where to look—and covered them. No one would come to check it out; that would be a dead giveaway that they were watching him. But in case the embassy really searched this room while he was gone, he wanted to retrieve the personal files that tied him in with Porter Deven and those trips to Prague and Sulzbach.

He went to the gunmetal gray cabinet. *Porter's file was gone.* Drew searched methodically; his perseverance paid off. The Prague file and Porter's were jammed together, the Aldrich Ames records squeezed between them. Lennie had no access to this cabinet, but someone did. He took out the Sulzbach report and the Bosnia-Moscow folder, thicker than he remembered it, and added them to his collection. Slapping the folders on top of the cabinet, he sent the drawer flying. It jammed on its rollers and took him another five minutes to get it closed and locked.

Back at his desk, Drew shed his coat and tried to focus on the opening line of the Bosnia-Moscow report, but he couldn't get Lennie out of his mind. Was Lennie being set up as Drew suspected, or had she willingly carried classified documents out of the embassy for a price? One persistent thought replayed itself. Why had Lennie never mentioned her Yugoslavian heritage?

Two years ago Lennie had been his last choice for a secretary, and she knew it. Shy and uncertain on her first day, she had said, "If you want to have someone else—"

"No. You'll do fine," he had told her. "Do you have children, Mrs. Applegate?"

"It's Miss, but please call me Lennie. I can stay overtime if you need. I'm a very good worker. You can ask Mr. Fairway."

"I already did." Looking at her troubled face, he had teased, "As long as you have a cup of cappuccino and the newspaper or a copy of the *U.S. News and World Report* on my desk every morning, we'll get on just fine."

The following morning she came into his office balancing a

brand-new mug spewing steam into the room, the *Evening Standard* under her arm. He had been too embarrassed to tell her he had already scoured the paper. Today's version wouldn't even be out until midafternoon, so he grinned and said, "Everything but the *U.S. News and World Report.*"

"They didn't have one at the book stand," she apologized.

When she reported in on the fourth day, he was blessing his computer. It had just crashed, and he had no idea how to rally technology to his side. "You don't have to swear, Mr. Gregory," she had said. "I'll show you how to use it."

As predicted, she scored zero on personal relationships, but she knew how to run an office and to deal discreetly with classified material. She was, he had decided, the only good thing that came out of his assignment to the London embassy. Each morning began the same way: the coffee on a coaster so it wouldn't stain his desk; the newspaper opened for him, sometimes to the sports page; the computer booted up, ready to go. By the third week he found a book on British history on top of the *Evening Standard*, a gem from some secondhand bookstore.

"You mentioned this one last week," she said shyly. "No British history buff should be without it."

He tried to repay her kindnesses. Two theater tickets now and again. Once to the Royal Ballet at Covent Garden. Another to the *Mikado* at the Coliseum. Twice to the Royal Opera House. It took her weeks before she could tell him, "One ticket is really enough, Mr. Gregory. Oh, I'm grateful, of course, for two, but—it's difficult to get someone to go with me at the last minute."

It was as close as she ever came to admitting that she had few friends, if any. That first Christmas—after she'd told him she'd never been to Scotland—he had given her a three-day rail pass to Edinburgh with her hotel reservation covered. He felt secure with his generosity. Lennie never discussed her personal life with the other secretaries at the embassy.

It was months before he dragged out of her that she was responsible for elderly parents, and then he hated himself for the locker-room jokes. He had often chuckled over Lennie's laced shoes and dowdy suits, all four of them. "She's not the latest fashion," he admitted to the boys. "She even rotates her blouses, regular as clockwork. The pink one on Monday, the green one . . ."

Ever since that trip to the mountains of Sulzbach—ever since he had made that firm decision to put God at the top of his priority list—the old locker-room jokes came back to haunt him. That's when he told his colleagues, "Lennie is not the cream of society, but she's a woman of integrity." That elusive characteristic that Drew's mother had drummed into him from boyhood.

Now Fairway and the ambassador wanted him to eat his own words. Had he misjudged Lennie? Had she really fooled him? Or had she become the scapegoat for the missing embassy files? He spent the rest of the afternoon reading the Bosnia-Moscow report, one ear cocked for Lennie's return from her luncheon date with Parker. She never came back.

Bosnia. Croatia. Zagreb. Tuzla. The names touched the old sore spot that had landed him the desk job in London. He had been on a covert assignment in Sarajevo, a civil war exploding all around him. Everything went well until he met his Croatian contact. Even now his mind went back to Leopold Bolav, a burly man with a definite leaning toward vodka and communism. Twenty men recognized Leopold as the leader of their guerrilla unit, but Drew disliked Bolav. With a white Persian cat balancing on the shoulder of his faded fatigues and the laces of his muddy army boots loose at the top, he didn't give the appearance of a leader.

The day before Drew was to slip out of Sarajevo, Leopold had called an early morning meeting in the basement of a bombed-out shelter. When Bolav failed to join the unit, Drew walked across the underground room and pulled down a wall map. That's when the explosion flattened him against the wall. It was better than what it had done to the other twenty men. Drew was the only survivor in the room. His code name Crisscross was blown as well, bringing his covert career to a sudden halt. Sometimes his personal loss depressed him, but the loss of the men who hadn't lived long enough to see the end of that bloody war still tore at his gut.

Back in Paris, Drew had said, "I think Leopold infiltrated the ranks. Mark my word, he's a Serbian Intelligence officer. That's why my cover was blown."

Porter Deven, the station-chief in Paris then, had laughed at the idea. "Admit it, Drew. There's been a clerical blunder. That's all. Be glad you got out of Sarajevo alive." And with that, Deven had shipped him off to London to wait out a safe return to covert action. Drew was still rotting away at the embassy, ticking off too many birthdays. He rubbed his forehead, pressing his fingers into the scowl grooves to ease the miserable pain thumping there.

Everything at the embassy was buried under mountains of paperwork. Well, he'd add to the confusion. He switched on his computer—surprised that Lennie had not turned it on this morning—and began to revise the Bosnia-Moscow report. He filled it with disinformation that would infuriate Glenn Fairway if he caught wind of what Drew was doing. Disinformation that would trap Lennie if she leaked it into other hands. Deliberately, he filled in half-truths, new names—some that existed, others that formed in his mind as he typed.

He paused at his keyboard, then pulled more facts and figures from the air about the peacekeeping forces in Bosnia—some that had succeeded, others that had gone awry. He remembered the name of the Russian officer who had headed up the 1,500-man crack paratrooper unit. Drew had seen a picture of the man once, so he added a mustache and height for good measure. He suggested a possible tie between war criminals who had escaped the borders and the reported uprising of the Phoenix-40 in Russia.

Satisfied with the results, he made photocopies, and then with a flick of his hand, he deleted the file he had just created. *No record for you to find, Fairway. Not in my computer files. The computer and I are totally innocent.*

He turned off the computer. Click. Hum. Buzz. Flashing lights. The darkened screen appeared. He went into Lennie's office. Her copy of the Bosnia-Moscow report was right where he expected to find it, not in alphabetical order, but according to Lennie's own geographical placement. He smiled as he slipped the extra pages neatly into the folder and put it back into Lennie's drawer. On impulse, he decided to check out the Parisian Terrorist report. With his scheduled three weeks in France, he might as well have facts at his fingertips: known terrorist organizations and right-wing Parisians, the exact sites for bombings in the '90s, and their devastating statistics. *The Parisian folder was missing.*

Drew blinked against the image of Lennie's hasty exit for lunch, her arm held tight to her body. Tightly enough to conceal a file under her raincoat? Lennie could have walked out of the embassy with Parker's security clearance covering them both.

Drew's jaw locked; the pain jabbed beneath his ears and ran a rapid course down his jaw. *Lennie, Lennie. What happened to you?* He was still squinting with eye fatigue when his wife poked her head around the door, a visitor's pass pinned to her dress.

Miriam was elegant as always. Lights and shadows fell across her oval face like the vivid strokes of a Rembrandt painting, yet softened with the delicate touch of Renoir. Her mellow voice matched the image. "Drew, darling, you haven't forgotten about dinner with Ian and Chase?"

"Oh, *Liebling*, it totally slipped my mind."

"You'd better hurry. Ian can't miss his plane." Miriam glanced toward Lennie's door. "I was hoping to catch Lennie."

"She's been at lunch for four hours."

"And obviously without your blessing, dear. I wanted to invite her and her gentleman friend to dinner this weekend."

"Can you put that off until after the Tour de France?"

Her eyes searched his as she stepped to the side of the desk and gave him a quick peck on the cheek. "You're going away?"

"For three weeks. Fairway and Carwell volunteered my services at the cycling race. Go with me, Miriam."

"No, but you can drop me off in Paris for a shopping spree."

"I'll keep the credit card with me."

"I have my own. Drew, while you're away, work up some enthusiasm for my dinner guests. Lennie is a lonely woman. You told me that yourself. Besides, you agreed, my life in London would include lots of company."

"I didn't expect our guests to include Radburn Parker."

"Lennie's love? What a fancy name."

"For a scoundrel." He stood. "How did your day go?" he asked as he stuffed the file folders into his briefcase.

"I spent all morning at Sotheby's auction with Rupert Townsend."

"One of those auctioneers?"

"One of their department heads. An old friend. A dear man actually. He showed me some marvelous paintings. One by Rubens that I really liked."

"I trust you left the checkbook home."

She laughed. "Don't worry. We didn't have enough in our account for that one."

He swung the briefcase into his hand. "Would your *dear man* at Sotheby's keep something for me?"

Her eyes traveled slowly to his briefcase and back to Drew's face. "In his vault?"

"Yes."

"Well, I did pay for lunch today, so he does owe me a favor. And he won't ask questions."

Chapter 5

Chase watched Ian's British Airway plane climb until it was less than a dot in the London sky, and then she turned to the Gregorys. "Drew, what do you think happened to Coach Skobla? Ian is really worried about him."

"Ludvik Skobla is not Ian's problem. But give me a few minutes, and I'll make some phone calls."

Drew took off with a wink, not giving them a chance to ask questions. As he made his way toward a public phone, Chase said, "Miriam, Ian is getting too serious."

Miriam's deep-set eyes filled with pleasure. "I thought so. You couldn't find a nicer young man."

Chase saw her own sadness reflected in the window glass. "But, Miriam, how can I be in love with someone I barely know? We've never really dated, and he's already proposing."

"That sounds like Ian. He was never one to waste time."

"But I want a courtship with flowers and candlelight dinners and time to get acquainted."

"That's what I wanted, Chase, but Drew persuaded me to run off and get married six weeks after we met." The airport lighting could not diminish Miriam's beauty or darken her magnificent smile. Her reddish-brown hair was swept back from her face in a striking chignon that highlighted her remarkable cheekbones. "Most of my husband's roses came after we were married."

"It just wouldn't work for me. I have unfinished business back home, completing my Ph.D., for one."

Miriam squeezed her hand. "Dear Chase, you have a brilliant

mind. Use it. But you also have a tender heart. Listen to it. Make certain your unfinished business in New York is not an excuse. It just might be that you and Ian need each other. Drew and I do."

A few stragglers kept their faces pressed against the airport window, the pain of farewell still marring their expressions. "Miriam, when I marry—if I marry—it will be in Long Island in June when Mother's roses are the most lovely."

"Oh, Chase, everyone goes for a June wedding."

"Not everyone has a rose garden of her own."

"June wouldn't work. Didn't Ian tell you? He competes in the Giro d'Italia in June, and a month later it's the Tour de France."

"Maybe he could spare me a few days between races."

Miriam's brows drew into an arch. "A young man like Ian would want more time than that to take his bride on a honeymoon."

Miriam picked up a bridal magazine in the airport waiting room. The torn cover page showed a smiling wedding party at the altar with groomsmen in winter black tuxes and bridesmaids in long red velvet. "Why not wed off season—a late winter wedding?"

"I'll be hard at work on my Ph.D. by then."

"With me it was my love of art. I'm afraid with you, it's your love of learning. Make certain that's what you really want."

The closeness that she had felt to Miriam faded. "Marriage isn't all that important to me. My grandmother Callie used to say, 'You marry them, bury them, and then you spend their money.'"

"That's frightfully unkind. What sort of a woman was she?"

"She was wonderful, but my grandfather was always busy working on his next million. Callie had everything, but she would have given it all up just to spend more time with him."

"Chase, a man has to provide for his family."

"The Bartholomews were one of the richest families in New York. It's just that my grandfather was married to his job."

"Like Ian is glued to bicycling?" she asked. Foreboding filled her voice. "Chase, don't wait as long as I did to discover those golden moments of sharing someone's life."

They were the only two at the boarding gate now, but they could still see Drew at the pay phone, pounding his fist against the wall. "That has to be Vic Wilson on the line," Miriam said. "They always argue—Drew suggesting one plan, Vic another."

"I thought they were such good friends."

"They are. Who wouldn't be with Drew? They are as different as two beet tops, but they work well together, those two."

"Will Vic know where Coach Skobla is?"

"Oh, my, no, but he'll be on it the minute Drew hangs up."

They moved toward Drew as though Miriam sensed his need of her. "You're so alike," Chase said. "Ian and I are so different."

"No, dear, Drew and I are opposites. The art gallery is my whole world, but he endures the galleries for my sake. Don't be so afraid of Ian's career that you're afraid to look at Ian."

"He'd be gone so much of the time, like my grandfather."

"So was Drew. I fought Drew's career and lost sixteen good years with him." Her smile caressed Chase. "I have a funny feeling we're a lot alike, my dear," she said.

Don't I wish. You have the grace and sophistication that Callie had. The absolute confidence that you chose the right man.

"Chase, Ian is a lot like Drew—a man quick to know what he wants." Their steps slowed to a crawl as Miriam glanced at her. "There must be things you like about him."

"He's a challenge on the tennis court and like a gazelle at the Jungfrau in Switzerland. Even on the lower slopes the higher we climbed, the more determined I was to keep up with him." As they reached Drew, she said, "We both like England and Beatrice Thorpe." As she thought of Bea, darkness settled over her. "Bea's afraid something will happen to Ian during the race."

"Don't worry, Chase. Bruises heal," Drew told her as they joined him.

"Is everything all right, Drew?" Miriam asked.

Drew shook off Miriam's concern and winked at Chase. "Vic will have Coach Skobla located and on a plane back to France before we reach the house. Now about you and Ian—Ian thinks the world is on a crash course to oblivion and that you plan to right the wrongs before that happens."

"We do get in our worst rows arguing over politics."

"Ouch," Drew said. "So do Miriam and I."

"You do? Well, I don't like being several months older."

Miriam's laughter was contagious as she leaned her head against Drew's shoulder. "Chase! Dear child, Drew is eleven years older than I am. What is age if you really love someone?"

"You'd be financially secure," Drew said. "Ian has negotiated some profitable contracts during his cycling career."

"I don't need Ian's money. I come into a large inheritance on my twenty-fifth birthday." Embarrassed at her outburst, she asked, "Drew, does he really have a chance to win the Tour?"

"There are high odds on him. A couple hundred riders will start the race, but only five are contenders for the big win at the finish line. Ian is right up there."

"And the other four?"

"All older, some of them more experienced riders than Ian. The Swiss favorite for one. And he's racing against last summer's winner—that's never easy." He took their arms and propelled them down the corridor toward the exit. "Jon Gainsborough is demanding a win if they expect him to sponsor the team again next year."

As they fought the crowd, Chase mused, "Just a handful with the chance to win—then why do the rest of them kill themselves in such a grueling race?"

"Probably for personal glory," Miriam said.

"No, *Liebling*. It's more than that. For any man who ever wanted to conquer a mountain, this Tour is the ultimate test."

"And I thought it was all for a yellow jersey."

"No, Chase. I'm afraid the stakes are higher this time."

She stopped abruptly, causing a chain reaction at the exit door. "Drew, Ian pooh-poohs the bomb threats against the Tour."

He squeezed her arm. "So you know about those?"

"I know about the international repercussions."

"I'm more concerned about the death threats against Ian."

"Against Ian? Then I must go to him. He needs me."

Miriam's eyes danced. "Nice to be needed! Drew's going. Go with him. I have no intention of standing in the heat watching a bunch of young men pedal themselves into nervous exhaustion."

"Not even for Ian?" Drew teased. "You won't reconsider?"

"My darling, you told me women don't ride in the team cars."

"Neither does Central Intelligence, but I'm still scheduled to ride in the Gainsborough team car. Things are different this year, but they're mostly security precautions." When they reached the Rolls Royce, he said, "Chase, if I pull the right strings, they might make room for you as an American journalist assigned to the Kendall race. Do you know anything about journalism?"

"Enough to bluff my way. But what New York paper would I represent?" She grinned. "Samuel Abt reports for the *New York Times*."

"Just give me the name of a Long Island paper. I'll make certain that Langley gets you an official press card."

"Won't Mr. Gainsborough have a fit about that?"

"Let me worry about Gainsborough and Coach Skobla."

In the growing darkness as Drew helped them into the car, Chase saw a frown forming at the corners of Miriam's eyes. "Drew, don't let the Company trick you into telling the old lies."

"I won't, Miriam." His gaze slid past her to Chase. "Having Chase on board will be good for Ian. He'll take fewer risks."

"But, Drew, aren't you risking Chase's safety?"

He tapped the steering wheel. "I won't let anything happen to her, Miriam. She can be a real asset to us. Ian trusts her. He'll confide in her."

Miriam turned away, her voice strained as she said, "Then you and Chase can go running around the French countryside looking for terrorists if you want. I'll be safer shopping in Paris."

🌑🌑🌑

On the other side of London, Jon Gainsborough checked the lock on his car door and rolled up the window as he turned his Audi A4 onto the narrow street. Night seemed darker here, the blackness broken only by old-fashioned lampposts and a flickering neon light on the corner pub. Jon was crunched in the compact car, the weight of his massive body pressed against his diaphragm. He mopped the back of his neck with his bare hand, hating himself for the fear that controlled him. An Opel Vectra had followed him for several kilometers—one of the boys from MI5 he was certain. Yet here in this back alley, when he would have been grateful for a tail, the Opel was no longer behind him.

Sweat formed on his temples and poured down the small of his back. He was on his own except for women traversing the sidewalks and two cars traveling slowly along the curb. This was not his part of town, not his way of life. He humped over the steering wheel, searching for the Maystead Inn, trying to imagine what kind of trouble Ludvik Skobla was in that demanded Jon's midnight ride to a seedy hotel with a thick packet of money in his pocket. If the London tabloids got wind of Coach Skobla's whereabouts, their chance at the Tour de France was over.

Jon couldn't handle more scandal. For weeks he had faced the accusations that he was involved in the sale of chemicals to Third World countries. Jarvoc, the steel plant near Prague, had already collapsed, his colleagues there held in custody. Now he worried about his own steel plant folding, a personal loss that would include his cycling team—the only joy that filled his life since his marriage had folded. He felt layered in humiliation, the latest one coming when the Parker Foundation pledged funds to keep the team solvent. He suspected that Dudley Perkins was behind the loan—Perkins, his old friend at MI5, his enemy now.

"Cheers, Jon," Perkins had said. "It's still the Gainsborough cycling team that Britain will root for. No one has to know that Radburn Parker is calling the shots now."

One humiliation after the other. And now this midnight run to bail the team's coach—the *directeur sportif*—out of trouble. At the first whiff of more scandal, Parker would back off and take his financial support with him. And that would be the demise of the Gainsborough team. Jon could never climb back from that disgrace; the chance at winning the Tour was the only thing holding him together these days.

In the middle of the second block, he pulled into the Maystead's sparsely filled parking lot. The office in the two-story building was darkened. The venetian blinds hung crooked at the windows. A dog howled nearby. Tree branches swayed. A train whistled in the distance. He patted the money envelope inside his pocket and waited another three minutes. When no Opel pulled in beside him, he heaved his massive form from the driver's seat.

He was an enormous three-hundred-pounder, who tried to compensate for his short stature and thick-set body by wearing fancy Savile suits and decked heels on his Italian footwear. In the dead of night no one would appreciate his expensive attire or admire the speed and stealth with which he moved his hulking frame along the side of the building to the garbage pit.

His breath still came in short, tight gasps as he hurried past the shadows in the open terrace and climbed the narrow steps to the second floor. "The third door," Skobla had told him.

He counted them like a schoolboy, half expecting the wrong

door to open and cameras to flash, bringing even more scandal to his name. Sweat trickled down his fat jowls as he knocked. He jerked back as the door swung open. Across the dingy room, Ludvik Skobla sat in the wingback chair looking haggard and unkempt, his clothes slovenly, his feet bare.

"You're drunk. I should have fired you on the phone."

"You know I don't drink," Skobla said through swollen lips.

Jon adjusted his eyes to the fluorescent lighting. It was true. Skobla was a strict disciplinarian with himself and with the cycling team, a man intolerant of drinking or seedy living. He seldom spoke of his family back in the Czech Republic; but he was always the epitome of the sports world hero—from his spotless sweat togs with the team logo to his stark white running shoes.

Right now the Gainsborough sweat top was smudged with dirt.

The musty smell of stale cigar smoke filled Jon's nostrils as he stepped into the room. A streak of light beneath the door to the adjoining room blurred and lit again as though someone stood there listening. Jon's gaze strayed back to Ludvik. "What are you doing in London? You should be in France with the team."

"But you sent for me, Jon."

"I what?"

Jon realized as the door slammed behind him that there was a third person in the room. "Sorry," Jiri Benak said. "I sent the message to force both of you to meet me here."

"You!"

"Me, Jon," Benak said. "Alive and safely out of Jarvoc."

In the poorly lit room, it was difficult to distinguish Jiri's features or his snow-blond hair; even his blue eyes looked like dark circles in his narrow face. He was not unattractive, but a neatly dressed thirty-nine-year-old with cigars protruding from his shirt pocket and a pistol in his hand. His beige raincoat was noticeable now at the foot of the bed. He showed little emotion; his power lay wrapped in the mind games he played on others.

Gainsborough had silenced more than one man with his barbed glances, but as he stared at Jiri Benak, he felt like marshmallows inside. Benak, for all of his mild appearance, was a violent madman who designed destructive weapons.

"What do you want, Benak?" Gainsborough asked.

"Chemicals. Money. Your expertise. A job after the Tour de France. I expect you to help me."

"I no longer work for the steel mill in Jarvoc."

"Of course not," Benak agreed amiably. "The Russelmann family and the plant in the Czech Republic are shut down, but I have some of the records from there—ones that will prove that you worked for us and knew about the sale of chemicals."

"I *didn't* know."

"But you suspected. It's good you didn't fire Ludvik. It's too late to find another *directeur sportif* with the race just days away." His forced cheerfulness slipped as he waved the pistol. "Sit down over there, Jon. We need to discuss the race."

Gainsborough backed toward the bed and made a concave in the mattress as he sat down. "What happened, Ludvik?" he asked.

Skobla looked miserable. "He wants us to throw the race—to disqualify the boys with drugs if we have to."

Throw the race? Then Benak doesn't understand Skobla or cycling or steroids, Jon thought. *He doesn't understand the overall points that build during the race. Or how hard we've worked for this.* Whatever Skobla's background, he was not a man to cheat. He thought too highly of coaching, of winning.

"That's impossible," Jon said for both of them.

"I'll be there to make certain you do."

In spite of the pistol in Jiri's hand, Jon raged back, "We won't shame our team by throwing the race. The Tour de France has nothing to do with you, Jiri."

"But it does. I've bailed you out at the steel plant more than once, Jon, with my blueprints. And you, Ludvik, it was my recommendation that secured you the coaching job with the team."

"The race isn't played that way," Skobla said.

Jiri patted his gun. "Don't you want to live long enough to see who wins? Or must I turn to Moscow to stop this race? Believe me, Jon, I've already contacted the Russians."

Gainsborough couldn't conceive of a Muscovite willing to help Jiri, not with the whole world searching for him. Benak was playing his mind games. Was he behind the bomb threats, too? He was an expert with semiautomatics and Saran gas and homemade bombs. Jon kept his voice even. "Interpol is looking for you."

"For blowing up the Jarvoc tunnels? Didn't I die in that explosion?" Jiri's mouth hardened. "Or did Drew Gregory announce to the world that I was still alive?"

Jon wiped his sweaty face with the corner of the bedspread. Was the explosion in the tunnel all that Jiri remembered? He was mad, insane. Had he blocked out the gassing of some of the Russelmann family, the theft of chemicals?

In a flat voice, Jiri said, "If it hadn't been for Gregory and that Kendall family, I'd be running the Jarvoc plant now."

"Forget them."

"They ruined my chances. I saw Kendall. Our paths crossed at the top of Mt. Ventoux." Jiri blew down the barrel of his gun and aimed it at Jon again. "I left Kendall a message on the Simpson memorial. I dislike people who stand in my way."

A streak of light still shone beneath the adjoining room, the threat of someone's presence ominous. Jon's mind cleared. Jiri didn't know that Gregory would ride in the team car. But he must know that Kendall had a good shot at winning. If Ian won, Jon's dwindling finances would spring back. His hope soared. His only chance to escape was to agree with Benak—to talk himself safely out of this hotel and back to the car. One anonymous call to Scotland Yard on his cellular phone would guarantee Jiri's arrest.

He exchanged glances with Ludvik Skobla. "We'll have to throw the race, but it's your call. Coach?"

Skobla came to life. "We can't risk anything at the beginning of the Tour. It would be too obvious, Jon."

"When then?" Jiri insisted.

"When we reach the Pyrenees. Stage seventeen."

"No, Skobla. That's five days before the end of the race."

"Riders are exhausted by then," Gainsborough assured him. *And if you elude Scotland Yard tonight, we'll alert the French authorities to pick you up before we reach the mountains.*

"Jon is right," Ludvik said, rubbing his hands on his knees. "If our team fails to reach the summit, no one will be surprised. A lot of riders have to quit the race in the mountains. We'll make certain Kendall is one of them," he lied.

"Grant us that much time, Jiri," Jon said. "We need to reach the mountains. By then we can win a stage or two of the Tour. That way we save face with the racing world and won't be excluded from future races." In spite of the pistol still waving in his direction, he took the packet of marked bills from his pocket. "Ludvik, why did you ask me to bring money?" he asked, knowing.

"The money is for me," Jiri said. "I'm low on funds."

"Then it's yours." Gainsborough laid the envelope on top of Benak's raincoat. "This should cover you for three weeks." *By then you will be arrested. And Kendall may ride to the finish line in a yellow jersey in spite of you.*

🏺🏺🏺

Jiri looked at the lumpish, overweight man, with his abdomen stretched by overeating. But Jon's fleshy hands were well-groomed as he kettle-drummed his fingers on the money envelope, reluctant to let it go. "Is it all there?" Jiri asked.

Gainsborough's answer boomed across the dimly lit room, blasting Jiri's ears. "You can count it if you want." He shoved Skobla's shoes toward him. "Put those on, Ludvik. We've got to get you back to the team by morning."

Sweat formed on Ludvik's upper lip as he glanced from Jiri's face to the bedside clock. "I missed my plane, Jon."

"There are others," he said as he urged Ludvik to the door.

As Gainsborough's fingers wrapped around the doorknob, Jiri brought the butt of the pistol down across those fat knuckles. "Don't cross me, Gainsborough. Don't cross me."

He opened the door himself, smiling as they walked out. In spite of the problems at the steel plant, Gainsborough was useful enough for Jiri to let him live for now. As the two men descended the stairs, he dropped into the chair and counted the money. *Enough to buy more ammonia nitrate and copper wire. More than ample.* He slapped the bills on his bony knees as he glanced toward the adjoining room. *And Moscow will more than triple this once we can come to terms.*

He had no desire to live in Moscow—the offer had been made—but he was willing to sell his weapons for money, one intricate design at a time. If these didn't please the Kremlin, he knew enough about chemicals and nerve gases to pique their interest. Jiri had better plans than life in the frozen north. He would make his home in the English countryside among the rolling hills of the

Cotswolds, periodically leaving the safety of his thatched cottage to meet his Russian contact in Vienna.

The door to the next room opened and a solemn-faced cyclist in a hooded Gainsborough jacket came in with a brisk stride. His hair was wet from showering, dark strands of it damp against his forehead. He was a muscular twenty-eight-year-old with classical European features and eyes that had not laughed for a long time.

"They're gone?" he asked, his angry gaze fixed on Jiri.

"Yes, five minutes ago."

"Will they throw the race?" he asked.

"Perhaps. But Gainsborough is more crafty than I expected."

The cyclist was quick-footed and sturdy-legged as he paced the room, his shrewd eyes taking in every shadow. As a Serbian Intelligence officer, he had outfoxed his enemies during four years of war. He had escaped out of Bosnia when the NATO forces moved in, and both his name and his code name Roadrunner appeared on the war criminals' list of those charged with crimes against humanity.

Roadrunner talked as he moved. "So they are going to do exactly what I thought—nothing. Why did you let them go?"

"They agreed to stop the team by the last mountain stage."

"That's too late, Jiri."

"Jon's a foolish man. He won't let Skobla throw the race. They'd rather risk Kendall's life than give up their best chance of winning. The purse strings on the Champs Elysees are too tempting. But we don't need them."

"Then you must carry out the threats against Kendall."

"Against the world," Jiri said. "I will devise a way to stop this race, and you must help me, Roadrunner. Kendall's death is up to you."

"You've never killed a man, Benak?"

Jiri patted his pistol. "A few. But you are guilty of genocide—of ethnic cleansing," he mocked.

"Your victims did not die in a war, Jiri. Mine did. But killing hundreds of fans along the Tour is unnecessary."

"Then Kendall remains my personal responsibility," Jiri said.

"Yes. I will race Kendall—nothing more. And he knows that if I see a chance for a breakaway from the peloton, I'll take it."

"You're not on the team to win."

"The fans won't know that."

"It's an unnecessary risk. The Russians won't like it if the U.N. Security Council discovers your whereabouts."

"I am still Serbian Intelligence, not just a courier for the Bosnia-Moscow operation. Take care of your end, Benak, and I will handle mine."

Jiri shrugged, unwilling to argue any longer. "You plan to return to your own country, don't you?"

"Everything depends on this race. Once the Serbians take over again, I will go back with full honors, not with war crimes hanging over my head."

Jiri sensed his frustration. "Take my warning. Coach Skobla may claim residence in the Czech Republic, but he may have a direct phone line to Moscow. He may already know who you are."

Alarm registered on Roadrunner's face as he said, "Impossible."

"When you get to s'Hertogenbosch in the morning, how will you explain your absence to Coach Skobla?"

"My girl will vouch that I was with her." He zipped his hooded jacket. "What am I to tell my friends, Jiri?"

"The Russians or your British handler? Parkovitch, wasn't it? Tell them that my weapons expertise comes with a high price. Nerve gas is the poor man's atomic bomb. And I can supply that, but only if I deal directly with your man in Moscow."

"Professor Ivanski is more interested in what you do for us during the Tour de France."

Jiri's laugh turned brittle. "Reassure him that I am working with you. What's the life of a cyclist or a few hundred fans along the way to me?" *And Ian Kendall will blow with the others.* "So tell your friend Parkovitch that I'll create a hostage situation during the race that will please the professor and divert the world's attention away from Bosnia and Moscow. When can I meet with Parkovitch?"

"He'll be watching you, Jiri. If he trusts what he sees, he'll contact you during the Tour."

Jiri was losing control. He flushed his cigar ashes down the sink as the Roadrunner stalked across the room and tore off the bedspread, rumpled the bedding, and thumped the pillow.

"You make it look like I tossed and turned," Jiri said.

"Any other man with a history like yours, would have."

Chapter 6

In Russia, not forty miles from Moscow, Yuri Ryskov stepped
from the bus three kilometers beyond his intended destination. He glanced around, his hooded eyes wary as he took in
the half-dozen rundown shops that filled the cobbled square.
Professor Boris Ivanski's country estate lay to the east beyond the
village center and scattered farmhouses. Yuri would approach in
a roundabout direction, circling the village and striking out
through the woods to reach it.

Before he could take a step, the bus driver leaned out the window. "Make up your mind. I am leaving."

Yuri waved him on. "This is the place," he said.

The driver shifted gears and pulled away, leaving Yuri in a
blinding dust cloud. As the dust settled, he stumbled to the water
pump to wash sand particles from his burning eyes. His throat
felt parched, his fetid breath tasting of garlic and onions. Ryskov
was a dark-haired, wiry man in his mid-thirties with pasty skin
and a nervous stomach that soured with every meal. Ever since
Alekos Golemis's death in Sulzbach, Yuri slept and showered with
his revolver close at hand. Even now it pressed against his ribs in
a shoulder holster.

As the pump water dripped from his chin, he saw Boris
Ivanski's housekeeper pushing her way to the head of the market
line and waving a fistful of rubles that would guarantee her the
best meat and vegetables in town. Few paid any attention to Yuri.
Stranger or not, as long as he did not crowd in front of them, he
could go about his business unhindered.

An old woman in a dark shawl sat on a stone bench, waiting her turn, her dark eyes turning curiously on him. In spite of the summer weather, she had tied a black head scarf beneath her sagging chin. Yuri pitied her. She was just another elderly pensioner with barely enough rubles to buy sugar, soap, and salt. As poorly dressed as she was, it was unlikely that she had money enough for vegetables and meat for a watered-down *borscht* soup for herself or for the listless grandson clinging to her side. Yuri pulled some fruit and hard candy from his pocket and went to them. Without a word, he put the fruit in her basket and the candy in the boy's hand. Impulsively, he touched the lines on her weathered face, and she shivered.

Almost July, Yuri thought, *and yet you are cold, as I am often cold, in this country of ours that never seems to be warm.*

Yuri moved on, afraid that her weary-worn smile would tear him apart. Inside, he wished her dead, but it was a merciful thought, for when he grew old, he would choose death, not the humiliation of poverty and scarcity. The woman couldn't know that Ivanski—the recluse in the estate outside her village—was ready to destroy the Tour de France so he could fuel and shape the Phoenix-40 into a powerful new regime in Moscow.

Ivanski had little concern for the poor. He wanted the old imperial leadership that would take them back to the days of the czars—to the old ways when only a few were rich. But what of the poor? Yuri hoped that in spite of the iron control of their lives, their stomachs might not seem as empty. But he knew that international cycling would be taboo and this woman and her grandson might well starve to death.

As he trudged through the woods of white birch trees, he snatched one of the bright green leaves and tore it into shreds. The heaviness in his gut was an unbearable knot. Fear. *Professor Ivanski would call it fear.* The professor had been his mentor, his friend. Six months ago Yuri had favored Ivanski's plan for a revolution; now he dreaded it. How could he still pretend to be heart and soul a part of the old Phoenix plan when all he wanted was a new life for himself in another country?

When he had last been here in the bleakness of winter, he had plowed through deep snow, the frozen crystals crunching beneath his boots. Now summer twigs snapped and bent beneath his weight, and fragrant wild flowers covered the rolling hills on Ivanski's property. Ivanski had guests, important guests, if Yuri could judge by the shiny vehicle parked by the house.

Yuri expected the housekeeper to answer when he knocked, but the professor opened the door himself. Curiosity filled Ivanski's dark, intelligent eyes as he greeted Yuri. "My housekeeper is upstairs—exhausted from pedaling her bicycle home so fast to warn me that you were in town. She doesn't know I sent for you."

He glanced beyond Yuri. "No one else saw you come?"

"No. No one."

"Come in. My other guests can wait."

He gave Yuri a welcoming thump on the arm, not the Muscovite embrace that he had always given during their years of friendship. With a wave of his smooth hand, he hurried Yuri into the library. A photograph of Ivanski's wife who had died in the bitter cold of a Moscow winter sat on the mantel, filling the room with her presence.

"Professor, your wife would have been proud of all your accomplishments, as Moscow is."

"Perhaps, but she did not live long enough to see them."

Long after her death, Yuri, a poor boy without rank or experience, found favor with the professor. Under his fatherly tutelage, Yuri became the youngest member of the Phoenix-40. The Phoenix rebellion had failed once, betrayed by one of their own, but the surviving revolutionaries were ready to strike again.

Ivanski waved his hand around the room. "Moscow expects me to spend the rest of my life completing a six-volume research work on Russian revolutions, dating back to the reign of the czars."

"A very great honor, Professor Ivanski."

There was no joy in Ivanski's face. He was brilliant, deeply respected in the intellectual circles of Moscow. He could quote Lenin, Stalin, Brezhnev, Gorbachev, and Nicholas Trotsky without displaying his utter dislike for them. Yet he was as fanatical and impassioned by revolutions as Vladimir Lenin had been.

Except for his full czarist beard, he was a plain sixty-four-year-old man in thick silver-rimmed glasses. His rumpled shirt sleeves were rolled up, his striped tie askew, and strands of his thinning umber hair unmanageable. As he sat down, a faint smile touched his lips. "What kept you so long when I sent for you? Are you still blaming yourself for the failed mission in Sulzbach?"

Yuri felt as though tart lemon juice had been poured on the raw lining of his stomach. Names came at him like darts: *Nicholas Trotsky. Alekos Golemis. Drew Gregory.* He hated thinking back to the dead Russian colonel, the murdered cyclist, the elusive CIA officer. "You sent me to find Colonel Trotsky's mother," he said.

"Oh—so I did." Absently, he stroked his beard. "You seem uneasy this morning, Yuri. Was this mission a failure, too?"

More acid burned Yuri's stomach. "The American CIA found her first, but she was already on a slab in the morgue."

"With no one willing to claim her body? Unfortunate, but these days families don't have enough rubles to bury their dead."

Yuri jammed his fists into his pockets. "How much worse will it get? In the old regime her pension would have been ample enough for a decent burial."

"Life changed with the collapse of communism," Boris reminded him. "Now our people have freedom of speech and empty stomachs. They are ready for another change, Yuri. Once we put the Phoenix plan into action, we will offer them a better life."

Will we? His dry mouth kept him from answering. He would end up like the old woman in the food line, just a hungry Muscovite waiting for a handout of runt potatoes and dark rye bread. He wanted more for himself—a land where he could lie down in a warm bed in the winters and fill his stomach with good food on a daily basis. Ever since he had tracked Drew Gregory in the mountains of Sulzbach, Yuri had contemplated defecting to America. He pictured himself slipping into an American embassy and seeking political asylum in exchange for—for what? He had nothing to barter with.

He fixed his eyes on the wood carving that hung on the wall beside the professor, Russian proverbs engraved on it. "Better to turn back than to lose your way. The tears of strangers are only water." *The professor believes he must turn the people back to the old ways,* Yuri thought, *before strangers in other nations overpower our land.*

Mentally, he ran down the list of Phoenix-40 names again: Jankowski, Kavin, Aleynik, Trotsky, Radbrazhensky, and

Parkovitch. Most of them were dead now. How had he and Professor Ivanski slipped through the net and gone undetected for so long? "Have you set a date for the revolution, Professor?"

"Soon." He tapped his hands together and rested his beard on the tips of his fingers. "History must reverse itself. It is time to bring back the days of the czars."

To that harsh, bloody rule of Nicholas I? Yuri wondered. He slumped into the chair across from Ivanski. *Or to Nicholas II, who was forced to abdicate?* "There are no royal descendants, sir."

"Then we will establish our own royalty. Some of our people have demonstrated in favor of going back to the monarchy. Why else would we still have a statue of our last czar? Why else do we sell pictures of Nicholas II in our marketplace?"

Because there are no meat or staples to buy, Yuri thought bitterly. *So we buy memories and worship a dead emperor.* "Not everyone is buying his picture, Professor."

"Imperial Russia must rise again. I plan a peaceful transfer of power. A diplomatic takeover. I am well-accepted, Yuri. The people will follow me back to the glory days of the past."

"Back to the palace in St. Petersburg?" Yuri asked.

"Yes, my grandfather was servant to the emperor there. Now I shall be the emperor." His voice grew curt. "But the men in the parlor believe a military takeover is the only answer."

"Ivar Noukov?"

"Yes. The general and his Serbian friend Leopold Bolav are here. They want me to step down so General Noukov can take my place." Ivanski's ghoulish laugh filled the room. "Bolav met with the president and the politburo to ask them to release an arsenal of weapons to them. He asked the Americans for money, but he comes to us for military aid."

"American money for weapons?" Yuri asked.

"No," the professor scoffed. "I don't know what excuse he used. Rebuilding perhaps. Or for agriculture. Yes, he asked the Americans for financial aid, but he comes to us for military aid. General Noukov insists that we help him."

"Let NATO help them again."

Ivanski's temples bulged. "Yuri, Mr. Bolav wants uranium. NATO won't supply that."

"Uranium? It would be five years or more before Bolav's people could come up with an atomic bomb."

"That's why I suggested nerve gas or biological warfare. I have a Czech supplier for this. Our hands would remain clean. For now," Ivanski said, "the availability of weapons or chemicals will serve Leopold's purpose. It will make the Bosnians and Muslims cautious. More importantly, it will take General Noukov out of Russia. I want the revolution to start in Moscow," the professor said calmly. "General Noukov and Leopold Bolav insist that we spread ourselves thin by striking in Bosnia first."

"With only one military unit there?"

"Noukov will delay the demobilization of our unit. The American president will protest—but he insisted on our being part of the peacekeeping forces in the first place."

Ivanski leaned back in his chair. "We will stage a chaotic disruption at the Tour de France. Within two hours—with the help of crack Russian troops and more planes, men, and equipment ready to go—there will be a Serbian coup in Bosnia." His eyes blazed. "While the NATO nations think that a Russian-Serbian rebellion has flared up in Bosnia—while the existing government in Moscow is condemned internationally for its involvement—the revived Phoenix-40 will march on Red Square and be firmly in control."

"It can only mean more bloodshed, Professor. The general will turn Bosnia and Red Square scarlet again."

Ivanski's confidence rose. "I do not care what happens in Bosnia, but I will offer our people here a peaceful solution—a return to the monarchy. Yuri, within hours of the tragedy at the Tour de France, Boris Ivanski will be the emperor. And you will serve with me."

Insane, Yuri thought. *His brilliant mind has snapped.*

Boris tapped his temple. "It is all worked out here. Once in power, I will demand an immediate withdrawal of our troops from Bosnia and bring General Noukov home in disgrace; he will be executed in Red Square." The professor glanced at his wife's picture again. "I want only what is best for my country."

Odd, Yuri thought. *I want nothing more than to leave it.*

The revival of the Phoenix plan would lead to death, and death was the one thing that Yuri feared more than failure. He yearned for the freedom that Colonel Trotsky had found in Sulzbach. Sixteen years ago Colonel Trotsky had been the mastermind behind the Phoenix-40, his leadership sound and calculated. In his own way, Professor Ivanski was as clever as Trotsky had been, another master of deceit, but was he brilliant enough to rule this country?

"The old Phoenix plan failed," Yuri warned.

"I will succeed because I know where Trotsky blundered."

No, Trotsky won, Yuri thought. *In the end, he won. He found his God there in Sulzbach and died a man at peace with himself. If only he had lived long enough to explain his God to me.*

A determined smile lit in Ivanski's eyes. "I know my plan will work. Noukov and Trotsky knew the strategies of war. I know the history of the Russian revolutions—the reasons why they succeeded or failed. I will not make the mistakes of other men."

Still Yuri argued, "Our people will not want another imperial Russia if it robs them of their religious freedom."

"What foolish nonsense, Comrade Ryskov."

Comrade to remind him of the old days and ways without God. Yuri snatched at courage. "Nicholas Trotsky believed in God."

"Comrade Trotsky is dead."

Granted. It was true. In the old days Colonel Trotsky had not believed in God, but Trotsky in the robes of a priest had spoken of peace, not just peace in the mountains of Sulzbach, but of an everlasting peace. The last time Yuri saw Trotsky, he was a dying man, but dying unafraid. Yuri said, "Our people can better die of starvation than to live without God again."

The professor gripped Yuri's knee. "I have lost General Noukov to my team. Am I losing you, too, Yuri? See me through this one. I need you as a courier one more time." He clapped his hands as though the matter were settled. "I have a man in London who will work with us. Do you remember Professor Parkovitch?"

"I thought he was dead, too."

"He has lived in England for years, supposedly as a Russian sleeper." Ivanski peered above the silver-rimmed glasses, past Yuri to a memory that rankled him. "Once Parkovitch was committed to helping us. I persuaded Colonel Trotsky to include him in the Phoenix-40, but I may have sent friends to their deaths because I trusted Parkovitch."

"If he was the British agent who betrayed the Phoenix-40, then why work with him again?"

Ivanski's eyes smiled. "According to my intelligence reports, he frequents the American embassy. That could be an advantage to us, Yuri. And he always had close ties with MI5. Once we saw that as a plus. Now—who knows?"

He seemed to be sifting his thoughts. "Parkovitch suggested that we use the Tour de France as a pivot point for passing messages. But I developed a better plan; a chaotic disturbance at the Tour will turn the world's eyes on France and away from Moscow. That's why I am sending you to Paris."

"To pass messages?"

"To check on Parkovitch. And to meet with a man called Jiri Benak. Benak is wanted by the International Police Force, another unsavory character who may be useful to us."

"But why use the Tour?"

"My dear Yuri, it adds a certain flare and style that no other revolution has had. A hundred years from now, we will be remembered for these glorious moments in history."

And you will be dead!

"We must test Benak. Not on our own soil, but there in France. If the Czechoslovakian proves himself worthy, then he will have a place in our new government—preparing weapons for us. He is a genius at that. And we have placed a cyclist on the British team. You will bring them all together, Yuri—Parkovitch, Benak, and the Serbian rider. You will test their loyalties to me. You will be my eyes and ears." A trace of a smile brightened his eyes. He tugged thoughtfully at his beard. "You won't mind going to Paris again, will you, Yuri?"

Paris! The taste in Yuri's mouth was suddenly sweet. He had walked past the American embassy on Avenue Gabriel more than once on his last trip to Paris, struggling to find the courage to ask for political asylum. If Yuri could get safely inside the embassy, he would refuse to answer any questions until they put him in contact with Drew Gregory, the American CIA officer.

Ivanski's words drew him back. "Find Parkovitch, Yuri. Play his cat-and-mouse game if you have to. If he betrayed us, he may not contact you, but he will be aware of your presence. You must be on guard." The mentor's eyes warmed for a millisecond. "The information you send back to me is crucial. Use coded information through the regular channels."

"The Moscow coup depends on me?"

"Yes, my young friend. Everything hinges on you. Imperial Russia will be grateful."

Yuri licked his parched lips. *And failure this time would be unforgivable.* The image of the American embassy on the Avenue Gabriel filled his mind again. Now he had something to barter with. What remained of the old Phoenix-40 definitely had plans to rise again in Bosnia and Moscow, and a British agent might be implicated. He could name names. Yuri had only to convince the French guards by the embassy gate to let him pass safely inside.

Boris swiveled in his chair and wrapped his thick hand around a bottle of Cognac. "Before we join General Noukov and his Serbian friend, Yuri, let us drink to our success and to the future when we rule from the old palace in St. Petersburg."

Yuri had no desire to celebrate a revolution. But he stood and lifted his glass. "Here's to that time when we have no rationing and we can bury our dead."

"And now, Yuri, let us go and deceive General Noukov and his friend. They believe we are working with them."

Yuri followed the professor into the modestly furnished sitting room. Something had amused Ivar Noukov as Yuri entered the room. A sneer still crinkled the general's ruddy features and tapered his dark eyes. He kept his hands on his lap, his thumbs spinning in perpetual twirls.

As Professor Ivanski took his seat behind the cluttered desk, his black cat sprang and landed on the other guest's shoulder. She pressed her fur against his cheek, purring. He scratched her neck, their potential for friendship obvious; but there was no welcome on his face for Yuri. "I'm Leopold Bolav," he said, not waiting to be introduced. "And you must be Yuri Ryskov. So, Professor, will he be joining us in Bosnia?"

"No, Paris has always been a city of intrigue, Leopold. I am sending him there to serve as your courier and perhaps to help negotiate a uranium transaction in the middle of the Tour de France. No one will be expecting that."

Leopold leaned forward, his cold black eyes shiny. "Then can you divert three or four hundred tons of uranium oxide my way?"

"I am certain we can help you. If not with uranium, then with Saran gas—or other useful weapons. We have contact with Jiri Benak, an expert in these areas. He assures me that he is in touch with a German chemical company that mines and processes uranium." The professor looked completely at ease as he said, "One of our British investors will determine whether Mr. Benak can help you without endangering our own security."

The Slav's cooperation wavered. He brushed the cat from his shoulder. "The fewer people aware—"

Ivanski cut him off. "If Mr. Benak and my British contact favor helping you, we will pass a message to you through the Serbian cyclist. I leave it to Yuri to work out the details."

"He is wearing the number 91 on his jersey. Do not forget that number, Mr. Ryskov, 91," Leopold repeated. Turning back to Ivanski, he asked, "What about General Noukov?"

"He can replace the general already there in Bosnia—"

Leopold cast a glance at Noukov. "It will be necessary to send the other man home in disgrace."

"A land mine would make a permanent exodus," Ivanski said. "And an acceptable reason for sending Noukov to replace him."

Noukov came out of his silence. "Leopold, I will be ready to leave as soon as you send back word—about the land mine. But, Professor, Paris is not a place for Yuri to meet Mr. Benak."

Ivanski's voice turned cold. "They will meet at Maxim's in Paris—out in the open, innocent fans at the Tour de France. And, Ivar, I will expect you to send word to me as soon as you secure a foothold in Tuzla or Sarajevo. Timing is essential. Send your messages through Paris. Yuri will make certain I get them."

The amusement in the professor's face never wavered. He was as certain of himself as Colonel Trotsky had been when he birthed the Phoenix plan. Once again the professor was in total charge.

Yuri pulled his chair to the desk and ran his hand over Ivanski's research notes on the Phoenix-40 and its failures. Parkovitch's name glared up at him. As the room emptied, leaving them alone, Yuri asked, "Why didn't you tell them that Parkovitch is your British investor?"

"There is no need for them to know."

"Professor, you have no intention of supplying the Serbians with uranium or Saran gas, do you?"

"Not if it risks my own security. But they are aware that Benak will set off a major bomb blast during the seventeenth stage of the race. Like I told them, timing is absolutely essential."

Ivanski walked briskly to a wall map and yanked it down, unveiling a well-marked world. London and Paris were boldly underscored. Small yellow flags outlined the Netherlands and France, each marking a stage in the Tour. He ran his hand clockwise. "This is the circuit that the Tour will take this year."

His hand stopped at the seventeenth stage. "I have been in touch with Jiri Benak and Parkovitch. Separately, of course."

Yuri waited, his eyes fixed on his mentor and the map.

"Benak is foolhardy, a madman no doubt. But we can depend on him to start a crisis situation at the seventeenth stage."

"While the whole world watches?" Yuri asked.

"Yes, while the whole world watches, Leopold can have his Serbian coup in Bosnia—and I will move into my palace. The people will follow me, Yuri. I know they will."

"What about Parkovitch and Benak?"

"If things go as I plan, they may eliminate each other."

He turned and smiled at Yuri, his finger still pointing to stage seventeen. "Yuri, this is what I want you to do. . . ."

Chapter 7

Grover Kendall left the District of Columbia and careened his Jaguar across the Maryland state line. As he sped toward his dad's construction site—an apartment complex this time—he knew he was destined for an argument. Ian, Grover concluded, had made a wise choice when he moved to Europe to avoid their father.

He parked unnoticed and sat in the convertible trying to interpret the mood on his father's sun-freckled face. Aubrey was taller than Grover and muscular, moving up and down the ladders with the agility of a bobcat. He expected hard work from his men, but no more than he was willing to do himself, which boiled over at 200 percent. For a man who seemed always at odds with himself, Aubrey Kendall had built an outstanding reputation. As advertised, Kendall construction jobs were done right and on schedule.

Aubrey's success had been a long time coming, delayed until wife number three appeared on the scene, stepmother number two for Grover. What blew Grover's mind was Jill's love for his father. Her love was reason enough for Aubrey to finally quit messing around and take the sobriety route. He had always pooh-poohed the twelve-step plan, but with Jill's support he would have gone for a fifty-step program. Jill had made a new man—a sober man— out of Grover's father.

But Aubrey struggled with other family relationships. He still harbored smoldering resentments against his mother for never being there when he needed her—for dying when he loved her. And he was bitter against his father for giving Olivia's grandson

Nedrick his rightful place in the family lineup. There had been little letup on Aubrey's violent fist-doubling against God—because
he couldn't blame anyone else for taking his first two wives.
Grover's mom with cancer and Ian's mother at childbirth. Lately
Aubrey's grudges were aimed at his youngest son. In Aubrey's
eyes, Ian's choice of cycling could never measure up to Grover's
junior partnership in a prestigious law firm.

Drumming the steering wheel with his car keys, Grover knew
he could put it off no longer. He eased from the car and picked
his way through the piles of lumber and steel rods and gravel to
the man barking orders—the man in the hard yellow hat with the
Kendall jawline and a surprised look on his face when he saw
Grover. "Son, watch your step," he called.

"How are you, Dad?"

Aubrey checked his watch. "Been dry six years, six weeks," he
said. He clapped Grover on the back. "What can I do for you?"

"I talked to Grandfather this morning."

"Uriah called from London? What did the old sot want?"

"The same thing."

"I've already told him—I'm not going to Europe. I can't leave
this construction project that long."

"I thought you sent for your passport."

"I changed my mind. I'm not going."

"But Gramps insists we back Ian as a family this time. The Tour
de France may be Ian's big win."

"It wasn't last year. I'll just catch the next one."

"Or the one after that?"

"Grover, if it's so all-fired important to you, go yourself. Maybe
Jill will fly to Paris with you."

"The timing is bad for me, Dad."

"Heavy date?"

"The firm asked me to represent them in Bosnia. One of the
congressmen is taking a group of investors to look over the eco-
nomic needs there. I'm to oversee the legal problems."

"What's wrong with the big boys? You lack experience in foreign law."

Grover kicked a mound of gravel. Aubrey always came up with
the downers, the negatives. "I guess the big boys don't want to
muddy their shoes," he said.

"Or get their feet blown off with a land mine."

"I was the logical choice. I'm good at Slavic languages." He risked reminding his father, "And I've been there before, Dad."

"When you were a kid."

And twice more after that, Grover thought. *During college, but you don't know about those two trips. You would have had my hide—called me a right-wing sympathizer.* "Dad, when I think of the Olympic Games in Sarajevo, I understand Ian and his international racing. It's a whole different, exciting world."

"Well, it's not my world."

"Sarajevo is one of my best memories. I'd just turned fourteen. And it was just Grams and me."

"I bet that was a first."

Grover's facial muscles tightened. "Ian couldn't tag along at the last minute. The flu or something."

"For months you talked about going back there to live."

"I still think about it sometimes."

"Maybe when one of those investors gets his business going over there, he can hire you on as his legal advisor."

No, Grover thought. *I made some bad moves there on my last visit—going in under the guise of a charitable organization to deliver food and bedding and coming out with propaganda pamphlets.* "I wouldn't be welcomed permanently," he said.

"Girl trouble?" his father asked.

"Yes, and I'd like to go back and find her." Five years was a long time to keep a pretty girl in his mind. She could well be one of those who died in that bitter conflict—fighting the war in her own way with an underground paper. He had handed her a wool blanket with the scratchy surface of army surplus.

"Charity," she had scoffed. "If you really want to do something, come back and fight alongside us."

He had mumbled something about finishing college. "All right," she had told him. "Then come once in a while and take my pamphlets back to America. Someone has to help us."

It had been the girl more than his own political views that had persuaded him to smuggle pamphlets out of the country with Serbian bombs exploding less than a mile away.

"Grover." His father's voice was sharp.

"Sorry, Dad. What were you saying?"

"I asked you to have dinner with Jill and me tonight."

Grover hated to say no. Aubrey would consider it a personal rejection. "Tonight is out, Dad. The firm signed me up for a refresher course in the Slavic languages."

"You expect to learn it overnight?"

"Enough to say 'hello,' 'good-bye,' 'how much?' And 'if my client here builds his business in your country, there will be no health benefits or retirement plan.' Legalese like that."

Aubrey surprised him and smiled. "You won't be a junior partner long. High school and college in three years each. The best law school—"

"Ian may have been Grandma's favorite, but she always provided for me, too. Her insistence on private tutors paid off."

Aubrey's smile vanished. "I suppose you think I let you down. It was always Olivia who was there for you while I hid behind my bottle. Is that it?"

"You said it, Dad. I didn't."

Aubrey shoved his hard hat back from his forehead. His eyes were as intensely blue as Ian's. It seemed to be all that the two men had in common.

"Dad, won't you reconsider going to the race?"

Aubrey shook his head. "It's not like Ian needed us. He's been on his own ever since he rode his first bicycle."

And the thing eating you is that Grandmother bought it for him. You were too stinking drunk to know that my brother wanted one.

But calmly he said, "Ian is going to win this one, Dad."

Aubrey wiped his palms on his jeans. "You always had a soft spot for that kid brother of yours."

Another jab at his father's old drinking days slipped from Grover's tongue. "We were both lonely growing up."

"How many times do I have to tell you I'm sorry? It was lonely for me, too. I buried two wives, remember?"

"That's over, Dad. Done with."

"Is it? You bring it up often enough. Either take me for who I am, Grover, or don't come around." Aubrey thumbed his sweatshirt. "I'm just an earthy sort of guy, son. Blue collar. That's me. At least you go to work in a business suit—smelling of Giorgio Armani for Men, Jill tells me. That's better than Ian has ever done." He almost spat the words on the ground. "Spending his life sweating in a cycling jersey and latex britches."

He flicked the lapel of Grover's designer suit, his mouth twisted into a crooked grin. "You're well-blended, Son, except for that mustard yellow tie. Better have Jill pick out your ties from now on."

"What about Europe, Dad? Gramps thinks we should go—"

"If Uriah wants to go, let him."

"He's not feeling well. The best he can do is be in Paris when the race ends."

"The rest is up to us? No. Have his stepgrandson go."

"Nedrick Russelmann isn't our problem, Dad."

"Sharing our inheritance with him is."

Jiri Benak stood alone in his rented house in the Basque village where he had found refuge. It lay on the French side of the Pyrenees; his window opened to a magnificent view of sheep grazing on the lower slopes with a craggy range of mountains rising behind them. He felt safe in this village, closed to outsiders. But it had opened to him—thanks to Ignasius.

Out on the slopes, Ignasius moved contentedly among the sheep. He wore dark knickers, knee-high wool socks, and a long-sleeved shirt-vest with bright multicolored designs on the lapel and cuffs. A royal-blue beret sat cocked on his head. Ignasius prodded his sheep with a staff as he herded them up one slope and down another; they disappeared into a valley, leaving only the mountains and sky for Jiri to enjoy.

Nature's beauty! And still Jiri could bring the face of Drew Gregory into focus at the snap of a finger, marring that beauty. He did so now, hating Gregory. Because of him, Jiri was a man without roots, without country, without money. All he had was his mind and his ability to design weapons of destruction.

The success of his mission depended on controlling his resentments. He fingered a piece of copper wire, carefully planning the bombs he would use on the Tour—homemade, not traceable to any company or location. Like his father and grandfather, Jiri was a designer of weapons. A brilliant man, he called himself. The key was fear. Strike fear into the thousands that lined the Tour route, and he could cause total pandemonium, accomplishing what he wanted with minimal deaths.

Abject fear. That was the key. Panic. He would create havoc, utter confusion that would disperse the crowds in a frantic dash for safety. First, he would continue the flow of typed notes to threaten the riders, and then by stage eleven, he would use an incendiary bomb to create a firestorm. Or a light-weight pipe bomb designed for minimal destruction. Or better yet, a plastic bomb to blow away the mountain. But he knew the invincible French mind. Nothing would stop the race. And then stage seventeen! Jiri thrilled at the thought of the explosion that would grab the world's attention and make what was happening simultaneously in Moscow and Bosnia seem small in comparison. Only after he proved his worth to the Russians by destroying the Tour de France could he plan the destruction of Drew Gregory.

The Basque village was a temporary solace—his invitation to life in Moscow intolerable even to consider. What he wanted was that cottage in the Cotswolds—a base from which he could work— where he could return. For now, he must remain in this village because of its proximity to stage seventeen on the Tour route. From here he could safely transport his bomb. Everything depended on an unhindered friendship with Ignasius.

They had met three years ago at a mercenary camp at the foot of the Pyrenees, the two men as different as a glacier from a golden wheat field. Jiri was a cold, cynical loner; Ignasius was warm and friendly. Jiri, blond and blue-eyed, was German-born, German-reared, an employee at the Jarvoc steel plant in the Czech Republic. Ignasius was a farmer. His narrow face had been so dark that Jiri thought him a Spaniard. He was of medium height, his prominent nose so large that it formed stretch wrinkles between his brows and across his forehead. An arrogant German and a swaggering Basque peasant! They proved kindred spirits, blood brothers—distrustful of authority, greedy for power and money.

In an unwritten pact with Ignasius, the villagers took Jiri in as part of their isolated community, and once he was accepted, they felt committed, obligated to protect him. That he came and went freely—disappearing for days at a time—did not alarm them at first. He was Ignasius's friend, a friend that must be protected from

Interpol and all outsiders. As long as Jiri danced with the people, drank with them, laughed with them, they found no fault in him.

He turned from the window and went back to his worktable, doing a mental rundown on the materials he had gathered. To his left stood the old battered typewriter with the faded ribbon and the packet of plain paper. To his right lay a spool of copper wire, a shoe box filled with new timers, and a rolled sheet of plastic. He toed the sack of silverware on the floor—the metal fragments that he needed when he built his bombs. A smirk narrowed his mouth as he thought about the locked shed behind the house where he had hidden bottles of ammonia nitrate and castor oil.

Not a week went by without his thoughts turning back to the steel plant in Jarvoc—and the explosion in the Jarvoc tunnels that had allowed him to put a safe distance between himself and Drew Gregory. He had never intended self-destruction, but the violence of that explosion had almost killed him. It had blown him against the shaft, sucking the wind from his lungs and blinding him with dust particles, cutting his face and hands with fragments. The whole horrendous experience had compelled him to hate Drew Gregory more.

🌼🌼🌼

Paris, 2 P.M. Drew Gregory and his wife stood outside the Hotel de Crillon at the Place de la Concorde, across the street from the American embassy. Drew glanced anxiously at his watch. "We're an hour later than I intended," he said.

"So why are we standing out here?"

"Carwell wants it to be a casual meeting and unrehearsed. And here they come, Maggie outrunning Troy as usual."

Maggie darted across the street from the embassy and pounced on them with a flourish, gushing, "Drew, dear, what a wonderful surprise! How nice to see you."

He accepted the kiss she planted on his cheek, grateful that it wasn't his lips. Their encounters had always been at the social level, mostly at embassy balls where she never sat out a dance. She had fought coming to Paris—had gone ballistic as Troy put it—but she had recovered enough to take on Paris with utter abandon. From her lovely, outrageous outfit, he could see that she had obviously found one of the wacky couture shops off the Champs Elysees.

Drew groaned. Troy's Agency salary could never cover Maggie's extravagance. And Miriam was going to be in Paris on a three-week shopping spree with Maggie Carwell! He'd be poverty-stricken the next time he saw Miriam.

As he turned to warn her, Miriam's head cocked slightly, amusement in those gorgeous eyes. She seemed braced for her own demonstrative greeting.

But Maggie said shyly, "I've so looked forward to meeting you, Miriam. I can hardly wait to hear about your art gallery in Beverly Hills." The ringed hands clasped. "Shopping and the galleries will be so much more fun with you here. Have you seen Paris before?"

She took a breath at last, waiting. Miriam obliged her and laughed. "On my honeymoon. Actually on both honeymoons."

"Then you don't know a thing about the city," Maggie told her. "We will have a perfectly marvelous time together."

"Not until I find a room."

"No reservation? Then you'll stay with us. No, I won't hear any arguments. There's plenty of room, isn't there, Troy, dear?"

He acquiesced, his brows arching. He gave Drew a brisk handshake, a nod to Miriam. Carwell was the CIA station-chief in Paris, a proper man groomed this morning in English tweeds and smelling of Tiffany cologne. His wife chose his wardrobe, but she could not hide the emerging bald spot in his thinning gray hair.

"Miriam will be comfortable with us," he agreed pleasantly.

Miriam will be exhausted, Drew thought, *but safe.*

Maggie glanced at her jeweled watch, another of Troy's bribes to keep her happy in France. "There's a fashion show in another hour. We mustn't miss it." She looked up at her husband. "Troy, love, be a dear. Have Drew transfer Miriam's luggage to the embassy limo. You can bring it home when you get there—at midnight." She turned a scolding glance on Drew. "I hope you don't detain my husband any longer than that."

So Maggie thinks I arranged this meeting, Drew thought. *Wrong!* He was here on Troy's orders for another behind-closed-doors meeting with Maurice Chambord, a time-gobbler that Troy had insisted upon. "We have more information," Troy had said on the phone. "Best discussed in person."

Drew slipped his arm around Miriam. "I was going to treat my wife to the Hotel de Crillon, but I'll feel better about her staying with friends. I didn't like the idea of her wandering around Paris alone for three weeks."

"Oh, we'll be together the whole time," Maggie promised.

"But what about you, Drew?" Miriam asked.

Troy was quick to avoid another invitation. "We'll get him a room here at the de Crillon. He leaves early in the morning."

By three at the latest, Drew thought. Tonight, if Troy's meeting ends sooner than planned.

Miriam squeezed his hand. "You haven't forgotten dinner with Robyn and Pierre this evening?"

Embarrassed at his memory lapse, he said, "I wish they hadn't insisted on flying over to Paris just for dinner."

"Pierre is here on business, a medical supply conference of some sort. Robyn came with him. Besides, Robyn has to see you, Drew, just to make certain you're all right."

"Nothing's going to happen to me."

"She's afraid for you. For herself actually."

He turned his face away from the Carwells and said, "Miriam, I'll never walk out of your lives again."

She whispered back, "Robyn knows that, but the fear of losing you is never far from her thoughts. She hates what you do for a living." She flashed him a warm smile. "Robyn said they have something important to tell us. Something that can't wait."

He gripped her shoulders. "They're all right?"

"Of course. They've never been happier." She turned to Troy. "Could Drew leave the meetings early? Say around seven."

Troy nodded. "It will give us an excuse to break early."

"That's settled then," Drew said. "I'll make reservations."

"Pierre made them at Maxim's. Meet us there at seven, Drew."

Carwell checked his Gucci watch. "Maggie and I will pick Miriam up at the restaurant at eleven. Is that late enough?"

"Ample time," Drew said. He glanced down at his suit. "I won't have time to change before dinner, Miriam."

"The children won't even notice, not with their good news."

She tilted her face toward him. Dismissing his own dislike of public affection, he kissed her with growing intensity at the thought of their three weeks apart.

With a quick wave to Troy, the women were off to the fashion show, Maggie talking at avalanche speed. Troy shook his head. "I hope your wife can keep up with Maggie's constant chatter."

"She'll keep you young, Troy."

"Or put me in an early grave. My sons warned me that I should think twice about marrying a woman so much younger, but Maggie is the joy of my life, Drew. I'd be lost without her."

As the pedestrian crowd thinned in front of the Hotel de Crillon, Drew asked, "Are we meeting at the embassy?"

"No, I wanted our meeting to be casual." He nodded behind them. "The Societe du Tour director agreed. Chambord and the other gentlemen are waiting for us in the private tearoom."

Drew whistled. "Not on my expense account."

"No. On the Agency's. Drew, before we go in—the less you tell your daughter about the problems at the Tour, the better."

"I won't lie to Robyn. I'll abbreviate the truth—but that's as much as I can promise." He restrained Troy as he moved toward the de Crillon. "Now you tell me—why did I make this unnecessary trip to Paris? What's wrong with using the phone?"

"Chambord is not too sure of you, Drew. He's afraid you'll go off and run things on your own during the race."

"Is that how you described me to him?"

"I guess something I said gave him that impression. Chambord thought your coming to Paris would give you a good view of the Champs Elysees."

They were steps from the boulevard. "I've seen it before."

He pulled Drew against the store front. "We wanted you to see it again so you could picture the avenue in your mind lined with half a million fans. It's up to you to make certain Kendall makes it all the way to the Arc de Triomphe."

His fingers pressed against Drew's arm. "I don't want any surprises in the meeting."

"Meaning?"

"Did Kendall tell you about the latest threat?" Drew raised one eyebrow. "At Mount Ventoux? He glazed over it. He didn't seem alarmed enough to warrant notifying Chambord."

"Or me. I still had to hear it from Chambord. That should have come from you, Drew. Kendall denied it, of course, so we're forced to go on the word of Basil Millard, one of his teammates."

"Maybe Millard wants Ian off the team," Drew said.

"No, they're friends. He photographed a chalk message at Mount Ventoux, the second or third threat against Kendall. Millard notified MI5; they notified Chambord. Without Millard's help we would be unaware that the problem was ongoing. Most of the threats are against the Tour. Now it's narrowed down to one team. One rider."

"We discussed it before—it could be someone with a personal grudge against the Kendall family."

"We've compared all the warnings. Some are typed. Others scrawled in ink. The signatures differ. After comparing the bomb threats and the warnings to Kendall, we're convinced that the problem is not limited to one organization or one man. We may be dealing with two separate terrorist groups, Drew."

"Tell Chambord to call off the race."

"The French don't bow down to threats."

"So no extremist group has taken credit?" Drew asked.

"They won't unless the bombs go off. The Palestinians and the IRA like to take credit after the fact. Or send a warning thirty minutes in advance." Carwell paused. "We've been checking, but young Kendall has no ties with any of these organizations, no political interests in them. His whole life is cycling."

"I could have told you that, Troy."

As people hurried by them, Carwell retreated into the hotel entryway. "I think the terrorist organization is using the international race to speak out politically, but we still don't know their terms or why they are targeting Kendall. Kendall's record comes up clean. Doesn't drink or carouse. Probably doesn't even vote absentee ballot." Carwell kept running at the mouth. "His grandfather hasn't been active in MI5 for years, and his grandmother's politics died with her."

"You've got to look beyond the family, Troy."

"We have." Carwell cleared his throat. "Chambord and I have discussed every terrorist group that has attacked France in the last twenty years. We turned over every name we could think of to Interpol. French Intelligence has increased security threefold."

"What about Coach Skobla? Maybe he's involved."

"What earthly reason would he have to stop the race, Drew? There's money in winning." He lowered his voice as he opened the hotel doors. "We don't have answers yet, but Chambord still insists there could be a Russian connection."

"Any specific reason?"

"None that makes sense unless you count the possibility of a political uprising that we're not onto yet. I lived in Moscow, Drew. Chambord's right. You can never outguess them."

Drew grimaced as they stepped inside the lobby. "It might be as simple as the Russians not having more cyclists in the race."

Troy's tired eyes darkened. "To pacify Chambord, we brought in a Russian handwriting expert, a rather likable chap."

As they walked over the glittering marble lobby floor in the luxurious eighteenth-century hotel, Troy said, "We've arranged for a team doctor to ride with you. Dr. Raunsted. He's French, knows the language. Spent years in sports medicine."

"Jon Gainsborough won't go for that added expense."

"We didn't ask him, and, based on your concerns, we didn't notify Radburn Parker either. The doctor has worked for us before, Drew. He'll be there to keep a close watch on Kendall and the team. And on you, too."

He put on a smile as they entered the private garden room, empty now except for a table of three. The man with the handlebar mustache grinned as they approached. Drew recognized Francois Pellier, the French commandant who had helped him on a previous assignment in Paris. Out of uniform, Pellier was casually dressed, yet a polite, articulate man as he rose to meet them. "Monsieur Gregory, how good to see you," he said with a warmth that twisted the whiskery ruffle on his upper lip.

The man to Commandant Pellier's right had fiery red hair; shocks of it stood straight out from his temples. He was thirty perhaps, certainly not more than thirty-five. This had to be the handwriting expert, the analyzer of an open o, an uncrossed t, the undotted i, or a poorly looped l. Drew didn't trust their theories, but then his own handwriting was nothing to brag about.

The expert's shoulders were stooped, either from long hours at the desk, Drew concluded, or as compensation for his gangly six-foot-four frame. He had a pleasant look on his face, a noted relief to Drew when he saw Maurice Chambord scowling up at him. Drew took the Frenchman's proffered hand in his, skin brushing against skin, Chambord's distance carefully maintained with the limp handshake.

Chapter 8

Drew arrived at 3 Rue Royale fifteen minutes late and passed under the awning into Maxim's legendary opulence. The interior of the restaurant glowed with mahogany and copper and full wall paintings—stylish enough to delight Miriam, masculine enough to please Drew. He strolled to the reservation desk. "I'm with the Courtland party," he said, glancing around.

The maitre d' led him through the crowded restaurant toward a secluded corner. Drew had anticipated a quiet dinner with his family, but he was bombarded with a steady hum of foreign languages as he wound around the tables. French. German. Spanish. Italian. The high-spirited clientele was as mixed as its one-hundred-year-old history, with tourists chattering nonstop and fashionable Parisian celebrities demanding attention. He sidestepped a chair as a diner stumbled to his feet, mumbling in Russian. Casting a preoccupied glance at the man, Drew turned his attention to his family, waving as he approached them.

"Don't get up, Pierre," he told his son-in-law as he placed a hurried kiss on Miriam's cheek. "Sorry, I'm late, *Liebling*."

"I'm used to it. It's your daughter who's been fretting."

He leaned down and whispered in Robyn's ear. "I've missed you, Princess." As he sat down between Miriam and Robyn, he asked, "Shall we go ahead and order? I'm starving."

"I gave the order," Pierre told him. "But I asked the waiter to hold off serving us so we could visit awhile."

"Oh! Guess the majority rules. What shall we talk about?"

"You, Daddy."

His guard went up. "You first, Princess. You're the one with the good news."

Her smile turned impish. "You remember the Prescotts?"

"You know I do. If it hadn't been for Andrea and Sherm, I never would have found you and your mother again."

"Sherm rang us up yesterday—with a birth announcement."

Drew felt disappointment. All through the meeting with Chambord and Troy Carwell, he had tried to guess Robyn's news. It had all gone back to the possibility of having a grandchild of his own. He managed a cheerful, "They've had a baby? A boy?"

"No."

"A girl then?"

"Well, not exactly."

Drew's face clouded. "What then? Has something gone wrong?"

"They had twin girls, Dad," she said excitedly. "Katrina and Kathryn. Katrina was named for Andrea's grandmother."

Drew tossed Robyn a wry smile. "I guessed as much. I met Katrina York. She was married to my superior officer in my army days." He fought off deep emotion. "I spoke with the captain's wife a few times before she died, and I'll never forget her."

"And the name Kathryn?" Miriam prompted, taking his hand.

"That would be for Ryan Ebsworth's aunt."

His thoughts spun back to Andrea York's flight to Canada after witnessing the assassination of the American ambassador in Paris. Andrea had sat in the jet a few rows in front of him, a beautiful girl in her chic Italian suit with Ryan, the spindly Canadian terrorist sitting beside her. Drew had followed them to Lake Harrison under orders to protect Andrea, but Sherm Prescott had complicated everything by falling in love with her.

As Miriam squeezed his hand, he said, "Ryan's aunt was a godly woman. She raised Ryan as her own son and loved him, but he broke her heart with the choices he made. He drowned in Hell's Gate Canyon with Andrea looking on."

Robyn's sea-blue eyes held his. "Were you involved, Dad?"

He twirled his glass and watched the lemon wedge swim around the rim. "I tried to capture him, but Ebsworth chose suicide."

"Dad, I didn't mean to upset you."

"It just brought back memories—not all of them bad." He watched his daughter in a detached mood as she blew against the wisps of auburn hair tumbling across her forehead. "Robyn, I thought Andrea might have told you about those days in Canada."

"A little bit, but not about Kathryn or Ryan."

"The Prescotts are good people. How like them to allow Kathryn to be a grandmother by proxy."

Robyn's fingers touched his, the wedding band and diamond on her finger still sparkling with newness. "Pierre is wiring flowers to them tomorrow—when we get back to Geneva."

"I can send them from Paris," Pierre offered. "Should we add your names, Drew?"

"Would you? Mother's and mine. And double whatever you plan to spend on baby gifts. Something really feminine," Drew suggested. "Katrina and Kathryn were both stylish women."

"Dad, will you be as excited when you're a grandfather?"

His neck snapped as he turned to her. "I'd be the proudest man on earth—except for Pierre here. I missed so much of your childhood, Princess. I want to be around for my grandchildren."

"How? You're always away on another assignment." Her finger locked around his. "Dad, don't get involved in the cycling tour."

"Has your mother been upsetting you?"

"She hasn't said much. It's what the news media say about the bomb threats that worries me. Why don't you just stick to tennis matches at the embassy, Dad? You'd stay safe that way."

"There's nothing to worry about, Princess. They have the Tour de France every year."

"Except for World War I and World War II," Pierre reminded him. "This is another time when they ought to cancel out."

"And give the terrorists a victory?" Drew's jaw clamped. "I'll be safe. Vic Wilson and Chase Evans are going with me."

"Ian Kendall's girlfriend?"

"Robbie, they're just friends," Miriam said. "Ian wishes for more, but he'll ride better knowing Chase is there for him." She ran her finger over Drew's wrist. "If anything happens during the race, your dad is counting on Ian confiding in Chase."

"The old theory that a woman keeps a man more focused?"

"It works for me, Princess." Drew groped for words to reassure

Robyn. "Honey, security is tight. We're just working with the Tour organizers to make certain the race runs smoothly."

Pierre leaned forward, hands clasped. "If they expect a smooth race, then why invite intelligence agents to ride along?"

Drew matched Pierre's cynical gaze. "Dealing with the threat of terrorism anywhere is part of our job."

Pierre's dislike of intelligence agencies showed in his sun-bronzed face; his gaze challenged Drew to defend Company honor. For a man with Swiss blood running in his veins, Pierre was good with statistics that defaulted the intelligence system. He could spew off the Agency history from Donavan to Colby almost as well as Drew could, and throw in Woolsey, Webster, and Deutch as though he kept a personal dossier on each one.

"You're a marksman, Drew. Is this what it's all about—the assassination of some foreign leader attending the Tour?"

Not some foreign leader, Drew thought, *but the assassination of a cyclist.* He sat stoically, determined to quell any argument that could put a wedge between his daughter and his son-in-law.

"What about it?" Pierre asked. "It's not up to me to explain your job to your daughter. She gets upset whenever I suggest your Company has a long history of questionable operations. This Tour business is just getting you involved again."

Drew didn't like locking horns with Pierre or risking their tenuous truce right here in Maxim's. He'd come to appreciate Pierre over the months—a young executive in his early thirties who loved Robyn more than anything else in life. He had a pleasant face—angry at the moment—strongly chiseled, honest, direct. But he wasn't budging an inch this time.

"Well, Drew? Is the Company up to its old tricks?"

Fortunately, Drew thought, *you only know what you read or hear.* The history was tainted, Drew had to admit. Bill Colby and men like him spilled the Company history into books; Ames and Porter Deven had sold its secrets, but the record wasn't all bad.

"Daddy?"

Miriam maintained her calm, her hand still resting on his. "Pierre—Robyn, dear, that's enough. This was supposed to be a family celebration. A happy time. Let's not quarrel."

"But Drew's job makes my wife unhappy."

"It doesn't have to, Pierre." She faced her daughter. "Robyn, dear, your father's life is a world unlike our own."

One beyond your comprehension, he thought ruefully. *A Company still trying to live down its assassination teams and government takeovers. A Company still tainted by the old days, the Cold War ways. But must I always apologize to my family?*

Miriam smiled, the half-smile that Drew dreaded. He knew that his Company loyalties still prickled her skin.

"Robbie," she said, "come to the powder room with me. Please."

In her own gentle way, Miriam would squelch the questions so that their dinner together could be special. *Colby's honorable men,* Drew thought as they walked away. The code of silence that Miriam had always hated. Drew's miserable world of intrigue left so little room for those who meant the most to him. Again he met the scathing in Pierre's eyes. "Truce," he suggested.

"Good idea—but how serious are the threats against the Tour? In Robyn's condition—"

"Is something wrong with my daughter?"

"Only with her worrying about you. I met this Maurice Chambord at a company dinner recently. He was our guest speaker, drumming up enthusiasm and funding for this year's Tour." Pierre paused and then said, "He was an impressive, well-dressed man, but not my kind of person. If you're working with him, Drew, it could mean trouble."

Tongue-in-cheek, Drew said, "Chambord did suggest an assassin to take out the man or organization threatening the Tour. He looked directly at me when he said it."

Pierre's face filled with disappointment. "I counted on your experience on the Sulzbach mountain to change your old tactics."

"I didn't take Chambord seriously, and I certainly didn't agree." Drew touched his chest. "Don't judge me too severely, Pierre. That moment on the mountain changed me in here. It didn't change Company policy. I'm needed. The terrorists are targeting Ian Kendall."

"Kendall? Let the British handle it. He's riding for them."

"He's an American, Pierre, and a personal friend."

"Stay out of it, Drew. A death at the race could put a shroud on the Tour for years to come."

"The Munich massacre didn't stop the Olympics." From the corner of Drew's eye, he saw the girls coming back. "Even when the militia threatened to disrupt the last games, they just beefed up security. That's what this is all about. Security."

Protection for Kendall and those other fine young men.

"You have enemies, Drew. Be careful—" Pierre's words hung in the air unfinished as Miriam and Robyn took their seats again.

Drew checked his watch. "Pierre, what happened to that meal you ordered? Did you ask them to roast a whole lamb?"

Pierre lifted his hand and a waiter stepped from the shadows, a massive tray balanced in his palm. He grinned as he served them bowls of creamed mussel soup with onions and parsley swimming on top. He turned to Drew, "Ground pepper, monsieur?"

"Please."

"Drew, we're having breaded Sole Albert for the main course," Miriam said as she tasted her soup. "That should please you."

"Did you remember the torte Tatins for dessert?"

"Exactly like our honeymoon."

"Even to the glasses of vermouth, *Liebling*?"

"We'll do what we did then—leave them."

"More lemon Evian?" the waiter asked. "Or anything else?"

As Pierre shook his linen napkin, Drew said, "I don't seem to have any silverware—or napkin."

The waiter turned to his tray and swung around again, placing a service setting by Drew's hand. He grinned as he waited.

"Did you run out of Maxim's napkins?" Drew grumbled.

"Oh, Daddy, don't make a fuss. Use what he brought you."

Drew unraveled the rough terry cloth and caught the silverware in his hand. The waiter hadn't moved. Miriam nudged closer to Drew. Robyn slipped her hand into Pierre's. Four pairs of eyes focused on him, the waiter's bulging with anticipation.

"What? It's not linen." He shook the terry cloth open and glanced at the waiter. "I don't understand."

The waiter shrugged, palms extended. "The monsieur, the madame want to surprise you."

At a signal from Miriam, the waiter lifted the cloth and tucked it around Drew's neck. "A bib for you, monsieur. I read it. 'I love my *grandpere*.' That's you, Mr. Gregory."

"It's true?" Drew asked, his grin matching the waiter's.

Robyn nodded, her face glowing. "I'm—we're—Pierre and I are going to have a baby. You're going to be a grandfather."

"And if you're going to be around as promised," Pierre said, "you had best plan on retirement by the end of March."

"March! You mean—"

"That's what she means, Drew. Our daughter is pregnant. That's why our kids insisted on dinner together this evening."

"You already knew, *Liebling?*"

"I guessed."

So did I, he thought, *but that Prescott news threw me.*

"Are you pleased?" Robyn asked anxiously.

With the bib still tucked beneath his chin, he pulled Robyn to her feet and into his arms. Across the top of her head, he winked at Pierre. "I'm pleased for you both, Princess. I can't believe you flew to Paris just to tell me."

"We thought you'd be more cautious during the Tour de France if you knew. You will be, won't you, Dad?" she asked as their dinner plates were served.

"I'll just be gone three weeks. I promise."

Promises! He was always making promises to Robyn. He had promised to climb Heidi's mountain with her a long time ago. "Princess, I guess we have to put off our trip to Heidi's mountain a little longer."

"I'm not crippled—just pregnant. You are happy for me?"

"As thrilled as I was the day I learned about you. I can still see your mother coming out of the doctor's office, saying, 'Yes. Yes. Yes.'"

"Then why do you look so worried?"

"I want everything to go right for you."

Miriam's pregnancy had not gone well. Toxemia. Swollen hands and feet. Periodic bed rest. Just as violent was the emotional upheaval as they fought about Drew's overseas assignment. They had agreed on the name Wallace for a boy, but the whole time Drew had wanted a girl, a girl baby as pretty as Miriam. He smiled at this grown daughter of his who favored the Gregory side of the family. No child had been more wanted. No child was missed more during those long years of separation from Miriam.

Pierre pushed back his dinner plate and slipped his arm

around Robyn. "Drew, if we have a son, we plan to name him Drew Wallace after you. Robyn's idea, but I concur."

Miriam's face glowed in the candlelight as she leaned over and kissed Drew's cheek. "Darling, we'd better pray for a little girl. I could never handle another Drew."

Drew Wallace! Wallace for the dad that Drew had loved and admired. "Wallace! Then my grandson will be a giant of a man. My father was."

Outside of Maxim's, as the Carwells pulled up to the curb, Drew hugged his daughter. "Princess, boy or girl, Mother and I will be pleased as long as the baby is healthy."

He kissed her on the forehead and released her. "March." He glanced at the Carwells standing politely by their car. "By then I should be retired." *The Tour will be over. And the trouble at the embassy—the trouble with Lennie—should be settled by then.*

Carwell frowned as Robyn asked, "Will you retire nearby?"

"I planned on Scotland until your mother came back into my life, but your mother wants to stay in London or Switzerland, close enough to be with you and Pierre now and then."

"And to bounce your grandchild on your knee." She leaned against him. "I'm so glad you two are back together again."

"I never wanted your mother to go away in the first place."

"Any more than I want you to go away now? I'm afraid you won't come back. Why don't you tell Mr. Carwell you can't go?"

Pierre stood by the open taxi door, waiting for Robyn. "I have no choice, Princess," Drew said. "I'm just doing my job."

Yuri Ryskov sat alone in the corner of Maxim's, unobserved by Drew and his family. The herbed sole still lay on his plate, half-eaten, bits of unfamiliar stringy greens beside it. He had drained a second glass of vermouth, and now the pain in his stomach rose to a new pitch, gnawing and tearing at his innards.

He had seen Gregory arrive—his good fortune unbelievable as he recognized the American CIA officer from Sulzbach. For a fleeting moment, hope rose in Yuri's breast. He stumbled to his feet as the waiter led Gregory past his table, intent on begging him for asylum. He cried out in Russian, but in the blaring cacophony of the foreign voices all around him, Gregory did not hear his cry for help.

He sank back down to his chair, defeated, the taste of mussels and onions filling his mouth. He yearned for someone to speak his native Russian so he could ask for the English words that would grant him entry into the American embassy.

He tried to sort out the discord of sounds that pressed all around him. Deep voices. Soft voices. No one turned his way. No one offered to sit at his table. Now the orchestra was playing "The Merry Widow," the notes of the song familiar to his ear.

Yuri watched Gregory slip his arm around the stunning woman beside him and saw the faces of the young couple animated and smiling as they spoke with Drew. Suddenly Gregory was on his feet, a strange piece of cloth tucked around his neck, his arms open to the young woman who looked so much like him.

Longing gripped Yuri as he watched Drew Gregory. Yuri had never known the love of a woman, never felt the touch of his own child's hand, never slept in Paris without fear of a gendarme knocking on his door. Perhaps in America he would no longer be alone, no longer be afraid. Peace. Yuri wanted peace.

But could there be any peace in the bronze glow of this room? Fear wrapped its tentacles around him. Here in Paris, he was following Professor Ivanski's orders. Somewhere in the shadows of Maxim's, Yuri's contact from the Czech Republic was surely aware of his presence. Why had he not made himself known?

Chapter 9

As the airliner stopped at the Schiphol terminal, Salvador Contoni vaulted from his seat and grabbed his luggage from the overhead rack. By the time the cabin door swung open, he was by the attendant's elbow winking. "Sorry, I'm in a hurry," he said.

She glanced at his suitcase. "You travel light."

"It avoids delays at the roundabout." *And the risk of the* politie *noticing me,* he thought. If he needed clothes, he would buy new ones, or when the race neared Isigny, he'd go to the farm and pick up the suits he had left at Monique's in March.

The flight attendant's dark eyes looked like brilliant saucers as she said, "Thanks for flying with us, but I thought you were going to show me Amsterdam this evening."

"Next time." He knuckled her cheek and deplaned while the other passengers still crowded the aisle.

First class had accommodated his last-minute arrival and now allowed for this quick departure. The moving walkways swept him through the terminal, past shops and car rentals; then with long strides he was out of the airport and boarding a hotel bus for the fifteen-kilometer ride into Amsterdam. For convenience he took a room at the Seven Bridges, grateful that at the peak of summer there was still space available. Monique preferred to stay at the elegant nineteenth-century Amstel that overlooked the river, but the Seven Bridges was more to Salvador's liking—not even a dozen rooms, but his had been tastefully furnished. The owners frowned upon credit cards, so there would be no surprise when he paid cash for his lodging. The bountiful breakfast would be served in his room, giving him the privacy he needed.

Once settled, he struck out for the diamond center to keep his appointment with Willem Christofels. When Sal reached the Singel Canal, he lingered on the bridge to take in the lights and shadows that might have inspired a Rembrandt painting—or the mystery of a Ruisdael landscape. He loved this hearty city. She was a capital of trade and finance that appealed to his love of money, a network of waterways and flower markets that delighted him, a unique metropolis filled with businessmen pedaling their one-speed bicycles to work. He wished Monique were by his side so she could enjoy these faces of Amsterdam set against a delft blue sky one moment and then darkened by the shifting clouds the next.

His mood swept to the gray of the clouds as the bells of the Westerkerk tower rang out the notes of "John Brown's Body." This was Amsterdam as Sal knew it—full of the unexpected, a city of carillon bells and gifted artists—a city tolerant of those with goals less noble than the painters. Ignoble was how Monique described his plans to find Ian Kendall. Did she not understand? It was not Kendall that he wanted to destroy, but Drew Gregory.

He pounded his anger against the pavement as he walked rapidly toward the diamond center. Any other man would be going there to buy a diamond for the woman he loved. Sal had other plans. He reached the glittering shop in ten minutes. A gloved attendant held the glass door open for him. Once inside, Sal gazed around and did a visual recheck. The grinding and polishing of diamonds was done in the rear of the store with a few professionals out front to impress the tourists and the potential buyers. Willem Christofels could usually be found front and center, overseeing his customers and his profitable business. This morning he was noticeably absent.

"*Goedemorgen.*" The pleasant voice belonged to the elegantly dressed receptionist, the pretty face and figure to someone in her early twenties. Christofels's daughter? The oldest one?

"Brunhilda?" he gambled.

Her curious eyes settled on him. Her voice lowered. "I didn't recognize you, Mr. Contoni."

"It's been four years—but your father is expecting me."

Her gaze shifted uneasily. "He left early."

"But we have an appointment."

She scanned the calendar. "*Gisteren*," she told him.

"No. It was not yesterday. This morning." He made a point of glancing at his watch. "Precisely at eleven, and I am on time."

"Perhaps you can reach him tomorrow, Mr. Contoni. If it is diamonds you want, I can—"

He left her still making excuses. The doorman swung the door back for him, preventing an enraged thrust of Sal's bare fist against the glass. Outside he looked back. She had picked up the telephone. *Go ahead. Warn your papa,* he thought.

It took him a fraction of a second to picture Christofels's home in his mind; it was just two or three blocks from the store beyond the ring of canals. No, he remembered. It was one of the charming canal houses off of Keizersgracht or Prinsengracht. The look-alike houses sat flush against a sidewalk lined with elm trees, typically Dutch, spotlessly clean, and tippy with age. They clung to their seventeenth-century charm, existing without benefit of yards or porches, yet having the glistening waters of the canal and the flowered houseboats in easy view from their front windows.

Salvador recognized Christofels's gabled home when he saw it—a narrow three-story house of stucco and brick leaning into its neighbor. The shutter-windows were open, and a flat portion of the red roof served as a hideaway for the potted geraniums. Sal strolled into the gift shop filled with curios and books, nodded briskly at Christofels's wife, and slipped past the lace curtain into the living quarters before she could stop him.

At the foot of the narrow, twisting stairs, he called, "Willem, it's Contoni. I must see you."

An unwelcoming grunt erupted as Willem filled the top of the stairwell. "Why did you come here, Contoni?"

"You didn't keep your appointment."

Christofels looked thirty pounds heavier. He was a hard-working family man, visibly unhappy with his unwanted guest. As Sal climbed the steep steps, he imagined Willem's bulging hips brushing the walls. He stopped two steps from the man's doubled fists, not risking a confrontation.

"Don't come here haunting me with past mistakes, Contoni."

"Relax, Christofels. No one knows that your polished diamonds helped fund the mercenary camp in the Pyrenees."

"Harland Smith lied to me about my investments."

"No, he fed into your right-wing sympathies."

"I thought we were running guns to help the Bosnians."

Sal shook his head. "You should have realized Harland had no political loyalties. He sold arms to anyone that wanted them."

"What a fool I was."

"That's over now and the camp shut down. But I still need your help, Willem. I need to borrow a bicycle."

Christofels visibly relaxed. "That's all? Your visit has nothing to do with—my old political views?"

"I don't care how a man votes," Sal said. "My whole association with Harland Smith was for money." *No, that's a lie,* he thought. *I stayed on, waiting for the day when something happened to Smith, and Monique was free to be mine.*

Christofels's glance strayed to his wife at the foot of the stairs. He turned abruptly and led Sal into the tidy sitting room. "Why bother me? I cannot risk loaning you a bike. The International Police Force is looking for you, Salvador."

"The black kettle speaks. What about you, my friend?"

Christofels overlapped the chair as he sat in it. "I have nothing to do with politics anymore."

"Nor do I. But, Willem, I need your bike and your car."

"You can rent them elsewhere. Don't involve my family."

"A privately owned Volkswagen will be safer—your wife's car perhaps—with a bike rack on top." He leaned forward. "And I need two cycling jerseys—one identical to what the British team is wearing, the other a duplicate of one of the Dutch team jerseys."

"How can I do that?" Christofels whined.

"How is your problem. Your contacts in s'Hertogenbosch will know where those teams are staying. Steal them if you have to."

"What are you into now, Contoni?" Alarm darkened the pouches beneath his eyes. "Are you involved in the bomb threats against the Tour de France?"

"Bomb threats?" Contoni asked. "Of course not. I'm not a fool. But I am attending the race, and I do need transportation."

Sal grew anxious as he heard footsteps on the stairs. "It's just for three weeks, Willem. After that, you won't see me again unless I come to buy a diamond for Harland Smith's widow."

Willem's jaw cracked. His mouth twitched involuntarily. "You always took a fancy to that woman. Get out. I can't help you. I won't—"

Christofels turned, startled, as his daughter ran into the room. "Mother is frightened, Father. Tell him to leave."

Salvador smiled at Brunhilda. "He just did, but I am not going until your father promises to help me."

"I can't do what he asks, Brunhilda." The whine twisted his mouth. "He wants shirts like the cycling teams are using."

Her eyes narrowed. "I'll help you get them."

"But I will not loan him your mother's car."

"Then let him have mine," she said.

Salvador welcomed his unexpected ally. "I will return it in three weeks, Brunhilda. With not a dent in it."

"Just leave before my mother's heart gives out again."

"I will trust you and your father to have everything ready for me by morning. . . . And no police—for your own good."

Christofels was too polite to ignore Dutch courtesy. He extended his hand. "*Dag meneer*, Mr. Contoni."

"Good day to you, too, sir." Contoni barely let their hands touch, and then he pulled out the press card that he would wear at the Tour de France. "Everything is legitimate this time."

"You're a journalist now?" Christofels asked.

"And why not? A man has to make an honest living."

🌀🌀🌀

At three Salvador spotted Monique slipping into one of the brown cafes not far from the art museums. She was seated at a wooden table by the time Sal reached her. "Where have you been, Monique? I waited for you at the Rijksmuseum for two hours."

"I thought you said the van Gogh gallery."

He let the excuse slip by. She was lying, but there was no need to confront her. Not now. Not yet. "There are 250 rooms in that place! I searched everywhere for you."

"I am sorry. I hope you saw Rembrandt's *Night Watch*."

"I stared at it so long I know every stroke on that canvas."

His fury abated as he saw her long-lashed eyes brim with tears. Even so, she was lovely to look at with that gentle softness to her mouth and her shiny dark hair brushed to a sheen. "It's all right, Monique. I'm just glad I found you."

She tried a smile, but it only pushed her tears to the edge.

"Are you hungry? Thirsty?" He rubbed the back of her hand. "Of course. Why else would you have come here? What will it be? Hot chocolate? The Amsterdammers smother it in whipped cream."

She wrinkled her nose. "Just coffee with milk."

He ordered *koffie verkeerd* for her and a glass of iced *jenever* for himself. He wanted to keep his mind clear; the juniper berries would give his drink a fruity taste without being intoxicating. "And ham and cheese *broodjes* for both of us," he told the waitress. "You can add liver sausage to mine."

While they waited, he said, "I took a room at the Seven Bridges. I want you to stay there with me."

"No." Her response was firm, a denial that there had ever been anything between them. "I already have a room, Salvador."

"At the Amstel?"

"Yes."

He glanced away, unable to laugh as the locals were doing. They were a happy lot, sitting on the plain, wooden furnishings, enjoying the congeniality of their companions as much as the drinks in their hands. The dark wood-paneled walls of the cafe had turned yellow from centuries of tobacco smoke; the fresh haze from smoke stung Sal's eyes—and yet it was a cozy atmosphere with the old prints hanging on the wall.

He faced her again. "Monique, did you bring the cycling helmet and placards with the number 190 and number 191 inscribed on them?"

She pointed to the sack beside her. "The fans will know there are only 189 riders," she said miserably.

"Few, if any, will notice."

She picked at her sandwich. "Salvador, I'm cold. Maybe I should try that hot chocolate after all."

Moments later he leaned over and blotted the whipped cream mustache that had formed on her upper lip. "There. That's better. Now—did you find us a room in s'Hertogenbosch?"

"Yes, in a private home a block from Kendall's hotel. You can walk to the starting point of the race from there."

He smiled. "If we can get through the crowds."

"I'm not going back there with you."

"What? When did you decide that?"

"When I visited the Anne Frank house this morning."

"No wonder you've been so depressed."

"She was so young, Salvador—like my sons. I cried when I saw that room where she spent two years of her childhood locked away with nothing to do but pin magazine pictures to her wall."

He wedged her hands free from the cup and held them. "When I build our home in Italy on my father's villa, there will be plenty of room for the boys. They will never feel locked away."

"But my boys are happy on the farm where they are."

"And you?"

"What makes them happy is enough for me."

"Monique, when the Tour leaves Belgium, I'll drive over to see you and the boys."

"No, Salvador, I don't want to see you again."

He glared at her. "But I promised Anzel that I would come."

She stopped arguing. She would never stand in the way of a promise to Anzel. Anzel with his dark eyes and thick black hair looked like his mother, but his face was chiseled in stone. He still struggled to come to grips with watching his father die—knowing that he had held the rifle and pulled the trigger.

"How much longer will he go on condemning himself for his father's death, Monique? Doesn't he realize it was an accident?"

"No," she said sadly. "Anzel knew what he was doing. But what choice did he have? Harland would have killed Gregory."

"Perhaps even his own son."

She shuddered. "Yes, I believe he would have. But I can't tell Anzel that."

"I'd like to spend time with Anzel. Let me take him to the race with me. I know he'd enjoy the excitement."

"That's madness. As crazy as my parents telling me that Anzel needs God's forgiveness to make everything right again."

He reflected. "Perhaps."

She chewed her lower lip. "How can I tell him about God's forgiveness? The truth is, I haven't forgiven my own son for killing his father. Poor Anzel. He is just beginning to take to his music again. Other than that, he has nothing left."

"Anzel has you, Monique. That is more than I have."

🌀🌀🌀

Chase Evans stood by the hotel window in s'Hertogenbosch and stared down at the ancient moat that ran along the old town wall. She was too excited to sleep. The first stages of the Tour de France would be played out in this city. As she tried to calm the erratic thudding of her heart, she kept her face to the window, fearful that Vic Wilson would read something in her expression and ask, "Are you that excited at seeing Ian Kendall again?"

Was she? *Focus on the town,* she told herself. *On anything but Ian.* The town lay little more than a leisurely drive from Amsterdam, but Vic had made it seem like a steeplechase run, allowing them only glimpses of the flat countryside that lay between the airport and this second-story hotel window. Her images of the Netherlands had been little snatches: a modern airport, the sparkling canals in Amsterdam, and small dairy farms with those unused windmills in the distance. As they drove into town, the carillon bells in the cathedral rang on the morning air.

Vic had grinned and said, "Someone knew you were coming."

She turned from the window as Vic slammed his suitcase on the bed.

"It's lovely here in Den Bosch, Vic."

"Thought you'd like it. But you can thank the Duke of Brabant, not me." He grabbed his shaving gear. "It all started with Brabant's twelfth-century hunting lodge and a bunch of sheep. I had nothing to do with it."

"And now all of this! Canals. Cathedrals. Ancient crumbling walls. Narrow three-story houses. It's all so charming."

"That's right," he said, picking up his bath towel. "It's twentieth-century people living in thirteenth-century houses."

"Vic, if you're going to take a shower, I'll go on down to the lobby and wait for Ian. I'll be safe there."

"No." His voice sharpened. "I'll take a quick shower, and then we'll go down together. Drew's orders! You're not to be out of my sight until he gets here."

"That could be midnight."

"Or six in the morning, but he'll be here." As he picked up a clean shirt and undershorts, he said, "Stay put. Don't even go to your own room."

As the bathroom door slammed, Vic's clutter tumbled from the mattress, spilling black-and-white photographs on the rug. She scooped up the mess and tossed it back on the bed, all except the pictures of a woman. These she scrutinized with growing interest as Vic whistled in the shower. At last the water was turned off, and Vic came back into the room, still whistling.

She held up the pictures. "Is this a friend of yours, Vic? Honest, you do make a lousy photographer."

"What are you doing with those?" He snatched them from her and dropped them in the suitcase along with his dirty clothes.

"Well, did you take them?"

"No."

"Then you are not the lousy photographer. I thought maybe she was your girl—so you cut off your competition."

"Lennie is not my girl. I don't have a girl anymore."

She heard the longing in his voice and remembered that he had sworn off dating since being diagnosed as HIV-positive. Embarrassed for them both, she glanced down at the photos again. "Are they surveillance?"

"Again, not mine. Lennie Applegate works at the embassy. She's Radburn Parker's lady friend. And before you ask, he's a Londoner, a thorn in the flesh to Drew. So don't press Drew for answers, and don't worry your pretty head about Lennie."

Vic was overcompensating. His attempt to kill her curiosity had aroused it. "What's wrong? Is her husband having her tailed?"

"There's no husband."

Chase took the risk of picking the pictures up again. "This Lennie is obviously with a man. The photographer cut him off."

"I told you. I am not a camera freak."

"Her companion is a big man."

He pivoted around, still tucking his fresh shirt in. "What makes you say that?"

"His hand is in the picture—and it's big. And this Miss Applegate of yours seems to be looking up at him."

"Observant, aren't you?"

"I had plenty of time. You took a long shower. So why is Drew having her photographed on so many different days?" To his frown, she said, "I think these were made from a video camera. Day and date provided."

He grabbed them from her and shuffled them like a deck of cards. "Any other information from that pretty head of yours?"

"Yes, it's the same man in each picture."

Again his brows shot up. "Go on with your rundown."

"He always wears the same jewelry—an expensive watch and diamond cuff links."

That seemed to surprise him. "I thought you would zero in on the onyx ring on the man's finger."

"That, too," she agreed. "But you wear one just like it."

As Vic shuffled the pictures for the third time, she said, "You've come up with something. I see it in your eyes, Vic."

"Those cuff links look familiar, but I can't quite get a grasp on why." Vic's face twisted with displeasure. "I think I'd better hold off showing these to Drew until I figure it out. Okay?"

"Okay." She eased them from his hand and placed them on the bed. "We'd better go," she urged. "I don't want to miss Ian."

An hour later—after repeated trips to the desk—Chase sank deeper into the chair in the hotel lobby, determined to wait out Ian's arrival. Vic dozed in the chair across from her. Sleep distorted his angular features. The sagging jaw line and gawking mouth made him seem vulnerable and older. She wondered how much of it was ill health or just physical exhaustion. With rumors of Vic's HIV status surfacing at the embassy, it seemed that Drew was Vic's only friend—unless they counted Miriam and herself.

They found Vic likable, but they worried about him. He had brushed off the bronchitis of a month ago and insisted that the unrelenting low-grade fever of the last few days would go away. It seemed to Chase that Drew Gregory lived under the pretense that Vic would live forever, at least until he was ninety. She tried to form an image of Vic a year ago—before she knew him—with an array of girlfriends at his beck and call. Somewhere along the way, one of them had given him more than a night of pleasure. She didn't know the girl—Vic didn't either—but Chase resented her for giving Vic the virus that could take his life.

He stirred and cast a sleepy eye her way. "No Kendall yet?"

"Not through that front door. Should I tell him about Drew?"

"Just enough."

She drummed her fingers on the arms of the cushioned chair. "I don't even know why Drew went to Paris."

"More high-level meetings. Just tell Ian Drew will be here when the race begins. Guaranteed." His words caught in a yawn. "Kendall is a smart boy. Once he knows we're riding in the team car, he'll figure out why."

Chase glanced toward the lobby doors again. "Vic, I wonder if Ian's staying at another hotel tonight."

"No, his team checked in here, and it's against the rules to overnight away from them. Otherwise the rider is disqualified."

"Really?"

"Really." He yawned again. "Let's give it another half hour and then call it quits. Tomorrow's a big day, Chase."

She fingered the press card in her pocket. "And I will be a blubbering novice with all those journalists."

"You'll do okay. Wake me when Kendall comes."

Six minutes later three cyclists charged through the lobby door—Ian, the fair-skinned Basil Millard, and the dark-eyed Orlando Gioceppi. Her eyes and smile focused on Ian. Damp strands of shiny red hair peeked out from beneath his cycling helmet. She stumbled from the chair, her numb legs almost toppling her.

"Ian!"

"Chase!"

She willed her feet to run to Ian as he bolted toward her. And then she was in his arms, pressed against his sticky jersey. He tilted her chin up and kissed her urgently.

"I wasn't expecting you," he said, still holding her.

"You invited me. Did your dad and brother come?"

"I told you—they never come." He nuzzled her hair, blowing softly through it. "Basil's wife can make room for you."

"Don't bother," Vic said, joining them. "We're booked here at the hotel. Let's go up to the room and fill you in on what's happening."

Pleasure drained from Ian's face. Jealousy rose in its place. "Sorry, " he said, releasing Chase. "I'd better turn in."

"Keep a cool head, Ian. You'll need it." Vic shot a warning glance toward the cyclist coming through the door. "Who's that?"

"Marcus Nash. Nash has been gone all day, off on his own."

"Ian, isn't that the man who followed us to London the other day?"

"He can't be, Chase. I would have recognized him."

"Not if he was wearing dark glasses and a wig," Vic said. "Let's get out of this lobby. Chase is here at great sacrifice. We don't want the two of you seen together very long. And, like it or not, Gregory and I are riding in the team car for your protection."

"Over Jon Gainsborough's dead body."

"We have his permission. We're to make sure you live through this race, Kendall. Now let's go up to the room and talk things over."

Chapter 10

Drew Gregory stood in the doorway to the press room looking down at Chase's angry face. The gold in her blouse heightened the sizzling luster in her wide brown eyes. Officially Chase was on her own now, name tag and all, one of the few female sports writers on hand for the outset of the Tour de France. But some of her spunk was gone this morning, that do-or-dare smile that he liked cut off by the stubborn tilt of her chin. Behind her came the clicking of computers, the murmur of voices, the flashing glare on the television screen as the Dutch commentator predicted more rain when the cyclists rolled down the ramp and started on their 2,495-mile journey toward Paris.

"Say something, Chase," Drew said.

Her expression remained as gloomy as the weather report as she stared beyond him toward the lively crowd outside.

"Listen to me, Chase. Thanks to Langley, you are here as a journalist. That means being in the press room."

She swept a strand of her burnished chestnut hair behind her ear. "It's not fair, Drew. I want to be out there by the starting ramp to see Ian off."

"Not today. You don't want to be caught in a thunderstorm."

Her gaze riveted on him now. "I've been in the rain before."

Did he dare argue with her? She was accustomed to having her own way, to making her own decisions. "You're my eyes in the press room, Chase. Keep a lookout."

"Do you expect me to find a terrorist in the press room?"

"I don't know where we'll find him. But stick close to some of the seasoned journalists. They'll be quick to spot a problem."

Drew wanted Chase out of harm's way as the 189 cyclists left the enclosed *Brabanthallen* and rolled down the ramp, a minute apart, one right after the other, racing against the clock in a time trial that would leave only milliseconds between the winner and the man in second place. He dreaded the moment when Kendall would be on the starter's ramp in full view of the cheering crowd and that lone terrorist determined to take him out.

He left Chase sulking in the newsroom and headed back to find Vic Wilson. Outside, grayness filled the Saturday sky. Trees along the boulevard still dripped from a midnight rain, leaving the pavements slick from the dampness. News commentators kept announcing their gloomy weather forecasts, but the rest of the citizens of s'Hertogenbosch were eager to show off their city to the riders and their fans with a *van harte welkom*.

Drew shared their excitement but more from the urgency of getting the race underway. As far as he was concerned, the sun and the hot stickiness of a summer morning would surely break through the thunderclouds.

Fans crammed the streets, closing in on a bigger guest list than s'Hertogenbosch had seen in decades. They were up to the task. The city sparkled with preparation, its clean and spotless streets scrubbed even cleaner, its shops that normally didn't open their doors until later in the morning already opened. Flowers in a rainbow of colors filled the windows. On one side of the street, vendors had set up a table of Indonesian *rijsttafel*, but the smell of currant and rye breads and sweet bakery goods that permeated the air broke down Drew's resistance. He bought pancakes for Vic and a tart stuffed with apples and cinnamon for himself. Everything was for sale. Tour trinkets and hats, *koffie* and tea, wine of French and German vintages, and one ingenious young man was selling thick slices of ham and cheese.

Drew leaped back as Maurice Chambord's official red car bounced over the sidewalk and back into the street, screeching to a stop near the starting ramp. Chambord stepped out and strutted about in his forest-green blazer and dark gray trousers. He seemed as nervous and jittery as the riders, but he managed a broad smile as he mingled among the neophytes who had never ridden a Tour. He offered a handshake to the cyclist standing beside his Lotus bike and a pat on the shoulder to the rider slumped on a chair waiting for that final medical clearance.

Chambord stopped short of greeting last year's winner. The Spaniard was aloof and confident, his most vocal competition two bikes from him and his strongest French rival with his back to the crowd. Despair swamped Drew's usual optimism. Ian Kendall was a superb cyclist. Hadn't he proved that in the Giro d'Italia? But what were Ian's chances against these other world champions?

Chambord's quick movements caught Drew's attention as the Frenchman brushed shoulders with the crowd and pushed his way to the nearest gendarme. *So that was what the stroll was all about—a final word to the constable in charge.* Chambord's gaze strayed slowly over the people, coming to a stop when he spotted Drew. Drew swallowed the last of the apple tart and went reluctantly to the Frenchman.

"Where's Vic Wilson?" Drew asked.

"Waiting for you in the team car. That gives him access to a cellular phone and small TV monitor."

"And Ian Kendall?"

Maurice nodded toward a square tent near the start-line. "In there warming up."

"Is he with Coach Skobla?"

Chambord shook his head. "That is one man I want you to watch closely. I don't trust him."

"And Jon Gainsborough?"

"They are two of a kind. It's good that you and Wilson will be riding with them."

"Any problem?"

"Nothing but this," Maurice said. He took an envelope from his blazer and handed it to Drew. It had been addressed to Chambord at the Societe du Tour de France and postmarked from Gascony days ago. *I'm waiting for the race to begin,* it said.

To Drew's arched brow, Maurice said, "Our handwriting expert checked it out. It was written on the same typewriter. Signed by the same man. He's somewhere in the crowd, Monsieur Gregory."

❦❦❦

Inside the wind-trainer tent, the wheels hummed and spun. The stifling acrid air smelled of sweat as another twenty riders sat on stationary bikes and pedaled with all fury.

Pearls of perspiration rolled down Ian's face. He brushed them away with his shoulder. The dampness made ringlets of his wavy hair and sent rivulets of water down his bare arms. His thoughts pedaled faster than his legs. Unlike many contenders in the race, Ian didn't seek a solo win in the prologue. That had been his strategy last year—win the prologue and stay on top of the overall standings for the first three stages.

It had been a dreamer's scenario, out of reach for a rider still new to the Tour. He laughed to himself. Young riders always felt invincible. Was that just a year ago? He had been twenty-two then, a man ready to take on the Tour de France. He was a mountain climber—had been even then, but he wanted a good show. The whole race or nothing at all. For his grandmother?

Yes, it had always been for his grandmother. He hadn't even made it into Paris and didn't know now whether he would have had the strength to run the full course, even if the crash hadn't put him out of the race. He'd done well, exceptionally well according to the *L'Equipe* write-ups the day after the race ended for him.

A year made a man wiser and older, old at twenty-three, going on twenty-four. He made his legs go faster, enjoying the exhilaration and safety of the wind-trainer. His helmet hung from the shoulder strap on the handlebars, swaying as he pedaled, his grandmother's message taped inside. He tried to focus on his grandmother so he could push Alekos Golemis from his memories. Alekos should be on the wind-trainer beside him. That big, grinning Greek should be alive, not buried on Corfu.

Once Ian left the tent—once he lined up on the ramp and started his time trial—he would give it his best, but he wasn't set on a win. With the shaky weather conditions outside, he knew better than to start out the long journey risking a win in the prologue and breaking an ankle like Chris Boardman had done in '95 on a slick, wet curve. Ian would settle for coming in with a good standing—top ten maybe. Or at least the top twenty-five. He'd make up time with wins in the Alps and Pyrenees. He was ready. He was an endurance man. This was his year. His race. With all due respect for last year's winner, Ian knew he had a chance for a place on the Paris podium. First place if he had his way.

His grandmother kept tapping his memory, pressing into his thoughts. *I'm still riding for you, Grandma,* he told her.

But I'm riding for Alekos Golemis, too. I owe him one, Grams. He wanted to be here riding with me. I should be riding for the team, but I'm riding for you and Alekos.

And, Grams, I'm riding for Chase Evans.

Here in this stinking tent he could almost see his grandmother as he had last seen her ten years ago sitting across from him in the Fox Hunt Restaurant in London, elegantly dressed, with her wide eyes full of love for him; and then hours later lying dead in the street outside of No. 10 Downing, her dress splattered with blood and her body motionless. As the sweat blinded him—or were they tears?—he knew that she would be pleased with Chase Evans.

Chase was his grandmother's kind of gal.

He saw someone coming through the tent flap and recognized Gainsborough's *directeur sportif,* a serious coach who believed in the team, a man who switched to his native Czech tongue when he was excited. Ian didn't break his rhythm as Ludvik Skobla approached. At forty-five, the coach kept his body trim, but this morning he looked tired, stressed out as he came slowly across the room in his stark white running shoes. Fringes of his hair had grayed at the temples, with the lines on his face adding a dozen years to his age.

"Something wrong, Coach?" Ian asked.

"Kendall, you're to get out there and take the race today."

"That wasn't the game plan."

"It is now. Jon Gainsborough wants you to win the prologue."

"It's not worth the risk in these poor weather conditions."

"Those are your orders, Ian."

Ian cast a glance down the row of riders. "Talk to Orlando, Coach. He's the one super motivated to win the prologue."

"You're the team leader—our best chance in this Tour."

"I can't waste my energy on the first day. I'm a mountain rider. That's where I can gain overall points and move ahead."

"You're a sprinter, too, Ian. The best all-around rider I have. Just ride hard for those seven kilometers."

Resentment took over. "Coach, there are eighteen turns—a couple of sharp curves to negotiate. No way am I going to risk my safety with a fast ride over wet roads."

Ludvik flexed his arms, his fists doubled. For a moment Ian was certain the coach would pull him bodily from the cycle. "Ride to win today or don't ride at all."

"Crash today and I'm out. . . . Or don't you and Gainsborough want me to finish this race?"

The vessels in Ludvik's neck throbbed. "I want you to live through it. God helping me, Ian, I want nothing more than for you to stand on the victor's podium in Paris. That's why I've worked so hard with this team. You're a good rider. I'm proud of you."

"As long as I beat everyone else's time trials today?"

"It's for the best." The haggard lines on Skobla's face deepened. "Ian, how are you getting along with Orlando now?"

"He still blames me for Alekos's death."

"Gregory talked to him about that this morning."

"It was none of Gregory's business."

"He seemed to think it was." Ludvik glanced across the tent at Orlando. "I think you and Orlando will be friends again now."

"Any fast cures for getting on with Marcus Nash? That man can never take Alekos's place with the team."

"Give him a chance."

"You should have given us a choice!"

"We needed the Parker Foundation funds. Nash riding with the team was part of the agreement."

The whir of the trainer-wheels screeched in protest as Ian braked. "I didn't know."

"You weren't supposed to know. But if he gets out of hand—"

"I can handle Nash."

"Stay away from him. That's our best advice. We're concerned about your safety." He moved closer and gripped Ian's handlebar. "If you see anything out of the ordinary today or anytime during the next three weeks, drop back to the team car and tell us."

"I don't go backwards in a race, Coach."

"Then send one of your support riders. We'll whip you into the security of the team car as quickly as possible."

"If you think you're trying to reassure me, Coach, you're doing the opposite. You are scaring me spitless."

"Then talk to your friend Gregory. He has his own way of dealing with fear. He insisted on us having prayer together before we left the room this morning. That's an experience I haven't had since I was in knee britches."

As he swung Ian's helmet, he fingered the paper taped inside. "Is that your rabbit's foot?" he asked.

"No, just some words I live by."

Skobla read aloud, "'Run with patience the race that is set before you.' Nice words—a quote from some Scottish poet?"

"No. Days before my grandmother died, she underlined those words in her Bible and wrote my name beside them."

Skobla's gaze mellowed. "Then run that race of yours well."

۞ ۞ ۞

An hour later Ian sat at the top of the starting ramp, his feet on the bike pedals, the strap of his riding helmet tight beneath his chin. The tower of St. Janskathedral loomed above the city, shrouded in a faint gray mist; but the clouds were lifting, the streets drier than when the first cyclists set off.

Only 7.3 kilometers to go, he told himself. *You can do it, man. You can do it.*

He waited for the signal to go and then rolled down the ramp into the sultry morning. Gripping the straight-up handlebars and bent in a tight aerodynamic tuck, he sped toward the center of s'Hertogenbosch. The faces in the crowd became a blur as people leaned over the steel barricades and urged him on.

He wiped Chase and his grandmother from his mind as he rode south along the seventeenth-century town wall into the suburbs. Zooming past more cafes and narrow three-story houses, he careened around the circuit in an explosive burst of speed. Negotiating the first of a dozen curves at seventy-six kilometers per hour, he passed the man who had left the starting ramp a minute ahead of him.

Fans held up placards. *Five kilometers to go. Four.* The last three rose on a slight incline. He pedaled hard as he swept back into the town square to the music of a noisy jazz band and the distinctive smell of the locally brewed beer tickling his nostrils. As he free-wheeled across the finish line in his sweat-soaked jersey, Ian slumped over the handlebars.

Minutes later, his head shot back, his eyes glued to the clock as the remaining riders came racing across the finish line. Orlando was beside him now, pouring a glass of water over Ian's head and shoving a bottle of juice into his hand. "The prologue favorite crashed halfway through the race," Orlando told him.

"In the rain?" Ian asked.

"He skidded out on the wet pavement."

There was no time to ask about last year's winner. Ian's name came over the loudspeaker. A deafening roar erupted. He had just a seventeen-second lead, but enough to make him the overall leader as the day's prologue ended.

From the large television screen in the press room, Chase watched Ian mount the podium and felt both pride and sympathy for him as he tugged the yellow jersey over his head. He looked so serious, handsome actually. He was no longer disheveled from the race, his face no longer sweaty. Somewhere after crossing the finish line and dismounting the bike, he had found time to splash his face and comb that thick red hair. *Smile,* she thought. *Your grandfather and Beatrice Thorpe are watching you on television.*

Ian had won the individual trials from a well-fought race, but the news commentator negated his victory, saying, "The last thirty racers had a distinct advantage riding over drier roads."

His voice droned on as he announced that the Netherlands champion racer had crashed when he skidded on the rain-slick street. "The American Ian Kendall won," he said, "by sheer luck."

As Chase's fist hit the table, the man beside her winked. "You must be covering the young American," he said.

He was a good-looking man, casually dressed in slacks and a white polo shirt, his mocking gray eyes laughing at her. "There's more than one American racing," she reminded him.

"But only one with the chance of holding on to the yellow jersey all the way to Paris."

"Do you really think Kendall will win?" Chase asked.

"I don't think much about it. I cheer the Italians myself."

She glanced at his thick blond hair. "The Italians?"

He grinned. "Born and reared in the vineyards near Milan."

"But I thought—"

"That all Italians had dark hair? Wrong."

She smothered her embarrassment. "Lesson number one," she said, smiling up at him.

His eyes and voice danced at the same time. "I'm Salvador Salatori—but just call me Sal."

"Chase. Chase Evans." Her hand seemed lost in his, his release of it taking longer than pleased her. She pulled free. "My hometown paper wants Ian Kendall to win. So do I."

He gave her a sly wink. "No matter who wears the yellow jersey, the long racing history of the Tour belongs to France."

"And today the glory belonged to s'Hertogenbosch."

"They did pay thousands for the privilege of being the host city—many more lire than I'd invest."

The stirring notes of the "Star Spangled Banner" on the TV drew Chase back to the screen. Ian looked relaxed now, and shy, as he held the bouquet of flowers and took the perfunctory kiss on both cheeks. He lifted the flowers and waved them. His smile started at the corners of his mouth, little indentations that added to his boyish confidence. Then the twinkle lines by his eyes deepened. *Now he will pour on all his charm,* she thought. She was beginning to know him, and the realization surprised her.

Her flesh prickled with pride as he tucked an American flag in with the flowers and waved them again. She squeezed her arms against her chest. "I love being an American," she said.

As Ian stepped from the podium, Sal's eyes narrowed. "Odd that they did not play the British anthem for the Gainsborough team, but it doesn't matter to me who wins the Tour. Like you, I cheer for my countrymen. But if we do not win, at least I hope it will not be the British team—or that American cyclist."

"Why do you dislike Americans?"

Salvador shoved his hands deep into his pockets. "I don't. Only a few of them."

Chase picked up her laptop computer and swung the strap over her shoulder. "I think I'd better go."

"Will I see you tomorrow?" he asked.

"I plan to be here."

"Then I will save you a work spot next to mine."

"Why bother? I'm still going to cheer for Ian Kendall." She left the press room, working her way gradually through the crowd back to the hotel where Drew and Wilson waited for her.

"Well," Vic asked when she came in view, "are you pleased with the outcome?"

"With Ian's win? Of course. But I didn't like being cooped up in the press room all day."

"Did you meet any seasoned journalists?" Drew asked.

"Just one pompous Italian who doesn't want an American to win."

Chapter 11

Stage two, day three—the Netherlands. Like the prologue, stage one had started and ended in Den Bosch. Tight curves on the slippery roads and traffic islands in the town had caused several crashes, ending the Tour for more than one rider as he looped through the countryside past gigantic windmills and winding streams. But nothing had slowed the sprinters or dampened the spirit of the cheering crowds in s'Hertogenbosch.

Now as Drew waited for the second stage to begin, his mood was as gloomy as the dark misty weather. He checked his Gucci watch for time and date, accurate as always: July, Monday—thirty minutes before the peloton rolled out of Holland and headed for Belgium. Ian still held a marginal lead, giving him a second day in the *maillot jaune* as the overall leader. As far as Drew was concerned, the yellow jersey put the spotlight on Ian, making him a vulnerable target for the madman determined to eliminate him.

Drew searched the pre-race crowd. The fans were eager to see the riders set out, yet reluctant to let them go. Journalists were catching last-minute interviews with the Tour favorites. Kids crawled under the barriers for autographs with the police looking the other way. The last rider stepped up to the sign-in chart, looking tired and jittery.

Drew didn't envy today's schedule—a 228-mile ride over narrow roads with torrential rains predicted before they rode up a steep, cobbled hill and finally reached Wasquehal. For Vic Wilson it meant breakfast in Holland, lunch at a sidewalk cafe in Belgium, and dinner in a historical setting in France. But as the peloton rode off, Drew planned to head to a small airfield outside Den Bosch where a private plane would whisk him off to Normandy.

As Drew looked over the crowd, a tall man in stone-washed denims sauntered toward him with a come-a-day, go-a-day bounce to his steps. His worn baseball cap sat backwards on his head, and a mammoth grease rag dangled from his hip pocket— a good cover for Brad O'Malloy, one of Troy Carwell's casually dressed bright boys from Paris.

O'Malloy stuck out his hand and flashed a brash grin. "I'm here for the duration of the race," he said, pointing to his I.D. badge. "I'm replacing one of the Gainsborough mechanics."

"It looks like you're replacing me."

"Just for a day or two. I'll keep Kendall's bike in good working order."

Brad was a ten-year man with the Agency, spoke French fluently, and in spite of his sleepy eyes, his alert mind clicked in every happening in his mental notebook. He hooked his thumbs in his belt and yanked his jeans a notch higher. "You can fly off to Isigny without giving security a second thought. But let me warn you before you see Madame Dupree—Salvador Contoni may be back in France planning rough moves against the Tour."

"I thought she came back from Italy without him."

His eyelids drooped at half mast. "Just go peacefully and check it out. The latest intelligence reports have them both here."

Drew balked. "Why don't you go in my place?"

"You'll recognize Contoni." He thumped Drew on the shoulder. "We've got things covered here, Drew. Vic's in the team car. I'm riding in that one with the bike rack on top."

"And Ian Kendall is riding out there in a yellow jersey."

His gloom deepened; the prayer that he tried to pray for Ian's safety drifted with the clouds. "Have you met Ian yet?" he asked.

"Over a flat tire. He thinks I'm a replacement for Nick who went down with the flu yesterday."

"Kendall isn't that trusting."

"Then we'll both be on the alert. I gave his cycle a once-over this morning. That way it passed safely from my hands to his." He gave another yank to his jeans. "Don't worry. I strip down car engines for relaxation. It's good for my stress level."

Drew had no doubt that O'Malloy could strip down a damaged cycle or fix a flat with equal efficiency and have it back running within seconds. Brad's office at the embassy in Paris was a clutter, but not his thought process and not those strong hands of his, greasy at the moment.

O'Malloy whipped the rag from his pocket and wiped his hands. "Carwell suggests that you bypass Nogent-sur-Oise and meet up with us in Soissons."

"Two days with Monique Dupree? I'd wear out my welcome."

"Just stay cool, Drew. One of the bomb warnings came from Soissons. French Intelligence is checking stores against the sale of timing devices and plastic explosives."

"That's like finding a pebble at the top of the Alps."

O'Malloy shrugged indifferently. "Carwell wants you to check out each day's route ahead of time."

"I'd need a bomb disposal unit for that."

"The French have one of those ROB devices. That robot's like a one-man bomb squad."

"You have your head in a turnip patch, Brad."

"No joke. It's a remote control unit built from spare parts." He wiped rain from his face with his grease rag, smearing the side of his cheek. "Even works on rainy days like this."

"What do you want to do—terrify the fans along the way?"

"Someone else plans to terrify them," he argued. "A bomb disposal unit was your idea. If you don't like a made-in-France label, ask the White House to send one of those state-of-the-art jobs from the air base in Turkey. Langley could check on it."

"The Tour will be over before we'd get through all that Washington red tape."

"We have Americans in the race, don't we?"

"Six of them, counting Kendall. All on different teams."

O'Malloy's sleepy eyes narrowed. "So we'll get you your bomb unit. Langley can speed things up. That or anger the White House because some American rider got himself killed in the Tour."

As the riders lined up at the start-line, Brad went back to his car, leaving Drew pressed against the steel barrier with rain washing over the bridge of his nose. The riders pedaled toward him, shoulder to shoulder. The streamlined bicycles glimmered in the rain, the many colors of their team uniforms brilliant in spite of the mist. As riders bent forward over the handlebars, helmets and dark goggles masked their faces, but Drew saw Ian toward the front of the pack. He gave Ian a thumbs up and then made his way through the crowd to the waiting taxi.

Thirty minutes later Drew was airborne, the pilot lapsing into silence after three aborted attempts at conversation. Still he pointed down to the peloton riding over the winding hills below them. Then he lifted the plane higher, swooping above the windmills and marshes of Holland as they headed into the strong winds above the Belgian countryside.

The wind currents snapped at the plane, bouncing them mercilessly into an air pocket as they crossed the border into France. They rode the French coast, speeding along the windswept beaches above the chalky cliffs, and came in for a rough landing in a lush pastoral region on the edge of Isigny.

Again Carwell had a car waiting for him.

Beech trees broke the heady winds as he drove past the high-hedged fields and half-timbered farmhouses. Finally, turning into the Duprees' driveway, he parked beside another car rental. The familiar weather-beaten house was set back from the rural road; brown-and-white Norman cattle grazed lazily in the rain. He welcomed the raindrops on his face and listened for the shouts of the boys' voices as he walked over the cobbled path toward the house. He saw no movement at the windows, heard no sounds, yet he sensed that someone was watching him. Before he could wrap his fingers around the old brass knocker, the thick wooden door swung wide. Monique Dupree's curious brown eyes were as dark as her shiny hair. The smile around her sensuous lips was forced, her eyes full of mistrust.

"I was in the area," he said, and then remembering his new covenant to be up front and honest, he added, "Actually I left the Tour de France to see you, Madame Dupree."

She stepped back, visibly shaken, and beckoned him in. "You should have called. I haven't much time to visit now."

He stopped in the middle of the room to glance around and then turned and faced her. There was an elegance to the way Monique stood there looking up at him, a delicate grace that seemed out of sync in this aged farmhouse with its stone fireplace and frayed throw rugs. Only the nervous twitch of her eyelid marred her outer beauty. She was uneasy in his presence, overly anxious to show him the way back to his car.

"Are the boys out?" he asked.

"They are down by the river with a friend."

A friend with a car rental. Contoni? Contoni and a boat. Salvador always left room for escape. "And your parents—are they here?"

Monique nodded toward the back of the house. "Just *Maman*."

He glanced up in time to see Monique's mother—a buxom, wide-hipped woman—escaping down the narrow hall to the safety of her blue-tiled kitchen with its cast-iron range and old-fashioned water pump. As the tantalizing smell of beef and vegetables reached the parlor, he felt an urgency to state his business, leave, and find the nearest cafe en route back to the plane.

"Your father?" Drew pressed.

"Working the fields."

Berger Dupree, as his name implied, was a tiller of the soil, a man who made his living off the land. Monique's parents were religious people, but they withheld their pleasantries with Drew, blaming him for the death of their son-in-law. Or was it their utter dislike for intelligence officers that made them so cold toward him?

She made no effort to offer him a chair. He held his ground. "Madame Dupree, I haven't heard from you since you came back from Italy. We had an agreement. You were to bring Contoni back to France with you."

She avoided his eyes, hesitating long enough for him to know that she was lying. "I never found him."

"But my Company kept their part of the bargain. The settling of your husband's estate is moving rapidly through the courts."

"Yes. I will soon be the sole owner of Harland's houses and land. Small comfort to my sons," she said. She folded her arms tightly against her chest. "I told you, I didn't find Sal."

Drew smiled patiently as he took some pictures from his pocket and spread the prints on the arm of the sofa. "These are proof of your times together. This one was taken in Milan—and this one from a helicopter above Contoni's yacht. And this on the island of Corfu—willingly in the arms of Salvador Contoni."

Her hands curled into tiny glacier-white balls as she sank into the safety of the cushioned sofa and stared down at the pictures. "Sal—Mr. Contoni would not come back with me."

"But you must have made some arrangement with him?"

"None." Her answer was too quick, too sharp.

He looked at the bowed head and gently lifted her chin. "Are you certain that Contoni is not here in France again, perhaps at the Tour de France? Or perhaps with your boys even now."

Her dark eyes blazed. "I told you—they're with a friend."

"He is a poor companion for young boys, Monique."

As she winced, Drew pressed his advantage. "Contoni shot a friend of mine—at your castle at the foot of the Pyrenees."

"Salvador never carries a gun."

Even in her anger, she was beautiful, desperately trying to protect Contoni. Drew knew the signs. Monique Dupree was in love with Contoni, involved in the one way that would destroy her.

"I was there, Monique. When my friend Jacques tried to escape, Contoni killed him."

"No, never. I've been with him. I know how kind he can be."

"To you, but he's not good company for your sons."

She bit her lip. He surprised himself with gentleness, saying, "Contoni always carries a gun, Monique."

She dabbed at the blood forming on her lip. "No. On his yacht—he carries a weapon for protection, but he knows there are to be no guns around my sons." She glanced toward the black cavernous fireplace. "Have you never killed a man, Mr. Gregory?"

In the army, he thought. *And on covert action with the Agency.* His gaze shifted to her clasped hands, the transparent skin tight enough to tear. Yes, he had killed men, but always in the line of duty. But he was redeemed now, forgiven for the past.

"Well, Mr. Gregory, have you ever killed anyone?"

His jaw slackened, then went taut again. "Yes."

He saw the triumph in her gaze and wondered if the blue-gray of his own eyes had turned to steel. "Contoni is a wanted man," he said. "Interpol, French Intelligence. We must stop him before he kills again. For your safety and the safety of your boys."

She turned toward the wide farm window. As she looked out over the fields, she chewed at her lip again. "He won't hurt my children. He is fond of them."

And more than fond of you.

Her face was easy to read. Anger. Fear. Motherly love. He pitied her for the loneliness that she must feel. Her husband had been twice her age—a powerful, secretive man. Contoni was younger, vibrant, perhaps genuinely in love with her. Drew picked up the snapshots from the chair, placing the one of Monique and Contoni on the island of Corfu on top. They were standing on the deck of his yacht, Contoni wearing his skipper's cap, Monique's dark head pressed against his broad chest.

"I'm sorry," Drew said. "If I had known there was anything between you, I would not have asked you to go to Milan for us."

He put the snapshots in her hands, the picture of Salvador and Monique on top. She folded her fingers around them. "I don't have a picture of us together," she said. "Thank you."

Outside the two car rentals were still parked side by side. Birds chattered in the tree by the window. Down the hall they could hear Monique's mother bustling about in the kitchen. "Are the boys with Salvador?" he asked.

"Their grandfather is out there."

But not with them, Drew thought. "I'm going after them."

"You must not hurt my boys."

He placed his broad hand over hers. "I would never hurt your sons. Anzel saved my life."

"I was afraid you'd forgotten."

"A man doesn't forget a sacrifice like that."

"Mr. Gregory, when Sal saw you coming, he forced the boys to go with him. Oh—they went willingly enough. He's good to them."

Tears washed over her high cheekbones. "Promise me you won't hurt any of them, Mr. Gregory. Promise me you won't take Sal on my father's land—not with the boys watching."

Drew glanced at the rental cars again.

"He didn't come that way," she said.

Was she lying? Or was she hiding another guest? "Contoni can't get too far." Drew reached for the phone.

"Don't bring the gendarmes here. Anzel is still terrified of the police. I'm certain Sal is gone by now."

"Then we need your help to find him."

"He's following the race—I know that much. But I won't help you find him, not when Salvador is my friend."

Down the hall, the back door closed. Drew moved swiftly to the window in time to see Monique's mother hurrying toward the barn. "So your *maman* goes to warn him?"

"She goes to protect her grandsons."

He spun around and caught her off guard. "Monique, what does Contoni have against Ian Kendall?"

The color drained from her face. "Ian Kendall?"

He had the urge to cross the room and shake those narrow shoulders. "Kendall is riding with the British team in the Tour de France with a good chance to take the prize on the Champs Elysees. But someone is trying to stop him. We've received several threats against Ian, even bomb threats against the Tour."

"Sal wouldn't do that. He wouldn't risk his own safety. Not that way. . . . And he doesn't even know Kendall," she whispered.

"Then why is he sending death threats?"

"Why would he do that? When we were in Corfu, someone paid him to stop Kendall from winning—but not to kill him."

Drew stared at her. Ian's friend Alekos Golemis came from the island of Corfu—was buried there. Alekos's father lived there and had met with Salvador at the family villa. "Someone in Corfu paid Contoni to go after Kendall?"

"Yes. A large amount of money."

And Vasille Golemis has money. "And you were there when he hired Contoni? You can identify him."

"I won't. I can't. He is a powerful man."

He glared down at her. She would never willingly help the Agency. She had spent too many years living with her husband's twisted thinking. "I don't need his name, Monique. I am certain I know it already." To confirm his suspicions, he added, "I knew his son. The boy was a friend of Ian Kendall's."

Her chin lifted defiantly. "Sal has nothing against Ian Kendall. It's you he hates, Mr. Gregory. Not the young cyclist."

As Drew walked back to his car, the boys ran across the fields toward him, Giles's short, stubby legs pumping. Drew held out his arms. Giles would arrive first, eager for the candy treats that Drew carried in his pocket. Anzel would come shyly behind his younger brother, asking for nothing, expecting nothing. They were just yards from him when rifle shots exploded, the bullets zinging over their heads.

"Get down," Drew shouted.

Anzel dropped flat on the ground with his arm around Giles. As Drew crawled to them, another round of bullets whizzed above them, lower this time. He lifted his head as he reached the boys and saw Monique start out the door toward them. She was yanked back inside. *Salvador Contoni? He's in there with her.*

A third volley split the air to the right of him. Drew wrapped his arms around the boys, keeping their faces to the gravel. "Who's out there, Anzel?"

"My grandfather."

"Not Salvador Contoni?"

"He left, Monsieur Gregory. An hour ago."

Drew lifted his head higher. Fifty yards from them, Berger Dupree stood in the open, his rifle aimed on Drew. An AK-47? Or one of those French jobs that would be just as deadly? Berger was a nationalist, apt to sport a French MAS service rifle even if it dated back to World War II.

As Berger moved steadily toward them, Anzel turned his head, a grass stain showing on his hollow cheek. "Grandfather will kill you if you don't leave," he said.

Giles's body quivered beneath Drew's arm. "Put the gun down, Berger," Drew called. "Your grandsons are here."

"I know," the stony voice called back. The old man was less than twenty yards away now. He was still handsome in spite of his seventy-plus years, but there was fire in those enormous mahogany eyes.

As Berger closed in, Anzel said tearfully, "He won't hurt you, Mr. Gregory, if you go away."

Drew touched Anzel's upturned face. "Put the rifle down, Berger," he shouted again. "You're frightening your grandsons."

Wisps of Berger's snow-white hair tumbled over his forehead; the bushy brows arched. His skin had been leathered by the sun and wind storms and by long hours in the fields. He was tall, bent slightly, his work pants tucked into high boots, his hands steady as a bar of steel as he kept his sights on Drew.

"Those were just warning shots," he thundered.

"I came here for Salvador Contoni."

"Didn't the boys tell you? He's gone. And I have another round to go. So get off my farm, Monsieur Gregory. I will not let you stand in the way of my daughter's happiness."

🟡🟡🟡

Inside the house Monique screamed as Thymous Golemis yanked her back into the entryway. She fought against his manacling grip.

"So that was Drew Gregory?" he fumed.

"Yes."

"He never even guessed that I was here."

"You stayed well hidden, but he parked beside your rented car. . . . Now, let me go, Thymous," she cried out. "Before something happens to my sons."

Thymous kept her in his grip as he leaned against the wall and stared out the window. He was breathing hard, wheezing. "Your boys are all right. The man with the rifle will not hurt them."

"My father?"

"Yes."

"Not Salvador?"

"Gone, I think."

"Did you hear everything we said, Thymous?"

"Enough to know that Gregory can ruin my father's career unless I can stop Contoni from carrying out my father's plan."

She stopped squirming, her thick lashes wet with tears. "I don't want you to find Sal," she whimpered. "I don't want anyone to find him."

His black eyes filled with pain. "You are so foolish. So foolish." Thymous relaxed his grip and lifted Monique's chin with the back of his hand until their eyes met. "You can't have both worlds, Monique. Someday you will have to choose. Salvador Contoni can only bring you unhappiness."

"And you, Thymous?"

"I would be good to both you and your boys."

Chapter 12

Jiri Benak left the Basque village at sunup and caught the nearest high-speed train to Paris for his meeting with the Russian agent. After deliberately delaying the meeting, Jiri felt pleased with himself. He could imagine Yuri Ryskov waiting for him at Maxim's five days in a row. But Jiri was following his own agenda, not Professor Ivanski's.

For Jiri, the deaths of Drew Gregory and Ian Kendall were priority; that it would cost the lives of fans and other young cyclists was of little concern to him. Within days he would strike against the Tour de France—before the riders even reached the Pyrenees. He smiled at the headlines of the newspaper in the hands of the man in front of him. Soon the eyes of the world would turn, not to the young riders racing toward Paris, but to Jiri—to what he would do along the way.

In Paris he stepped from the train as rested as when he had boarded. The depot was swarming with gendarmes. Approaching one of them, he boldly asked the way to Notre Dame. Then he sauntered to the curb, cocksure and smug, and hailed a taxi in the opposite direction. Wanted as he was by French Intelligence and Interpol, why could he move about so freely?

You will never find me, he thought. *I am too visible.*

Danger nurtured Jiri, satisfying him like morsels of a thick, rare steak. He chewed on danger, survived by it. Yet taking Ivanski's warning, Jiri hired three separate taxis, riding switchback across both banks of the Seine as unhurried as he had been when he laid his plans for this day. He had given himself ample time for his noon appointment. If the French taxi drivers remembered him at all, it would be as that fare whose face had been masked by thick, dark glasses and a wide ash-blond mustache.

Benak left the third taxi a block from the Arc de Triomphe, and as the driver merged with the traffic, he pocketed the glasses and removed the false mustache that irritated his upper lip. From here it was an easy walk up the Champs Elysees to Maxim's. If today's meeting with Yuri Ryskov turned sour—if Ryskov had set a trap for him—Jiri would outsmart the Russian.

Paris was too crowded for Jiri, too filled with antiquity and historical buildings. But now as he made his way through the heart of the city, he found himself acutely aware of the Arc de Triomphe, viewing it as little more than a crumbling war memorial in need of repair. Even the modern Pompidou Center annoyed him with its ducts and cables. He shaded his eyes for the same critical gaze toward the city's most famous landmark; to Jiri the distant Eiffel Tower was a mass of scrap iron. Except at night. Illuminated at night, the tower was as eye-catching as the floodlit domes of the Sacre-Coeur, brilliant against the night sky. For a moment his eyes went back to the distant tower. He wondered what size bomb he would need to destroy it and then shrugged. No, he had no real desire to destroy these remarkable structures—these landmarks. Let the Parisians have their city. Jiri's sights were set on the Cotswolds and a peaceful thatched cottage of his own.

Halfway down the boulevard, he slid into the empty chair at a sidewalk cafe, grateful for the bright red umbrella that shaded him from the glaring sun. As he quenched his thirst with a lager, he watched the maddening throng of tourists, wondering if Yuri Ryskov or Parkovitch walked among them. Work with these men? Why should he? Create weapons for them? At the right price, yes. What did it matter to Jiri if Ryskov and Parkovitch came into disfavor with the professor? Jiri did not like dealing with little men.

And you, Professor Ivanski, you remain an elusive leader, a shrewd man that I already despise. Refuse to meet me personally? he thought. *Belittle me, will you? No, not for long.*

Help Ivanski in the Tour and what guarantee did Jiri have that his Russian connection would work to his advantage afterwards? He must go slowly and not bow to the professor's demands, no matter how well Ryskov presented them. He wiped the lager foam from his lips, then pushed back the cuff of his sleeve with his finger. Just ten minutes to reach the far end of the tree-lined Champs Elysees.

🕭🕭🕭

For hours Yuri Ryskov wandered around Paris, finally reaching the Hotel de Crillon for the third time that morning. Across the narrow street lay the ghostlike embassy with the American flag flapping atop the building. Yuri passed the entrance to the hotel and stopped at the corner to light his last cigarette. He puffed nervously, his shrewd eyes wary of the strangers shoving past him. Yuri had only to cross the narrow street to speak to the American Drew Gregory.

A block from him lay the Rue Royale, the way to the Church of the Madeleine and Maxim's restaurant. To his left a nineteenth-century fountain spewed its waters on the Place de la Concorde. He had sat there for an hour this morning with the sound of traffic throbbing in his ears and his thoughts on the reign of terror that had once filled the square. Two hundred years ago, Louis XVI had been executed in almost the very spot where the sun now filtered through the fountain waters.

The French Revolution. Yuri wanted no part in any revolution. Not here in this picturesque square, nor in Moscow. Professor Ivanski's plans would lead to another reign of terror. The stub of the cigarette burned against his fingers. He flicked it into the air and watched the ashes form tiny gray specks. *Ashes. Nothingness. Like my life.* He wanted to be free. He wanted to know the deep peace that Nicholas Trotsky had known. Trotsky, dead now, was once a revolutionary, but in the end he was a man at peace. Yuri must find Drew Gregory, for surely all Americans knew about this God whom Trotsky worshiped. Or was Yuri's mentor, Professor Ivanski, right? God did not exist.

Thoughts of immortality haunted him. The tragic deaths of Nicholas Trotsky and the young cyclist Alekos Golemis hung like a canopy of black clouds over him. To contemplate the destruction of other riders seemed hideous. These were innocent young men who had no interest in the old glory days of Russia.

Yuri's mouth went dry; the sour taste of garlic and onions and stale cigarettes coated his tongue. He must break with Professor Ivanski and disappear as Trotsky had done. But he dreaded the consequences, feared the cowardice of dying without peace and facing that unknown tomorrow. Across the street lay his one hope for freedom, for answers. He took a step toward the curb, the tips of his shoes dipping precariously. He tried another step. Thoughts of his mentor in Russia sent cold sweat running the full length of his spine. Dare he betray Ivanski? Dare he seek political asylum?

Somewhere behind him, cathedral chimes began to ring. The Church of the Madeleine? He could not be sure. The ringing that surely brought joy to others pierced his ears. *Twelve noon. Maxim's.* Time to meet with the Czechoslovakian and finalize the plans that would disrupt the Tour de France and quite possibly set off another revolution in Moscow. Ivanski longed to go back to the old Imperial Russia, but Yuri knew there could be no going back, no bloodless coup. No, his people—and they were still his people—would die by the thousands in a bloody massacre that would start in Red Square. He lifted his eyes toward the embassy once more, his throat so constricted he could hardly breathe.

Move, he told himself. *Run. Seek freedom.*

Above his own strangled cry, he heard the voice of his mentor saying, *Yuri, am I losing you, too? See me through this one, Yuri. The people will follow me.*

🐚🐚🐚

Radburn Parker moved briskly through the city of Paris with total disregard for others. He cut a straight path, his large frame forcing the Parisians to break rank and go around him. His sense of superior worth—if currently not in his thoughts—was visible in his strides. When he took the time, as he did now, he admired his reflection in the store windows. He was a man of great height, as ramrod straight as any Burmese Army Ranger.

His father had been a British ranger in the 1940s, sowing his wild oats abroad and living out much of his life on the northeast frontier far from the family residence in London. On one of his infrequent trips home, he had married unexpectedly. Forty-five at the time, he soon grew restless to go back to the Far East. Radburn was born in his absence. Memories of his father were sparse and bitter—a stranger on brief leaves, an authoritative figure with his Burmese walking stick coming down hard on Radburn's knuckles or stinging across his buttocks at the slightest provocation; but his father was an impressive man, tall and striking in his uniform, with a raucous laugh and sunburned skin. The Parker Foundation money would have been his if he had not chosen a military career. Instead, it had passed down to Radburn.

They had never liked each other, yet Radburn had his father's sense of pride, his gift for languages, his hidden cruelty in dealing with others. And he had something his father never had—outward charm. The very words caused Radburn to stop and smile at the store window. The reflection came back as that of a happy, pleasant-faced man. He lifted his hand to brush down a few wild strands of his thick crowning glory. He considered himself handsome, a gentleman, gratefully rid of his wife—thanks to the British courts—and free now even of Lennie Applegate.

Thoughts of his family seldom pressed him. They did now. He considered it prophetic, a warning of trouble ahead or a premonition of danger. He rarely carried a weapon, depending on his own ingenuity to protect himself. He set out again with quick strides, his mind unwillingly turning back to his father's swagger stick. "The perfect weapon," his father had called it.

On impulse, Radburn made his way to the back streets of Paris to a quaint specialty shop where he had twice found relics of war for his son's collection. "Monsieur Parker," the owner greeted him, "you've come back. How can I help you?"

Parker moved slowly along the aisles. "Just browsing."

"For that boy of yours?"

Radburn smiled. "Hardly a boy. He's seventeen now."

"And still interested in military school?"

"Unless I find him suitable employment at the Parker Foundation."

"You should bring your son with you sometime."

Radburn cared not a wit about any of his children, but he said, "I'll do that. But I warn you, he leans heavily toward John Major's political views."

"That should please you."

No, Radburn thought. *It has set us at odds.* From his own Cambridge days on, Radburn never wavered from his communistic convictions: universal power, universal control. His roots of dissatisfaction had smoldered in his boyhood, but it was his forced education at his father's schools that had spurred his sudden interest in the writings of Karl Marx, a philosophy that was nurtured during his days in Moscow.

He found the counter he wanted toward the back of the store, a marvelous display of solid canes and sharp-pointed walking sticks. "My son would like one of these."

The shopkeeper grabbed up the gold-handled one and raised it toward Radburn. "What about this trekking stick?" he asked.

Radburn winced as he had done when his father came down hard against his knuckles. "That's a Burmese Army stick, isn't it?"

"Just a good imitation," the owner admitted. "The original was issued exclusively to the Burmese Army Rangers."

"I know. My father owned one."

He took it in his hand now, noting the sturdy construction and solid rowboat handle. Like the original, it was made from baby bamboo. It had possibilities. A man like Jiri Benak could use it to take Kendall down in stage seventeen. He ran his fingers down the hollow stick, feeling for the bolt and nut mechanism that allowed the cane to fold in two. *The perfect weapon.*

"Does your boy mountain hike?" the man asked.

"Around London? Hardly."

"It rains there. This would be good for fording streams."

Parker chuckled. "That was one of the purposes for it when Sir Jeffery Hillpig Smyth designed it. I'll take it."

Carrying the parcel under his arm, he reached the Champs Elysees without even noticing the turns he had taken. He stopped mid-boulevard and went inside a sidewalk cafe. He was sitting there sipping coffee when Jiri Benak took up a table outside, the red patio umbrella casting an odd tinge on his snow-blond hair. In less than three weeks the street in front of them would be blocked off for the final day of the Tour de France when the cyclists rode into Paris, if they rode in. They were counting on Benak, but Parker had misgivings. He held little hope for the meeting between Yuri Ryskov and this Czechoslovakian madman.

He sat back in his chair as Benak lifted a second lager. Until recently, life had been dull, too routine, Radburn's every need met through the Parker Foundation. He had become bored living as a sleeper in London for a dozen years or more, constantly waiting for someone to pick up the reins of the old Phoenix-40. But

Ivanski as a leader with his wild imperialistic dreams? His plan was mad, but because of the uncertain state of the Russian leadership, it held the possibility for success. And then Lennie Applegate had come his way feeding American secrets to him, documents that assured his position once again with Ivanski and the old Phoenix-40.

Parker had the best of both worlds—the intriguing possibility of working both sides as a double agent. He had his high social status in London and his close ties with British Intelligence that had swung the doors wide open at the American embassy. And now he would be an active participant in the most unexpected coup in Moscow. But if the need arose to protect himself, intelligence agencies around the world would pay him well just to know what Ivanski planned.

Benak stood and left the cafe. Radburn followed him at a safe distance up the Champs Elysees, down through the underground passage beneath the Place de la Concorde and back up into the sun, still heading toward his appointment at Maxim's.

As Radburn paused to shift his package to his other arm, he noticed Yuri Ryskov walking alone, walking unsteadily. *He didn't even see me. Drunk?* Parker wondered. *At noon? No, Ryskov is having trouble with his stomach and is staying away from hard liquor.*

Something was wrong. He switched surveillance and lagged behind Ryskov, expecting him to turn right on the Rue Royale. He walked straight on. At the corner near the Hotel de Crillon, Yuri hesitated at the curb, waiting to cross the narrow alley in the direction of the Avenue Gabriel. Across the street lay the somber-looking American embassy. "Ryskov," Parker called softly.

Yuri turned, startled. He licked his lips as their eyes met. Seconds passed and then recognition. "Parkovitch!" he said.

Parker pulled Yuri back from the curb and glanced at the embassy. He kept his voice low, calm. "That's the wrong way, Yuri. We still need you. You have a meeting with Benak."

"I know. About the Tour." His eyes looked sunken, his sallow skin tight against his cheeks.

He's sick, Parker thought. He edged Yuri away from the pressing crowd to the side of the colonnaded building. "Have you talked to Professor Ivanski lately?" he asked.

Yuri nodded. The cold stone wall against his back seemed to rally him. "Yesterday. I tried to warn him that our plans won't work unless Benak cooperates with us. And there's a girl," he said. "Ian Kendall has a girlfriend. She could cause trouble for us—she's one of the journalists at the Tour. Her family has political connections."

"Yuri, we know about the girl." The wary eyes turned back at the sharpness in Parker's voice. "Yuri," Parker continued, "our plans are set in motion. Forget Miss Evans. Everything depends on you getting the message to Ivanski at exactly the right moment."

"I know. Trust me. Stage seventeen," Yuri said. He pushed his shoulders hard against the wall and sighed. "But can we trust Jiri Benak?" he asked.

Can we depend on you? Parker wondered. It was too late to move another agent into position. "You know your way to Maxim's. You're late. You'd better hurry."

"Are you not meeting with us, Parkovitch?"

"Not yet. It is best that Benak not be able to identify me. You size him up. Report back to me." *And in the meantime, I will decide your fate, Yuri Ryskov. I will not allow you to ruin it for all of us. For me.*

Yuri's gaze strayed back toward the Avenue Gabriel. For a moment, Parker was impressed with the short distance to the embassy. He had only to cross the narrow alleyway himself. Perhaps it was safer to bow out now before Ryskov did something foolish. Americans would pay Radburn well for any information that would stop the threats against the Tour de France.

On a whim, he said, "Give Benak this package for me. . . . Here, Yuri, do as I say. Take this to Benak."

Ryskov took it. "It's light."

"It's a Burmese walking stick. It may prove valuable for stage seventeen. . . . He will know what to do with it."

"Do I promise Benak anything if he succeeds?"

"Tell him I have our tickets to Moscow. We're booked on a flight the day after the race."

"What happens if the plan fails—if our timing is off?"

He gripped Ryskov's shoulder. "We won't fail."

But if we do, you will have nowhere to go, Radburn thought. *But I will tear up my ticket to Moscow and go back to London and call British Intelligence.*

There was only one thing wrong with going back to London. Lennie Applegate would be there.

Chapter 13

Chase waited until Ian's roommate left the room, and then
she winked at Drew. "Thanks, Drew. I won't be long."
"Good. Anyone catching you coming out of Ian's room
might misunderstand."

"You won't. That's what matters." She paused, her cheeks
flushing. "I want Ian to know I miss him when I don't see him."

"Get going. I'll hang around until you leave."

Chase hurried down the hall, turned the knob, and slipped in.
"Ian," she whispered. "It's Chase."

He propped himself up on his elbow, looking groggy, his chest
bare, his sheet tucked against his waist. One bare foot poked out
at the end of the bedding. "You shouldn't be here," he warned.
"It's against the rules."

"I had to see you. Are you all right?"

"I'm fine." With his gaze still on her, he shoved a crumpled
sheet of paper under his pillow. "You look nice." He eyed her curiously. "What's wrong, Chase?"

"I don't know why I came on this Tour. I never see you."

"I didn't want it to be this way. But the rest day is coming
before we ride into the Pyrenees. We'll spend that day together. I
promise." He struggled with the sheet to free his other foot. "I feel
like I'm under house arrest. This is the first morning I didn't have
Vic or Drew standing guard at the bathroom door."

"Is it that bad?"

"Worse," he grumbled, "now that this O'Malloy fellow is sniffing around like a third hound dog."

"I thought he was the new Gainsborough mechanic."

"You think they'd pull in some unknown with security as tight as it is? He knows the mechanic's jargon, but ten-to-one, he's with the CIA." His voice deepened. "Come here, Chase."

She crossed the room and sat on the edge of his bed, suddenly shy at their nearness. Embarrassed, she thought, *If I marry him, this is what I will awaken to for the rest of my life: that quizzical boyishness that is creeping into his expression, that unrelenting gaze in those blue eyes, tender as he looks at me now. That curly mop of sleep-tousled hair.*

"I love you, Chase," he said.

"Please don't, Ian. I have to be sure."

His shoulders were strong and muscular, but his upper torso was lean, the thumping beat in his chest visible as he searched her face. "I forgot," he said. "I have to win the race before you can make up your mind about marrying me."

"Oh, Ian, I was only teasing when I said that." An overnight growth of beard had formed a shadow on his face. The reddish bristles felt rough to her fingers as she traced his jawbone. "I don't just champion winners," she said. "I've been interviewing the exhausted riders who abandoned the race. To me, it counts that they started—that they gave it everything they had."

He grinned slowly. "No street corners here. You'll have to do your political campaigning from the mountaintop. What will it be this time—the riders who don't make it to Paris?"

"No—my same old soap box. AIDS victims and the elderly."

He sobered. "You're a funny girl. Sophisticated one moment. Out to conquer the world the next."

"Just my small part of the world." Her throat tightened. "My mother called me last evening. My friend Jeff is dead."

"The young man with AIDS?"

"Yes. I really liked him, Ian. Jeff's nurse called asking for me, so Mother went in my place."

"Your mom sounds like a great lady."

"She is, Ian. The greatest. But I think it's the only time in her marriage when Daddy threatened to leave her. Mom's visit to Halverson House made the society page. So she won't go back."

"To keep your father happy?"

"No, because it was so depressing. But she's asking her bridge club to send care packages to the residents there."

"Nice gesture."

"It's more than that. Mother saw beyond the illness to the person dying. That's what happened to me when I visited Jeff. I really wanted to see him again. I didn't want him to die."

"We all have to die sometime, Chase."

"But not that way, with his body wasted and his life snuffed out before his time."

Ian's mouth twisted. "How then?"

"Jeff's brother said he'd understand if Jeff had died in a war. Even an accident would have been better—"

"We'd know how that way," Ian agreed. "But not why. I don't think we ever understand why a young person has to die."

"Whatever you do, Ian Kendall, don't you leave me."

"Wouldn't think of it. Now—you'd better go and give me time to get dressed and signed in before the race."

She reached under his pillow and snatched the crumpled sheet of paper from its hiding place. "Tell me about this first."

"It's not from another girl, if that's what you think."

She spread the embossed hotel stationery out on the bed and read: *Remember Simpson, Kendall. You will never make it to the top of your mountain.*

"Oh, not another threat on your life. I can't bear it."

For an instant, he forgot the covers he was clutching and wrapped his broad hand around hers. "I'll be all right."

"But he's here in the hotel."

"We don't know that for certain." He eased the paper from her fist. "Someone slipped it under the door this morning."

She glanced toward Marcus Nash's side of the room. "I suppose Marcus found it?"

"Come on, Chase. He's my roommate."

"I don't trust him. And Drew definitely doesn't."

"If it makes you feel better, neither do I. But I'm stuck with him until we reach the Pyrenees. Then we switch again."

If you reach the Pyrenees Mountains without being hurt, she thought. "What do you know about him, Ian?"

"Not much. He was a last-minute replacement for our team."

"I'll do a profile on him and see what I can find out."

"Stay out of trouble, Chase."

"You, too."

"I fight my own battles. You stick to your old folks and sick boys." She stood. "I'm going before the coach finds me here."

"Or worse, Drew or Vic. Chase, what do you do with your spare time?"

"I spend it with a journalist. He's thirtyish. Italian. And frightfully attractive," she teased. "It gets me out of that hotel room full of women."

"I thought you liked rooming with Basil Millard's wife."

"I do. I did. But her baby is fretful, and Marcus Nash's fiancée—who is prying and curious—gets dibs on the bathroom first, blares the TV at all hours, and takes the best bed."

"She sounds like Marcus. Considerate and kindly." As she backed away, he pursed his lips. "You've forgotten something."

She started to laugh and then in spite of herself leaned down and kissed him soundly on the lips.

When she reached the door, he called across the room, "Have you told your folks about you and me yet?"

"Bits and pieces. We talk on the phone every day. Mom says they are actually printing my articles in the town paper. Imagine, I'm making it big-time back in Long Island."

"Great!"

"Well, the editor and Dad are good friends. But Mom doesn't think it's just that. She thinks I'm good."

"You are."

She flushed happily. "I'm doing profiles on the riders."

"What about me?"

"I'm saving you for the grand finale." She blew him another kiss. "I'll write you up when you win."

"Don't wait that long, Chase."

Salvador Contoni had learned long ago never to sneak around but to go boldly to his task. He did so on Friday morning under the canopy of a charcoal-gray sky, whistling cheerfully in spite of the weather and the weight in his knapsack. If anyone stopped him, he would cockily point to his I.D. badge clearly labeling him as a journalist. But if the search went further, they would find he was carrying a laptop computer, some wire, and a few hand tools. A hollowed log—fifteen inches long—lay at the bottom of his knapsack, completely concealing the Contoni Interceptor.

Without breaking his stride, he stepped from the major walkway and eased alongside the thirty-foot TV Mobile unit. He could hear muffled voices coming from inside the truck where the communications equipment with its control panels and a row of television monitors were being manned. In another thirty to forty minutes, there would be bedlam inside the truck when their monitors went blank.

Sal stepped carefully around the satellite dish and over the numerous cables that fed into the TV screen in the press room. He moved more cautiously now toward the rear wheels where he slipped his knapsack to the sodden ground and emptied the contents: the intercept box, wire, his tools. He worked quickly—no longer whistling—as he tapped into the main line that ran directly into the press tent. Placing the black intercept box against the trunk of a tree, he secured it to the side of the cables with gleaming bolts. Deftly he connected the wires, the frequencies already modified to French television. Back in the press room, he would activate the switch with a remote control; the click of a second button on the keyboard would send the warning over the huge screen, a message for Maurice Chambord and the world to read. Sal would have five seconds, ten at most, to neutralize the main lines, blackening the truck monitors. It was all the time he needed to block out the regular Tour transmissions. A third click of a button, and the startled journalists and the world would be forced to remember Bottecchia. Ottavio Bottecchia—the man who could have become the greatest Italian rider.

Chase was crossing the street, helping a stranger find her way in the rain, when she saw Sal come from behind the cable truck and hurry toward the press room. She pointed the woman toward the hotel and then darted inside, hesitating just past the doorway, wondering where Sal could have gone. Images flashed across the huge television screen. Hundreds of journalists occupied the folding chairs. Long tables were cluttered with paperwork, blinking monitors, laptops, and computers with cellular phones attached. Phone cubicles stood on the sides of the room; with their constant audiovisual linkups, journalists could spin their transmissions around the world within seconds.

From where Chase stood, the summer drizzle sounded like the pelting of a violent storm against the thick canvas tent. She shook the rain from her blouse and hand-wiped her damp hair. The journalist beside her rubbed his bifocals with his handkerchief and grinned. "Love, you look lost," he said. "Can I help you?"

"Cycling journalism is still all new to me."

"Can't be timid in this business." Putting his glasses on, he peered at the press card pinned to her blouse. "Evans, eh? I'm Galleger. You haven't seen Samuel Abt this morning, have you?"

She shook her head. "I don't know him."

"Right. You're a novice then. Better get acquainted with Abt. He's one of the seasoned journalists at these Tours. Writes for the *Herald Tribune* and the *New York Times*." He brushed some more rain from his sleeve. "But I got my start in Tour journalism with a Belgian writer, Harry Van den Bremt. Ever hear of him?"

"I'm a novice, remember?"

"Big name to Tour journalism. Bronzed. Overweight. Always smoking. A wide grin that showed the gap between his front teeth. But I liked the chap. Harry always said the only way to taste the race was to be out there watching up close."

She thought of Drew's opposition. "I'd like to do that."

"Then take a day on the sidelines. Sometimes I think the monitors give us distorted images. We never see the pain and courage of the riders up close." He glanced at his waterlogged shoes. "But this is one time I'm glad for an indoor press room."

"But it's not the same as being on hand at the finish line."

"You sound like Harry. This is different from the early days of Tour journalism, Miss Evans, but that's what the big tele screen is all about. It lets us know what's happening and gives us the official results without us drowning in a rainstorm. Well, cheers! Gotta run." He gave her a comradely thump on the arm. "See you about town, love. And if not again this year, then next. Cycling events are my permanent beat until I cash in."

As she watched him make his way to the back of the room, she saw Salvador and waved. He pointed to the empty chair beside him.

"Nice to see a familiar face," she said as she reached him.

"Especially when it's yours. Where were you last evening?"

"Interviewing the young man who rode in the Broom Wagon."

"That's like leaving the race in a hearse, Chase. Why waste your time with a quitter? What's he hanging around for?"

"His doctor's clearance. He was hurt when he hit that wall."

Sal booted up his computer. "Chase, stick with the winners."

She thought of Ian. "I am."

The computer buzzed like a turbojet warming up. Now Sal seemed preoccupied. Checking his watch and the monitor. Running the mouse over the pad. Glancing furtively at the screen. Chase kicked his sodden knapsack, questions rising in her mind.

"Sal, I saw you out by the television truck climbing around all those cables. Can't you read signs?"

"Not if they're not in Italian. Tell me, what did they say?"

Her gaze went from his face to his hand as he clicked the mouse again. "It said, 'no trespassing,' Salvador."

His voice came back sharp. "Who was the old lady you helped across the street?"

"She wasn't an old woman, Salvador. She was my grandmother's age. Still rational. Still able to get around. She just needed directions to the hotel. She reminded me of the Willowglen."

"The what?"

"A senior residence—a place for the elderly in my hometown. I have several friends there."

"What are you—some kind of a crusader?"

"I just like to help people."

"Then help me." His eyes were cold as he glanced at the wall clock and said with a hint of irony, "Help me find a way to stop the American from winning, and then maybe one of my countrymen will come in first."

As the screen saver danced with rainbows, she ran her hand over Sal's cellular phone.

His hand clamped hers. "Don't use that."

She winced at the pressure on her wrist. "Sorry. I wasn't planning to use it, Sal. Can't you be a bit more pleasant?"

"It's too early," he said irritably. "Sit down, Chase. Turn on your own computer."

She slumped into her chair, determined to lash back. Before she could say more, there was a flashing light in the front of the room as the giant screen went blank. Laptop computers crashed. A rumble of discontent filled the room. A technician ran toward the light switch. . . . expletives . . . grumbling journalists.

"What's going on?" Sal asked, clicking his mouse again.

And then a warning flashed across the big screen: *Remember Bottecchia! It will happen again this year.*

Vic fell into step with Drew as they walked along the road. "Did you hear about the glitch in the computer system?"

"I didn't like it. What's this Bottecchia business?"

"Ottavio Bottecchia. A rider back in the twenties. Won the Tour twice. The Italians pinned their hopes on him. Found him dead along the side of the road three years later."

Drew frowned. "And the computer hacker was sending a message that we'd find one of our riders the same way? This Bottecchia fellow, was he killed in a race?"

"Who knows? Chase can ask her Italian journalist friend. From what I hear, Bottecchia died of a skull fracture. His bike was intact. None of his clothing ripped. Political maybe. He was anti-Fascist. Not popular back then perhaps."

"Then ask Chase to check some more."

Vic rubbed his angular jaw. "She did tell me she saw this Sal—Salatori—whatever his name is—prowling around the cable truck shortly before the glitch showed up."

"Is she connecting him to the problem?"

"If she is, she's not saying." Vic's jaw rub had reached beneath his chin, his hand resting now against his Adam's apple. "Chambord's boys found an intercept box out by the cable lines."

"Did it cause the malfunction?"

"Could have. Some journalists lost everything on their hard drives. All it needed was someone pushing a remote control and whamo—a five-second interruption to the regular transmission."

Drew groaned. "And all Chambord will do is call it a small problem in the electrical system."

🌢🌢🌢

On Saturday Drew sat sideways in Maurice Chambord's official red car wishing in a month of Sundays that he had stayed in England. He missed Miriam, worried about her shopping spree in Paris, and longed simply to sit down with her and talk about the baby that would make them grandparents.

"I'm anxious to get home," he had said in their last phone call, and Miriam had replied, "Take all the time you want, darling. Maggie and I are having a marvelous time shopping."

The voice thundering in his ears now didn't belong to Miriam. "No security measures take place in the Tour without my approval," Chambord said. "Do you understand, Monsieur Gregory?"

What Drew understood was that he was running interference for Troy Carwell. Carwell had stepped out of line by contacting Langley about a bomb disposal unit without going through Chambord. Drew controlled his own anger and waited for the showdown, his lanky legs cramped as he faced the Frenchman. Working for Chambord was difficult, taking his orders unbearable.

Chambord's narrow lips were tight, bloodless. "We do not want Washington involved in this." A tremor vibrated his words. "Washington contacted President Chirac—"

He tented his fingers—the nail beds turning blue—as though by the very act he could keep his fury in check. "We have a thousand international journalists at the race, Mr. Gregory. If they get wind of this, the public outcry would be worse than the bomb threats. Panic worldwide. Bedlam. It would ruin us."

Drew could guess the rest. Global acceptance mattered to Jacques Chirac's presidency. Chirac would have chewed out the Tour leaders. And now it was Drew's turn. "You didn't think you could get the French robot," Drew reminded him.

"I didn't want that robot unit. I have my reputation to consider. The entire Tour is my responsibility." He leaned forward. "I have called off my order for the robot bomb unit."

"It's not available?"

"We have no need for it."

"Mr. Chambord, we have another twelve days in the race."

"I know. I know. But we're halfway through. Our internal security is good. Nothing has happened." He recanted that with, "Except for some injuries and ruffled feathers among the riders. These bomb threats have all been a hoax. Don't you agree?"

Drew didn't agree, never had. But he held his tongue.

In spite of the weather reports and the contest that loomed ahead in the Alps, Maurice Chambord's confidence had grown with each passing stage. The bomb threats had become routine for him. Excitedly, he said, "As President Chirac pointed out, the only real problem we've had is bad weather."

And plenty of that, Drew thought. He'd quit many a picnic for less rain than they'd suffered in the Tour. Bolts of lightning and thunderstorms with torrential rains. Streets and villages awash with rain water. Temperatures dipping until they wondered whether they were hitting an early fall in July. The cyclists had been constantly buffeted by head winds as they raced over the narrow winding roads and past windblown wheat fields.

Drew waited for the ax to split the heavy air between them. Days ago he had tried to force a confrontation with Chambord, insisting on an all-out search for Salvador Contoni; his concern fell on deaf ears. But Interpol and Drew's old friend Pellier, that polite, articulate police commander in the city of Paris, welcomed the latest news on Contoni.

Within hours, Pellier had distributed a police sketch, a good likeness of the handsome Italian. "He's ours now," the commandant had said, twisting the tip of his handlebar mustache. "What do you Americans call it—a feather in my cap?"

Drew was certain that Chambord had managed forty seconds of silence before the ax fell again. Chambord's eyes were shiny pinpoints when he said, "Mr. Gregory, you were absent from the Tour for two days without permission."

Drew shrugged. "I didn't cherish riding the flatlands of Belgium in a torrential rain. Thought it might make me car sick."

"So you settled for a choppy ride in a chartered plane."

"I guess I did. Had a friend to see in Normandy."

"A wealthy widow," Chambord snapped.

"The wealthy widow who informed on Salvador Contoni."

Drew reached for the door handle, unraveled his long legs, and stepped from the shiny car. He turned and leaned into the open door. "I have a report to make to Troy Carwell in Paris. Should I make reference to this little exchange?"

"I tell you, everything is under control, Mr. Gregory, except you. Tell him that! The person behind these threats is just some crackpot who gets his fancy by frightening others."

"I still think the threats are real, Monsieur Chambord."

Chambord looked at Drew as though he were a schoolboy failing to comprehend his lessons. "Every race has had its threats," he said. "Don't you see, Mr. Gregory? We went across the flatlands of Belgium. Where was our terrorist? Up those magnificent streets of Antwerp. No problems. Soissons and Chambery—nothing happened. We are safe."

"Safe because we've taken precautions," Drew argued.

Chambord tapped the steering wheel. "Here we are at the foot of the Col de la Madeleine ready for our first alpine climb. Where could a terrorist hide along these mountain ridges?"

Just behind the parapet wall, Drew thought.

Chambord's forced smile eased his facial muscles. "Gregory, we will get you safely up to the Alpine Ski resort. Such beauty. And over the Galibier Pass. Have you ever been there?"

"Never."

"Two or three days in the Alps, my friend—that's where the race begins. You will see some of the greatest riders ever. Even you will forget about the terrorists up there."

But Maurice Chambord's optimism was premature. On the eve of stage eleven, the first bomb exploded.

Chapter 14

Drew pushed his morning coffee aside and came out from behind the newspaper as Ian joined him. Ian was ready for the race, right on down to the helmet strap secured snugly beneath his chin. His thigh-hugging shorts bore the Gainsborough logo. The stem of his riding goggles was tucked at the top of his jersey. It struck Drew again that Ian had grown from a lanky, awkward kid into a handsome, athletic young man, with his grandmother's sensitivities and Uriah Kendall's stubborn jaw. He had, after all, known Ian all his life, but he felt closer to him now, more like an uncle to his favorite nephew.

If Drew could bypass Troy Carwell's orders, he'd have Ian on the first flight back to the Cotswolds. As far as Drew was concerned, there wasn't a cycling race in the world worth losing your life over.

"You wanted to see me," Ian said.

"Just to wish you well on today's ride."

"It's an easy one. We head east for a while over some rolling hills. We should have a good tailwind to speed us along."

"What're your chances, Ian?"

"I'm going to pace myself. I have my eyes on stage eleven."

"Climbing in the mountains? That's where you shine."

"Expect to." He slid into the chair across from Drew and removed his head gear. "So don't ask me to quit now."

"And risk disfavor with your grandfather? It crossed my mind." Drew flattened the newsprint. "You look good, Ian."

"I felt good until I saw the headlines. How do you tolerate a daily diet of coffee and news? It's the same old thing. Bomb threats. The assassination of prime ministers. Nuclear power. Train derailments. Intelligence communities blowing it again."

Drew checked his irritation. "Don't remind me about Aldrich Ames and Porter Deven. Granted—the world's a mess. But it's nothing more than a warning, a trumpet call from a coming King."

"You sound like my grandmother and Beatrice Thorpe."

Drew gave him a reluctant morning grin. "For the first time in my life, I'm beginning to think like them."

"I run on my grandmother's steam. She taught me to run my race well. Got her challenge taped inside my helmet here."

Drew pointed to Ian's chest, heart-level. "Make sure that truth gets inside. Wow! I really do sound like your grandmother."

"I've got it stowed away. I wouldn't be out riding in that pack today if I didn't believe God rode with me."

Vic sauntered up to their table, his face looking gaunt as he sat down uninvited. "You two solving the world's problems?"

Drew nodded. "Been talking about the King's business."

Vic held up both hands. "Hold off, Drew. I'd rather talk about the race. What do you say, Ian? Is it still your burning ambition to ride up the Champs Elysees in the winner's jersey?"

"Right on. For me, July is meant for Paris with half a million fans cheering me on."

"I thought you just wanted to impress Chase."

"I want to marry her, but it's not what she has in mind."

"Just another 1,000 miles to go. If you win, maybe you can pick up a bride as well as the torch from Greg LeMond."

"I'm not picking up anyone's torch, Vic. I'm riding my own race." His face clouded as he turned to meet Drew's gaze. "The threats are coming against me. At least put me in the picture."

Drew refolded the newspaper, the edges even, and laid it on the table. "We've made little progress. Each time we lay out our strategy for stopping the terrorist, Chambord insists that it is simply a madman out there angered over unemployment."

"Thanks, Drew. That's really comforting."

"Chambord won't hear it, but a man named Salvador Contoni may be out there in that sea of faces along the Tour route." Drew slid Contoni's police sketch across the table. "It's a long shot, Ian, but I'm convinced that this man was hired by a Greek millionaire to stop you from winning."

The effect was explosive. "Alekos's father?" he blurted. "He still blames me for his son's death? Alekos and I were friends."

His mouth opened, then clamped shut. "Does Mr. Golemis hate me that much?" The words were too repugnant for Ian. He snatched up the police photo and his helmet and stalked from the room.

"Was that wise to tell him about Golemis?" Vic asked.

"I can't worry him with unconfirmed reports about a Bosnia-Moscow connection or a Serbian war criminal riding beside him."

"He ought to know all the risks."

"He's too close to them. He could be rooming with the Serbian. . . . Yes, that's right. Marcus Nash may be Dudley Perkins's Roadrunner. We've sent Nash's fingerprints to Paris."

"And they're bunking together night after night?"

"The coach arranged it for me. We have to know the truth. If Carwell is right, Nash is quite possibly a Serbian Intelligence officer. If he is, then he knows every move we're making."

"You'd do better checking out Coach Skobla, not some poor rider who made the team at the last minute."

"His name never appeared on any major race this year, yet he qualified for the biggest race of all. Nash is clever, too interested in self-preservation to harm Ian in the room. Vic, whatever happens will be along the Tour route."

"And we're in trouble if we picked the wrong man. Let's just pull Ian out of the race and be safe."

"Troy Carwell said no! The Serbian's London contact is here in the crowd, too. Sooner or later Nash will make a mistake."

"If we haven't made the mistake—"

Drew ignored Vic. "If we're right, we can deliver the Lily-Trotter right back into Dudley Perkins's hands—some double agent who's sitting right under our noses."

"Drew, you're not trying to finger Fairway? That stinks."

"So does treason."

🪲🪲🪲

Four hours later Maurice Chambord's shiny red car pulled alongside the Gainsborough vehicle. Drew rolled down the rear window as straggling cyclists pedaled past them.

"Morning," Drew said.

"It is afternoon," Chambord grumbled. "We had reports that someone was riding Kendall's rear wheel wearing placard number 190."

Drew grabbed his list. "What's his name?"

"How would I know?" Chambord shot back. "There's no rider registered with that number."

"Is Kendall all right?"

"He is now. But number 190 ran him into a brick wall. Cost Kendall a few seconds, so he'll lose points in today's stage."

"Pick the man up, Chambord."

"Impossible. It's every fan's fantasy to ride in the Tour. When the gendarmes rushed him, the cheering crowds just opened a path and let the man slip away. Then they closed ranks again. Happens like this every year. Some fan taking a glory ride."

"It's the wrong year for jokes, Chambord."

❦❦❦

In southwest France, Jiri Benak hiked through the fields toward his friend tending sheep on the hillside. Ignasius was wearing his patched knickers and knee-high socks, a red beret cocked on his head, and boots laced tightly against his ankles. He turned as Jiri approached, his face wreathed in smiles.

"My friend," Ignasius said, "you are back."

"In from Paris late last night."

"I thought you might sleep the morning away."

"I have always been an early riser, Ignasius."

The man leaned against the crook of his staff. "More so when you are troubled. You should be as I am. The past is put away. I am back where I belong—with my people, with my land."

"I have no people," Jiri said. He envied Ignasius for that unearthly calm, that simplicity of life.

"Did everything go well?" Ignasius asked. "Did you keep your appointment?"

"As planned. I left before the Tour reached Paris."

Ignasius grinned slyly. "But it comes our way soon. I think you knew this. That's why you came here a few weeks ago—so you would be here when the cyclists climbed the Pyrenees."

You have been in my cabin, Jiri thought. *Seen my equipment. Sifted through the box of timers and nails. Found the copper wires and bottles of ammonium nitrate hidden in the shed. And guessed my purpose.* "I will move on in another month," he said.

The weather wrinkles in Ignasius's face deepened. "Some of my people are anxious for you to go on now. But what of the race, my friend? Will you see it with me? We have a young rider who makes his home in one of the Basque villages."

"You want him to win?"

A raucous laugh rose from his belly. "It makes no matter to me who wins. But you, my friend, I think it matters to you."

"And does that shock you?"

"You never shock me, Jiri. We no longer think alike. Someday perhaps you will find a village like this and settle down."

"But not in this one?"

Jiri's thoughts traversed the continent, winging to the Cotswolds and the stone cottage that would be his one day. He was yanked back by Ignasius's next words. "I think not. A Basque way of life is too basic, too modest for you."

Ignasius stooped down by the lamb nibbling grass by his feet and ran his rough hand behind the woolly ear. "We would do better to part as friends," he said.

"Will you help me once more before I go?"

The black eyes met Jiri's, guardedly, amusement beginning to creep in. "And what do you have in mind?"

"You've used avalaunchers—blown away rock slides."

"And you want me to create a rock slide? No," he said flatly. "The cyclists will ride through my village peacefully."

"Before that—before they get here."

"Then you will move on?"

"As soon as the race is over."

"And where is this mountain that you want to blow away?"

"At the beginning of stage eleven—and I want only to block the roadway. To send a warning."

"I know you well. To destroy it is more likely, my friend."

He no longer trusts me, Jiri thought. *That part of our friendship is dead, gone.* The nostalgia of the loss dug at him. "Just go with me. Carry one of the knapsacks. Help me."

"So the launch site looks like the work of a peasant?"

"Show me how to pack the plastic explosives against the rocks. I will set the timer. I will blow the mountain."

"A moment ago it was nothing but the road. No lives lost."

"None. We must leave soon. I can hire a private plane."

The peasant's face brightened. "I have never flown before."

"Then you will tonight. And you will be back here on your land and with your people by morning."

"Perhaps you could be gone from our village by then?"

"Not until after the race."

Ignasius shifted uneasily. "What purpose is all of this?"

For a flash, the thought of Drew Gregory blurred Jiri's rugged features. "I am trying to stop an old enemy," Jiri said.

"Was he once a friend?"

"No, you are my only friend." He spoke confidently now. "There's a steep place along the mountain curve. The slope has been stripped of timber. Or an old avalanche left it barren. There are massive boulders and tree stumps left. We can bring them down and dam up the route."

"You are quite mad, Benak," Ignasius said. "Quite mad." But he smiled, a curious mischief awakening in those dark eyes.

He turned and prodded his sheep with his staff as he swaggered off to climb his beloved hills. Jiri watched him go.

I am not mad, Ignasius, he thought.

Jiri was driven by anger. Drew Gregory had robbed him of his livelihood at the steel factory in Jarvoc. Even Boris Ivanski's offer of opportunities in Russia or his own obsession with the illegal sale of weapons meant nothing to Jiri as long as Drew Gregory lived. Yet, in a strange, compelling way he knew that killing Gregory would not satisfy him. He could inflict a far greater wound on Gregory by exploding a bomb along stage eleven and sending the warning message direct to Gregory: *Your friend Ian Kendall will never stand on the winner's podium in Paris.*

When Jiri looked again, Ignasius and his sheep had dipped below the crest of the first hill. He gazed higher to the craggy mountains above him where the gigantic peaks of the Pyrenees were snow-capped and the lower slopes stripped of their timber.

Wednesday, 9 P.M. Jiri and Ignasius balanced the heavy rucksacks on their backs and climbed three kilometers up the mountain, their shadowy movements like part of the rock formation. Ignasius stayed in the lead, Benak behind him. A lone figure in a hooded Gainsborough jacket followed them, his steps so stealthy that only Ignasius had heard him. Ignasius rounded a boulder and held up his hand. When the third man came around the boulder, the shepherd secured him with a choke hold.

As the two struggled, Benak demanded, "What are you doing here?"

With reluctance, Ignasius released him. The young man rubbed his neck, saying, "Benak, I came to ask you the same thing."

"Then come with us, Roadrunner. And watch us blow away the mountain."

Ignasius led the way again around the rock wall. Five minutes later, he reached the area of an old rock slide where a whole section of mountain lay bare. He struck out straight up the cliff, losing his footing on the stones as he went, clawing to keep from tumbling back to the road. Finally, he signaled to the others and set down his rucksack.

They worked deftly, silently. Across the road, there was no barrier—just a straight drop-off down into the valley. Some of the tumbling mountain would soar off the cliff. Jiri found a V-shaped recess that pleased him, one that was set against gnarled tree roots. They worked quickly, piling layers of rocks around on the ground. They positioned two cone-shaped cylinders filled with explosives at the base of the rocks, leaving part of the charges exposed. Jiri took over now, inserting a detonating cap into one end of each cartridge. Wires were attached. Screws tightened. The delayed timers set. Five minutes apart.

It will work, Ignasius told himself. *It will blow part of this mountain away. It will create another avalanche.*

He bent down again to pile more rocks and earth around the cylinders. And then as stealthily as they had come, they slid back to the road, creating a small rock slide as they went. "We separate here," Ignasius said. "It will be safer that way."

❦❦❦

Long after Sal and Chase left the press room, the sun plunged behind the mountain, leaving only darkness and a hazy moon. Case studied the Italian as he capped his pen and stared out the cafe window.

"Are you all right, Salvador?" she asked.

He sighed as he turned back to her. He was a handsome, moody man, talkative one moment, sullen the next. He seemed to brood more as darkness set in. "Well, are you?"

"I should be content. Good meal. Good company. You didn't even give me your usual excuse about getting back to your friends."

"They were busy," she admitted.

"That was to my advantage. Thank you for having dinner with me, Chase. I hate eating alone—and my hotel accommodations get worse."

She laughed. "Mine get more crowded—and Millard's baby cries constantly. But I really must go so they don't worry about me."

"I have a better idea. Why don't we cycle up the mountain a short distance and check out tomorrow's route?"

"In the dark? I don't think it's a good idea, Sal."

He gave her his cocky grin as they left the restaurant. "You're not afraid of me?"

She wasn't really afraid, but she didn't want to be alone with him on the mountainside—and Drew Gregory would have fits. But she said, "Of course not. But without streetlights, we'd ride right off the mountain."

"At least we could stretch our legs and walk a bit. I will have you back at your hotel in an hour."

"I'll hold you to that."

She struck out guardedly, afraid that he might attempt to take her hand. Half an hour up the slope, Salvador said, "Chase, I keep seeing you with that American rider."

"Ian Kendall? We're friends."

"I thought *we* were friends."

She laughed uneasily. "Can't I have more than one friend?"

"You should have told me. You know what I think of him."

"You don't even know him. He's special to me. Don't you have someone really important to you, Sal? You never mention your wife and family. Aren't you married?"

"I'd like to be."

"Does she have a name?"

"Monique."

"That's pretty."

"So is she."

"Sal, where were you this morning? You missed that crazy fan who rode in the Tour today."

"Did I?" he asked.

"He wore number 190 pinned to his jersey. He forced Ian into a brick wall; it could have cost Ian the race."

"Probably an accident," Sal said indifferently.

In the moonlight she noticed his bandaged fingers, and her suspicions rose again. And then like the dawn breaking, realization came. She said, "Sal, you know there's no rider registered with that number."

"Are you suggesting that I wore that number?" he teased.

"It could have been you, Sal. You never showed up in the press room. And you have a bike. . . . You didn't, did you?"

"Ride into Kendall? What do you think?"

She didn't like what she was thinking. Not Sal. Not her friend. "What did Ian ever do to you?"

"Nothing," he admitted. "But if he wins the race, he gets rich. If he loses, I do."

She shivered. The implication of Sal's words chilled her. Or maybe it was the mountain air putting goose bumps on her arms. Then they saw a young man in a hooded jacket coming toward them from higher up on the slope. When he spotted them, he hesitated, and then slipped over the edge of the road, scrambling into the darkness.

Chase went another step or two, then felt the earth tremble beneath her feet. As she tried to steady herself, a shock wave rocked the mountain. A split-second stillness followed before the mountain rumbled like a gigantic earthquake.

The groan turned into a deafening roar as the hillside exploded. Sal threw Chase to the ground and covered her with his own body. Sand and gravel began to fall, building momentum until it roared down the slopes like a waterfall. Rocks and tree stumps soared and plunged to earth. Metal fragments from the explosives broke into jagged pieces, scattering with a tremendous force, the metal shards cutting Chase's cheek and hands. And then the massive boulders broke free, pitching and lurching as they tumbled down, twisting and somersaulting like cannon-balls, forming craters in the road as they landed. A quarter of a mile away, the swoosh of fire cut the brush along the side of the road. The flames threaded their way across the road, over the cliff, and down toward the valley. They danced and snaked along the ravine and over the gutted path of an old avalanche where they would burn out. In the semidarkness an eerie gray funnel of smoke rose from the mountain. And then utter stillness as the rock dust choked them.

Chapter 15

Thursday, *8 P.M.* Outside the restaurant window, dusk chased away the pink and gold streamers in the night sky, leaving the snowcaps at the top of the Alps draped in darkness—as silent and mute as Drew had been with Vic sitting across from him. Drew couldn't sleep—hadn't slept—for twenty-four hours. Last night's explosion at the foot of the mountains kept playing in his mind. The smoke cloud rising in the night sky. The second detonation. The rocks and boulders soaring like war missiles. Somebody had set that explosion. Somebody had gotten away with it.

He tried to block out their frantic search for Chase, but it kept flashing back. As well, he recalled the utter relief when they found her. She had been sitting alone, terrified that the mountain might explode again. Her hands like ice. A cut on her cheek. Even in the darkness, her eyes looked like saucers. Aftershocks shook the foundation beneath them. Then the procession came—trucks and people on foot. Walking. Running. Climbing. Shovels and picks in their hands. Dogs barking by their sides. Women carrying buckets. And singing. The people were singing.

"They're singing," Chase had said.

"Yeah, off-key." He squeezed her hand and said lightly, "Maybe they're just scaring the terrorists away."

"Then they didn't find them?"

"Not yet. But the terrorists didn't defeat the people in this village. They're fighting back. Everything is going to be okay, Chase."

They had stumbled down the mountain together, leaving the

townspeople with their torches and lanterns, their picks and shovels, an all-night crew determined to clear a narrow path in that rubble so the cyclists could ride up their mountain.

The Italian journalist had been nowhere in sight, but Drew hadn't thought about that last night. He thought about it now, realizing how gladly he could strangle the man for deserting Chase. Now he allowed himself to question why the man had fled into the darkness without her. Drew's mind stayed on standby, too numb to rehash the events even with Vic Wilson.

"I still want Chase to go back to London," he said aloud.

"She refuses. Insists on going back to the press room to make sure her friend is all right."

"It's more than he did. Leaving her alone like that."

"But, Gregory, he stayed with her until he saw help coming." As Drew rubbed his eyes, Vic reached across the table and poked him with a fork. "Don't look, but trouble is on its way."

"Chase and the Italian journalist?" Drew asked.

"No, Chase was turning in early. Marcus Nash just came in." Vic frowned, his dusky face hard like granite. "That was quick. He's already leaving. Stopped at the reception desk, turned around, and walked out."

"Did he leave anything?"

"Can't tell. Want me to check it out?"

"Too obvious. I'm just glad he left. Brad O'Malloy is on it. I told him to keep an eye on Nash."

"Cancel that one. Jon Gainsborough ordered his mechanics to keep a twenty-four-hour vigil on the equipment."

"So Nash is out there wandering around on his own."

"So is Salvador Contoni. When are you going to show Chase that police sketch?" Vic stretched his vision beyond Drew, and a smirky grin twisted his mouth to the left. "Brace yourself, Drew. You aren't going to like this one bit."

Drew flattened Vic's hand. "No games tonight, Wilson. I'm dog-tired."

"Edgy is more like it. Radburn Parker just walked in, looking sporty in his London tweeds and hiking boots."

"Is Lennie with him?"

"No, but he sure put on the charm for the receptionist."

Drew hid his displeasure when Parker walked up to them. The

man's thick, wavy hair appeared more wheat-colored than blond, the skin of his squared face pocked in the flickering candlelight.

"Gentlemen, Jon Gainsborough told me I'd find you here."

"What are you doing up here, Parker?"

He put his handkerchief to his runny nose and said, "I have a personal interest in the British team. Or have you forgotten?"

"Oh," Drew said. "I try to keep that on the back burner."

Parker remained unshakable like a miserable cold, his bullish-eyed gaze unblinking. He twisted the band on his Zodiac watch. "I have an hour to spare. May I join you for dinner?"

"The chair's empty. Take it."

Even sitting, he looked massive, composed. He flung his ruck-sack on top of the tablecloth—barely missing Vic's elbow—and pulled out some photographs. "Obviously Glenn Fairway didn't tell you I was coming, Gregory."

"I haven't been in touch with him."

"Which displeases Fairway."

"Nothing to report. So far the race is going well."

Parker's sharklike smile deepened. "Are you discounting last evening's mishap? Plastic explosives, wasn't it?"

"The gendarmerie handled it."

"But I thought half the mountain came down."

"Only part of it. What's happening at the embassy?"

"Nothing but stolen memorandums. Fairway ordered a twenty-four hour surveillance on Lennie. She won't get very far."

"Does she know you're in France?"

"She knows I'm away on a business trip. I had to leave. I couldn't face what was happening to her. It's been difficult for me, Gregory. I am quite fond of her."

I bet, Drew thought.

Parker pointed to the photos. "Fairway asked me to deliver these to you, Gregory."

Drew slid his hand across the linen and spread them out. "These are all of you and Lennie."

"We have had some great times together. The opera. The theater. She is well-informed about literature and music."

One by one Drew picked up the pictures—seeing, yet not seeing the old Lennie in fashionable clothes, a love-sick expression on her face as she looked up at Parker. His broad hand rested on hers. Involuntarily, Drew glanced at Parker and was startled to see a wedding band on his finger.

No, Drew thought. *You didn't go that far! You didn't marry Lennie.* "You're married?" he asked.

"The ring? I wear it when I travel. My wife and I are divorced—long before Lennie," he volunteered.

"Why bring these to me? I'm not interested in your affair with Lennie—if you two have a problem, let Fairway handle it."

"He wants to avoid your arguments on your return to London. No surprises that way. He insisted on these surveillance photos. I agreed—but all of that was before she meant so much to me."

You lie well, Drew thought. He pulled his pen from his shirt pocket, uncapped and recapped it. These were places that would have delighted Lennie. St. James Park, the Victorian Room at Geffrye's Museum, the two of them strolling arm in arm by the docklands, a close-up one on the steps at 16 Oakley Street, and a fifth one of them browsing at Vanbrugh's Rare Book Store.

"None of these prove her guilt," Drew said.

Parker's smile was condescending. "But when we dated, she insisted on taking the tube home alone. Sometimes it would take her hours to get home after that. I'd keep calling and calling—"

Maybe she just didn't answer her phone after midnight. But traveling alone—well, why not? Drew wondered. Lennie was too timid to arouse questions in the minds of neighbors by arriving home in the company of a man. Drew's aggravation mounted as Parker shoved a second set of photos across the table.

"Fairway persuaded me to follow Lennie," Parker said. "Once to Gabriel's Wharf, another time to Waterloo Station. These are the result."

Drew frowned. *Waterloo Station! Isn't that the route she took to her parents' residence?*

Parker's tone became urgent. "The woman in both sets of photographs is the same person, Gregory. There is no mistaking that this is your Lennie Applegate. Those computer disks in her hands were taken from the embassy and passed to her handler."

"What kind of a fool photographer are you? You left out the man's face."

Parker's wide lips sealed for a moment and then opened again.

"There is another problem, Gregory. Fairway insisted that I tell you. . . . Lennie has a brain tumor. Inoperable by now."

Drew felt as if a cold wind had swept in off the Alps and engulfed him. "Lennie ill?" His fists clenched around the uncapped pen. "You're talking a tumor—a brain tumor?"

"Right on. It is terminal, old man," he said, his gunmetal gaze steady. "Gregory, surely you knew about her headaches?"

"She was squinting a lot lately," Drew admitted, "but I thought it was her new contact lenses."

"Then your lack of concern may have cost Lennie her life."

Drew had the urge to plow his fist straight into Parker's Roman nose. "She's dying? My secretary is dying?"

"That's what the doctors say."

"Parker, if Lennie has a brain tumor, no wonder she got into this mess. She's confused—not thinking clearly."

Across the table, anger flared in Vic's eyes. "A terminal illness doesn't mean a person's not in charge of her faculties."

"What—"

"Drew, you know I'm a walking time bomb, a body waiting to test positive to AIDS this year, next year. But I can still think. The medical odds are against Lennie and me, but we're still responsible for our actions." Vic shuffled through the pictures. "Face it, Drew. Lennie knew what she was doing. She was well paid for every memo, every secret that left the embassy."

Drew couldn't equate the mousy, shy Lennie with a shrewd spy who could walk boldly out of the embassy with American secrets. "She wasn't after Jaguars and mansions, Vic. She just wanted to help her parents. They're old and ill."

"There are government agencies for that," Parker said.

Vic shook Drew's arm. "Don't let your loyalty blind you."

No, Parker and Fairway are trying to take Lennie down, and it's up to me to stop them. He brushed Vic's hand away. "I'm okay."

Parker's thick brows lowered, forming dark awnings above his eyes. "I admit, in the beginning, dating Lennie was part of the surveillance. I never expected to care about her." He drew his shirt cuff over his watch band. "But it was all over between us before we discovered that Lennie had helped the Serbian cause."

Another lie, Drew thought.

"According to Fairway, she sent money every month—a pittance to be sure—but what she intended for her family was used by the rebels. The truth is Lennie helped in the barbaric war effort without knowing it. That didn't sit well with Fairway nor with me. We both felt that with Lennie's employment at the embassy, we should have been informed about her personal ties with Serbia."

"What about the brain tumor, Parker? Surely this has something to do with what's happened."

"I've urged Lennie to consent to the surgery. She refused. So I convinced the doctors to increase her medications to help her get through the rough spots. What else can I do, Gregory?"

You're a good actor, Drew thought as Parker's voice wavered. "Why doesn't Fairway detain her—and insist on medical care?"

"Fairway feels that the important thing is to catch her taking a classified document from the embassy. And that's it. She's ours."

"And where will you be, Parker, when that happens?"

"I fly back to London in the morning. I will want to stand by her, of course."

Of course.

The smirk on Parker's face tightened the lines around his mouth. "Gregory, do you question Glenn Fairway's time frame? Ah! I see that you do. But you Americans took a long time tracking Porter Deven and Aldrich Ames."

Drew winced. "I don't feel much like dinner, Parker. I think I'll ask the waiter to send a tray up to my room."

"I'll join you, Drew," Vic offered. "You don't mind eating alone, do you, Radburn?"

"Under the circumstances, no." He ran his hand over his burlap skin, barely controlling the twitch at the corner of his mouth. "I don't like this any better than you do, Gregory. Neither does Fairway."

Back in their hotel room, Drew paced back and forth, pounding his fist against his palm. "Why this pictorial sham? Parker doesn't care about Lennie any more than Fairway does."

Vic loosened his tie. "Parker seems genuinely fond of her."

"As attached as a Siamese cat befriending a bulldog."

Drew covered his eyes, hoping to shut the miserable pictures from his mind. Why was he so uneasy about Parker? They were on the same side, weren't they? He was helping them, wasn't he?

"It's not Parker we're after, Drew. This is takedown time for

Lennie. She's played a high-stakes chess game and lost." He tossed Parker's pictures on the bed and dropped another set beside them. "Here are the photos from Glenn Fairway's vault."

"And you're just now giving them to me?"

"I held off—I've been trying to put it all together myself, but there's nothing we can do about them until we get back to London. They're just like Parker's photos."

Drew spread them out. The old Lennie with the new look was clearly evident, but again the camera had caught only a man's arm, a cuff link visible on his sleeve, an expensive ring on his finger, a computer disk in his hand. What kind of a dud was Parker with a camera? A schoolboy would have had enough smarts to include the man's face. "Vic, what if Parker faked these pictures on Fairway's orders?"

"Then we're about to hang Lennie on Parker's photography."

Drew scrutinized the photo where Lennie's fingers rested on the man's broad wrist. Mousy Lennie overtly touching someone? "That's it," Drew said. "There's a blue Zodiac watch like the one Parker wears. I saw it on his wrist again this evening."

Vic's shrill whistle blasted through the room. "That's it then. Lennie gave Parker a watch like that for his birthday. But how? She couldn't afford an expense like that on her embassy salary."

"She could if she's selling embassy secrets." Drew leaned over the bed and with a wild brush of his hand swept the pictures onto the floor. "If Parker didn't take these pictures, maybe Glenn Fairway did. They're in it together, Vic. Mark my word."

🏵🏵🏵

Parker glanced at his watch and cursed himself for wearing it. He had removed his Cambridge ring before leaving London and even remembered to leave his favorite diamond cuff links at home. But automatically he had worn the Zodiac—Lennie's birthday gift to him. He had in truth been flattered by her gift, but wearing the watch this evening had been a careless mistake.

He knew it the moment Drew Gregory thumped one of the photos, his finger actually pointing at the Zodiac. "What kind of a photographer are you, Parker? You left out the man's face." Parker had felt the heat rise in his neck, yet Gregory made no mention of the watch. Would he, once he studied the photos again?

Parker swallowed his drink. Gregory and Wilson would be in their room by now. He shouldered his empty rucksack and left the restaurant without ordering dinner. Outside, he glanced around. Even at night the chateau was as gleaming white as the snow-covered glaciers above him. He strolled over the cobblestone path and disappeared into the shadowed darkness of the evergreens that climbed the mountain slopes. As he inched deeper into the foliage, he smothered a sneeze with his handkerchief.

He moved more cautiously now, avoiding the marked trails and listening for sounds of snapping twigs behind him. He felt the rawness of the mountain air against his cheeks. His nose ran from the annoying scent of the wild alpine blooms that clung to the granite rocks. It had to be their pollen or the last of the Martagon lilies giving him fits; they were beautiful in the chateau gardens, disastrous for his allergies. The shadows grew longer, darker, with only fading streaks of light from the chateau windows to guide his steps. He kept his handkerchief to his face and muffled another sneeze.

"Over here. What kept you so long, Parkovitch? I left word with the receptionist."

He stopped, waited. The shadowy figure remained hidden among trees, forcing Parker to take the first step. "Roadrunner?"

The cyclist stepped forward, sullen and dark like the night, his handsome features partly hidden behind the hooded jacket. Parker saw the glint of the knife in the young man's hand and felt contempt as he faced him. "Put that away," he said.

"I had to be certain it was you. Jiri Benak must be somewhere nearby. Did he contact you?"

Parker took the handkerchief from his face long enough to answer. "I don't intend for him to identify me. Not yet. But I've been watching him. Benak is a clever man, most useful to us."

"What's wrong with you, Parkovitch?"

"Flowers make me sneeze."

With a throaty laugh he said, "You must be allergic to the lilies or thistledown."

"I'll live," Parker told him. "But I need to get back inside the chateau. And you should be resting for tomorrow's race."

"I had to see you first."

"Risky with Gregory and Wilson staying in the same hotel."

"Did they tell you about last night's bombing?"

"It made the news. A bloody good show."

"You call a botched job successful? Benak is running his own timetable. I don't think we can trust him."

"You worry too much. We can still use him."

"The villagers spent all night clearing the debris, forming a path for us to ride over. It slowed the race considerably. Two of the riders dropped out—refused to ride the stage."

"I know. I know. And there was destruction in the valley along the burned hillsides. But no deaths. Few injuries."

"You knew about it, didn't you, Parkovitch? Knew it was going to happen. You and Benak should keep me better informed."

No, I didn't know. He said, "You're safe. Nothing happened to you. The major plan is still the same. Stage seventeen."

"Are there any more bombings before that? The timing has to be perfect. When do I alert my people in Bosnia, Parkovitch?"

You won't live to do that, Parker thought. *Professor Ivanski has no lasting interest in Bosnia or a Serbian uprising. You are useful and expendable, Roadrunner—my job, according to Ivanski—but I will arrange to have someone else take care of it.*

He blew his nose and with a nasal twang said, "It's all arranged. Benak sets off the bombs. You create an accident for Kendall—a pileup of cyclists that will plow into the bystanders. Ryskov contacts Ivanski. And Ivanski notifies the Serbs."

"So everything hinges on Ryskov getting his message through to Moscow. Let me take care of Kendall before then."

"Ivanski insists that everything must happen at once."

Roadrunner shrank deep into his jacket, his resistance as dark as the night. Parker pitied him. He was young, but he was accustomed to giving orders, not obeying them.

"Nothing will go wrong," Parker assured him.

"Ivanski will end up with a bloodbath in Moscow."

"What would it matter? The rich Mafia will still be wealthy. The elderly poor still hungry. It's time for the Russian people to do more than just dream of the past." *Time,* he thought, *for the remnants of the Phoenix-40 to rise to power.*

"You seem more Russian than British, Parkovitch."

Yes. His pulse quickened; he sensed excitement in his own voice. "The present Kremlin regime is unpopular. The last elections didn't solve a thing. Many men still covet the presidency. Yavlinsky. Zyuganov. Zhirinovsky. Even Gorbachev still yearns for a comeback. All of them former party members," Parker scoffed. "Only Ivanski has the answers."

"The blood in Red Square will turn a deep purple before this is over."

"Unless Ivanski's plans for an Imperial Russia are put into play. It will be a bloodless coup, but once in office, he will disband nuclear disarmament and build a strong military backup."

"A strange mix of peace and power. And you believe he will succeed?" The young man bent his head back, his face to the starless sky. "If everything goes wrong—for you, for all of us—where will you go, Parkovitch? Back to London?"

"I can always go to Moscow. Ivanski has promised me a position in the new leadership—as second in command."

"With your British ties? You are as crazy as the professor." He started to slip away along the unmarked trail.

"You haven't asked about your aunt," Parker called.

As Nash faced Parker again, a patch of light from the chateau windows fell across his high cheekbone. "Aunt Lennie?" he asked sadly. "Poor woman. Does she really believe I am her nephew?"

"The longer she does, the safer it is for you."

At midnight Drew patched a phone call through to Glenn Fairway in London. "Sorry to call you so late, Glenn. I'm worried about Lennie Applegate. How is she?"

Drew heard Fairway tapping his fingers on his desk before he said, "You know her. Never misses a day at work."

"In spite of the brain tumor?"

"What tumor? No one told me she's sick."

"Fairway, she gets headaches a lot lately."

The finger tapping grew louder. "Not since you've been gone. The only thing strange about Lennie is the portable radio on her desk. She keeps it tuned low to the BBC reports on the Tour."

Drew tried to sort it out, but he said, "Is she that interested in the race?"

"She is since Radburn Parker left."

"I saw Parker this evening up here at the Alpine Ski resort. We—almost had dinner together."

"He's there already? I'm surprised. He had a business appointment in Paris. Something to do with the Parker Foundation. . . . I didn't realize he was joining the Tour so quickly."

"He's the one who told me about Lennie."

Fairway sounded disgruntled. "Well, he should have told me."

"About those pictures—"

"What pictures?"

Didn't Parker show them to Fairway? Wait. He remembered Parker's exact words, *"Fairway asked me to deliver these to you, Gregory."*

"Look, have Parker call me. He said he was heading back to London tomorrow."

"No, he took a two-week holiday to the continent."

"Switch to scramble. I need to know what's going on with Lennie. What evidence—"

Fairway's tone sharpened. "That's not the thing to discuss over the phone." The switch hollowed the sound of Fairway's voice as he said, "The last couple of days, nothing has turned up missing. She's back to her old routine. Comes to work. Goes home. Never leaves the apartment except to visit her parents."

"I have to get in touch with Parker, Glenn."

Fairway chortled. "If he's not staying at your hotel, scan the fans. He'll be there somewhere. He's sticking with the Tour until Paris. He's quite a cycling fan. Been following it for years. Now with a team of his own—"

Drew wanted to yank the phone from the wall and toss it across the room. Parker had lied to him. Or was Fairway doing the snow job? "Doesn't Lennie have a nephew in the race, Glenn?"

"You've got me. Never heard that."

Surely Fairway knew. Drew allowed the memories to flash back to Lennie's loyalties right on down to a cup of steaming cappuccino on his desk first thing in the morning. Had he ever thanked her for her efficiency or that impossible filing system of hers that never failed? His thoughts raced from the dowdy suits to a grateful Lennie with an opera ticket in her hand and her shy way of telling him about her parents, yet never asking for sympathy. But he didn't like recalling his own wedding, with Lennie sobbing and dabbing her eyes during the ceremony.

Where had it gone wrong? Where had he missed Lennie's cry for help? Everything pointed back to Parker coming into Lennie's life. Drew pictured clearly that last moment with her—Lennie going off to lunch with Parker, her shiny laced shoes tapping rhythmically down the embassy corridor. She had turned and called back, "My nephew will be riding in the Tour, too, Mr. Gregory."

"You're running up the phone charges, Gregory. If you have something else to say, say it, or let's cut this exchange short."

"Glenn, Lennie has a nephew riding in the Tour. Check it out for me in the morning. Name. Team. I have to find him."

Drew sensed Fairway's resistance and hated his hard-nosed way of not answering. "You can reach me tomorrow night at the Reims Couette, a bed and breakfast just outside of Gap. Try the name Marcus Nash on her. He's on the Gainsborough team."

"Should I tell Lennie you need the information, Drew?"

"Not yet. She still trusts me. Let's leave it that way. But squeeze the information out of her. Parker would."

Drew slammed the handset down and disentangled his fingers from the cord as he dropped into the chair. Lennie Applegate was walking a thin line at the London embassy. Her health was threatened if he could believe Radburn Parker, and her safety in London was endangered by a station-chief whom Drew no longer trusted.

Chapter 16

Greece. On the island of Corfu, Vasille Golemis stood on the edge of the cliff overlooking the tranquil sea. Far below the vertical drop-off, the waters were radiant, peaceful. Inside, he felt nothing but turmoil. He stepped closer to the precipice, his toes flush with the overhanging cliff. Life seemed so empty, the villa too quiet, the ache in his chest unbearable. He was due back in Athens in a week, his extended leave over. But still he grieved. Still he longed to see the face of his son again. Vasille wanted to die. He wanted to be done with Parliament and politics; he wanted to see his son—wanted to tell him that he loved him.

These days he kept wondering whether he had ever told his son how much he loved him. Or had he left those words for Olympia to convey to their children? There was a rustle behind him, the thud of familiar footsteps on the path as the gardener came through the rose arbor to stand beside him.

"Are you all right, sir?" he asked.

Golemis turned his head, a faint smile on his lips. "I was thinking about my son," he said.

"Thymous?"

"No, Alekos."

Andreas Savo fingered his hoe like a flute, as though the melody had eluded him. He was an old man—with the family for thirty years now. Deep facial ridges were sun-baked into his skin, his hands callused from long years in the gardens. His dark eyes were scolding. "Try to remember the good things, my friend," he admonished. "You can never bring Alekos back."

Vasille would have word-whipped his political opponents for less than that, but he considered Andreas a trustworthy friend. "Andreas, I miss him."

The caretaker patted Vasille's arm and gently pulled him back from the rocky ledge. Vasille glanced at the rippling bay again. "It is so peaceful down there, Andreas."

"But you have your wife. Let her comfort you."

"My wife does not understand. All she does is pray."

"Your wife prays because she understands."

"Where is she, Andreas?"

"Cutting back the grass and weeds from Alekos's grave and polishing his tombstone."

"Olympia does that every week." Vasille's voice filled with despair. "That won't bring Alekos back. Our son is gone."

"But it comforts her, sir."

"And my other children? What comfort are they? Thymous and Zoe have been gone for days."

Andreas removed his straw hat and brushed the garden dirt from his trouser leg. The wrinkled face was filled with concern, the eyes still reproving.

He is growing old, Vasille thought. *I cannot bear to lose him, too.* "Do you know where Thymous and Zoe are?" he asked.

"They have gone to France." He covered his sun-toasted bald head again. "They had promised Alekos they would go to the race."

Golemis felt no surprise. "Then they have betrayed me by going. Do they intend to cheer Mr. Kendall on to victory?"

"No, they love you. They want only to stop Mr. Contoni before something worse happens."

"So you know about him? Did Thymous tell you? He always confided in you even as a child."

"No, I overheard you speaking to Mr. Contoni in the library. Forgive me, sir, but what you asked him to do broke Zoe's heart."

"Ah! I had forgotten. Zoe has always liked young Kendall. But he is wrong for her. She will get over him."

"That is not why she went to France."

Vasille looked at the bay again. "So Zoe confides in you, too."

"Only when her father is unaware that she is hurting."

His mouth twisted as he asked, "Have I been so neglectful?"

Andreas nodded. "You are sad. Your children understand."

"There was an accident at the Tour de France yesterday, Andreas. Do you think my children understood that?"

The old man shook his head. "A bombing," he said. "How could they understand that?"

"Surely they know that is not what I asked Contoni to do. He was to stop Ian Kendall from winning." Slowly he turned again and met the old man's watery gaze. "Was I wrong when I hired him, Andreas? Have I done the wrong thing?"

🐞🐞🐞

In Russia Boris Ivanski unlocked the top desk drawer and took out Yuri Ryskov's last transmission. He shoved pencils and the Phoenix-40 papers aside and smoothed it out against the desktop. Running his finger under each word, he read it again: "Lunched at Maxim's. Met an acquaintance of yours. His next planned events: eleventh and seventeenth. Unable to change plans. Major competitor uncooperative. Advise friends."

An acquaintance? The Czechoslovakian? Ivanski wondered. *Or Parkovitch? Or both?*

His housekeeper stood in the center of the room gripping a coffee tray. She was a square-faced woman with sulky features and black unfeeling eyes who had come to his employ after his wife's death. He tried to recall the occasion for employing her and could not—tried to remember who had recommended her, but that memory was lost too.

"Do you want something?" he asked.

"Do you? Something to eat? More coffee?"

"Nothing. Has Ryskov called?" he asked.

"There have been no phone calls, Professor. You were here all morning—"

She cut her words short. She seemed to look straight through him—seemed to be severing the phone cord with her gaze. It was as though at this moment she hated him. But she had not hated General Noukov. She had respected him. Was it Ivar Noukov who had recommended her? Or Yuri? No, Yuri had never trusted her.

"That will be all," he said curtly.

For an instant, she stayed unmoving, her big scrubbed hands

balancing the tray. Then she turned abruptly and left him to his misery. He folded his hand over Yuri's coded message. He faced the truth now. The Czech was following his own agenda with no concern for the original plans. Without Jiri Benak's cooperation, the planned coup in Moscow could fail.

"Competitor uncooperative." In opposition to them all, Benak had chosen the dates with a plan of his own. He had tried to blow away a portion of a mountain in some unknown French village. Was he trying to stop the race before it even reached the Pyrenees?

"Unable to change plans." Yuri had lost contact with the Czech. "Advise friends." Advise Noukov and Leopold Bolav, and all of Ivanski's plans would crumble. He reached for the phone. Pulled away. Reached again. His fingers caught in the cord. Noukov would be waiting for his report. How could he tell the general that something had gone drastically wrong in France? Or warn him that something worse could happen before the seventeenth?

◉◉◉

In Bosnia that morning, two men sat high on the hillside overlooking the shelled city, the Serbian with a stray cat purring in his lap and the Russian general with a half-filled vodka glass at his feet.

"What do you see?" Leopold asked, brushing the cat's fur.

General Noukov peered through his binoculars. "Soldiers."

"The French? Americans?"

"Here. See for yourself." He handed the binoculars to the other man, the cat hissing at the intrusion.

He grunted, his voice gravelly. "Will they ever leave?"

"Some have." Ivar Noukov wiped his hand across his bushy mustache and reached for his glass. "If they all do—if even the covering forces leave—then the Russian contingency goes as well. I would have no reason for keeping them on."

"Our time is running short then. And no word from Ivanski."

"It will come. He never admits defeat." Noukov smiled. "He will call. If he doesn't, his housekeeper will get word to me."

"Can we trust her?"

"I don't," the general said. "But I trust her more than the professor. Ivanski is brilliant, but I question his methods."

"His methods no longer include you, do they, General? Is that why you chose to come to my country?"

"A man obtains his freedom in any way he can. Ivanski and I covet the same position. His was a mad scheme from the beginning. And now—" He palmed the sky and shrugged. "Stage eleven has gone sour, and the professor will see it as my strategy gone wrong."

"But nothing unusual has happened since then."

"Except some nails on the road that caused a number of flats. A few stiff hills to climb. A photographer with a broken leg. And at least another dozen men have abandoned the race."

"None of Mr. Benak's doings. Nor yours."

He chortled. "How can you be so certain, Leopold?"

"My men watch you closely, and Benak—he takes pride in destruction. According to Marcus Nash, Benak still has plans for stage seventeen. I just trust they agree with our own."

"And if they don't?"

Leopold sighed. "My country was at war so long that I felt defensive when the peacekeeping forces came. And now I am remembering how it was six years ago. Living in peace. I'm not certain I want to go back to killing my neighbors again."

"Then will you go back to your village and your work?"

"As an engineer? It is all that I know except soldiering. But to go back is no longer my choice. I am on the wanted list."

The general studied the man beside him. "And Marcus Nash was one of your men—the only one who could betray you?"

"Yes, that is why I made certain he left Bosnia. War criminals, they call us. Poor lad! He was simply carrying out my orders. But, Ivar, if only one of us survives, I intend for it to be me. Nash can only return here if Ivanski's plan works."

"Do you plan to betray me as well, Leopold?"

"Survival is a strong instinct. We expect more American businessmen to grapple for the rights to rebuild this land. I could probably get more help from them than from Ivanski."

"You are fortunate. The Americans will need engineers who can speak the language."

"And you, General, what will you do if our plans fail?"

"Stay on with you," he said, smiling. "It would never do to go back to Moscow. Ivanski can turn on a man very quickly."

At the onset of stage fourteen, four cups of steaming black coffee and the sports page did little to alleviate Drew's black mood. He had not seen Radburn Parker since that evening in the Alps. If Parker was riding with the Tour, he was keeping out of sight, a strange disappearing act since he had such a heavy investment in the Gainsborough team. Drew poked at the rubbery scrambled eggs and scowled up at Vic as he joined him for a late breakfast.

"Where have you been, Wilson?" he asked.

"Seeing Chase safely to the press room. Either she starts taking a hotel room alone or she's packing it in."

"Back to London? Doesn't she like her accommodations?"

Vic chuckled. "I would, but it's a problem for Chase. She has five women in one room. She's sick of climbing over suitcases and listening to Millard's little girl cry half the night."

"I thought she liked Millard's wife and daughter. Chase can't go first class all her life. Sharing a room is good for her."

"You're in your usual morning grouch. Here, have some more coffee." Vic filled Drew's cup. "Sugar?"

"Black. Just black."

"That's how Chase feels. She caught Marcus Nash's fiancée going through her luggage last evening. I'm telling you, Chase is out of here unless we find her another place to stay."

"Brigette is just jealous of Chase's fine luggage."

"I don't buy that—not the way you mistrust Nash."

"So keep them both under surveillance. And let's give up our hotel reservation to Chase and sleep in the lobby."

"I'll scout around and see what else we can do. But when Ian finds out about Brigette's luggage inspection, he'll have a cow."

"Let's send them all home!" Drew tossed a crumpled note across the table. "Chambord got this an hour ago. Read it."

Vic smoothed out the note and read: *Take care in stage seventeen. Next time it won't be a bomb.*

"Wow! This accounts for your foul mood."

Drew wrapped his fist around the warning note. "Chambord brought us here because of the threat of terrorism. Now he insists that we've been mistaken; no terrorist group has taken credit—so none exists. Just a crackpot out there. Logical, eh?"

"Ian doesn't put much stock in the threats either."

"None that he's admitting. He says if we force him to quit the race, we may lose our terrorists. He's right, of course."

"Ian checked out okay this morning, Drew. He's not talking terrorists—just grumbling about another bowl of muesli mixed with yogurt. He'd eat steak for breakfast if they'd let him."

Drew poked his cold eggs again. "Smart boy."

"Last night in the therapy room, Ian looked wiped out even with his head pillowed on that yellow jersey, but Kendall recovers quickly. These last few days would have done me in."

"That's why Carwell has you riding in the team car."

"Guess so. After the beating he took in the Alps, what does Ian do today? Holds on to the jersey for one more day."

"I hope he can hold on to his life." Drew swallowed hard and went back to burying his face in the sports page. He had started the Belgian reporter's article three times and still found his thoughts drifting back to London. To Glenn Fairway and Lennie.

Drew gave up on the article and signaled for more coffee. "Vic, I can't keep my mind on the race; all I can think about are the problems back at the embassy."

"You usually lay out the puzzle pieces."

"They don't fit together this time."

"Name them."

"Here in a public dining room?"

"Someone could bug our room and report back to Fairway. But no one knew we'd eat here at this table at this precise hour."

Drew glanced down at the sports page again and mumbled, "Troy Carwell delayed my retirement because of a problem at the London embassy. And suddenly Fairway wanted me out of London, and Carwell wanted me back in France."

"Monsieur Chambord asked for your services."

"At Carwell's suggestion." Drew kept his voice low-key. "Chambord didn't know I existed. With the problem with Lennie, the logical thing would have been to keep me in London."

"The threats here are greater."

"Greater than national security?"

"This one has an international twist. Besides, Ian Kendall is your friend."

"So was Lennie."

"You suggesting a connection, Drew?"

"No, they don't even know each other." He smashed the paper together and dropped it on an empty chair. "We're dealing with two separate problems. Lennie possibly turning traitor. Ian trying to do the ride of his career."

"And someone trying to stop them both."

"Vic, maybe I'm being set up. These are people close to me—my secretary and the grandson of a good friend. And the more lies Parker and Fairway throw at me, the more convinced I am that Lennie and Ian are nothing but scapegoats, a couple of innocents taking the blame for something I did."

"Possible," Vic said. "But not likely. If you were the target, you'd be dead by now. Let's just stick with the two scapegoats— but two separate problems? I can help you with one problem, Drew. If we believe Parker, Lennie is sick and dying. If we believe Fairway, she never misses a day of work. Do you want my cousin Brianna to check it out?"

"How?"

"Do we have a doctor's name? A clinic? The hospital?"

"Brianna can't just walk in and take medical records."

"I don't question Brianna's methods. She knows her way around a hospital better than the nurses do." Vic gave his tongue-in-cheek grin. "When they wouldn't be up front with her about my case, she put on a volunteer's smock and marched right down to the records department. Made copies of all my papers. Even ordered copies of my X-rays before they caught on."

"Sounds like Brianna."

"Great gal. My best friend." As Vic tried to glide over the catch in his voice, he wiped the back of his hand across his mouth. "Brianna will fall apart when I check out. We go back to our preschool days—throwing sand at each other one minute and best pals the next. Been that way all our lives. Drew . . . when the time comes, if this AIDS thing takes me out, will you stand with Brianna for me?"

"Miriam and I will be there. Count on us."

Vic made a quick comeback. "If Parker's story about Lennie's brain tumor is a hoax, Brianna will be on top of it right away."

"Glenn Fairway won't thank us for getting your cousin mixed up in this."

"Brianna likes taking chances."

"Warn her. Lennie's under twenty-four-hour surveillance. That's one thing Parker said that I believe."

"Lennie takes the tube home each night, doesn't she, Drew?"

"Catches the Bakerloo Underground."

"Brianna can post herself at the ticket window until Lennie pops up. It won't matter who's following her, Brianna will make a good show. She'll have the information we want by the time they reach Lennie's station."

"Too risky. What if it's a short run? Someone is bound to recognize Brianna—she's been at the embassy enough."

Vic snapped his fingers. "Brianna will have to quiz Lennie the first time out. She'll make like a ventriloquist and fool anyone watching her. If it's standing room only, she can stand beside Lennie. If there's a seat, she'll grab it. Trust Brianna. She loves playing cat-and-mouse. We did it all through our childhood." Vic's eyes sparked with the memory. "If she has to, she'll play nurse or doctor and ask some pertinent questions."

"Tell her to be careful. Lennie could turn on her."

"Trust Brianna. She'll get the answers we need with the surveillance team totally in the dark. We'd better go, Drew," Vic said. "Gainsborough has fits when we're late. But Ian would ride off happier if Chase were in the team car under our care."

Drew checked the bill and counted out the French francs, leaving in spite of his gloom, a sizable tip. "Ian should be happy just having her nearby."

Vic grinned. "He didn't like that Italian journalist paying so much attention to Chase. Ian likes to protect his own territory."

As they reached the crowded sidewalk, Drew said, "The press room would have been a perfect place for Contoni to hide out. He's clever enough to have developed that intercept box that threw the glitch in the television system. And maybe even clever enough to have set the explosions on the mountain."

"You're wrong on that one, Drew, if you're still trying to line up Contoni and the Italian journalist. The journalist was with Chase when the hillside exploded. He protected her with his own body."

"But why the sudden disappearing act right afterwards? Check it out for me, will you, Vic?"

"I did. He didn't show up in the press room. Hasn't for the last five days. His computer—everything gone, his spot beside Chase cleared off."

Drew thrust his hands into his trouser pockets and struck out for the hotel. "We have to find him, Vic. Chase's safety depends on it."

Chapter 17

London. Lennie Applegate peered into the cracked mirror in her desk drawer. Her eyes and face looked as peaked and dull as her gray linen suit. She fluffed the sides of her hair, but they felt limp and lifeless in her fingers. *Lipstick! I need lipstick.*

Her hand trembled as she applied it. What was the use? Radburn was gone. On a business trip, he had said.

Radburn had walked out of her life. Had he ever been in it? *Gone. Gone. Everything gone. It's only a matter of time before they arrest me.* But Radburn Parker would go free. Were the ambassador and Mr. Fairway so blind—so unwilling to see what a deceiver Radburn really was? Like the Third Man, he had wedged himself into the embassy life and secrets. And still they trusted him. Was she the only one who knew the truth?

Lennie tidied the clutter on the desktop and stood. She left the room and walked slowly down the embassy corridor, taking petite steps as she passed her old office still ribboned off for redecorating. She could see the painters in Mr. Gregory's room, whistling as they rolled the fresh cream paint over the walls. She wondered if Mr. Gregory would like that color—he was so particular about satisfying his wife's aesthetic tastes.

Her eyes downcast, she counted her own steps.

One. Two. Three.

They will arrest me now. She stole a glance down the long corridor. *That young marine ahead—perhaps he will stop me, handcuff me, search me. Go ahead,* she thought. *I want to be caught. Do you hear that, Mr. Gregory? I want to be punished. I'm guilty, but I am not a traitor.* She licked her lips and tasted the ruby red lipstick. *My loyalties are to Britain, Mr. Gregory, but I did not betray the Americans.*

Four-five. Six-seven.

Other secretaries—other employees—hurried around her. A girl from the ambassador's secretarial pool smiled, a friendly smile. *Oh, Mr. Gregory, did you see that? Someone just smiled at me.* Her forehead felt damp. And why not? It was July and hot even in this air-conditioned hallway. *Radburn said that I would ruin your career, but I would never hurt you, Mr. Gregory. You are my friend. I wanted you to notice me. To like me.*

Mechanically, she moved down the corridor, one step at a time. Muted. Frightened. *Eight*—that was her left foot.

Nine-ten . . . twelve-thirteen.

Tears brushed at her lashes. She wiped them away with her gloved hand. *You are a traitor, Lennie Applegate. You are a traitor.* The words thundering in her mind sounded like Mr. Gregory's voice; the iron-gripping vise set off a sudden violent headache, churning her stomach until she felt her insides would spew out on the embassy floor.

Yes, I have sold secrets to the enemy. I did it for my nephew, Mr. Gregory. You will understand, won't you? I did it for my nephew—and for my beloved Radburn. But, Mr. Gregory, I am not a traitor. I am not a spy. I am Lennie Applegate, remember? I am not an undercover agent like the Countess of Romanones.

A broad shoulder bumped hers. "Good night, Miss Applegate."

She looked up, stunned. "Good evening, Mr. Fairway."

Her steps dragged behind his. *Fifteen-sixteen. Seventeen. Eighteen.* Mr. Fairway stopped and glanced back her way as he spoke to the marine. She could see the marine's facial features now—so young, so handsome in his uniform, his profile rigid beneath that visor. *He sees me now. And I am afraid. I must prove to him that I am not carrying secrets from the embassy.*

She slid her right foot forward. *Nineteen . . . twenty.* Several steps from the exit Lennie pitched forward, her purse and its contents spilling on the floor. The marine was at her side at once, kneeling beside her, his hand firm at her elbow. "Are you all right, Miss Applegate?"

So you know my name? She nodded up into his handsome face and fought the tears pricking behind her eyelids. He was young enough to be her son with a wash of freckles across the bridge of his narrow nose and a crew cut so stubby that it barely showed its flaming red. *See,* she thought as he helped scoop the articles back into her purse, *I have nothing more than my wallet. My comb. My lipstick—the ruby red that Radburn likes. My vial of perfume.*

"Oh, no," she cried. "The lens in my sunglasses popped out."

He tried to replace it. Their eyes met, his sparkling with youth. "I'm sorry, Miss Applegate." He ran his hand over the floor. "You'll have to have them repaired. The screw is missing."

As a tear made its way down her cheek, she brushed it away. Always, she had wanted a son, a boy named Michael with red hair and blue eyes, like this young man had. He was on his feet, pulling her gently up beside him. "Be careful, hear."

She saw the microphone wire attached behind his ear and knew he would report the incident the minute she left the embassy. She could imagine him saying, "1700. Miss Applegate leaving embassy. Fell deliberately. Purse contents normal. No computer disks."

She marched stiffly through the door, out into the glaring light of a summer day, a brilliance that could not touch the utter midnight of her soul. Down the steps she lurched, past two London bobbies who tipped their hats to her. One of them steadied her on the last step. She smiled back, wondering if he was aware of who she was. Of course. For the first time in her life, her every move was under scrutiny. She, a Miss Nobody for so long, had become important enough to follow twenty-four hours a day.

Don't you understand? I did it all for Radburn.

As she squinted against the glare of the late afternoon sun, the rolling waves of her visual migraine forced her to grope blindly for her dark glasses. She fumbled with the broken lens, but could not attach it. It remained clutched in her hand as she wound around the stone barricades and through the iron gate to the sidewalk. *See, I am in no hurry tonight. I have nothing to hide. See, I am going one step at a time.*

As she put her left laced shoe on the rough pavement, the terrible pain in her head struck with pounding intensity. She stopped again without looking back. Was the man who had followed her yesterday and the day before and the day before that in position to follow her again? Was he British or American? A friend of Radburn's or an acquaintance of Mr. Gregory? She had resigned herself to the final outcome. They would arrest her, but when would the police car pull up and an officer invite her inside? Would she have her wrists shackled behind her? Tonight when she reached her flat, would she find it ransacked?

That day would come as surely as Radburn Parker had walked into her life and out of it. She had loved him, but he had used her, and she had let him. She hated his vain promises now: freedom for her nephew, her nephew's name removed from the war criminal list in Bosnia, her parents well cared for. She had trusted Radburn and had been thrilled at the arrival of her nephew—the young man she had not seen since he was a baby. Handsome. Dark. So frightening with his black moods. So unlike what she had expected.

"We must help him. He's our blood," her father had said.

And she had obeyed. What had it mattered to her father that she must betray the Americans? Family was what mattered to him.

Footsteps behind her pounded like the beat of drums between her temples. She fumbled for her change purse at the train ticket window. "My money," she cried. "It's back on the embassy floor."

Tears streaked her makeup. A young woman's hand reached out. "Here," she said. "Take my travel card. I have two." Her voice was kind, her face blurred by the exploding stars in Lennie's eye. The girl lagged behind, lost in the crowd again, but the sweet fragrance of her Arpege lingered.

Down the steps to the underground Lennie went, gripping the iron railing because the rolling waves in her left eye would not go away. If she could reach her flat, she would lie down with cold packs on her face and pray that the awful pain would let up. It would take another hour before the waving pattern would stop altogether. She must not vomit in the underground this time. She must control that terrible feeling. *Get home. Get home. Everything will be all right if you can only reach the flat.*

Lennie ran for the train, stumbling in her haste. She shoved her way through the crowd and collapsed on a seat. As she closed her eyes, the visual waves changed to deep purples and black; the subway car spun around her. A passenger climbed over her legs and sat down beside her. The smell of Arpege was strong again.

As the young woman flipped open her newspaper, she said, "I'm Brianna. I'm a friend of Drew Gregory and Vic Wilson."

Lennie's eyes flew open. The woman was pretty, coolly dressed in a sleeveless frock. She wore a narrow gold band on her wrist, another around her ankle. There was a deep gloss to her lips and a high sheen to her shoulder-length hair. The newspaper rattled as the girl turned the pages. Softly, she said, "Don't look at me, Lennie. Just listen. I'm here to help you."

"No, don't. I'm being followed."

"I know. He's an attractive brute, but he found standing room only. He can't hear what we're saying." Brianna folded the paper in half. "Drew is worried about your tumor, Lennie."

Lennie's spine seemed to fuse. If she turned squarely and looked at this stranger, surely her ribs would crack. Her voice was as rigid as her back. "I have no tumor," she whispered.

"But Mr. Parker—"

"Radburn? What does he know? Lies. All he tells are lies."

The newspaper rattled as the girl turned to the theater page. "He told Drew about the CAT scan and the X-rays. When are you going to have the brain surgery, Lennie?"

"I refuse to have surgery."

"But the doctor said . . ."

The tube roared to another stop. The standing passengers swayed with the car, scrambling to keep their balance. The man who had followed Lennie took a seat two rows behind them. Lennie clutched her purse. "Are you from the doctor's office?"

"I told you. I'm Brianna—Drew's friend. Vic's cousin."

Lennie did not remember Brianna, but she had smelled the sweet fragrance of Arpege in Mr. Wilson's office once, moments after his cousin had been there. Could she trust her? If only the terrible headache would go away so she could think more clearly.

"Are you all right, Lennie?"

"I'm in pain. And the vision in my left eye is blurred."

"Then let me see you home."

"No. That man has been following me for days. And when he disappears, someone else takes his place." She feigned interest in Brianna's newspaper and pointed to the second column, her eyes too blurred to see the words. "Tell Mr. Gregory I don't have a tumor—but the wall of an artery in my brain is wearing thin."

"An aneurysm?"

She heard alarm and sympathy in Brianna's voice and felt a strange sense of comfort in finally telling someone what was happening to her. "Yes, when it breaks—"

"Lennie, you could bleed to death."

Brianna faced Lennie. "Lennie, I know my way around hospitals and doctor's offices. Let me go with you to your next appointment. If you need surgery, I can be there for you."

"No. No surgery. It could be a slow bleed, even weeks before something happens, but when it explodes, I will be free."

"You'll be dead. Drew Gregory won't like that."

"Radburn will."

"Whose side is Radburn Parker on?" Brianna asked.

"I thought he was on my side. And no one at the embassy is really sure which side I'm on." The London tube was pulling into Lennie's station. "Don't follow me," she begged. "I only have a short way to go."

"Give me your doctor's name, Lennie. Perhaps Drew can help."

Lennie fumbled in her purse and took out a business card. She dropped it on the seat between them. Brianna kept her eyes on the paper as she palmed the card and slipped it into her pocket.

"Don't follow me, Brianna. I won't be alone." She nodded toward the man already making his way toward the exit doors.

"I'll run interference for you so you can go home in peace."

🦋🦋🦋

On the platform, Brianna made straight for the stranger. He was a muscular hunk, attractive in a tough sort of way with his sharp jawline and eyes that looked right through her. She barreled into him and groaned as her narrow shoulder collided against his rock-hard chest.

"Get out of my way," he demanded, his gaze on the crowd heading for the stairs.

She massaged her shoulder. "You almost knocked me down, and now you're going to be rude on top of it?"

He tried to step around her, his broad shoulders pushing against her. "Move," he ordered.

She blocked his way again, thinking, *You're just one of the hot-*

shots from the embassy, too bullish to do anything but frighten peo-ple. You're doing a good job on me. She brushed her long hair back from her face. "I expect an apology."

"Apologize to you? Look what you've gone and done."

"What?" she asked innocently.

"I was trying to catch up with a friend."

Brianna glanced around, praying that Lennie had the needed head start. The crowd on the stairs had thinned, but Lennie had just now dragged herself to the top step. Brianna looked back at the stranger just as his elbow slammed against her.

She stumbled backward, grabbing at his arm. "What about your apology, mister?" she insisted.

"I'm sorry." His gray eyes hardened. "I've seen you before."

"In your dreams maybe."

"No, at the embassy."

"What embassy?"

He seemed unsure now. "Are you with security?" he asked.

"Obviously, I don't know what you're talking about."

He took off running, taking the steps two at a time. She sashayed up the steps behind him and lingered on top for twenty minutes wondering which direction Lennie and the man had taken. At last she went back down the steps, through the turnstile and boarded the train headed back to the heart of London. Easing into the first unoccupied seat, she swung one slender leg over the other and took refuge in staring out the murky window.

Only when the train picked up speed and roared along the track did she take the business card from her pocket and read it: "Dr. Kirk Hammerill, Neurology."

It was an appointment card from the outpatient desk of a char-ity hospital for 7 A.M. the following day. *Okay, Lennie. I'll see you there.* She leaned back in her seat, lulled by the swaying of the train. *And now, my sweet cousin Victor, I'll see if I can get through to your hotel room.*

She had nothing but bad news regarding Lennie, but they had to know the truth. A brain tumor? No. An aneurysm? Quite pos-sibly. The outlook for Lennie was grave either way. But there was one more thing. Brianna wanted the whole truth from Vic. The embassy wouldn't put someone under surveillance for ill health. No, Lennie Applegate was in trouble. Deep, serious trouble.

Chapter 18

The next afternoon while Brianna Wilson waited for her, Lennie sat in Glenn Fairway's private office in an uncomfortable straight-back chair, her hands folded tightly on her lap, the toes of her laced shoes turned inward. She pressed her knees together to keep her legs from shaking.

Fairway's stubby fingers tapped impatiently against the desktop. His eyes—gray or blue, she couldn't tell—looked directly at her. His movements were deliberate. He tilted his head, avoiding the glare from the window. The tapping stopped long enough for him to take a thick manila folder from his desk.

This is it, she thought. *I am not to be arrested on the streets of London, nor to be handcuffed and torn from my apartment with my neighbors watching. I am to be detained by security before I leave the embassy this evening.* She shuddered, dreading the words he would use. Spy. Traitor. Foreign agent.

But I did it all for Radburn.

She allowed her gaze to stray over Fairway's spacious mahogany desk with the latest state-of-the-art computer to the rich brown swivel chair where he sat. Veiled sunlight from the window marked a clear path to his bookcase lined with thick leather-bound volumes. In one corner, two Queen Anne chairs faced the aquarium with its colorful squirrel and butterfly fish. The walls of the room were crowded with diplomas and awards and two framed mountain scenes, one of Mont Blanc at dawn. But everything came back to the man who controlled this room—back to her own portable radio centered on his desk so she could see it.

Mr. Fairway was solidly built. A lock of curly gray hair hung down on his bony forehead. Other than that, his features—pleasant enough—were nondescript. No aquiline nose nor moles, no scars nor laugh wrinkles to remember. He was someone who had wormed his way through the crowds unnoticed, yet noticing everything himself. Still his silver hair and well-cut suit gave him an air of dignity, but Lennie knew he was greedy for power. Even a slight insult could spark his anger.

He seemed to be waiting for her to speak, to confess. She avoided his eyes and focused on the bridge of his nose. Fairway was charming to women, a quick-witted man who wanted to possess the good-looking ones who worked for him and to consign the less attractive to out-of-the-way cubicles in the embassy.

Two years ago he had dumped her back into the secretarial pool. If Mr. Gregory had not taken her as his assistant, she would have been jobless. Jobless and fiftyish. She never quite admitted to her real age, but to be tossed out into London to tread the rain-soaked pavements in search of another job had been terrifying. She was too uncertain of her own abilities. Mr. Gregory had been a godsend—a formidable boss to be sure, but he proved to be a kind man. A single man back then. She blushed at the remembered fantasies that had gripped her those first months.

When Fairway finally broke their silence, his voice was stern. "Miss Applegate, my secretary tells me that Brianna Wilson is waiting for you."

"Yes. We're having tea together before I go home." To cover her concern, she added, "She's Mr. Wilson's cousin."

"I'm aware of that, but I didn't know you knew each other."

He was forcing her to make an excuse.

"She's been to the embassy many times, Mr. Fairway."

"Has she?" He scowled as he said, "Miss Applegate, I understand your nephew is riding in the Tour. I need to know his name—and the team he's riding for."

Her stomach muscles tightened. *You sent for me to ask my nephew's name?* She wanted to laugh out loud. Radburn knew his name. Radburn had placed him on the Gainsborough team. "My nephew, Mr. Fairway?" she asked.

"Is your nephew's name Marcus Nash, Miss Applegate?"

Give that away and they could trace her heritage back to Bosnia. She risked lying. "I have no nephew, Mr. Fairway."

He reached out, flicked on her radio, and twirled the dial. "You have followed the Tour de France quite closely," he said.

You took my radio. "So has half of London," she countered.

"Very well." He turned back to the folder and opened it. "Lennie, are you planning to go away with Mr. Parker?"

Involuntarily her head jerked back until she met his gaze. His eyes seemed green now, the gleaming glow of a Balinese cat. In silence, he shouted at her, *Traitor. Traitor.*

She wanted to scream. "Radburn—Mr. Parker is out of town."

"And you don't have plans to go somewhere together?"

He was confusing her—accusing her of a romantic getaway.

"Mr. Parker is in Paris on business, Mr. Fairway."

"Are you to meet him there after the race, Miss Applegate?"

"No," she said faintly.

"Speak up."

"No, Mr. Fairway, I don't expect to see him again. Ever."

"Then you knew he was going away for good when he left London?"

If he left the prominent social and familial position that was his in London, where would he go? He would never forsake the wealth and pleasurable life that the Parker Foundation provided. Mr. Fairway was mistaken. "He never told me he was moving away, if that is what you mean."

"But you suspected?"

"He talked of visiting Moscow again. On holiday, I think. He taught there, you know. Some years ago."

"The historical philosophies of ancient leaders, if I recall correctly. A modern Plato."

"Radburn was a history or science professor," she corrected. "There on an exchange professorship."

"A rare invitation."

Had Fairway discovered the truth about Radburn's past? About his plans for the future? Fairway's catlike eyes demanded an answer. "He was friends with one of the university professors," she said.

"Which university, Miss Applegate?"

"Radburn never said. I never asked. It never seemed important. . . . It was such a long time ago."

Fairway thumped the folder. And now she wondered whose folder was on his desk. Hers? Radburn's? Or was Fairway trying to corner her? She could never betray Radburn. He had warned her against it. "I wouldn't want something to happen to your parents," he had said. "Or to your nephew."

"Miss Applegate, how long have you been working for Radburn Parker?" Fairway asked.

Meekly, she said, "I thought he was working for you."

Fairway's eyes blazed. As his neck vessels bulged, he wedged his finger into his shirt collar and tugged. "It would seem that he has deceived us both."

She rubbed her eyes, trying to block out the tension headache that was building. "Why are you asking me about Radburn?"

"Because I need answers." His chin pressed against his folded hands. He looked like a man betrayed.

Arrest me, she thought. *Don't taunt me like this. Don't force me to say things that I dare not tell you. I can't let anything happen to my parents. They are old—*

"I have your medical reports here," he said, his eyes not unsympathetic. "You are ill."

"I am seeing a doctor for my headaches."

"Yes, we know. Your reports are all here."

Brianna! Brianna had betrayed her. Or Radburn. Anger gave her courage. "How dare you look into my personal life," she said.

"When it involves our security, we have no choice."

She gazed down at her clasped hands and watched her knuckles turn a chalky white. *It is coming now. He will arrest me. He will speak of the secrets I have taken from the embassy.*

She felt a sharp jabbing in her eye, intense heat and pain as a black speck swam in her visual path. Her eyelids fluttered as the speck spread like spilled ink, its dark, weblike tentacles clouding her vision. The headache broke, acute, piercing like a sharp spike driven through her temples.

"Miss Applegate."

She opened her eyes. The room spun, the desk and chairs riding in pinwheels around the ceiling. Fairway's face blurred. He tilted with the room.

"Are you all right?" He was standing over her now. Touching her. She flinched, but his hand remained firm on her wrist.

The aneurysm? No, she would have already drifted into unconsciousness. She was in pain, but she could still reason. "I must go home, Mr. Fairway," she whispered.

"I need your answer first. Give me your nephew's name."

"Please. I am ill."

She was aware of him leaning back across the desk and striking the intercom button. He spoke urgently, but his words were meaningless to her. Silence. And then his fingers were tapping again—the back of her chair this time.

"Take a deep breath, Miss Applegate," he told her.

Behind them his office door opened, and light steps came tripping across the carpet. "Miss Wilson," he said, "Miss Applegate is ill."

Brianna knelt beside Lennie and gently took her clammy hand. "Hi," she said. "We've sent for the ambulance, Lennie."

"No . . ."

"You're not well."

"I can't see you with my left eye, Brianna."

"One of the hemorrhages that the doctor warned us about." Lightly she added, "Besides, I'm not worth looking at."

Brianna—attractive, fun-loving. Fragrant with Arpege perfume. Casual and carefree. "You're young. Pretty."

Brianna pushed a lock of her shiny hair from her face and smiled. "I'm older than you think. Thirtyish like my cousin Vic."

"But better looking," Lennie whispered.

"I'd better not tell him that."

The pain came fierce again. "Am I dying, Brianna?"

"Shhh!" Brianna patted her arm. "Don't say that."

"She can't leave the embassy yet," Fairway announced. "I have questions to ask her."

About the missing disks? Lennie wondered. *And the bank accounts?*

"Ask her tomorrow," Brianna snapped, "when she can think more clearly."

"Now," Fairway demanded, "before the ambulance comes."

"If I have to call the ambassador, I will," Brianna warned. "Miss Applegate is too sick to question right now."

"I have to know what she did with the embassy disks."

"She's not going far, Mr. Fairway. Can't you see? She's ill. If she lives long enough, you can question her again. Tomorrow maybe. I'll take full responsibility—"

"You'll take more than that if she escapes."

Commotion filled the office as a stretcher was rolled into the room. Ambulance attendants. A marine guard. The ambassador's secretary who had smiled at Lennie. Lennie felt herself lifted from the chair, her body limp as they laid her on the hard surface. The leather strap tightened around her, securing her arms against her body. "My purse," she cried.

Through her blurred vision, she saw Brianna snatch it from Fairway's hand.

"I'll keep that," Fairway said.

Brianna outshouted him. "We'll need her medical cards."

Someone was listening to Lennie's chest. Someone else was ripping the sleeve of her new gray suit and placing a cuff there. She squirmed against the pressure and heard the attendant whistle. "The diastolic and systolic are about to converge."

She thrashed, frightened. *My blood pressure is running wild,* she thought.

"Forget that IV," Fairway ordered. "Just get that woman out of here."

As they rolled Lennie from the room with the IV running, she heard Fairway on the phone. "Get me a full report on Parker—everything you can on his background, especially his years in Russia," he demanded, his tone razor-sharp. "I want to know who his chief contacts were when he lived there."

You won't like what you learn, Lennie thought. She strained to hear Fairway's words as the stretcher jammed in the doorway. His voice seemed distant now, but still she was certain he said, "Call Dudley Perkins over at MI5 and tell him to get over here. And get the station-chief in Paris on the line. . . . Of course, I mean Troy Carwell, you idiot. I want to ask him about his old posting in Moscow."

Brianna leaned over the stretcher as they hurried down the corridor. "I'm here, Lennie. I'll ride in the ambulance with you."

"That's not allowed, miss."

"It is this time," Brianna told the attendant.

Lennie tried to pull away as Brianna squeezed her arm. Brianna Wilson was not her friend. She was working for Fairway.

❦ ❦ ❦

An hour later Fairway's rage was under control, his outright suspicions of Parker hidden, when he met with Dudley Perkins. As they sat in the Queen Anne chairs facing the aquarium, he made his inquiries sound casual. "We are wondering whether Radburn Parker could be passing information to old friends from his Moscow days. Innocently. Do you think that's possible, Dudley?"

"Mr. Parker comes from a well-established family, Glenn."

"So did Kim Philby—and Anthony Blunt, the queen's art historian."

"Let's not do battle," the Englishman said. "You Americans have your shameful history, too."

"Yes, Porter Deven and Aldrich Ames. And now we have Harold Nicholson's betrayal to contend with."

"Not easy," Perkins said quietly. He was a gaunt, spindly man with a pinched face and thin smile. Fairway knew him to be uncompromising, inflexible, a strong defender of his country and countrymen. His pale, inquisitive eyes focused on the aquarium as a brown-spotted eel slithered around the coral, causing the Yellow Tang to swim in the opposite direction.

"You've added a Trigger Blue Throat since I was last here."

"Yes, that one with the yellow-tipped fins. And the calico—that one's new, too."

"Colorful," Perkins said, his voice passive.

"Dudley, we have a problem at the American embassy."

"I am aware of that. The young woman, Gregory's secretary."

Fairway smiled. "She's fiftyish, middle-aged. And she's been in the company of Radburn Parker a lot lately."

"We agreed to that, Glenn."

"But we were lax in our security check on Parker. He slipped in without a thorough investigation on our part."

"We've been over that, too. What are you suggesting?"

Fairway soft-pedaled the blow. "We need your help over at MI5. Parker was quite political in his youth, wasn't he?"

The grave smile was discerning. "So was I."

"Dudley, it is quite possible that Parker made serious friendships in Russia that might be useful to us now. That's all we're asking for—a bit of background on his time in Moscow."

"I know you too well, Fairway. Your implications are more serious. You're not accusing Parker of espionage within these sacred American halls? Parker and Miss Applegate—I won't hear of it."

"Someone has been her handler, her contact person."

With controlled rage, Dudley said, "Is that what this is all about—throwing suspicion on a member of a prominent British family?"

"His social status is not the issue, Dudley."

"The Parkers are friends of the queen. They were her guests at the Royal Ascot races recently. Don't bring scandal to the Parkers."

"I saw it all on TV—the Parkers riding in an open landau behind the queen's carriage. Radburn seemed a bit tipsy."

"Probably embarrassed in the company of Miss Applegate. It did take it a bit far. There's just so much fancy fixing you can do with a woman like Applegate. But she wore a stunning hat."

"Quite impressive," Fairway agreed, chuckling to himself.

Perkins refused to be humored. "If what you are suggesting reaches the news media, the tabloids will tear the Parkers apart."

"What if Parker is not really on a holiday? Perhaps he had another reason for going away—like catching the Red Express to Moscow," suggested Fairway.

"You won't let up, will you? What do you want from me, Fairway?"

"A full report on Radburn Parker's time in Russia."

"Those records belong to MI6."

Perkins sat quietly for several minutes, blotting his face with a starched white handkerchief, a scowl forming between his bushy brows. Without conviction, he said, "I think you are wrong, Fairway."

"Prove it."

At last Perkins said, "At the risk of the boy's safety—at the risk of my own position—MI6 has a contact person studying in Moscow. Vladimir Wecker was born in London of Russian immigrant parents and speaks the language fluently."

"Studying at the University of Moscow?"

"No, at the Academy of Sciences. He majors in earth sciences—geology and mining. It allows him a number of field trips throughout Russia. For a while he sent my wife postcards."

"Have him look into Parker for me."

"MI6 won't thank me for interfering. Wecker is a touchy subject with them. Three months ago they contacted my wife and advised her not to write to him again."

"Hard to do for an organization that doesn't exist."

He laughed dryly. "Molly thought that if they wanted to be so secretive about their existence, she could ignore them. But they paid us a midnight visit in our home, warning us that Wecker's safety was at stake. It was a shame—Molly and the boy have always been close, especially since Joel's death." He blotted his face again. "Wecker's mother worked for my wife's family for years. You will go carefully?"

Dudley seemed intrigued with the fish again, his gangly fingers tapping the glass. "But I must warn you—Wecker tends to make friends with political dissidents."

"Risky."

"That's the business we're in, Fairway. MI6 has no real ties to Wecker. He's on his own with no official contacts with our people in Moscow. He's just a student abroad who sends reports at irregular intervals at prearranged drop points. That's the only way they know he's still alive. But I will see what I can do—if for no other reason than to clear Parker's name. If you ruin Parker's reputation, the queen will have my job."

"When we searched Parker's flat this morning, we found a number of scholarly articles by the Russian Boris Ivanski."

"The Nobel prize winner? He's quite a controversial figure, well-known in Moscow. Parker would find his writings most interesting."

"Have Wecker check on Professor Ivanski, will you? Just in case Parker knew him personally."

Dudley stood—a tall and distinguished English gentleman. "Wecker reminds me of my son. Fearless. Adventuresome. Molly worries about him. If anything happened—"

Fairway shrugged. "Dudley, why don't you and your wife have dinner with me soon? My treat. Your wife likes the Le Gavroche's or The Connaught, doesn't she?"

"My wife is still in the Greek Islands." He tipped his hat, his smile somber. "If M16 agrees to help, I will get back to you in the morning, Glenn."

No reconciliation yet, Fairway thought as Perkins left the room. Perkins's social position had come through his marriage to Molly, a gracious woman who had too often taken second place in Perkins's life. Sadly, their only son was one of the casualties of the Falklands crisis. He was dead—the same direction in which their marriage seemed to be heading.

As Fairway tapped the aquarium, the fish shimmied to the top. "Hungry little critters, aren't you?" he asked.

He teased them, delighting in their playful cavorting. Then he sprinkled food into their tank, laughing at the marvelous blend of colors as they swam hungrily to the water's surface. He sobered as he watched the shimmering fish gulp down the confetti-like morsels. Was he being duped, suckered in as fair game by Perkins? With the rivalry that still existed between MI6 and MI5, would there be any chance of Dudley unraveling Parker's days in Moscow? If not, Fairway was dependent on Troy Carwell pulling strings with his old associates in Moscow. But it was easier on a man's pride to turn to Perkins—to take his chances with the Englishman.

Chapter 19

For two days Professor Ivanski stayed at his research work and took light meals in his study, barely going inches from his desk lest the phone ring and he miss Yuri Ryskov's call. His calendar was clearly marked: "July 17, Stage 17." He dozed in his chair, his mood deteriorating with the weather and the silent phone. He wanted action, but today dragged as the riders took a rest day at the foot of the Pyrenees. But in twenty-four hours he could march triumphantly into Red Square with the people chanting his name as he returned them to the golden days of imperialism. But everything depended on Yuri Ryskov's signal, his phone call.

Ivanski spun in his swivel chair and gazed at the picture of his dead wife on the mantel, her presence as real to him as if she had just gone from the room. "Have I trusted the wrong man?" he asked her.

He wondered how she would have looked in the palace as the wife of an emperor or whether she would have approved of his deep desire to rule this land. He pictured her in a long sequined gown, her delicate hands held out to him. If only she had lived to share the days ahead with him. As he mused, a sound disturbed his reverie. A stone thrown against the house? Company? No, his housekeeper would tell him if guests had come to the door.

He spun his chair until he faced the open window. Soon dusk would settle over the forest behind his property. He demanded privacy, thrived on it. It had not taken the villagers long to know that they were unwelcome on his estate; yet at the edge of the woods he saw a young man limping toward the farmhouse. The man met Ivanski's stare, making no effort to be secretive. Perhaps he was lost, simply in need of direction back to the village.

Ivanski opened the window and called out in Russian, "Get off my property!"

The stranger hesitated, his weight on his good leg. In fluent Russian he said, "I would if I could walk, sir."

It was a friendly voice. He limped forward, obviously in pain, his empty hands hanging limply at his side now. *No weapon!* Then he paused again, recognition on his face. "You're Professor Ivanski," he said pleasantly. "Imagine finding you out here."

"This is my home. What are *you* doing here?"

"I was on a field trip. Came alone." He had limped another yard closer. "I'm majoring in earth sciences." He pointed toward the mountains. "I've been in the old mine shaft."

"And you injured yourself?"

"I slid in the loose gravel. I sprained my ankle, I'm sure."

"You are not from the village."

"No. Moscow. I am Vladimir Wecker," he volunteered. "I missed the late afternoon bus. It left early."

Ivanski reflected. Yes, he had heard the bus for Moscow grinding up the road ten minutes off schedule. He looked down into the guileless, unblinking eyes, daring the young man to come closer. "You must go. I am busy."

Wecker shrugged, running one dirt-smudged hand through his thick hair. The rucksack on his back was as caked with dust as the shoes on his feet. "If I could just rest first, Professor."

Without invitation he traversed the last three yards to the side porch, sat on the bottom step, and rubbed his swollen ankle. "I heard you lecture at the Academy of Sciences a few months ago," he said. "It was marvelous."

"The lecture on intercontinental missiles?" he challenged.

Wecker twisted his neck to glance sharply back at the professor. "No, sir. You spoke on the history of Russian imperialism and the revolutions against our country. The Phoenix-30 or -40—something like that."

Russian imperialism and the revolutions had been his topic; they always were. But he was certain that he had never mentioned the Phoenix-40. And strangers never came this way unless someone sent them. Someone like Parkovitch. Sheltered by the forest, the farmhouse was not even visible from the main road. No, Wecker had come deliberately, but was it safe to let him leave?

The young man's eyes sparked with curiosity. "You seem to know all about the old Russia, Professor."

"Yes," Ivanski admitted, not without pride.

"My grandfather thinks the revolutions in our country date back to the Decembrist. He called it the seedbed of Marxism."

"Did he?" Ivanski asked. Marxists, Bolsheviks, Bloody Sunday—what did it matter? They were part of the past; Ivanski was about to make history by restoring the old imperialistic days of the czars. "Vladimir, I must get back to my work," he said.

"If I could just use your phone first—to call a friend. There's not another bus back to Moscow for hours."

For a flicker of a second, he wondered if the young man had strayed from the trail and stumbled on his property accidentally. He scoped the forest with his sharp eyes and detected nothing, not even the flutter of leaves as dusk crept in. Could Wecker be an innocent Muscovite, as he claimed? But why would he have left the bus stop on an injured leg? No, he must lure Wecker inside and into the basement before the call from Ryskov came through.

Wecker no longer rubbed his swollen ankle. He was balancing on his good leg, looking wary. "I better go before it gets dark."

Ivanski's housekeeper peered around his shoulder. "He's hurt, Professor. He can't walk on that leg. I can help him."

She has guessed my plan and will not allow me to harm this stranger. Reluctantly he stepped back from the window. "Bring him in then and tend to that ankle. And allow him one phone call."

"But you are expecting—"

He silenced her with a scowl. "Help him, and then I want him out of here as quickly as possible." *I want him silenced.*

All Vladimir Wecker could think about was beating it back to the safety of the village even if he had to crawl. But there was no turning back. The door was open. He followed the housekeeper inside. She led him down the hall past the professor's library. He had only a second to glance inside. No time to check it out.

She was urging him to hurry as she led him into the kitchen. She was a strange woman, her shifty eyes never meeting his, and yet she gave him a scalding cup of black coffee before going off and bustling about her stove.

As he watched her, he tried to decide where he had gone wrong. When he had approached the farm, he sensed no danger. It was a well-kept house, isolated and shuttered and nestled against the forest. He found no stone or wire fence high enough to keep strangers out. No armed guards stopped him. No attack dogs snarled and nipped at his heels.

The MI6 request from London had been urgent. Wecker was to report back on Boris Ivanski and his possible association with the Englishman, Radburn Parker. And wasn't that Wecker's whole purpose in living in Moscow—of actually studying at the Academy of Sciences—to be available for the good of England? He had felt supercharged when the assignment came. He didn't mention his sprained ankle—just packed up his knapsack and caught the bus out of Moscow. Professor Ivanski! He knew the man's reputation. What could be so important that he had sparked MI6's interest?

Even as he had limped across the grounds, he was certain that Ivanski was just an eccentric recluse who liked his privacy. But he knew he had misjudged the professor the minute he said the words "Phoenix-40." He had blown it.

The housekeeper was back now with a steaming basin of water, smelling medicinal. In spite of her gruff appearance, she bent down and eased off his shoe and stocking, her eyes finally meeting his. "You should not be here," she told him. "Professor Ivanski does not like company."

Gently she turned Vladimir's discolored foot in her hand, examining it. Alarm filled her dark eyes. "This is an old injury," she whispered.

He could taste the fear. "I know. I thought it was healing—but I twisted it again out in the mine."

"But you injured it even more by coming out here."

She plunged his foot into the basin and held it there until he felt his skin burning, but he bit his tongue and held on, and moments later she seemed grieved for what she had done. "Do you still want to make that call?" she asked.

Vladimir nodded. As his foot soaked, she pulled the cord free and dragged the kitchen phone to him. He knew now that the chance of leaving the farm was minimal. He had overstepped his boundary and, feeling cocky and sure of himself, had gone beyond the MI6 orders to check out the farm. Slowly, as though he were trying to retrieve the number by memory, he dialed a pre-arranged number.

The cheerful operator stationed in a small wing of the British embassy said, "Academy of Sciences."

Good so far, he thought, *especially with the professor listening on the other end.* "This is Vladimir Wecker." He spoke distinctly, willing himself to think clearly. To use his ingenuity to leave this farmhouse alive. "I need to get a message to my housemate, Sergei Glass."

Both names were traceable, registered students at the academy. Authentic right on down to biographies that would pass Professor Ivanski's scrutiny. "Tell him I missed the bus back, and I'm out with a bad ankle." *Deliberately missed it.*

Surely Sergei would read into his words and know that Vladimir was out on a limb. In trouble.

"No," he told the operator. "It was a field trip."

"And was it worth it?" she asked.

"I found what I wanted," he said. *Are you listening? Are you writing down what I'm saying? I found what Sergei expected me to find—trouble at the Ivanski farm.* Did the operator hear the professor's heavy breathing on the other end of the phone? Or did she think it was Vladimir?

"My location? A farmhouse forty miles from Moscow." He glanced at the housekeeper. "Boris Ivanski's place, right?"

She frowned.

"No, I believe he lives alone—except for his housekeeper." The operator was a trained agent, taught to pick up bits and pieces from his words. *Are you reading me right?* he wondered. *Are you understanding that there is no visible security?*

"His housekeeper is helping me. My foot is really bad." He winced as she dragged his ankle from the basin and wrapped it snugly. As he said, "The farm is isolated, but I'm sure Sergei can find it," she gave another severe tug to the bandage.

The woman on the other end came back apologetically. "Sergei is gone for the evening. Is there anyone else?"

"No, Sergei's the only one with a car." A double meaning. Transportation out was urgent. The message for Sergei's ears only. That would put it straight through to British Intelligence. Straight to London maybe.

"When he comes back—"

The housekeeper was glaring at him now. "I guess I'd better go back to the village. I've worn out my welcome here."

Did you understand me? he wondered. *I've got problems here.*

His words had reached her. "Wecker," she said, "you should never have gone so far on that bad ankle of yours."

It was a gentle reprimand. "It will be easier for Sergei to find you in the village, so go there as quickly as you dare."

You don't think you are going to see me again, he thought. He cradled the phone, setting it down as though it were china.

"Go," the housekeeper said. "Go while you have the chance."

"Thank you," he told her. He risked one final remark. "I thought Radburn Parker lived here with the professor."

"Professor Parkovitch?" She winced. "Go," she said. "Now."

He had sent the message to the embassy as clearly as he dared, using the right words to alert the others, a message that might even now be going out in an embassy pouch to London. He had found Ivanski, and he was unwelcome. If the place was secured, he had seen no one. He was going back to the village for his own safety. And he needed transportation out of here as quickly as they could get it to him. Something was going on. And, yes, the well-known Professor Ivanski bore watching. But he had not been able to convey the housekeeper's reaction to the name Parker.

His foot barely fit into the shoe, but he forced it on and made his way down the steps. He didn't look back but limped steadily toward the forest, determined to beat the race against total darkness, to distance himself from Ivanski.

He had just reached the edge of the forest when he heard the footsteps tracking across the moss-covered ground behind him. There was no time to dive for safety, not even a second to spare to spin around and face his assailant.

It was a single shot at close range, the sound and the pain hitting Vladimir at the same time as the bullet pierced between his shoulder blades. He pitched forward without even a cry.

♛♛♛

At noon Glenn Fairway found Dudley Perkins strolling in St. James Park. Perkins was carrying his umbrella like a walking stick, tapping along the path, deep in thought. He was a rangy chap, a somber man with languid eyes, his homely face and thick skin giving him a morose appearance. Yet he was highly respected, a member of the British think-tank. He had worked himself up through the intelligence ranks, a man committed to his job and country.

Fairway didn't relish the job at hand. He was about to tell him that Vladimir Wecker was dead. He signaled Perkins off the walkway to the nearest empty bench and sat down beside him. He was startled at the pinched gauntness in Perkins's face. Dudley never required more than five hours sleep, but the deep half moons under his eyes suggested that he was going on less than that now.

"Glenn, have you heard from Vladimir?" Perkins asked.

"Indirectly. We had a call from MI6."

"About Vladimir? They didn't call me."

"I know. It's bad news. Vladimir Wecker is dead."

"He can't be!"

Perkins's eyes closed. Fairway gave the man another five minutes to recover. "His friend Sergei Glass found him in the mine shaft several miles from Professor Ivanski's place."

"Then Wecker never reached the Ivanski farm?"

"He found Ivanski's place all right. Even managed a phone call from the farmhouse."

"But you said Wecker died in the mine shaft."

"His body was dumped there. He was shot. I'm sorry, Dudley."

"What have we accomplished?" he asked. "A young man wasted."

"He went beyond what he was instructed to do. He confronted Ivanski face to face. But we have no proof, of course. So it's still a waiting game. We do know that Radburn Parker and Boris

Ivanski taught at the same university. Parker often dined in the Ivanski home and may have shared the man's ideology."

Perkins dug the ground with his shiny black shoe. "I can hardly believe that Vladimir sent you that kind of information. Parker and Ivanski may have been working colleagues but not conspirators. Have you told this nonsense to Drew Gregory?"

"There's no need to yet. Personally, I don't think this has anything to do with the Tour de France—apart from the fact that Radburn is in partnership with the Gainsborough team. This is embassy business. And Lennie Applegate is right in the thick of it." Fairway rested his arm on the back of the bench and glanced at the swans in the pond. "The information is based on our own intelligence reports. The possibility exists that Ivanski was part of the old Phoenix-40. We are working under the assumption that they both held membership. We can't pick them up on guesses, but we're keeping surveillance."

"That's outrageous. Parker is the British citizen who first exposed the Phoenix-40 rebellion."

"Before or after some of their leaders were executed?"

"Before, I think. Keep in mind that Ivanski is a Russian historian. Of course, he would be well versed on the Phoenix-40."

"Dudley, Parker is supposedly on holiday, yet when we examined his flat here in London, we found no personal papers. No canceled checks left behind. No letters. No receipts or files. His books are packed away."

Not a muscle twitched. "So he isn't coming back to London?"

"If he senses danger, he may catch a Red Eye to Moscow."

"And leave Miss Applegate behind? Embarrassing for your reputation, Fairway."

"We have all been quite duped, Miss Applegate most of all. For now, we sit tight. We've arranged for Parker to ride in Maurice Chambord's official car. That way we know where he is." He shrugged. "The Russian, of course, is not our responsibility."

For an instant his attention riveted on the swans again, and then he said, quite kindly, "I'm sorry about Wecker." They stood at the same time. "Dudley, when is your wife coming home?"

"I'm afraid to ask her. But it will be a while yet. Her hostess persuaded her to spend a few days on the island of Corfu. Seems that the woman has an old school friend living there. Lost her son a few months ago." His face was reflective. "Molly thought she might be able to help the woman."

"Believe me, Dudley, I hate adding to Molly's pain. Will you tell her about Vladimir?"

"No. It would be like losing our son all over again. She was fond of Vladimir Wecker."

"How can you keep the news from her?"

"If I say nothing, she will think of him as alive. She won't grieve that way—not until his family gets in touch with her."

The villa at Corfu. Even on the veranda where she sat, Molly Perkins could see the portrait of Alekos Golemis—a handsome young man, his features dark and striking, and those marvelous hooded eyes full of life. She could not have endured seeing the likeness of her own son staring down from the barren wall—and be forced to grieve as the woman across from her was still doing.

Molly crossed her long legs and sipped the light wine that Olympia Golemis had offered her. She swallowed but did not taste it. She wondered now why she had allowed Marcella to persuade her to fly to Corfu. "We'll just spend a couple of days with my dear friend, Olympia and her husband. They have only recently lost their son. Oh, darling Molly, you will do them so much good."

How? Molly wondered now. *Do I tell her about my own grief, my own loss so many years ago? Do I tell her about Joel? Joel as a little boy and the shared disappointment that there never was a brother for him to play with? The wretched way I felt when he went off to boarding school, my secret fears as he learned to fly, and my thoughts of suicide when I knew he was dead? Do I tell her that the girl Joel was going to marry married somebody else? Do I tell her how Dudley packed away every picture of Joel in the house, taking even that small comfort from me?*

She groped for words and found them in the spectacular Grecian setting. "Olympia, you have a lovely view here."

"Didn't I tell you?" Marcella asked. "Absolutely gorgeous view. Why do you ever go back to Athens, Olympia?"

"We haven't, not since Alekos died. His father insists on being here . . . with Alekos."

Molly shivered. She could not have borne having her son's grave on the family estate as this dear woman had done. This morning she had stood in the guest room watching from the window. She saw Olympia down on her knees. *Praying,* she had thought. Then she had realized that Olympia was cutting back the weeds and polishing her son's tombstone. Molly had slipped into her shorts and pink tunic and gone out to her, extending her hands without a word.

It had been no easy task to help Olympia to her feet. She was a heavyset woman, not the once-glamorous schoolgirl that Marcella had described. But her hostess had a very gentle face, even with the grief lines around her eyes and mouth. Olympia had put the tools in the large pocket of her wraparound skirt and dusted the dirt from her fingers. And then they had linked arms and walked back to the house without speaking.

"Marcella tells me that you lost your son, too," Olympia said as she rocked her empty glass.

"Yes. In the Falklands. Joel was a pilot. He crashed at the San Carlos bridgehead." She sounded like a schoolgirl again, answering a question in history class. The more facts she could give, the better the grade. Barren rocks. An isolated mass of land off the coast of Argentina. In defense of the queen. Dead Brits. Dead Argentines. Her beloved son. Her only son.

"Afterwards, Joel's wing commander came to tell us what he could. Mercifully, Joel died quickly." *Mercifully.*

"He was young," Olympia said.

"Older than your son. Joel always wanted a younger brother."

Marcella had brought her to Corfu to comfort Olympia. Instead they were both about to dissolve into tears, the death of their sons as raw as the day they had occurred. "I'm sorry," Molly said, "I didn't mean to burden you with my own sorrows."

"On the contrary, we need each other. Was he an only child?"

Molly nodded and felt the tears prick her eyes, the way they had the day the news came. She thought of Joel's childhood and said out loud, "We spent long hours together, Joel and I."

"Where was Mr. Perkins?" Olympia asked gently.

"Building his career." Her words were sharp, bitter. She set her wine glass down, fearful that Olymbia would see her trembling fingers. Fearful that she would ask again, *Where is Mr. Perkins?* She couldn't bear to admit that she had left Dudley—that she did not know when she would go back to him because she waited for the impossible. She waited for Dudley to beg her to come home again.

"I would never have survived Alekos's death without Vasille."

"Seems to me," Marcella protested, "it's the other way around. Vasille would utterly fall apart without you."

"Vasille needs me. That's why I will never leave him."

I will never leave him. Molly choked at the words. She had run out on Dudley, and yet she knew he still needed her. Across the veranda their eyes met and held, Olymbia's kind and sympathetic. "Will you holiday much longer?" Olymbia asked. "Or will you be going home again soon?"

Marcella opened her mouth to comment, but Molly quickly said, "I suppose you're right. It is time to think about going home again. But Dudley rarely misses me. He's so busy."

"Marcella tells me your husband is in politics, like Vasille. Vasille's whole life was politics until Alekos died."

Marcella was on her second glass of wine. "Vasille is in Parliament," she said. "Dudley can't match that one, can he?"

Molly smiled at them both over the brim of her glass. She did not want Olymbia to know—any more than Marcella knew—that Dudley was in intelligence work. She looked beyond the porch railing over the vast Golemis property. The gated land swept down over the verdant hillside to the magnificent bay below. "I thought this lovely olive orchard was your husband's job."

"A family business," Olymbia said. "Handed down for generations. Vasille feels obligated to keep it going."

"And he has," Marcella chirped, "quite successfully." Her expression did not change, but envy colored her words. "Vasille hoped that one of his sons would take it over."

"I'd forgotten about your other children, Olymbia," Molly said apologetically. "Older? Younger?"

"Older. Our son Thymous and our daughter Zoe."

"And a handsome pair they are," Marcella said. "If I were a younger woman, I would give that Thymous a run for his money."

And it would be for his money, Molly thought. As wealthy as

Marcella was, rich after two divorces, she would never have enough.

Olympia smiled, and now the sweetness of her face unveiled her beauty. "Someday he will meet the right woman, Marcella."

Marcella put her hand to her chest. "If only I were younger. And Zoe—does she still carry the torch for the young American?"

As swiftly as Olympia's smile had come, it disappeared, the lines on her face anguished over something. "Marcella, don't mention him in front of Vasille. He despises that young man."

"Whatever for? Such a nice young man and so eligible."

Molly wanted to kick Marcella, to warn her away from troubled waters, but Marcella plunged on. "A cyclist, wasn't he? A friend of—"

Her words caught up with her. "I am sorry. I never meant—"

"They were friends." Olympia turned to face Molly. "Alekos and the American rode on the same cycling team. And now Zoe and Thymous—in spite of their father's objection—have gone to France to watch the Tour de France."

"How heavenly!" Marcella exclaimed, trying for lightness again. "So Zoe's flame grows brighter?"

Tears brimmed in Olympia's eyes, one tear slipping over her rounded cheek. "They went to keep their promise to Alekos."

Chapter 20

Ian came out of his troubled sleep with a start, grasping at the dream already slipping from his mind. Someone had been waving at him. Chase? No, the dream was coming back now—fading, coming back: a pileup on the mountain curve and his grandmother dressed in white smiling down on him, her blue eyes brilliant beneath the dark velvet lashes. She waved, beckoning him to follow. The same premonition of tragedy that had come to Ian on the day of her death stalked him now like an alarm that couldn't be turned off.

He groaned and tossed on his narrow hotel bed, the top sheet twisted and knotted around his bare legs, the flimsy floral spread spilling onto the floor. His upper torso was covered with sweat, his innards cramping violently.

It has to be last night's upset stomach, he reasoned.

Miserable abdominal cramps had accompanied him to bed and had driven him to the bathroom every hour. His gaze wandered across the room, returning to the makeshift IV pole in the corner. He remembered now—Chase coming to his room shortly before midnight just to say good night.

Alarm registered on her face when she saw him. "I'm getting Drew," she said.

"Don't. Vic and Drew slipped out of the hotel hours ago to scout around."

"Scouting for what?"

He didn't know. He was too worried about the cramps that

were tearing at his gut, threatening his chances in the Tour. He tried to grip Chase's hand and felt too weak even to do that.

"I think someone poisoned me."

"The cook," she said. "You're not the only one ill."

He actually smiled at her. "Thank God," he said, meaning it.

Her eyes grew misty. "Well, according to Drew and Beatrice Thorpe, that's the right person to thank."

"Can you just sit with me for a while, Chase?"

"No. If anyone catches me here, they'll disqualify you. You know Gainsborough's rules. No wives. No girls. No fraternizing."

And no illicit affairs, he thought. That was always Gainsborough's final word to the team before every race. In the middle of the conversation with Chase, he had to make a beeline for the bathroom. The cramps were getting worse. Embarrassed, he said, "You'd better go, Chase."

"I'll go, but I'm going to wake the doctor. You're sick."

Dr. Raunsted made his appearance moments later, barely thrown together with his shirt hanging free, his black bag in his hand and his hairy toes jammed into ill-fitting sandals. The doctor reached out and steadied Ian as he groped his way back to bed.

"I think I have the stomach flu, doc."

"Half the guests in the hotel do."

The doctor's examination was quick and precise, Ian wincing as Raunsted palpated his stomach. Then Raunsted chuckled. "After tonight's meal, a number of you are crying for mercy. I'd say the cook added a bit of bacteria to his stew."

Ian doubled his legs to his chest. "The pain is terrible."

"You have ridden more than 2,900 kilometers. You've worn your immune system down."

The doctor was a good man, into athletics, a runner himself. In his jeans and rumpled shirt, he didn't look much like a doctor, but Ian was grateful to have him on board.

"Am I washed up?" he asked.

"It's your call, Ian. You have today to rest up. I will check you tonight and again in the morning. You will live. Gregory insists on it. You're just dehydrated, Kendall."

"I've got to keep racing, doctor, but I'll never make it the way I feel now."

"Kendall, if anyone can be back on that bike in twenty-four hours, you can. If you're lucky, this is just the twenty-four hour bug. You have that long to recover. The rest day will help."

He ignored Ian's arguments as he strung up the makeshift IV pole. "You need a glucose drip."

"No drugs, doc. They'll disqualify me."

"If the food poisoning doesn't."

As Raunsted uncapped the needle, Ian practically backed into the wall. "No medicine."

"It's not a steroid. It's okay. We have to settle your stomach so you can ride again. Everything is legitimate, Kendall. We just have to get some fluids in you."

۞۞۞

That had been hours ago. Now Ian's gaze went from the pole in the corner to the door. He willed Chase to reappear, to be up and about like the dawn. From the corner of his eye, he caught a glimpse of a sheet of paper sliding under the door. The sour taste in his mouth turned to fear. He forced himself to sit up and fought the dizziness as he calculated the steps. Six? Seven? Could he make it? He was sweating, weak as a newborn kitten as he stood. He risked one step and fell back against the pillows.

The doorknob turned. Basil Millard poked his head into the room. "Morning, old top. How are you?"

"I've felt better. But how will I ever ride today?"

"You won't have to, except for our training run. It's a rest day, remember?" As Basil stepped into the room, his foot crushed the sheet of paper. Their eyes met.

"Bring it to me, will you, Basil?"

Millard hesitated. "Wait until the doctor gets here. He's with Drew Gregory right now."

"Is Drew sick, too?"

"He cut himself."

"Shaving?"

"Out scouting, he called it. Tracking Nash probably. Drew has a nasty gash in his arm. He will explain when he sees you."

Ian held out his clammy hand for the paper. "Is it another warning?" he asked.

"Just like the one at Mount Ventoux. It's the only kind of mail you've been getting this trip."

Ian's thoughts raced back to the Tom Simpson memorial. *You will never make it to the summit, Kendall.*

"I'm going to turn this over to Drew. You have enough on your mind." Basil's freshly scrubbed face was full of concern. "You're sick, and you need the rest. So enjoy it."

Ian swung his legs to the side of the bed again, his head spinning as he did so. "I promised to spend today with Chase."

Millard pushed him back down. "You are not going anywhere until the doctor checks you out." He tucked the warning in his pocket. "Ian, the team and I have been talking. You have to drop out of the race. A win isn't worth your life."

Ian glanced out the window at the Pyrenees, the mountain chain that rose like an impassable barrier to his dreams. Rangy peaks and barren rocks awakened him to the challenge of the climb. Or, after all his training, was this remote terrain that towered above the lush hills out of reach for him?

"Are you listening?" Basil asked. "We want you to abandon the race. You have a stomach upset. It's a good excuse."

"I'm not looking for excuses—just for the chance to climb that mountain."

"Don't push yourself too far. Tom Simpson did."

They both knew that the lonely ride toward the crest of Mount Ventoux had been a final mountain climb for Simpson, his heart unable to take any more physical beating in the blistering hot sun. "This is not Ventoux," Ian reminded Basil. "I won't quit."

Millard's breathing sounded as labored as Ian's as he thumped the warning in his pocket. "You do not have a choice."

"You've met my grandfather, Basil?"

"Good man. I admire him."

"In his younger days, he served with British Intelligence. Did you know that?" Without waiting for Millard's answer, he said, "Gramps never gave in to terrorists. I won't either."

Millard's jaw locked. "I wonder what drove Simpson?"

"Maybe he rode for the glory of it, like the rest of us. Summer glory! Autumn glory!" Ian's fist struck the damp mattress. "Call it what you want, but I have to finish this race."

Millard's eyes were sympathetic. "Simpson's grasp for the top left a young widow and two little girls who didn't have their dad around as they grew up. Is that the legacy you want to leave behind, Ian?"

"My legacy is wrapped up in winning."

Basil took the note from his pocket and shook it in Ian's face. "If this were addressed to me, I'd take my wife and child and fly back to Birmingham today."

"You're not me. And I don't have a wife and child."

"You have Chase."

Ian looked away, unwilling to voice his fears. If he missed the top of the mountain as the threats warned, only Chase and his grandfather Uriah would grieve if something happened to him. And Drew and Miriam. It all boiled down to having nothing to leave behind except a handful of mourners. *Chase, Chase,* he thought miserably, *I love you. Will you ever know how much you mean to me?*

"Ian," Basil said, "you won't make it up the mountain unless you do a conditional run today."

"My poor body says no, but maybe we can go later."

"I'll check back after lunch to see how you're doing." Millard slapped the paper in his palm. "I'm going to turn this over to Gregory. Why don't you talk with him about it?"

"I don't want to bother Drew again."

"You better talk to someone—and Gregory seems to have a direct line with heaven."

Ian managed a smile. "I think they call that praying."

🌀🌀🌀

When Basil reached Raunsted's room, Gregory was ready to leave. "You okay, Mr. Gregory?" Basil asked.

"Just tripped in the dark. Nasty cut, that's all."

"Then could I talk to you two?" Millard asked as he stepped into the room. He unfolded the paper and handed it to Drew. "The team wants Ian to go home."

Raunsted's eyes were as dark as his hair. He rubbed his jaw and said, "That's Ian's decision. How is he this morning?"

"Weak."

"Still vomiting?"

"Not while I was there."

"He may not get his strength back to ride the mountains. But he'll make the first twenty kilometers from sheer determination."

"And after that?" Drew asked.

"I won't destroy the man's spirit. I don't know why winning is so important to him, but Kendall has to make the decision." He gave them a wry smile. "But in my mind he will never make it to Paris. The boy is knackered with fatigue. He'll have to abandon somewhere along the way. I'll go by and give him another slow glucose drip. That will keep him resting for the morning. After that it's up to Ian's body to recover."

"That's your medical opinion?" Drew asked.

"Are you questioning my training, Gregory?"

"You came on board for the Tour at the invitation of Troy Carwell. I wasn't sure you even had a medical degree."

He smiled. "You thought all I did was collect blood and urine samples and report in to Carwell?" Raunsted's smile turned into a deep chuckle. "No, I come with full credentials. I did my medical training in France and graduate study in sports medicine. That's when I discovered my first love—the value of exercise physiology on team sports. I even throw in a bit of fatherly counsel now and then."

"You're only a dozen years older than the team."

"Old enough. And you, Basil, you need to get some rest yourself before tomorrow. Your red blood cells are down, your iron store depleted. You need your strength if you're going to ride support for Ian all the way."

"But you don't think he'll go all the way?"

"No, but you will."

"Doctor, can you have someone stay with Ian so he rests?"

"Are you volunteering someone?"

"If you give the order, Chase Evans could be there."

"I'll arrange it as soon as I see Kendall."

He smiled at Drew as Millard left the room. "I'm glad Carwell asked me to come. These threats have affected the whole

Gainsborough team. They race hard. Orlando Gioceppi's toxins are high, his liver overworked. Robbie has the start of an infection that could take him out of the race. I ordered Ramon back on the exercise bike for another thirty minutes to clear up the lactic excess. The team is plagued with exhaustion."

"And Kendall?"

"I expected him to break under the stress. But he's a tough one. Stubborn. The stomach bug might do what nothing else could."

"Put him out of commission?"

"I'd rather see him go out that way than risk another tragedy in the mountains. We've had enough of those in the past."

🟤🟤🟤

It was just past noon when Ian awakened again. He stretched and felt better. He reached out for his water glass and saw Chase curled in a chair near his bedside, reading. She lowered the book and smiled. "Hi, sleepyhead," she said.

"Chase!" he said groggily. "What time is it?"

"Almost one."

"I've been asleep for four hours?"

"Your body needed the rest."

"But I promised to spend the whole day with you."

"You did. You just didn't know it. The doctor insisted that someone stay with you. Millard volunteered me. How do you feel?"

"I think I'm better."

She felt as surprised as he looked. "Then my praying really worked."

"What do you mean by that?"

She was embarrassed. "Well, Drew told me we should pray for you to get better."

Ian laughed at her. "Did you?"

"Did I what?"

"Pray."

"I'm not really sure. I don't have any experience in it."

"Drew didn't either until recently. My grandfather always said Drew was not a very religious fellow. Oh, he was an altar boy—but he outgrew all of that."

"Well, he talks about heaven like he's going to be there some-day."

"He is. He did a turnaround in the mountains at Sulzbach, ran the whole nine yards, from there to eternity."

She curled a strand of hair behind her ear. "My family never talks about things like that. We only pray at weddings and funer-als, and I can't even be sure about that."

"You should talk to Drew."

"And not to you?"

"I believe all that stuff. I just don't know how to put it into words. About all I can do is hand you my grandmother's Bible. Other than that, I never know what to say. But you could talk to Beatrice Thorpe when we get back to England."

"But, Ian, she's confused."

"Not about things that matter. She's a straight-shooter then."

"Then go with me—as soon as we get back to London."

"I'll do that. I'll even hold your hand while we're there. Right now, I'm trying to decide whether I feel strong enough to take you to dinner. But I don't think I'd better go that far."

"What about the patio gardens? It's restful out there. We could have tea. I could go down and get a table for us."

He sat up. Slowly. "Okay so far," he said. He wet his lips with the water and began to whistle.

"I don't recognize the song," she said.

"It was a favorite with my grandmother. 'I've Got a Date with an Angel.'"

She flushed, pleased.

He grabbed his robe and slipped into it. "So far so good," he said. "Now if I can take nourishment."

"Just take it easy," she warned.

"I will. I'll shower and dress. And if I'm not down there in the patio in twenty minutes, come looking for me."

He pressed his cheek against hers, and she pushed him away. "Oh, Ian, make that thirty minutes. You need to shave."

She waited until he crossed the room to the bathroom and dis-appeared behind the closed door. *So far, so good,* she thought. *At least you're still standing.*

Still she lingered, waiting for the sound of the shower running. When she heard it, she fluffed her hair in the mirror, applied fresh makeup, and left. Above the running water she could still hear him whistling "I've Got a Date with an Angel."

The infusion of light and color in the scented chateaux gardens was like surveying a Thomas Kinkade painting. Striking red flowers grew against the stone wall, their brilliance softened by the delicate hues of blue and pink flowers. A family of ducks waddled around the flower pots and under the white iron benches. Sun rays cut through the high trees and across the rippling pond. Nearby a string quartet played softly.

The maitre d' led her to an empty table. She was seated facing the chateaux, waiting for Ian, when she noticed the guests at a table for two. Sal had dropped from the Tour since the night of the bombing, but there he was, as ruggedly good-looking as ever, caressing the hand of a beautiful, young woman. The girl's dark red-brown hair was swept back from her face, silken strands of it falling softly over her left shoulder.

For a moment, Chase wanted to rush over and demand answers from Sal. How dare he disappear as he had done without a word to her! But then perhaps the girl was the reason he had gone away. He was smiling, but the girl looked near tears, those wide eyes reproachful. She looked up and caught Chase staring.

At a nod from the girl, Sal turned. He recovered quickly and beckoned Chase over. He stood when she reached them and gave her a quick hug. "I missed you, Chase."

"You are the one who went away."

"And I'm leaving again this afternoon," he said with a wink. "For Nordlune this time." He turned back to his companion. "Zoe, this is Chase Evans, a journalist friend of mine. Zoe Golemis. Chase reports on the Tour for her hometown paper."

"Sal and I met in the press room."

Zoe seemed surprised. "In the press room?"

"They have a special place for journalists," Chase said.

"Then it is no place for Salvador. For all I know, he is the one responsible for the bombing on stage eleven."

Shocked, Chase said, "He couldn't be. He was with me. Actually, I think he saved my life."

At closer inspection, Chase saw that the girl had been crying. Her complexion was dark, her skin lovely, and now her long lashes brimmed with more tears.

"The two of you will like each other," Sal said. "You are both rooting for the American."

Zoe turned back to Chase. "You know Ian Kendall?"

"She knows him quite well," Sal announced.

Again Chase saw pain cross the girl's face. Gently she said, "I know the Kendall family, Zoe."

"The whole family? You didn't tell me that." Salvador's voice danced, but his eyes had turned cynical. "I have just been telling Zoe that I am still against the American winning."

"Mr. Contoni, please go," Zoe begged. "Please."

Mr. Contoni? Not Salatori. She was about to ask him when he said, "Zoe, I thought we were going to have lunch together."

"I'm not hungry, Sal, but if you change your mind—"

"I do not want your money. Your father already paid me."

Zoe flinched as he touched her cheek, her expression angry enough to push him away. Sal took no notice, his tone arrogant as he turned to Chase. "Her brother was a friend of Kendall's. They rode together once—but her father dislikes Ian intensely."

Was a friend. Golemis. Chase felt sick. *Alekos Golemis.*

"I'm sorry, Zoe," she said as Salvador left them. "How can you bear to be here at the race?"

"You know who I am?" She dabbed her eyes. "I promised my brother Alekos that I would be here for him."

"You called Sal Contoni, not Salatori, the name he gave me."

"Salvador Contoni—that's his real name, and, Chase, he is not a journalist. He never has been."

Zoe was looking beyond her, and Chase knew without looking up that Ian was making his way slowly to them. He was cleanly shaven, casually dressed, and scented with French cologne. His eyes were bright, or had they brightened when he saw Zoe Golemis?

"Zoe," he said—and there was affection in his voice, "why are you here? This is too painful for you."

"I promised Alekos I would be here for him. You are riding very well, Ian. He would be proud of you."

"I never got to tell you how sorry I was."

"My father wouldn't let you. It was shameful for him to send you away. But you mustn't stay at the race. You must go home."

"I have to ride to the finish line."

"Oh, Ian, you were always a bird in flight. I thought nothing would ever bring you down to earth. But I think maybe Miss Evans has done that for you." She stood hastily.

"Don't go," he begged. "Have tea with Chase and me."

Zoe reached up and kissed Ian on the cheek. "Some other time," she said.

Ian was quiet long after Zoe walked away. Finally, when their tea was served, Chase asked, "Were you with Alekos when he had his accident in the Sulzbach mountains?"

His eyes glazed over. "That was no accident, Chase. Alekos was strangled by a Russian agent."

"Killed? . . . Murdered! How awful—for all of you. But why didn't you go to his funeral? Orlando and Basil did."

He gave her a ghost of a smile. "I tried. But Zoe's dad told me to get off the island of Corfu." He reached across the table and took her hand. "I've come to terms with that, Chase."

"Have you come to terms about Zoe?"

His hand tightened over hers. "Alekos wanted Zoe and me to get together. Permanently."

"And what did you want?"

"For a while I thought the chemistry was there. The spark. But that was all. The only person I really want is you. You're all I think about."

"If you're going to win, you can't be thinking about me."

"I can't stop thinking about you."

Chapter 21

S tage seventeen. Ian Kendall awakened to the challenge of the Pyrenees. This was the day he had waited for, a climber's dream. He felt better, refreshed, unwilling to quit. Downing his muesli and yogurt, he felt confident that it would stay down. He eyed the fruit and unbuttered pasta and omelet more cautiously. The omelet only reminded him of the misery of the last twenty-four hours. He grinned to himself and voted for his grandmother's challenge: *You can steel your mind to anything.*

He stuffed the pasta in, swallowed, prayed, and kept his thoughts on the race. Day after day, six to seven hours each day, Ian and the other cyclists had ridden the roller-coaster roads and cobbled streets of France, dipping into Italy and until yesterday racing through rainstorms or tiny villages in 90-degree heat. Ian had sweated up the steep mountain slopes of the Alps with the world's best riders and cruised over the lower lands to the Pyrenees. The 189 racers had dropped in number, ill and exhausted. Two days ago one Spaniard had raced to his physical limit and been carried away on a stretcher. One Italian had crashed out. The Australian had slipped from his sweaty saddle and dropped by the wayside in a heat stroke. Franz, the square-jawed German on the Gainsborough team, abandoned the Tour in tears, a respiratory infection wracking his body. The rest of the pack rode on, too goal-oriented to notice their fallen competitors or to see the medieval castles or golden fields of sunflowers. They were guilty of seeing only the riders in front of them or the road beneath them and always waiting for the red kite that would signal a kilometer to the finish line or listening eagerly for the roar of the fans cheering them on.

As he reached the sign-in podium, Ian looked around for Chase and saw her running toward him. He held out his arms, and she allowed herself to be swept up in them. He twirled her around once and knew that a second turn around would send him spinning.

"I love you," he said, setting her down.

"Is that all you can say?"

"It's all I can think about. How come you're not in the press tent?" he asked.

"Drew insisted that I stay with him today after showing me the police sketch of Salvador Contoni. I don't like thinking about my friend Salatori deceiving me—"

Ian touched her lips. "Just think about me."

She nodded. "We borrowed a car for the drive to Nordlune."

"That's the third mountain pass—at least four hours into today's stage. So you're on official business?"

"The helicopter will check the race course from the sky."

"The helicopters are part of the press corps every day."

"There's an extra one today," she whispered. "Sal Contoni drove up to Nordlune last evening. That's why we're going."

"So you can take any bomb meant for me?"

"Drew wouldn't take me if he thought it wasn't safe."

"Funny girl, how could he stop you once you made up your mind to ride with him?"

Chase touched his cheek. "Ian, nothing will go wrong. I will be there when you come over the crest of your mountain."

For an instant he rubbed his eye, feigning a visual irritation. In his recurrent dream, his grandmother was always at the top of the ridge beckoning to him. "You'll miss my starting out," he said. "This is my big day."

This rugged mountain was his challenge. His foe. His dream. A single summit could determine the outcome of the race and the man who would wear the yellow jersey in Paris. He wanted to be that man. Ian flattened his jersey against his muscled stomach. Yesterday's pains were gone. He felt strong. This was his chance to grab a piece of glory for himself. He didn't dare dwell on the warning: *You'll never make it to the top of your mountain.*

Chase ran her finger over his wrist. "Be careful today."

He felt her shudder and said quickly, "I'll be fine. After the Pyrenees, the roads are flat along the Garonne River. And after the rolling hills of the wine country, we head straight on to Paris. We're going to make it."

"Oh, no," she said, "I think Chambord is heading our way."

He strutted toward them in his forest-green blazer and dark gray trousers, the level of his mood hidden behind dark glasses. But his voice was pleasant. "*Bonjour*, Kendall." His smile broadened to include Chase. "Beautiful day. Beautiful day. Don't worry about a thing. Our gendarmes and escort motorcycles will protect your young man the whole way."

His gaze remained on Chase. "Gregory tells me you're chasing the wind to Nordlune. Lovely Basque village. Used to be a way station for pilgrims, but hardly a place for terrorists." He rattled on. "If you stand down the hill from the Chateau de Arceson, you will have an excellent view of the race."

Chambord stared off at the towering Pyrenees with their craggy, snow-capped peaks. "It's a formidable challenge, my boy. I dreamed of being a cycling champion once. Rode with Eddy Merckx back in the seventies."

"I didn't know that," Chase told him.

"Glad you didn't. I had the humiliation of riding the Broom Wagon when I abandoned the race. I was never a winner, Miss Evans, but I can recognize a champion when I see one. I saw this young man of yours ride four years ago—just a young man then."

Chase smiled back. "That's when you turned professional, wasn't it, Ian—just before your nineteenth birthday?"

"You'd better go," Ian cautioned. "Drew hates waiting."

۞ ۞ ۞

Yuri Ryskov had to warn the Serbian rider that Jiri Benak was quite possibly following his own agenda. Stage eleven had been proof of that. Yuri had no idea what the Serbian looked like, only that he wore a Gainsborough jersey. *Number 19. Or was it number 91?* He tried to remember back to the meeting at Professor Ivanski's farm with Leopold Bolav and General Noukov. "Remember that number," they had told him.

Number 19? Or 91?

He pushed his way through the crowds toward the host of riders gathering around the start-ramp. Team uniforms in every color. Endless numbers—139 riders left, 139 numbers . . . 6 . . . 30 . . . 88 . . . 99 . . . 111. He kept searching, more frantic now as the twenty-one teams mounted their bikes. His message—blocked out in a childlike scrawl—was burned in his mind:

> *Benak foiled plans. Moscow alerted. Advise General Noukov. Will attempt to salvage project in Paris. Meet Parkovitch there.*

Yuri studied the faces again, finally recognizing three Gainsborough riders. One with a bushy blond mustache. The darker one called Orlando—Orlando Gioceppi, if he remembered correctly. And the cyclist with strands of red hair poking out beneath his helmet and wearing the placard number 19.

A gendarme yanked Yuri back, but Yuri pulled free and ran. He was short of breath when he reached the rider with 19 on his bike and jersey. He shoved his message at the startled man.

"Take it," he ordered in broken English.

A broad hand wrapped around it. "What's this?" the young man asked.

"Read it. Be careful," Yuri warned.

Before he could explain, Yuri was pulled back behind the yellow barrier, the gendarme cursing him in French. But he smiled complacently. The red-headed Serbian was reading the message, a frown cutting across his youthful face.

Number 19 folded the note, tucked it into his headgear, and looked around. Across the yellow barricade their eyes met. And then the whistle blew. It was time to ride into the Pyrenees.

As Ian rode off, Chase thought, *He's recovered. He'll make it.* She was still smiling when she reached Drew. Even Drew's usual morning grumpiness failed to squelch her happiness. She didn't quite understand what was happening, but she knew deep inside that Ian Kendall—number 19—was part of her future plans.

Chase and Drew barely spoke on their drive to Nordlune. She

preferred thinking about Ian and how important he had become to her. But when they reached the Basque village at high noon, even Drew had to come out of his sour morning mood. Nordlune was like stepping into the last remaining wilderness in the mountains. What had once been a way station for pilgrims had emerged as a flourishing spa town, serviced by people in Basque costumes and black berets. Sheep grazed the lush hillsides beneath the remote terrain and jagged peaks of the Pyrenees range.

Drew and Chase wandered through the seventeenth-century chateau with its beamed dining room, enjoying the delicate aroma of Basque cuisine coming from the kitchen. But later, when Drew came out of the loo, she startled him by grabbing his arm, her face ashen. "I—I just saw Jiri Benak walk through the lobby," she gasped.

"Don't joke, Chase. It had to be someone who looked like him. Benak would never attend a sporting event like this."

Her tears brimmed over. "But, Drew, I will never forget Jiri's face. Remember, he tried to take my life in the tunnels of Jarvoc."

He took her hands in his and rubbed the warmth back into them. "Leave him to Interpol."

"But, Drew, how can I? I have nightmares about him still." She pulled away from him. "That man really did look like Benak."

He nodded. "Don't think about those days in Prague, Chase. We're to keep our eyes open for Salvador Contoni."

"Well, maybe I was mistaken." She began to relax.

"Now let's find ourselves a spot on the mountain to wait for Ian," Drew suggested.

Beyond the chateau lay the scented garden and a gushing mountain stream, and farther down the hillside the turbulent, fast-flowing river. The town was filled with whitewashed houses with red-tiled roofs and a lone twin-steepled cathedral. Standing with Drew just below the crest of the mountain, Chase felt peaceful, content, Jiri Benak all but forgotten. She felt invigorated by the mountain air, fascinated by the jagged mountains. She couldn't imagine a more lovely setting to wait for Ian.

Jiri Benak left his three homemade plastic bombs and the bottles of ammonium nitrate hidden in the trunk of his car, and then he took up his post on the ascending side of the mountain with Yuri Ryskov standing begrudgingly beside him. Benak had already taken notice of the beautiful young Athenian in the crowd on his other side, a stunning dresser who wouldn't even give him the eye. But it was all right. He was too preoccupied thinking about his friend Ignasius. They had quarreled as he left the village.

"Go," Ignasius had told him. "And don't come back."

A wise move, as he considered it, for if by some small chance he were traced back to Ignasius's village, they could deny his presence or at best deny knowledge of where he had gone.

The girl finger-brushed her dark hair behind her ear, a quick feminine gesture. Still she would not look at him. He tossed his beige raincoat over his other shoulder, feeling miserable with the sun beating down on him. He would be grateful when the cyclists rode by and he could make his way safely out of Nordlune—without Yuri Ryskov. Let Ryskov send whatever signal he must; Jiri was not interested in the planned coup in Moscow. He would take refuge in the Cotswolds. Still he worried. What about the bombs hidden in the car? Nordlune was an isolated town with only one main road for an escape route. No, he would not set them off here. His own safety came first. He would save them for Paris. The tighter his chest felt, the more grateful he was for the cane. He leaned on it, his trigger finger going automatically to the nut-and-bolt mechanism that would allow him to fire at Kendall as he crested the mountain pass. But it was up to Marcus Nash to edge Kendall toward the crowd, putting Kendall within firing range.

He gave a hint of a smile to the girl and then turned to Ryskov. "You were late arriving, Yuri," he said. "What kept you?"

"I made certain that Kendall was well enough to ride today."

The fractional smile cut at the corners of Benak's mouth again. "It won't be long now, Yuri."

"What if something goes wrong? Marcus Nash may not be able to keep up with Kendall. He's never ridden in a race before."

"He's riding well in this one. He spent years riding a bike in the mountains in Bosnia with mortar equipment on his back."

Benak looked down in disgust at the Russian, wondering what cowardice drove him. Or was it fear? He was a reluctant revolutionary. The girl seemed to be listening now. Jiri kept his voice low, confidential. "Once Kendall crashes, it is up to you to call the professor."

"I will use the phone at the chateau."

And while you place your call, Jiri thought, *I will drive away, and you will not see me again. And if you cross me, Ryskov, there is a second pellet in my cane, and I will use it.*

🦂🦂🦂

In the broiling heat, the stranger beside Zoe Golemis had chosen to carry a beige trench coat and a walking stick. Zoe had paid little attention to him until she heard him mention the name Ian Kendall. He spoke in an unfamiliar dialect. *Slavic,* she guessed. But the name Kendall came across clear, distinct.

He was attractive, but far too serious, like her brother Thymous. Unlike Thymous, this man's hair was so blond that it looked snow-white; his eyes—whatever their color—were shaded by dark glasses. He was much older than Thymous but still too young to be carrying the Burmese walking stick with its handsome gold handle. He must have sensed her studying him, for he turned now and looked down at her; in spite of the sunglasses, she could see that his eyes were cold and disdainful. As he tossed his trench coat over his shoulder, she felt a hard bulge in its pocket and cringed.

A gun. She was certain the man was carrying a gun.

She inched away, glancing around for a gendarme, but saw Thymous instead pushing his way through the crowd toward her. She tried to tell him about the gun, but Thymous distracted her.

"Have you seen Salvador Contoni?" he asked.

"No, he probably didn't come to this village after all."

"Town," Thymous corrected wearily. "And I don't even know why we came."

Zoe didn't risk telling him that it was Salvador who told her about Nordlune. And she still hadn't found the courage to tell Thymous about her meeting with Ian. Talking about Ian would only open old wounds for her, as seeing him had done.

"Yesterday when I lunched in the gardens, I overheard someone mention Nordlune. I'm glad we came. It's lovely up here, Thymous, so please don't fuss. Don't be disagreeable—"

"I won't," he promised, "but we don't have to stand in the sun. I rented a room in the chateau with a balcony and a coffee urn. It will be an hour or two before the riders reach the pass."

"Long enough for you to call Monique Dupree?" she asked.

His dark eyes flashed. "She refuses to take my calls, Zoe."

She linked her arm with his. "Does she matter to you?"

"A little," he admitted. He squeezed her fingers. "But coming here to France has been harder on you, Zoe. I should never have let you come."

"There was no way to stop me."

As they ran up the steps of the chateau, she looked up at him and realized afresh how handsome he was. Yet his dark eyes were sad—and had been ever since their brother's death. These days Thymous never smiled. She feared he would never smile again.

Salvador Contoni stood behind the steel barricade, his press I.D. badge visible on his lapel. As he waited for the riders to come around that last curve and scale the hill, he opened the box of nails in his hands, his muscles flexing in anticipation as he wrapped his fingers around them. He would throw them. There was nothing to it. It would be like tossing a ball to Anzel Dupree. Sal felt powerful, invincible, like the craggy Pyrenees that rose before him. The mountains were majestic, but to Sal they didn't begin to match the Italian Alps. No, the mountain ranges of his homeland were far more spectacular, the terrain more fierce.

Idly he studied the faces of the Frenchmen and foreigners around him, some of them tipsy with wine after a chilling overnight in the mountains. The Chateau de Arceson lay directly behind them, situated near a fast-flowing river with the mountain road beside it as the only way out of town.

Again his gaze swept the people around him, and he was struck by two men—one a towhead like himself, with a manacle grip on a hand-carved cane; the other gentleman was pasty-skinned, his eyes sunken in a gaunt face. They stood in silence, like strangers, but Sal was certain that they traveled together. His attention had been drawn to them because Zoe Golemis had been standing there beside them. At the sight of Zoe, he shrank behind other spectators. Sal saw no need to strike up yesterday's argument. Zoe had humiliated him in front of the American journalist.

"For all I know," Zoe had said, "he is the one responsible for the bombing on stage eleven."

But he remembered with pleasure Chase Evans's quick defense. "He couldn't be. He was with me."

Because of Chase's loyalty, he no longer wanted to harm Ian Kendall, but he would stop him from winning by filling the narrow road with nails. It didn't matter how many young riders piled up on the mountain curve. Nothing mattered as long as he could puncture Kendall's tires and rob him of that marginal lead that he was clinging to so desperately. Delay him on this stage of the race, and Kendall would lose the chance to ride into Paris in a yellow jersey. Once the loudspeaker announced that the riders were almost to the summit, Salvador would toss his sharp nails on the road and walk away whistling.

What did it matter if Zoe Golemis saw him? She had made a fool of him—and no one ever made a fool of Salvador Contoni.

۞۞۞

As Ian rode the flat section of the high valley, he battled through his pain, calculating each kilometer in the steep climb to the third mountain pass. He was driven by Chase's promise, "I'll be there when you come over the crest of the mountain."

The blistering sun made him sweat. Or was his feverish body still reaping the toll of twenty-four hours of illness? The sun seemed to melt the tar on the roads and the rubber on his wheels. And yet the mountain air chilled him, sucking at his already blowtorched lungs. His throat felt dry and raw like sandpaper, his legs threatening to cramp.

The first ascent had taken little more than an hour, the wild descent less than twenty minutes. The second summit was another well-fought battle, won in segments with its 6,000 feet of vertical climb; but this legendary pass in front of him towered much higher, with twenty-nine hairpin turns to the top. He did not allow his thoughts to wander toward the finish line nor to think about quitting. Twice he found himself humming "I've Got a Date with an Angel." Even this distracted him, so he pushed the song from his mind, forcing himself to count one kilometer at a time.

ᛒᛒᛒ

Salvador Contoni's mouth soured. The nails stuck to his clammy palm as the riders winged around that last hairpin turn and hit a straight course toward the peak. There were two Gainsborough riders, Ian Kendall in the lead. Or was it three of them ascending the steep hill as though they were one?

Now, Salvador told himself. *Throw the nails and then split. Get out of here.*

Sal saw the agony on Ian's face, the strain of the ride visible in his eyes. Sweat poured down the athlete's face. The muscles in his legs and arms were wired tight as he pedaled against the wind. The greater the pain, the harder he rode, swaying and lurching his bike to keep his balance.

The cheers were deafening. Flags waved. Bottles were emptied in celebration. Little children screamed without knowing why. Sal dropped the nails back into the box and brushed his damp palm against his trouser leg. He was sweating like the riders.

Something was wrong! One rider pushed hard against Ian, shoving him toward the crowd. The shouting turned to cries of dismay as Kendall grasped his neck and began to ride erratically. Alerted now and Argus-eyed, Sal saw the man with the gold-handled cane lower it to his side. For an instant, his gaze locked contemptuously with Sal's, and then the two men were swallowed up in the crowd. They were leaving. Escaping! The box of nails dropped from Sal's hand and clattered at his ankles. He knew with the instinct of a man bent on survival that he would be blamed for whatever was happening.

ᛒᛒᛒ

To Ian's left lay the rock wall and a steep drop-off. Every part of his body ached, each breath filled with pain. He drove himself forward, his eyes barely focused on the crest of the mountain. Today's eight-hour stage was too long to have nothing but a thin layer of spandex between his skin and the saddle. He accelerated, riding out of the saddle to relieve the pressure; and then for the last of the long climb he sat toward the back of the seat and pedaled, his arms spread wide to ease his breathing.

Behind him, the peloton rode together along the narrow road; in minutes some of the pack would launch an attack and try to sprint past him. Marcus Nash rode on Ian's wheel, forcing Ian to take the brunt of the wind. Ian flew over the cobbles, trying to out-distance him; finally in sheer exhaustion he dropped to twenty-five kilometers per hour at the steepest incline.

Just ahead he saw the top of the mountain pass, the three rid-ers ahead of him mounting it even now. The crowds were elec-trifying. He accelerated again, borne on by their cheering. Still Nash kept doggedly at his back wheel. He tried to warn Nash off as they sped toward the top, wheel to wheel.

"Get back," he shouted.

Nash kept coming. Suddenly, he swerved toward Kendall, forc-ing Ian toward the crowd.

The jab struck Ian's neck. Stunned him. A violent pain that came from nowhere. The numbing rode down his arm. Tingled his fingers. Cut off his windpipe. He grasped his neck. Nothing. A small welt. Only a drop or two of blood. Sweat poured over his eyes, fogging his wraparound goggles, blurring his vision.

Ian tried to warn Nash off again. Now he could no longer form words. They were descending the mountain, the momentum building. His body crouched over the handlebars, his knees locked in a fixed position. His head spun. He was drifting into darkness. Lurching. Swaying. Veering across the path of the oncoming peloton. And then he saw his grandmother. She seemed to be part of the fleecy clouds, but the face was her own, the radiant smile the one he remembered. She said nothing but simply beckoned to him. And then he was catapulting over the stone wall, soaring like a bird in flight, his body twisting, spin-ning, plunging, his legs and arms flailing like broken wings. He felt his body lurch forward, shudder on impact, and then the light dwindled to darkness, emptiness.

🌀🌀🌀

Just before the accident, Drew and Chase had stood in the swel-tering sun, jammed in the flag-waving crowd. Drew knew from "Tour Radio" that a Banesto rider and two men from the Telekom team were in the lead. A six-man breakaway had launched an attack on their wheels, Ian Kendall and Marcus Nash among them. According to the commentator, the men rode with only seconds dividing them.

The roar of the crowd turned boisterous. The deafening shout of the fans came simultaneously with the riders scaling the top of the pass. Drew raised his fist in a triumphant thrust toward the sky and said, "Here they come, Chase."

For an instant the cycles skimmed above the surface of the narrow mountain road, bounced, and were riding rubber to rubber again, building momentum as they raced down the mountain. Drew recognized the lead riders: Mario wearing the polka dot jersey in this stage of the journey; Nicholas the Greek riding in his first Tour de France; and Conan, the Irishman, expressionless as he rode by. Behind them came Ian and Marcus Nash and, surprisingly, Orlando Gioceppi, the Italian whose friendship with Ian was back into full swing. The rest of the Gainsborough team were nowhere to be seen, struggling no doubt in the pack not yet coming over the hill. Nash was like a wild card, a last-minute selection to the team, still riding Ian's back wheel, laughing, jeering. Now they rode side by side, shoulder to shoulder.

"Drew," Chase cried, "he's forcing Ian into the crowd."

Drew was still beating the air with his fist when Ian's bike jerked out of control. He stifled the soundless, sickening fear in his throat as bike and rider veered erratically across the road in front of the oncoming peloton. Ian tugged at Nash's hand before his own bike slammed wildly into the stone wall.

For an instant it remained airborne, and then bike and rider disappeared down the sun-splashed cliff. Silence. Dead silence before the screams erupted around Drew, Chase's cry jarring, ear-splitting. More cries meshed with hers as a pileup of young bodies and bikes scraped the gravel. Photographers emerged from among the fans. Bulbs flashed. Video cameras rolled.

Nash smashed his bare hand into one of the cameras as he waited for the team mechanic to replace his cycle. Then he rode off, not even giving a fragmented glance at the cliff where the medical staff was already scrambling down the slope toward Ian.

"We're family," Drew told the gendarme as he and Chase broke through the police barrier and dashed across the road. He kept his hand tight on her icy fingers as they vaulted over the stone wall.

They could see Ian's twisted body lying down the mountainside, his bike in ruins a few yards from him.

"Wait here, Chase," Drew told her.

But she kept stumbling down the rocky cliff behind him. Midway down, she grabbed an overhanging tree limb and hung on. "I can't go," she cried. "I'm frightened."

He knuckled her chin and stumbled on, slipping and sliding over the rocks and bracing his own fall with the heels of his hands. Ian's body was battered, his face bloody. Thatches of red hair poked out from his high-tech cycling helmet and fell across his forehead. The bloody bare fingers of his hands lay limp. Brad O'Malloy and Dr. Raunsted were already kneeling beside Ian, Raunsted with a stethoscope in his ears. O'Malloy offered a sympathetic nod to Drew.

As Drew called Ian's name, Ian gasped and lay still.

Raunsted yanked the helmet free, exposing a raw red gash beneath Ian's chin—and a round two-millimeter puncture mark on his neck. As Raunsted initiated CPR, the rescue helicopter hovered above them.

Drew didn't even try to forestall the tears as a flood of memories swept over him. A scrawny kid on a swing. An awkward schoolboy dropping ice cream on the red leather seat of Drew's car. Ian with his beloved grandmother. Ian with Uriah. Ian and Chase and the dreams that were ending. And now this. Drew couldn't watch. He stared down instead at the Giro helmet and the white sheet of paper that had fallen beside it. He picked it up, startled at the frightening message it contained:

> *Benak foiled plans. Moscow alerted. Advise General Noukov. Will attempt to salvage project in Paris. Meet Parkovitch there.*

He caught O'Malloy's eye and handed the note to him. "Go with Ian—and get this to Carwell in Paris."

"Is it important?"

"It may have cost Ian his life. Awhile ago Chase told me she thought she saw Jiri Benak in the crowd, and I brushed it off."

As the helicopter lowered, Drew bent down and touched Ian's limp hand once more. Drew turned and brushed shoulders with

Radburn Parker. As their eyes held, Drew calculated, remembered, condemned—and wondered. Within inches from where Parker stood, Drew saw the fingerless glove caught beneath the rear wheel of the twisted bike, a different-colored glove than the ones Ian wore. It had been torn, ripped from its rider's hand. Drew stowed it in his pocket and dug his way back up the cliff to Chase.

She was still clinging to the overhanging limb. Frozen. Frightened. "I must go with Ian," she said.

Drew pressed her head against his shoulder. "Don't look anymore," he told her gently. "Just remember Ian the way you saw him yesterday. That's the way he'd want you to remember him."

Chapter 22

Only seconds, moments, an eternity for Salvador Contoni. He stood transfixed, detached, riveted to the mountain as though he had been impaled on the slopes of Nordlune by the very nails he had intended to throw across Ian Kendall's path. Confusion! Hysteria! The crowd was breaking up, many surging toward the descending side of the mountain. Their frenzy startled Sal. He was galvanized, electrified. Driven by his own need to escape, he bolted toward the chateau in pursuit of the two strangers—the pasty-skinned man and the one with the golden hand-carved cane.

As he ran, someone cried above the din, "Stop him."

Hands reached out ripping the sleeve of Sal's jacket, tearing at his polo shirt, grabbing at his skipper's cap. He wrestled for his freedom. "You idiots," he said in Italian. "You have the wrong man."

An angry woman tore the press card from his lapel. What did it matter? Salvador Salatori did not exist! A muscled young man jumped him, tugging Sal to the ground. In the brief time since he had dropped the nails, the shouting on the other side of the mountain had turned to piercing cries. Sal was forgotten, the hold on his shoulders loosened.

He ran toward the chateau parking lot, determined to be on the narrow mountain road before someone else attacked him. *Paris. Freedom. Monique.* As he reached in his pocket for the car keys, he saw the stranger—the taller one with the gold-handled cane aimed at him. The man was like marble standing there, his expression cold like the rocks around them.

Salvador ducked down and crawled like a child on his belly, his heart pumping wildly. He tried to reach up with his hand to unlock the car door, but he sensed the man creeping closer.

"Jiri." The call came from the chateau. "Jiri!"

The cane lowered. The steps that had dogged Sal retreated as the man sprinted toward his friend. Salvador lay motionless on the ground. Their car accelerated, wheels screeching as the driver put distance between them. Then came another cry, the same despairing voice by the chateau. "Jiri, don't go without me."

Salvador rolled over, facedown, and used the palms of his hands to push himself cautiously to a standing position. Stark fear gnawed at his gut. He needed a drink, needed something to steady himself before he faced that drive down the mountain. But did he dare follow so closely behind the stranger? The man could be waiting for Salvador on the next hairpin curve, waiting with his finger on the firing mechanism. Sal leaned down and retrieved his skipper's cap and dusted himself off. *The drink.* He would go inside the chateau and calmly order a drink. He cocked his cap on his head and forced himself to assume his usual jaunty stride as he entered the chateau and made his way briskly into the bar.

"Did you hear?" the bartender asked. "They just lifted one of the riders out by helicopter." He pointed to the radio wedged in among the rows of glasses. "Dead, they say."

"Ian Kendall?"

"No name released yet. But there is more than one rider down. Big pileup."

Sal ordered a whiskey and took it straight down. He plunked the glass on the counter and without a word between them, the bartender filled two whiskey glasses, and they drank in silence.

Sal feared that whatever had happened out there would be blamed on him. He shrank back from the icy tentacles clawing at his gut. He felt trapped with nowhere to run, nowhere to hide. He would go back to Milan, home to Mama as he had done as a small boy and find comfort in those strong arms—and he would ask Monique to go with him. But would Monique condemn him for the accident here on the mountain without ever knowing the truth?

He feared the Golemis family as well. They would read the

headlines and see the accident on television with news reporters blowing everything out of proportion. If Golemis had stooped to hiring Sal to stop Kendall from winning the Tour de France, what would prevent Golemis from hiring someone else to eliminate Salvador?

He wanted to phone Monique. "I have to make a phone call," he told the bartender, and his words were calm, decisive.

The bartender went on polishing a glass to a crystal-clear shine. "Phone on the wall," he said, "if that man over there is through with it."

Sal allowed a sweeping glance of the room over the brim of his glass. The man with the pasty skin sat at a corner table, staring down at the wine goblet in his hand. When Sal reached the phone, the receiver was off the hook, the cord dangling.

He snatched it up and heard an angry voice on the other end demanding, "Yuri Ryskov. Yuri Ryskov, are you there?"

An odd accent, Sal thought, *and the crackling, wavering sounds of a poor connection. Not French, definitely not French.* The words were shouted this time, "Yuri Ryskov."

Sal hung the receiver in place, silencing the growing fury of the man on the other end. He walked slowly to the corner table. "Yuri Ryskov?" he asked as he took the seat across from him. He could see that Ryskov was carrying a weapon, a Russian model 9mm, but he was too distraught to aim it. "My name is Salvador Contoni," Sal said. "I believe we can help each other."

Ryskov's eyes looked like sunken holes in his gaunt face; the skin stretched too tightly over the bony cheeks. An empty goblet and a half bottle of wine sat on the table in front of him, but he was not drunk. Ryskov belched without apology, and the stench of garlic and onions blew across the table at Sal.

You are not just frightened, Sal thought, *you are ill.*

"What do you want?" Ryskov asked.

"I saw your friend in the crowd—the one with the gold-handled cane. Perhaps we should have a drink together," Sal suggested.

Ryskov winced, blinked, and filled his glass again. "Shall we drink to bombs?" he asked. "And Red Square bathed in blood? The death of fans and riders won't stop."

The man's accent was Russian. He rambled on. "My friend went off without me. . . . Are you American?"

"No," Sal said. "Italian."

"Benak won't stop. He'll meet the others in Paris."

"Someone wanted you on the phone, Ryskov."

Ryskov's gaze veered away. "Is Professor Ivanski still waiting?" he asked.

Ivanski. Sal tucked the name away. "I severed the connection."

Ryskov tilted his third glass of wine. "Professor Ivanski. Bombs. Death. Paris. Red Square. It won't stop."

If Ryskov was joking, Salvador wasn't laughing. Sal stood. "I'm leaving," he said.

"Take me with you," Ryskov begged. "I need to get to Paris."

So do I, Sal thought. *To Monique's condominium on the River Seine.* But he would stay out of sight for a day or two in Bordeaux. Rest. Wait. Have the car checked. Once the Tour passed through Bordeaux, he would move on. "I'm driving toward Paris in a day or two," he said. "Would that help?"

Yuri Ryskov wiped his mouth and shoved his goblet aside. "I want to go to the American embassy."

So Sal had a defector on his hands. The man was crazy. Beside himself. "To the Avenue Gabriel? Why there?" Sal asked.

A glint of hope lit the dark eyes. "I want to be free," Ryskov told him.

🦂🦂🦂

As the helicopter airlifted Ian Kendall's battered body above the slopes of Nordlune, Radburn Parker made his way back up the sheer cliff behind Gregory. He allowed a safe distance between them, unwilling to face the man head-on. Silently, Parker was counting his losses, chalking up his advantages.

As Parker mounted the stone wall, Maurice Chambord met him. "I think we lost him, Chambord," Parker said.

The Frenchman's mouth twitched. He turned and led the way to his official red car. For three days, Parker had ridden in style with Chambord, sitting beside the tour director and hearing first-hand reports on the race and its riders. He had become the confidant to Chambord, commiserating with him on the terrorist threats and advising Chambord to keep a sharp eye on Gregory.

Now they rode in silence for miles, Chambord drumming his fingers on the window—waiting for the cellular phone to ring.

"Maurice, what happens if—"

"If he dies?" Chambord asked coldly. "I will have to announce it over the 'Radio Tour.'"

"It has happened before," Parker said.

"Does that make it any easier? They were all good men. Francesco Cepeda sixty years ago. And Tom Simpson and Fabio Casartelli. I was there for that one."

"What about Ottavio Bottecchia?" Parker asked.

"His death was different. And there have always been the accidents. Men missing the twists and turns on the road. Some plunging over the cliffs in the mist—one paralyzed for life."

"There was no mist today, Chambord."

"I know. I know."

Parker lapsed into another silence, calculating, recalculating. He was safest in the car with Chambord, the shiny red car like a wall of protection for him. Always before, Parker had used humor to work his way through difficult situations. But this was no time to joke, not with Kendall's life hanging in the balance. But the truth was, Radburn wanted Kendall dead. It would be one less worry when he reached Paris. For now he fretted, wondering whether Yuri Ryskov had sent the signal to Moscow. He kept hoping that the commentator on "Radio Tour" would interrupt the program with the announcement of a successful coup in Moscow—and Professor Ivanski's triumphant entry into Red Square.

At dawn Parker had placed a long distance call to Ivanski's residence. A stranger had answered, not the professor. And not that housekeeper of his. Perhaps just a friend, but it had been a brusque, authoritative voice, saying, "The professor is not in."

Radburn closed his eyes as he pressed his head against the cushioned seat. *Had the professor fled?* he wondered. He must know. Otherwise, he dared not risk flying to Moscow to join him. He still had two tickets for the morning after the race, first class out of Charles de Gaulle. One for himself. One for Benak. But where was the Czechoslovakian at this moment? Other than Ivanski, only three men knew that Radburn was part of the uprising. If Ryskov or the Czechoslovakian or the Serbian rider on the Gainsborough team betrayed him, he would execute them.

Radburn Parker! A good name. A well-established reputation in London. A man acquainted with the royal family and some of the hierarchy in British Intelligence. He would maintain these privileges at all costs, suppressing his own political views if he had to. Yes, if their plan failed, Parkovitch would slip into anonymity, but Radburn Parker could still go back to London and hold his head high. He might even get back in time to see Lennie Applegate arrested and put on trial. And he would most certainly soak up the sympathy extended to him as the financial arm behind the Gainsborough team and its lost rider.

The cellular phone rang. Chambord didn't move. *Answer it, you fool,* Parker thought. *It might be good news.* Yes, the death of Ian Kendall would be good news to Parker.

Chapter 23

Washington, D.C. As Grover Kendall crossed the Maryland line into Washington, his cellular phone rang. He put his coffee cup down and answered it. The hysterical voice on the other end had to be calmed. "Jill, what is it?" he asked sharply.

"We've got to get to Aubrey," she cried. "Before someone else tells him."

"Tells him what, Jill?"

"There's been a horrible accident at the Tour. Oh, Grover, the news commentator said—"

"What, Jill? Tell me."

"Ian is dead."

Grover's car swerved, spilling his coffee over the leather seat. He gripped the wheel, struggling to steady himself. Cradling the phone, he groped for the knob, trying to tune in the news station. Static. Nothing. Music. Everything. Everything but what he wanted.

"Grover, say something."

"You're certain?" he demanded of his stepmother.

"I'm not sure of anything. I pray there's been a mistake. Oh, Grover, your father left for work at dawn. We've got to get to him before he hears it from someone else."

"It won't change his work schedule," Grover said bitterly.

"Don't say that. You know this will break your father's heart. Are you going to help me or aren't you?"

"I'm on my way."

"I'll shower and dress and come, too."

"Drive carefully," he admonished as he roared down the off-ramp and rerouted his vehicle back toward Maryland.

He was sweating, speeding when the news station repeated the story. "Tragedy has struck the Tour de France again. . . . The American cyclist Ian Kendall is believed dead. . . ."

Grover worked out the time difference between the Pyrenees and Maryland. The accident had occurred hours ago. Why hadn't they been notified? Why the delay? Dead. His brother. That kid brother who lived for cycling. *No, Ian,* he cried. *This was to be your big win.*

For the second time in two weeks, he pulled the Jaguar into his dad's construction site. His hands felt frozen to the steering wheel. July, and he felt cold inside, lifeless, sick—the way he did the time he fell into the Delaware River in the middle of winter. Ian had screamed from the riverbank, "Don't die, Grover. Dad will be mad at you."

"Don't die, Ian," he cried. "Dad will be mad at you."

Grover felt dead inside, dead like his brother. He parked by the edge of the yellow ribbon.

"Move on," a worker warned. "This spot ain't for parking."

"Where's Mr. Kendall?"

There was a generalized wave of the man's hand. Grover stepped defiantly from the car and plunged forward—past the piles of lumber, the gravel hills, the rows of iron rods.

He found Aubrey high on the scaffolding, fearlessly balancing on a two-foot plank. The sun had freckled his father's face even more, its blistering rays turning that full mustache to a golden hue. Without benefit of a hard hat, Grover shaded his eyes and called, "Dad, I need to talk to you."

"It's a busy time, son. Call me this evening."

A man sauntered by with a crackling portable radio. He turned toward Grover. "Did you hear the news? The boss's son—"

Grover tore the radio from the worker's hand and snapped it off. "I'll tell him," he said.

"Okay. Okay. Have it your own way."

Grover squinted up at his dad again. Aubrey stood on the edge of the plank, youthful in spite of his forty-six years, one hand in

his jeans pocket, the company name Kendall Construction emblazoned on his polo shirt.

"Dad, it's important," Grover said.

Aubrey saluted him with an empty coffee cup. "Then climb up
here and get it off your chest."

Grover calculated the distance between the scaffolding and the
mounds of gravel on the ground. He couldn't risk his father
falling if he told him now. Behind him a car door slammed, and
Jill's soft voice asked, "Grover, have you told him yet?"

"Not yet."

"Jill. Jill, what are you doing here?" Aubrey stared down at
them, his face beneath his hard hat visibly shaken. "It's Dad, isn't
it?" he asked.

He began working his way down, one hand on the ladder, the
other on his cup. His muscular body moved with the speed of a
bobcat on a reverse run. As his feet hit the ground, he turned and
faced them, his probing eyes an intense blue like Ian's. As he
searched their faces, the coffee cup slipped from his hand and
shattered on the rock pile. His red-freckled face turned ashen.
"Has something happened to Dad?" he asked.

Jill fell into his arms weeping before Grover had time to whisper, "It's not Gramps, Dad. It's Ian."

🥀🥀🥀

Long Island, New York. Ten minutes after Nola Evans fell asleep,
Seymour's snoring awakened her. She came to with a start, her
body in a cold sweat in spite of the summer heat wave that had
hit the east coast. She poked Seymour. For a moment the room
went quiet, terrifying her even more as she thought of the children. Shivering, she slipped out of bed and into her robe and
went into her dressing room to phone.

"Tad, are you all right?" she asked as her son answered.

"Mom, it's midnight. Of course, I'm all right."

"I called earlier this evening."

He laughed. "Checking up on me? I had a heavy date. Nice
blonde. Just got in—haven't even showered yet."

Nola could hear the water running. "Are you alone, Tad?"

"Not lately."

"I think I'll call Adele."

"Talked to that old thing a couple hours ago about a legal matter. She's her old self. Almost bit my head off. So your little flock is just fine. How's Chase?"

"I was hoping she had written to you."

"Chase and me? We don't keep in touch. She's probably cooped up in some library corner. That's not my style."

"No, Tad. She went to the Tour de France." She hesitated. "As a journalist."

"That's a laugh. Didn't think she could get her head out of the books long enough for something practical and fun."

Nola went limp. Would the children never come to terms? Never speak kindly of each other? The sound of running water in Tad's bathroom ceased. She knew that Tad was not alone.

"Good night, son," she said.

"Hey, Mom. Tell the old man I'd like to go sailing this Saturday. Hope he doesn't need the boat."

"Your father is not an old man."

"Sorry, sweetheart."

"Tad, make your own arrangements with your father."

Nola went back to the bedroom and paced, finally stopping by the wall where the portraits of the children hung. She couldn't see their faces in the darkness, but she knew they had been happy, spoiled children. Seymour had always demanded more of them than they could give. She had never demanded enough. Three spoiled children. Three self-centered adults. What kind of selfish monsters had they reared? Adele haughty and thoughtless, never calling. Tad slipping from one unstable relationship to another with no regrets over a failed marriage. And sweet, caring Chase traipsing around the world chasing after the wind—this time chasing a young cyclist born with the wind against him. Her sigh was so deep it felt like a chest pain. Dear, dear Chase. She would always be special to Nola and worth defending.

The bedside clock glowed in the darkness, its hands moving toward 3:15. Nola felt lightheaded, exhausted from lack of sleep. Pacing back to the window, she stared into the night sky, willing it to streak with dawn. She wanted morning to come and disperse the shadows—wanted the alarm to awaken Seymour. She needed him. She knew that something had happened to Chase.

It was 3:30 when Seymour's own snoring awakened him. "Nola," he said groggily, "what are you doing over there?"

"Praying that you'd wake up so I wouldn't feel so alone."

"I'm here. What's wrong? Is it your hot flashes again?"

"It's Chase. Something has happened to Chase."

He practically fell out of bed trying to reach her. As his arms went around her, she cried, "Oh, Seymour, I've been awake all night just worrying about her. I know she's in trouble."

He pulled back and laughed. "Nola, she's always in trouble."

"That's not true."

He stood there in his rumpled pajamas and bare feet, his uncombed hair making him look boyish. In the youthfulness she saw Chase. The two of them were so much alike, so often at odds.

Amusement replaced his grogginess. "By now she's marching in Piccadilly Circus on behalf of a British labor union. No, that wouldn't be right. This month she's tooting around France." His chest vibrated with his chuckle. "Give her time, Nola dear, and she'll hook a ride with one of those cyclists right into Paris."

He led Nola to the bed and turned on the bedside lamp. "Sit down, honey. I'm going to make us a pot of tea."

"I'm not thirsty."

"I am. I need a drink before I call the American ambassador in Paris. I'm going to tell him you need to get back to sleep."

"You can't get the ambassador out of bed at this hour."

"Why not? We're friends. I met him at the White House on his last trip to Washington. Besides, there's a time difference. Four here. At least mid-morning there. He'll know where the Tour is." He knuckled her chin. "Chase will be all right."

As Nola waited, the room felt suffocating. Still she shivered. Her bloodshot eyes burned from the winds blowing in from the Long Island Sound. She hugged her body trying to calm herself as Seymour came back to the room.

He framed the doorway, suddenly unable to come across the room to her. "I forgot your tea," he said.

For a second she thought her heart had quit beating. Now it raced uncontrollably. "Seymour, what did the ambassador say?"

It didn't look like Seymour standing there. It didn't sound like him when he spoke. "Chase's young man—that cyclist—has just met with a tragic accident. He was killed . . . yesterday . . . today. I don't know exactly with the time change."

Nola gripped her pillow and rocked on the edge of the bed. Chase was all right. Tad. Adele. Her children were alive. But she felt as if one of her own children had just been ripped from her. "Ian?" she cried. "Not Ian Kendall?" When Seymour didn't answer, she said, "Poor Chase. We've got to go to her, Seymour."

"It's not like catching the subway, Nola." His hands ran frantically through his thick gray hair. "I can't get away. We have a deadline on a government contract."

She wanted to slap him. To throw the pillow at him. To disown him. "I hate your job," she said, her voice rising. "It's driven wedges between us before, but never like this. Chase needs us, Seymour Evans. Do you hear me?" She was screaming now. "For once in your life forget that job and think of your family."

"Honey, stop yelling. Think of the neighbors," he warned. "Your daughter is all right."

"Chase may have just had her heart torn out, Seymour. Doesn't that matter to you?"

His hand went unsteadily to the dresser top. "I'm so sorry, Nola, but there's no way to get in touch with Chase. We don't have the racing schedule. We don't know where she's staying. Cities. Villages. Who knows where?"

"The press room," she said, her voice quieting. "There has to be a central place for the journalists."

"I'll have my secretary check."

"No, Seymour. Just this once, do it yourself." She held out her arms. "Chase needs you. . . . I need you."

He came across the room, his hands like ice as he touched her. "I promise you, Nola, I'll turn Europe upside down to locate her." He would, she knew. She felt his tears against her cheek. "Do you think she really cared about him?" he asked.

"I think she loved him, Seymour."

It was time for Seymour to get ready for work, but he kept on holding her. "I'll make reservations for the first flight out to Paris. We will find our daughter, Nola, and comfort her." He smiled grimly. "Or there will be the devil to pay."

On the island of Corfu, Vasille Golemis was overcome with grief. Unconfirmed media reports indicated that the American rider had died in a tragic accident on the mountainside. He knew better. He snapped off the radio. The villa sitting room never seemed darker, even with all the sunlight flooding through the windows. His legs buckled as he made his way around the room, forcing him to clutch the chairs until he reached his desk.

He lifted his face to his son's portrait. Alekos! The thick lips seemed pursed to speak, but Vasille clapped his ears, dreading his son's condemnation. For a moment he wished that the sea behind Alekos would wash the portrait away and take the reproving look in those dark eyes away forever. *Forever*. That's how long his son would be gone. That's how long Ian Kendall would be gone. He reached up and tried to yank the portrait from the wall.

"Don't, Vasille. It would not change things."

His wife's ponderous steps came up behind him. He turned to face her. She looked straight at him as she had always done.

"Molly and Marcella have gone, Vasille," she said.

"Because of me?"

"Molly is going home because her husband needs her."

"I need you, Olympia." He wanted her to smile, to hold him against that massive bosom of hers, to put her chin against his shoulder. She made no effort to come to him.

He had to make her understand. "You were here when I hired Salvador Contoni to stop Kendall from winning."

"And I told you it would dishonor your son's name."

"Olympia, I didn't hire Contoni to kill Ian Kendall."

When she answered, her voice was barely a whisper. "But you chose a man who thought nothing of killing."

"I was wrong." Her gaze never faltered. He weakened under it. Looking around, he said, "I wish Thymous were here."

"He is in France with Zoe."

"I know. They are there against my wishes."

"They wanted to stop Mr. Contoni from harming Alekos's friend . . . but obviously they were too late."

Vasille stared at his wife. "What have I done?" he asked her. "What have I done?"

"You have had your revenge. That should comfort you."

He palmed his hands to his cheeks, the tips of his mustache touching them. "Forgive me, Olymbia. Forgive me."

As she opened her mouth, her crooked front tooth caught at her lip. "You are asking the wrong person for forgiveness." She lifted the shawl from her shoulder and formed a crown around her head, highlighting her sad, empty eyes.

"Where are you going?" he asked.

"To church. To pray."

His legs went wobbly. "Take me with you, Olymbia."

She shrugged indifferently. "Why now, Vasille? You have not entered the church for years."

"Then surely it is time for me to go." His knuckles went white as he pressed his hands against the desk. "Please, Olymbia, take me with you. I cannot bear to be alone."

Now she allowed herself to look up at her son's portrait. Vasille saw her tears brim over and watched helplessly as she dabbed at them with the corner of her shawl. "He was so young," she said. "So alive—like Ian Kendall. But perhaps they are together now. That would be a blessing."

As she turned back to Vasille, the hard glint in her eyes softened. "Come, Vasille. Alekos would never want us to be at odds." She held out her hand, and he took three halting steps toward her to grasp her fingers.

◉◉◉

In Isigny Monique Dupree and her father stared at the television as the unconfirmed media reports echoed through the farmhouse. They kept their eyes fastened on the screen as the scene was repeated over and over. The pileup. The injuries. And the helicopter lifting and carrying the young man's body with it. Her father's face was troubled, creased with wrinkles, suddenly old. He pointed to the screen. "There—there. Look, Monique."

She panicked. Had he seen Salvador among the fans? "Turn it off. Turn it off," she begged.

"That rider beside Kendall—who is he?"

She forced herself to look again. "They all look alike."

"His name, Monique. You have watched this race every day. What is that man's name—the one riding closest to Kendall?"

"Marcus Nash," she whispered. "He was a last-minute replacement on the British team."

"He caused that accident."

"Oh, *pere*," she cried. "I begged Sal not to get involved."

He gripped her arms. "Salvador Contoni? What do you mean?"

She shrank away from her father's grip, cold, numbing fear paralyzing her. Her father shook her, his lined face scornful, his voice harsh as he said, "Speak up. What about Contoni?"

"He—he was hired—hired to stop Kendall—any way he could."

"You knew this?" Her father's face turned purple with rage. "You knew and you didn't stop him?"

"How could I? He has been good to me—good to my sons."

"Oh, Monique, you are such a foolish woman. We thought you had learned your lessons with Harland Smith. But you grow more like him every day. . . . You won't change. You will never change. You are a disgrace to all of us, a failure to your sons."

As he reached for the phone, her fingernails dug into his wrist. "*Pere*, what are you doing?"

"I'm calling that American in Paris. What was his name? The American—the man I tried to frighten off the farm."

Her lip trembled. "Gregory. Drew Gregory."

"He may not be in Paris, Grandpa."

They whirled around. Anzel stood in the door, his boyish face taut, his body wispy-thin, his eyes staring coldly at them.

"Then who do I ask for, Anzel? Someone who can speak French. Someone who will listen to this poor peasant."

"Tell him, *Maman*," Anzel told her, his tone high-pitched. "If you and my friend Sal are in trouble, tell my *grandpere*."

Monique's gaze went back to her father. She was losing Anzel. Losing Salvador. "Mr. Carwell. Troy Carwell." Her father waited, his eyes demanding more. "He's the head of the American CIA in Paris. Their station-chief. The man over Mr. Gregory."

Strands of thin gray hair fell across her father's forehead as he dialed. He shoved blindly at them, his voice crackling as he said, "It is my duty to call. You won't, Monique, but Monsieur Carwell will want a full description of Salvador Contoni."

"Please, Father. Don't. I can't risk being involved. What if something happens to me? Please think of the boys."

He stared across the room and held out his hand to Anzel. "I am thinking of them, Monique."

"Salvador promised me not to come back here. Ever."

"But you will go to him. To Paris. Milan. Greece. Where will it be this time, Monique?"

"It does not matter, *grandpere*," Anzel said as he crossed the room. "Giles and I will be safe here with you."

🏵️🏵️🏵️

In London Lennie Applegate stared in horror at the television screen as Ian Kendall careened wildly toward the stone wall. And then he was airborne, his body and bicycle soaring over the wall and spiraling down out of sight.

The riders kept coming. Three of them racing together. A pack of six behind them. The peloton in the distance. One by one they crashed, a massive pileup of young bodies and cycles. Fifteen at least. For a second even the commentator said nothing. Thousands of fans stood gawking, speechless. Lennie screamed, breaking the stillness of her quiet neighborhood. And then a second later, panic and bedlam erupted on that road in France. Lennie's eyes remained fixed on the television. Motorcycles and bicycles. Team cars and fans. Others were scaling the wall and disappearing out of sight as they scrambled down toward Kendall. The cameraman swung away from the wall and zoomed in on the twisted cycles and on the young faces contorted with pain.

Lennie clasped her mouth, shutting off the scream that tore at her throat. Only moments before the accident, she had seen her nephew pull up, pedaling furiously alongside of Kendall as they crested the steep mountain. She saw the astonishment on Kendall's face turn to shock as Marcus edged him toward the crowd. The cameras were on them as they took the descent at fifty miles an hour. A second later Kendall reached out to ward off Marcus's attack. Kendall's bike began to weave. Just before the impact, he made a dramatic effort to correct his wheel as he veered across the path of the oncoming peloton.

As Lennie's nephew descended the mountain, his wheel locked with the rider ahead of him. Marcus skidded out of control. She watched in alarm as he fell, his leg scraping across the surface of the road. As he crawled out from under his twisted bike and stood, the cameraman caught a close-up of the fury on Marcus's face. He adjusted his helmet, his mood as black as his hair. As he brushed the dust from his hands, she noticed the missing glove and cringed for the pain he must be feeling with gravel embedded in his palm. He exchanged cycles with one of the team mechanics and rode off as others lay bleeding. And then—as Lennie brushed the tears from her eyes—the camera switched from Marcus, swept once more over the pileup behind him, and panned down the mountain to the limp body of Ian Kendall.

Marcus. Why, Marcus? Is winning that important to you that you can ride away and not look back at Ian Kendall? She had been so proud to have her nephew riding on the Gainsborough team, and now the love she had felt for Marcus turned to loathing.

Lennie backed away from the television and called in sick for the third time in her embassy employment. She sounded sick. She felt sick. Nausea welled up from deep inside her. Her temples throbbed. The receptionist said, "But, Miss Applegate, I have you listed as coming in late after a medical appointment."

I changed my mind, Lennie thought, and for the third time in ten days, she said, "I am having trouble with my eye."

"You're alone. Do you want me to call the doctor for you?"

"No."

"Should I give Brianna Wilson a jingle?"

Brianna? No. "I am quite all right. I just need rest. I want to put a cold pack to my eye." *Don't you understand?* she wondered. *My eyelids are swollen from crying. There's been an accident—a horrible accident.*

"I worry about you, Miss Applegate. Ever since the other—"

Lennie still cringed over that humiliating exodus from Mr. Fairway's office strapped to a stretcher. The laser treatment at the hospital had stopped the hemorrhage, but she would have permanent cloudiness in that eye.

"Let me send someone to be with you."

Lennie dropped the receiver in place. As she hung up the phone, she glanced through the crack in the lace curtain and stared out the front window. Mr. Fairway already had a man on duty. The same man was there again this morning. Watching. Observing. Keeping her under surveillance. Should she burn the memo in her briefcase? No, it no longer mattered. Radburn had called her from France and asked her, no, demanded that she take one more memorandum—the one that would clear his name. Not hers.

She considered going out to the country to her parents' home, out where there was no television, but even there she would be followed. Behind her the radio and television blared out the news again, the commentator's grave voice saying, "The helicopter bearing the body of Ian Kendall—"

Dead! He's dead? Someday it would be her name on the lips of the journalists. But not yet. Right now it was Ian Kendall's moment to be remembered. She tried to remember him coming to the embassy to see Mr. Gregory, a handsome young man with sandy red hair. But she couldn't fill in Ian's features. It was as though they had been blotted out when his cycle crashed over the stone barrier in the Pyrenees Mountains.

Chapter 24

In Paris Miriam Gregory and Maggie Carwell spent the afternoon browsing in one of the elegant couture shops just off the Champs Elysees. Collette's Couture Shoppe was scented with Chanel No 5 and mirrored on three sides, giving the room depth. One corner was comfortably arranged with two blue velvet wing chairs, a bound volume of the latest fashions on the table between them.

The instant they walked through the door, the manager rushed up, hands outstretched. Within minutes she was showing them the fall evening dresses in baldacin and crepe de chine and the last of the summer sheaths in the brightest of colors. The racks bulged with the latest fashions, feminine and overpriced. Maggie insisted on trying on everything that caught her fancy. They giggled like schoolgirls, the saleslady standing patiently by, confident that Maggie would not go away empty-handed. Finally she made her selections.

As she waited for her parcel, Maggie tried on another dress and was examining herself in the mirror when the door was thrust open, jarring the usual lilting melody of the chimes. In the mirror they could see Troy Carwell striding briskly toward them.

"Maggie, put that dress back on the rack and go home."

"I have to change first, darling," she said lightly.

Troy did not smile but said sternly, "Change then—and go home and wait for me. I must talk to Miriam alone."

"Drew?" Miriam gasped. "Has something happened to Drew?"

As Maggie darted into the curtained dressing room, Troy

reached out and steadied Miriam. "We have to talk," he said, spiriting her out of the shop.

Outside, she saw the long gray embassy limousine waiting by the curb, a small flag fluttering from the chrome ornament. She stopped. "I won't go another step until you tell me. Is it Drew?"

His face was ashen. "Drew is all right. It's young Kendall. There's been an accident in the Pyrenees."

He propelled her toward the car. She moved, her legs numb as the embassy driver opened the door for her.

"To St. Mercy Hospital," Troy told the driver.

Not to the morgue. Then Ian was still alive. She dared to hope, to pray. She fell against the seat back, her eyes closed as though she could block out what was happening. Troy comforted her with his hand gently over hers. She opened her eyes again and fixed her gaze on the fine red hairs on his hand. "I'm ready," she said. "Tell me."

He squeezed her fingers. "The news media already announced the accident, but within an hour they will report a fatality from that tragedy in the mountains." His grip tightened. "Several were involved. Only Ian careened over the parapet."

"Was it bad?"

"They almost lost Ian twice en route to the hospital. Once there, we arranged for an immediate medi-evac on to Paris."

Her furtive glance went to the tinted bullet-proof window and then back to Troy. "You took a chance moving him," she said.

"The plane was fully equipped, trained staff on board. We feared a spinal injury or, worse, head trauma. We had to get Ian to a place where he'd get the best medical attention available."

She shuddered.

"We had to move him, Miriam. The news media reported that Ian's body was transferred to London."

"They think Ian is—dead?"

She fought her old revulsion of the CIA. The Agency was controlling a dying boy. She pulled her hand from Troy's and pressed her eyes to keep the tears from coming. "Is the news media in on your deception?"

"No. We just want the terrorists to think he's dead—"

His words sank in. "Then it wasn't an accident, Troy?"

"No. Ian's status is very guarded. His grandfather insisted that the family needs you. We had no choice but to involve you."

"And Ian's father and brother?"

"Aubrey and Grover are flying in early in the morning." He crossed his lanky legs, his cap-toed oxfords polished to a shine. "We are keeping the truth from them until they arrive."

"That is cruel, Troy. Aubrey is flying here expecting to take his son's body home? How could you be so cruel?" She glared at him. "What about Nedrick Russelmann? Is he with Uriah?"

"Uriah's stepgrandson? He won't leave Uriah's side."

"He may when Aubrey gets here," she cautioned. "Aubrey and Nedrick never got on well."

Troy reached up and spread strands of gray across his bald spot. Miriam felt overpowered by the scent of his cologne and knew that always in the future when she thought of this day and the tragedy on the mountain, she would remember the smell of Tiffany and hate it.

As the driver switched lanes, Troy said, "Kendall may not make it out of surgery." He touched her hand again. "We can only hope Ian lives long enough to reach the recovery room—long enough for his father to reach his bedside."

"Have you told Drew?"

"Not yet. We saw no need—"

"Of course not," she snapped. "Hold the truth from him, and he'll stay with the race and come up with answers for you."

Troy nodded, his face still ashen. "And now who is being cruel?" he asked. "Not knowing may keep your husband alive."

She quieted, forcing the words, "And the girl? Dear Chase. We have to send for her. She will want to be with Ian."

Troy patted her hand. "Please, Miriam, try to understand. We want Miss Evans to stay with the race. If we allowed her to come here and see Ian, the terrorists might get wind of it."

"What makes you think you can persuade her to stay with the race? Do you expect her to go on as though nothing happened?"

Carwell shifted uneasily. "There's no official engagement." He avoided Miriam's gaze. "And right now there's no reason for the terrorists to think that Kendall and Miss Evans were more than friends. I think she will help us."

He twisted his shoulder against the seat back and faced her.

"Drew and Chase saw the accident. Kendall was in the breakaway group, riding well, wearing his yellow jersey."

Bitter tears stung Miriam's eyes. She wondered if she would ever like the color yellow again. "They saw everything?"

"Yes. We're gathering information from film and video cameras. Photographers and fans began shooting the minute the crash occurred. We want to know who rode beside him."

She wanted to shake him. What did it matter where Ian rode or who rode beside him? "What good will all that do, Troy?"

"Faces in the crowd. We're looking for one face in particular—and anyone else that looks suspicious."

She pressed her fingers to her lips. She would not break down and cry, would not crumble in front of this man. Nor did she want her eyes to be red-rimmed when she faced Uriah.

Troy sounded more confident now. "Some terrorist group will probably take credit, but nothing yet. We do know one thing—they have an accomplice among the riders, someone Ian trusted. Possibly someone on his team."

He hesitated as though weighing his words again. "Ian took a poison pellet at close range. That's what made him lose control."

Troy took a lingering look out the tinted window as they sped through the snarled traffic, weighing his confidences again. "If Drew's theory is right, the terrorist who fired that pellet was in that group of fans. We hope the films will help us."

The driver took the exit off the motorway, barely slowing to the speed limit. The wheels squealed. He glanced at them through his rearview mirror, and then, with the car in control, he turned to the right. Three blocks later, they pulled up in front of a flagstone hospital on the edge of Paris.

"Miriam, if you make me a list, Maggie can pack a suitcase for you."

"I'm to stay here—at the hospital?"

"That's what Uriah wants—you here with the family." He smiled wanly. "Apparently you have always been close friends. And, Miriam, we've cordoned off an entire wing for Ian's safety."

He helped her from the car. With his hand to her elbow, they went staunchly up the steps and through the plate glass doors of St. Mercy's Hospital. A uniformed gendarme stood just inside the doors, an indiscernible smile on his lips as they passed him. *You know Troy,* she thought, and felt a measure of comfort that he would not be the only police officer on hand.

No one stopped them. No one questioned them as they walked through the lobby down the main corridor. One or two people nodded briskly at Troy. When they reached an elevator marked emergencies only, he stopped. "Ian won't be out of surgery for an hour or two, but Uriah is waiting in his room."

"Which room?"

He nodded to a nurse who had come up beside them. "She will take you up, Miriam. If you need me, let the gendarme on duty know. He will get in touch with his own commandant, Francois Pellier, or with me. I'll stay in touch with Drew. I promise."

"Will you tell him the truth?"

"As soon as I dare."

"Please, don't let anything happen to Drew or Chase."

She knew he could not promise safety for them any more than he had been able to provide safety for Ian. She ached for Chase. Chase's pain must be unbearable. Young love. First love. Miriam had guessed all along that Chase cared deeply about Ian. But no one should have to think that the man she loved was dead—not for a minute, not even for the CIA. Yet knowing her own fickle heart, Miriam knew that Chase would leave the Tour and fly to Ian's bedside—alerting the terrorist that he was alive. Right now Chase was in a key position to help Drew and to help Ian's team, but at what price?

She turned her anger on Troy. "If Ian doesn't make it, Troy Carwell, I will never forgive myself for not calling Chase."

"We will all bear your guilt," he said.

Seeing the pain in Troy's face, she sought safer ground. "What will you tell Maggie when I don't return to the house?"

"Absolutely nothing. She will have heard the news reports."

"Then she will clamor for details."

"Which I won't be able to give. She will sulk, but Maggie knows better than to question me." He sighed wearily. "We will take our meals at separate tables tonight—me in the dining room and Maggie in the kitchen with our house girl, Maggie chatting aimlessly about the latest fashions."

"And in the morning, will you be speaking again?" Miriam asked softly.

He smiled. "Our truce will come long before that. We need each other, and that will bring us together."

She watched him go, so striking in his familiar rich brown suit—a kind, practical man, not unmindful of the woman he loved. He did not look back. Miriam smiled faintly up at the nurse. "I'm ready," she said.

They stepped into the lift and pressed the button for the fourth floor. As the door opened, she saw Uriah Kendall and Nedrick standing behind him, both of them exhausted and uncertain. Uriah called out, "Oh, Miriam. Thank God you have come."

They ran to each other, arms outstretched, their tears unchecked.

❦❦❦

At the American embassy that night, Brad O'Malloy sat slouched in the chair across from Carwell's desk. He was wearing his tight stone-washed denims and threadbare gray sweater in spite of Carwell's rules that called for a strict dress code. It was after hours, the sun long set, and O'Malloy was more interested in going back to his apartment for a good night's sleep.

With his eyes at half-mast, he gambled on speaking first. "Have you notified Gregory that Kendall made it out of surgery?"

"He doesn't know Kendall is alive. Someone might risk another assassination attempt if he thought Ian had survived." Wearily he said, "We have to keep it under wraps."

"Carwell, Gregory saw the wound on Ian's neck. He's smart enough to know what happened. And if you don't—"

"Don't threaten me, O'Malloy."

"Just waving a caution flag. Miriam Gregory didn't sign a loyalty oath to this Agency. Her husband comes first."

Carwell eased back his shirt cuff and glanced at his Gucci watch. "One in the morning! It's too late to call him back. I'll call him later this morning."

"Before the riders leave the start-ramp? I think Mrs. Gregory will give you that long."

"Forget the Gregorys. My job is to interpret the message that Ian Kendall carried. We can't question Kendall yet—he's still unconscious, but as soon as we can—"

O'Malloy shook his head. "You don't trust the kid. I met him, Carwell. Kept his bike in shape. I was with him when he headed for the start-ramp, and I swear he wasn't carrying anything but his grandmother's Bible verse taped inside his helmet."

"Whether he's involved or not," Carwell said stubbornly, "as a result of that message, we know that Jiri Benak may be in the middle of the race somewhere. The terrorist threats are still coming. The latest promises to finish the job in Paris—here in the City of Lights before the riders cross the finish line."

"A threat like that in Paris—how can we stop him?"

"French Intelligence traced him to a Basque village. They arrested a friend of his named Ignasius. We'll get Benak."

"Before he gets to Paris? Poor Kendall. He never had a chance, did he?"

Carwell agreed. "But things are coming together, Brad. Langley is taking the threats seriously and working under the assumption that the man called Parkovitch will be in Paris. They aren't ruling out the possibility of an international crisis."

"So far the threats are being poorly executed."

"Or deliberately thwarted, O'Malloy. The red phone lines between Washington and Moscow have been hot for the last twelve hours. The president in Moscow is denying any knowledge of a plot to disrupt the race. The White House is pushing hard for answers."

"With any results?"

"Orders from the White House were to interrogate Kendall. We told them we can't interrogate a dead man."

"They think he's dead, too? They'll have your head, Troy."

"Langley is handling it. It still took three phone calls before Moscow acknowledged the existence of an Ivar Noukov. He's head of a Russian contingency in Bosnia—a recent replacement for a general killed in a traffic accident in Tusla."

"Another untimely accident? Do you plan to arrest him?"

"The Russian president will have something to say about that, if he's well enough. If necessary, Brad, we'll take old Ivar out with an accident of his own, but only as a last resort."

"And Parkovitch?" O'Malloy asked.

"Outright denials. Nothing more. So far Parkovitch is just a name, but our own agents are at work, trying to get a line on any of Noukov's old cronies. Or on why he was sent to Bosnia."

"Exiled there maybe. You don't have long to find answers, Carwell. If you want the best out of Gregory, tell him the truth."

"Aubrey and Grover Kendall are due at Charles de Gaulle in a few hours. Grover is booked on a flight to Bosnia four hours later."

"The grieving brother. And the wayward general. I have a feeling I'm flying to Bosnia. Right?"

"We booked you on the same plane with Kendall. First class, the seat right beside him."

"Do I shake his hand or ignore him?"

"You decide. Just keep your eye on him. And you'll contact two of our agents there. They'll put you in touch with Noukov."

"So my work is cut out for me? Guess I miss the end of the Tour de France. Shame. I was getting so I liked it. And getting really good at fixing the bikes while the riders were pedaling."

O'Malloy crossed his legs, and the worn sole of his walking shoe irritated Carwell. "Any report back on Nash's fingerprints?"

"A match." With an uncommon smirk, Troy added, "We'll send copies to Bosnia and The Hague but not until the race ends."

"So the Serbian war criminal rides all the way to Paris?"

"All the way."

"What about Gregory?" O'Malloy asked as he stood. "He needs to know about Nash and Ian Kendall."

Troy glanced at his watch again. "I can't wake the man up."

"Gregory won't be sleeping. Wait until later and you'll miss him. He'll be in some out-of-the-way cafe drowning himself in coffee. Ten cups and the sports page, and then he's approachable."

His flippant approach alienated Carwell. Carwell allowed silence to fill the room, and then veering his gaze away from O'Malloy, he patched through a call to Drew. Moments later, his words stormed across the wires. "I don't care what your hotel rules are. This is an emergency. Ring Mr. Gregory's room now."

Chapter 25

Drew lay on top of his bed fully dressed, wondering why he had been unable to reach Miriam. He wanted to pack it all in and go immediately to Paris to be with her. When the phone rang, he grabbed it before Vic awakened. "Drew speaking," he said.

"Carwell here. I have news for you."

Drew bolted to a sitting position. "Is it about Kendall? Have they done the autopsy?"

"That won't be necessary. Ian was shot with a poison pellet, but he's alive—at a private hospital with police protection."

"Alive?" Drew shouted. "But it's been broadcast all over the world that he's dead. His father is flying over to claim his body."

"We had no choice, Drew. The fewer who know the truth, the better. The threats are still coming in, more bizarre than ever."

Alive! Drew felt raw rage, rage that at this moment not even a prayer could mellow. "We've talked twice before, Carwell, and you've known this all along? Why have you kept us in the dark?"

Vic swung his lanky legs over the side of his bed, his eyes wide. Drew held up his hand to silence any questions.

"Drew, Ian is critical. At first we weren't certain he'd make it out of surgery. But that wife of yours is one terrific lady. Miriam is spending every minute with the Kendalls. She's like a rock."

"Then Chase and I are heading for Paris right now."

"No, Gregory, you can't tell Miss Evans. And you and Vic stay with the Gainsborough team. You're there to find a terrorist."

Carwell hesitated. "Washington and Langley are handling the

message that O'Malloy brought out. The search for Jiri Benak has intensified. We have no lead on Parkovitch, but Moscow has a General Noukov stationed in Bosnia."

"Is Nedrick Russelmann at the hospital with Uriah?"

"Uriah depends on that young man. He accepts Russelmann as flesh and blood, but we expect trouble when Aubrey and Grover get here."

"The old sibling rivalry," Drew said.

"Maybe that's why Grover has a reservation to take him right on out to Bosnia. He's traveling with some businessmen."

"Bosnia? Troy, can you keep him there for me? I want him to check on Lennie Applegate's family, especially her nephew."

"If you mean Marcus Nash, we've done that, and he's not Lennie's nephew. That's straight from Glenn Fairway in London. Seems Miss Applegate saw the accident on television and blamed it on her nephew. She says he ran Ian off the road. The sad thing is, he's not really her relative, but she doesn't know that yet."

"Then who's the man riding with the Gainsborough team?"

"A Serbian Intelligence officer wanted for war crimes. Lennie's real nephew was killed in the war. The town records were destroyed, but the men and boys in the village were killed execution style. Nash simply took over his identity."

"So I'm to keep my eye on Nash?"

"All the way to Paris. We want to know every move he makes. In the meantime, O'Malloy is on his way to Bosnia to get a line on General Noukov. He can check on what happened to Applegate's family for you."

"That means O'Malloy is sitting in your office right now. When does he leave?"

"On the same plane with Grover Kendall."

"Will Grover come out unscathed?" Drew asked.

"It depends on whether he's involved politically—"

The line in Paris went dead before Drew could slam the receiver in Carwell's ear.

"What was that all about?" Vic asked

"The biggest medical hoax I've ever been involved in. And Carwell, blast that man, has involved my wife in his deception."

"Miriam? Wow! So Kendall's really alive," Vic said.

"And we can't tell anyone, not even Chase. Carwell's orders.

And we're to stay on and ride to the finish line. But we're to make certain Chase stays with us so the terrorists don't get wind of Ian's condition. Everybody plays dead."

"Where are you going, Drew?"

"To see Chase."

"It's two in the morning."

"She'll be awake. She thinks the man she loves is dead. Not very conducive to counting sheep."

With a faint smile on her chubby face, Basil Millard's wife drew back the door and allowed Drew to enter. She nodded toward the bedroom across the hall. Chase was snapping her luggage shut; the rest of her clothes lay in neat piles on the bed. Basil Millard sat there straddling a straight-back chair, his arms braced on the chair back. Neither of them seemed aware of Drew leaning against the door frame.

"I wish I could say something to help you," Basil said. "My wife and I hate to see you go. We may never see you again."

"My reason for staying is gone."

Millard's face shadowed. "I called Franz in London. He already knew. Heard it on the BBC news."

"Is his lung infection better?" she asked.

"Yes. Said to tell you he was sorry—about the accident. He apologized for abandoning the race—said maybe if he had stayed with the team, that all of us together might have protected Ian."

"That's sweet." Her voice faded. "Franz is not responsible for what happened. None of you were. It was an accident."

Wrong, Drew thought.

Millard licked his upper lip, the tip of his tongue swiping across his thin blond mustache. Without his helmet and goggles, Millard's face looked rounded like his wife's. "The team may be pulling out of the race," he said quietly. "It doesn't seem right to go on without him."

"Oh, Basil, Ian wouldn't want you to do that." She toyed with a blouse, her face turned from him. "You knew Ian so well. Do you think he's with God? If—" Her voice faltered again, and Drew ached for her. "If I knew that for certain, maybe—"

"I'm not much on things like that," Basil admitted. "But I rather imagine if you want to ask God something, you can just talk to Him. Maybe my wife knows."

Chase began throwing her things into another suitcase.

"So you're really leaving?" Drew said from the doorway.

They turned, startled to see him.

"Oh, Drew. I told you I was going. Vic offered to drive me to Paris."

"I need him here. And I want your help, too, Chase. Ian would want you to stay. The race meant everything to him."

She tossed her head, her chestnut hair shimmering in the lamplight. "I thought *I* meant everything to him," she said softly.

"You do—you did." Drew crossed the room and lifted her chin, forcing her to look at him. "Ian would want you to see it through to the end—for him."

"Don't ask me to do that, Drew Gregory. I can't. . . . I won't. I'm going to Paris to find Mr. Kendall."

"Ian's grandfather? The Kendalls are private people. You know that, Chase."

She crumbled visibly. "All right then," she whispered. "I'll talk to your wife, Drew, before I fly on to London."

"Are you going on to New York after that?" he asked.

"I want to say good-bye to Beatrice Thorpe before I leave. . . . I should tell her what happened. . . . Drew, I suppose you're staying on? Everything for the race and Monsieur Chambord."

"The problems are still here, Chase. They didn't go away." He waited until she faced him again. "I've been on the line with Paris," he told her. "Talking to Carwell. They tried to bring Ian back on the flight in." It sounded so hopeless, but it was all he could offer. Part of the truth.

The floodgates opened again. A fresh flow of tears washed down that already puffy face. "During this whole race terrorists threatened Ian, and then a stupid accident—"

"It was no accident," he told her.

She collapsed on the edge of the bed, her back against the suitcase. "What do you mean, Drew?"

"Ian was injured before his cycle went out of control." He watched Basil from the corner of his eye and saw his scowl deepen. "He was injured with a pellet gun, Basil."

Drew didn't say a poison pellet. He spared them that, but he couldn't throw off the sight of that puncture wound in Ian's neck. "Ian was stunned before he went over that wall."

Millard's fingers dug into the chair back. "That's impossible, Gregory, at the speed we ride those bikes. People tried to stop the riders in the old days with nails and tacks when the Tour first started but not in our modern-day races. We don't try to put each other out of the competition."

"Someone did."

Drew glanced at Chase, not wanting to add to her pain. "Ian had a wound on his neck—" Drew hated the tremor in his own voice. He could not allow his personal involvement with Ian and his family to color the job that lay before him. "There was the wound," he repeated, "and a scrap of paper that tumbled from Ian's helmet during the accident."

"Another terrorist threat?" Millard asked.

"We think this message was given to Ian by mistake. I sent it to Paris with Brad O'Malloy."

"The Gainsborough mechanic? Don't tell me he's another intelligence officer." Millard knocked the chair over as he stood, and in his anger he left it toppled. "Ian carrying a code of some sort? I don't like what you're suggesting, Drew."

"And I didn't like Troy Carwell's report when I talked to him on the phone. Ian was definitely shot with a pellet gun. Metal fragments penetrated just beneath his skin."

"No," Basil cried. "That means ricin poison in his bloodstream. Then he was dead before he ever went over that cliff." He shook his head, his voice shaking with anger. "Isn't that how they took down a BBC broadcaster some years back?"

"The Bulgarian exile? Yes, the same scenario. But he was jabbed by a sharp point carried in the ferrule of an umbrella."

Millard's gaze turned cynical. "Drew, we just carry bottles of water on our bikes. There's no place to conceal a weapon. The pellet had to be fired by someone in the crowd."

Uneasiness crept over Drew. He had fixed his suspicions on Marcus Nash, convinced of the link between Lennie and her "nephew." Nash had ridden Ian's back wheel just before the crash. But the video films that Drew and Vic had played over and over pointed to another unwanted possibility. A pack of six men

had been riding together, Ian's friend Orlando Gioceppi riding
among them.

Now, facing Millard and that round cherub innocence and the
guileless blue eyes, Drew's questions ran wild. Basil Millard had
gone to the top of Mt. Ventoux with Ian—and Millard knew too
much about poisoned pellets. Had the whole Gainsborough team
conspired against Ian? Franz was the only member of the team
who had dropped from the race, his body racked by a lung infection—yet abandoning sooner than they had expected. Had Franz
disagreed with the plans to stop Ian?

Drew forced his attention back to Chase and Millard, but the
doubts kept coming. Jiri Benak and Coach Skobla had known each
other in Czechoslovakia. Were they in this together? Or was the accident only one step in a plot that went beyond the Tour to Moscow
and to General Noukov and Parkovitch, whoever they were?

"Millard," he said, and his voice turned gruff and unkind, "do
you know someone by the name of Parkovitch?"

"No."

"Or General Noukov?"

Millard's tone sharpened. "I don't know any generals. Is this
some kind of joke, Gregory?"

"I don't think the note in Ian's helmet was intended as a joke.
It named names. Suggested problems all the way to Paris."

All color drained from Chase's face. "Ian never had a chance.
The terrorists won."

"No," Drew said. "The terrorists only win if we all quit the race."

Drew gathered Chase against his chest much as he would have
done with Robyn if she had been there. He let Chase cry, wondering why he himself had not shed a tear. The stoic Drew Gregory
holding his own, sloughing off emotion, being the invincible one.

"What do you want from us, Gregory?" Millard asked. "Alekos
Golemis and now Ian—and still you want us to ride? Didn't you
hear the news reports? The whole world believes it was a fatal
accident. Accident, Gregory. How can you ask us to finish the race
as though nothing happened?"

"Fold it in now, and we will never know the truth." He had to
keep the team in the race. Carwell's orders. And by some miracle,
he still had to convince Chase to unpack her suitcases and ride
with the Tour to the finish line—all because something bigger was

about to happen, quite possibly with a terrorist riding on the Gainsborough team.

Chase's convulsive sobs were quieting now. Still he held her as though he himself might find comfort in hugging Ian's girl. He took his handkerchief from his pocket and wiped the tears from her cheeks. "Blow," he said.

He almost smiled. She sounded like a baritone horn blown through dry lips.

"Chase, I know you want to leave. I understand. But we'd be in Paris in just a few days. By then the investigation will be over. Carwell will have answers for us."

"I can't—"

"Would you do it for me? Would you just trust me and stay?"

"Drew," Basil said, "I may have seen the man who gave that note to Ian—right after we signed in this morning."

Chase caught her breath. "Not Salatori?"

"No, it wasn't the journalist."

Benak then, Drew thought. "Fortyish. Medium build. Blond. Beige raincoat. Perhaps even smoking a cigar."

"Late thirties or forties, all right. But this man was not a particularly strong-looking man." He held up his hands. "I don't think Ian knew him. When they told us to line up, Ian tucked the note under his headgear."

"What happened to the man?"

"I don't know. I didn't pay that much attention. Orlando was there. He might remember more."

Basil's wife stood in the door now, their crying baby in her arms. In four long strides Millard was at her side, wrapping his arm around them. Above the top of his wife's head, he met Drew's gaze. "The man spoke in broken English—an accent of some sort. He warned Ian to be careful."

"Did Ian seem alarmed? Frightened?"

"Not afraid. Startled."

As Drew left the room, he said, "Chase, I'll try to reach Miriam tonight and let her know you're coming to Paris."

"Don't bother calling her, Drew. I changed my mind." She began emptying her suitcase. "Without Ian, it doesn't matter where I am. I'm going to stay and help you if I can. Ian would want me to do that."

Chapter 26

Bosnia. Two days later, Leopold Bolav tossed his khaki fatigues and his worn turtleneck sweater on the narrow unmade bed, stowed his gun beneath the pillow, and then dressed with great care. For the first time in months, he wore a white dress shirt and tie and the best of his serge suits, the only one salvaged from the war years. The shirt was frayed at the collar, one button missing, but tucked into his trousers, the missing button did not show. Four years ago, his wife would have used the shirt for a dust rag, but that was the distant past when she and his family and his job were his whole life.

He gave himself a final inspection in a cracked mirror and was startled at the emptiness in his eyes hooded by bushy gray brows and at the sulky protrusion of his thick lip. At forty-seven he had grown old. The war had done that. He could do nothing about the ravages of war any more than he could undo the killings that he had ordered. Now there was little he could do with his face or his bulbous nose, but he brushed his bowl-cut gray-blond hair to the left and slicked it down with water.

His Persian cat had taken possession of his sweater and lay curled in its armpit. He leaned down and scratched her neck, smiling as she purred back. "Your dish is empty," he said, apologizing for the watery milk that she had licked dry. It was time. Past time. He left the small quarters where he and General Noukov were housed and made his way to the town meeting.

Leopold entered the conference room, mingling among the foreigners and engineers and town officials who wanted only to forget the war and build their cities again. No one spoke of the Tour de France. No one seemed to care who raced or who won. Not one man in the room mentioned the rider who had died. Aimlessly Leopold picked up a coffee cup brimming with thick black coffee, the strong aroma filling his nostrils and scalding his throat. He clung to the cup for confidence, and when the others took their places at the table, he joined them.

The count would be accurate. He was there to replace another engineer, a man he had once worked with, a man too sick to make his appearance. Leopold had been part of conferences like this long years ago, sitting with a Muslim neighbor to his right and a Croatian across the table from him. Friends then. Drinking and smoking together and rolling out the blueprints for the 1984 Olympic Winter Games in Sarajevo. They had laughed back then, making jokes about the venues going up on the site of the assassination that had led to World War I. In those days of planning for the Winter Games, the turmoil and chaos was in Beirut—not Bosnia, Yuri Andropov was dead, and Professor Ivanski was unheard of in Russia.

And now they were here again, not to plan luge or bobsled runs or ski lifts, but to speak of foreign investments and foreign corporations controlling some of the rebuilding projects in his own country. He hated them, these strangers with names he didn't even know—unwilling to come four years ago to help stop the killings, but here now to grab at the opportunities to build up their own coffers. But no matter how clever or rich these men were, they could not erase the pockmarks and bullet holes in the conference table or plaster over the memory of the cracked walls, the broken windows, the shattered lives in their war-torn towns.

He folded his big hands on the tabletop to stop the tremor in his left hand and to help force the fury inside of him back down into the pit where it belonged. The town mayor was introducing the foreign guests now, the interpreters coming to the rescue of the Americans when language failed them. Pompous, well-dressed businessmen with their cuff links and silk ties. Portly gentlemen. Pleasant ones. And then his eyes settled on the American lawyer who had accompanied them, the name plucked from memory before the executive officer could say, "Grover Kendall."

"Sir," Kendall said, "it is good to see you again."

Their gaze locked. Kendall was well-groomed, smartly dressed. He wore no wedding band on his finger, just an expensive watch that he kept twisting. His voice was calm, unemotional as he asked, "Your daughter Ozella—how is she?"

As Leopold stared at the young man, memory tunneled back through the war years to five years ago when his daughter had come home with Grover Kendall. Kendall had traveled to Yugoslavia—it was still Yugoslavia then—and had left the country carrying propaganda pamphlets, not because he was political, but because he was smitten with Ozella.

She had been beautiful, convincing, bewitching. "Ozella." There he had said her name aloud. His only child. The room had gone silent as though everyone hung on Leopold's answer. He lifted his chin defiantly. "My daughter is dead," he said. "My whole family is dead."

The young man's expression crumbled. "I'm sorry. Truly sorry. I was hoping to find her on this trip."

And marry her? Leopold wondered. *Or did you plan to smuggle more political pamphlets out of the country?* He saw sympathy in the young man's eyes, as though he had stepped back in time and memory to that bursting joy of youth and first love.

Leopold looked away. *You know who I am,* he thought. *And it will not take you long to realize that I am the Leopold Bolav wanted on the war criminal list. Yet you will not interfere because of my dead daughter—and because you are here to help rebuild my country, to be part of a foreign takeover.*

When you discover where I live, will you knock on my door, or will you betray me? Or will you go back to The Hague and report where I am and who I am? Leopold was weary, too tired to think of fleeing. The seventeenth stage of the Tour de France had come and gone. That was the day when their plans should have come together— when Professor Ivanski was to have his imperial kingdom and the Serbs of Bosnia could go back to the battle line. But was that what he really wanted? Or was this—this chance to rebuild the cities of his country—what goaded him?

Three hours later the meeting ended, and Leopold rose stiffly from his chair. He braced his hands on the pocked surface of the table and risked a final glance at Grover Kendall, framed by the cracked walls of the room. Kendall avoided his gaze, but as

Leopold left the conference hall, he was certain that the footsteps behind him were youthful and determined. Yes, his daughter's first love was following him.

۞ ۞ ۞

Bordeaux. That same evening, Drew found Chase by the side of the road. She sat with her legs drawn to her chest, her face buried against bent knees, a solemn dejected silhouette in the moonlight. Shock was giving way to grief.

"Chase, it's Drew." He slipped up quietly and dropped down beside her. "You shouldn't be out here alone."

She lifted her face, the tears sparkling in the light of the moon. "Nothing happened these last two days of the race. And my hotel room is so crowded. . . . Everyone is so concerned about me. Drew, I can't stand all the questions and sympathy."

"You could have called me."

"At two in the morning?"

"It wouldn't matter. I keep late hours. Besides, I'm always grumpy in the morning. But honestly, Chase, you shouldn't be out here alone. It isn't safe."

"I speak French."

He laughed gently. "You're still in a foreign country." He handed her his handkerchief. "Can I help?"

"If you know how to scream," she said.

"I could give it a try. Are you just wanting the hills to echo back?"

"No, I've been screaming at God."

"Did He holler back?"

"He didn't say anything, Drew. My grandmother Callie was right—He doesn't even exist. In spite of what Ian used to say."

Drew's throat tightened. "What did Ian say?"

"He was quoting his grandmother, I think. He said, 'You can never be alone in the moonlight, not with God looking down on you.'"

"That's why you came out here?"

She opened her mouth to scream.

"Better not," he said. "You'll have the whole town awake. That's why I'm here. I heard that screeching noise—thought it was some wild animal."

Meekly she said, "Just me. Trying to get God's attention."

God had Drew's attention. The moon and stars lighting the vastness of the night, the whole universe cried out to Drew, convincing him once again that Someone had it all together. But how could he convince Chase? He said, "It was like this for me, too, Chase, when I settled things with God in the mountains of Sulzbach. 'Cept I didn't have a brilliant moon like that. But I had a canopy of clouds and the trunk of an evergreen to lean against." He chuckled lightly. "I would have fallen over without that tree for support. . . . I kept trying to swallow my heartbeat and make excuses."

"You were all alone?"

"Yes. I figured it didn't concern anyone else."

"Is that when Ian was in Sulzbach with you?"

"Yes. The day after his friend Alekos died."

"Were you angry at God?"

"Then? No. Just scared without Him. And my son-in-law was smart enough to give me space. In fact he gave me the whole mountain."

"Don't leave me, Drew. I'm scared. I didn't get to say all those things to Ian that I wanted to say. On the rest day when I met Zoe Golemis, she told Ian that he was always like a bird in flight, always wandering. Drew, I'm like that. My father says I'm always chasing the wind."

She held up her hands to the evening breeze. "Dad says I'm never earthbound. I was just beginning to think the wind was blowing with me—that I had found in Ian all I'd ever wanted."

Drew squeezed her hand, icy cold in his. It was the wrong moment to tell her that what she wanted was inner peace. "I think Ian knew that you cared about him," he said.

"But, Drew, he didn't know—Ian didn't know I loved him."

He watched her in the darkness. Saw her tears. Felt her pain. Gently, he asked, "You're sure you loved him? It's not what happened? You're not confusing grief for a friend with love?"

"I think I knew all along. He was different from all my other dates, even in the hills of Gascony. But it was just my pride. My degrees. My selfishness. My infatuation with Luke Breckenridge. I even wondered if Ian were good enough for me."

"He wondered the same."

"Did he tell you that, Drew?"

"A couple of times. I told him if it was meant to be—it would happen."

She rolled her hands over the path, clutching at a stone lying there. "So God didn't mean it to be?"

"I'm not wise in God's purposes, Chase."

She tossed the stone. They watched in silence as it disappeared over the cliff, soundlessly—as Ian had disappeared. "Do you think about where Ian is now?" she asked.

What could he say? He couldn't tell her that Ian was still in a coma, fighting for life. Alive, but barely. When she finally knew, she would hate Drew, hate the Agency, hate all of the lies and betrayal. This fragile moment with her—this moonlight night when she was sitting here doing some real heart-searching would come crashing down on her. Crashing down on him. It would be okay for her to hate him. But to hate God because they had all betrayed her! Drew could not tell her the truth, and Ian had no way of telling her. He was still in a deep sleep from which he might not wake up.

She turned her head to face him. "Well, Drew, do you know where Ian is? Can you promise me he's all right?"

"Chase, I try not to make promises that I can't keep. I don't always have answers—and even when I do, I can't always share them."

"Did Ian tell you about his dream?"

"His dream?"

"On the rest day—the day before—before the accident he told me that he kept dreaming about his grandmother. All in white. Waving to him. Beckoning Ian to come to her."

Drew blinked hard, shutting out the moonlight, trying desperately to escape the moment. What if Ian never awakened from his coma? What if they robbed Chase of the chance to go to his bedside while he was still alive? He agonized inside, shifting slightly.

"Drew, if I thought Ian were with Olivia, it might not hurt as much. Oh, Drew, if only I knew God existed."

"Try Him."

"How?" she whispered.

"No big deal," he said huskily. "That day on the mountain at

Sulzbach, I just told Him who I was—just in case He didn't know. And I told Him what I wanted. I figured God knew what a mess I had made out of my life without giving Him a rerun." He counted stars for a few seconds before saying, "Funny thing, I didn't think much about the blackness of my life—just the void and the emptiness."

As she leaned her head against his shoulder, he said, "I ended up thinking that God saw me for what I would be—could be—not for what I was. Chase, He's got the whole canvas of our life in full vivid color. That's the way He views us."

Another soft chuckle slipped past his lips. For a moment he wondered whether he had turned the confessional back to his own needs. "God saw me as worthwhile, Chase. Had to. He was dumping all of eternity into my lap."

"You don't sound much like a preacher, Drew."

"Deliver me. My son-in-law does a better job at that."

She pushed away and stared up at him in the darkness. "You really believe there's an eternity?"

"Positive." He reached over and cupped his hand over hers. "The way I have it figured out now is that God's Son sits on the right side of the Father kicking in a lot of prayers for us. I keep Him pretty busy."

"Do you think He is praying for me?" Chase asked, marveling.

"Yeah, you too. You can't go wrong on that. I'll leave you, Chase—I'll just go a shouting distance away. Your moonlight protector. But you're not alone. This is a private matter between you and God."

"But I'm mad at Him—if He does exist. Oh, Drew, He didn't have to take Ian."

Drew went cold inside. Truth mocked him. He couldn't tell her that Ian was still alive. Drew squeezed her hand. "Sometimes God asks us to trust Him with pretty big things. Not just our own lives—but with those we love as well."

He felt her shoulders convulse, heard the deep sob well up within her. He stood—tears in his own eyes—and smiled down at her. "You won't even have to scream—unless you're calling me."

Chapter 27

S *tage twenty: The day before Paris.* A morning mist rose from the river, the city veiled by the sweeping ash-gray fog. Drew could have done with seeing the sun this morning. The coffee at the hostel had been bitter, and the pot was empty before he could pour his third cup. The fine drizzle and this thick haze added to his unrelenting headache. A dull pain pressed his temples, and spasms tugged at the back of his neck. He couldn't shake it—hadn't since the tragedy in the Pyrenees.

Two days had gone by without incident, but he didn't trust the terrorists. The morning after Ian's accident, the Gainsborough team had turned up at the start-ramp, seven somber faces showing the stress they were under. Millard had looked crestfallen, his jaw twitching nervously. Nash remained aloof, several feet from the others, a sneer catching the corners of his mouth.

Drew could still hear himself—not Jon Gainsborough or Coach Skobla—but Drew choking on his lie as he stood before the international press, saying, "The Gainsborough team has made the decision to finish the Tour in memory of their teammate."

Basil Millard rode off full throttle with a skill he'd never demonstrated before. Even today Basil was no longer riding support to Ian, but riding to win, doing better than Orlando Gioceppi. For twenty-four hours there had been no warnings, and now one had arrived along with the morning mist—the terrorist promising the riders a big surprise in the City of Lights.

"Call the race off, Chambord," Drew had urged.

With meticulous care, Chambord pocketed the message in his

blazer and walked off. In spite of his indifference and the inclement weather, stage twenty was going well. There had been no unexpected attacks. No daring breakaway by unknowns. No pileups along the ravine. No major injuries. The remaining 133 cyclists rode cautiously with the mist hanging low over them and the heady aroma of grapes surrounding them as they rode through wine country.

Drew was in the Fiat when Orlando Gioceppi pulled to the side of the road and waited for the team car to reach him.

"I can't go on," he said when they slowed and stopped.

"A flat?" Skobla called out impatiently.

"No. I'm quitting the race."

"You must not quit."

"I'm sorry, Coach. I'm sick."

Gioceppi looked more troubled than ill, his eyes dark and shadowed. When he caught Drew's eyes on him, his gaze veered ahead to the bike mounted on top Chambord's car; Ian's helmet was strapped to its handlebars and the number 19 boldly attached. The tendon in Orlando's neck throbbed as someone tore the placards from his shirt and bike. He turned back to the way they had come, cycling off and disappearing around the curve into the mist.

For a meeting with Jiri Benak? Drew wondered.

Drew had no one to follow him. He glanced at Raunsted. "Gioceppi is refusing the Broom Wagon. But I don't understand. Why would he abandon now? He could have made it."

Dr. Raunsted nodded. "Delayed depression or exhaustion. No other medical reason. Guess he just didn't want to go on."

For the next six hours Drew's thoughts centered in on the terrorists. He couldn't even recall who took the stage win. Drew did not like Salvador Contoni, but he could not in his wildest imagination continue to link him to the bombing of stage eleven or even to the accident in the Pyrenees. It was not like Contoni to work with a man like Jiri Benak. They worked best alone. Benak was greedy for power, a destructive madman. Contoni was more of a survivalist, bent on his own safety and the lure of the sea.

It was true that Contoni had worked for Monique Dupree's husband—had even sailed the yacht where arms deals had been negotiated—but Drew could not picture Contoni disrupting an international cycling event for mere pleasure. It was not Contoni's style. Yet where was the man? He had not returned to the press room since the bombing—had not even been seen since that horrible moment in Nordlune. It sounded crazy—even to Drew himself—but he saw some good in Contoni. He had come from good roots in Milan, and in his own gruff way he'd been kind to Monique Dupree's sons.

Even as Drew pondered over the threats against the Tour and over the possible surprise attack that awaited them in the City of Lights, Salvador Contoni and Yuri Ryskov were back in the car with the Amsterdam license plate belting down the motorway toward Paris.

For two days Sal had kept his ears tuned to the television, expecting to see his name blasted across the screen by the media. But neither Salvador Salatori or Salvador Contoni made the headlines. With the car serviced and his fears subsiding, he left the hotel in Bordeaux and struck out for Paris. Sal was surprised that the Russian had stayed with him; but he rather liked a man who could speak of nothing more than freedom.

Yuri had slept for the last 100 kilometers, his breathing as raspy as a sick man's. Now as Yuri rallied and shook sleep from his eyes, Sal took note of the car three lengths behind them. They were being followed. On impulse he took the cutoff toward Orly Airport. It was time to dump the Russian. Together, they would be taken. Alone, they each had a chance to escape.

Sal pulled into the terminal parking lot, pocketed the keys, and whipped out a flask of whiskey. He poured two small shots and handed one to Yuri. "To freedom, Yuri. Yours and mine."

Ryskov took it and swallowed. "To freedom. It appears that we have come to the end of our journey together." Wiping his lips, he asked, "Where will you go, Contoni?"

"A night in Paris and then to Italy." He capped the flask and put it back in the glove compartment. They walked inside the terminal and up the steps to the viewing balcony to watch the jets coming and going. The planes were specks in the sky on takeoff, a blur of unchecked speed as they landed.

"Can you find your own way from here, Yuri?"

Yuri nodded. "There is always a plane back to Moscow."

"Paris is fourteen kilometers south. Your call, Ryskov."

On the spur of the moment, Sal took out his father's business card and handed it to Ryskov. "This is an open invitation if you are ever in Italy. The Contoni Vineyards are just outside Milan . . . in case you don't go back to Moscow."

Sal saluted and disappeared toward the stairs.

🜚🜚🜚

Yuri crossed the wide corridor to the massive plate windows at the front of the building. Lifting his mini-binoculars, he watched Contoni move stealthily through the parking lot to the car with the Dutch license plate. No one followed him.

Yuri smiled. *Italy, Mr. Contoni? Or Amsterdam? Or do you have other plans?* Disappointment stole his smile. He would never see Contoni again, a man who had understood his cry for freedom.

He waited. Still the car did not move. Car trouble? No, Salvador was stepping from the vehicle and striding briskly back toward the terminal.

Maybe he is coming back for me, Yuri thought. *He will take me all the way to the Avenue Gabriel.*

"Ryskov," said a harsh voice in Russian.

The binoculars slipped from Yuri's hand and dangled from the strap around his neck. Guardedly, he turned to face a tall, wiry man in his thirties with a half-inch black beard. His almond eyes were cold. "Mr. Parkovitch is waiting in the car for you."

Yuri's death warrant. The crowd had thinned, his escape route already denied. "Why are you at the airport, Ryskov?"

"I am catching a flight to Moscow."

The man's smile turned cunning. "Is Professor Ivanski waiting for you on the other end? You know what happens to traitors in Moscow." He jerked his head toward the stairwell. "We must not keep Parkovitch waiting."

As Yuri looked around, the man said, "Let me warn you, I am armed with a silencer in place. Walk ahead of me."

Yuri's insides felt on fire as the whiskey burned his stomach. He was fourteen kilometers from Paris—fourteen kilometers from the American embassy. He broke into a run, crashing toward the stairs, the man's steps thundering behind him.

As Yuri slid down the railing toward the landing, Salvador looked up and grinned. "Something told me you needed my help."

Sal stepped aside as the Russian sprinted toward them, his gun aimed at Yuri. Sal was still grinning as he tripped the assailant. The man lost his balance and rolled down the cement steps, the back of his head cracking against the bottom.

Yuri tore his binocular strap free and twisted it in his hands. He reached out to wrap it around the man's neck. "No need for that," Contoni warned. "He is out cold. Bleeding. Go. Take a taxi. You will be in Paris before he wakes up."

Yuri glanced around the empty stairwell. They were still alone. "Parkovitch is waiting outside for me."

Sal kicked the inert body. "Parkovitch expects you to appear with this bodyguard." He touched his fingers to his brow in a salute. "To freedom, Yuri," he said, stepping over the man.

۞۞۞

As he neared Paris, Salvador thought about Monique. Without her, life was meaningless. Without his freedom, she would never agree to move to Milan to live with him on his father's estate.

Since Kendall's accident, Salvador had grieved for the young man, grieved even more that Monique would blame him for it. But if Ryskov could be believed, there was more danger ahead, the risk of more deaths on the Champs Elysees. If Sal could send out a warning—if he could convince Monique that he had done so—it would awaken her sympathies and increase his chances with her.

He picked up the cellular phone. It was one of those European models that could cut across the boundary lines, giving him distant access. He toyed with an idea and counted the risks. With his decision clear, he asked the operator to help him. His French was weak. He risked Italian. "*Puo aiutarmi?*"

"You want my help?" the operator repeated. But silence followed except for her persistent, "*Bonjour. Bonjour.*"

"*Parla inglese?*"

"*Oui.* Yes, I speak English."

He enunciated each word. "I must speak to Drew Gregory at the American embassy. This is an emergency. *Per favore.*"

"Monsieur Greeg-or-i. American embassy."

"On Avenue Gabriel."

The phone line crackled and hissed. For a moment, Sal thought it had gone dead, and then a deep voice said, "Gregory is unavailable. This is Troy Carwell. How may I help you?"

Sal said, "I am Salvador Contoni. I want to barter for my freedom."

He relished the boldness of his own words. Carwell's silence slapped at him. He held on, putting his elbow to the horn and weaving through the traffic with one hand. Carwell would try to tap into the line and signal someone to start recording.

Go ahead, Sal thought. *It's a rented phone. Under an assumed name. It will take you precious time to trace the number to Amsterdam. But you don't know I'm in a private vehicle, thanks to the diamond cutter in Amsterdam.* "Carwell, I'm in a hurry."

"So am I," Carwell answered. "I'm a busy man."

"And a smart man. I have information on the Tour de France, on tomorrow's glory ride down the Champs Elysees."

He sensed the man bristling on the other end, but his voice remained calm. "I'm listening, Mr. Contoni."

As much as he hated Drew Gregory, if Gregory guaranteed Sal's freedom, there would be no doubting him. But could he trust Carwell? He had to risk it. "Signor Carwell, I have a reliable informant. I can give you names. The threats against the Tour are not over. One signal from the men in that crowd, and a coup in Moscow will go off as planned. Late, but it will take place."

Renewed interest filled Carwell's voice. He no longer acted as though he had a crackpot on the other end. "I'm listening."

"Don't trace this call," Sal warned. "You'll never find me."

Carwell chortled. "The traffic around you is heavy. But the names, Mr. Contoni. If lives are at risk, give me the names."

"You must remove my name from Interpol's wanted list!"

"I'll leave that up to Gregory."

"Good." He could trust Gregory. "The Russian's name is Boris Ivanski. He has a British contact here in Paris."

"So you are in Paris, Mr. Contoni."

He had blundered. He kept talking. "There's a Serbian point man. The two may connect tomorrow in Paris." Urgently, he filled in the details. What Carwell did with the information was up to the American embassy. "And you will want to contact the covering forces in Bosnia. Advice them to pick up General Ivar Noukov, the ranking Russian military officer in Bosnia."

Sal could hear sirens behind him. Two lanes over. A police vehicle riding the fast lane with its lights flashing.

"You see, Mr. Contoni, we have traced your call."

But the police car sped by him, racing toward Paris, looking undoubtedly for a rented vehicle. "No more tricks, Carwell," he cautioned. "Do you want my information or not?"

"Why should I believe you?" Carwell asked.

"You cannot risk doubting me. There's another Russian agent. Less than an hour ago we drank to freedom." Sal paused. "He sees the American embassy as his only hope for that freedom. If he shows up there—and I think that he might—he will confirm the names and places that I gave you."

He severed the connection and picked up speed. Had he won his right to freedom? His mouth was still dry as he began to whistle. He licked his lips, and the music improved, muffled a bit by the truck riding his bumper.

Sal had gone six kilometers when the phone rang. He smiled as he rolled down the car window, grabbed the phone, and dropped it on the pavement while it was still ringing. In his rearview mirror, he saw it smash on the motorway and disappear beneath a huge truck's grinding wheel.

"That's to my liberation from Interpol," he said aloud, and then he went on his way whistling, his tune quite merry.

👐👐👐

Yuri was breathing rapidly when he tumbled into the back of the taxicab at the Orly Airport. "Paris," he told the driver. "The American embassy."

The Frenchman shrugged. "Avenue Gabriel is a one-way street. I will take you as close as I can," he offered.

Seven kilometers into Paris the driver announced, "We are being followed."

Yuri glanced back. Parkovitch was at the wheel, two car lengths behind them. Yuri turned his gaze back to the meter. Six kilometers away. Five. Three. One. They had reached the Champs Elysees. Yuri took a fistful of francs from his wallet and dropped them over the back of the seat beside the driver. The taxi wheels scraped the curb as the vehicle screeched to a stop.

"Go through the park. The embassy is on the other end."

The driver roared off before Yuri could slam the door.

Sweat formed on Yuri's upper lip. He took off. Glancing back, he saw Parkovitch pull to the curb. Step from the car. Run.

Yuri raced over the walkway that wound through the trees. He shoved past couples walking leisurely through the park. The gun! He must not be found with a weapon on him. He released it from his holster and tossed it. Parkovitch called out behind him, but he kept running toward the Avenue Gabriel, his long legs stretching double time toward freedom.

He reached the narrow one-way street and was midway across when he heard the gunfire erupt. It came from behind him like an explosion in his ears. His neck snapped. The back of his head throbbed. He felt the sudden dampness on his shirt.

He tried desperately to pick up speed, but his feet would not obey his commands. His arms and legs flailed in slow motion. They clawed at nothingness above the pavement, a pavement smeared with blood. The deafening roar of the traffic on the Place de la Concorde merged with his muffled cry for help. Yuri no longer heard Parkovitch behind him. He blinked at the blurred image of French guards rushing toward him with firearms cocked. Screaming, commanding him to stop. The French sounds thundered in Yuri's ears. High-pitched. Indistinguishable. Meaningless.

More gunfire split the air. More blood, his own blood splattered on the curb. He spun and stumbled toward the gendarmes as pain caught every nerve fiber along his spine. For a millisecond, the dullness of the embassy beyond the iron gate turned to the glowing white of the chapel on the Sulzbach mountain. Colonel Trotsky's mountain. As suddenly, it was the mute gray of a distant building again, an American flag flapping above it. Yuri fell forward, facedown, his fingers stretched toward the American embassy, freedom too far away for him to grasp.

🦎🦎🦎

Monique Dupree parked behind the honey-colored stone complex and walked around to the front entrance that overlooked the River Seine. As she put her key in the brass lock, someone pulled the door open. She stepped inside and looked up into Sal's troubled face. "I thought I would find you here," she said, smiling.

"Your father hung up on me when I telephoned."

"I know. That's why I came to Paris."

"Go away with me, Monique."

"Not without my boys—"

"We can take them with us. I will be good to them."

She went to him and allowed him to hold her, her thoughts on the sea that would lure him away from her. As Sal held her, she thought about Anzel refusing to go with her—of her father saying that she would always make the wrong choices.

"I can't go, Sal," she whispered.

"Is that why you came here—to send me away? We can go to my parents' home in the vineyards near Milan. We will be safe there, Monique. My mama is fond of you; she would be fond of the boys."

Her palm covered the stubble of beard on his well-chiseled chin. "We would be bad for each other," she said softly.

"I would be good to you, Monique. I love you."

He nuzzled the top of her head. She wanted to believe him—wanted to run away with him. "You must go, Sal. My father will guess that I came here. He will notify the Surete. He knows about Ian Kendall—knows that you . . ."

He clasped her shoulders, his eyes piercing. "But I didn't hurt Kendall."

"You killed him," she said quietly.

"No, no. Someone else did it."

"You were there in the crowd. I saw you on the television."

"Thousands of people lined the race. How could you see me?"

"I would know your face anywhere. I see it all the time. In my dreams. When I'm alone or reading to Giles just before he falls asleep. And I see your face when Anzel glares at me."

"So you cannot get me out of your blood. Go away with me."

"Sal, don't force me to choose between you and my sons."

"You know I have always loved you—even when your husband

Harland was alive." He pulled her against him, his muscles tensing. Despair filled his voice. "And now you are a widow. But Anzel has you, and I do not. Why must it be this way between us?"

"Go, please."

Slowly, he released her and stepped back, his eyes hardening. Then he turned and snatched up his car keys.

"Drive carefully, Salvador."

"I am always careful."

"Where will you go? So many of the streets are already blocked off for tomorrow's race."

"I will find a way out and drive straight through to Milan."

"But it's not your car."

"There's no time to think about that. My father will reimburse the man in Amsterdam—"

"Take my car instead," she offered.

"And leave you stranded? No."

For a moment their eyes held. *Go,* she thought. *Before I change my mind.*

The weather-lines around his mouth deepened, his gray eyes wistful. "If you change your mind, Monique, I will be in Milan."

No, she thought. *The sea will lure you back.* She wanted to say, *I tried to love you. I wanted to love you.* But the words did not, would not come.

Without speaking again, he strode across the room, stepped outside, and slammed the door behind him. She stood motionless, yearning to run after him. No man had ever excited her as he had. Her knees buckled. She slid to the floor with tears running down her cheeks. "Salvador. Salvador."

For an hour she sat collapsed on the floor, rocking back and forth, her face puffy from the tear-wash. Salvador would stay a few steps ahead of the law, but not forever. She would never know when they found him, so he would always be alive to her. She would think of him standing tall and handsome with droplets from the Mediterranean Sea kissing his suntanned face, his skipper's cap pushed back revealing those marvelous cool gray eyes. *Just keep that memory of Sal in your heart,* she told herself. *Remember him at the helm of his ship, his wild and windblown spirit free as he sails over the chicory waters.* She still tasted the sweetness of his lips against hers. And yet he would never be hers. He would always belong to the sea.

Thirty more minutes ticked away. Still she sat hunched over the hardwood floor. As if awaking from a dream, she gradually became aware of her surroundings—her uncluttered apartment tastefully decorated with its seventeenth-century antiquity. She had chosen each piece of furniture with care and always with Harland's approval. Now it seemed so unimportant, so meaningless. Even the private garden off the bedroom that she had shared with her husband—that she had even dared share with Salvador—had filled with weeds and wilted flowers. All through her marriage to Harland, she had been at home working the soil, delighting in her garden. Now it was overgrown with thorns and deadwood like her life, a life cluttered with poor choices.

Outside, she heard the distant chimes of the cathedral, like a clarion call to her soul. She possessed everything, more houses and lands than she needed. But in the restless chamber of her heart, she possessed nothing. Her father—a poor peasant farmer at best—had refused the tainted wealth she offered him, choosing instead the simple honest way of life that she had known as a child. Back then, she had been barefoot and free, a rosary her only true possession. Then Harland walked into her life offering an eighteen-year-old the glitter of Paris.

Her parents had fought her leaving home. Even now they had everything Monique wanted—the old stone farmhouse where she had grown up, the land that they had plowed year after year. And they had what Monique wanted most—peace and the affection of her own sons. The pealing of bells in the cathedral tower stilled, but the ringing in Monique's ear persisted. She cupped her ears and tried to stop the noise before she realized that it was the telephone.

She crawled across the room on her numb legs and grabbed it. "Salvador?" she whispered.

"No, Monique. This is Thymous."

Thymous Golemis. She brushed her straggly hair back from her tear-stained face. "Thymous, where are you?"

"My sister Zoe and I are in Paris until after the race."

He doesn't know, she thought. *He doesn't know that Ian Kendall is dead.* "Thymous, Kendall isn't—"

"I know. I was there when it happened. And I cannot face my father unless I know the truth about Kendall's accident."

"He's dead, Thymous."

"Is he? I will know more after my appointment with the Surete this afternoon. I'm meeting with Officer Pellier."

"Will you tell him that your father hired Salvador?"

"If I have to. My sister and I promised our brother that we would be here for him." Thymous paused. "After Ian Kendall's accident—we felt compelled to stay on for Alekos and Ian both. Once they were good friends, you know."

Monique eased into a chair, her heart pounding unevenly. "Are you all right, Thymous?"

"I would be if I could see you."

"You wouldn't want to—not if you could see the way I look now." *Limp from crying. Puffy cheeks. Swollen eyelids. My skin blotched.* "Thymous, go back to Corfu with your sister. Be with your family. You need one another."

"I can't forget you, Monique. Come with me. I want you and your sons to visit the villa. I want my family to know you better." *They wouldn't like me. I've made such a mess of my life.*

"Monique, come for a week or ten days or a month. My mother says it takes a month to dig deep roots. The rest would do you good. You can relax and sunbathe. I will take the boys swimming and boating and show them how we work the olive orchards."

"You don't even know my sons."

"I want to know them. I want to know everything about you, Monique."

"But your parents—"

"It would do them good to have children around." His voice wavered. "They need someone to help fill the void that Alekos left behind."

She felt his pain across the telephone connection and gave him a moment to recover.

"Monique," he said, his voice still unsteady, "you will bring gladness to my mother. She will take you to market on Saturdays and to church on Sundays. Father Papanikos considers her one of the faithful."

"And would your father welcome me? I don't think he liked me very much on my first visit."

"Give him time. . . . Will you come? Come for a month, Monique. Come forever."

"Thymous, would you still want me if you knew that Salvador Contoni was just here?"

It took him thirty seconds to answer. "I must confess—I was parked in a taxi across the street. I saw him leave, Monique."

"And you didn't try to stop him?"

"I am not Contoni's conscience. When I saw him, I thought there was no chance for me. I went back to my hotel." He managed a weak laugh. "It took me two hours to find the courage to call you. Will you have dinner with me tomorrow evening so we can talk about Corfu?"

"Not tomorrow. Paris will be teeming with people."

"The crowds will thin out by nine. The race will be over. We can have a late meal. Can you be ready by then?"

She twisted the phone cord. Her answer should be no, and yet, unlike Salvador, Thymous had made the right choices in life. The faithful son. Stalwart. Gentle. She couldn't make him any promises, but she wanted to know him better. She remembered her first impressions of him—a handsome Greek with black hair and sad, dark eyes that mirrored his own deep pain. She thought of the cleft in his chin, the strength in the unbroken lines in his face, the respect that he had for his family. She pictured Thymous doing what Harland had rarely done—carrying Giles on his broad shoulders or tossing a ball to Anzel.

"Are you certain you want all three of us to visit your villa? I must tell you—Anzel is a picky eater. Like I am."

"I will tell the cook."

"Giles is afraid of bugs."

"I will teach him not to be afraid."

"He's spoiled."

"So was Alekos, and we loved him."

"I'll ask them. The boys might come for a little while."

"Come for as long as you will stay. Forever, I hope."

I won't live with you, she thought. *I won't do anything else to embarrass my family. And once you know me, you won't want it to be forever.* "I can't make any more wrong choices," she said.

"My mother won't let you. What about dinner tomorrow?"

Monique closed her eyes and pictured Salvador—his white

skipper's cap pushed back, long strands of his sun-bleached hair blowing freely. *Dear Salvador—wild and free.*

"Monique," Thymous said anxiously, "are you still there?"

"Yes, Thymous. And dinner tomorrow sounds wonderful."

Chapter 28

Paris. Across town from the Arc de Triomphe, Jiri Benak continued his relentless drive through the streets of Paris in a stolen florist van filled with carnations, gladioli, baby's breath, and delphiniums. The gas tank moved toward empty. He must fill it again before he rode the Champs Elysees to deliver his floral tribute to the Tour de France.

Another man's white coveralls stretched tightly across his chest, and a cap emblazoned with "Pierre's Flowers" sat jauntily on his head. How eagerly the young florist had agreed to weave two massive floral wreaths together and wire them to their stands with special wire provided by Jiri. Jiri had helped him carry the flowers to the shiny blue van. As the man turned back, smiling, Jiri's gun smashed down on his skull. Quickly, he shoved the florist into the back of the van and took his check from the man's pocket. Then climbing into the truck, he attached a cone-shaped plastic bomb to each wreath, positioning a third one snugly behind the passenger's seat.

With the bombs in place, he drove through the inky blackness of night on toward the dusky gray that came just before dawn. Drawn at last to the quiet street that led to St. Mercy's Hospital, he slowed to a creeping crawl as he reached the somber facility. For a moment he considered dumping the florist off at the emergency room, but right now, it was too risky to enter St. Mercy's.

Racing the dawn, he drove on to an isolated spot a few blocks from the hospital and pulled to the side of the road. He circled round to the back of the van and opened the doors. There among the floral pieces lay the three cone-shaped cylinders filled with explosives. He checked the detonating caps at the end of each cartridge, saw the fine wires extending from them, and felt satisfied at how neatly he had made them part of the iron stands.

As he hauled the man's inert body from among the floral pieces, blood seeped from his head wound. Without remorse, Jiri dragged the florist to the cliff and lowered him over the hillside. He stood there, lighting a cigar and smiling as the man's body rolled down the slope and jammed against the rocks.

The pale pink rays of dawn broke at last, spreading across the horizon—the metal frame of the Eiffel Tower and the domes of Sacre-Coeur still darkened silhouettes. Now faint streamers of coral and melon jabbed the charcoal sky, piercing through the rippled clouds and turning to the glorious golden glow of day. Jiri's big day! He flicked his cigar down the hill toward the injured man, and at the same relaxed pace climbed into the van and drove away. He still had plenty of time to make his delivery.

Troy Carwell and Miriam Gregory rode the emergency elevator from the fourth floor down to the lobby of St. Mercy's. In spite of the dark circles beneath her vivid deep-set eyes, Miriam looked elegant. How she managed her stunning appearance he could not imagine. She had run on catnaps for the last three days. This was day four, and she was still going strong.

"Miriam, I never meant for you to get so exhausted," Troy said. "But Uriah says that Aubrey listens to you—that with you there, he's calmed down quite a bit since arriving in Paris."

She laughed. "Aubrey still wants to sue the U.S. government, the French president, and the directors of the Tour. He may have added others while I showered this morning."

"Will he follow through on his threats?"

"All Aubrey wants is for his son to get better. Besides, his wife won't let him sue anyone. Jill's very good for Aubrey."

Taking Miriam's hand was like gripping an icicle. Troy knew at that moment that much of her outer strength was a facade. She was nearing exhaustion. "Miriam," he said as they reached the lobby, "I can have Drew back here by six or seven this evening.

Just as soon as the race is over, Francois Pellier has promised to send Drew and Chase by police car. Sirens wailing."

"Does Chase know yet?"

"She will soon." He squeezed her icy fingers again. "There's a beauty salon down the block. Why don't you go have a manicure—or whatever you women do?"

"I can't leave Ian that long."

He grinned. "I think the nurses can handle it in your absence."

"So you want me away from the hospital?"

"Yes, for an hour or so."

She glanced at her nails. "All right."

"Good girl. By the time you get back, we'll have Ian moved down to the regular Intensive Care Unit."

"Moved? From the fourth floor?"

"We just—well, we thought it would be easier on Drew and Miss Evans to see him in a normal setting."

"Intensive Care is not a normal setting."

He shrugged, leaned down, and kissed her on the forehead. "Ian's nurses will transfer with him. Everything will be okay."

"Troy, are you expecting more trouble?"

He met her question honestly. "In the last memo from the terrorist—postmarked here in Paris—he promised us one final surprise in the City of Lights." Her grip on his wrist sent a chill down his spine. "Miriam, if anyone on staff leaked out information on Ian's hospitalization, the terrorist could find him. But if something happens, it will be on the fourth floor, not down in Intensive Care. Now go—and get beautiful for Drew."

She started toward the glass-plate entryway. He pulled her back. "We'll use the emergency exit. I have a police escort waiting there for you."

Outside the hospital, his attention was drawn to the unconscious patient being wheeled into the emergency room: skin colorless, scalp bloody, the code paddles balanced on the stretcher beside him. Troy glanced toward the policeman waiting for them. "An accident case?" he asked.

"Some vagrant. Found him dumped down a hillside nearby."

"Is he a candidate for intensive care?" Troy asked sharply.

"Where else? The man's fighting for his life."

Troy turned back to Miriam. "Sorry you had to hear that."

She sent him a trace of a smile. "After my last fours days here at St. Mercy's, nothing shocks me."

"Then I'll leave you in this officer's care. Any message for Drew? He's meeting me at the embassy in another thirty minutes."

"Oh, Troy, give him a big hug for me."

Carwell chuckled. "I won't go that far, but I'll tell him you sent your love."

In the heart of Paris the Champs Elysees was being cleared of all unofficial traffic. Steel barriers marked the dividing line between riders and fans. French flags and banners snapped above the Arc de Triomphe. A three-tiered platform stood to the left of the monument with an empty bandstand in close proximity. The twelve main arteries that fed into the Place Charles de Gaulle were secured with police cars. Robot bomb disposal units lay on either side of the Arc—one near the Avenue Kleber, the other looking like the British Marauder on the Avenue de Wagram. McDonald's restaurant was doing a booming business with the first of the half-million spectators already lined up on the tree-lined boulevard. A half-million people—and only a few aware that a contact between enemy agents was about to take place.

Francois Pellier's blue-uniformed gendarmes were ready and alert for whatever might happen—stoic young officers determined to keep the crowd back, to keep them safe. Motorcycle police roared up and down the avenue, clearing the remaining truculent drivers out of the area on threat of arrest. Pellier scowled as a florist vehicle drove up the Avenue Victor Hugo and parked near one of the bomb units. Armed police ran toward the driver as he stepped down. But he waved amiably as he opened the back of the van.

Pellier grabbed the walkie-talkie from his belt and flipped it on. "Get that truck out of here," he yelled.

"Looks clean," came the answer. "Proper I.D.—just a last-minute delivery. . . . Two floral wreaths ordered by the tour director the driver tells me. . . . Yes, Maurice Chambord."

"Then get them delivered and get that truck out of here."

Still he felt uneasy as two of the gendarmes helped lift the flowers from the truck. They balanced one of the wreaths between them and carried it to the Tomb of the Unknown Soldier sheltered beneath the Arc. The driver bore the second massive wreath in his own hands. At the Arc the driver paused, still pleasant as he thanked the officers. He knelt to adjust the wreath, but they waved him away. He hesitated, still touching the flowers, and then Pellier watched him whip off his cap, his hair snow-blond in the sun. For an instant, the man stood reverently before the eternal flame as the honor guard marched rigidly past him.

"Get him out of there," Pellier mumbled to himself.

The driver picked up the second wreath again and went alone to the platform and secured the flowers against the podium. The man's fingers moved deftly, Pellier noted. *Adjusting the arrangement perhaps,* he thought.

Within seconds the commandant paced in front of the podium, admiring the flowers, giving his orders, thumping the palm of his gloved hand with his walking stick. Now he noted with pleasure that the flowers were the brilliant colors of the French flag! Red carnations, white gladioli, and deep blue delphiniums! As he touched a carnation with his stick, the wires that held them gleamed. Uneasiness swept over him. Pellier wanted the race to be over with, not hours from ending. He just wanted to hear the national anthems of the winners—he didn't care who won—and be free to disperse the crowd. The terrorists had threatened a surprise for Paris, and no matter how he had protested, the race had not been canceled. His mustache twitched in agitation. He strode to the police van. "Where is Monsieur Gregory?" he demanded. "And where are the cyclists?"

"On the outskirts of Paris, sir. The man in the yellow jersey is leading a pack of 127 riders."

"Are they all right?"

"So far, sir. Just had a report that a train filled with Dutch passengers is racing them into Paris. Half of Holland should be here."

Pellier sighed. So in this first leg of their ceremonial ride into the city, the outcome was already decided; the Dutchman had held on to his overall points. The tense competition of the last three weeks had given way to celebration for at least 127 of them. They had made it all the way, and Pellier wanted nothing more than to have them beat the terrorists to the finish line. These riders were still his responsibility.

He groaned and paced again.

❂❂❂

Five hours earlier and forty miles from Moscow, Professor Ivanski watched the television coverage in his library, his mind distracted by the silent phone and the haunting face of his wife staring down at him from the picture on the mantel. Dead, and yet her image pricked at his conscience, filling him with doubts, condemning his dream to take Russia back into imperialism. *You would have opposed me,* he thought. *You whom I loved and wanted to reign by my side. You would have disapproved.*

Outside a commotion shattered the quiet. He flicked the curtain back an inch and peered out. Unmarked vehicles roared across the lawn, stopping yards from the farmhouse. Men tumbled from the vehicles in riot gear. Behind them other *Militsia* stood guard—sharp-looking young men in their blue and gray uniforms.

Ivanski shouted for his housekeeper. She appeared at once, her dish-reddened hands fingering her apron pockets.

"What's going on?" he demanded.

Before she could answer, the police charged through the front entry. "You didn't lock the door," he shouted.

A smile twisted her lips. "General Noukov's orders."

You and General Noukov! He gave a defeated shudder, and then he closed the file of the Phoenix-40 and met the gaze of the man standing across the desk from him. He was dressed in a plain dark suit, his face ruthless, his eyes burning like dark coals.

"You will come with us," the man said.

To Moscow? Ivanski wondered. He had planned to drive to Moscow today—in triumph, not in custody. *Or to the notorious Lubyanka prison, the old KGB headquarters? No, the KGB was abolished by Yeltsin. To the Gulag then,* he thought bitterly, *to one of the labor camps in the wastelands of Siberia.* Weariness engulfed him as he rose from his leather chair. The room filled with men. His books were torn from the shelves, his desk drawers dumped upside down. He stared transfixed as his wife's picture swayed on the mantel, her shrewd eyes gazing down at him.

The police did not allow Ivanski the courtesy of reaching for his jacket or changing from his slippers into his shoes. A soldier in riot gear shoved Ivanski's face against the wall.

"What do you want? I am Boris Ivanski. I'm a national hero."

"You are under arrest," the man said as he shackled Ivanski's wrists and thrust him out of the farmhouse and down the steps to the waiting black car.

He had only seconds to glance back at his home. Another dozen young men crashed through the front door. He felt himself slammed against the backseat and trammeled inside the car. He watched in terror as the man in the black suit climbed in beside him. But he spoke out once more. "We must go back to the days of the czar, back to an Imperial Russia," he shouted.

The man flicked a shred of lint off his trousers and gave Ivanski an ingratiating smile. The car lurched forward. The professor closed his eyes. It was over. He had lost everything.

۞ ۞ ۞

At the American embassy, Drew Gregory barged into Troy Carwell's office. "Troy, I'm pressed for time," he said. "I'm meeting Chase and Pellier within the hour. So tell me and tell me fast— Ian, how is he?"

Carwell's brows furrowed. "He's alive. Responsive off and on. Don't worry. Gendarmes are all over the hospital."

"And they're also in full force on the Champs Elysees?"

"They are. Bomb squads included with their canine units sniffing out every building on the boulevard, even McDonald's." He tried to coax a smile from Drew, saying, "The canine unit may have wiped out the hamburgers."

"Troy, the second this race is over, I'm going to tell Chase that Ian is alive, and she won't thank us for deceiving her."

"We'll give you a police escort to his bedside. Guaranteed. Now sit down, Gregory. We need to talk."

"I prefer standing."

"Just take a look at this." Troy handed Drew a police photograph. "This man died outside the embassy gates yesterday."

The grotesque features in the police photo were barely discernible. And yet something in the gray face stirred a memory in Drew. "Who was he?" Drew asked.

"Yuri Ryskov. The Russians haven't claimed him yet. But he was shot in the back with a Russian model 9mm. He carried little I.D.—just a postcard of Notre Dame in his pocket and some religious beads. Do Russian Orthodox have rosaries, Drew?"

"Don't ask me."

"He also had a detailed map of the Tour. The Alps marked off. Stage seventeen circled. And five stars on today's stage."

"More trouble?"

"That's how Pellier and I read it. The terrorist promised us a big surprise here in Paris. We also found a scratch pad with your name on it. Misspelled, but clearly your name, Gregory."

Drew stared at the picture again. "Why me?"

"Pellier thinks he was targeting you. I think the poor devil was just trying to defect. If he was, he wouldn't have enjoyed his freedom very long." He handed Drew the preliminary autopsy report. "Not much to go on. Male. Late thirties. Poor dental care. Gastric contents, half-digested breakfast—and carcinoma cells. He would have been dead within a year. He was a sick man."

"Ryskov. Yuri Ryskov. That name sticks in my craw." Drew frowned. "Sulzbach! That's it, Troy. He was part of the Russian team sent there to take Colonel Nicholas Trotsky back to Moscow."

"A friend of Colonel Trotsky?"

"Hardly friends. More like part of an assassin team. If he's one of the men from Sulzbach, he'd have reason to hate me. I know that someone in Ryskov's team murdered Alekos Golemis."

Troy whistled, startling Drew. Carwell was a stickler for good impressions. Whistling was out of character for him. "Ian Kendall's friend Alekos! Could that be our Russian connection?"

"You tell me. Ryskov could have taken Ian or me out without the elaborate plans to disrupt an international cycling race."

"At least we can breathe easier about Professor Ivanski. The Russians picked him up early this morning and took him to Moscow for questioning."

"Not to Siberia?"

"What they do with him is not our problem, Drew."

"Sweep it under Red Square, eh?"

"Whatever," Carwell said. "But they did confiscate Ivanski's records on the Phoenix-40. Dudley Perkins had a good man there, risking his life for good old England. Sacrificed it actually."

"I was foolish enough to think the Phoenix-40 died on the Sulzbach mountain." Drew looked down at the gray mask of death in the photo. "It ties in. This Ryskov was part of the Phoenix-40. One of the old hardliners. So he could have worked with Ivanski."

"The red lines in Washington and Moscow have been ringing off the hook. Chances are with Ivanski out of the running, we've stopped a major crisis." He jabbed his finger under his collar. "A toppled government would be too risky for America and the world."

"They're a formidable foe, Troy."

"Politically and militarily perhaps. They have a capable air force. But come in out of the Cold War, Drew. That's over. Forget the past. I was posted to Russia for a few years. They're a good people. They want peace and friendship, a chance at the good life. But a few men like Ivanski can ruin it for all of them."

"Apparently Ryskov feared another revolution." He glanced at his watch. "Sorry. Time to leave. I promised to meet Pellier."

"Before you go," Troy said, "if Parkovitch is here in Paris—if he exists—he won't know that Ivanski was arrested or that Ryskov is dead. But he may be waiting for someone else."

"That's why I still have my eye on our Serbian rider."

"Marcus Nash rides well," Troy reflected.

"Too well."

Troy walked Drew to the door. "We had a phone call from an old friend of yours. Salvador Contoni offered us some answers in exchange for his freedom—including Ivanski's name."

"He called the embassy?" Drew asked.

"Talked to him myself. Told him his freedom was up to you."

"I don't give freedom to any man."

"Is that a sermon coming? Or do I just accept that as your agreement to keep Contoni on Interpol's list."

"Both," Drew said.

In Bosnia the Americans had been placed on tactical alert. Grover Kendall and a Humvee full of men in military fatigues pulled up in front of Leopold Bolav's small apartment. They clamored out of the jeep, but the apartment stood empty, Leopold and General Noukov both gone. Only a scrawny Persian cat hissed back at them as they broke down the door.

"All right, Kendall," the officer in charge snapped. "You said they would be here. So where are they?"

Grover stared back with sleepless eyes. His clothes looked rumpled after an all-night interrogation. "Mr. Bolav would never allow you to take him," Grover said.

"You warned him?"

"No, Lieutenant, I have no personal interest in Mr. Bolav."

They were back in the Humvee, the motor running. "Where to next?" the lieutenant asked as he pulled his lanky legs into the vehicle.

"There's an old war shelter on the edge of town. Bolav told me he'd go there if he had to and fight it out to the finish."

The lieutenant patted his rifle. "If that's what the man wants, we can accommodate him. It would save us the expense of another trial for a war criminal."

"Bolav lost everything. His daughter. His whole family."

"You can weep for him, Kendall. I won't." The lieutenant turned his attention to a radio communication with his headquarters and asked for backup. That accomplished, he turned and said, "Get out here and go back to your nice, fancy hotel room."

Kendall jumped down and faced the officer. "I thought when you asked me to help you, that you would just arrest him."

For a flash the lieutenant was sympathetic. "I know about Bolav's daughter, Kendall, and I'm sorry." He offered a casual salute. "We will do what it takes. If Bolav and General Noukov choose death over capture, we will battle it out with them."

Another civilian rode in the back of the Humvee in oversized fatigues and white running shoes, hardly military issue. "I'll get out here, too," he said, and with unexpected agility sprinted out of the backseat to stand beside Grover.

"Take care, O'Malloy," the lieutenant said.

"Was just going to tell you the same thing. It's a big one, Lieutenant. Just sorry we can't tell you any more."

"I just take orders, sir. Glad to be of help." He saluted again and with a nod to his driver sped off in the direction of the bombed-out shelter.

"Kendall," Brad O'Malloy said, "I know it's tough trying to separate the father of a friend from the man Leopold Bolav became. Don't blame yourself. War does strange things to men."

Grover brushed angrily at the wrinkles in his suit. "That's right, we can blame the war."

O'Malloy shrugged. "Are you staying on in Bosnia?"

"Our group heads back to the States tomorrow to write up our proposals and throw in our bids. After that we wait to see what happens. But first I'm flying into Paris to be with my family, if they'll still have me."

O'Malloy's brash grin was self-assured. "Funny thing, I'm heading back there myself. Catching a military flight out. Maybe I can get you on board. I'll call you, but pack up and be ready."

O'Malloy took off at a sprint, rounding the corner and disappearing from sight. Seconds later Grover heard the hum of another jeep and knew that someone had been waiting there for O'Malloy. He shoved his hands deep into his pockets and turned in the direction of the hotel. It wasn't fancy or first class, but it was all that was left for tourists in this war-torn city.

Grover walked block after block, down the empty streets, past the silent houses to the corner store where he had first met Ozella Bolav. He paused with a lump in his throat too big to swallow, and then he went on facing the future alone.

Paris at last. The 127 riders rode past the Eiffel Tower and through the streets of Paris, pedaling steadily. As they reached the Place de la Concorde, their competitive spirit emerged again. Sly glances passed between the riders. The eight laps on the Champs Elysees offered that final chance for individual glory. The Dutchman tightened his grip on the handlebars. Marcus Nash sprinted ahead, Basil Millard riding his wheel. Others took up the chase. It was time to steal a final victory before someone else sprinted across the finish line first. Time for Ian's teammates to race with everything in them.

Chapter 29

Drew edged Chase toward the podium where Parker, Chambord, and Pellier were standing. He nodded to the French commandant as they reached him. "Pellier," he said, "this is Chase Evans."

Pellier, an articulate man with a handlebar mustache, lifted Chase's hand to his lips. "We're ready, my dear," he said. "We're just waiting for Monsieur Gregory's signal."

Drew said, "Let the Serbian ride all the way to the finish line—just in case he contacts Parkovitch before the race ends."

"If such a man exists, Gregory," Parker said.

Drew kept his eyes on Pellier. "You'll take him—even if he's the man in the yellow jersey?"

"We will be discreet," the commandant said. He smiled kindly down at Chase. "I'm sorry about your young friend. He rode well."

Drew broke in. "Francois, why is that florist van parked by the bomb unit? I thought—"

Pellier's gaze swept over the crowd. He grabbed his walkie-talkie. "What is that truck doing there again?" he shouted. "Check it out. Bring in the canine units. Patrol the boulevard." He waved his arms. "Get rid of that truck. Where's the driver?"

"Gone, sir."

The first of the cyclists barreled down the Champs Elysees to the cheering of the thousands. Still distraught, Pellier said, "It looks like your Marcus Nash is riding well."

"That's our man," Drew told him.

Pellier scowled at Parker. "One of the Gainsborough team?"

Drew ignored Parker's fury as he replied, "Nash is Yugoslavian by birth. Serbian Intelligence by profession. I'm certain he's our man."

Radburn snapped back, "That's the first I heard of this."

On the second floor of a building not far from the McDonald's restaurant, Jiri Benak watched the riders pedaling over the hot pavement. He adjusted the field glasses strapped around his neck and glanced down for the third time at the attaché case braced between his feet. His beige raincoat lay neatly inside it with the Burmese walking stick folded in two and the firing mechanism and ricin pellets easily retrievable. He felt growing anger. Where were his Russian contacts—Ryskov and the elusive Parkovitch? Had they really betrayed him?

His resentment smoldered as he glanced toward the Arc and the podium where the floral wreaths stood. Gendarmes guarded the bottom of the steps, keeping the excited fans at bay. Standing room on the three-tiered platform was reserved for three young men, strangers to Jiri. Once the Tour winners stepped on the platform, their weight would activate the sensor timing device. Jiri imagined the band conductor lifting his baton and the triumphant notes of the Dutch national anthem filling the air. And then the blast. Death and chaos would follow. Within seconds the wreath beneath the Arc would blow, and fifteen minutes later the van would be sky high—Jiri's final tribute to the race, and his mocking message to the men who betrayed him. If the blast took their lives as well, all the better.

He must leave before the last rider crossed the finish line, five or ten minutes before the winners mounted the podium. Jiri needed that margin of safety, but he regretted that this final surprise would not have his trademark. A blast as destructive as this one should bear a man's signature.

The excitement of the half-million fans on the sidewalks below him peaked. Six laps to go. Marcus Nash was riding well. Jiri shoved the last bite of a McDonald's hamburger into his mouth and washed it down with the chocolate milk shake. He preferred a Czechoslovakian dish, a plate of *veprovy rizek* or even a bowl of *polevka* and a *salat*, but the American fast food, French version, had satisfied his gnawing hunger. He lifted his binoculars. The faces in the crowd sprang toward him, their features brought so closely into focus that he saw the mole on the fat man's cheek and the hair on the upper lip of the woman beside him. Out there in that crowd was the man called Parkovitch, the man who had guaranteed Jiri safe passage to Moscow.

۞۞۞

"Drew," Chase said, "that's Orlando Gioceppi over there."

Orlando. Every nerve fiber in Drew's body tingled. Orlando Gioceppi, not Marcus Nash. "We were wrong then. It wasn't the man posing as Lennie's nephew. Chase, stay right here. I'll be back."

He pushed through the throng and made his way to Ian's teammate. "Orlando," Drew said.

Orlando spun around, surprise in his jet-black eyes. "What are you doing here, Gregory?"

"I was just about to ask you the same thing. When a rider abandons the race, he heads home. What brought you here?"

"I'm waiting for someone."

Drew felt sick. "Waiting to meet Parkovitch?"

"What? I don't know anyone named Parkovitch. Take off, Gregory. You'll ruin everything. You have to get out of here."

"It's over, Orlando."

"For Ian, yes. But Basil and I figured out what happened. We know who caused Ian's accident. We have an account to settle."

"You were riding well. Why did you abandon?"

He smiled ruefully. "I agreed to drop out and come here to keep my eye on Nash and any contacts he made. Basil's overall points were high enough to stay in the race and try for one of the first seven positions. It was the best we could do for Ian."

Orlando's gaze drifted back toward the boulevard. Marcus Nash and Orlando seemed to spot each other at the same time. Nash spun around on his bike, almost causing a pileup as he rode like a salmon going against the stream. Before Drew could stop him, Orlando hooked Nash's bike with the crook of his umbrella and sent the man sprawling. He was on Nash before he could crawl away, throttling him with his bare hands. "This is for Ian," he said, pounding Nash's face again.

Drew pulled them apart. "Let the gendarmes handle this."

As they waited for the police, Drew took the shredded glove from his pocket and thrust it in Nash's face. "I found this by Ian's body. It wasn't his."

Nash focused on the glove with total indifference.

"Do you recognize it, Marcus?" Drew asked. "Because I do. I saw the video films, and you were wearing this glove just before you sent Ian crashing over that cliff."

Two gendarmes stood politely, waiting for Drew's orders, as 126 riders took another lap up the Champs Elysees. Orlando wrenched Nash's arm behind his back. "Gregory asked you a question." He twisted again. "Answer him, Nash."

Nash winced in pain; sweat and blood coated his face. "I warned Ian off my bike. Otherwise, he would have taken us both over the cliff." He held up his free hand, the bruised fingers still swollen. "My glove was threadbare. Kendall ripped it from my hand just before he careened over the stone wall."

As they marched Nash back toward Pellier, the crowd made a path for them, their eyes curious. When they reached the others, Drew saw the cunning smile on Radburn Parker's face fade. At the sight of Marcus Nash, Parker shrank back.

Nash's fury erupted as he glared at Parker. "Parkovitch, you ... you ... This was all your doing, Parkovitch."

Nash! Parker! Drew had no doubt that the Serbian Roadrunner and the British Lily-trotter had just come face to face!

❂❂❂

Five laps to go! Jiri Benak was certain that the Serbian rider strove for a stage win. Now on the fourth lap, he watched in horror as Marcus Nash turned in the opposite direction and rode against the traffic. Seconds later he was wrestled off his bike and dropped to the ground. Without Nash, Jiri would never identify Parkovitch. The McDonald's hamburger knotted in his stomach. Yes, that was Drew Gregory confronting Nash and Orlando Gioceppi securing Nash's hands behind him in a manacle grip.

Leave now while you have a chance, he told himself. *Take your margin of safety.* But he kept his binoculars on the scene below him and watched Gregory manhandle Nash toward the podium.

Lap three. Lap two. Jiri kept his binoculars on Nash's face. And then a uniformed man with a whiskery ruffle on his upper lip stepped forward, smiling. Nash was obviously screaming out in protest, his fury directed at a big man in a tweed jacket.

Parkovitch! It could be no one else. Jiri focused his binoculars on the square, self-assured face and watched the man's arrogance turn to fear. Parkovitch lifted his umbrella in self-defense. As the umbrella was snatched from his hands, he grabbed the young woman standing beside him. Chase Evans! Yes, that was Chase Evans, and Parkovitch had taken her as a human shield.

Jiri did not wait for them to be arrested, handcuffed, marched off to a police wagon—and he dared not wait for the winners to step up to the podium. He grabbed his attaché case and made his way back to the pavement below. The noisy crowd pressed against him as he worked his way along the storefronts, moving rapidly away from the Arc de Triomphe.

۞ ۞ ۞

"Let Chase go, Parker," Drew demanded.

As Parker locked Chase against him and dragged her backward toward the podium, he waved a gun in his free hand.

A Russian model, Drew thought as he inched toward them. *A double-action 9mm. Possibly a Makarov. The kind of gun that killed Yuri Ryskov.*

By the cheers erupting around them, Drew knew the race was over. Maurice Chambord strutted forward, his green blazer splitting at the seam. His mind was so occupied that he was unaware of the gun in Parker's hand. "Parker," he shouted, "stop fooling around. Let Miss Evans go. We must get on with the ceremony."

Chambord waved the three Tour winners toward the platform and nodded to the band conductor. The man lifted his baton.

Drew grabbed Chambord's arm as he reached the platform. "Parker is not fooling, Maurice," Drew cautioned.

Chambord's agitation turned to astonishment. "What—what's going on?"

From the corner of his eye, Drew looked at Basil Millard moving toward the steps. "Don't let those young men on the platform," he cried out.

Chambord gaped. "Why not, Gregory?"

"I don't know why. Just keep them off. Something isn't right." He nudged Pellier as he shot a glance toward the bomb unit. The unmanned florist van was still there. "These flowers—where did they come from?" he asked.

"Monsieur Chambord sent them," Pellier said.

"I never send flowers."

Drew winced at the fear in Chase's eyes. He peered down at the wreath. His mouth went dry as he spotted the fine wires extending up from a cone-shaped cartridge. "There may be a bomb in that wreath," he warned. "We've got to get the people away from the podium."

Pellier shouted more orders. "Bring in more dogs. Move the robots in. That blue van delivered two wreaths—"

The mass of people seemed mesmerized, unwilling to turn and run. They gawked in disbelief as the robot unit rolled in.

Parker swung Chase around. Her skirt brushed across the massive wreath. A sniffing canine rounded the steps, tugging at its leash. As the German shepherd neared the flowers, it sniffed and snarled and then began barking furiously, pawing the ground where Parker was standing.

Parker recoiled. "Get those dogs off of us."

The police officers braced to a standstill. The barking turned to a low growl. There was no color left in Chase's face. Her eyes were dark and hollow; emptiness and fear filled them. The old spunk had gone out of Chase. She no longer struggled. She had given up. As far as she knew, Ian was dead. In Bordeaux she had said she wanted to be with him. "Chase, don't you dare give up," Drew yelled. "Hang in there. Ian is alive. Ian is alive."

❂❂❂

"Ian?" Chase's voice was barely a whisper. "Ian is alive?"

Across the barren space between them, their gaze held. "He's in the hospital," Drew said. "He needs you."

Her tears brimmed over.

Drew inched closer, infuriating Parker. "Let her go, Parker. Take me instead."

Parker's grip tightened around Chase, his fist catching her beneath the chin. She gasped for air. "Stay back," he warned. "All of you. I want transportation out of here, Gregory. Now."

"You won't get very far, Parkovitch."

"But Miss Evans goes with me." His viselike grip hardened. "Don't believe Gregory," Parker whispered. "Kendall is dead."

No, Ian is alive! I feel it, but Drew lied to me. She hated him. She loved him. Some of the gendarmerie stood with guns drawn, powerless to help her. If they used their weapons, Drew was in the line of fire. Drew would die. She would die.

Oh, God, she cried inwardly. *Where are You? You were there on the hillside in Bordeaux. Where are You now?*

With each step Drew risked, Parker's rage mushroomed. He placed his cold revolver against her neck. "Tell them to clear a path for me, Miss Evans. Or you are dead."

She could not utter a word. She looked frantically at Drew. His gaze veered off, came back. He mouthed the words again, "Ian is alive. He needs you."

Ian is alive! Other voices assailed her. *Nola, dear, she is always chasing the wind.* Her father's disapproval. *I love you, Chase. I can't think about anything else.* Ian's voice close, tender as though he were there. *They tried to bring Ian back on the flight in.* That was Drew Gregory lying again.

Parker swung Chase around, trying to keep the dogs at bay. Her skirt snagged on a wire in the floral arrangement He yanked it free, and then his eyes fixed on the wreath.

"A bomb," he said. "It *is* a bomb!"

For an instant his grip loosened as someone in the mesmerized crowd took up the cry. "A bomb. The man has a bomb!"

The word echoed through the crowd. "A bomb! A bomb!"

"I want safe passage to the airport," Parkovitch called. "Or she is dead, Gregory. We're all dead. There's a plastic cylinder in that wreath. Jiri Benak's work. We'll all blow any minute."

"I know. I saw it." Drew glanced around at the people, thick as a stone fortress, unmovable. "Pellier, evacuate everyone," he urged.

Pellier shouted another order. The robot bomb units moved

forward, away from the Tomb of the Unknown Soldier, advancing steadily toward the people.

"A bomb!" someone shouted again.

Numbing fear swept over Chase. Her throat went dry. The robot unit moved toward them looking like a marauder in battleship gray, its iron jaws and hooklike tentacles extended. Chase watched its caterpillar tires make tracks across the lawn, coming in slow motion, coming relentlessly. Her tongue felt too thick and dry to wet her lips. For an instant she thought the iron claws were reaching down for her. But its X-ray eye was aimed at the floral wreath.

The voices assailed her again. *Chase can do anything she sets her mind to do*. Her father's voice coming out of the past. And over and over, Drew's words, *Ian is alive!*

She wanted to go to Ian. She felt the fire come back into her spirit. She dug her long, lanky legs into the ground, and then she kicked backwards wildly. She hit the podium first and then landed a good one on Parker's shin. He groaned. The dogs kept barking.

A bomb! The words rolled like a wave over the people. They tumbled over each other, a frenzied mob blindly rushing toward the Place de la Concorde. As Parker's hold tightened, Chase bit his wrist just above the Zodiac watch, and then she put her narrow heel into his shin again. She kicked him a third time and cried out hoarsely, "That one is for Lennie Applegate, Mr. Parker."

🌀🌀🌀

Sweat ran down Drew's face as the arm of the iron robot swept past Chase and scooped the floral wreath up into its jaws. Now the wreath was lowered gently into the metal container. Sand poured over the flowers. The massive lid lowered and clamped shut. The robot retreated. Slowly. Slowly backing away. Minutes passed. Eternity rushed past for Drew.

He nodded to the cyclist creeping up behind Parker. Millard took a flying leap onto Parker's back. The Makarov 9mm exploded as it went sailing through the air. Drew saw Chase stumble forward and fall facedown. One of the dogs stood guard over her, gently licking her outstretched hand. Drew was there now—without remembering the steps he had taken. "Are you shot?"

"I don't think so. Just scared."

He lifted her up and rocked her. "Chase," he said, "Ian is alive. He was injured severely, but he is alive."

As the gendarme restrained Parker, the robots disappeared behind the Arc de Triomphe, moving their cargo slowly away to a safe area. The commandant smiled. "Chambord, in another hour you can go on with your ceremony."

"But the crowd is gone."

"We'll put out word over the television. They'll come back." Pellier turned from Chambord and tapped Radburn Parker with his stick. "That was foolish, Comrade Parkovitch," he said, "frightening Miss Chase like that."

"The name is Parker," Radburn said stiffly.

"Very good, monsieur. Whatever. But first some questions for you about the Phoenix-40. And you two," he said to Drew and Chase pointing his stick, toward a waiting car, "be off."

As they raced to the waiting police car, Chase cried out, "I don't even know who won."

Drew grinned. "Basil Millard came in third. That's what matters. He did it for Ian."

Jiri Benak crossed over to the back streets and passed by the first three subway stations. But where was the blast? He had heard nothing. The fury of failure rose like bile in his mouth. He had failed, but he would survive. *Just keep going,* he told himself.

As he boarded the Metro, he felt less oppressed. The mission had failed, but for now, he must think only of escaping to the Normandy coast, to Dieppe or Calais. From there he would cross the Channel, riding the Stena Sealink Line or the Hoverspeed. Or perhaps he would catch the Eurostar through the tunnel to England and from there on to the Cotswolds. How he would live, he did not know, but for a while he would hire out like Ignasius as a sheepherder. And then? Well, time enough to think about that later as he sat by his cozy fireplace in the Cotswolds. As far as Jiri

Benak was concerned, he had all the time in the world to think about his future.

❧❧❧

Chase sat in silence as the police car sped toward the hospital. Forty minutes later, she stood in the door of Intensive Care, afraid to go in. In the cubicle by the nurses' station, Ian lay on his back, his long arms limp against the spread, his face a chalky gray, those piercing blue eyes closed. There was no movement, no sound except the steady drumming of his heart monitor and the grind of a machine rotating his knee joint, forward, backward. She tried to see beyond the bottles and machines, tried to shut out the deafening beat of the monitor, to block out the erratic green and red lines on the wall screen above Ian's head.

She gasped as a couple peered around the cubicle curtain, two well-remembered faces. Nola Evans ran toward Chase, Seymour right behind her. Nola opened her arms wide, and Chase tumbled into them. Her father ruffled her hair and cried out gently, "Oh, baby, baby, are you all right? We wanted to come to you, but Mr. Carwell insisted that we wait here in Paris for you."

"I would have come days ago—" Chase took a deep breath and glared up at Drew. "How can I ever forgive you for not telling me that Ian was alive? I should have been here with him."

"No, dear, Mr. Gregory did what he thought was best. There's no time for regrets now," Nola said soothingly. "Ian needs you."

"But I'm afraid—afraid of all those machines."

"It's still Ian. Go on. Go to him." She hugged her daughter again. "We'll have lots of time to talk later."

Her father patted her rump, the way he had done when she was a child and he wanted her to brave the diving board or the ski run for the first time. "Do what your mother says. We'll be here waiting for you," he said, his voice still choked with emotion.

"No, we'll be waiting by that other bedside," Nola told him. "That patient has no one. They don't even know his name. And no one, not even a vagrant should suffer alone." Nola kissed Chase's forehead. "Go on, darling. Go to Ian. And remember, we love you."

Chase ran across the room. She took Ian's hand and tenderly

kissed those bruised, skinned knuckles. His face was swollen, a purplish bruise ran across his cheek; one arm was thickly bandaged. *But he's alive,* she kept thinking. *That's what matters.*

She leaned over the side rail. "Ian," she cried as she kissed the dry, white lips, "it's Chase. I'm here with you now."

A nurse stole into the cubicle on soft soles to check the IV pump that fed into Ian's upper chest. Chase bit her lip. She had to look into Ian's beautiful eyes, had to convince him that life was still worth living.

"He's been asleep like this most of the time, in and out of consciousness." The nurse's long, tapered fingers touched Ian's brow. "He's only said a few words since the accident. . . . Calls out for his grandmother every now and then."

A quiver shook Chase's body. The dream again. Ian's grandmother beckoning for him to come. "Lord," Chase cried, "don't take him from me, not when I've discovered how much he means to me."

"I should have been here with Ian," she told the nurse.

"He hasn't been alone. His family—your family—have been with him the whole time. They made a great fuss, especially his father. And all of them refusing to leave Ian by himself." Her eyes twinkled. "So the doctor wrote an order to cover them being here twenty-four hours a day. We just work around them."

"Did he ever ask for me?" Chase whispered.

Across Ian's hospital bed, their eyes met. "You must be Chase! He's asked for you more than anyone." She smiled across at Chase, a comforting human gesture, and then she was gone.

Alone, Chase brushed the locks of tousled hair from Ian's forehead and ran her fingers gently over the swollen face. She willed him to hear her. "Ian, it's Chase. I love you."

The seconds dragged by with unbearable stillness. And then painfully, with the muscles of his neck taut, Ian's face turned toward her. His eyes blinked open. His wandering gaze focused on her. He struggled to make sounds and then whispered hoarsely, "I thought . . . you . . . would never come."

Chapter 30

August 1, London. The streets narrowed as Drew neared Lennie's address. When he turned onto Ivershire, the homes were crowded together, the shingles cracked and weather-beaten, the lawns nothing but tiny strips between the pavement and the five stone steps. Dowdy white curtains hung at the windows, blocking out the summer breeze. He checked the number in his address book. It was Lennie's place, but where was the garden she had bragged about? One chipped flower pot sat on the top step filled with pink begonias; a twisted vine of string beans dragged across the worm-gnawed tomato plant that grew against the railing.

He hesitated, not wanting to intrude on Lennie's private life. This modest dwelling—not her acts of betrayal—must have been the reason she refused his rides home even on cold winter evenings. He knocked. The door creaked open, and she stared out at him, a 9mm gun gripped in her hand.

"Oh, Mr. Gregory, it's you." She looked frazzled, her eyes darting, the gun still aimed at him. "I was afraid Radburn would come back now that the race is over."

"He won't be able to, Lennie."

She glanced beyond Drew, her eyes wary. "Where is he?"

"Lennie," he said quietly, "quit pointing that thing at me."

She looked down at her hand, surprise registering on her face. She lowered it. "Oh, I'm sorry, Mr. Gregory."

"Please, may I come in?" he asked.

She used the door for a shield as he stepped inside. "Did Mr. Fairway send you?"

"I volunteered to come." He took the gun without any resistance from her. *Another Russian 9mm Makarov,* he noted, *almost too big for her to handle.* She clasped her hands in front of her. Now she looked like the old Lennie in a straight skirt and old-fashioned blouse, her skin as white as flour.

"Mr. Fairway promised that I could talk with you first—to tell you about Parker," Drew said.

"Is he dead?" There was relief in her voice at the prospect.

"No, Lennie. The gendarmes arrested him in Paris at the close of the Tour de France."

"I didn't see that happen, and I was watching the television."

"The cameras were on the riders, Lennie."

"Yes, I suppose you're right." Her words sounded pinched, flat as she said, "The gendarmes, you say? Then they saved me the trouble. I would have shot him with his own gun if he had come back here. Radburn taught me to fire it."

Drew tried to picture this mousy woman at a firing range, missing the target. He followed her into her cracker-box sitting room— drab and colorless except for the potted plants in every corner. From the center of the room, he saw a tiny kitchen in one direction, Lennie's tidy bedroom in the other. The sitting room sofa was faded; a shattered picture frame lay on the worn rug beside it. Lennie's typing table had been drawn close to the desk, a half-filled sheet of paper fed into the typewriter. Several medicine bottles were lined up in a row on the top of the desk, a vase of dying red roses beside them. The Bible that Miriam had given her lay open on the desk. He emptied the chamber, pocketed the bullets, and placed the Makarov beside it.

"Parker should never have given this to you."

Glancing at it, she said, "I was terrified in the beginning, but I'm a good shot now, Mr. Gregory. Radburn always said if I had to, I'd know what to do with it."

He focused on the emptiness in her eyes as she said, "I wanted to go mountain climbing, too. I'll never get to do that now."

"I suppose not," he said. "But it isn't fun climbing alone."

"I have always done things alone—all my life." Before he could sympathize, she rubbed her forehead. "I'm sorry about your Mr. Kendall. I really wanted him to win the race."

He wanted to tell her that Kendall was still alive, but she might take refuge in that and hold back the information they needed. "You didn't ask why Parker was arrested."

A faint twist of her lips allowed that familiar prim and proper smile. "I already know. Did *you* have him arrested?"

"I was there."

"Did Radburn still have the Bosnian file?"

"Not on him." *No,* Drew thought, *we found that in the boot of his car along with the folder on Prague and copies of my own personal records of the Phoenix-40. And two one-way air fares from Paris to Moscow. Did Lennie plan to go all the way to Moscow with him? Or was Marcus Nash to be his traveling companion?*

"Lennie, were you planning on a plane trip?"

Her eyes widened. "Oh, no. I'm terrified of flying."

"That sounds like Miriam. My wife hates flying, too."

Lennie's cold finger touched the back of his hand. "Was my name in your Bosnian report?"

"It is now—a coded reference only. But all along we knew a British family was tied in with a Serbian war criminal."

"Family roots go deep, Mr. Gregory."

"I know, Lennie." It was impossible to hate her.

Miriam had said, "Pray with her. At least offer her hope."

The thought of praying for Lennie left him tongue-tied. He should confront her with a long account of what her deception had cost America. How many Russian agents and Bosnian *assets* would still die because of it? How much had they paid her for working for them? "Don't judge her," Miriam had warned. "If you must go see her, Drew, don't judge her."

He felt weak-kneed. What had he expected to accomplish by coming here? Assume her guilt? Hear her confession? "Lennie, did Porter Deven recruit you?"

"Radburn recruited me, Mr. Gregory." In the tiny kitchen the kettle kept whistling. "Would you like some tea, Mr. Gregory?"

"Only if you're having some."

She shuffled off to the kitchen like an old woman, her bedroom slippers flapping at her nude heels. It was the only time he had ever seen her in anything but dark lace-up shoes. He looked again. Were there blood stains on her slippers?

As she stood at the stove, he took three quick strides to the desk to check the labels on the medicine containers. *Enough sleeping pills for a permanent rest.* He dropped the bottles into his pocket beside the bullets, thinking, *Not this way, Lennie.*

When she came back into the room empty-handed, he led her to the sofa and urged her to sit down. As they sank onto the broken springs, she hunched over like a rag doll, her face as white as the curtains. She was thinner; he was certain of that. Eating poorly. Not sleeping. Already serving her life sentence.

"Lennie, I think you cut your heel."

"I did that yesterday when I stomped on Radburn's picture."

He could see the deep gash now, dried blood caked around it. "You may need stitches."

"Right. I will have it looked after later."

"Lennie, why didn't you tell me you needed money? I could have loaned you some."

The rag doll stiffened. "I never borrow money or take loans, Mr. Gregory. I would have no way to pay them back."

"But your family was ill."

"Just my mother. Radburn helped me find a less expensive nursing residence for my parents out in the country."

"Will they be all right?"

"Not when they find out what I've done."

She wrung her hands, her upper torso rocking back and forth. Drew half expected her to creak like the rocker in the corner.

She saw him eyeing it and said, "I promised Mums that I'd take that old chair to her. And now—"

"I'll make sure she gets it if you give me the address."

She pointed toward the desk—and seemed suddenly aware that something was missing. "My medicine," she cried out.

"I have the pills," Drew said. "It's not the answer."

She lifted her face. "Is that what you thought I would do?"

"I couldn't take a chance, Lennie."

"I never meant to steal the memorandums, Mr. Gregory."

He stared at the faded wallpaper again, dull against the bright gloxinia in the corner. "Lennie, why did you do it?"

"For my family," she said simply. "Mr. Fairway introduced me to Radburn. Radburn flattered me—took me to dinner, bought me flowers. And then he came to my apartment late one night and told me my nephew was on the war criminal list in Bosnia—that he'd be executed if they found him. Radburn guaranteed my nephew's safety if I copied the Bosnia file for him."

"And after that, it was one file or disk after the other?"

"Yes," she whispered. "You can't imagine how frightened I was at hearing all the rumors about the thefts at the embassy—you hear things like that in the powder room—and knowing that I was the one they were talking about."

Her face remained solemn. "He made me so many promises, Mr. Gregory. By then I was in too deep. He told me if I stopped bringing the files, he would break off seeing me and turn me over to Mr. Fairway." Her gaze strayed to the shattered picture of Radburn lying on the floor. "I loved him. When that no longer mattered, he threatened to hurt my parents or ruin your career. I couldn't let that happen. I had to find every file, every disk he wanted. . . . You always told me I could find anything. Better than Sherlock Holmes, you used to tell me."

"I did tell you that, didn't I, Lennie?"

The chalky face turned a cherry red. "I never thought you'd marry Miriam again. I always liked you, Mr. Gregory. I thought . . . when you sent me on that trip to Scotland, I half expected you to be there waiting for me."

Drew's stomach turned, and for a second he thought he might vomit right there on Lennie's threadbare rug. Had this poor woman been in love with him? What had he done to give the wrong impression? A couple of opera tickets. A holiday ticket to Scotland—a nice Christmas bonus. "Lennie, for me it was always Miriam," he said gently.

"I know. It's just—you were so kind to me. Such a gentleman." The cherry coloring touched her cheeks again. "That's why I turned to Radburn while you were on your honeymoon."

You were lonely and vulnerable, he thought miserably. *No wonder you fell for everything Parker said and did.* Drew took Lennie's icy hands in his; it seemed to be what Miriam would expect him to do. The heat from his own hands barely penetrated the chill. "Did he ask you to steal the memos?" he asked.

"Just to copy them." She pulled free, her hands dropping limply to her lap. "But we both had security clearance, so taking the folders from the embassy was my idea." She hesitated. "At least Radburn told me it was my idea. Sometimes with my awful headaches, I can't remember clearly."

"And after that?" he asked.

"I put the files back the next day. 'No harm done that way,' Radburn told me. And then he convinced me to just use the copier machine. It eliminated the risk of returning the files, but it seemed more like stealing—not just borrowing." She rubbed her fingers together. "You're ashamed of me, aren't you, Mr. Gregory?"

"Would it matter?" Drew asked.

"What you thought of me always mattered."

He was certain that she would tear the skin from her fingers if she rubbed them anymore. "I knew he was using me when he accused me of stealing useless reports. He boasted that the others were copying much more sensitive material for him."

Others? Was the whole embassy infiltrated with traitors? "Who are they, Lennie? Tell me. We must know."

"I never knew. Radburn wouldn't tell me."

"Why?" Drew asked wearily. "Why, Lennie? I trusted you."

"Radburn told me I owed him everything for bringing my nephew out of Bosnia alive. So many of my father's family had died during the war. But saving my nephew's life was one of the nicest things Radburn did for me."

One of Parker's charming tricks, like sending you flowers, Drew thought as he noticed the dying roses again. "Lennie, your nephew is dead. The rider on Jon Gainsborough's team was not the real Marcus Nash. He took your nephew's papers and I.D. when your nephew was killed during a Serbian attack on his village."

"That can't be. . . . It all started with my nephew. He was a nice young man. Dark and handsome. Frightening, but so polite."

And so deceptive, Drew thought.

"Marcus had all the right papers when Radburn brought him to the house. And pictures of my father's family."

"That nice young man was a Serbian Intelligence officer. He stole your nephew's identity in order to get out of Bosnia before the NATO forces moved in. Radburn helped him."

She collapsed against Drew, sobbing. Drew patted her shoulder and did what Miriam had told him to do. He prayed for mercy for both of them, prayed for peace.

Her muffled words cut off his prayer. "Don't. I'm not worth it. My father told me that we had to help Marcus. He was all we had left—what can I tell my father? He trusted that young man."

Drew wiped the tears from her cheeks. "Someday, Lennie, I'll get to Bosnia when things are more settled there. I'll find out what I can about your family. Maybe arrange for a proper burial."

"You would do that for me—after all I've done?"

"Everyone needs a friend." He stood. "If Miriam and I can help you in any way—"

"No, we'd better say good-bye here. I'm sorry, Mr. Gregory."

"I am, too, Lennie."

"Will they come for me soon?"

He reached out and helped her stand. "Soon. They can't risk waiting any longer. Parkovitch didn't work alone."

"Parkovitch? Who is Parkovitch?" she asked.

"That's what the Phoenix-40 called Radburn Parker in Moscow." He saw by her expression that she had not known the extent of Radburn's contacts—didn't know that he was a member of the Russian Phoenix-40. "Lennie, Parker had other agents here in London who will want to silence you."

"What will happen to me?" she cried.

"You will be arrested and tried for espionage—a bit tricky since you were selling U.S. secrets, but the British government will back us." His fears were as deep as her own. "I don't think it will be a long trial, Lennie. Parker will be interested in saving his own neck, and he has the money to back him—unless you are willing to testify against him."

"Oh, I couldn't do that, but if all this gets back to my parents, it will kill them."

It won't, he thought, *if I arrange to have them transferred to the isolation of the Eagle's Nest—to Margot Hampton's care.* "I'll see what I can do," he said.

"Mr. Gregory, would you thank your wife for the dinner invitation? She invited us for after the Tour. Tell her that Radburn and I won't be able to make it now." Her voice was empty, detached. "Tell her some other time."

He nodded. "She'll understand."

"It's the first time I was ever invited to a private home in Chelsea. I was so looking forward to it."

"So was Miriam," he said.

A police car cruised by as Drew went down the five stone steps. He glanced back and saw Lennie's curtain fall into place. *She knows,* he thought. *Knows that they are coming for her now.*

Five minutes later three cars pulled to a stop in front of him. Perkins and Fairway stepped from the first limousine. "Is she all right?" Fairway asked.

"She's frightened."

As Perkins nodded to the officers in the first car, police in plain clothes, Drew asked, "Dudley, could they let her walk out on her own, unassisted, unrestrained?"

"No handcuffs? Of course." Perkins turned and barked some instructions.

Drew watched the police climb the steps. As they reached the flower pot, they heard the gun go off, the first blast so violent that it blew out the window. As a second shot rang out, Drew and Fairway ran, Perkins puffing behind them. They found Lennie sitting at the desk, alone as she had always been, her fingers still locked around the Makarov. Her loose hair draped across the box of extra bullets. Drew had emptied the chamber, but Lennie had outwitted him.

She had known exactly what she was doing. One shot to the window to warn them to stay clear and a single shot to the temple leaving her colorless cheek streaked with blood. Lennie's distorted face lay against the shattered frame with Radburn Parker's picture in it. A letter was braced against her open Bible, Drew Gregory's name in bold print on the envelope.

He took out her unfinished letter—knowing that it would contain the highlights they had already shared—the pathetic confession of a lonely, misguided spy. He leaned over Lennie's lifeless body and read the eleven words that she had underlined in the Bible that Miriam had given her: "Have mercy upon me, O God . . . for I acknowledge my transgressions."

The next morning as Drew passed the checkpoint at the embassy, he saw Old Glory flying at half mast. He was still frowning as he reached his office. The room had been freshly painted, the carpet newly laid. Even the desk had been replaced, the deliberate water damage completely obliterated. Vic Wilson stood in front of Lennie's cubbyhole office, the room completely sealed off. "What's going on in there?" Drew asked.

"They're giving the room another once-over."

"Lennie didn't know how to plant bugs or any of the trick espionage techniques."

"No, but Parker was an expert at those things."

Drew glanced out the window, grateful that he could see through the tinted windows. "What's with the flag, Vic?"

"Glenn Fairway's idea. The ambassador agreed."

"A cover-up?"

"The good kind, Drew. We couldn't afford the scandal so soon after the Porter Deven betrayal, especially with your uncovering Deven and Lennie being—well, your secretary. Fairway concocted this forty-eight-hour salute to an employee who met her untimely death when her revolver discharged accidentally."

Drew whirled around. "That's a new definition for suicide, a new excuse for espionage, and a blatant misuse of the rules for flying the American flag."

Vic shrugged. "We're a crazy lot here at this embassy. But only a few of us knew that Lennie was under investigation."

"She was a British subject, Vic."

"But our employee."

The wind outside snapped at the flag. It fluttered and unfurled to its full colors, a touch of America on foreign soil. The brilliant red stripes were like scarlet ribbons hiding Lennie's betrayal. Perhaps it was the least he could do for failing her. "Tell Fairway thanks, will you, Vic?"

"I'll do that. Are you heading back to Paris again today?"

"Yes, Miriam's picking me up. I'm scheduled to meet with Carwell and French Intelligence for a full report. After that, Carwell told me to take ten days. Miriam and I will spend part of that time at the hospital visiting Ian."

"Fairway says there's talk of flying Ian back to Maryland for treatment. Does that mean a lifetime in a wheelchair?"

"No, you old fool," Drew said, giving a solid, playful punch to Vic's arm. "For rehabilitation. Another year or two, and there's going to be a Kendall back in the Tour de France."

"And Chase Evans?"

"I'd say she'll be in the crowd somewhere, cheering him on."

"And wearing a yellow jersey herself?"

"Yes, Vic, that sounds like her, doesn't it?"

Epilogue

Wednesday, August 6, Paris. Chase reached Ian's hospital room wearing a sleeveless powder blue sheath cinched at her narrow waist and a stylish floppy-brimmed hat that accented her dark velvet-lashed eyes.

"Ian, I'm here. Did you miss me?" She stopped in the doorway, surprised to see Miriam and Drew Gregory standing by Ian's bedside. "Miriam! Drew! I didn't know you were here."

"We're just leaving, aren't we, darling?"

Drew tilted his head and frowned. "Leaving? We just came."

Miriam tucked her arm in his. "And we're just leaving."

"Oh, yes. I see. Guess you kids want to be alone. Miriam and I did have some things to do—a late lunch with Ian's grandfather for one."

"Huh?" Ian peered around and winked at Chase. "Oh, yes, Uriah will like that. . . . Chase, come here."

"In a minute. Let me see the Gregorys off."

As Miriam pulled Drew toward the door, he grabbed an orange and peeled back the rind with his teeth. "Your folks brought the fruit basket, Chase," he said.

"I'm amazed that they're still here. Dad's never been away from the office that long before."

Miriam laughed. "Your mother threatened to leave him if they went home before Ian was really out of the woods."

"Drew, is everything ready?" Chase whispered.

"Your father and Aubrey Kendall have the phone line set up. Everything is ready to go."

"What do I do?"

"Push the speaker button. Ian won't have to hold the phone."

"That's good—because I'll be holding his hand. You're certain everything is set up."

"Positive."

"Trust Drew," Miriam said. "At least trust him this time."

Across the room, Ian was growing restless. He held out his bandaged hand toward Chase. "What's all the secrecy?"

Chase blew him a kiss. "Be right there." Still she stayed by the door, tears welling in her eyes as Miriam hugged her.

Miriam said, "Ian had a steady stream of visitors this morning. Even Jon Gainsborough and Maurice Chambord put in an appearance. And his team brought Ian the winner's silver bowl."

"But a Dutchman won. He's not on the Gainsborough team."

Miriam said gently, "The accident brought all of the riders together."

"And made them generous," Drew said. "A check for half the winnings came with the bowl for Ian's medical expenses."

"And Ian is so much better. You're good medicine for him."

Chase blushed. "His eyes are brighter now."

"And yours," Miriam said. They hugged again. "Will we see you before you leave for the States?"

"If you have some free time. I'm flying back to New York with my parents this weekend. On the Concorde." She glanced at Ian and tried to smile, but knew that it was little more than a tearful grimace. "I had no choice, Ian. Dad took his credit card back. And graduate school begins in ten days."

Ian's face looked white against the backdrop of hospital linens, strands of his unruly red hair falling against the pillow. "It's okay," he said flatly. "I understand."

"I don't," Drew grumbled, his voice low. "You can't walk out on Ian now. You're his major chance for a full recovery."

She whispered again, "I'm taking him with me. He just doesn't know it yet." She stood on tiptoe and kissed Drew before he could give her news away.

"You're serious? He won't be well enough to leave."

"And he won't get well here by himself. I'll explain later."

"Over dinner?" Drew insisted.

"All right. Over dinner. But I'm not leaving Ian until the hospital puts me out tonight."

"That's eight o'clock," Miriam said. "I fought the staff on that every night."

"Did you win?"

"Usually."

"Then we'll have dinner at nine." Drew checked his watch. "We'll wait for you in the hospital lobby, Chase. Nine sharp."

Chase watched them leave arm in arm. When they reached the end of the corridor, they turned and waved, Miriam's enormous dark eyes bright with laughter. Chase would miss them when she left Paris. She faced the closed door for a moment, and then with a warm smile walked across the room to Ian. "Do you think we will be as happy as the Gregorys twenty years from now?" she asked.

"What chance do we have?"

"None if you keep a gloomy look on your face."

"Where have you been for the last two days, Chase? I kept waiting for you to come."

She touched Bea's necklace at the hollow of her neck. "I flew to London and drove up to the Eagle's Nest. You told me to visit Beatrice Thorpe the first chance I had. Bea's worried about you, Ian. She said it wasn't like you not to come and see her."

"Poor Beatrice."

"She thought you were dead."

"So did half the world," he said.

"She saw the accident on the TV screen, so the staff snatched her television out of her room and wouldn't tell her what happened. After that, she refused to eat. She's very frail, Ian."

"She's very old. Ninety-five on the last count."

She squeezed his two unbandaged fingers. "Bea cried for five straight minutes when I told her you were alive—and how sick you had been." Chase leaned down and kissed him. "She sent her love. Now rest for a while, Ian. I'll be here."

She sat at his bedside, holding his hand as he dozed. Twenty minutes later when he opened his eyes, she said, "Are you finally awake, sleepyhead?"

"I was dreaming about the beautiful girl at my bedside."

She flushed with pleasure. "Ian, do you want to talk about the Tour yet?"

"How can I? I really wanted to win," he said.

"Do you know one of the Gainsborough riders came in third?"

"No one told me. Oh, not Marcus Nash?" he asked miserably.

"No, Basil Millard."

"That's impossible, Chase. He was here this morning. He never said a word. Basil never came in third in his life."

"He was never so inspired before. He did it for you. Besides, you told him he had never ridden to his full potential."

"He's a great guy."

"That's the way he feels about you. He couldn't even speak when we told him you were alive. Your teammates supported Basil—against Marcus Nash's better judgment—and then they gave it everything to try to win that race for you."

"But they couldn't beat out the favorites?"

"Not this year's winner. . . . But I don't want to talk about the team anymore, Ian. It's time to talk about us."

"Us? Is there anything left to say?"

"Everything!" She fluffed her hair and locked some strands behind her ear. Their eyes met and held. "Ian Kendall, will you marry me?"

He bit his lip, his face pensive, his blue eyes piercing. "Don't, Chase. You don't have to do that. I didn't keep my end of the bargain. I didn't win the race. I didn't even finish."

"There will be other races."

"For me? I might not walk normally again, let alone ride."

"Is that what your doctors said?"

"Not exactly, but I doubled over and fainted the first time they got me up."

"So you're quitting?"

"No, they tried again, and I screamed the whole five steps."

"Well, I'll be with you today, and we'll scream together."

He touched her, the gauze wrap on his hand rough against her cheek. "You can't gamble your life away on me. Not now."

"Four weeks ago you were willing to take a chance with me."

"Chase, four weeks ago I planned on winning a race for you. Look at me now, a physical wreck."

"I'm looking—you're still a handsome hunk to me. Ian, get used to it. I always make up my own mind. I want you in one piece, too. So we need a second medical opinion. That's why my dad flew in two orthopedic specialists from Columbia Presbyterian."

"Not those two doctors who woke me up this morning? One of them said he was a neurologist."

"Possibly. I get specialists like that mixed up."

"What good can they do?"

"Well, they won't pamper you. That's my job. They specialize in nerves and bones. My dad told them they'd better earn their money." She laughed as she ran her finger across his lip. "You may not like my dad, but you'll have to tolerate the doctors. One of them is a cycling enthusiast who lost money on you this time. He expects you to race again—so he can recoup his losses."

"That will never happen. I think I've lost twenty pounds."

"Then you'll have less weight to carry up the mountain." She tapped his IV monitor. "Just blame your weight on your transfusion diet."

"My legs still feel numb—useless when I try to stand up."

"Ian Kendall, your cycling hero Greg LeMond came back from a near-fatal hunting accident—he won the Tour after that, too."

"That was an incredible comeback."

"Yours will be, too." She kept Ian's hand against her cheek. "LeMond didn't ride a marathon a week later, you know. It was weeks before he could stay on a bike for twenty minutes a day."

"How would you know, Chase?"

"I called him from my hotel room." *At least I dialed his stateside number. Oh, dear Lord, forgive me. I'm already stretching the truth . . . and I've just been with Bea.*

"From here in Paris? LeMond took your call?" Ian asked.

She hesitated. "He's human, you know."

"Chase, I don't want to be a second-rate rider."

"LeMond didn't either. And he didn't succeed by frowning."

Ian's tired eyes smiled wanly. It seemed to take all his energy to work up a smile. Next month when he finally rode his first mile again, she would tell him the truth—the complete truth. Or by then—or even this afternoon—maybe she would find the courage to really dial Greg LeMond. Right now, Ian believed her. She saw hope spark in his eyes.

"My gut hurts, Chase, worse than the broken bones."

His spleen or his liver, the doctor had said; but in the joy of finding him still alive, she couldn't remember for certain. "Pretend like it's a stomach virus. Flu always goes away."

"These miracle doctors of yours—what did they say?"

"That any more surgery will have to be done in the States. They've studied your X-rays. They have big egos and reputations to live up to. They'll have you out of here by this weekend."

"Sounds like I've got a great team behind me."

"Well, there are a couple of feisty players. Your dad and mine are having a go at it. But it's only because they care."

"Tell your father that my dad can be a tiger."

"Your brother Grover calls them both bobcats. My dad has to help you. He says when he gives me away, the man I marry has to be standing at the church altar." Ian's eyes brightened; she took courage. "It was the wrong time to remind Dad that I plan to marry in mother's rose garden with you standing at the arbor."

"You're crazy. What about finishing your doctorate, Chase?"

"I'll work on that while you're in rehab. That's why I have to fly back to New York so soon—but you're going with us, Ian."

"Like this?"

"Well, I hope you don't wear that ugly hospital gown."

"I can't even take five steps on my own."

"You ever hear of stretchers? They'll carry you on board."

"Absolutely no stretcher—or I won't go."

"A wheelchair then—or they won't release you from here."

"What would I do in New York, Chase?"

"My dad wants you in the best rehab hospital in New York City—so I'd be home on weekends. Oh, Ian, New York will be in all of its autumn glory right after we arrive."

"So will Maryland," he said wistfully.

She felt his longing. "Then you're not going to New York?"

"I can't. Not if my dad wants me hospitalized near home."

"He does," she said. "Your dad and Uriah have been burning the wires to Maryland trying to find a better rehab center there. If you go there, I'd have to fly to Maryland each weekend."

"Can you get your father's credit card back?" he teased.

"He promised me one of my own."

"I love you, funny girl."

She choked up. "I thought you'd forgotten—"

"How could I? You are in my mind all the time. I thought about you when Marcus Nash rode against my cycle. That's when I realized I might not see you again. . . . I remember the stab in my neck—and then my bike started to weave, and after that—" He ran his bandaged hand through her hair, the gauze catching several strands. "After that I don't remember anything until I woke up in the hospital screaming with pain."

She forced tears away and said softly, "Oh, Ian, I should have been here with you."

"My grandfather was here . . . and my father. Yes, my dad! They just held me down until Miriam could run and get the nurse."

"And then the nurse came and gave you a shot?" Chase asked.

"One that put me back to sleep—but at least I could dream about you and forget that awful pain."

His bruised face broke into another smile. He reached up and pulled her to him. "I love you, funny girl," he said again.

As she rested against his shoulder, she heard the pulsating beat of his heart through the thin hospital gown. "Ian, I'm serious. Will you marry me?"

She felt his heartbeat race. Huskily, he said, "Let me think about it. Give me a second."

She pushed away, just far enough for their lips to be touching and whispered, "Well, what did you decide?"

He was so somber that she laid her head against his chest again, ready to tell him she understood, perhaps was even ready to let him go, if it came to that.

He blew on her ear. "Could you give me a year to be back on my feet—back on my cycle and racing again?"

Chase blinked back happy tears. "What about next July—after the Tour de France, darling?" she suggested.

"Sounds about right to me."

"That gives Mother time to get her rose garden ready for our wedding."

The phone rang. Chase pushed away from Ian and reached blindly behind her for the speaker button. "Hmm," she mumbled.

"Ian!" The crackling sound was not the phone line, but the wavering voice of Beatrice Thorpe.

"Beatrice," Chase cried. "Ian is right here."

Ian tried propping himself up on his elbow with Chase still leaning against him. "Bea," he said. "Bea."

"Oh, dear boy, are you all right?"

His bandaged arm tightened around Chase. "I'm fine, Bea. I'm going to be all right. And I've got good news."

"Tell me at once."

"It's about Chase and me."

"I guessed as much, you ninny."

Chase smothered a chuckle and brushed her cheek against his. The thumping of his heart pulsated as one with her own.

He smiled. "Bea, we're going to be married . . . next summer in New York."

"New York." Wistfulness filled Bea's quavering voice. "I've always wanted to see New York."

"Then come to our wedding," Ian urged. "We'll put you on the front pew as part of the family."

"I don't have a proper birth certificate. These folks at the Eagle's Nest don't seem to know where it is." Her sigh vibrated over the speaker. "And I certainly don't remember."

"We'll work it out," Ian promised, his gaze on Chase.

"Cherish each other," she said. "Keep on loving each other. And, Ian, dear boy—"

"Yes."

"Give Chase a great big tender kiss for me."

"I'll do that," he said.

And he did. Ian was still smiling, his lips parted, his azure eyes bright and lively. Chase slipped her arms around his neck as their lips met, the sweetness of that kiss fervent with the promise of years to come.